ROYAL POWER

By Andrea Blythe Liebman

Authors Note: *Please note that this book depicts issues of sexual assault, emotional abuse, death, violence, emotional torture and incarceration, and sexual content.*

PART ONE

ONE

LIV

"You may be immortal and all, but I still cannot fully support this amount of caffeine intake."

The sun was shining brightly; his eyes sparkled deviously.

Liv huffed playfully, taking a dangerous sip from her beverage, daring to push the limits of her ruler's boundaries. He looked dazzling in a green crewneck sweater and slim denim jeans, accompanied by white and neon yellow sneakers, playing the role of college student miraculously.

"I kept my mouth closed for the first two coffee beverages, but a third cold brew..." He pressed.

"...Over half a day of exploring *and* two meals." Liv interjected with a smile.

The trees rustled in the distance. The fresh scent of pine filled her body, reminding her of the many wonders from the earth's beauty. Similar to her golden, coffee regulator, she too donned an outfit from her past life, a grey hoodie stamped with her college mascot layered beneath a black leather jacket.

"You are going to have so much energy by the time the basketball game starts, you will practically be dunking on the court, instead of the team."

"So long as they count those earned points toward our school." Liv hummed, her grin slowly growing around the straw clenched between her teeth.

"I said, no more coffee."

He flashed a monstrous growl, firmly yanking the cup from her grip and throwing it across the pavilion. Brown liquid stained the sparkling concrete, muting it with disgust.

Liv looked back at her boyfriend, eyes wide.

He had turned again.

He grabbed her arm and ripped Liv from her seat before catapulting her against the tree.

Her body hit the cold stone wall.

Darkness.

No longer was the sun dazzling on her tanned skin but instead a cold fog hovered over her ghostly existence.

She breathed deeply, assessing the damage. Her shoulder had been pulled out of her socket. It was the second time that week.

Or night?

To her, it was all becoming one never-ending nightmare.

Liv tried to ground herself in her surroundings. She felt tired. Weak.

"And you were honestly enjoying that pathetic banter?" The cruel statement judged from afar.

"Where am I?" Liv mumbled, trying to see clearly.

Only a blurred vision of darkness could be obscurely identified. It smelled of basil verveina, cedar wood, cardamom and leather.

Her head hurt. She was so cold. She wanted to go back to sleep, return to her dreams of the outside world. Go anywhere from this hell.

"I could not let you escape for too long, *Ollie*." The softened voice whispered; a hint of dry sarcasm soothed her conscience.

Hayden. He was here. He would rescue her. She was safe.

She would be all right.

Liv exhaled a sigh of relief, trying to minimize the distance between them by lifting herself up. But she fell to the cold, relentless floor. She had been out for too long, drugged too often and tormented too much.

How long *had* it been?

To her, it felt like eternity, but it was over now.

"Thank god you're finally here." She cried, starting to shake with relief, finally allowing her guard to come down and instead rely on his strength.

She yearned for his warmth. She was so tired.

But Hayden was here. She would be all right.

"Oh, Ollie." He purred, "You should not use that descriptor – *god* - so loosely," before kicking her stomach and knocking her unconscious once again.

PEYTON

"I can't find her. Why am I unable to find her?"

Hayden hadn't stopped pacing in his loft.

It had been two days. His anxiety was starting to make Peyton delusional.

He had already asked this question one hundred times, receiving the same answer in return. But Hayden was her king, and although he was hurting, he was also testing Peyton's patience.

If only Peyton could convince Hayden to change out of his navy suit and white collared shirt, both worn to exhaustion since Liv's capture.

With a deep breath, Peyton firmly repeated again, "Tristan said Arlo made sure the headquarters would be untraceable, and we suspect with Kronos's additional support, they've ensured that no one will find it, unless you know where it's located-"

"And they want you to find it."

A door slammed shut behind her.

Thank Zeus. Peyton huffed, turning to find Tristan with Piper right behind him. Maybe Tristan could pacify Hayden's growing and almost intolerable restlessness with *some* intel from his Dark God connections. It had only been a couple weeks since Tristan had publicly declared his loyalty to Liv and the Pure God cause, so she had hoped he would be able to leverage any pre-existing relationships to help them discover where his Element Elite had been taken captive.

Peyton turned to Piper, her eyes mentally demanding she take on their royal highness, Hayden. Ever since Rei had left them the morning before on a mission to secure an army to backup the inevitable rescue, Peyton was slowly joining Hayden's level of 'losing her shit entirely,' because of Hayden's level of having already lost *his* shit entirely.

"We came back as quickly as we could." Piper squeaked.

Keep your composure. Breathe. Peyton reminded herself. *This is not the time to bitch out your friends...*

Peyton forced a smile and nodded, finally walking over to greet them.

"Thank you."

On the other hand, Hayden had no time for salutations.

"I felt her." He whispered, turning to Tristan. "I could feel her."

"That's why you summoned us back." Tristan confirmed with a nod.

"Two days ago." Hayden hissed. "What took you so long!?"

"Because we were on the border of *Scotland*," Tristan explained, unsuccessfully masking his irritation as he sat on the couch. "That's easily a week's journey for a common deity. We made it back in *two days*."

"Did you run into any Dark Gods?" Peyton asked, genuinely concerned. She ran her fingers through her wavy beach blonde hair to ease her apprehension.

She had to recognize her immediate gratitude for Hayden's anxiety being directed toward new targets. So, Peyton started to make coffee in the kitchen for both of their friends – a journey like that would not have been easy, especially with the current circumstances their world faced between extreme viewpoints of government policy.

Now, it was no longer safe, whether you were a Pure God *or* a Dark God.

"We were able to deter them." Piper confirmed, albeit weakly. She walked over to the crackling fireplace and fell onto the black leather sofa nearby.

Peyton took a better look at Piper, whose midnight bob appeared tousled and stunning navy blazer was ripped into a grungy vest, revealing her silver long-sleeved blouse underneath. Peyton turned to Tristan, her arms crossed over her blue, floral laced dress. He certainly looked less injured in his staple leather jacket and black denim jeans paired with a suspiciously textured, coif hairstyle too relaxed for indifference.

"Piper blew them off our path before they could spot us, and made the entire manipulation look natural." Tristan clarified, his voice tired, but with pride sparkling from his eyes.

Peyton and Piper's eyes both mirrored his dazzle.

My girl!

"The clothes' state is more so from colliding into a tree during the process." Piper admitted embarrassingly.

Peyton laughed, thankful these friends were safe - she could breathe a little lighter, for the time being.

The door opened and slammed again, this time presenting Rei looking worse for the wear. He too, had not rested since Hayden commanded that he rally an army immediately after Liv's disappearance.

"Silas has granted permission for five troops to accompany us on our mission." He bluntly stated, heading straight toward the liquor cabinet.

Clearly everyone was set on testing the *"if you don't love me at my worst..."* sentiment, today. Peyton fumed, rolled her eyes and joined Piper on the couch, ignoring Tristan's speculation.

"Over one thousand deities?" Tristan's eyes grew wide, "That will slow us down. We need to be able to take them by surprise, slip into their head-quarters undetected." He turned back to Hayden, challenging him. "Less will be more with this fortress. Unless you want to start another war. And if that's the case, five troops will not suffice for a full-blown battle."

Rei sighed, as if already anticipating this conflict. He calmly poured himself a whisky and took a deep sip. Peyton felt for him, so stood back up and walked over, massaging his shoulders in support. She hugged him from behind; appreciative for the soft velvet, olive green jacket he wore - she had felt cold and lifeless while standing still and watching over the ghostly Hayden.

"There is no way I'm not going." Hayden protested, staring Rei down with exasperated eyes.

Tristan looked confused and turned to Rei for an explanation.

"As we discussed, I will not allow the king to journey into Arlo and Kronos's territory without security. It's too dangerous." The Security Elite declared, taking another sip of his whisky.

His glass now empty, Rei reached to refill his beverage.

Peyton got to the bottle first, pouring herself a glass before replenishing his. If she had to hear this argument one more time… she needed to be drunk enough to *not* remember it once she sobered up. Although her time was infinite, her patience for hearing this debate had infinitely dissolved.

"I've been stuck here doing nothing while they do Zeus knows what to her!" Hayden slammed his fist against the pole, breaking it in half.

Piper gasped, watching the beam crack into two, its effects trickling like dominoes as the entire ceiling structure began caving through.

She leaped toward the pole, holding it upright with all of her concentration. Finally, she managed to beg aloud, "A little help, please!?"

Peyton jogged over immediately, cursing under her breath about babysitting children, before reconstructing the beam. She nodded to Piper, giving permission to relieve the burden of holding the entire loft together, before muttering, "A band-aid, until we can get Thyo to repair the infrastructure properly."

But she had enough.

Peyton turned toward her king, skin turning purple as she began to blow up and reprimand him. "If you-"

Rei had already calmly set down his drink, stepping in to diffuse his hotheaded girlfriend, and alas, the entire room.

"We all need to take a moment. Can we at least agree to that?" He stated, nodding to innocent Piper as a grounding example. "Piper almost exploded there because of us. If anything, can we keep it together for her sake?" He turned to Hayden, wisely choosing his words. "Your highness, you need to keep your sensibility. Outbursts like this will not help get her back."

"It will do the exact opposite. Get us all killed." Tristan huffed, rolling his eyes.

Hayden sighed, clearly wanting to throttle Tristan, but thankfully also understanding that they needed him.

"It won't happen again." He turned to Tristan; his eyes clear once again. "Unless prompted."

"I am not going to risk my life, and consequently Liv's, if you're going to behave like a child." Tristan declared calmly; the subtle reprimand done tastefully to keep the peace. At least for the time being.

"Even if all Hades breaks loose, I'll still be able to handle that kidnapping traitor." Hayden challenged.

"And Kronos?" Tristan reminded him. "You may be more powerful than Arlo, but did you forget about your ancestor? With his ancient magic and eternal knowledge?" Tristan darkly smiled. "Not a chance. And as much as I would love to witness that downfall, I suggest you don't push your luck, princeling."

"King." Hayden reminded him, disturbingly composed.

Well, at least they were acting more civil. Peyton rolled her eyes.

Tristan took a breath, before matching Hayden's gaze. "I'll start calling you that when you start acting like one."

"How dare you defy the king." Rei snarled, his eyes wide.

Well fuck. The only civil one in this room just turned. Peyton sighed, preparing to tap back into ringmaster, praying Piper would grow some balls to give her a well-deserved break.

"How dare you all coddle *him*?!" Tristan pushed back. "We all want her back. End of story. So, why is he the only one who's allowed to lose his god-damned mind over it?"

There was silence. Nobody disagreed, even Hayden.

"Grow up." Tristan stared Hayden down in conclusion, before turning to Peyton and Rei. "Either accept my counsel, or don't. I'm not going to risk my life knowing our plan will be a failure."

And with that, he ran out and slammed the door.

Piper turned to her friends with a weak shrug.

"I'll go." She offered with a sigh and then left the loft to put together the broken pieces.

LIV

Her brain felt foggy, immobile.

Liv focused on the cold stone freezing her cheek, offering the only solace to her aching, bruised body. Feeling numb offered reprieve so she tried to remain unconscious, disconnected to her reality, for as long as she could.

She wanted to move, but was afraid of the pain. Or worse, the discovery of no pain at all, a body truly broken and functional no more.

No.

Instead, she remained still, relishing in the comfort of the cool stone. Determined not to recognize how disparaging it was to only have the consolation of a floor tether her composure.

It was all she had.

She had nothing else.

When her consciousness eventually reached a fraction of clarity, her heart started beating fast, naturally recognizing the danger that dwelled in the surrounding darkness.

Just focus on the cool stone.

Liv's mouth started to tremble; it was all she had to give. She scrunched her eyelids closed even tighter, begging it would help keep her determined resolve.

No. She reminded herself. *No.*

But her heart kept beating quickly. She tried to take a deep breath through her lungs, but after the first inhale, her bruised ribs ached, causing an unforeseen pressure on her right side to cut her breath immediately.

Liv coughed, causing more pain to spike through her right ribcage.

Smaller breaths.

Only able to hold the air for a moment, she attempted the coping mechanism again, and again, inhaling a short breath before gently exhaling through her nose.

If anything, she was grateful for the distraction.

TWO

PIPER

How could all of her friends disgustingly hate each other?

She needed Liv – her best friend was the only person to who this all made sense, who would have been able to reprimand and get everyone in line.

Or at least on the same plane.

Stupid.

Piper shook her head.

Liv wasn't here.

Puerdios echoed of loneliness. As Piper hurried down the hall, it was as if she had been transported back in time, returning to a place unwelcoming to someone like her, someone who didn't belong.

She felt *worthless.*

Only Liv understood that feeling and could appreciate the beauty of having friends.

Having one friend.

But the entire world that they had spent so long building was quickly crumbling, a kingdom breaking down as if Liv had never ruled, never existed.

Piper didn't have her one friend anymore. What was she defending now?

Stop thinking like that.

She fought her conscience, a constant battle between insecurity and self-worth.

Don't revert back to who you were.

Who you *are*. A voice reminded her.

Piper knew it would take longer than a couple months to combat a lifetime of being lame. So, she had to keep reminding herself that one battle took priority for now: the fight for Liv.

It was all she had.

She approached his door, bolted and intimidating; exactly how Tristan wanted the world to view him. She hoped that unlike her, he was still the same deity that Liv had transformed. She prayed he would listen to her and not cast her aside like he had always done before.

Piper gently knocked on the door, fiddling with her fingers as she looked around the shadowed halls. It was almost 180° SR, and the sun would set yet again.

Piper dreaded seeing the moonlight because it meant it would be almost morning again.

Almost five days since Liv had been captured.

And at least three more days, at minimum, until Liv could be rescued.

A chill crept down Piper's spine as the door slowly creaked open.

Three days of godly torture easily equaled *weeks* of intense mortal torture, dark abuse mechanisms only the cruelest and evilest of beings could imagine. And who knew where Liv was in the process of transitioning from human to deity, how much her body could take before it crashed. Was she fully immortal yet or only temporarily able to withstand Kronos's powers? Either outcome, they were losing the game against time.

Piper took a deep breath. She needed all the strength she could muster if she were to survive within the ruling society of the most powerful deities. Many of which were her close acquaintances, starting with the one she went to see now. She stared at the uninviting door, mentally preparing herself to accomplish what she came to achieve.

Stepping into the doorway, she quickly announced, "It's me. Piper," before gently closing the door.

Silence responded.

Piper took a step further.

"Can I come in?" She asked softly, surprised when her high-pitched voice echoed down the hallway.

Tristan peaked his head around the corner, looking a little stunned.

"Of course." He breezily confirmed, waving her in.

Piper quickly walked to the kitchen area, finding Tristan steering toward his whisky bar.

He had changed out of his dirt-stained travel attire of black jeans, an ink collared shirt and brown leather jacket, showered, and now looked crisp in a plaid flannel and grey leather pants. Piper's eyes went wide at the realization she was still in her torn, tarnished attire, most likely with her night sky choppy bob looking unruly and uncaged. She quietly commanded, "Cristam," and quickly added, "Emendo," to first return her snarly hair back to silk and then stitch her blazer-turned-vest into a newly altered garment. She had started whispering, "Detergeo," to quickly clean her body and dust her clothes, but instead jumped and accomplished nothing at the sound of Tristan's voice. Fortunately, he was facing the cabinet when Piper reacted to the noise, but she had an inclination it was only to save her from further embarrassment.

"Usually my friends aren't as polite as you, Piper. They barge in and ask for forgiveness later." He turned back to his guest, "Can I interest you in a drink?"

Piper looked first at Tristan, then registered what he had asked, so followed her gaze to the cabinet full of golden liquid, dread penetrating her core as she tried to ignore the terrible memories of drinking whisky and combat her urge to run away.

Finally, she squeaked, "Sure."

Be there for him. Be strong. She reminded herself.

Tristan tried to contain his laughter at the sight, but failed.

"Not a fan of the dram?" He hollered with a grin.

Piper smiled shyly as she tried to compose her reasoning, "Not particularly. I've only had a couple though… with Liv."

As soon as she said the name aloud, she regretted it.

It clearly pained both of them to hear Liv's name in memory.

Tristan finally broke the silence.

"You're a good friend." He nodded and grabbed two whisky glasses and a wine glass. "I'll make us Old Fashioneds, and if you still don't care for the taste, I have a red wine bottle that one might call, 'the deep stuff,' for you."

"Thanks." Piper smiled, finally sitting down at the counter bar with a kind smile.

Tristan lit the fireplace across the room while summoning all of the ingredients needed for his alcoholic potion. He began peeling the orange and nodded to the bottle of Four Roses he had sitting on the counter for Piper to study.

"The key to a good Old Fashioned is selection and precision. You need to know the right whiskey to use – not too fancy or complicated where it'll hinder the taste, but not too weak that the flavors will be overtaken by the mixers and become lost in the final product."

"You make concocting cocktails sound like war strategy." Piper joked shyly, grabbing the bottle and reading about the whiskey.

"You'll learn that with my life, everything is strategy." Tristan laughed, but it didn't genuinely deliver. "A strategy for survival."

Piper put down the bottle. "A bourbon from Kentucky… I take it you weren't in the mood to sip on something Scotland-related?"

Tristan shrugged, muddling a sugar cube with bitters.

"I understand this world is brutal." Piper sighed, "I, more than anybody. But don't you see? You have us-" Piper paused, correcting herself. "Me."

Tristan remained quiet, giving the timid girl time to find her platform. From the past four days together, he had learned only good came from listening to her genuinely and carefully constructed advice.

"We're all surviving, but you don't have to strategize around us. We aren't cruel, like Arlo or Kai."

"You." Tristan clarified, plopping an ice cube into her drink and topping it off with the Kentucky bourbon. "Liv... Zeus forbid anything happens to her before she's back with us." He added an orange peel and repeated the same in his own glass, starting the following names with each added ingredient. "Dylan, Zayne and Kyril."

He handed Piper her drink, ignoring her opposition as he clinked her glass and sipped.

"And the jury says...?"

Piper took a first sip, her palette shocked by the mix of citrus, spice, pear and maple syrup erupting in her mouth. With the second swig, her taste buds had adapted to the concoction, enjoying a sweeter, smoother finish.

"Surprisingly good." She hummed, taking another sip, before continuing on with her argument. "You know Peyton, Rei or Hayden wouldn't do anything to deliberately hurt you."

Tristan contemplated the proposal with another sip of his own drink before countering, "Peyton and Rei are loyal to Hayden. Hayden is loyal to Liv. Liv is the common denominator to our peaceful co-existence."

"Peaceful?" Piper challenged with a huff, taking another sip.

Tristan laughed, genuinely this time.

"Liv is loyal to me, as I am to her." Tristan's voice turned melancholy with his explanation of the circumstantial reality of their situation, "If Liv is out of the equation, Hayden's tolerance turns, and Peyton and Rei won't lift a finger against his crusade against me."

The Old Fashioned was beginning to affect Piper's conscience. Wanting to make the conversation a bit more lighthearted, like how her mind was feeling, she darkly joked, "If Liv is out of the picture, you're no longer a threat."

Tristan eyed Piper, acknowledging the risky assessment about his feelings toward her friend, but wanting to keep that buried where it needed to stay.

He finished his Old Fashioned, and before beginning the process of making the next, clarified, "If Liv is out of the picture, then that means I failed."

Piper finished her drink in unison, sliding it back to Tristan's working mini bar.

"If Liv is out of the picture, Tristan, that means we all failed. You, me, Peyton, Rei and Hayden." She stood up, walked over to him and grabbed the orange before he could get to the fruit, and began peeling. "We are a team. We do this as a team. Just like your drink and all of its ingredients. We work together and make this mission a damn delicious cocktail."

LIV

Hours later... perhaps days... or possibly no time passed at all, Liv stirred again, blinking her eyes as she woke to the smell of basil verveina, cedarwood, cardamom and leather.

Her body tensed and eyes went wide as she mentally cried.

No. No. Not again.

Liv gulped.

What torment was Hayden going to put her through this time?

After holding her breath, praying Zeus to spare her and imagining all the ways he could destroy her soul, she caught a stronger whiff of his fragrance.

She *dreaded* the smell, what it did to her. What *he* did to her.

The pain.

Hayden wasn't the hero.

He was the enemy.

PIPER

"Do you mind making three more of those cocktails and maybe inviting the Pure Gods into your territory?" Piper asked after they had completed their second round of drinks. "As much as I would love to just drink away our sorrows, there are some pretty important decisions to be made tonight."

Tristan eyed Piper before returning to his libation creations.

Well, at least he didn't exactly decline the ask...

Holding her breath, she watched as he sauntered over once again to his liquor cabinet, this time grabbing three more cocktail glasses and bringing them back to the counter with a sigh.

"There's another orange in the refrigerator." He bluntly stated, before grabbing more whiskey and beginning the cocktail concocting again, three times over.

"Thank you." Piper mouthed, tiptoeing across the kitchen to grab an orange.

"Sorry, I'm being a dick." Tristan spat, sighing as he leaned against the counter. "With everything going on, this should be the least concern, but today's a traditionally hard day for me."

"A traditionally hard day?" Piper asked, placing the orange in front of Tristan, facing him directly with only the kitchen counter in between. "Are 2's typically your nemesis? A what's-the-point, existential crisis sort of thing?"

Tristan smiled, his eyes gleaming with amusement.

Piper continued, "Not-the-beginning-of-the-week, not the end, not the glorious hump day 3, nor 5-yay or even the eve of the weekend… should we all go back to sleep? Sleep through all future pointless 2's? Am I right? I can probably get Hayden to make a royal proclamation…"

Tristan broke into laughter. Piper mirrored his delight like a Vulcan Mirror.

Anything he needed.

Tristan wiped a tear of joy from his eye as he took a deep breath.

"That was impressive, Piper. I didn't realize you had it in you." He sighed, "It feels odd to laugh about it. I haven't been able to laugh about it for almost twenty years."

"That's a long grudge against 2." Piper added with a sincere smile, gently grabbing Tristan's hand on the counter. "What's the real reason you're upset?"

Tristan looked at Piper, his façade dropping. He looked younger, more innocent, more vulnerable to pain as he remembered the reason for his outburst.

Unexpectedly, he first took a swig of the whiskey bottle near the counter, grimacing at the bold choice in shot.

Piper squeezed his hand, prodding him to share and not try to numb his pain. They'd never survive if everyone confined their struggles within.

"Today's my sister's birthday." He finally whispered, staring at the kitchen counter, before solemnly clarifying, "Or, *was* my sister's birthday."

Piper nodded in acknowledgement, "Giselle."

"Yeah. Giselle." Tristan confirmed, remaining quiet after.

The silence hovered over as memories of the Goddess of Water and her rustic beauty penetrated their minds. Piper and Tristan were both only infants when she disappeared, yet Piper could vividly remember when she had entered the Elements Pillar, lighting up the room with her stunning beauty and generous spirit. Her soul glistened like freshly fallen snow below a sparkling sun.

Tristan had nobody to remember his sister with – both of his parents had been sent to the Underworld by Kai and Arlo's wrath, his grandmother's death the same reason his sister mysteriously vanished quickly after.

Piper curled around the kitchen counter, grabbed the bottle of whiskey and poured two glasses respectively. And although she absolutely dreaded the taste of the liquid gold, she raised her glass in the air, Tristan following suit.

"To Giselle." Piper declared, "She was lost too soon, but may she prosper and find peace, wherever she be."

And with a warm smile, their eyes locked for a brief eternity, before Piper closed her lids and knocked back the drink, trying her best to maintain composure out of respect for the Underworld.

And to make sure she avoided giving Tristan any inclination to how miserable that ode to his sister actually felt, Piper immediately pulled Tristan into an embrace, hiding her alcohol-induced shivers.

Yet, that action was the best distraction from the whiskey shot Piper could have hoped for. She froze, wondering if Tristan was secretly freaking out internally like she was.

His arms wrapped firmly around her waist as he whispered, "Thank you, Piper."

The vibrations from his voice sent chills down Piper's spine. Thank Zeus Tristan held onto her for a moment longer, bringing her in for a tight hug and allowing her to recover her composure before letting go.

"Right." Piper nodded with a forced smile, "Now, time to round-up the Pures."

And with that, she departed. The smile dropping into a worried grimace as she ran down the hall.

Shit. Shit. Shit. What the Hades was that?!

When Piper arrived back with Hayden, Rei and Peyton, she was surprised and relieved to find Dylan, Kyril and Zayne at Tristan's loft, too.

"I've told them everything." Tristan admitted immediately. "We need their intel. They've been closer to Arlo more recently than myself."

Hayden remained calm, to Piper's relief.

"What can you tell us?" He asked politely.

Dylan eyed Tristan, almost as if asking permission to continue.

Tristan rolled his eyes, cutting in on her behalf. "They're loyal to Liv and the Elements Pillar, I'll vouch for them. I'm not sure exactly how they can help yet, but as we determine a plan, it doesn't hurt to have them here to provide insight and counsel to any ideas we propose as we finalize a course of action."

"I'll vouch for them too." Piper added, softly smiling to Tristan before turning her gratitude to his friends.

"First, you should have told us Liv had been kidnapped." Dylan said tartly to both Piper and Tristan, ignoring Piper's appreciation before turning to Hayden and adding earnestly, "But now that we do know, we're happy to help, however we can."

She pulled off her maroon fur coat and effortlessly laid it on the couch behind her, revealing her auburn locks gently curled over a sequined mosaic maxi-dress. She levitated the three glasses of Merlot that Tristan had poured, sending two to her friends and grabbing her own; the hue perfectly matching her lips as she took control of the glass.

There was another knock at the door.

All eight deities looked at each other with confusion.

"Anybody else you've invited along on our rescue mission?" Peyton sarcastically called out while walking to the door. "Oprah? Heracles? The Pope?"

The Goddess of Discovery couldn't help but add with a Tristan-inspired mimic, "*Over one thousand deities? That's too many!* Instead, I'll invite… *nine hundred ninety-nine deities in the room… nine hundred ninety-nine deities… take one down…interrogate it around… until there's nine hundred ninety-eight deities in the room…*"

But even her dry humor couldn't mask her underlying edge. Aside from Silas, who else knew of Liv's capture?

When she opened the door, Peyton sighed in relief, stopping her song in tandem.

"We came as soon as we could." Daphne explained, Jocelyn following right behind her. They both looked worse for the wear too, with visible dark bags under both sets of eyes. Daphne wore a grey turtleneck sweater over a silk skirt. Jocelyn dazzled in a lavender lace gown and gold headband, albeit looking exhausted.

"She's been gone for more than four days, Mother!" Hayden roared, exasperated.

"Be thankful we arrived, at all." Jocelyn snapped back, falling into Tristan's black leather couch and rubbing her temples as if she had a migraine.

Daphne remained stoic, standing tall and tilting her head, silencing both children in a heartbeat. After a moment of pause and when she understood everything was under control, Daphne walked over to her son to explain.

"You know I had to play through every choice, every circumstance and every outcome before deciding whether or not to interfere."

Hayden started mirroring his sister, rubbing his head to keep his temper under control. "Well, where is she?" He finally asked, with a forced politeness. His agitation was growing, and it had been slim to begin with.

Daphne showed the first break of strength, looking to Tristan warily. "She is where you suspect."

"And where is that?" Hayden reiterated.

Daphne turned to her son, pleading. "You know I cannot tell you, or else I would."

"So, you expect all of us to put Liv's life in the hands of conveniently turned Pure Gods of recent?"

"Precisely. And not expecting it, but demanding it of you." Daphne confirmed, ignoring her son's concerns. "And Hayden, you do not want to command otherwise. As your mother, I am begging you."

Hayden stared at his mother, his jaw clenched, and finally huffed before taking a sip of his Old Fashioned.

Piper warily looked between mother and son, the dowager queen and king, and felt the tension in the air rising.

"You know I would tell you if the result ended favorably," Daphne whispered. "I implore you to trust me, and consequently, Liv's appointed advisor."

Silence ensued as Hayden continued contemplating his mother's words.

Deities were groomed *not* to trust other deities, for it usually ended in one's demise. And the more powerful you were, the more others would be tempted to betray you. Sure, Piper was certainly struggling, but Zeus was she relieved not to be in Hayden's position.

"Can you just agree so we can get on with it?!"

Jocelyn broke the silence, to Piper's relief.

Hayden turned shockingly to his older sister, prompting her to explain with a yawn.

"Processing the potential future is exhausting, never mind the trek to get here so urgently after. And we all need a break to rest before we dive into action. So, the sooner you agree, the sooner we can establish the plan and prepare for it accordingly."

Hayden sighed, looking to his mother, and finally nodded. He turned around to Tristan, Dylan, Kyril and Zayne, decision finally made.

"We are at your disposal."

LIV

They had been drugging her.

Even that revelation took too long to string together. Her mind refused to contemplate the equivalent of the malicious action in the immortal sense any further.

She hadn't compiled one coherent thought in a while.

It hurt her skull to even comprehend that.

Accepting her need to keep her eyes closed and conserve her strength, Liv powered through. This meant it was soon time for her captors to once again poison her, do whatever they were doing to keep her immobile, and soon.

She didn't have much time left before she re-entered oblivion.

At the revelation and acceptance of her impending doom, one small tear slid down Liv's cheek.

Avoiding panic, instead she tried to absorb any power she had to give, to preserve it, when a small twinkle flashed through her bracelet.

She saw home.

Liv managed to smile, delusion forcing her memory to glue the vision in her mind.

But she couldn't remember it. She was too weak.

Liv fought again, draining one more ounce of power for the light. Sparingly used, but just enough for another twinkle.

Stars sparkled momentarily before falling off the wall.

Liv wasn't able to absorb the stag's crest before it disappeared.

She was so depleted. Another tear slid down her face as she closed her eyes and tried to imagine the crest that had just flashed across the wall, in hopes of remembering it for strength in the future.

For anything to leverage in the future, if she had one at all.

Liv knew it would require anything and everything to help her survive this battle, needing to be reminded of her little piece of home, purity among such dark savages in an unrecognizable world.

REI

Rei never thought he'd see the day that he, Elite of the Security Pillar, would be listening to Dark Gods for strategy and guidance in his position.

Did they count as Dark Gods if they supported a Pure Elite?

Their appearances certainly disqualified them from that luxury.

Rei studied Tristan, practically identical to his sister, Giselle. The only differences were their mischevious eyes, where his gleamed amber while hers had sparkled aquamarine, and being separated by shadowed hair where hers had shone.

He had once been tasked to protect her like he had been assigned Liv. Now, he had failed twice.

Rei shook his head, refusing to follow the dark path of regret. That didn't bring Giselle back and it certainly would not bring Liv back, either.

The only difference was that he had survived Tristan's scowls and mistrust over the years – for Tristan was a child at the beginning and a stranger in his adult years until this past season.

And now he was listening to this stranger-child's advice.

But Hayden?

Rei would send himself to the Underworld, beg Hades to grant him entrance, before he allowed himself to exist with the mistrust of his brother, his king.

Peyton placed a warm hand on his shoulder, bringing him back to the room filled with leather, whiskey and anxiety. She knew how Tristan haunted him.

She raised a brow, insinuating the unspoken question – *are you okay?*

Rei gulped before nodding 'yes' but grabbed her hand anyways.

Holding it kept him anchored to the present, instead of running through a past filled with mistakes.

"As we've agreed, the hardest part will be finding an entrance. Especially if trying to herd a large army of thousands." Kyril stated, pulling his hand out of his leather jacket's pocket to accept a hot cup of coffee from Dylan.

It was almost sunrise. The deities had switched from whiskey and wine to coffee and tea.

Only Joss had slept. And even still, she tossed and turned in an angry slumber.

"So, we keep the troops at a distance and send a limited search party to determine the exact whereabouts of the entrance." Peyton proposed, taking a sip of her latte.

"Who goes in the search party?" Rei agreed, taking a breath and hoping for dear Zeus, Hayden would accept what the majority ruled.

"Tristan and Rei." Daphne interjected first. Her monotone decision acted as if she were back in a trance.

Everyone turned to Hayden except Tristan – his eyes remained on Rei.

Rei knew if Daphne had proactively participated, it was for a deliberate reason and opposing would ensure consequences. But he also knew her participation could not alter the natural response from others, so he had to express his hesitation either way.

Hayden began to object; Rei could see the angst swirling in the king's mind. But before his highness could begin his deposition for being included in the search party, the Security Elite cut him off.

"Daphne, if Kronos is residing with Arlo at the Dark Gods' headquarters, surely Hayden should be present? His powers are the closest in match?"

Rei saw Tristan roll his eyes in response, setting his reasonable demeanor on defense.

"Kronos is the most powerful deity in our history. Do you think you could defeat him, Tristan?"

Joss rolled up from the couch, lazily. "If all goes to plan, neither Tristan or you will need to confront Kronos during this rescue."

"If all goes to plan," Rei reiterated before adding sarcastically, "*that* sounds promising."

"If all does *not* go to plan," Tristan added with a challenge, "I would be *honored* to sacrifice myself against Kronos on behalf of my Element Elite. You can run free, Rei."

Rei glared at Tristan, refusing to accept the bait, so added lightheartedly, "And when you are inevitably sent to the Underworld, Tristan, I will happily step in and finish the job for you on behalf of your Element Elite, and Hayden, our king…we'll serve crème brulee and whisky at your memorial."

"Well, at least a 'Hail Mary' plan has been established." Tristan rebutted jokingly.

To others in the room, a kindhearted banter took place. Yet for these two, it rooted much deeper.

LIV

Did she actually have a hangover?

Liv groaned, although she really wanted to scream.

A hue of green penetrated the darkness of her mind.

Panic and terror filled her core to find out why.

Liv took a breath, focusing first on the cool stone against her pounding headache before opening her eye.

Her gaze followed the light to a pair of lantern green eyes.

A snake.

The eyes penetrated her own, burning the cornia before she slammed her lid closed. She was too weak to cover her head with her arm.

Her weakness would be her demise.

A bolt of pain grasped onto her skull and green filled the room, brighter, and demanding Liv's attention, even through her masked sight.

The burn was constant, and after the shock of the initial intensity, Liv discovered it wasn't much more than what she already felt, just another level of pain to tolerate.

Who was it?

The smell was familiar.

Liv had smelled it before.

Cardamom…

Trembling, Liv whispered, "Who are you?"

She wasn't sure if she had meant to direct it loud enough for her captor to respond. She was past control of her thoughts, actions and bodily moment.

But as soon as she heard the voice vibrate toward her, she regretted the question, the uncontrollable wonder, immediately.

Melodically and seductively, the snake replied to her outburst with a low growl.

"Your worst nightmare."

THREE

LIV

When the image of a lakeside cabin flashed in her mind, Liv silently screamed herself awake.

And when she came to consciousness, Liv saw green, the most terrifying green – an alert and a warning.

Not the serene green found in nature, painted on moss and crystalizing from fir trees, but a vibrant, cruel green – that of weeds, of a poison draining the plants and its roots into nothingness.

Liv yearned for blackness – any other desolate, dark hue would be preferred to this.

Monsters were angels in masks compared to this.

She felt a golden warmth from beyond, but she knew light would only bring pain.

Liv tried to lift her head only to drop it against the concrete floor immediately after, begging for the impact to knock her into the abyss again. But upon attempt, she couldn't move an inch above the ground.

Instead, she crushed her eyelids together, fighting against the light.

Because now, Liv preferred the obscurity.

TRISTAN

Rei and Tristan had circled the last known landmark identified as the entrance to the Dark Gods' quarters, confirmed true by Zayne's use no more than three days ago.

Since then, it had been relocated.

With more Dark Gods proving untrustworthy, the frequency with which Arlo would want and be able to move the headquarters, especially with Kronos's powers by his side, was unknown, becoming an endless chase.

They were so royally fucked.

After a sleepless night hosting more Pure Gods than Tristan ever wished to entertain under his roof, he had set off for Scotland once again.

This time, he brought more allies than he wanted.

Meaning all from the night before accompanied him but Peyton, who flew directly to Silas so the two could organize the troops and bring them across the Loch to set up camp.

Meaning after several tantrums from Hayden and promises made to the king to report back before any actions were taken, Rei and Tristan had finally ventured to investigate the standing stones and determine if Zayne's reports were accurate.

Tristan originally hoped they would be able to establish an entrance *and* report back before the troops arrived. He had not stopped believing it was in their best interest to keep numbers small. But alas, now having failed to open the Dark God's quarters, let alone *find* the entrance, his mind was shifting – perhaps they would need the bodies simply to re-locate the fortress in this mystical land.

He refused to believe that *the world* would become an optional development.

Tristan re-tied his grey and maroon plaid scarf around his neck, zipping his leather jacket up as the wind cursed against his skin. It was as if he heard Kronos's personal whispers through the howling air, demanding he leave at once. He pulled his beanie down further over his ears as he walked over to Rei.

"Any luck?" Tristan asked out of social obligation; he already knew the answer.

Rei shook his head, before looking back one last time at the standing stones.

Tristan noticed Rei also received some sort of chill, or warning, because the Security Elite pulled his pale blue trench tighter before turning back and walking past him, away from the landmark. Tristan followed.

"We'll have to figure out a way to find the entrance, reveal it, and break through to the castle without alerting any guards." Tristan observed, trailing behind Rei down the hill. "Clearly, I've been banned from the premise or worse it's been relocated, but either way, those we can trust are no longer receiving the invitations to the Dark Gods' headquarters."

"So, what do you propose we do?" Rei asked, still marching back toward camp.

Tristan picked up his pace to keep up with his conspirator before deliberating their next move.

"We'll need to inquire about the new location and determine where it's located." Tristan considered aloud.

"And if it still does not reveal itself?" Rei challenged, yet again picking up his pace.

Tristan understood, so did not complain. They had wasted a day with this unsuccessful venture. They could not waste another.

A day, *a minute,* could be the difference between Liv existing in this world or the Under one.

"Then we'll need to find a Dark God to let us in." Tristan stated, although he did not like the last-resort option. With a sigh, he ran his hand through his messy ink hair and whispered doubtfully, "But, Zeus knows who would be desperate enough for that…"

Rei turned back with a smirk, a mischievous thought forming in his mind.

"Cleo? If you or Hayden convinced her of your love. Or both. A simple 'blame it on the hypnosis done by Liv' should suffice…"

"Haha, funny." Tristan joked, rolling his eyes.

However, a pause comfortably settled into the land, long enough for Tristan to contemplate the absurd proposition.

She was his cousin, but they *had* been friends, *genuine* friends, to an extent outside of obligatory family relations. At least what he suspected was true on her end, since he always bore the guilty conscience of survival instincts as his true motive. And if not Cleo, perhaps one of her best friends, Elsa or Brie.

Tristan turned back to glance at the ancient standing stones one last time. The dark rocks planted horizontally into the ground looked ominous with the dark, cloudy sky surrounding the massive structures. They always represented terror, guise and despair, and for him, a cruel obligation to endure.

He was almost thankful they no longer symbolized the entrance. At least one terrible part of his life could remain in the past.

Don't think that. Tristan scowled. *Don't be happy that we aren't closer to helping Liv.*

And that was the ongoing battle that would now take part in his head.

Could he return to the dark soul he once was for the sake of the pure woman he now loved?

LIV

Her eyes flittered half-open.

She looked around the darkness, trying to distinguish any clues to determine where she woke up but all she saw was black. She felt as if still in a deep sleep, a piece of herself somehow missing in this cruel dreamland.

Fighting the agony, Liv stretched her right arm, trying to reach some-thing, *anything,* that might shed light to what was happening to her. Upon finding nothing, she took a breath and stretched her fingers out with a wince, hoping to find a wall to help guide her sight.

Had she always felt this way? Disoriented and with no memory of her days? It seemed a lifetime ago she had been at Puerdios with her friends. How she longed to once again reunite with Peyton, Rei, Piper and Tristan. Hades, she would even be thankful to be stuck in a classroom with Cleo, if it meant she didn't reside in this darker version of the Underworld.

Something was missing. In this dungeon, she knew a piece of her was missing.

Obscurity blurred her thoughts when she tried to remember what part was lost.

She was so tired. Her head ached with her minimal thoughts, but she needed clarity.

Green eyes caught her attention. Whether in the flesh, an illusion or a memory, they flashed at the other end of the space – the cell.

Dark Gods.

Radical Dark Gods.

Like two buckles fastening together, something clicked. A bridge connected two distant lands over a sea.

This wasn't a dream. This was a nightmare.

And with her obvious frailty, they must have been poisoning her – diluting her strength, her power, her being, her soul.

Could she cast a protective spell? At the first attempt, her head pounded as if she had been struck in the skull with a hammer.

Liv needed air. She needed to clear her mind. She needed a break from this never-ending hell.

She refused to look back toward the green eyes, because imaginary or not, she didn't want to risk it if that magic was the influence to her weakness. But she knew there was nowhere else to look in the darkness.

Instead, Liv closed her eyes and imagined being outside, a sense of calm erupting as she pretended to lie in a hilly field under the night sky.

The clammy, cold stone faded away. She smelled the sweet scent of grass, forcing her body to believe it was gently supported by the earth's terrain. With a soft breeze passing by, grasshoppers, crickets and birds softly chirped nature's tune in the ambient background. And above her, sparkled the most mesmerizing artwork of all – stars and constellations painted in the sky – telling the stories of heroic deities and myths of the past with each pattern. Her favorite, the brightest star of all, shining so loudly so it could be the light Liv needed to guide her out of the darkness.

Liv gasped, eyes breaking open.

A connection.

She felt a connection.

A connection Liv didn't realize was there before.

HAYDEN

Ollie.

Outside of his tent, looking at her constellation, Hayden could feel her.

She's alive.

And he could *locate* her.

Liv's in Scotland, near the Storr.

Hayden took his first true breath of relief since her capture. But the peace did not last long as he launched himself toward Rei's juxtaposing tent immediately after.

"Rei, Liv signaled to me. She's near the Storr. I have her location now, we can send troops to rescue her..."

"Hayden, one moment." Rei yawned, motioning to light his quarters before standing up. "You've located Liv? That's great news."

With the light, Hayden could make out another sun-kissed blonde head in Rei's bed.

Hayden coughed. "Apologies, Peyton."

"We've been through way too much to qualify *this* as a flustered moment." Peyton replied unfazed, swiftly jumping out of her bed with a mocking smile, "Feel better now, your majesty? Officially reporting for duty."

"The Storr you said?" Rei clarified, "Did her signal include an entrance?"

"That's not how it works." Hayden replied. "But that's where she is. We're on the wrong island."

"I'll grab Tristan." Peyton offered, "He might already know the entrance to that location."

She grabbed her navy and green tartan printed coat to cover her matching flannel pajamas and flew off into the night.

Peyton had only arrived that evening with Silas's troops. He knew she was exhausted, they *all* were. Yet, he hoped this rush of adrenaline would help them push through another day.

Hayden sighed, anticipation building in his core as he sat down on Rei's leather stool, near a mahogany wood table with maps of the world piled across it.

Rei took his cue and removed all maps but one. As Rei efficiently organized the spare maps back into the cabinet behind him, Hayden stared at the one that remained: Isle of the Skye.

"Perhaps we don't give Arlo enough credit." Rei stated dryly. "Visiting the last-known camp is sleuth enough – we would have never expected them to return to a previous headquarters after vacating it."

"This screams Kronos." Hayden replied, explaining with one concept as he tapped his head and whispered, "Mindgames."

The two stared at the map in silence, both dreading the possibilities of what they could soon face.

Finally, Hayden exhaled, taking off his olive-green field jacket and revealing a grey henley that complemented his navy jeans and bronze combat boots. Sitting down, he massaged his temples trying to process the newest lead.

"Care for coffee?" Rei sighed, throwing on a mustard yellow sweater to cover his shirtless choice of sleepwear, although it matched his sweats of the same color. "It's going to be another long night."

"Yes, thank you." Hayden whispered.

He could still feel Liv, a connection tying him to her – and yet it didn't help his topography skills in the least. As Rei handed him a warm mug, Hayden continued penetrating any form of power down the line to his soul mate, whatever remained in his growing depletion, while still unsuccessfully trying to find the Storr on the map before him. If they would simply let him guide them to her…

"Here." Peyton tapped, popping up from behind.

"Why should I have even bothered searching without you?" Hayden muttered with a sigh, smiling with appreciation. "Thank you."

He looked around the room to find Tristan leaning across the table in his go-to leather jacket, accompanied by Piper peaking over his shoulder and wearing a metallic gold suit.

"Even if it's the same location, they've definitely created a different entrance for security measures." Tristan scoffed. "Without that confirmed, our hands are strapped."

Silence filled the room.

Piper nudged Tristan.

"… Your majesty." He added with a sneer.

Ignoring Tristan's clearly heartfelt loyalty, Hayden returned his eyes to the map.

"They moved their campground within three days. What if they continue to move at such a rapid pace? Now is our best chance of attack." Delusion spread over the king's eyes as he repeatedly looked around the location for an entrance clue, a never-ending circle growing increasingly more frustrating with each round.

"Hayden, don't make Liv a new martyr to launch one thousand ships." Rei softly advised. "Not today."

Hayden stared at Rei, knowing his Elite made a valid point. He couldn't selfishly send his men on a suicide mission for Ollie. And worse, if the Dark Gods sensed an attack, they could easily send her to the Underworld in spite.

"So we don't send an army." Hayden conceded. "Instead, we sneak into the fortress."

"And how do you propose we do that, without knowledge of any entrance?" Tristan challenged.

"Well, it seems it's time to prove yourself useful, Tristan."

PIPER

As soon as they had been dismissed, she chased after Tristan as he departed the tent. The wind howled, as if calling to wolves that would never come.

"Hey. Hey!" She squealed, trying to keep his pace. "Tristan, wait!"

Had her king just served Tristan a death wish? Was losing him really equivalent to an army squad?

She shook her head, aghast that she could have such a thought. Of course, one body was better than twenty – but Tristan, he was worth more than that.

His council and connections had to be worth more to them, she clarified in her mind.

She could feel the kettle ready to boil as she watched him simultaneously try to extinguish the flame as he paced ahead. Piper started jogging to clear the growing distance.

Finally running up to him, Piper grabbed his shoulder. "Tristan…"

He swung his arm to remove her grasp, but fortunately stopped to hear her out – or more so to see what she wanted.

Piper took a deep breath, trying to summon the courage to say something. To figure out how she may be able to help Tristan, or at least try and be there for her friend before he ventured off into the unknown. She gulped, ignoring her last thought that this might be the last time she saw him.

Unsteadily, Piper tried to lower her body to make eye contact with his gaze on the ground. When she caught it, she couldn't help but shyly grin.

And oh, to see a spark of mischief sparkle in his eyes, made her sadly chuckle as she stood back up, bringing his gaze along with her to eye level.

"Are you okay?" She finally whispered, taking a cautious step toward him.

He allowed it, but his jaw tensed at the question. He looked off into the distance again.

"Hey," Piper finally filled the space between him, pulling him into a hug. "We'll figure this out. We can handle this." She hoped her trembling voice sounded strong enough to mask the worry and fear. And she was too thankful he couldn't see her wide eyes.

"Piper," he whispered melodically, "Piper, thank you."

He sighed and held her close. She felt protected within his arms – the worry seemed to fade away in his embrace. She closed her eyes, taking a deep breath and absorbing his scent – cinnamon and peat.

Piper could almost hear the soothing sound of a crackling fire emanating from his touch.

Tristan began to remove Piper's arms from around his neck, "But, you cannot come with me, this is something I must do on my own."

Piper's eyes went wide again.

"But what if Cleo-"

"Cleo can do many things. It's not worth your time to craft up nightmares of the unknown." Tristan kept Piper's hand in his own, radiating heat to burn her doubts away.

"If I'm there, even in the shadows, at least I could help if anything went wrong. Or, be aware of a starting point of where to look for you. Or know what happened, that something happened, *if* something happened..."

"You are starting to make me doubt my own powers. Do you really think I'll be so badly equipped to protect myself against *Cleo?*" Tristan's eyes sparkled with humor, but Piper could see that underneath was sooted kindling trying to remain strong.

"I know you can defeat Cleo." Piper stated blankly. "I worry that Cleo won't remain true to her word and instead of meeting independently, may bring reinforcements to outnumber you..."

"That's crafting up nightmares again Piper, which I thought we had already discussed."

Piper bit her lip, fighting against the insecurities that grew from her own self-doubt to worry for her friend.

Tristan put both hands on her shoulders, "We both know the best way to find Cleo and get her to share the information we need is for me to go alone."

"I don't have to be *there* when you meet up with her, Tristan…" Piper stared at the ground, knowing she wouldn't get Tristan to change his mind, but needing to make sure she tried every angle and offered any alternative to convince him nonetheless, so she would have no doubts in her efforts if he never came back…

A gentle hand lifted her chin, fiery eyes met her glacier ones, melting them instantly.

"In order to convince Cleo of anything Piper, I'm going to have to turn into someone I'm not proud of – a deity I don't want you seeing or ever associating with me."

"Tristan-"

"No, Piper. You don't get it. I may have to push boundaries, do unthinkable things and say untrue words poisoned with darkness. I can't have you see this side of me."

Piper darkly laughed.

Tristan cocked his head curiously.

"I was only going to remind you that we've known each other for years, Tristan… so I already know that you can be a huge dick."

Tristan eyes went wide with a brief pause before he started chuckling and replied calmly, "Perhaps I'm a bad influence on you after all – you just insulted me and enjoyed it."

Even when caught off guard, his voice was intoxicating. His hand still remained on her shoulders. They were only a few inches apart.

Before thinking, Piper whispered the first thought that came to her head. "Perhaps I'm still in need of a bad influence."

Her jaw dropped as soon as the words left her mouth. She immediately looked up, anxious to see Tristan's response. Her heart was pounding so hard, she worried it would erupt from her chest.

But Tristan's face looked raw, genuine, sad and confused. Before she could apologize or explain that she was kidding, he pulled her into a desperate hug.

And she understood.

With a sad smile, Piper whispered, "Please be safe. And come back."

HAYDEN

He heard light steps gently glide closer behind him – elegant, soft and gentle.

He also knew that if he showed any recognition of Piper behind him, she very well would trip, freeze or topple over. So instead, he stared into the night sky, praying that whatever he had would be enough for Ollie to survive.

And Hayden continued to focus on the view above until he felt heat to his left and gold silk accommodating itself to the rocky-surfaced seat. He smiled. Piper was always her best form when nobody was watching – a true rarity – and he was positive he would never find another genuine soul like her for his eternal life.

"Tristan left." Piper nodded, following Hayden's gaze to the sky. Her high-pitched voice remained quiet with the statement.

"He'll be back." Hayden confirmed, still focusing on the world above.

"I know." Piper replied, although not as confidently as her previous statement. "I have a favor to ask – possibly not even a favor and I, I don't ask for much – and I know this is not the right time…"

"Piper, we're friends. I would be happy to oblige." Hayden gently interrupted. "What can I do?"

He felt her wrestle with the idea.

"If Tristan succeeds, is there any way you could promise to… treat him like our inner circle – not necessarily nice, but just like one of us?" She blurted out.

Hayden froze. He wasn't sure if he should chuckle at the request or seriously contemplate whether he could realistically be respectful toward Tristan before making a promise to the purest deity he knew.

"It would make my life much easier, and Liv's – when she returns."

Hayden tensed at the following statement.

"Your majesty…" Piper started sadly, grabbing Hayden's arm.

"Hayden." Hayden corrected, only briefly turning to look at Piper before returning to the stars. "And yes. I'll try."

Out of the corner of his eyes, he saw Piper nod to herself in accomplishment. Another moment passed before he heard her mousy voice once again.

"You felt her tonight." Piper stated, not succumbing to the offer of using his majesty's informal name, but moving forward cordially. "Can you still feel her?"

"Yes." Hayden whispered. He continued pulsing feelings, power, emotion, and strength – anything and everything that he could – through the bond. It was diminishing, dissolving once again. And he was weakening, clawing onto a tie that was breaking. He had sent all of his power to her – and did not have much more to share before he too, would be depleted.

He felt Piper's gaze move back up to the night sky. Her arm still remained encircled around his for support.

This time, she remained quiet.

With all of his might, Hayden sent one final blast of power to Ollie, praying to Zeus that it be the last thing he had control of doing for now to ensure his love's survival.

Reactively, he grabbed his torso and curled over, vomiting onto the grassy field. Beads of sweat glistened down his temple.

Hayden gratefully realized Piper hadn't let go of his arm, acting as an anchor he desperately needed to remain connected to this land while fighting the darkness. And as he pathetically leaned against his legs, head between his knees, fighting his pounding headache and trying to focus on recovering, he witnessed the debris of his sickness below vanish when a cold compress pressed gently against his neck.

After some time, Hayden finally regained enough strength to sit upright once again. Piper was already staring back up at the sky, so he mimicked her gaze to the only other sight that could soothe him as much as Piper tried – Ollie's constellation.

The cold compress dissolved, but her arm remained sturdily around his for support.

And they sat in silence, together, yet still individually alone.

LIV

"Did she ever tell you about our affair, our child?"

Liv gasped awake.

She was in a cell. She had been captured by the Dark Gods. She needed to escape. She…

She was more cognizant than she had felt in… months.

Liv could feel power drumming in her body. For once, she wasn't deplenished of power. But how?

"Oh, look who's finally awake." A tartly sweet voice echoed through the cave.

Liv knew that voice. She held back a tear.

She wanted to *spit* at her uncle.

"Why are you even doing this!?" She cried.

"Eat." Arlo pushed an untouched plate in Liv's direction.

Instead of accepting the much-needed nutrition, Liv sat upright and ignored it. She needed answers – or at least any clues that could help her escape. She ignored the green glow that emitted behind her uncle, knowing she didn't have much time of clarity.

"We're much nicer to our prisoners – look, tonight you're getting steak, vegetables and potatoes – would you prefer we feed you only bread instead?"

Arlo's smile was laced with venom, his eyes looking down to her as his Roman nose remained high in the air.

"Answer my questions and I'll enjoy my meal." Liv proposed weakly. "One bite per answer."

"Okay, I'll assuage your request. But only because I'm curious how many questions you'll be able to get to after the first bite."

"Why are you doing this?" Liv repeated.

"Kidnap you? I wanted a nice family reunion. Get to know my niece." Arlo dryly retorted. He nodded to Liv's plate. "Eat."

"You didn't answer my question." Liv challenged.

"I did. You'll have to ask another question to clarify what you *really* want to know."

Liv contemplated his response, deciding it didn't sound *too* unreasonable. She took a small bite. A tiny bite for an insignificant response.

"I mean the Dark Gods. Why are you a radical supporter? You have no legacy. Once you're defeated…"

Even with the small bite, Liv could already feel the poison begin to seep through her veins, she didn't have much time. She started feeling sick to her stomach, a new development to the never-ending potential of her captor's cruelty.

"You won't have anyone to continue the family's dark pastime…. it'll be as if you and your cause-never-existed…" Liv slurred the last part. It was getting tougher to keep her eyes open.

"That is exactly why I am doing this!" Arlo roared. "Do you not know?"

"What?" Liv murmured, swaying. She was so tired.

"Another bite."

She obliged, she was too weak to fight.

"Did your beloved's mother not tell you about our affair, *our child*?"

Liv tried with all of her non-existent strength to stay awake, to stay strong. She wanted to ask what Arlo meant by a child, but more about the term beloved. Why had he dared to use such a ambiguous term before her?

So, amidst the story or falsehoods Arlo was eager to tell, Liv succumbed to the darkness once again.

And in her dreams, Liv continued to see the lantern green eyes of the snake, subconsciously knowing he was watching her, constantly seeping poison into her veins.

DAPHNE

Hayden abruptly entered his mother's tent.

However, the action could never *truly* be unexpected when Daphne was involved. Fortunately as a boy, he had learned to knock for others from his father's chidings.

"We are *losing* her." He clenched his jaw, moving in closer to where Daphne sat at her desk, patiently waiting for her son's arrival.

She remained silent, instead focusing on writing correspondence to her Pillar Heads.

"How much longer until we move, Mother?" He commanded.

Daphne finally sighed, turning to her son.

He *knew* she couldn't tell him. For the outcome she saw, Daphne couldn't venture away from her visions – this one included.

"Hayden, we've been over this..."

"To leave me in the dark? To leave Ollie in the dark?" Hayden shouted. "How am I supposed to trust your visions if I don't know what they entail?"

"You have to trust that I love you." Daphne pushed, already knowing the internal struggle he faced. The next thought that would leave his mouth.

"I trusted you to keep us safe once before." Hayden spat. "And then I was forced to become king."

"It was the best possible outcome." Daphne whispered after a pause, a stoned poise taking over her body, emotionless. She couldn't give any insights or clues away now.

Even with the anticipation of it coming, hearing her son's doubt in her abilities stung. Instead, she reminded herself she should be proud.

Because trusting a deity was the same as befriending your enemy. *She* had taught him that.

And if it weren't for falling in love with a mortal, Hayden would have had greater darkness within him if he had nobody to turn to, like herself. Their paths had paralleled, she knew precisely what pain he was going through. She had experienced it two-fold, and worse.

But that mortal was a deity now. And she had been captured.

So, he was alone again, allowing an opportunity for the darkness to return and take over his soul.

And only Daphne had control of the outcome now.

REI

He couldn't sleep.

Peyton was snoring.

Nothing felt right.

With a sigh, Rei gently kissed his sleeping beauty on the forehead, holding in a laugh as he took her current state, mouth wide open.

Only Peyton would manage to discover how to snore with her mouth *open.*

If she were ever kidnapped...

His fists clenched at the thought. He could only imagine the hell his friend was currently living in.

And that's why he got out of bed.

He grabbed his brown anorak and headed outside.

The one thing Rei hated was being static. Unable to act on what he *really* wanted to do. He took it as a growing mechanism, a life challenge at the irony of his position – mostly taking orders, needing to be strategic with all tasks assigned.

Precisely the reason why he was so irritated his entire time in Oregon while secretly watching over Liv.

Rei laughed aloud. How he would kill a Chimera to return to that time. Liv had been safe, Hayden was only mildly cautious and mostly naive, and Peyton enjoyed the same mission.

How he longed to return to the ease of her nighttime visits, when anytime she had wanted to spend time with Rei, all she needed to do was claim she was staying at the sorority house but instead meet him in the tree outside her dorm as he watched over Liv. Those nights had single handedly healed them.

And the only considerate threat was Finn – sand compared to rocky cliffs on a storming beach.

Now, they were dealing with Kronos. Their maker. Their destroyer.

And their plan was to hope an infant deity could swoon another infant deity into stupidly revealing the entrance to her people's fortress.

The whole thing was idiotic.

Rei sighed, continuing to walk downhill.

But he too, was once idiotic. When he had actually believed Cleo was innocent from her blind admiration for Hayden, that she would remain loyal to the crown despite her crush's heart belonging to another. He had blackened out what it felt like to be heartbrokenly destroyed.

When Peyton had hinted to a growing affiliation to the Dark God cause, Rei essentially escorted her to the Dark ones himself by casting her out and becoming an extreme Pure God. Never trying once to understand why she was leaning toward their morals.

Another mistake at his cost.

Thank Zeus Peyton had a more forgiving heart than he and could always see the bigger picture as opposed to black and white.

For the remainder of his walk, Rei wandered mindlessly, until he stumbled upon Hayden's tent and the owner sitting outside, staring at the stars.

"You look like shit." Rei dryly observed, sitting next to his friend, his brother, his king.

"I'll improve my wellness routine once Liv's back." Hayden retorted back, before sighing and rubbing his eyes. "It's been a *night*."

"No, it's been a *week*." Rei corrected, offering Hayden a flask. "But, you're depleted. You have to take care of yourself."

Hayden took a swig, passing it back to Rei to sip as well.

The whisky immediately warmed his body as it burned down his throat.

"Silver lining, the alcohol is good here." Rei joked, taking another dose before shifting his gaze to Hayden after a silent response.

Hayden had returned to staring at the night sky.

His eyes were hollow, skin pale. If Kronos arrived now, he could essentially pinch Hayden and get their king to submit to whatever he desired.

"Hayden. You have to rein it in." Rei sighed, "I say this not only as your Elite, but as your brother."

"I have to give Liv her best chance of survival." Hayden replied, his voice monotone.

"Exactly. You have to give Liv her best chance of survival." Rei agreed, "And as the only one who can defeat Kronos, you being unable to fight him really unbalances our success rate for this rescue."

Hayden remained silent, still focusing on Ollie's constellation.

Rei paused to give his friend the time to process his internal demons.

Finally, Hayden spoke.

"You remember when you and Peyton were apart?"

"I, like you, was not my best self." Rei admitted curtly.

"I granted you years of cutting down trees and gallivanting in the wilderness – whatever you needed. A distraction, a way to exert pent-up anger, think, reflect, heal. Time… to figure things out."

"I, and the Pacific Northwest, thank Zeus she came to her senses." Rei turned to Hayden. "But I remember those times. The struggle, the pain, the inability to control the other being and circumstance."

Another pause.

"Sometimes, I wish I was normal." Hayden admitted.

He whispered it so quietly that Rei had to take a moment to make sure he had actually heard the words leave his friend's mouth.

"Don't all good leaders?" Rei huffed.

If he let Hayden give in to the sinking sand, it would be much harder to pull him out.

Hayden finally left the stars and came back down to earth, eyeing Rei while simultaneously ignoring him.

"I don't have the opportunity to run away for a month – do reckless shit to numb the pain. I can't even run off and feel like I'm doing something to get her back. And I already know you'd have my head if I asked again for a personal rescue attempt."

"You're finally catching on." Rei observed dryly, with a soft laugh.

Well, at least one thing had cemented in his thick, royal brain.

Hayden looked at the ground, gently kicking a rock from the dirt into the grass ahead. "Sometimes I wonder how it would be, if I weren't king. If we weren't gods and our powers were stripped." He looked off to the edge of a forest on his right, the birch trees softly bristling with branches moving from a light breeze. "Would we stop kidnapping one another's loved ones or refrain from destroying good people by tearing apart their communities? I'm not saying peace, I'm not naive. But the deception, backstabbing, the massacre – would it be reduced among equals?"

Rei amused the notion, if anything for the sanity of his king, before his conscience reminded him that it wasn't the world they existed in, so theoretically there wasn't a point in wasting time debating dreams.

"It would be a lovely sight, a world where everyone was treated with respect." He faced Hayden, unsure how his friend would react to the harsh reality, "But even then, you wouldn't be able to guarantee Liv's safety."

Hayden nodded hesitantly in agreement.

In these moments, Rei was reminded that his king was still just a boy – a young man looking for guidance, influenced by those around him – someone with an open mind but who also lost his father too soon.

"I guess I should appreciate the ability to worry about her for now. That's better than having nobody to worry about at all." Hayden finally admitted, shrugging as he ran his hand through his hair.

"Now, that's the Hayden I adore and loathe." Rei smiled, slapping his king on the back. "Let's go."

LIV

"You need to eat." Arlo spat.

"Why?" Liv replied, hoarse. Her body looked like a corpse. She was stronger, yet weaker all the same.

"You aren't fully immortal yet, niece." Arlo hissed. "You need sustenance or else you will wither away, demi-god."

"Then, I wither away." Liv coughed. She couldn't remember the last meal she had that involved more than two bites, anyway.

"Have you already no fight left?" Arlo asked, approaching Liv and slamming his face into her sight. "You're weaker than I hoped, Olivia. Once upon a time, you showed such bravery. Is it no longer worth our time holding you hostage?"

"Was it ever worth your time?" Liv asked aloud, rhetorically.

She remained on the floor. Arlo didn't respond.

"Aside from torturing your niece, of course – which obviously cannot be the reason since this is only the second time I have seen you since my arrival." Liv rolled onto her back, closing her eyes first and pausing, until slowly her eyebrows scrunched together as she thought about it more.

Her question was met with silence.

Perhaps she was finally getting under her uncle's skin. Perhaps she no longer cared.

"Do you have someone else do your bidding so you can watch without consequence?" Liv tried to lift herself up, away from Arlo, but she was too weak to move more than merely propping her body weight against an angled arm.

The motion seemed to please Arlo, because he stood up before her. He was wearing a tailored brown suit layered with a leather bomber jacket. Liv's clothes were now of the same color, although originally the fabric had been cream. She despised to find such a repulsing commonality with her kin. Disgust began flaming in her core.

She looked up and met his gaze with pure hatred, "If that's the case, my uncle is a sadistic coward."

"Perhaps a coward, and perhaps a sadist – but not combined." Arlo replied with a wicked grin. "And it ruins the fun of torturing my niece if she willingly chooses to kill herself. So eat." He kicked the plate closer to Liv, watching as she first winced before slowly recoiling away from the food.

"Ah, you still think the food is poisoned. Magically enchanted to weaken you." Arlo concluded with a clap. "Perhaps you do have some fight left in you, after all."

And with a malicious chuckle, he departed the cell.

Liv took a look at the plated meal before her, and after taking a whiff of the stew she immediately retched before passing out once again.

A sliver of light grew in the distance.

Liv cracked open one eye to find a torched flame floating through the air, with a hooded head behind it. As it approached, the thing appeared to have white eyes, but no irises or pupils – just an eerily glowing blank canvas for means of sight.

"You've been invited to dinner." Echoed a voice near the door.

Liv had become so enchanted by the hooded figure; she hadn't noticed Arlo standing by the entrance. He had changed into a silk burgundy suit with a massive fur-trimmed, suede black coat.

"By who?" She sneered, before turning her attention back to the dark creature. It was leaning over her, foreboding. Heat radiated from it, and flames began forming inside her body, as if she were becoming an eternal inferno.

"Does it really matter?" Arlo challenged back, "You'd be too weak to fight them anyway – which by the way, I wouldn't try tonight – or with your little friend." He nodded to the gremlin figure.

The hooded creature stuck its finger into Liv's lock and turned it until her chains clicked and dissolved.

She was free.

Liv lifted her hands in front of her, trying to make out her limbs. She was weak, but her arms felt like feathers now that they no longer carried the weight of the metal cuffs.

"Come now. We don't have all night." Arlo waved impatiently.

Liv cautiously put her hand to the cell's stone wall, using it as leverage to support her body weight as she attempted to stand.

The last she time she had fully stood upright had been the last day she saw the sun.

Liv took an apprehensive step forward, making sure she remained balanced. Her legs felt like twigs.

When I do build my strength, I'll need to start doing leg lifts or squats if I ever want to escape... she dryly reminded herself. *Where's Rei for grueling training when I actually need him.*

Another step.

And another.

Two steps.

And another two.

Until she finally made it to Arlo by the entrance, stepping into the torched light.

He didn't move. He didn't say a word. He just stood there.

And after a moment of silence, Liv thought this had to be another sick trick of her uncle's and that he would send her back to her chains after a laugh.

She waited for his mouth to curl upward, but it remained stoic. Not until looking her up and down when Arlo's facial reaction turned into wicked loathing.

"Olivia, do you have any etiquette?" He finally asked, cruelly. "You cannot dine with Kronos himself looking like a dead weed."

"Apologies, it seems I was too preoccupied to visit the garden for a rose." Liv sarcastically replied. But her tone didn't deliver as she had imagined in her mind.

Even her voice sounded like dirt.

Instead, she continued to stare at Arlo, challenging him to care – because she sure in Hades didn't.

"Fine." Arlo opened the door to lead the way to dinner.

Liv stepped through the door wearily, anxiously – it took everything in her control to appear discontented while eagerly beginning to build a map of the prison inside her head.

What would Rei notice?

As Liv went through the threshold, an invisible cool breeze misted over her body. The heavier weight in fabric gave her the first signal that Arlo had enchanted her. She looked down, now sporting an olive-green silk gown with a matching colored long-sleeved bandeau wrap with black leather details. Her hand now had a decorative black metal glove – or was it a bracelet?

Or was it a newer, chiquer version of her chains to this prison?

Liv looked questioningly to Arlo.

"At least your bruises are covered." He replied tersely, "Come along."

Still moving slower than usual, Liv attempted to keep Arlo's pace as he marched through the dungeon, proving to be excruciating conditioning for her.

Focus. Liv reminded herself.

At the first crossway, Arlo turned right.

He led her down another cold tunnel, where Liv tripped over her foot and crashed to the floor. Arlo only paused for an annoyed moment while his niece crawled back to standing before he turned left up a flight of spinning stairs

To her right, the staircase went back down – to blackness.

At the top of the stairs, Liv passed a massive metal door. She was panting, her heart pumping quickly from the incline, but she heard faint chanting coming from the closed barrier.

It didn't sound like a chant of peace.

Dread encompassed Liv's body.

Naturally, Liv placed her hand on the stonewall to help balance her feeble body and continue on after her uncle.

Suddenly, a hiss cut through to her right ear, making Liv jump to find another head desperately trying to grab her through a cell door that she certainly had not noticed earlier. She stumbled in fear, colliding into the opposing stone wall.

"Olivia!" Arlo yelled angrily. "What is taking so long?!"

Heart pounding, Liv eagerly moved away from the two doors and toward her uncle, but she was unable to get the most disturbing image from her mind.

The eyes – or the non-existence of eyes – on the prisoner's head were fully white.

Right, left, left, left, right, left.

Liv repeated the sequence in her head while Arlo led her to the dining room.

From all of the historical movies and shows involving an estate or castle, one thing remained consistent – the formal dining room would connect to the kitchen.

And the kitchen would connect to an outdoor loading area.

It was a stretch, and for all Liv knew this enchanted fortress could reset to a new maze everyday, or worse, the kitchen's staff didn't need proximity with magic, but it was a start. While conscious and outside of her cell, Liv knew she needed to take advantage of observing her surroundings so she could prepare an escape.

Arlo sighed – Liv sensed with slight relief – as he showed her to the dining table in a midieval inspired room, decorated with rich bannisters, large wooden fixtures and silver dinnerware.

A pair of brown eyes and an evil smirk unwelcomed her to the table.

"Ollie, how *great* it is to see you." The blonde bitch smugly said, her voice laced with sweetness more fitting to sour candy.

"Cleo." Liv's eyes glared.

Arlo coughed, so Liv nodded tersely and added an insincere smile.

As her uncle led Liv to sit down at the table across from her scholastic arch-nemesis, Liv's hands clenched. Arlo followed suit, sitting at the head of the table and to her right.

Liv naturally turned to the woman sitting next to Cleo. At this point, anyone would be better to chat with than Cleo or Arlo.

"Hello, I don't believe we've been introduced? I'm Liv."

"I know who you are, darling." The woman replied curtly. "I am more surprised that you do not know who I am. You returned a precious artifact to me only a full moon ago."

Liv observed the stranger, trying to recollect any history of meeting her before. She dawned a silk, mustard yellow dress with abstract floral prints, paired with a large black fur coat and black leather boots. Her feathered bangs and overall 70's-inspired look was reminiscent of Cleo's style, in fact – *she* reminded Liv of a more seasoned version of Cleo, but with chocolate hair.

Kai's hair.

Klarya. The Art Pillar Elite.

Well shit.

Perhaps Cleo inevitably would be the best deity to battle conversing with through dinner.

Liv smiled smugly, although internally she was scared shitless.

"Of course, Klarya, the Art Pillar Elite, I'm so sorry to have misplaced you earlier. I hope you are enjoying the Athena statue?"

…That got me kidnapped by Arlo, the first time.

"Oh, it's marvelous." Klarya spoke with an east coast accent, like she descended from Maine or Connecticut. And money. "Restoring our original collections with pieces that rightfully belong to the gods is truly a rewarding mission as an Elite. In fact, Cleo will be starting her own projects for our Pillar this summer."

Yet, when Klarya placed her hands on Cleo's shoulder, Cleo flinched.

She turned to her daughter, with what Liv suspected to be the most intimidating warning a mother could give, because Cleo nearly crumbled.

But instead, Cleo readjusted herself and met Liv's gaze once again, with poison in her eyes.

Apparently, apples didn't fall far from the tree in the Art Pillar.

And if Cleo couldn't take revenge on her monstrous mother, it was clear her next attack would be to take it out on the weakest, most outnumbered guest in the vicinity.

"We were going to launch an initiative with Kai to reclaim artifacts made by our kind through various elements, for what would have been a rewarding installation. But now, that particular program is on hold." Klarya glared at Liv with a subtle smirk.

A game. She actually was using her son's death as a power-play.

Liv took a deep breath, more from judgment than composure.

"My deepest condolences." Liv awkwardly replied, "Perhaps my uncle, Arlo, could be of service. He has a knack for leading Element Pillar initiatives against the Elite's will."

Arlo pressed his foot onto Liv's boot, a subtle warning to hold her tongue.

At first, Liv rolled her eyes, but then she saw Cleo across the table, her eyes glazed as she numbly and obediently stared at the empty plate before her. Whether also playing into her mother's tactics or exposing raw pain to the topic, her sadness made Liv pause.

"I am truly sorry." Liv reiterated in a whisper, "Kai was once my friend – my only friend at Puerdios for a time." She turned to Cleo, "I only wish for peace – a world where all gods can respectfully discuss and resolve issues without tyrannical manipulation and constant war."

"You wish for nothing." Klarya spit.

"The impossible." Cleo whispered, her eyes finally lifting to meet Liv, dead with disgust.

The dining room door opened once again, revealing the most beautiful, statuesque God Liv had ever seen. Her heart started pounding, she clenched the side of her chairs, feeling beads of sweat cooling her body as it started trembling.

His golden skin perfectly complimented his sun-kissed hair. His square jaw spread into a cruel smile as he finally noticed the new guest dining among the others. He had radiant green eyes, and when Liv locked hers with his, a flash of green amongst darkness penetrated her mind.

Yet, he looked so *normal*. Nothing like Hades, where you could feel his ancient years upon this earth. And for someone who had so recently returned from the Underworld, he definitely didn't look like a corpse anymore.

Instead, he looked like *a man* – a jaw-dropping, drool-worthy, gorgeous specimen. But beauty could be cruel and his had exponential potential for disaster.

"Kronos, we're so happy you could join." Arlo announced, standing up immediately to greet his maker.

Klarya and Cleo stood up quickly after; Liv followed suit, albeit slower and much less gracefully than the others due to the raging battle of pain her body continued to thwart her way.

Her heart hadn't stopped pounding against her chest. Liv was fairly positive she hadn't breathed since he entered the room. Perhaps that was his ancient power, bestowing customized daunt to all he met. After a gulp, she repeatedly commanded her body to breathe in, breathe out, gulp, breathe in, and breathe out...

"Olivia, it is such an honor to have you dine with us tonight"

His voice was velvet, liquid ecstasy. A drug, claiming its addict.

And although he only sported a casual, black cashmere crewneck sweater with simple, yet sleek indigo denim pants, his unspoken, assertive power hovered over the room. Liv finally understood she was not the only one in chains. He controlled any and all of his descendants – for his power was ancient, rich and all-encompassing.

Each step he took toward her felt like she was sinking further into an accident about to crash – heavily aware the scenario was not ideal but having no control in pivoting paths.

Finally, he approached her. His head loomed over hers as she slowly looked up to meet his gaze.

Stop shaking...

He gently grabbed her hand, bringing it up to his lips to kiss in greeting. The maneuver felt forced, slimy. She smelled a hint of basil verveina, cedarwood, cardamom and leather. Too familiar, yet everything about him felt cold and distant, from his touch to his stance. She wished there was more space between them; Kronos's presence was suffocating her.

A thought penetrated her core, that when everyone so easily fell in love with a person, it was natural for that person to inevitably become heartless.

A dark chill spread to her bones. She was crashing.

"Thank you for the invitation." Liv bleakly replied, trying to appear poised.

She had stopped breathing again.

Kronos smiled, a wicked sight before he moved on to Klarya and Cleo.

"My darling duo…"

Liv took a deep breath, composing herself, and sat back down. She tried to bask in momentary refuge; wholeheartedly knowing this terrifying monster would soon be back in proximity with a crystallized focus on his prey.

She lifted a glass before her, mentally procuring a test to see if the wine before her was safe to drink.

Salvum test bibendum. Salvum test bibendum.

Liv nearly fainted from the use of her depleted power source as she repeated the koine phrase to summon the protective spell. She felt a bead of sweat roll down her temple, immediately wiping it, grateful Kronos's attention was still entranced with the Art Pillar and Arlo's gaze was obediently watching over his master like a dog.

Yet, the drink remained red, so Liv gathered it must be safe to drink.

Or… your command didn't work properly.

Liv shuttered, selecting the glass half full, both literally and perceptively.

When Kronos finally sat at the head of the table opposite from Arlo, Cleo and Klara followed suit.

A deathly silence hovered over the table.

Liv defaulted to looking at Cleo for guidance, witnessing her take a sip of her own beverage, and then another.

Liv mimicked the gesture, taking another sip of her own glass.

"Olivia, you must be wondering why we are all here." Kronos finally offered.

Liv didn't reply, instead she stared at her wine glass.

Kronos did not seem to mind, as he continued on, unfazed. "We thought you would appreciate seeing a friendly face from school." He nodded toward Cleo. "And that you, Cleo, would be appreciative of the progress we have made with Olivia."

"Yes, clad me in leather and call me a Dark God." Liv dryly commented, rolling her eyes. She took another sip of her wine for it seemed to be the only way she would survive this dinner.

Klarya's jaw dropped, Cleo wearily sank further into her chair.

Arlo immediately stood up and grabbed his niece's arm, hitting her with a blast of electrocution. Liv's head slammed against the table when Arlo finally let go.

Kronos nodded to Arlo to sit down, putting his dog at bay.

"We would be far from proud of *that*, Olivia." Kronos brushed off Liv's comment, acting as if nothing happened, "And I would be more skeptical if you did not resist."

Liv's head remained against the table. She focused on her breathing, taking another moment to compose herself against the tears swirling behind her eyes, waiting to be undammed.

Be strong.

She finally sat up, instinctively going for her wine glass in hopes of numbing her pain, her trembling body, her mind.

"Olivia, is the wine to your liking?" Kronos finally asked, as if oblivious to the torture which just took place before him.

Play nice, Liv. Survive.

Liv loosened her clenched jaw, set down her glass and turned to her host, smiling sweetly. "Yes, it's quite complex. I… always enjoy Cabs from Northern California."

Kronos's eyebrows raised in surprise, "Dionysus would be impressed."

Liv forced an awkward laugh, shaking her head. "I assure you, it would not last long. I simply have an advantage of growing up in California." *And a mortal mother obsessed with black currant, blackberry, tobacco and mint notes.*

How she *wished* she were home with her mom right now.

Organically, Liv grabbed the wine glass and took another sip, feeling caged under a microscope as Kronos continued to study her.

"Fascinating. And tell me how *was* your upbringing in the mortal world?"

Liv gulped a large quantity of wine, quickly trying to determine what would be safe to talk about. She didn't want to reveal *too* much information about her mom or Lacey to risk sparking any dark ideas at their expense. Yet, she didn't necessarily have any immortal connections to focus on, so at least the being cast into the spotlight could stand a chance with defense.

She set the glass down.

"It was quite normal. I attended school and played volleyball, enjoyed dancing. The only huge difference was my mother raised me on her own, but I was raised with love."

"No incidents with your powers as a child?" Kronos prompted, "So, you had no knowledge or connection to the deity world during your youth?"

"None." Liv confirmed, "Well… at least until I was attacked in college." Liv paused to scowl at her uncle before continuing, "In result, Rei and Peyton brought me to Puerdios University for my safety, and it seems that being immersed in the deity world and surrounded by our kind finally ignited my powers to surface."

"Curious." Kronos replied smoothly, before moving his attention to Arlo. "It seems your niece had a very remote upbringing. What a miracle that you were able to be reunited with her in spite of it all."

"You call this reunion a miracle?" Liv replied dryly. "Let's agree to disagree."

"Olivia!" Arlo snapped, hitting his hand against the table, forcing the wooden structure, metal instruments and glass objects to jump. "You will not disgrace Kronos with such words."

Liv recoiled.

Perhaps her tongue was getting *too* loose from the California Cab.

"It is okay, Arlo." Kronos replied calmly, "Your niece's honesty humors me."

The dining room doors opened, to Liv's initial relief, revealing corpse-like beings that carried dishes to serve each guest. As they approached closer, Liv's eyes grew wide at the recognition of the white eyeballs – these were the monsters she had found locked up downstairs, clones to the hooded figure that had sent chills down her spine as it released her from the chains earlier.

A chilly breeze went through her soul, like an icicle piercing her core, as an expression-less server delivered her meal and glided away.

"Ah, Olivia – my newest experiment." Kronos explained, passively waving toward the servants, but ending with a demonic smile so malicious that Liv's skin became gooseflesh, reminding her once again that this entity at the table was not natural. He too, was a monster caged within a relative vessel.

"An… experiment?" Liv slowly asked, trying to calculate how many different creations she had seen during her limited time outside her cell and assess how destructive they could be.

"I will issue a warning in lieu of an explanation, so listen carefully darling." Kronos's crisp, melodic song paired with black bombs igniting joy behind his eyes. "My unique position in having returned to the living world allowed me to discover a new species, far more powerful than my previous experiment with the Olympians and incomparable to my father's contribution with the Titans."

"They are more powerful than any present-day deity?" Liv clarified, studying a creature as it obediently refilled Cleo's empty wine glass, noticing how her rival froze during the entire interaction, yet appeared to be getting sick. The creature, dressed in grunge leathers reminiscent of a suit and with coarse peppered hair, moved robotically, but perhaps once could have been a woman, a goddess, in a previous life.

"Precisely." Kronos smiled darkly. "The Dark Gods are very fortunate to have them supporting our cause – The Pure Gods' army is no match for the one we are creating."

Creating. Not building, not recruiting.

A heavy weight pressed against Liv as she sunk into her chair.

Kronos and the Dark Gods were playing with an unlimited number of soldiers.

Liv dropped her fork, pushing her plate away in unison with her appetite.

Kronos clapped with a rueful smile, as if he had been waiting for this gruesome revelation all along.

"Now that you are done with your dinner Olivia, shall we demonstrate?"

Liv couldn't believe that she once thought Hades to be the master player of games. He had nothing compared to this mindfuckery.

Kronos stared cruelly at Liv, as a new monster approached her. The Soulless looked oddly familiar, Liv studied him for a moment longer, before her jaw dropped.

No longer in glasses, and now a zombie version of himself, Finn's corpse drew nearer, unaware of the victim he now approached.

Without moving a muscle, Kronos commanded the Soulless deity to do his bidding. Chains erupted from Finn's corpse, re-cuffing Liv's wrists together in a heartbeat.

Kronos nodded swiftly to Cleo, "Cleo, pay attention. This demonstration is for you, too."

Liv immediately glanced over to her nemesis, who looked like she was going to be sick with dread. Klarya elbowed Cleo with a stern look and immediately, darkness returned to Cleo's eyes as she smirked toward Liv. She too, had been trained to take part in a charade.

Instinctively, Liv tried to readjust her seating to find comfort amidst the chains.

"Of course, how rude, let us help you with those." Kronos admitted, walking over to Liv and causing her to revolt in fear.

Flashbacks of black and green took over her mind.

He nodded to Finn – but it *wasn't* Finn – he nodded to the monster, who reacted by lifting chains from the floor and formulating a metal corset, clasping it around Liv's waist immediately upon completion.

Kronos smirked as he stared at the contraption, watching as he commanded it to grow tighter and tighter.

Liv couldn't breathe; it was cutting off her airway. She gasped for air, but nothing resolved her body's needs.

"The best way to determine whether or not her immortality has sunk in." Kronos nonchalantly observed. "Sometimes, I hate for the Soulless to have all the fun."

Immediately following his vile declaration, Kronos produced a knife, gutting Liv in the core.

The corset broke and Liv screamed in pain, coughing as air returned through her lungs.

"And even better, watch this." Kronos smirked, impressed by Liv's state before turning to Cleo, "Here is the grand finale to showcase our progress."

He turned to Liv with a devastating smile.

"Ollie."

Liv recoiled, crying in pain and *hating* to hear that spiteful word. That *noise*.

As if the corset had reattached, Liv was back in the darkness, in the cage that would forever suffocate her until there was no light left. She couldn't breathe again. The darkness was taking over infinitely.

Kronos grabbed Liv's hair, forcing her to sit upright, consequently re-opening the cut from her core in the process. Blood started pooling the floor.

"Ollie, where is Hayden?"

Liv stared blankly at Kronos, in a daze.

Everything hurt. Her body was trying to the use any remaining power it had to heal her exposed torso, but she had none. Instead, her natural attempts to cure caused more pain. Her head pounded and her stomach grew even more queasy. She began shaking, fighting off the sweats as if her body was reacting to alcohol withdrawal. But this time, it was a reaction to depletion – power withdrawal, a drug that dangerously and exponentially fueled her vessels, a lifeline to her destruction.

She wanted to enter back into the dark abyss. She still couldn't breathe.

"Answer me, Ollie."

"I don't know!" Liv cried, shaking her head. The word Ollie sounded like mandrakes exposed above ground and emitting their lethal shrieks in her mind. She started choking; air still unable to pass through her body. Liv started turning purple.

"That's not what I want to hear, Ollie. Tell me where Hayden is?!"

Liv screamed, pulling her cuffed hands toward her face and stretching her fingers to plug her ears from the noise.

"Hayden?! Who's Hayden?!" She cried in a panic, explaining anxiously, "I swear I don't know where he is, I don't even know who he is…" Liv curled up into a ball, rocking back and forth slightly on the chair. She prayed to Rei, Peyton, anyone to get her out of this living nightmare.

Cleo's eyes went wide as she stood up from the table. "She's forgotten Hayden?"

"One of the many layers of her transformation. Soon enough, she will be the rallying cry for our cause… in time."

And with one grand finale, Kronos kicked Liv directly in her wound, forcing her to topple off the chair and slam against the floor, skull first. Air immediately returned to Liv as she coughed, finally vomiting in response to her body's power source eliminated once again. Her retching was a welcome respite, although it made her head pound more relentlessly.

Kronos turned to Arlo and dryly commanded, "Clean this up," before departing the room.

When the door slammed, Liv could only hear her quivering sniffles, could only feel the final tear slide down her cheek and could only focus on watching it drop to the floor.

Nobody else moved.

Liv may have passed out. She may have only blinked. Time no longer existed in this hell. But nevertheless, she awoke to Klarya's voice, cursing her returned consciousness.

"Well, you heard Kronos." She announced smoothly, "Cleo and I will leave you to… your niece."

Liv heard heels rhythmically click away, echoing in the grandiose space, the sound reducing with each step, until the steady beat paused.

"Cleo?" Klarya questioned from across the room.

"I'll be right there, Mom." Cleo replied smoothly. "Just indulging in this victorious moment of seeing Olivia Monaco, finally broken."

Lighter heels glided softly toward Liv, where a body shadowed over her.

Cleo smirked before stabbing Liv across her already exposed wound.

Her skin boiled while she cried in pain.

"Cleo!" Arlo shouted, "What the Hades are you doing?!"

"Leave me be, Arlo! Or you shall regret denying me my sweet revenge." Cleo's jaw clenched, as she continued torturing her enemy.

Liv started crying, the continuous stabbing was like one thousand needles penetrating her flesh at once – outside *and* from within her skin.

And then it stopped.

Liv took an exasperated sigh of relief, already beginning to shake in anticipation for what cruelty was to come next. She could only make out Cleo drawing another target on her torso for her next torture play.

Yet, before Cleo unexpectedly stood with satisfaction, cold hands had gently touched Liv's arm, instantly numbing her pain in a domino effect throughout her body.

"She's all yours, Arlo." Cleo declared.

Liv heard the lighter heels click across the room, slowly fading out to nothingness. Quickly, she dared to look at the remains of Cleo's abuse to determine how much more retching her body would endure with the inevitable healing.

But instead, she found a web of silk thickly stitched across what had previously been her gruesome cut. And right beside it, the most accurate trompe l'oeil of a deep, bloody gash intricately painted across her torso.

FOUR

LIV

Arlo dragged Liv back to her cell.

But before heading down into the dungeon, Liv caught sight of a black and foreboding steel door, the one she had passed before in terror. And as they walked by threshold, she could feel the darkness erupting from below.

Liv knew they would erase her memory of this sight tonight. Most likely of the entire dinner. The entire day. She would wake up once again with bruises and nausea and not remember how it came to be. The entire time spent in this personal hell had been a messy, unknown blur of reoccurring nightmares. Who knew how many times she had dined with Kronos before? How many times her maker had sadistically gotten off by introducing the Soulless to her?

How many times the encounters had been erased – like a crashing wave instantly removing footprints upon the shore, whisky evaporating into thin air? Quickly and aggressively demanding her mind to be in control while slowly destroying her being over time.

Think neutrally, she begged of herself. Liv still knew who she was, her general life history, most koine phrases of power commands and common mythology – that had been proved over dinner. Perhaps Kronos was only erasing the emotional memories, destroying selective parts of her brain. The triggering pieces, the ones that meant the most to her.

This is boring – a history lesson – deity history with Piper, Liv passively observed and with each step, came up with neutral facts to store in a part of her brain that she prayed wouldn't be alluring enough to attack. *I need to remember this, if I ever escape…*

So, she rethought and compartamentalized the details. Working in tandem with the brain's intricate, sometimes unknown beauty, as her only hope.

In the twenty first century, Kronos created the Soulless. A new species deriving from deceased deities, brought back to life to serve as a mindless army to act on his account. Most common identifications include solid white eyeballs without pupils and irises, zombie-like mannerisms. and loss of speech.

Liv repeated the facts in her head the entire way down, intertwining it with the castle's blueprint and her own circumstances, until her uncle finally tossed her back into the prison cell.

When Arlo finally let go of her arm, Liv felt his fingers' imprint still lingering atop her skin. The blood slowly circulated back to her tingling limb.

He slammed the cell door shut, remaining on the interior.

"You don't have to stay." Liv spat, stretching out her arm as far as her newly adorned chains would allow, attempting any movement to help increase its blood flow. "I'll be fine."

Arlo ignored his niece's request and instead turned to her.

"I want to give you one last opportunity to declare your loyalty to the Dark Gods."

"What?" Liv coughed.

She stopped moving her arm – the aching motion was worse than the prickling, anyway.

Arlo commanded a stone to rise from the cemented fortress, walking toward Liv in unison before sitting on it.

"You saw the Soulless today," Arlo proclaimed. "You experienced first-hand what Kronos is capable of, and if you continue to fight against him, it will only get *worse*."

Liv's jaw dropped, speechless at his proposal, but her uncle was completely serious.

"Which is exactly why I can't *stop* fighting..."

"Olivia, because I released Kronos without Hades's permission – he upsets the cosmic balance. He's essentially a demonic god, although powerful. You are no match for him."

"I'm the Element Elite." Liv challenged back, with as much grace and dignity her weak state would allow. "If not me, who? If not now, when?"

Arlo remained silenced.

"Kronos clearly considers me a threat. He went out of his way to kidnap me and apparently enlisted you to persuade me to switch my loyalty to him," Liv pressed.

"He did not send me." Arlo admitted, "And I'm not sure how much longer he'll find your captivity of interest..."

"So, he'll try to kill me." Liv declared, with such a nonchalance assertiveness that she could only thank the shock of the day's already dark festivities that death failed to evoke emotion in comparison. Perhaps she'd remember this, too.

"At least you're still alive." Arlo pleaded. "I had hoped you would have had a change of heart..."

"You. Call. This. Alive?" Liv growled through her teeth.

"Wouldn't you prefer this over the Soulless's fate?" Arlo roared back. "Or would you rather exist as an entity completely under Kronos's control – with your soul, your heart, your being permanently stripped from your body? That's what Kronos will do when he no longer finds value in your hostage. That's your fate if you keep fighting him. Can you not agree that declaring loyalty to the Dark Gods triumphs over losing all self-control?"

"And if I do join your cause, do I still get knocked unconscious anytime I disagree? Don't I remain in chains either way?" Liv challenged, holding her head high with as much expendable energy she could exhaust. "Dark God or not, I'll remain imprisoned."

And it was true. She knew her opinion and choice would get stripped away, and without them, she'd still lose herself. So, for now, the dark reality hovered over the words she was too exhausted to say. Imprisonment welcomed her future either way. But she'd rather face it with dignity, knowing that she fought for what was right and that she fought for it because she chose to.

Arlo grabbed her hand. "You don't understand, it's the only opportunity to avoid the fate of the Soulless. Once he controls you, he'll be able to override your sealed protection of the Underworld. Either way, he'll be able to release the Soulless so they are no longer bound to death, have access to Dark Gods of his choosing…"

"Why are you telling me this?" Liv pleaded, she stared blankly at the ground. Her full body was numb – it was too much to process.

Arlo sighed, stood up once again and returned the stone back into the concrete fortress. He opened the cell door and glared back at his stupid kin.

"Because, naive niece, tonight Kronos will enter once again and continue to erase any pertinent memories, including this one, until you have nothing left."

He slammed the door, leaving Liv once again in the darkness.

The glowing green eyes returned.

Liv started trembling immediately, her heart rate spiking instinctively at the cruel inevitability of Kronos's arrival. He was the hunter and she, his prey.

The eyes penetrated her mind, forcing her head to follow the rhythmic hypnotization of its gaze looking left and right.

Liv sighed, wincing in pain as she heard her cell door creak open and tried to make out Kronos's form, to finally face her torture head on.

"Ollie." His melodic voice scraped against Liv's skull.

"No!" Liv screamed, plugging her ears. "Stop! You want to control me, but you cannot! I won't let you!"

She hummed in her head the first song that came to mind, fighting the external noise. Liv had to get him out of her head and purge the green from her subconscious – it was the only way she could challenge the coercion.

Kisses of fire, burning, burning, I'm at the point of no returning…

She could smell a hint of verveina, cedarwood, cardamom and leather growing stronger as he approached her.

Don't smell him. Liv reminded herself, plugging her nose with her pinkies as her pointer fingers remained in her ears.

Kisses of fire, sweet devotions, caught in a landslide of emotions...

"You're practically doing the tormenting for me." Kronos's velvety voice smirked with pleasure as he slowly removed Liv's hands away from her face, holding them above her.

Liv kept her eyes closed, desperately singing the next tune that came to her mind.

I was cheated by you and I think you know when...

She felt his breath on her cheek before he slammed her against the cell wall and nailed her handcuffs above her head, restricting her limbs even more.

So I made up my mind, this must come to an end.

The song in her mind started becoming subdued with tears.

"Look at me now...Ollie."

The timeliness of his request with the coordinating lyrics threw her off, making her tremble as her silent jukebox began malfunctioning.

She was so tired...

"Olivia." Kronos prompted.

Liv wavered, her lips quivering as she began crying in fear. She shook her head sadly but slowly accepted her fate.

"So be it." Kronos drawled.

Suddenly, something sharp penetrated her leg.

Liv screamed, her eyes instinctively opening wide to examine her leg.

A sword had been lodged through her thigh.

"Now that I have your attention..." Kronos smiled, "If you close your eyes, the pain will intensify, so I suggest you stay awake, Ollie."

Liv whimpered, weakly hanging against the wall, desperately wishing she could clutch her destroyed limb and offer it solace.

"Why are you doing this?" Liv sobbed.

"Because, despite my brilliant efforts, you appear to be getting stronger."

"That's not possible." Liv choked. She was starting to see dark spots. Her head ached and now her skull had a new tender bump that stung against the cool cellar stone. Her body was falling apart.

"The prophecy cannot come true. I'm afraid the shared bond you have with my dear descendent is causing troubles with the seal you've created for the Underworld and hindering progress with my ultimate plans for you."

Kronos's usually temperamental tone crescendoed into an aggravated hiss, "I need to break it so your powers weaken and in result, the Pure God King's, too. And in order to break it, you see – I need to break *you*, Ollie."

Kronos leaned over Liv, grabbing her jaw with his fingers and forcibly bringing her lips up to his in a passionate kiss.

She was absorbed in his painfully intoxicating scent, and for whatever reason, he felt so familiar to her, as if in another lifetime, she had kissed him before. Liv began to relax, enjoying the momentary distraction. She had no clue what prophecy Kronos spoke of – or bond – but if this was how he wished to break it, she could oblige. She was still exhausted, but this surpassed inflicting pain and trauma that bordered death.

Suddenly, Kronos paused with a melodic chuckle. He kissed her neck, causing Liv to quietly moan before he drew the sword out of her thigh, tossing it across the stone floor. The metal clattered, protesting the maneuver, its anguish matching Liv's. She winced, her jaw growing tense as she fought the impending pain of the now exposed wound. Her dull blue eyes connected with Kronos's bright green ones, pleading he continue distracting her from the pain. He grabbed her neck with one hand and locked her hair in the other, bringing her back to his mouth.

Yet, as soon as Kronos saw a hint of a pleasured smile flicker across his captive's mouth, he punched her in the jaw – slamming Liv's face against the stonewall and from the impact, forced her unconscious once again.

PEYTON

"Hayden!" Peyton screamed, running down the hill to her king.

Hayden was curled up on the ground, grimacing with pain. Peyton shuttered as she bent down beside him; he looked as if induced with a raging fever yet battling a terrible nightmare all at once.

After Rei returned to their tent with bloodshot eyes from staying with Hayden through the night, Peyton volunteered to look after their king while he rested. That had been morning, but when she had visited his tent – he was no longer there.

It had taken the God of Discovery a full fucking day to find her king's whereabouts. And he could have been lost forever, on *her* watch. Holy shit, the Security Pillar would have disowned her. She would have been casted to become a toothless hobo living under a bridge...

When she finally reached him – her inner crisis vanished and reattached to Hayden, especially as she fully absorbed what dangerous state her friend was in.

"Hayden. Hayden! Can you hear me?!" Peyton grabbed his face – which was burning hot – before opening his eyelids to see if his pupils would dilate as she cast light in their direction.

He was shaking, terrorizing against her grasp.

"Come on, come on, come on, think Peyton!" She commanded herself.

Peyton desperately searched for a solution in her mind, navigating ancient textbooks, medicine alternatives, relative mythologies... until she quickly went on a limb and tried something unknown to their universe.

"Okay Hayden, I need you to be receptive to my powers..." Peyton concentrated, blasting a part of her to the heart of the king. Nothing happened – he remained in turmoil. "Ugh, like he could actually hear me, and a mortal TV drama could be my savior, anyway..." Peyton admitted in defeat, kicking a nearby stone before beginning to jump around. "But *you* can hear you, Peyton. And you are awesome. And powerful. And beautiful. – Why THANK YOU Peyton! – But most importantly, *you* can help Hayden find himself. Why? Because *you're* the motha-fucking God of Discovery!"

She turned back to Hayden, still jumping, and feeling a little more confident.

"Okay focus, Peyton."

She took a deep breath and with her entire being, willed Hayden to discover himself – to come back to the light and find himself again.

Peyton closed her eyes, blasting all that she could to her friend, praying to Zeus it would be enough to bring him back.

And when Hayden's eyes opened wide in a frantic alert of his surroundings, Peyton immediately pushed him over with all of her might.

"Idiot!" Peyton screamed, hitting him again so he toppled over once more.

"Whoa, Peyton!" Hayden yelled, scrambling back in defense, albeit slowly.

"You asshole!" She continued, marching in his direction, seeing red.

"Peyton, what happened!?" Hayden asked loudly, still keeping the distance between the two of them.

"Why don't you enlighten *me!?*" Peyton cried, "I only found you in comatose, you selfish piece of shit!"

Finally, Peyton crumbled to the ground, burying her hands in her face. It was too much, It was all too much.

Hayden ran over to her, pulling her into an embrace. Peyton appreciated the unconditional support and leaned against Hayden's chest, unable to contain her emotion. She couldn't remain mad at him for trying to give Liv her best fighting chance. She would have done the same.

"It's okay…" Hayden calmly repeated, rocking Peyton to soothe his friend as she caught her composure.

"It's not okay." Peyton finally admitted with a sob. "Nothing… is… okay. None of it."

Hayden continued his rhythmic movements with his friend, but instead began calmly repeating, "Okay then, life is shit…life is shit…"

Peyton chuckled between her sniffles as he continued on.

"Okay, okay…" She finally pulled herself up, hitting Hayden one last time, albeit less passionately, before pointing to him. "But you're still an idiot."

"I never said otherwise." Hayden agreed, lifting his hands in surrender.

"Why did you exhaust yourself past replenishment?" She cried, summoning water from a nearby loch for Hayden to drink. Peyton forced him to take the full canteen, demanding he consume it immediately.

Hayden obliged, but dropped his head.

"I couldn't sleep, so I went for a walk. And then I felt her again."

"Hayden, you have to take care of yourself." Peyton insisted.

"I've been feeling her less and less, Peyton. She's in pain, excruciating pain. But, she's confused – something isn't right." Hayden raised his head with determination and met Peyton's gaze straight on. "We *have* to go get her."

"I know, Hayden…" Peyton put her hand on his shoulder.

"No, you don't Peyton. *Life is shit.*" He challenged, reminding her not to gloss over the realities of their present circumstance. "I truly worry we don't have much time left before she never comes back."

Peyton smiled sadly, "Then you must give her everything you have – help her break through whatever barriers they're drowning her in. Keep sending her strength, but most importantly help keep her alive." Peyton rested her chin upon her hand that lay gently on Hayden's shoulder, "But you *have* to be more careful about your limits. You're depleted. If you can't feel her now, you must rest. We stick to the plan."

"You're right. I'm sorry." Hayden admitted, leaning his head against Peyton's. "Thank you."

"Don't mention it. Life is shit." Peyton chirped back with a smirk.

PIPER

"Are you actually doing homework right now?" Hayden teased, glancing over Piper's shoulder.

She glanced up, finding the king in better spirits, before returning to her studies.

"Someone has to keep up with the curriculum, so his majesty doesn't fail out of Puerdios University." Piper retorted back, with more sass than she had ever imagined possible.

Oh shit.

"I mean..."

Hayden laughed, waving her terror away nonchalantly. He sat down next to Piper outside of her tent and extended his hands toward her flaming fire.

"I'm not sure what is more impressive – that you have remained in touch with the staff at Puerdios to receive these weekly homework assignments, or that you choose to work on them outside, during the winter, in Scotland."

"It's not too bad," Piper explained, staring at the embers, "it calms me."

"At least your fire is warm." Hayden smiled politely, all too knowingly.

"She's waiting for Tristan's arrival." Peyton chimed in, sitting on the opposite side of Piper, bringing her in for a comforting hug. "And this heat feels amazing. Hayden nearly froze me to the Underworld with his shenanigans today."

"I am *not*," Piper squeaked, "waiting for Tristan. I mean, I... just find my tent too lonely for my liking. Out here, there's action. Things to see. Deities to talk to."

As soon as the last reason left her mouth, Piper knew she had made a mistake.

"What deities do you 'talk to'?" Peyton asked smugly, wholeheartedly trying to conceal the smile growing on her face. "You only talk to Hayden, Rei and me – and that's because you have no choice, we practically force ourselves upon you and make you be our friend. So, just admit it... you're waiting for Tristan."

"I'm not waiting for him." Piper reiterated with a soft voice, weakly. "It's not like I've been pining away, anxiously awaiting his return, imagining a romantic reunion where he runs up that hill and sees I'm the first to greet him when he comes back, so he lifts me up and twirls me around in excitement, because he's charged with information to help rescue Liv, but then pauses, catching my eye, realizing just how much he's missed me during his arduous journey, so he cups my face..."

Hayden politely coughed, looking at Piper mischievously.

Piper's eyes went wide in horror as her jaw dropped mid-sentence.

"Like I stated, I'm *not* waiting for him." She returned to her notebook, scribbling down some more notes, rather aggressively.

"With that set-up, *I'm* now waiting for Tristsan. I want to discover what happens next!" Peyton joked, unable to contain herself.

Piper rolled her eyes, dropping her notebook and pen with a defeated sigh. She turned toward the hill, looking out into the mist because something caught her eye. To see better through the fog, Piper stood up and covered the fire's flame momentarily.

She saw a man. A dark figure, slowly becoming clearer through the Scottish Highlands.

Tristan.

Without a second thought, she immediately dropped all of her educational materials to the ground and sprinted out into the unknown.

"Well, should we go after her?" Hayden asked Peyton, still in shock at their peculiar friend.

"Well, since she was clearly *not* waiting for Tristan, I don't think it's necessary." Peyton shrugged with a smirk. "But Zeus, Trellis – that timing was insane."

Piper flew down the hill, until she collided with the man and felt his cold leather against her cheek. She held him closer, unable to contain her excitement.

"Piper!" Tristan laughed, pulling her into a deeper embrace. "What an unexpected way to be welcomed back."

How she missed his voice, its rich melody that calmed her every nerve instantaneously.

Well, except for some...

She pulled back, with the purest smile radiating.

"You found Cleo." Piper confirmed in a whisper.

"Strangely enough, Cleo found *me*." Tristan replied.

"Oh Zeus…" Piper's eyes grew wide. She instinctively pulled him back into an embrace. "I'm so sorry…"

Had he been captured? Tortured? How had he escaped?

She clung on tighter.

"No, no – it wasn't like that. It was cordial. Strangely enough, I think she was more freaked than I was about the entire encounter. But Piper, she revealed the entrance. We can rescue Liv."

Piper was already hugging Tristan, but she hugged him *more*. A can't breathe, don't care, break-my-ribs-and-I'll-be-glad-of-it type of embrace.

They'd be returning to Puerdios soon.

Thank Zeus she had kept up with the curriculum.

TRISTAN

"You were correct Hayden, she's still at the Old Storr, but we have to move quickly. Cleo confirmed they've been switching entry protocol sporadically with location changes at minimum every week – it could change tonight or in a few days."

"And Cleo's demeanor?" Rei interrogated, "Do you believe her intentions were pure? She's tricked us before."

Tristan sighed, running his hand through his hair before shaking his head.

He had felt Cleo's terror beneath her stoic demeanor. He could pretty accurately call out Cleo's bullshit ways – she usually emitted no emotion behind her crueler intentions, bordering sociopathic. This time around, she was pretending to be strong, and had refused his offer to return to the Pure Gods forces with such painful regret that Tristan believed her internal conflict was similar to one who battled a self-injury disorder.

"Cleo's our friend. She's capable of petty nonsense and social humiliation, but you can't believe she would actually want to inflict pain upon someone – on one of us." Hayden defended, supporting Tristan with a nod, to his surprise.

"But would she realistically ever want to *proactively help* Liv?" Peyton challenged, rightfully playing devil's advocate.

Everyone instinctively turned to Daphne and Jocelyn, who remained silent in the corner.

Jocelyn started to speak, but Daphne stopped her before she could get the first word in, warningly placing her hand onto her daughter's knee, shaking her head in dismissal.

"We cannot confirm her intentions. Not today." She stated indifferently.

Jocelyn sighed, sincere apology emerging across her face.

Silence filled the room, until Tristan finally spoke.

"I don't believe it's not about Liv." Tristan explained, "I spent my entire travels back weighing the options. Cleo didn't give much to work off and I have no facts to support my intuition, but ultimately I think Cleo must have seen something darker, more dangerous… and finally realized that we *need* the prophecy to come true in order to have any chance of defeating Kronos and whatever terrible things he has planned."

Hayden studied Tristan for a moment and then the mapped plan in front of him, trying to weigh the options.

"It's decided. We head to the Isle of Skye at dusk." Hayden commanded. "Pack your things and be ready before nightfall."

After Rei, Peyton, Jocelyn and Daphne exited the room, Tristan stayed back, nodding first to Piper to follow the others. He finally asked for the update he had been craving since encountering a terrorized Cleo.

Cleo, who was possibly one of the most favored Dark Gods of Kronos, frozen with fear. He sensed it, even through her stoic façade.

A whisper emerged from his breath.

"Have you felt her?"

Hayden paused, sighing deeply before responding and beginning to pack his things for the next destination.

"Not since this morning."

HAYDEN

He stared at his belongings, wondering if it was worth unpacking again. The task in itself seemed daunting, and possibly pointless if they were to uproot again and move to another location by dawn. Still drained from the morning's power depletion, flying across the sea felt not like the first, but the *second* work out after a long hiatus from the gym, and now what Hayden really wanted to do, was sleep. Fall into a deep, mindless sleep where he could rebuild his strength without worry. But that was and would be impossible, when fear kept him up at night and monsters threatened his dreams.

He had spared his divine powers earlier, instead dispensing physical energy by hand-placing each item into his bags, taking infinitely longer if it hadn't been for Rei checking in and immediately packing the remaining royal campsite with one snap.

Instead, he chose to be selective with his unpacking, only looking for his most valuable item among the campground – the only thing that brought him consolation these days.

He slowly walked over to a bag atop his bed and groaned – his entire body ached. His right leg felt like it was constantly asleep, so he dragged the limb stubbornly while trying to maneuver the majority of his weight to his left, even though that side was not immune to being worse for wear, either.

By the time he reached his bed, Hayden sighed heavily and dropped onto the mattress, temporary relief flooding his body as it relaxed for a moment before continuing on its mission. At least he was starting to feel *better* – less like a record-breaking hangover and more like a sinus infection after a grueling workout. He couldn't wait until he entered the recovery phase of 'a bad cold.'

Hayden zipped open the bag, digging through its contents. Tossing aside his lucky football and filing through various policy agreements that he *eventually* needed to sort through, he passed his father's royal-crested ring and his own highschool yearbook, until finally, he found it and released a sigh of relief.

The soft grey fabric relaxed against his grip as he pulled the sweatshirt out of the bag, putting it on immediately. It still smelled like her – hints of strawberry, daisy, white violet and velvety jasmine lingered on the fabric. It had been months since Ollie had teasingly gifted him the Oregon sweatshirt, apart of the façade they had created for her mortal mother.

Now, it was as if the bold pine green block letters across the garment were beginning to taunt him.

"For all the games we'll be attending..."

Her voice echoed in his head. Her infectious smile radiated across her mesmerizing face, implanting in his mind, while her eyes mischievously sparkled, as if hiding a secret only shared between them.

Zeus, she was beautiful.

He prayed, begged to the ancient Olympian deities that she remained alive outside of his mind, too – and once again, gave her all he had – focusing more on her enticing blue eyes, which invited him into her soul as he collapsed to the ground.

LIV

Her eyes opened wide.

A surge of power infiltrated her corpse – she was breathing, she was energized, she was *alive*. But to what expense?

Instantly, Liv willed a protective shield around her body, preserving her alertness from any poison seeping through air, food, skin or cursed command of this prison.

Cognizance was all she needed.

A simple step and her mind already felt clearer.

Stronger.

And soon, she could unleash fury.

JOCELYN

"Nice sweatshirt, bro."

Jocelyn couldn't help but deliver the line with her frattiest voice. She grinned proudly as Hayden stirred awake. Zeus, he looked terrible. But she gathered he already knew that.

Without missing a beat, Hayden challenged back, "How's Demetrius, sis?"

Jocelyn quieted immediately.

"That's what I thought." Hayden smirked, pulling off his Oregon sweatshirt. He walked over to his duffle bag and carefully placed it back inside.

As soon as it dropped and hit the interior, Hayden froze.

Jocelyn tilted her head, jaw dropping.

"Ollie."

She whispered the name in unison with her brother, who had already sprinted outside.

She followed, finding Hayden staring up at the sky within moments.

At least he's rested. Jocelyn assured herself, knowing he once again sent Liv energy, power and clarity to assist her potentially-fatal-survival.

Jocelyn wanted to tell her brother what she had seen, what might come – but her mother had reiterated that until there were only two paths, their mingling would only cause more frustration and unpredicted courses. Uncontrollable possibilities that would result in *more* fatalities. As the voices of reason, they needed to remain calm and constrain chaos.

Before, when she had only recently inherited her powers – she used to hate her lack of knowledge. Now, as her Elite powers strengthened, she wished to be on the other side – unaware, unburdened.

If only she had been able to predict *that* in the past.

And now, a veil separated Jocelyn from her loved ones, a darkened lens of the world that made it more challenging to connect with her unknowing friends. She constantly worried she would say the wrong word and change the future's course for the worse.

She had even pushed Demetrius away because of it.

As soon as her powers expanded to the galaxy, she could see everything in his path – the good and the bad. On their second official date, vivid images of his potential future crossed her mind – making love, a wedding, baby deities, arguments, a mysterious woman of an ancient land, pain, death…

She had seen his entire life begin and end, without knowing when, how and who.

But it always ended in death.

And that *terrified* her.

She couldn't accept Demetrius falling in love with another, the thought broke her. Yet, she wouldn't allow herself to be the cause of such pain, to be there for his downfall – helpless through it all and with only a constant reminder of the end for vicious consolation.

Jocelyn snapped out of her spiral, adjusting her light blue and gold cloak, pulling it tighter against the Scotland night chill. Her brother was none the wiser to her seemingly daily tormenting ritual, as he continued staring at the sparkling sky with a clenched jaw.

Casually, Jocelyn followed his gaze to the constellation he was desperately commanding to do his bidding. And, if he succeeded…

Suddenly, a vision flashed across her mind.

Jocelyn grabbed Hayden's arm in response.

"Oh no, oh no." Jocelyn's eyes went wide, turning to Hayden. "Liv's changed her course."

"Joss?" Hayden pressed, turning to her.

"You must go. Now!" Jocelyn pressed, "She's going to attempt escaping, tonight."

"Attempt?" Hayden's brow raised.

Zeus. It all came out too quickly. *Did she say something wrong?*

"I don't know, I may have said too much." Jocelyn panicked, searching through her divine images to see if anything changed, any clues as to what she should say. She was so unsure, she started crying. "Zeus, Hayden. I'm sorry. You need to talk to Mother, I – I can't say anything, I've already changed the future, I can't say anything else."

Before Jocelyn ran away, back to the safety of her tented solitude where she could fully break down, she heard her brother curse under his breath.

And as she sprinted, wiping the tears down her cheek, she felt Hayden summoning Tristan, Rei, Peyton and Piper before returning his focus to the stars, giving Liv all that he could once again.

FIVE

LIV

She was awake.

She was capable.

Liv lifted herself up, walked over to the far wall and, taking a page out of her captor's book, willed the tiniest stone out of the structure. Liv pushed her face against the opening, big enough for only one eye to see out, and stared up to the night sky.

Liv could feel the resistance of the tiny stone fight against her powers, *draining* her powers, but the sight gave her clarity. Feeling more lost than ever, for whatever reason, the stars called to her. She wasn't sure why, but now staring at the stars, she felt stronger – and it was improbable that another opportunity like this would present itself again.

Kronos has already ripped her apart today, so he wouldn't return until morning. She had already seen Arlo when he served her dinner, so odds were she'd receive no more visits from either of her cruel hosts.

And like clockwork, when she locked eyes with the brightest star in the sky, she felt renewed, empowered.

Liv needed to leave, and now was her chance.

HAYDEN

"We need to get her now. She's attempting to escape."

They were hours away. He had already calculated the best routes while waiting for his friends to join him in his tent, the designated war room. Maps had been scattered, highlighted and outlined for the impromptu plan of attack.

"Now?" Tristan's eyes went wide as he anxiously swore under his breath.

"Tonight." Hayden reiterated.

"*When* tonight?" Rei clarified.

"I don't know. Joss cracked and without thinking, told me."

"Shit." Tristan huffed.

"Care to add any value to this discussion other than curse words?" Hayden snapped, pointing to the maps, "If we take one troop through the Bioda Buidhe, that can provide cover for our numbers..."

Daphne burst into the tent, interrupting her son.

"Go. You'll be faster with just the five of you. I'll control the troops in your absence."

For once, she looked *worried*.

Hayden furrowed his brow; it was unlike his mother to show discomposure.

"What about entering?" Tristan sighed. "We still haven't confirmed if we can get *into* the headquarters with Cleo's intel..."

"She's there. Tonight." Daphne pressed. "All you need to do is catch her attention, and when she meets you, the entrance will be revealed for a moment."

Hayden looked through the tent's ceiling to the sky. Whether or not he trusted his mother's intention, even he knew something felt different. There was a new energy in their connection for the first time since she went missing.

"That's all we need." Hayden finally confirmed, grabbing his navy bomber jacket as he departed the tent. His friends followed without hesitation.

As he willed his pearl wings to expand and attach to his back – an extension to his soul, Peyton ran over.

"Hayden, are you sure about this? You're rested, but not fully recovered." She whispered, attaching her glistening, diamond-like wings in tandem.

"For Ollie, I will sacrifice no less than my life. She is my soul mate. Without her, I don't exist."

In that moment, Hayden realized the sentiments had been playing on repeat in his head, making the delivery resemble that of a broken robot. He was certainly broken, and without Ollie, it appeared his heart was missing, too.

"Okay." Peyton agreed, although clearly not convinced.

Like him and the others, she prepared to take off, running across the harsh Scottish terrain, each muddy step accelerating her further off the land and into the cloudy abyss.

With Tristan at the helm, his fiery flames igniting the endless path before them, Piper's silver wings and Rei's light blue metallic feathers flew strong at Hayden's side and Peyton reared the protective diamond from behind.

Now above the mystical clouds, Hayden found the moon, bright and compelling, and stared at it while determinedly whispering his own prayer.

"Trellis - give me your strength for this mission. Time is of the essence."

Hayden felt winded from the flight and he *hated* admitting that to himself.

The five deities had landed in the Quirang, hidden behind a rock structure but with the Old Storr in sight. They huddled in a close circle as Peyton immediately placed protection spells around them.

Rei kicked off the plan synopsis. "If the entrance to the Old Storr has changed, Tristan will go back alone, send a message to Cleo, beckon for her time and say he's made a huge mistake and needs counsel on how to get back into Arlo and Kronos's good graces."

"That should pass if the message gets accidentally intercepted." Tristan agreed. "And if it doesn't, hopefully Cleo will still be willing to meet."

"*When* Cleo comes," Peyton clarified, glaring at Tristan.

"Hayden will pause time, allowing Peyton to knock Cleo out and hide her. Rei and Tristan will then venture inside the castle." Piper quickly continued, breaking any potential tension.

"With me." Hayden added.

"You know having the King of the Pure Gods enter Dark God territory is ridiculous." Rei hissed, before muttering in disbelief, "We've only cemented this idea in your head for a week!"

"If Arlo is there, you both could defeat him and escape. But Kronos? I am the only one who can defeat him." Hayden pressed. "You need my powers."

"Not this argument, again." Tristan rolled his eyes. "We're leaving, now. We don't have time to circle around the topic." He turned and walked down the hill.

"What about the plan?" Piper squeaked, jumping in front of Hayden to block his path.

"Oh, the sole reason Piper and I are here?" Peyton added, glossing over Hayden's internal battle and explaining, "To keep Hayden from *blowing* up the world with rage and giving away our hideaway? Hayden, you must stay here or else Piper and I become disposable."

"Stop." Hayden whispered, a deathly tone that made Peyton's eyes go wide, but forced his friends to be silent.

"Sorry-" Piper squeaked, taking a step back.

"No, it's... okay, Piper." Hayden recovered, before fisting his knuckle and turning to Rei. "But you forget your place, Elite. I amuse it, because you're my brother and mean well, but today you *do not* command your king. Especially when you are risking your life for Ollie and we both know the better plan is to be prepared for the worst scenario – Kronos. I'm not trying to be heroic. I'm not trying to recklessly throw myself into danger. I'm thinking strategically and have been platonically troubleshooting this plan. You need me to ensure the goal is met – to free Ollie. Without me, you and Tristan will join the cells with Ollie and we'd be back at square one with less collateral. With me, you stand a chance for all of us to exit."

"Hayden-" Peyton interjected, with sad eyes.

"No." Hayden commanded.

Peyton's mouth snapped shut.

Hayden faced Rei to challenge his command.

After a moment of consideration, Rei finally asked dryly, "And if anything goes wrong in this mission?"

"Then, I personally give you all permission to eternally reprimand my mother for not telling me Ollie's location in the first place." Hayden added, marching toward the Old Storr and casting his own protection powers to become invisible.

With a devilish smile, he turned back towards his friends, knowing they could no longer see him and added, "If you survive, that is."

TRISTAN

His heart was racing with adrenaline, as if the frozen organ had finally melted back into an overload of functionality.

"Here goes nothing." Tristan hesitantly approached the black rock facing west below the Old Storr and whispered, "Di superi mortalium."

The black rock expanded, growing larger and transforming into a new shape, until it revealed staggered steps descending into a black abyss.

He turned back to the others, they all looked at one another unconvincingly.

"That's it?" Peyton finally asked. "That's the entrance? It worked?"

"It seems so." Hayden confirmed, still studying the entrance. He turned to Rei. "...Shall we?"

"I wasn't expecting it to work." Piper admitted in a whisper, turning to Tristan.

"Because of Cleo?" Tristan teased, trying to mask his terror.

"Because it was too easy." Piper replied speculatively, pausing a moment before taking a small step toward the entrance, peeking her head above the staircase. "Shouldn't it be harder?"

"From here on it will be harder, that's guaranteed." Rei offered, passing Piper. "I'll take any assistance while it's provided."

"You'll be careful?" Peyton stated aloud, her eyebrows raised at all three males.

None of them nodded in return.

"We'll survive." Rei corrected.

Peyton rolled her eyes, cursing under her breath.

But before she could begin her lecture, a bright white creature approached them, its hooves delicately prancing on the wet soil.

"Pegasus!" Piper shrieked, "That's a good sign, right?"

None of them nodded in return.

"Right." Piper whispered, pouting as she walked toward the beast and began gently petting its neck.

Tristan didn't run after her although he wanted to, but everything had already been said.

"The longer we wait, the more suspicious they'll get." Rei pointed out, already descending the staircase.

Hayden turned to Tristan and shrugged, following his Security Elite down the dark steps.

Only Peyton remained. Tristan glanced her way briefly before he nodded and ignited a torch, turning to trail the others through the entrance.

As soon as his foot crossed the threshold, the rocky substance knowingly reformulated. From within, Tristan watched the night sky slowly evaporate into blackness.

And then all became nothing.

"How long do you think this tunnel goes?" Rei finally whispered in the silence.

They had easily been walking for fifteen degrees.

"Perhaps the location never changes after all, just the means to enter," Tristan speculated, angling his torch toward the wall to see if any clues would present themselves regarding their destination. "We could be crossing the North Sea as we speak."

"There. Ahead." Hayden interrupted, ignoring Tristan, and moved onward.

Two mahogany doors revealed themselves, large and powerful, an invitation to destroy.

Tristan reached for the door, but it wouldn't budge.

"Try the password again." Rei commanded.

"Cleo didn't mention a second door..." Tristan argued, but finally succumbed to Rei's request and whispered, "Di superi mortalium."

Rei tried to open the door again, but nothing happened.

"Summon her." Rei demanded.

"I can't just summon her." Tristan retorted, "I can try to communicate to her by firelight, but that's risky. I don't know where she is in the castle and I can feel over a dozen flames..."

"Maybe there's a hideaway key around here..." Hayden offered, aiming his luminescent light around the door for any clues.

"And while he does that, you *flicker.*" Rei snapped.

Zeus. Tristan internally cursed.

He gazed into his portable fire, following the spark to a nearby room. The fire was too large, too risky. Tristan maneuvered to a smaller circuit, a simple flame – a candle. It smelled of burning lavender...

If Cleo was still in terror, she would want to soothe her worries with a relaxing atmosphere...

Tristan trailed through additional fires lit throughout the castle, finding a handful of burning logs heating large spaces to lamplights for central heating. None of the other flames felt purposeful like the second one he encountered.

If Cleo knew Tristan was coming, she may have intended for him to find her, distinguishing her flame to capture his attention.

Tristan paused, returning to the lavender room and writing in soot from the candle's flame with what he determined as the best cryptic message for her:

Whisky onsite.

He emerged from the flames, returning to his physical vessel among Rei and Hayden and the darkness.

"Message sent. Now we wait."

LIV

"Come on…"

Liv desperately tugged on her white druzy. She could *feel* the metallic weapon wanting to grow bigger but remained caged behind the mask of her original command.

"Excresco!" She commanded.

Nothing happened.

Liv stared more intently at the medieval miniature attached behind her stone, biting her lip.

"…Exsolvo!"

Finally, the object formed into a miniature dagger, clinking against the cool stone between her legs.

Liv huffed triumphantly, swiping off her forehead's perspiration with the back of her hand.

"This, I can work with."

She picked up the dagger, its tip sharp and tiny – the perfect size to fit into the lock binding her chains. She maneuvered the tool into the space, twisting and applying pressure throughout the intricate metal pattern until she heard a 'click!' and the lock broke free.

Liv smiled with delight.

She stared at the mechanism, sprawled lifeless on the stone floor, probably laced with protection spells that only a fool would try to combat with their own powers. Yet, deities were always so focused on power – Arlo and Kronos specifically – that even the greatest were too daft to consider the ramifications of how a once mortal without magic would attempt to break free, if she dared.

Fortunately for Liv, Rei too had mastered the craft of manipulating every angle for the best chance of survival, understanding and teaching her to not always rely solely on her limited powers.

Clearing herself of all bondages and chains, Liv stood up. Slowly, she creeped over to the bolted door and inspected its lock. Ignoring her lingering exhaustion, she looked down at her extravagant, metal toothpick resting easily within her palm.

"I'm going to need a bigger sword," she whispered with a sigh.

Sitting down, she began once again concentrating on her weapon.

You can't always rely on your powers to get the job done...

Hearing Rei's condescending tone echo in her mind made Liv angry.

"I know! But you never thought through the storage conundrum, now did you, asshole?" Liv hissed, continuing to focus on *Exsolvo* in her mind.

Yes, Rei had been a clever teacher, but his lectures – particularly in this situation – still drove her mad.

Liv ignored the reprimanding Elite, tossing his advice from her mind – she was starting to feel lightheaded and her skull began to ache.

Liv didn't have much time.

And yet, her Security Elite perservered, clawing back to claim her attention.

You can. You will. You can. You will.

"I am NOT weak!" She screamed in reply to her trainer's mental prying. Even thousands of miles away, Rei's fake simulation was of equal annoyance.

"Focus, Liv. God damnit!" She cursed, her body trembling with stubbornness.

On queue, the Viking sword returned to its formal glory, glittering against Liv's hand.

"Time for battle." Liv sighed in relief, standing up and piercing it through the lock.

The razor edges of the sword scraped against the lock's interior, undoing its purpose immediately. The door clicked open.

"Holy shit." Liv stared, eyes wide at her accomplishment. She paused, waiting to hear *someone* march toward her, to interfere with her escape and return her to her misery. But alas, there was no sound.

Bordering insanity, a dangerous glimmer of hope penetrated her thoughts.

She might actually pull this off.

With a deep breath, Liv pulled the door slowly open and exhaled.

Right.

She peaked out into the hallway and froze.

It became evidently clear that nobody came to stop her in her cell because nobody *needed* to stop her.

Guarding the hall was a golden snake, so large it towered over Liv. She immediately covered her eyes, she had only heard tales of a snake this size – of Ophion – whose fatal eyes could hypnotize one to any bidding, even to death.

Even among the darkness of her closed lids, a flash of bright green eyes penetrated her mind.

His eyes may blind but his mouth can't bite.

Piper's mousy voice echoed in Liv's head as an image of Puerdios's cozy library appeared in solace from the day Piper helped Liv with her serpent assignment for her Mythological Creatures class last winter.

Ophion has no teeth.

With her eyes still covered, Liv sprinted toward the monster, sword out and ready to attack. When she heard a hiss and quick movement to her right, Liv lunged with all of her might and pierced the monster in front of her with her mighty sword.

The snake cried, recoiling as Liv hesitantly opened one eye to witness the destruction she caused. She pulled the sword out only to replunge it back into her victim, noticing the sword illuminated a bright green as it sucked the life from the mystical creature.

With a final hiss, the snake finally fell over with its eyes no longer bright, but a dull grey. It could hypnotize and torture her no more.

Liv dropped her sword and collapsed to the ground beside the reptile corpse, her body trembling in relief.

HAYDEN

It felt like hours. The waiting.

They were *so* close to Ollie. Yet, still so far away with so much further to go.

The door's lock clicked. Slowly, it opened.

Hayden held his breath as a head peaked around the mahogany door.

"Tristan!" Cleo whispered, desperately crashing into Tristan with a hug.

When her eyes opened and found Hayden, her demeanor quickly changed from humor to horror.

"You two are already acquainted?" Cleo murmured, stiffening as she stepped back from her friend and dutifully extended her hand to Hayden. "I mean, it's lovely to see you… Kronos."

"Kronos?" Hayden asked in surprise. "Cleo, it's me. Hayden."

"Still an interesting acquaintance, either way." Rei popped out from behind the shadows and into the flamed light.

"Hayden?" Cleo whispered, her hand clutching her chest, she eyed Rei momentarily with disbelief before returning her gaze to the Pure God King. "Oh, thank Zeus!" She ran into his arms, before realizing what their reunion truly entailed. "You shouldn't be here, Hayden. None of you should be here, really."

"We're here for Liv." Hayden explained. "We won't leave without her."

Cleo shifted to Tristan, pleading reason. "I can get you in, but I cannot promise to get you out."

"Cleo, you've already helped us enough, we don't expect you to involve yourself any further." Tristan replied.

Knowing defeat with the three stubborn mules, she sighed, but then returned her gaze to Hayden, studying him curiously, "If you change your clothes, you could pass as Kronos. Nearly gave me a heart attack when I initially saw you."

"I look like Kronos?" Hayden questioned, staring himself down.

"Kronos looks like you." She clarified, "And almost identical, too. Might be genetics, might be mind fuckery." Cleo shivered before observing Hayden further. "But you have pure blue eyes, Kronos has poisonous green."

Cleo turned to Rei, scowling. "You will be tougher to disguise."

"There's the Cleo we know and love." Rei retorted back dryly.

Cleo studied the three of them, an idea formulating in her mind. "If you bind Rei, Tristan – it will look like you captured and brought him back to gain favor with Kronos." She nodded to Hayden. "I can dye your clothes to reflect Kronos's wardrobe and let you all into the Dark God Headquarters, but that's all I can offer today."

Hayden nodded, allowing Cleo to cast powers over his wardrobe – transforming his typical grey cashmere sweater to ink, and brown suede boots to matte black leather.

In the meantime, Tristan cast a spell that linked Rei's wrists together in a fiery rope.

Hayden ignored Tristan's glum smirk, first needing to understand his friend's shift in heart.

"Why are you helping us?" Hayden finally asked. "…I thought you hated Liv."

"Oh trust me, I still do." Cleo replied, not missing a beat.

"Then… why?" Hayden asked again.

"I…" Cleo grew quiet, shifting the weight between her feet. "I fear Kronos more."

When she looked up, gone was the smug entitled Elite, instead surfaced a broken, beaten girl.

"How bad is it?" Hayden whispered.

"Worse." Cleo studdered softly but delivered the word with a painful bite.

It was terrible leaving the extent to the imagination. But perhaps that was the circumstantial truth, as horrible as it might be.

"You can come with us." Tristan offered, dropping Rei's fiery bondages and grabbing her arms.

"No... my place is here. With my family." She explained, turning with a sad smile to her friends, "And so you'll always have a friend on the Dark side, if you should need it again."

Although appreciative to Cleo, her loyalty made Hayden wonder if there were any on the Pure side acting as a similar conduit. An image of his mother flashed across his mind – his doubts and untrustworthiness coming to the surface uncontrollably. He would ignore the thought for the time being, knowing the next crucial minutes of his immortality would definitively decide his future.

There was no turning back now, no matter where loyalties lay.

LIV

After what felt like forever, or in reality one minute, Liv began commanding herself to get up.

One movement at a time. First, just stand.

She leaned against the cold stone wall, finding balance among her weak limbs.

Just breathe.

Liv knew she was breathing, with the pounding of her heart rapidly bouncing against her chest and demanding attention.

Breathe slower.

She took a heavy step toward the golden beast; worried the snake was blessed with immortality and would spring to life with one hypnotizing hiss.

Be prepared for it to jump at you.

Another breath.

Another step.

A slow pattern that slowly calmed her into only slight terror until she reached her Viking sword. Liv carefully lowered her body, reaching for it while keeping her eyes on the deceased, or sleeping, monster. With both hands, she grabbed the bow of the weapon, leaning her entire body away from the snake, as the blade slowly emerged from its scaly flesh.

She didn't remember the sword being this heavy before.

Liv was panting.

She was thirsty.

She was *everything.*

Stay calm.

Keep going.

Commanding composure, Liv returned to the corridor's wall, leaning against it as she continued creeping down the tunnel until she reached the base of the stairs. Looking up, the staircase looked daunting. Keeping herself upright on the flat surface had already caused her legs to shake, muscles twitching in protest for rest. Relying on her legs for an incline would be a nearly impossible task.

Liv sat at the base, using her arms to lift her body to the next stair. She paused, catching her breath. Would it be more efficient if she crawled? Her legs felt like jello. Her arms hurt. Every muscle felt as if it were torn to its max and raging fury. Her body was a burning pit with no water to heal the hovering smoke.

Just keep going *up.*

So slowly, she dragged upward, step by step, moving backwards, laterally and crawling to keep the quiet ascension. Sideways, forward, backward – a rotating motion to engage all willing and able muscles to work, for she was facing her own personal Mt. Everest.

And when she reached the top, she cried with sad joy.

If anyone found her, she would have nothing to give. Without a fight, she would be carried back to her cell, starting at square one but with an even more challenging escape facing her ahead. She had barely made it out with this level of barriers, she would not be able to perservere through a stronger hold.

She would rot in this prison.

And so, she could not fail.

Liv looked up, finding a door handle on her right. She grabbed it for leverage to lift her body to a standing position and instead went swinging when the door blasted open.

She heard footsteps approaching.

Fuck. Fuck. Fuck.

Without thinking, Liv jumped behind the door, slamming it quietly shut behind her.

She closed her eyes, begging that no one noticed the activity. She still heard a faint march growing louder, but no unusual yells or alerts through the barrier. Liv opened her eyes, turning around to assess her options to temporarily hide until the marching succumbed. Studying her surroundings, Liv gasped.

Below her, she found a factory, creating... the Soulless?

Many lines, a pot full of lava, a contraption with spirits wailing within, bodies emerging and being transfused with its soul-less mass. Liv tried to count, it seemed monsters were being created by the dozen every minute.

Compartmentalize. This is a tomorrow issue.

Liv forced her focus to return to her escape and fortuitously found a burrow in the rock wall a few stairs down. As soon as she slid inside of the crevice, the exit door swung open again. Two deities passed by, both laughing as one told a tale of a recent trip to the Arts Pillar.

When their chatter disappeared into the darkness, Liv finally exhaled.

And as she looked back up the few stairs she'd need to ascend, she told herself she should make sure it was truly clear by waiting a moment. Although, in the back of her mind, she knew she was really just postponing the inevitable of having to go up *more* stairs again.

TRISTAN

It felt strange casually walking through the Dark God headquarters, as if he actually belonged there once again.

Cleo had departed before they entered, leaving the door cracked open for them. She had left them with instructions of how to access the dungeons and a prayer that Zeus be with them if they successfully found Liv.

Anyone they walked by followed a similar pattern when they spotted Hayden. Most froze, nodded politely and would curiously trail to find out any gossip about Tristan's return and capture of the Security Elite.

They were all fools.

The three Pure Gods passed the dining room on the right, praying nobody of status was enjoying a meal to witness their attendance. But that wasn't the challenging part, according to Cleo, only a precaution. The main hallway would be the trickiest part to maneuver through.

After four doors, they turned left to another corridor and collided into an ancient deity.

"Apologies…" Tristan immediately offered, but before he could look up, Hayden had already reacted.

He, along with Rei, Tristan and the mystery man, were thrown into the room that the deity had originally emerged from.

"Non sonus!" Hayden commanded. "Confinium!"

A low chuckle emerged from the darkness.

Tristan finally spotted the trapped deity. He looked exactly like Hayden, but his green eyes boiled in the darkness.

"You and Rei, go NOW." Hayden yelled, swiftly pushing them out of the room while simultaneously blocking another attack.

"We cannot leave you!" Rei growled.

"We stick to the plan – this is why I'm here. Save her!" Hayden yelled, before slamming the door.

Tristan went back to the door, trying to unjam its stubborn handle. They were locked out.

"Shit!" Rei roared, kicking the door, fiery bonds still coiled around his wrists.

"We don't have much time." Tristan proclaimed, with an internal 'shit' on repeat in his head. "Hayden can only hold off Kronos for so long – he's already depleted. We need to go. Now."

Tristan worriedly looked around. With Hayden's competent transition and impressive sound-proof barriers, it was impossible to tell what was going on within the confined room, so nobody had stirred to inquire what happened to their esteemed leader.

"We need to find Liv." Tristan pleaded.

And when Rei didn't move, Tristan used his fiery ropes to drag Rei behind him as he continued on with the plan, whether or not the Security Elite approved of ditching the Pure God King.

LIV

One more step.

Liv grudgingly lifted her foot on top of the last stair with a sigh of relief.

Looking around, it seemed the previous visitors were long gone within the depths of the monstrous factory.

She cracked open the door, looking both ways to make sure she wouldn't encounter anyone. The hallway was clear. She could persist.

Liv slithered through the exit and quietly closed the door behind her. Recognizing the next cell entrance ahead, she purposely steered herself across the hallway to the left side of the wall. Leaning her fragile body against the stone for balance, she needed to avoid the Soulless dungeon door she encountered before, because instigating their desperate cries would easily alarm the entire wing. Fortunately, by slowly pressing her back on the opposite wall, she was able to slide by without waking up the zombie deities.

She crawled to the end of the hallway, finding yet again her newest arch-nemesis – more stairs. Liv clenched her teeth together and made her way up, step by step. Slowly ascending, she grabbed on desperately for the metal handrail with her left hand, holding her sword in her right.

When she reached the top, she sighed. Now was the hardest part. She would need to blend in, be agile, possibly run, and execute all flawlessly in order to avoid getting caught.

Liv leaned over, bracing herself for what was to come. She gave into her beating heart, letting her mortal adrenaline take its course. She had remained calm for too long and now it was time to succumb to fear and her survival instincts.

When she went to grab the handle, the door flew open and a body slammed into her own.

Immediately, she blasted him against the wall, before realizing whom she had attacked and who had followed him into the dungeon.

They could be illusions, masterfully developed to bait her into recapture. Or they could be real.

But she could take no risks here.

Using the last ounce of power in her being, she attacked the second deity and thwarted him to join the first.

"The first whisky we drank together." She commanded to Tristan. By power alone she could tell the other was Rei, her weak state only able to hold him a moment longer. She turned to Rei, wild eyes demanding an answer. "The first book Joss loaned you."

He broke free first with a smirk shortly after. "You're fortunate that it's me. Moby Dick."

Liv turned back to Tristan.

"Do you really think I wouldn't run a security check on this fool before entering this concrete trap?" Rei cut in defensively.

Liv didn't concern herself with Rei's anger, maintaining a cutthroat glare to his companion.

"Talisker." Tristan dryly confirmed. "And you should *both* thank Zeus that I'm here with you, too."

Liv sighed as she broke Tristan's invisible bonds and he crashed to the ground. "I'll not be offering my gratitude to any ancient gods for some time." Liv snarled through her teeth. "Let's go. This way."

Before she turned to open the door, Liv heard Rei murmur, "Invisibilia Clypeus," to her relief, and entered protected and armed into a dimly lit hallway amongst millions in a maze. Liv wanted to feel grateful to have Tristan and Rei as supporting guides, but wouldn't allow herself to feel at ease until she saw the night sky without stone framing it.

After turning right into the main hallway and moving toward the dining room, Tristan grabbed Liv's arm.

"WHAT!?" Liv hissed with wild eyes, a predator attacking its prey.

"This way." Tristan calmly whispered, nodding further down the hall.

She contemplated his proposal. In her mind, she had concreted her escape process that it felt almost like a betrayal going against her determined and repetitive 'right, left, left, left, right, left' plan.

"There are deities dining in there." Rei explained, but with a terse tone that demanded Liv to follow their orders, or else.

She obliged, her heart pounding harder with each step, feeling as if she were fighting a magnetic pull for her conscience's desire to stick to *her* strategy. She wanted to rely on her friends, but she no longer could trust anyone but herself.

When they finally approached a grand mahogany entrance, Rei and Tristan opened one of the two doors and threw Liv into darkness.

After minutes of silence, Tristan lit a torch and came closer, wearily assessing Liv's current state.

"Zeus, Livy, you look like shit. What did they do to you!?"

Liv shushed him immediately. She would not let her mind think about those horrors. Not now. Not ever. She would crash and burn and never return if she allowed it.

SIX

LIV

The world was bright.

She covered her squinted lids, giving her sight time to readjust. A dull grey sky masked the sun, but even still, the clouds hurt her eyes.

"Liv!"

Her two best friends collided into her at once for a brief hug before pulling her back to safety, corralling her to their secret hideaway distanced from the stone entrance.

Liv dropped to the ground, placing her hand against the cool, moist soil. Rocks glistened from the dewy mist.

She was outside. She was free.

"Zeus, Liv. You're shaking." Piper squealed, taking off her navy dégradé wool coat and wrapping it around Liv's shoulders, encompassing her in a heat bubble.

Liv paid no attention to the striking warmth against her chilled bones. Instead, she trailed her fingers across a blade of grass.

Life.

Piper stepped away, joining the other three as they spoke in low voices, glancing over in Liv's direction every few moments. Every so often, a voice carried.

"WHAT happened?"

"You LET him!?..."

"He's still?!"

"Are we supposed to wait?"

All of the hushed whispers silenced.

Liv finally looked up from her grounded sanctuary to find all her friends worriedly staring at her amidst the bright backdrop. She immediately returned her gaze to the rocks – they were much less creepy. And didn't make her feel ashamed.

She heard footsteps approaching her. Liv knew she would need to *be* eventually, but she wasn't yet ready to return to life. She wanted to sit here and not move, and appreciate it on her terms from afar...

Peyton crouched down beside her, gently placing her hand on Liv's shoulder.

"Liv? We need to return to our campsite. Can you stand?"

Peyton had a naturally soothing voice, but it sounded strange with no hint of sass laced between words. Even stranger, never had she heard her previous roommate request, not demand, an action.

"Yes. I think so." Liv grabbed Peyton's extended hand to help lift her up. "But don't coddle me, it's getting weird."

Peyton smirked. "That's my girl."

Yet, her eyes still glimmered with appreciation, reducing the compliment's intended delivery. Liv sighed, accepting it would take everyone time to process the horror from the past weeks. If it had even been that long. Before automatically clarifying her imprisonment time, Liv caught herself and refrained – that would certainly ensue a frenzy with her rescuers, so instead she stood and found Piper pleading with Tristan.

"*Be careful.*"

Absorbing the intensity in Piper's words, Liv asked speculatively, "What's going on?"

Tristan coughed as he took a step back from Piper and explained, "Rei and I are going back. We can't leave-"

"No." Liv demanded, spiraling with fury, "You CANNOT go back. Why on earth would you risk your lives again?! Are you INSANE!?"

"You can't be serious?" Tristan huffed, eyes wide in surprise.

Rei jogged past Liv, nudging Tristan to turn around, and pointed down the hill.

Peyton ran after Rei, sighing in relief and muttering praise.

Liv took a small, weak step forward, feeling lightheaded. She wanted to return to the ground, but pursued forward. Yet, before she could move again, a statuesque structure collided with her, pulling her into his arms.

The movement was too sudden, and speckled dots penetrated Liv's vision, a flash of green echoing in torment, before everything melted into black.

HAYDEN

"Ollie!" Hayden gasped, pulling her into his arms with his heart racing fast.

She fell unconscious, limp against his body which now held her up. As he absorbed what condition she was in, he could only take it as a concrete block dropping on his soul, unable to be dosed. She was so bloody, frail, a complete wreck. *His* beautiful wreck. Alive and whole.

"Hayden, how did you…" Peyton interjected.

"She needs help." Hayden ignored Peyton, as he gently stroked a lock of Liv's hair away from her face, tears welling in his eyes with sad joy as he cradled her and commanded his wings to attach to his back. Hayden turned to his friends, commanding, "We return to the castle tonight."

"Hayden, you'll never make it…" Peyton pleaded, eyes growing wider when Hayden commanded Piper ride Pegasus on their behalf.

He ignored the loyal beast's transportation offer, only because he wasn't certain he'd be able to stay upright on the horse and hold Liv simultaneously without crashing. Flying would exhaust more energy, but it was simpler.

Instead, Hayden summoned Rhys, praying the Medicine Elite would be able to oblige the urgent demand.

She had so many bruises, growing darker while whatever poison ran through her body settled smugly into place.

Zeus Ollie... just hold on a little longer.

With Liv in his arms, Hayden ran down the hill, effortlessly taking to the sky. For all of the sick days, weak moments and anxious terror he encountered these weeks, Liv had it dealt ten-fold. She was stronger than he would ever be. And he needed to be strong enough for her now.

So, he fought the deplenishment once more, ignoring his crying vessel demanding reprieve and instead focused on two things: keeping Liv safe in his arms and delivering her to the royal palace as quickly as possible.

When Hayden burst through the castle doors, he practically stumbled in relief when he found find Rhys, Daphne and Jocelyn already in the parlour, ready to examine her. He raced her up to his royal headquarters and gently placed Liv on the four-poster bed. She still dozed, but not peacefully. Even unconscious, she looked as if she dreamt of nightmares.

He could feel the darkness penetrating her soul but was unsure if waking her from a much-needed sleep was the best call – their connection had weakened to a point where he no longer anticipated her desires. Instead of deliberating the unknown, he turned to Rhys for an immediate evaluation,

"You should leave us." Rhys kindly commanded, nodding to Joss to pull Hayden away.

At first, he fought his sister, desperately holding onto Liv's hand. But as emotion overcame him, he nodded and gave in, realizing his manic state of mind would not be ideal for Liv's recovery, conscious or not. He could barely keep his eyes open now – they stung from the icy wind. His head felt heavy with an unseemingly large pressure growing within, and proved from his mediocre protest against his tiny older sister, his limbs were no longer controllable, no longer his own, and succumbed to her grip almost immediately.

He needed to rein it in – be a source of composure, solidarity for Liv to lean on. She would need him to be strong for the two of them, until she could be strong enough for herself once again.

After pacing for what seemed like eternity, Hayden breathed when Rhys finally emerged from his headquarters and entered the parlour.

"She'll be okay." He nodded, letting Hayden pass him to visit her immediately and without objection.

With every step, Hayden felt more weight lifting off his shoulder. He felt lighter and finally saw hope rise above the horizon once again.

When he quietly opened the door, he found Liv resting peacefully. Her face no longer looked in pain, but as his gaze dropped lower, his heart sunk.

So many bandages, he observed woefully.

So much damage, and she had been *so* strong.

With a heavy heart, he sat down on the bed next to her, grabbed her hand and kissed her knuckle.

She was safe. He could breathe.

Hayden watched Liv sleep for an hour, finding comfort in the sight of her chest peacefully moving up and down – all that he needed for reassurance.

After some time, the door creaked open. Peyton, Rei, Piper and Tristan tiptoed in and stood beside the bed.

"How is she doing?" Peyton whispered, placing a kind hand upon Hayden's shoulder.

"Still sleeping." Hayden replied, gently rubbing his thumb in circles across her knuckle.

"Good. Now can you tell us how you managed to escape Kronos?" Rei tersely asked.

Hayden tensed, wishing this conversation could take place another time. But he refused to leave Liv and knew his stubborn Security Elite would not depart without answers.

"Trellis. I slowed time in the room – Kronos barely took two steps before I departed." Hayden nonchalantly but quickly explained in a whisper.

His watch did not leave Liv while he spoke, and the report instantly concluded once he saw Liv's eyes began to flutter.

"Ollie." Hayden leaned forward, hovering over her, protectively – ready to serve his soul mate, and help with anything she might need.

When Liv opened her eyes, she confusedly looked around the room, trying to determine her surroundings.

"Ollie, you're safe." Hayden assured, kissing her hand again.

Liv's eyes registered back to Hayden, alert and wide.

"Get off me!" Liv screamed, jumping away from him, crawling to the other side of the bed. She looked behind him, to Tristan.

Her eyes were wide with terror; she was trembling. Curled into a ball, her body had immediately closed him off.

Looking back to Hayden, as if she were imagining him, she whispered, "What are you doing here?" She looked around, confused. "Is this another nightmare?"

"Ollie, no, you're awake. What's wrong?" Hayden murmured, standing up and walking around to the other side of the bed.

"No, you… you stay away from me." She pointed at him, still shaking. Liv turned to her friends, aghast. "Where am I!? What is *he* doing here!?"

"Ollie, it's me…." Hayden pressed.

"Get away from me!" She screamed. A cry so loud, her panic took the form of a blade and penetrated his soul directly.

Hayden couldn't move another step. His heart broke at the reaction, but he would do as she commanded, always.

"Liv, this is Hayden." Peyton calmly interjected, testing the waters as she approached. When her presence only triggered silence, no terrifying alarm, she added, "Your boyfriend. The King."

"My boyfriend?" Liv shrieked, shaking her head in confusion, before declaring, "No, that's insanity. I want nothing to do with him." She narrowed her eyes on Hayden, cursing him under her breath, and repeated clearly, "I want nothing to do with you."

The words pierced his heart. Hayden couldn't breathe, it was as if his lungs collapsed. He took a step back, holding onto the bedpost for strength.

Liv found Tristan, her features still stoic, but voice softer as she requested, "Take me to Puerdios, please." She reached her hand to him, slowly forcing herself out of bed once she was securely held by the Fire God. It took all that Hayden had not to leap forward and assist her. Everything within him to refrain from begging her to stay.

After an initial struggle, Tristan finally lifted her into his arms obligingly, sharing an apologetic look toward Hayden. Liv followed his gaze, turning to Hayden with a stranger's glare and sending one cold shiver down his spine before the two departed the room.

What the hell had happened to her?

PIPER

Her friend had been rescued.

They had actually succeeded in bringing Liv back to Puerdios.

Yet, Piper worried if the Liv that first attended Puerdios was the same Liv who now returned.

She shivered at the sad tragedy they had all witnessed at the Royal Palace the day before.

Tristan had escorted Liv almost immediately after her command, leaving all of their friends, including her, speechless and with mouths drawn open.

Since then, Liv had stayed alone in her room, with Tristan her only visitor.

Piper did not know what to expect now that she was heading down the same corridors they had normally frequented together. Back to Liv's old loft – and into a past that felt decades old.

Upon arriving at the large wooden door, Piper straightened out her mixed grey, double-breasted, tweed peacoat dress out of habit and took a deep breath to compose herself before finally knocking.

After a moment, it opened to reveal Tristan.

He looked gorgeous, sporting a classic black t-shirt and ink denim. But alas, when did he not?

Piper beamed, her smile uncontainable, until she saw Tristan's blank face in return, met with silence. She cocked her head, furrowed her brows and immediately coughed as she instinctively looked down to her black combat booties to recover, to clear the familiarity from her mind, and return back to the shyer form she used to be.

"I'm here to see Liv." She explained, passing by him without making eye contact again.

She *wished* her voice didn't squeak so high that time.

Shaking her head and with an ache in her stomach from that awkward interaction, Piper marched forward determinedly, although not entirely looking forward to the next stop aboard this unknown train, either.

Piper found Liv on her velvet purple couch, drinking coffee by the blazing fire. She paused, taking in her best friend – hollowed eyes, bruises lingering on her neck, a bloody gash that that cut across her collar bone. Beneath the grey cashmere sweater and blanket, Piper could only imagine the additional remnants that scarred Liv's past.

"I dread this part." Liv growled above her coffee. "The first reunion. I shall be very excited for the next time we meet, after the shock of this one is far behind us."

Piper silently sat down, across from her friend.

"I don't need to make it weird." She whispered, trying to avoid gazing upon Liv again. Her eyes were already watery.

"You always make it weird." Liv darkly laughed, adding wholeheartedly, "Which is exactly why you are my best friend. Come here."

Piper looked up, beaming. Quicker than lightening, Piper was beside Liv, gently pulling her into a hug.

"I missed you." She smiled.

"I missed you, too." Liv croaked.

It felt good to be near her best friend, however whole or broken she may be.

When she pulled away, she noticed Liv mirroring her own actions of trying to subtly wipe tears from her eyes.

"I really do hate these reunions." Liv chuckled with a sniffle.

"It's over now." Piper smiled, before sighing deeply and summoning the materials Liv needed to catch up on her Puerdios curriculum. Normalcy. It was what Liv desired.

Even with the amount of schoolwork Piper had worked on during their journeys, she was behind; Liv wasn't even on the same track anymore.

Her Element Elite's eyes grew wide.

"I know." Piper agreed, spreading the curriculum across the couch in organized piles. "But I've already read half of it so I can tutor you and share my notes, but the assignments are another story…"

"No, no – not that." Liv waved the books off, pausing after she glanced over to the tall pile with dread. "I mean, we'll get to that shit show eventually…" Liv shook her head, turning her attention back to Piper, grabbing her hands.

"What are you doing? We already did the weird reunion thing…" Piper speculatively eyed her friend, who now psychotically smiled at their grasp.

"Piper," Liv looked up with a grin, "I need you to blow something up."

"What? You can't be serious!" Piper squeaked, releasing her grip and backing away from Liv. She finally looked up to Tristan, who had been lingering in the kitchen. He shrugged, turning away to refill his coffee cup.

"Okay, don't act like I'm crazy, please." Liv rolled her eyes. If they were going to pretend everything was okay, Piper needed the reassurance that Liv one hundred percent acknowledged that *nothing* was okay. "I mean, a lot of shit happened to me. I'll admit it. And I'm probably not okay. But I'm still sane. I'm still me."

"You just asked me to blow up something in your apartment." Piper reiterated blankly.

"I have theories." Liv retorted back, sinking back into the couch and taking another sip of coffee.

"You went AWOL at the sight of Hayden." Piper pushed, "Whether you like it or not. Things are not the same."

"King Hayden." Liv sneered, as if his name were propaganda. "Tristan already tried to explain. But frankly, I don't know how I could have loved somebody that I have no memory of."

"You don't remember anything about Hayden?" Piper whispered, dread filling her soul.

If the prophecy was their best chance of defeating the Dark Gods, Kronos must have manipulated her friend's mind to break the soul mate connection, weakening both Liv and Hayden simultaneously.

Much darker forces were at play.

"All I know is that his face haunts my mind and when I think of him…" Liv shivered, taking a deep breath before shaking her head. "NO. I can't." She closed her eyes, taking deep breaths. "Distract me. What's my first written assignment?"

"Er, a thesis on mythical creatures that reveal humanity's deepest fears." Piper spurted out quickly. "It also leads into the next assignment about depicting mythological creatures and stories from the constellations."

"Ugh." Liv's head was buried in her hands. "Monsters. Monsters are in the stars. Monsters reveal humanity's deepest fears."

Piper stared at her morbid friend. She knew she couldn't coddle Liv, but Hades, what were the demons her friend really faced at night? What happened to her while she was captured?

Instead, Piper went with a simple and nonchalant, "sure," before getting up and excusing herself, promising to return once she got more reading materials from the library.

She shyly nodded to Tristan, barely making eye contact, before leaving the apartment and sprinted toward Hayden's loft.

The king needed to know all of this, whether Liv knew him or not.

Piper mumbled, "Eugene," the new password to enter the royal loft at Puerdios University, and immediately regretted entering without permission as she overheard Hayden and Rei in the midst of a heated argument.

Hayden tossed his hands up in the air.

"Puerdios is not as safe as the royal palace! What do you expect – for Tristan to stay with Ollie as her personal bodyguard?"

Piper froze when Hayden pointed toward Liv's apartment, where she stood in direct line of the King's accusation.

"Piper, over here." Peyton called over, chewing on popcorn as she watched from the couch.

Piper mumbled an apology to both Hayden and Rei, before scrambling over to the safety zone Peyton had identified behind the black leather couch across the room.

"Popcorn?" Peyton munched, holding out the bowl without removing her eyes from the scene. Piper grabbed a handful, appreciative for the nervous outlet of chewing.

"You cannot control her, Hayden." Rei advised calmly.

Hayden ran his hand through his hair, "What am I supposed to do?"

"You have to let her heal." Rei offered sadly. "On her own terms."

"Then I'll camp at Puerdios." Hayden resolved, "There is no way I'm leaving my soul mate in this condition, defenseless."

"And risk smothering her?" Rei asked dryly.

Hayden glared at his Security Elite, ignoring the comment. "We'll have the next Elite meeting here at my loft. Thursday."

"So that's it? You're going to reside at Puerdios University? And what? Attend classes?" Rei growled. "You are the king, Hayden. Need I remind you of that?"

"Yes, Rei. Please do. I clearly forgot." Hayden sarcastically replied.

"This is ridiculous. I am dealing with an infant!" Rei yelled, turning to Peyton for support, finding both she and Piper with handfuls of popcorn halfway shoved in their mouths.

Piper could see Rei's skin boiling, about to explode.

"Really!? All of you… ARE INFANTS!" He concluded, directing his anger back to Hayden and pointing. "Two weeks. You get two weeks at Puerdios. I will tolerate this for two weeks." He turned to Peyton, reiterating, "TWO WEEKS!" before marching out of the apartment and slamming the door.

The silence that echoed was painful. Piper almost wished she had stayed with crazy Liv.

Peyton coughed, raising her bowl in the air toward Hayden.

"Popcorn?"

The glare she received from Hayden in return made both Piper and Peyton recoil further behind the couch. Piper grabbed another handful as it seemed they would be stuck there for quite some time.

LIV

It had been three days.

A blur of worried side glances, calculated responses and strategic check-ins, all in efforts to keep the glass from breaking.

It had been three days since she returned to her bright and cheery apartment, to Puerdios, to the life she had before *he* had captured her.

Liv rolled over in her bed, squinting out to the window and determining just how much longer she had until her first class.

She sighed.

Liv dreaded getting out of her bed.

And the most ironic part was that she had been unable to sleep while within it, yet still cursed when the sun finally rose, signaling the eventuality of facing the day.

She felt numb and incomplete. She knew a piece of her was missing, but she accepted there was a good chance she would never be getting that part of her back – it had been stolen from her in the dungeons, tortured with every evil glance from her captors, and killed when she pierced her sword into the golden snake's neck, never to return.

Liv was different. She *felt* different.

She once believed in hope, that with hard work and determination, good would triumph.

Not anymore.

By the cruel sun's position, she knew it was almost 240 degrees, and in 30 degrees she would need to meet her fate on the East Lawn for Warfare & Defense.

But if Liv thought about what she was going to wear, she could stay in bed for a couple degrees longer…

She knew she had a new gold corset with a burgundy silk skirt that Piper's aunt had delivered over the weekend, claiming the metal detailing served as the perfect armor for her first day back. It would pair well with the beige suede sandals Liv wore the day before, so they were already out and broken in…

And makeup. She would keep it simple, matching her lip to the bold hue of the silk skirt.

Well shit.

Liv groaned, trying to think of any additional details to help her stay in the warm confines of her bed and avoid the inevitable day ahead.

Finally, the ultimate alarm went off when she heard a knock at the door.

"I'll get it." Tristan jumped up from her couch, probably awake and bored but too worried to tease Liv about her irresponsible sleeping patterns.

…Another reason why Liv dreaded her return to reality.

She heard Tristan answer the door, Piper stutter as she stumbled into the kitchen and immediately offered to make coffee, cabinets swinging and water running before Tristan coughed and yelled of his departure to Liv.

Again, Liv felt the pounding turn from flames to wind penetrate her apartment – the simple handoff for Liv's newest babysitter.

She had felt wind gusting within Piper when she visited the day before, stronger than she had ever experienced with her best friend. Again, Piper's presence today only reinstated Liv's curiosity to whether her prayers to the Element Gods came true.

But, she wouldn't go down that path again. Even Liv understood how her recent request for Piper to prove the inclination only added weariness toward the question of Liv's psychological well-being.

She hated the tip toeing around. The second-guessing of her every move.

She hated it all.

"Liv, you up?" Piper called from the kitchen. "Coffee's brewing!"

"I'm up." Liv called back, her voice low and hoarse.

The sweet smell of fresh caramel, honey and chocolate infiltrated the apartment, giving Liv the motivation she needed to drag herself out of bed, change out of her silk pajamas and throw on her corset attire. She ran to the bathroom, quickly dutch braiding her hair into one long and messy Mohawk behind her skull, ending the thick braid by her ribs.

She quickly applied eyeliner and mascara, before painting her lips a deep rich mauve. It didn't entirely mask the hollowness of her gaunt face but if it weren't for her dead soul inside, Liv would have believed she passed for a normal, non-traumatized deity. Liv shrugged; it would have to do.

She slipped on her nude heels and joined Piper in the kitchen, plastering a forced smile to her face.

She was fine. She would be fine.

"You speak my language." Liv joked, gratuitously grabbing the coffee for something to focus on other than her well-being.

"I figured we could go to Warfare and Defense together." Piper shrugged, taking a sip of coffee herself. "I didn't realize Tristan was staying the night, or else I wouldn't have come so abruptly…"

Liv waved her off. "I'm sure he appreciates the break. I'm not the most lively of company these days."

Piper bit her lip, "But at least you can talk to him? Or feel a sense of security? It's probably good that he's here. And I was wondering why I hadn't seen him since you returned, so that explains it…"

Liv raised a brow, studying Piper's rambling reaction. She better cut her friend off before Piper hyperventalated.

"I promise you, it's nothing. We don't talk much. He sleeps with me. Although I don't really sleep…" Liv admitted, embarrassingly.

Piper's eyes grew wide, dropping her coffee mug on the counter, splashing it all over her deep jade two-piece ensemble.

"Zeus!" Piper shrieked, grabbing the kitchen towel and dampening it with water before patting her skirt down.

"Piper, you okay?" Liv finally asked.

"I- I'm fine." Piper squeaked, continuing to wipe down her skirt.

Liv sighed deeply, secretly happy for once, the concern wasn't directed toward her.

"If you dry the skirt, it should be salvageable." Liv advised, secretly wondering if this small maneuver could help confirm her speculation.

"Done." Piper exhaled, dropping the towel on the kitchen.

It happened so quickly. Liv lifted herself up to inspect the skirts remnants – but alas, it was good as new, dry-cleaned and without a flinch from Piper.

"The fashion gods smile upon you." Liv joked, unable to control the natural smile creeping onto her face. The muscles felt strange, unused, as her mouth organically curved upward.

"My fashion aunt would have cursed me otherwise." Piper sighed, laughing at her clumsiness. "No wonder she saves her best creations for you."

Liv stood up, spinning in response. "Your aunt simply creates gowns that help protect my body from running into inanimate objects. Next time, she's going to gift me an actual knight's armor and call it fashion."

Piper laughed, "I would *love* to see Rei's face if you walked up in that get up for Warfare and Defense."

"Speaking of which…" Liv groaned.

"Are you ready?" Piper asked quietly.

"It's amusing you think Rei would let me have a choice." Liv retorted back, grabbing her books. "Let's go."

Piper followed her out, as Liv took a look down the main hallway of her beloved university with a deep breath.

First day back.

She could do this.

Even in the morning, the candles glowed down the stone hallway, creating a warm and inviting atmosphere against the medieval architecture. Original baroque paintings decorated the hall behind stunning marble statues of mythological gods of the past.

The rococco, majestic decorations served as inspiration to the students, alluding to the mighty, great deities whose footsteps they had the 'honor' and 'responsibility' to follow with their academic learnings. But, as Liv looked around with contempt, she only saw a mockery of her heroes. To her, the once glorified figures were now merely *monsters* inadequately memorialized in the school, taunting her every step. There were two sides to every story, and now her inspirational surroundings depicting history felt more like propaganda.

Fellow students passed her and Piper as they glided down the hall, sequins glistening and tailored suits shining below the candlelight. Whispers followed, surrounding them with side glances and gossip.

"Now would be a great time for Tristan to blow up a statue or for Kyril to throw up in the quad so I become yesterday's news…" Liv muttered under her breath, before begging to Piper, "Can you cause a scene? Throw a drink at Dylan?"

"I don't think any of those circumstances will carry weight compared to the Elemental Elite being captured by Kronos and escaping the Dark God headquarters…" Piper apologized softly.

"Worth a shot." Liv mumbled discouragedly, as they turned a corner to exit into the pavilion.

Liv froze.

He was there.

Green flashed across her mind, momentarily blinding her. She could feel the blade cutting across her skin and reopening her wounds, a pounding sensation knocking into her stomache and stealing all the air from her lungs upon impact.

"Liv!" Piper yelled, steadying Liv with worried eyes. Her mousy nose intensified the genuine concern when paired with her high-pitched squeak. She looked to see what caused the sudden outbreak, finding Hayden still as well, with an apologetic and pained expression on his face as he kept his distance, completely helpless. "That's Hayden. Not Kronos." Piper clarified, grabbing Liv's face and making her look into her own eyes. "Liv it's me. You're okay. You're okay."

Liv nodded blindly, blinking as she came back to the present.

Hayden quickly passed by, ducking his head down.

"I *hate* him." Liv hissed, taking a step back as she caught her breath.

"That's Hayden. Not Kronos." Piper reiterated.

"They are the same to me." Liv panted, shaking her head. "And if what Tristan says is true, that he's the king, then *why* is he lurking around Puerdios University? Doesn't he have somewhere more important to be?"

"Liv, he's our age. He's a student here, too." Piper explained.

"He's what!?" Liv's eyes grew wide. "Why haven't I seen him here before?"

"Come on, let's keep going."

Piper led Liv away from the stone wall and out into the pavilion.

"I was preparing to face him for council meetings, but school as well? Is there anywhere I can be free of him?" Liv sighed.

"I'll put in a word." Tristan chimed in from behind, walking alongside Liv. "Until then, I offer the sanctuary of my cabin."

"Please." Liv pleaded, before turning to Tristan, surprised to see he no longer donned his classic black tee and had changed into a grey double-breasted suit and brown leather jacket with a shearling collar. "You clean up nice, Tristan."

"All thanks to Piper." Tristan casually explained, sharing a wicked grin to both girls.

Piper turned immediately away, blushing.

Liv pondered her friend's shy reaction until she heard her name in the distance, finding Kyril and Zayne greeting them at the edge of the East Lawn.

"Liv!"

Kyril embraced Liv into a powerful hug.

"Where is everyone? Aren't we technically late?" Liv observed over her friend's shoulder.

"Dark Gods outside of the Elements, Security and Defense, Candor and Medicine Pillar no longer attend Puerdios." Kyril explained sadly. "Radical Darks across all pillars have dropped out of school as well. Kronos's orders executed by Dark Elite decrees."

"That's a bit extreme, no?" Liv challenged while embracing him in a hug, before moving on to Zayne. "The best way to find compromise and work through issues is through conversation, connection and debate, not separation and isolation. That will only make the divide worse."

"They want control. It seems pretty in line with their agenda to us." Zayne sighed. "It's good to have you back, Liv."

Shortly after, his gaze glazed over Liv and up to the sky where their instructor was descending.

"I'm sure my father went easy on you lot while I was away, so plan on making up for loss time today." Rei commanded over ground as he flew into the East Lawn. "Partner up for training."

Liv instinctively nodded toward Piper, when Rei cut in politely.

"Piper, warm up with Zayne for the time being." He turned to Liv, "Liv, can I have a word?"

"Of course." Liv shrugged, walking away from the warmup field with Rei. "What's up?"

"I have another assignment for you to work on this week." Rei offered, handing Liv a notebook and pen. "Call it a PTSD assignment – I want you to analyze your experience with the Dark Gods, reflect and theorize on it."

Liv reluctantly took the notebook from her instructor. "You seriously want me to 'Dear diary' through Warfare and Defense class?"

Even stranger, Rei didn't resort to his automatic retort about 'always being serious' but instead remained calm.

"I'm sure you have a lot you're still processing, Liv." Rei stated bluntly, "Any good warrior thinks about past battles and learns from them. I want you to do the same."

"And what about the actual curriculum being taught this week?" Liv raised an eyebrow.

"We'll continue our personal training sessions tomorrow morning. We'll work on it then."

Liv nodded, albeit still slightly confused, but as soon as Rei glared with a 'well, what are you waiting for?' look, she immediately obeyed, turning around to find a nice tree to set up camp and… reflect.

She knew she should have just stayed in bed.

When the class concluded, Liv had drawn a beautiful flower and counted 62 rocks surrounding the general area.

"I'm just… not a writer." Liv admitted, recoiling under Rei's judgmental stare.

"Apparently, an artist. Shall we frame this?" Rei retorted, turning the notebook back to Liv so the flower could laugh in her face.

She ignored his asshole comment, standing herself up and brushing up any dirt or leaves from her gown.

"Tomorrow morning, then." Rei crossed his arms, with a speculative invitation.

Liv waved him off, ignoring his dull-bladed glare, and ran away to catch up with Piper and head off to Meteorology II.

"Hello my darling class!" Professor Deligne dramatically glided into the room, to Liv's never-ending amusement. Besides Piper's anxious correspondence to stay caught up on curriculum, Professor Deligne's mighty class of two must have taken a hard hiatus when her only students in Meteorology II weren't at Puerdios University.

"Hello Professor Deligne." Liv called back, resisting the urge to giggle.

"We have much to catch up on, you're cruelly behind in the semester." Professor Deligne sat on her desk, lowering her glasses below her eyes to interrogate her students, an act Liv gathered she had practiced numerous times to an empty classroom. "I expect you have already reviewed our materials on heat transfer and the Coriolis Effect?"

Piper's hand shot up in the air. "We have. Which group would you like to focus on for today's lesson? Conduction? Radiation? Convection?"

"All of them." Professor Deligne smugly replied. "And dear me," she lowered her gaze back down to her syllabus, "we'll need to scurry through our Astronomy concentration – please simultaneously pull out your focus books on constellations and their storytelling benefits."

Dramatically, Professor Deligne sighed, trying to extend her attempt to problem-solve the apparently dire educational situation her two students faced. "But perhaps we move that to a theory assignment – due our next class for discussion."

"For all classifications?" Piper clarified, her voice growing higher pitched and more anxious by each homework assignment and class progression. "Zodiac, heavenly waters, *and* deities?"

"Correct." Professor Deligne nodded. Liv was certain she spotted a hint of sinister amusement in their professor's eyes.

And it was only her *first* day back.

Liv prayed to the stars her reading would suffice for today's pop-quiz as she sank further into her chair, hoping Professor Deligne simply missed conversing with another interested deity on the subject versus actually testing how much Piper and Liv knew between the two.

Deity Power II went by equally as challenging as her previous classes for her first day back. On one hand, it was an actual class, so she more easily blended in with her fellow students – not cast out as the healing warrior or receiving desperate attention with a grueling test. But after missing weeks' worth of lessons, Liv relied heavily on Piper to carry her through the unknown subjects or sneak context into the current curriculum. Especially when the class pivoted from power lessons to theory and covering the phases of substance conversions, which proved more difficult with Liv's lack of attendance and expected knowledge from her previously missed Chemistry II classes.

Alas, she only caused one accidental steam explosion by not neutralizing the reactor in time, which in hindsight wasn't the worst-case scenario. Although during the incident, Liv turned an entirely new degree of red where she almost steam exploded herself.

The only plus to the entire day, was that she managed to royally avoid her 'fellow classmate,' King Hayden. When she returned to the sanctuary of her apartment with Piper, she collapsed on the couch and summoned a bottle of red wine.

"Tell me everything I need to know to survive Chemistry II, Mythological Creatures and Environmental Science tomorrow." Liv pleaded, handing Piper a glass of Merlot.

"Hayden might be in Mytho Creatures and Envi-Sci." Piper squeaked before taking a deep sip of her glass.

"Really?" Liv sighed.

Piper ignored Liv's unenthusiastic response with an apologetic look as she continued to drink the wine from her glass.

"Okay, got it. He's your 'friend,' so no complaining. Thank you for the warning." Liv batted her eyelashes as she primly smiled and over-exaggerated her gratitude. "Any tips on how to prepare for it? You saw how I froze today. He terrifies me."

"Did you ever think that's what Kronos and Arlo wanted?" Piper finally offered. "To manipulate your mind so you couldn't recognize your soul mate?"

"Soul mate?" Liv spit out her wine. "You've got to be fucking joking."

"I'm not going to tell you how to *be* Liv. After the hell you've been through, you deserve to process this as you need." Piper set down her wine glass. "I only suggest you try to keep an open mind. You don't find it at all strange that while all of your closest friends think only the best of Hayden and want only the best for you, you on the other hand recoil at the sound of his name? You're so willing to curse a man you claim to have no recollection of?"

Liv took a sip of her wine glass, contemplating the possibility. She desperately searched for any memory involving him, but all she felt was fear. That she had blacked something *terrible* out of her mind in association with him.

"I know Kronos and Arlo are the enemy." Liv reiterated, trying to control her shaking hands as she set down her wine glass. "But I know there's something missing with Hayden, something I don't trust. Call it a gut feeling, I guess."

Piper nodded, understanding Liv had a lot to sort through. "You're allowed to have those suspicions, it's not my place to tell you otherwise."

Piper summoned their Chemistry books, when Liv felt the overburdening wind gusting through the apartment. Something was different with Piper, she knew it.

"The first thing we should cover is neutralizing reactors, since you should have known that today…" Piper began flipping through her textbook when a knock sounded at the door.

Liv unlocked the door and swung it open, revealing Tristan reporting for duty.

"Hey ladies." Tristan greeted, no longer in his suit and leather jacket, but back to a black hoodie and matching sweats.

"Hi." Piper whispered, slamming her book shut. "Shoot, I forgot I… promised Peyton we'd grab dinner tonight."

"She can come over here. I'll make pizza or something." Liv offered, heading toward the kitchen.

"No, no – it's okay. She has a whole thing planned at her loft. Brined the pork chops and everything…" Strangely, or not so strangely for Piper, her friend gathered her belongings and ran to the exit before Liv could oppose again. "I'll see you both… tomorrow." She called out by the door, pausing to look sadly back at Tristan before shutting it behind her.

"So… pizza?" Tristan offered, getting up from the couch and following Liv into the kitchen, lesser the wise as he poured himself a glass of wine. "Pepperoni or combo?"

HAYDEN

The way she recoiled at his gaze.

How she dropped into a frenzied stupor at his presence.

And he hadn't even *approached* her. In fact, he stayed as far as he possibly could in the situation.

Which was worse? Liv not remembering him, or casting him as a villain in her story?

How had he been dealt both hands in this losing card game?

She was *terrified* of him.

He shuttered at the thought, focusing instead on opening the vintage Malbec for his mother.

Finally, the cork popped out and Hayden streamed the wine through an aerator and into a carafe before pouring the delicious substance into their respective glasses.

"Thank you." Daphne gently smiled, although the gesture did not reach her eyes.

A silence hovered between mother and son.

Daphne adjusted her white pleated skirt, "So, how was your return to education? Learn anything interesting?"

Hayden eyed her as he grabbed an onion and began chopping. Flashes of Liv doing the same action from the very same place haunted his mind. Yet, it was all he knew of the kitchen.

"Is Joss joining us tonight?"

"Sadly no – Demetrius showed up to the royal palace so she's a bit occupied." Daphne shared, taking another sip of her wine. "Can I help with anything?"

"You already know the answer to that." Hayden snapped, pushing the onions aside and grabbing a clove of garlic.

Liv's ghost lingered, mirroring his move.

"Clearly, we need to address something on your mind." Daphne sighed, placing her glass down on the counter. "What is it?"

"Why don't you tell me, for once." Hayden retorted, putting down the knife and stepping away from the counter.

"You know how this works." Daphne reiterated as she stood up. "I tell you what I can."

"What's the point of having two Candor Elites on your side, *in your family*, if both are silenced the entire time?" Hayden finally yelled.

Daphne sat back down, taking another sip of wine.

More silence.

"I tried to seed the dream of Liv's kidnapping in her slumber, so she could combat it in her sleep…" Daphne started to explain.

"Yet, you didn't tell her you were doing that so she could actually prepare. You *saw* that she would be kidnapped, didn't you?"

"That's not how it works, and you know it." Daphne pleaded, taking another sip of her wine. "I can't always tell when something will happen. And what would you do, have Liv live in fear? I tried to keep her safe to the best of my ability."

"You tried to keep her safe and you *failed*." Hayden sneered. "I failed. We all failed. And now she doesn't even remember me, mother."

"Oh, I'm sorry Hayden." Daphne eyes saddened, but the delivery could never be genuine. She already knew. Daphne already anticipated he was angry with her; it was exactly why she came.

He'd learned long ago that however pure his mother's intentions may have seemed, they were also precisely calculated.

Dinner continued on uncomfortably.

After Hayden finished sautéing the garlic and onion in olive oil while boiling the pasta, he mixed all together in tomato sauce and served the dish, alongside a Caesar salad, to his mother.

Liv's memory never left his side – a tormenting echo of a previous time.

"When did you learn your way around the kitchen?" Daphne asked politely, taking a bite of her entrée and humming, "This is delicious."

Hayden politely smiled, taking a bite of his own meal, remembering his many cooking trials in the loft while trying to impress Liv so she wouldn't feel homesick. Fortunately, this simple and easy dish became one of her favorites, mostly because it was the first he had successfully served unburnt.

"Of course." Daphne smiled, reading the thoughts that ran through her son's mind.

There was nothing more to say.

They ate their dinner together, in silence. A comfortable silence. An uncomfortable silence. A rollercoaster of read thoughts and controlled actions. Until Daphne finally stood from the counter and thanked Hayden for the wonderful meal.

"I'll see you on Thursday, my darling."

Hayden stood in response, walked his mother to the door and hugged her as she stood near the doorway.

"I'll have word from the sirens by then." Hayden finally said, unnecessarily reporting his upcoming whereabouts to a mother who already knew.

"Good luck with Calithya. Don't get drowned by the sea." Daphne sternly advised.

Hayden brushed off her concern. For his mom – it was only words.

"Safe travels back home, mother. Please send Joss my love."

"I love you, darling. Hang in there." Daphne released her embrace and paused in the doorway, staring at her son with empathy and sad eyes. "I did what I could, Hayden."

Yet, with his mother's burst of honesty and consolation, weakened with a rare emotion emitting from her eyes, his own truth surfaced in respite.

"You didn't do enough."

Suddenly his mother pulled him into another hug, a true hug, a deep embrace that consumed him, decorum be damned.

"Rely on the bond Hayden, she'll come around."

Daphne pulled back, her face once again stoic, masked – as if her emotional lapse had never occurred.

But before Hayden could ask any further questions, his mother was gone.

LIV

"Well, if it's not the little ray of fucking sunshine herself." Rei grunted, "You're late."

Liv rolled her eyes. She was exactly on time. And brought coffee.

"It's 210 degrees. You said 210 degrees." She handed Rei an Americano. "And you're welcome."

"I said we start training at 210 degrees, not drink coffee and exchange pleasantries at 210 degrees." Rei clarified, "And even if I said thank you, which I didn't, replying with 'you're welcome' drives me nuts. It doesn't even make sense."

"Who's the little ray of fucking sunshine now?" Liv smirked. "Wake up on the wrong side of the bed this morning, Elite?"

He took a sip of his coffee, ignoring the comment.

"So, what are we working on today?" Liv took a sip of her own brew before she set it down and began to stretch.

"You're weirdly chipper. You're never this eager in the morning." Rei glared at Liv, "Stop doing that."

At that moment, Liv was mid-lunge with her arm across her torso and although internally hilarious, it was proving harder to execute successfully due to her navy, long-sleeved, laced short dress with an accompanying back train.

Once she stood and faced Rei, he seemed to relax.

"So, what's with the creepy energy?"

Liv looked at the ground, shifting her weight on her navy platform booties.

"This is the closest return to my previous life, so it's more enjoyable than everything else… to date." She finally admitted.

"Well, let's change that, then." Rei maliciously grinned. "Let's start with a run – down the mountain and back. Hope you broke in your ridiculous hiking boots."

She was dying. Her body had weakened to an embarrassing state while in chains. All of the endurance she had spent months building, gone.

As Rei continued pushing her to the brink of her strength, her limits – Liv wasn't sure if she wanted to murder him or cry.

She hung onto her sword, an extended limb that made her weak arm want to chop the dead weight off. If he got close enough to her, the duel between the two would be no fair match at this point.

Panting, her only choice would be keep the distance so it would not come to swordplay.

"You can't run forever, Liv." Rei's voice echoed within the trees.

Liv rolled her eyes, she only had to run until 265 degrees – when training would conclude and Rei would have to release her to Chemistry. It was a cheap strategy, but she was in cheap condition for training.

"Distance won't make a difference when I do this – get ready, Liv!"

She heard her friend's evil cackle echo through the forest as he enjoyed making her life a living hell.

And she brought him coffee today. The nerve.

When Liv turned to jokingly flip him off, she saw two bright green eyes in the distance.

Liv screamed, her eyes wide in terror as she immediately ran in the opposite direction but instead collided headfirst into a tree, sending it timbering upon impact.

"Liv! What the Hades?" Rei hollered from afar, jogging over to his now frozen target.

Liv desperately searched the forest, trying to locate the green eyes, when Rei's form came into focus and brought her back to the present.

She was okay. He wasn't here.

"I'm fine." Liv coughed, walking toward Rei determinedly, and commanded, "Again."

"Not yet." Rei instructed. "Are you sure you're okay? You've been different all morning."

"I said *I'm fine*." Liv tersely replied, ignoring the question and not wanting to release the demons she held within. "Can we continue with training, now?"

Rei held his gaze, studying her more closely for details than a microscope could pick up.

Liv bit her lip, looking away. That was the worst – being with someone who welcomed silence, who knew it could drain her stubbornness and unplug whatever it was she was trying to contain inside.

"Clearly, you're not fine." Rei observed tartly.

"Okay, clearly I'm not!" Liv screamed, raising her hands up in surrender. "Happy now? I admit it! And what can you do about it? Nothing! So, CAN WE *PLEASE* GO BACK TO TRAINING?"

Rei sighed, dropping his sword and gracefully fell to the ground alongside it. He crossed his leg and patted the spot next to him on the grass.

Liv furrowed her brows but didn't argue. It was hard continuing to angrily pick a fight with a deity who didn't want one.

Still holding her sword, she sat down beside him.

The two both looked out to the field, watching the sun sparkle between the trees in the horizon, including the one she had just knocked over. Light glittered between the branches, as if each limb had been speckled with gold dust.

"It's the middle of winter and yet snow hasn't fallen in weeks." Rei stated. Not an accusation, but an observation. "One might think the Element Elite no longer likes the cold."

The stone floors. Shivering flesh against the relentless surface determined to keep Liv's fingers stiff and blue. Icy chill among nothingness.

Liv shook her head out of the memory, moving her fingers around the handle of her sword. Ignoring the connotation, she replied poignantly, "One might also discover global warming truly does exist."

But it didn't feel like a joke, and Rei didn't laugh.

"Liv, there are other forms of training required to maintain your strength." Rei pressed. "Physically, you're more powerful than ever. But you will not walk away from this war whole unless you acknowledge and exercise your mental state."

"Do you think I'm weak?" Liv stood up defensively, and hissed, "Are you insinuating my mind is not sound?"

"No, of course not." Rei stood up too, dropping his sword. "I'm telling you that there is something different and you are not the same. And that's okay, people change. But, I am here if you want to talk about whatever it is that is rotting your soul."

Liv huffed in amazement, more so at his accurate assessment.

"My soul?" She asked weakly, her hand naturally landed on top of her chest. "I feel like a part of it is missing – that it is *gone*. Whether rotted or torn away, half of me already no longer exists. It was left, *stolen*, in that cruel, stoned ice of hell. I am different because I am no longer me. I am a shadow. A missing piece of the girl who was elected the Element Elite. How am I supposed to heal a part of me that has disappeared? That no longer *exists*?"

Liv swore if Rei suggested his stupid journaling assignment…

But instead, more shocking words dispersed from her counsel's mouth.

"If you gave Hayden a chance-"

"No!" Liv's eyes grew frantic. "How *dare* you suggest *he* is a part of this healing process? He is *evil*." Flashes of wicked green eyes penetrated her skull, memories of the darkness surfacing in green glory. "He… tormented me for *pleasure*. He has you all fooled!"

"Liv, I *saw* Kronos. He looks identical to Hayden…"

Liv shook her head, fighting the embers desperate to release chaos in order to protect the remnants of her soul. She turned around, needing to walk away and literally cool off the steam emitting from her body.

"Okay! Okay." Rei commanded, still unable to tame his intolerance for dramatics. He was only proud he didn't hiss this time around. "If you won't listen to me, then listen to the stars."

Liv turned around, tilted her head in surprise and retorted, "The stars? Yeah, right…"

Yet, she still looked up to the sky in wonder. The soft fiery clouds were gradient, slowly transforming into a soft peach that blended from a light blue and purple on the other end of the spectrum toward the castle, where stars still sparkled from the night. Following the slow progression with her sight, she already felt calmer than before. The stars held ancient, unknown powers, awaiting to be harnessed. Perhaps there was a star meant just for her to conquer. But it didn't seem to be a sentiment that matched Rei's persona.

And when Rei remained silent, without providing a sarcastic mockery, Liv looked back to him, intrigued at the suggestion. "What do you mean?"

Rei stared blankly back, before processing the question, understanding the breakthrough value even Liv could not identify.

"Look to the stars the guidance?"

Liv raised an eyebrow in confusion.

"You've got to be fucking kidding me." He muttered in disbelief, running his hand roughly through his caramel hair, realizing just how much *had* been taken from Liv. Any grain connected to Hayden had been swiped from her memory and replaced with skewed, tormented ones.

He turned back to Liv. "Next training lesson, go to your room. Stare at the stars. You once believed they could help you, so maybe this exercise will allow you to do some literal soul searching."

Liv looked back up to the sky, still intrigued and already more at peace. Maybe it *was* working.

She nodded to Rei, thanking him for the lesson, and wandered aimlessly back toward the castle, never letting her sight go below the skyline.

SEVEN

PIPER

Between trying to catch up on schoolwork, avoid Tristan *and* Hayden, and keep a considerate eye on her best friend, Puerdios had become Piper's own strategic warzone.

She had been relieved to hear Hayden went to visit the Sirens and negotiate with Calithya during the week – easing one of her burdens but also making her feel equally guilty for having the initial reaction. Sure, the king was her friend, but it was also exhausting trying to maneuver routes and ignore Liv's ruthless commentary. Not even to mention the overwhelming amount of curriculum Piper was responsible to catch up *and* tutor Liv on. And finally, Hayden most pertently served as an unwanted distraction for Piper's biggest mission of all: steering clear of any and all interactions with Tristan. The Whisky God put her on edge, made her feel unruly things, and most of all, question *everything*.

Liv had been cast out yet again to therapy writing for Warfare and Defense, so Piper had nearly glued herself to Zayne during class. The only strange part with her action was that this particular class wasn't focused on pairs, but individual performance.

And when Tristan offered to help her cross a canyon, Piper instead overreacted, bumped into Zayne and almost accidentally forced him off the cliff.

Piper felt like *she* needed therapy writing. It was all becoming too much.

It wasn't that she didn't like Tristan, it was the complete opposite. Yet, she hated feeling like his second choice. And with Liv's return, it cemented the feeling that he was only nice to her because of her friendship with the Element Elite. Their time together had rooted from a common interest – both missing their friend – and now the sowed relationship had rotted into weeds, especially with the new, sparkling blossom returned abloom.

Piper had spent her entire life feeling like she was second choice in everything, and it pained her to live it again between two people she truly cared for.

So, she determined to separate herself from Tristan. To ignore the chills his devious grin gave her, to not allow his dazzling caramel eyes take her breath away, and definitely to remain at minimum, five feet away from his intoxicating scent.

Yet, she still secretly yearned that he would eliminate her will with three words.

And that was the biggest problem of it all.

After their simulation, Piper jogged over to Liv and Rei, overhearing their Security Elite reprimand Liv for drawing a stag instead of writing words again.

Piper froze, knowing she shouldn't eavesdrop on the conversation. She turned around, finding Tristan in her direct path should she take the polite route.

She tapped her foot, desperately looking around for any escape.

"Hey! Piper."

Zeus. He saw me.

Piper turned back toward Tristan, dreading the next encounter. She knew he was just en route to walk with Liv to the North Tower for Meteorology and Piper was simply a landmark on the way.

"Are you okay? You look like you're in pain. Did you hurt yourself in class?"

Piper looked down at her navy strapless gown with silver beading, wishing a bloodstain would appear for something to focus on rather than this. Alas, she was fine.

Tristan's hand gently landed on her arm in concern.

He was definitely within five feet and he smelled so good. Smoky embers, amber and spice, blended with the natural outdoor fir for a dangerously alluring combination.

She was breaking every rule.

"No, I'm fine. Just realized I... forgot to discuss Andromeda in my written assignment for Meteorology." Piper's mouth was speaking faster than her brain. She paused to remember what she had read about Andromeda in the first place, but she couldn't stop now, she just had to go with it. "It's a key example of mythology depicted in the stars that celebrates mortals as equals."

"Ah, Andromeda. A loss. How ever will Professor Deligne give you perfect marks now? The Perseus family will certainly never forgive you."

Piper turned to Tristan, speechless. "How...?"

"I like the notion of our past documented in the stars. It's a beautiful way to tell history." Tristan explained, his voice musical and crisp. "If you were looking for extra credit – Zeus knows we all need it from being gone – you could offer to write another theme on love depicted in the stars."

"Love?" Piper whispered. Her fingers began tingling as she combatted another wave of lightheadedness.

She was thankful to hear Rei behind her yell, "And then seriously, you drew a stag during class today?!"

But soon, Tristan's melodic voice captured her within his hold once again, a delicious poison absorbing into her soul and making her crave more of the addictive substance with each word.

"You heard correctly. Love has always been a powerful, motivating force. To the ancient greeks, it was a magical energy that could be harnessed for all essences of life. I like the constellations in the Perseus family because they depict different kinds of love."

Tristan turned to Liv and Rei; Piper followed his gaze. Deliberate words continued to be exchanged from afar. Piper felt for *both* of the Elites in that moment, each struggling to move forward to a mutually acceptable path.

"You aren't taking any of this seriously!"

Rei was pointing to Liv's drawings, but then spoke quieter, fortunately and unfortunately for Piper, for she could no longer hear his much-needed interruptions.

"They look like they'll be a while. Want to head back?" Tristan offered, his velvety voice hypnotizing her once again.

"…Head back where?" Piper squeaked after a brief pause, realizing he hadn't asked a rhetorical question. She cringed as the words left her mouth and regretted them instantly. She sounded anxious and sharp compared to his velvety vocals.

"The North Tower? You have to meet your doom in Meteorology, right?" Tristan joked, his smile dazzling.

Two for three.

"It's on the way to my Humanities class…" Tristan added, starting to lead the way back to the main castle.

Piper turned back toward Liv, debating. Rei and her friend still looked to be in deep conversation.

Say something.

She hadn't spoken for the past fifteen seconds.

Zeus, she hadn't spoken in fifteen seconds!

"Okay." Piper choked out, following Tristan like a magnet finding its pole.

After a few steps in silence, she sighed, realizing it was going to be much harder to avoid Tristan than she had suspected.

"Are you *that* worried about Meteorology?" Tristan asked, wrapping his arm around Piper's shoulder, and pulled her into a friendly embrace, squeezing her encouragingly as they walked. Yet, his arm lingered, and he didn't move away as they continued uphill toward the castle.

Piper looked at his hand on her shoulder, astounded.

"Meteorology is the least of my concern," she finally breathed.

She turned to look at Tristan, immediately locking eyes with his beautiful caramel irises, and accepted that there was no way she would be able to battle those dazzling eyes.

Three for three. Check. Mate.

But Piper refused to accept defeat. Not yet. So instead, she not-so-elegantly shook her head and blurted out, "Cassiopeia."

Tristan chuckled, and without missing a beat, replied, "Narcissistic queen of Ethiopia whose heartless vanity condemned her to the skies where she spends half of the year hanging upside down from her starry prison."

Piper grinned. Tristan really did know his stuff.

"Perseus." He countered.

"Named after the legendary greek hero, Perseus." Piper responded smugly.

"Obviously." Tristan smirked.

Piper turned, her mouth open. She playfully hit Tristan's chest.

"I wasn't finished!"

Tristan remained quiet, letting Piper make her case.

"The constellation lays claim to Algol, a bright red star to represent the head of Medusa, whom he famously killed using his shield to avoid her direct gaze. And, he saved the selfless Andromeda from the grisly sea monster Cetus, wed her and they happily had seven children."

Tristan nodded, impressed.

"Auriga." Piper then challenged.

"Too easy." Tristan swiftly replied. "Charioteer's helmet, linked to the Greek hero Erichthonius, who was created by a mysterious encounter between Hephaestus, my elder," Tristan dramatically placed his hand on his chest to emphasize the connection, "and Athena. He was known for his ability to tame and harness wild steeds and impressed Zeus by creating the four-horse chariot."

Piper wouldn't dare mention how she idolized Hephaestus in her youth, it would only fuel Tristan's flame to terrorize her more.

So instead, she fired back.

"The four-horse chariot," Piper picked up quickly, "love through care and innovation for one's passion."

As they entered back into the castle and headed up the stairs toward the North Tower, Piper realized the latter half of their conversation picked up speed, a comfortable acceleration, and yet now she didn't want to get to the destination so quickly.

"You're welcome. Now you can finally impress Professor Deligne with knowledge," Tristan joked. "It's about time you show her you're more than a pretty face."

Piper tripped on the stairs in response. She would have collided head-first with the granite step if it weren't for Tristan, who caught her arm and leveled her back to standing instantly.

"Ss-sorry, I must have tripped on my dress." Piper squeaked.

"Don't apologize." Tristan immediately corrected her, before reassessing her condition with care. "All good?"

"Yeah, I'm fine. Just clumsy." Piper nervously laughed it off, trying to hide her blushing cheeks.

She finally looked up at Tristan, unprepared for the beautiful sight that weakened her knees. His black henley and jade scarf perfectly complemented his brown suede field jacket, intensifying his piercing eyes and stunning beige complexion. Piper's heart melted and pulsed all at once.

Her gaze moved to his lips, only inches apart from hers.

She looked back up to him, curious to understand what was rolling through his mind.

Piper watched Tristan's eyes casted upon her lips – it felt like he was moving in slow motion. The world surrounding them a blur. It was only the two of them, gravitating closer and closer…

"There you are!"

Piper jumped back at the sound of Liv's voice.

Her heart was pounding. She tried to calm down her jumpy soul, looking everywhere, at the statue of Zeus at Olympia, Pegasus's statue, the above murals painted across the ceiling of their histories. Anywhere other than her best friend's glance that would see right through her and especially the heavenly eyes of the man who made her heart burn with fire in the first place.

"Liv. Hi! Sorry we left without you-"

"Don't apologize." Tristan whispered, again.

Piper ignored him and continued, "We weren't sure how long Rei was going to be…"

Liv glided up the stairs, her stunningly gold-embroidered, long-sleeved gown that slowly transitioned to a feathered skirt not holding her elegance back in any way. Even a darkened version of Liv was more poised than Piper could ever imagine being.

"No worries, I caught up." She shrugged nonchalantly but with a forced smile. "But we're definitely late, so let's keep the pace? Professor Deligne will not like to return to an empty class once again."

"Would she even notice?" Tristan quipped, immediately following Liv, once again mesmerized by her spell – the same one he unknowingly cast over Piper.

So, with that lovely assessment, Piper followed her friends, tailing behind the two, where she belonged.

HAYDEN

Hayden landed back on Puerdios property, surprised to see Rei waiting for him in the courtyard and sitting on the fountain.

Calithya and the sirens were not happy with the news of his reunion with Liv. It had taken three full days of bribery and ass kissing to keep them allied with the Pure Gods. Not to mention a daily flight from the Aegean Sea to Puerdios, with stops at the royal palace for meetings in between.

He was *exhausted*.

And fighting on behalf of a relationship that didn't exist anymore.

The irony of it all made Hayden delusional. Painfully delirious.

He acknowledged the dark humor in it, declaring his love for one who despised him, fighting for a rebel to his rule at the expense of an ally. Was this the custom, sadistic hell he had created for his own personal torture? Did he wish to exist in misery while his ex-soulmate fared the same fate?

Approaching Rei, Hayden snapped himself out of his never-ending mindless wanders. Instead, he briefly departed hell to temporarily visit this earth and those who grounded him to his vicious reality.

"What do I owe the pleasure?" Hayden asked, sounding too tired than he would have wished to display.

But in all honesty, he hadn't felt strong since that last horrifying morning. He could still tormentuously smell Liv's last cup of coffee lingering in his apartment – notes of wood, caramel, milk chocolate and lilies. That's how strong he had been. Now, he could barely smell the grass he stood upon. All senses were bleak. Nothing was distinct.

Rei jumped off the statue and wearily glanced over to Liv's loft window, before answering. "A revelation, your highness. During combat training."

"What?" Hayden said quickly, again sounding too anxious than he wished to display.

He shouldn't have been getting his hopes up. That had been the most brutal pawn of the game.

"She doesn't even remember parts of herself that could even remotely tie back to you." Rei whispered, worried of being overheard. "As a joke, I told her to look to the stars for guidance, and she had no idea what I was talking about. It was as if *she* was the one mocking *me*." His final statement revered with disdain.

Hayden looked up to their constellations, his heart breaking as he realized the possibility of Liv observing it for mindful impact had been eliminated.

Too much pain. It had been too much pain. Even more suffering. Could he bear any more?

No assurance came to comfort his dangerous thoughts. He bowed his head in weakness.

"I can't go through this again, Rei."

Rei's jaw dropped, but apparently he still had enough feeling to amass anger. He grabbed Hayden shoulders and shook him, willing to burden and fight this battle for his best friend only until he could again on his own.

"That's what Kronos wants you to do, Hayden. Don't you see? That's why he did this! To break you and Liv."

Rei forced Hayden to look him in the eye and register the manipulation behind their reality. He needed his friend to realize there was somebody to blame other than he and Liv. That the fates did not torment them, but an evil, singular soul.

But instead, Hayden sighed and looked longingly up at the sky, lost among all the other competing constellations, including those invisible to sight.

"I was going to propose to her, Rei." Hayden admitted, huffing at the shock at how different they were a month ago. He pulled away, turning his back toward Rei. "And now, she doesn't even remember who I am." Hayden kicked a rock, propelling it through the sky. "Worse. She's haunted by me. I'm now the monster in her story."

He darkly laughed, reminiscing on a conversation he once had with her a lifetime ago. When Liv had clearly laid out the same likelihood. Perhaps it was foretelling. Perhaps a cruel fate.

"What if I'm not the main character in her love story?"

Hayden swore he heard her rejecting whisper echo along with his question in unison. Her ghost from that night lingered behind him. Equally distraught and in despair.

"You are soul mates." Rei reiterated, ignoring the possibility. "You will find a way back to each other."

Liv's ghost vanished. Hayden already missed her presence, cursing for the memory to return and comfort him in his darkness. But she was gone.

Hayden shook his head. Instead, he looked up to their constellation, hoping for guidance or consolation. The stars sparkled back – a dazzling, unattainable optimism, making him fall apart on the inside once again, his hope crashing at an accelerated rate.

"What if she doesn't want to find a way back, Rei? What if I have absolutely no fucking control?"

He kicked the fountain, trying to release his anger. The stone exploded upon impact.

LIV

Hayden.

Liv opened her eyes in the dead of night.

She blinked, looking around her room, trying to recall the vision that appeared in her dream of the night sky. It was terrifying, but only because it felt as if it went against her entire being, a challenging perception she did not understand. Something connected to her, although she did not know why. Confused, she crawled out of bed, curious if she could follow the trail of her fogged memory. If the stars could lead her through the blackout like Rei had suggested.

Liv opened the window and cast a protective spell surrounding the open space. She climbed through the window, hoping to find a clue to the missing piece of her soul. She felt so lost, but maybe the stars could guide her home once again.

She looked to the right, smiling at the luminescent glow of Puerdios, but frowned when she only discovered Aquarius to be seen in the sky above. She searched directly overhead, and then behind her, pleading for a fragment of that vivid snapshot that called to her core.

And finally, she spotted it. The formation of stars, sparkling with secrets to the unknown.

Calling to her.

Ollie.

HAYDEN

Hayden snapped his head, instinctively turning behind him to Ollie's room. A powerful force directed him to her, pushing his boundaries of control.

There she was, stunning as ever, glowing on the rooftop.

Summoning him.

He wanted to run to her but held back. She looked so lost, and he felt a blend of her feeling scared and yet, finally at peace. He could not ruin this moment for her.

In all truth, he was too ashamed to face her now.

He had given up hope. For a moment in desperation, had given up on them.

But Ollie was still fighting, whether she knew it or not. She was still there, somewhere, and called for him to remain strong.

She still needed him.

Hayden looked up at the night sky, thankful for this remaining connection, and thanked Demetrius for giving them their little piece of eternity among the stars. Something that was only theirs and would forever be. A symbol of their soulmate connection that Kronos would never be able to break.

"Ollie just summoned me." Hayden chuckled in relief. The first genuine smile he had shared since that terrible morning of her disappearance.

"Liv? Why aren't you going to her, then!?" Rei exclaimed.

"She doesn't understand she's doing it." Hayden explained, still grinning shyly. "But she figured out a piece of our connection, without even knowing it."

"Well, that's something." Rei said. "Then there's hope."

"Then there's hope." Hayden confirmed, returning his gaze back to the night sky.

EIGHT

LIV

She had been dreading Thursday all week.

By royal decree, she had been invited, *summoned*, for the Elite meeting. Not to be hosted at the palace, where his highness should reside, but instead his personal loft at Puerdios.

It felt even more territorial than if she had to go to the standard location, where both the Candor Pillar Elites Daphne and Jocelyn resided, a neutral spot for all attendees. This was his personal space and therefore, made it personal.

Every time Liv thought about the forced situation, she felt sick to her stomach. Every time she thought of *him*, it was even worse.

Environmental Science dragged on. In any other scenario, Liv would have been thrilled to learn about the climates and ecosystems of Greenland, but as she blankly stared at her textbook and instead focused on the sundial in her mind, the degrees crept slowly through class. At that moment, Liv wondered what was worse – the slow ticking of a clock or a never-moving shadow.

To lock in the unfortunate predicament, the lecture was the last geographical location the class would review, moving onto histories of natural disasters the following week.

They had approached midterms for the second semester at Puerdios and in two weeks she would not only have to catch up on all climates and ecosystems of the world, but write a thesis to determine her mark.

And she couldn't even help herself by paying attention to one of the lessons in class.

As if her world couldn't get any darker...

When Professor Claredon finally dismissed the class, every step toward the door and to her final destination felt heavier. Even with a planned stop at her dormitory, she was fully aware of the inevitable, simply waiting to meet her doom.

Piper bid her a silent farewell as she returned to her own loft for the night, empathy emulating from her long stare with recognition of the unspeakable that Liv would soon face. The muted acknowledgement intensified her own dread.

Setting down her textbooks, Liv calculated she had 60 degrees before she had to attend the meeting. In efforts to distract her mind, she cooked her favorite spaghetti dish – a simple option with garlic and onions sautéed in oil and blended with tomato sauce.

In hindsight, wearing a white gown with crystal embellishments on the sleeve may not have been the outfit of choice for spaghetti and red wine, but tonight Liv was going to selectively choose her battles. Worst case, she could leverage a dinner stain to feign injury and escape if it all became too much.

Liv laughed at the irony, recognizing her unrequired need for an injury decoy, considering her body's tarnished state. A stain was the least of her concern against her evergrowing neglected battles.

And even though the garment she wore revealed many of the bandages covering her unhealed wounds, Liv refused to compensate for her past. It had taken a couple of days of guilt, but finally Liv had accepted that she had escaped – she was not in the Underworld. She was a survivor. And allowing the other Elites and allies to really *see* what had happened to her might help her argument.

But, if you spill your spaghetti, aim for the left leg with the thigh slit...

As she chuckled at her own thoughts, someone knocked on her door.

She opened it and found Tristan in the doorway.

"Just in time, want dinner?"

Tristan nodded, joining her at the counter after serving himself a dish.

"What do I owe the visit?" Liv inquired, wrapping her fork with noodles and taking a bite, brushing over how he stared painfully at her exposed and destroyed skin. "You know I have to leave in 15 degrees for the Elite Meeting."

"That's why I'm here." Tristan explained, "Do you want me to go to the meeting on your behalf?"

While Liv's body recovered from her torment, Tristan had been making daily visits to the Elements Pillar on her behalf, switching out correspondence and mail while checking in on those within the Pillar who dutifully remained loyal to the Pure God rule.

She owed Tristan everything. He was exquisitively too good for her.

Liv took a sip of her wine, actually considering the offering. She felt a sense of relief at the opportunity to hide from her fears.

To hide from her fears.

Was this who she had become? Welcoming weakness?

No, she was a survivor.

The weight returned, but she needed to learn how to function with the heavy monster.

"Thank you," Liv sighed "But, unfortunately I think I need to face this one."

"Of course, just concerned about how you'll react. Are you sure you don't want to head over there early?" Tristan offered, "Might be best to handle re-introductions in private. In case you flip out at the sight of him, again."

She knew Tristan was being considerate and overly protective, but she couldn't ignore the hint of mockery in his voice.

Do you want to play a game, Ollie?

"You don't understand, the things he *did* to me." Liv admitted, with a shiver, blocking out the darkest memories from her mind. "He *tormented* me for pleasure. He played games – corrupted righteousness and vindicated masochism – where I could only win if I lost. But I still lost when I won, nonetheless. He made sure I always lost."

"Kronos. Not Hayden." Tristan reiterated.

"They're one in the same to me." Liv took another sip of wine. She could not see one without seeing the other.

"If that's how you feel, it might be best to stay back. It's a strict sentence to openly pledge disloyalty to the king."

"No, I'm the Element Elite and this is my duty. I appreciate all that you have done while I…was away." Liv always stumbled at the descriptor. She hoped for the day where it would more naturally flow from her mouth. Or never need to be said again. "But I'm back. And need to lead by example. Being afraid of the Pure God King should not influence the responsibility, the duty, I have to my pillar."

"Do you want me to accompany you, at the least?" Tristan offered.

"Please." Liv whispered.

The silence in the Puerdios hall dramatized every echoed step Liv and Tristan took toward the Pure King's loft.

Where was everyone? It wasn't even 180 degrees…

When they arrived upon two foreboding, overtly sized, industrial-style antique oak doors, Liv took a deep breath, willing herself to remain calm and composed. She prompted Tristan to speak the password for entrance.

"Eugene." Tristan commanded.

The lock clicked open.

"Oregon?" Liv wondered aloud.

"Not my story to tell." Tristan admitted, opening the door.

As soon as they crossed the barrier into his territory, Liv was struck with a delicious aroma of wood, caramel, milk chocolate and lilies. At least the cruel king was a practical and knowledgeable host – or, perhaps it was Peyton's touch, as the goddess of Discovery greeted them immediately upon arrival.

"Liv! You made it. Looking stunning as always." She hooked her arm into Liv's and guided her into the open concept loft.

"You as well." Liv gulped, her heart pounding faster than it had all day.

She appreciated Peyton's playful gold beaded romper, casual yet still mesmerizing. The long sleeves draped low on her arm and attached to a revealing deep v-neckline, meeting a thick gold belt around her waist.

Peyton seemed at ease; perhaps Liv should take a cue from her best friend.

Daphne and Silas sat at the kitchen, both enjoying wine as they laughed casually. Liv was surprised to find Demetrius sitting with Jocelyn on the couch by the lit fireplace, apparently deep in a serious conversation as Joss hadn't acknowledged Liv's arrival in any capacity.

At the long table, Calithya of the Sirens and her brother Ammiras joined Rhys, the Medicine Pillar Elite.

Dyoedi of the Centaurs had not yet arrived.

So few remained on the Pure side, Liv sadly observed. They now fought against Kronos, The Arts Pillar, The Humanities Pillar, The Commerce Pillar and Agricultural Pillar, plus any Radical Dark Gods who voluntarily defied their Pillar Elite's lead, driven by unattainable power, and the support from the Cyclops and Minotaurs.

And now the Soulless.

Kronos and Arlo were not only creating an army. They were creating a destruction.

And the leader of the Pure Gods, King Hayden, was the worst of them all.

With that cruel perspective, Liv dragged both Peyton and Tristan to the bar and poured them all glasses of wine. It was going to be a long night.

After exchanging friendly greetings with Silas and Daphne, Liv decided it was best to strategize seating while there was still a chance to control the battle. She walked over to Calithya and sat next to her in the far corner of the table. As Rhys politely excused himself, Liv desperately eyed Tristan to sit at the head. That would naturally force to Hayden to sit at the opposite head table, and as far away from Liv as physically possible.

As Rhys passed behind her, he kindly paused and greeted her, naturally inspecting his previous artwork on her arms and chest. "Your wounds seem to be healing magnificently at first glance."

"I love hearing that." Liv smiled, "It's great to see you here tonight in support of the Pure Gods."

"I still remain neutral, our Pillar simply won't turn out those in need of medical attention, part of the Hippocratic Oath derived from our ancestors." Rhys explained softly, "But I hope to help however I can. And looking at your progress, I'll plan to stop by in a couple of days to take another look at your wounds."

He nodded with a gentle touch before he walked over to Daphne and Silas.

Liv returned to the table, smiling at her new allies, the sirens, when Calithya's eyes shot daggers at her new table guest. Liv coughed, turning her attention to Ammiras, who looked slightly more welcoming.

"Olivia, what a surprise to see you here tonight."

Ammiras's Spanish accent reminded Liv that he and his sister were not of their world, but instead of the sea. Perhaps that was the cause of Calithya's hostility, a different cultural norm. Even still, Liv wasn't entirely sure how to respond to the controversial conversation starter. She turned to Tristan, prompting him to jump in at any time.

"I was essentially counting down the days until her return." Tristan began, "Liv is much more capable of representing the Elements Pillar than I could ever give myself credit for."

Calithya's eyes dazzled at Tristan's silky voice.

Never underestimate the power of eye candy. Liv joked within her mind.

"And yet, you're still here?" Calithya prompted.

"As long as Liv requests it." Tristan smiled demurely.

"Similar to why we have a new location for our meeting tonight." Calithya continued, glaring at Liv again as if she were mentally determining how to murder the Element Elite in her sleep. Or worse, *kidnap her.* Liv flinched at her own sarcastic joke, a bad effort in trying to make light of the situation and find comfort in the awkward. But it was too soon, even for her internal thoughts to process.

And yet, Calithya's voice was melodic, musical and mesmerizing. Relentless in her delivery. Strong.

"On the contrary, this was not by my request." Liv finally spoke, concluding the declaration with a laugh.

The sirens did not laugh with her. Or ask for further explanation.

Liv turned to Calithya, moving onto another tactic: compliments.

"Calithya, I must say, your gown is stunning."

And Liv wasn't lying. The Queen of Sirens wore a stunning blush and purple dégradé gown with intricate slits woven into the bodice, exposing a tasteful amount of skin.

"I do not care for small talk and weak topics for conversation. Nor do I want to be amounted to what I wear." Calithya hissed.

Liv took a sip of her wine, trying to figure out *what the Hades was Calithya's deal.*

"Then, how about we not talk. Sound good?" Liv offered sweetly, turning to Tristan with astonished eyes.

"Oh, don't mind my sister." Ammiras cut in with a lighthearted laugh, "Calithya swam on the wrong side of the sea this morning. She holds grudges, but will move on eventually. Right, sister?" Ammiras nudged his sister with his purple silk jacquard suit.

"Yes. Eventually." Calithya rolled her eyes at her brother, "I shall go grab wine. Okay?"

She got up and left the table, but fortunately Ammiras took her seat as he scooted closer to Liv.

"I'm impressed you decided to go into the lion's den rather than shy away from it." Ammiras observed, nodding to his sister. "She's a beast on the exterior, but loyal and kind underneath. Although conversation lacked, I'm sure you impressed her with your audacity. Calithya will be debating whether she shall rival your no-nonsense approach as she drinks a full glass of wine before returning."

"Can't wait." Liv dryly commented.

The door opened again, revealing a large creature who almost took up the whole hallway. Peyton shyly approached, formally greeting their guest.

She was stunning, half female and half horse. The hair on her sandy skin matched the tail and hooves of her brown backside, piercing silver and glowing.

"Dyoedi, we're so honored you are able to join us." Peyton smiled, leading the centaur into the main area.

"Where is the King?" Dyoedi inquired, her voice penetrating the whole loft. Not accusingly or negative, just commanding to be heard.

On cue, Hayden descended the stairs, Rei trailing behind him.

His gaze first met Liv's, their eyes locking instinctively, instantly, before he forced his attention toward his newest guest.

One look, and all of her breath had been stolen from her. That's all it took to send her into a frenzy of darkness.

"Dyoedi, I hope I did not keep you waiting…" His voice echoed in the distant background.

The dark, stonecold cell. The beating. The cruel, sadistic fulfillment of her captor…

"Olivia, let's play a game…"

No. The pain is too much…

Her wounded leg desperately cried with throbbing discomfort.

"Livy?" Tristan nudged Liv, whispering, "You okay?" He cautiously looked over to Hayden who still spoke with Dyoedi.

Warmth. Light. Kind caramel eyes.

"I'm not sure." She breathed.

"Focus on me." Tristan grabbed her hand, squeezing it. "I'm here. You're safe."

Liv breathed, this time preparing for the presence she could anticipate. Returning her gaze back to the host, she found Hayden had been looking her way, but he immediately turned his attention back to Dyoedi again. Somehow, she knew that although he focused on his newest guest, Hayden still had Liv on his mind. She needed to choose her words carefully, play the loyal subject.

"I know Hayden isn't Kronos." Liv admitted, turning back to Tristan. "I know that you, Rei, Peyton and Piper have all told me so – but it's just a hard adjustment when he looks so much like my captor. The resemblance is hard for my mind to process."

Liv weakly smiled, taking another sip of her wine, hoping that would keep her in the king's good graces, ease his suspicion that she was on to him.

Just as he was acting, fooling them all – she could act too, and conduct the ultimate heist.

"Now that everyone is here, I welcome you all to join me at the table to begin our meeting." Hayden commanded kindly, but sternly.

He waited until everyone arranged themselves and settled in, before sitting down at the head of the table himself, across from Tristan as Liv had planned.

Liv - 1, Hayden - 0.

However, she was here in his loft to begin with – so perhaps they were at a draw.

For now.

Jocelyn sat across from Liv with a quiet smile. She donned a beautiful, purple velvet, Victorian-inspired gown, with lace covering her neckline and through her long sleeves, and buttons trailing the entire front of her dress.

Her eyes looked red, puffy. She quickly ducked her head when Liv tilted her own and wanted to ask her what was wrong.

Demetrius followed suit, nodding to Liv sternly. Far gone was the flamboyant character filled with charm, replaced by a man whose color had been stolen in a grey-scaled world.

"Olivia. It's good to see you again." Demetrius politely stated.

He wore a simple gold cashmere sweater layered under his heather grey suit. Even with the bright color of his metallic accent, it was the most reserved Liv had ever seen him. It appeared she was not the only one dealing with inner demons at present.

"As always, lovely to see you. Do you plan to stay in our realm for long?" Liv offered warmly.

"Sadly, I must return back to Jupiter tonight." Demetrius declared, stealing quick glances from Jocelyn before sighing and finally turning fully toward Hayden.

Murmurs quieted as everyone directed to the head of the table. Liv followed suit, the entire time repeating, 'don't freak out,' in her mind as she practiced steadied breathing.

Hayden smiled warmly at those who remained in the Elite Pure Council, quickly passing over Liv's gaze before leaning down to Rei and whispering in his ear.

With his attention captured away from Liv, it gave her the opportunity to finally observe him. He had a strong jawline, golden skin and bronzed hair. The navy crewneck sweater perfectly sculpted his torso, but the silk olive green bomber jacket he wore covered his arms, restraining Liv's mind from straying too far.

His beauty was painful.

"Liv." Rei finally stated, catching her attention immediately. "We want to start tonight's discussion with what you discovered while you were in the Dark Gods' custody. Do you feel comfortable speaking to it?"

Liv felt her heart pounding faster as all eyes gazed upon her. All, except King Hayden's – who remained focused on the whisky glass he held in his hand.

"Of course." Liv bit her lip, trying to determine where to start. The most important discovery was of the Soulless, no doubt. But how could she describe them? What information could help understand how to defeat this new species?

"Kronos has created a new breed – the Soulless – from the corpses of deities who have passed onto the Underworld." Liv whispered, wishing she spoke more eloquently.

"Impossible." Dyoedi declared.

Centaurs were known to be wise creatures, with inherited powers resembling that of the Candor Pillar. Strong-willed and stubborn-minded, having such an influential source disagree with her immediately was not a good sign.

Silence filled the table, before Silas finally spoke.

"How?"

"I don't know. Kronos helped create the Olympians, he's capable of creating other species. He could be proactively sending deities to the Underworld after securing their bodies to help build numbers for his army. All I know is that they're a lesser form, like a... zombie-version of Gods."

"Zombie?" Ammiras questioned.

Shit.

Nobody here was from her world nor understood the cultural phenomenon of the monster. And explaining a fantastical mortal reference would only weaken Liv's position, reminding all who sat the table that she was a demigod, only a newcomer to this dangerous world.

"Zombies are the undead. Trained to kill or reduce the mind to convert others into zombies, with no emotion of humanity intact."

But instead of her words, she heard the king's. His voice was velvet, assuring, supportive and direct.

Nobody questioned him in return.

Liv uneasily glanced over to Hayden, wondering how he was familiar with such a concept from her world. He simply nodded in support, before quickly addressing Rei – who had already forgotten about zombies and had moved onto the next monster – her uncle.

"If Arlo can't coerce mortals into slavery, or access the Underworld to bring supporters back into our realm, he's willing to risk it all for the next best thing." Rei pounded his fist on the table in frustration.

"The Soulless are illegal. No deity has ever treaded into such dark magic to bring back the dead." Hayden affirmed, rubbing his temple.

"How many?" Demetrius warily prompted Liv.

"Increasing by the hour, er – I mean thirty degrees. At least a hundred a day." Liv's voice trembled, "When I was... there," she choked on the memory, "I had limited exposure outside of my cell, but during those few minutes, I witnessed at least a dozen trained as servants, a dozen unkempt ones in a nearby cell and I'm sure countless more locked up throughout the fortress unseen to my eye."

"We'll begin researching how they can be defeated." Silas confirmed.

Coming from the Security & Warfare pillar, Silas did not mean tame, or capture them. He meant eradicate.

"I'll summon Piper. She can help with research so you can oversee testing." Hayden suggested, before pausing, "That is, if her pillar Elite grants permission?"

For the first time during the entire meeting, his voice sounded unsure, weary.

Liv couldn't look at him. Not when she knew he cautiously glanced her way. The green glare would be her undoing.

Instead, she gulped and nodded to Rei. "Yes. Piper can help you."

She hoped it wasn't too obvious that she meticulously had not granted Piper permission to help Hayden. It didn't feel right succumbing her best friend to her nemesis's control and Liv would never forgive herself if he pushed Piper to be at his mercy.

"Before we start wasting our energy and resources on this project, can someone please explain why we should blindly trust this demi-god's word, without any proof?" Calithya interjected with a hiss. "For all we know, Olivia saw a mythical creature her kind is simply not familiar with."

"I must agree with Queen Calithya's trepidations." Dyoedi stated, although at least giving Liv the courtesy of recognition before providing reason. "She is a newcomer to this world, only recently appointed to her status as Elite and has attended less than a few Elite meetings. Tonight was the first time I have been formally introduced to her, so you all must understand why I have my reservations before submitting my entire clan to your disposal at the word of a stranger."

"Eloquently stated, Dyoedi." Calithya devilishly smiled. She was just pleased someone supported her unjustifiable vendetta against Liv. "Except I have been formally acquainted with her and can claim she did not impress."

"Calithya." Ammiras warned.

"I support Hayden." Calithya reiterated, smiling sweetly at the king before darting her eyes back to Liv. "I never pledged my alliance to this inconsistent, man-stealing seahorse."

"How dare you!?" Liv stood up, her jaw clenched.

She stared the siren down, her eyes demanding justice from the slanderous accusation.

"Calithya, I suggest you apologize. Immediately." Hayden's voice commanded the table, he sounded angry, boiling Liv even more.

"Keep out of this, your highness. I can fight my own battles." Liv sat herself down, practicing composure as she glared at Calithya. "I'm not scared of a petty siren."

Calithya looked smugly at her newest nemesis, "Well, that naivety explains it all – why you have the audacity to act as if you didn't break off my formal engagement with the king or even acknowledge that you only showed interest in him when he had no interest in you." Calithya crossed her arms, huffing with discontempt before continuing against Liv's perplexed silence. "As soon as he came crawling back to you, risking his kingdom's alliances, you don't even show remorse for tossing him aside, nor apologize for forcing all of your superiors at this table to work around this ridiculous, immature drama."

Liv was speechless. Was she dreaming?

Ammiras grabbed his sister's arm, but Calithya pulled out of the warning to continue on.

"We're not in one of your teen fantasy movies, dear girl – this is real. Your actions have impact. And I for one, am not going to risk my people to take part in your little game."

Do you want to play a game, Ollie?

Liv recoiled, the darkest memories with Kronos penetrating her mind. No light could guide her out of this attack…

"Calithya." Hayden stood, commanding the room.

Liv couldn't look up at him, but she held onto his presence in the now. She focused on him instead of the monster in her mind.

"Let me make myself clear. You do not want to make an enemy out of Liv, because if I have to choose between the two – I will *always* choose Liv."

Liv looked up in surprise at the declaration.

Hayden was staring at Calithya to her right, glaring with undistinguished superiority, but not in a condescending way. He didn't yell, didn't raise his voice, but controlled the room in a way that made him more respected, more powerful.

Hesitantly, he checked to see if Liv was okay, needed his help or wanted him to hold back. And she finally saw the difference.

He had piercing blue eyes. Beautiful, kind, blue eyes.

Bright enough to light up the sky. Dazzling enough to compete against stars sparkling against the backdrop of a dark night.

As Liv pictured the soothing vision of the constellations in which she found herself gaping at every night, a calm took over as she listened to Hayden's speech continue in tandem.

"Dyoedi, Calithya and Ammiras – for as long as I have known Liv, she has proven her loyalty to justice and fighting for good, no matter the costs. She's already shown her willingness to sacrifice herself for the benefit of the Pure God rule, but more importantly – her people. She does not shy away from the challenges these beliefs present, but meets them head-on and with determination. I will forever be in her debt as long as she chooses to stand and fight by my side. If you cannot trust my word, then I interpret that as you do not trust me. And if that is the case, I have no desire for an alliance with those who do not truly support me. You can see yourself out now, if this is how you truly feel."

He was going to let them leave? Freely?

Liv expected imprisonment, tyranny, a sentence, *something* she would need to combat against, but instead, she remained seated at the table, more shocked from that than all that had transpired at the meeting. Was this just an act? Words easily stated for show?

And yet, something pushed against her mind to challenge that immediate inclination.

Calithya stood up; Ammiras remained seated.

"The sirens will take this into consideration. My brother will stay for the remainder of the meeting and we will reassess our pledge. Good night."

Calithya's flowing gown cascaded across the hard-wood floor as she showed herself out.

The door slammed, echoing through the quiet room.

Finally, Hayden broke the silence as he sat back down at the table.

"Well, Ammiras, we're glad that you are able to stay with us and report back to your sister."

"Of course, your highness." Ammiras nodded. "I think with the recent news of your relationship status, Calithya silently dreamed of a stronger alliance potential; she will need a couple days to process the destruction of her dream, but she'll come around."

"And if she doesn't?" Peyton spat out, the worry weighing heavy on her grimace. "That cuts our numbers by a third."

"While Kronos continues to grow his army." Rei added.

"What's right and wrong, getting blocked by a marriage proposal," Jocelyn stuttered in disbelief.

"Precisely the inverse of your justification." Demetrius retorted with disdain back to Jocelyn, whispering only loud enough for Tristan and Liv to hear at their end of the table.

"I will not jump into anything binding for the sake of an alliance, especially if the alliance evaporates without marriage on the table." Hayden clarified, "No marriage proposals will be discussed or advised from this council again. Not until I say so."

Truthfully, Liv didn't understand why he didn't just propose to Calithya again, but with the earlier revelation, figured it would be best to remain mum until she put those pieces together with Piper's help later that night.

"Have we considered seeking new alliances?" Liv proposed instead.

"All potential allies are accounted for." Silas replied.

"No." Liv countered, "With the numbers of demon gods, we're outnumbered – with or without the Sirens' support." She turned to Rei, prompting him to chime in when she added, "Rei spent time with the Norse Gods, why don't we try to find bigger alliances with them, and consider the Celtic, Egyptian and Buddhist Gods?"

"With the introduction of the Soulless, Kronos's wrath becomes a worldly issue." Rei agreed. "It may prove time to reignite alliances with those we once shared the burden of guiding the earth."

"They haven't been heard of for ages. We discussed..." Hayden countered contemplatively, turning to Liv, before he stopped himself. "Perhaps it's worth re-exploring."

"Liv and I can head the initiative." Rei offered, nodding to Liv with a proud smile.

"I'll help." Jocelyn added.

"Is that a good idea?" Daphne cut in, worried.

"Re-establishing relationships with other deity communities can only strengthen our chance of defeating Kronos." Jocelyn challenged. "If my powers help reveal truths about their locations, provide opportunities to reconnect, or at the very least cancel out leads faster, I don't see any consequences that would hinder the outcome if I weren't to help."

"Enlist me to assist as well." Demetrius offered, "As ruler of the Solar System, my powers may weigh heavy to help persuasion."

Liv beamed at the couple. In addition to Piper, Tristan and Peyton's unspoken support – they had developed a dream team for the cause in a matter of minutes.

"Rei, you focus on that committee. I'll head the battle of the Soulless." Silas agreed, "We shall report any updates at our next meeting."

"The centaurs will lead capturing a test-subject for your trials." Dyoedi offered. "I must admit, I'm curious to see one in the flesh and on my own terms."

"Thank you, Dyoedi." Hayden nodded.

Soon, the table grew silent at the conclusion of their eventful meeting. Hayden stood to bid his farewell, when Daphne finally whispered, "I'll help you, Silas."

Liv could tell the offer even took Hayden by surprise. He paused before thanking his mother and then expressed gratitude to everyone for their time. At the conclusion of all pleasantries exchanged, Hayden gracefully departed to the balcony.

"Tristan." Liv turned to her friend, "Excuse me for a moment."

It was now or never.

"This is the best choice you have made all week." Tristan joked, reading her intentions immediately.

"Keep an eye out for me, please?" She begged, already losing her courage.

"Okay. You'll be fine, but sure." Tristan rolled his eyes, but repositioned himself closer to the kitchen bar so he could see more of the outdoor area.

Liv trepidly walked out onto the patio, her heart beating more rapidly with every step.

But she fought the terror. Her stubbornness and curiosity battling the fear. She caught a whiff of his scent, causing her to stop. Verveina, cedarwood, cardamom and leather.

It chained her to her horror.

Focus. Focus. Liv chided herself. *You're okay.* Instinctively, she looked up to the sky, finding a welcoming peace in its beauty, the constellation assuring her all would be fine.

Remember his eyes, bright as the starry sky.

So, with another breath, she took a step, keeping focus on the stars with Hayden in her peripheral vision. Keeping a safe distance between the two.

HAYDEN

It had been challenging to minimize his staring. She practically *glowed* compared to the other deities.

But Rei had counseled Hayden prior to the meeting on the best way to accommodate Liv's fears. Eliminate direct contact with her, reduce interaction when possible and allow Rei to be the one to address her when absolutely necessary.

Yet, it had been too hard. His soul magnetized to her, ripping it from the necessity to be apart as he proactively combatted his natural inclinations, reworking his muscle memory that had spent a decade by her side.

And when he quickly glanced over to assess her cut and bruised skin, the speed of her physical recovery, he understood it only represented a fraction of the real pain that remained to heal, both externally and internally.

So, as he stood up from their testing Elite meeting, it pained him to see her so comfortably speaking with Tristan. To be the one who brought joy to Liv was all he desired, to be anything to her other than a cruel, powerhungry king. And the notion that she thought of him as such hurt him even more. She was the farthest she could be from proud of him, and her opinion mattered most. It was the only one that mattered.

He politely excused himself, weakly getting away from the sight as quickly as possible. Selfishly, it hurt him to witness Liv so happy from the action and support of another man, when his presence only brought her pain. And he hated himself for feeling that way.

He had been instructed to not make eye contact, yet Hayden had snuck in glances throughout the night – noticing how she reacted anytime he spoke, how she recoiled further into a shadow of the progress she had made since her kidnap. It was gut-wretching to see her so trusting of Tristan and so speculative of him, her soul mate.

Time and space. That's what she needed. And he would support her however he could.

And, he had meant what he said earlier. Even if she inevitably chose another, he would still support her, even if it killed him. It had always been Liv. It would only be Liv.

"Hi." She breathed beside him, her hands clinging to the patio balcony as she announced her presence.

Hayden turned to Liv, knowing the strength and effort it must have taken her to come this close to him. But why?

Fighting against all of the pain and suffering, Hayden made sure he showed her only pure joy and kindness when he replied with a smile.

"Hi."

He didn't want to push her. So, he looked up at the sky, observing their constellation, remaining focused on what little remained, but still existed.

Liv stared at her hands, trying to garner the courage to ask a question, yet was clearly still frightened of him. Hayden restrained himself from moving, breathing, *existing*, trying to summon strength and courage to allow Liv to speak the words frantically running through her mind.

She looked up and took a breath.

"...You called me Ollie when we first encountered each other." Liv stated blankly. "Why?"

Hayden looked down from the stars, daring to catch a glimpse of her. Seeing first-hand how terrified she was from being so close to him, when she believed him to be a soul-less monster, not her other half.

If only his embrace could console her, protect her, instead of sending her away with more nightmares. If only. So, he considered the question at hand, although unexpected, and answered it honestly.

"I used to call you that, before you were captured." Hayden offered kindly, although his focus remained on the stars. "It was a term of endearment."

"Ollie." Liv whispered the name to herself, brows furrowing.

"Yes, Ollie." Hayden smiled, sadly.

Liv's head snapped toward him. Something triggered within her mind. She snapped her eyes closed and creased her forehead, trying to process what she had just experienced, understand what her aching head was trying to communicate to her.

"Rhys said if I lost any memories during my torture… that they could resurface. I mean, if there are any parts to salvage." Liv confessed, staring back at her constellation.

Beckoning to Hayden. Without even knowing she called for his help.

He remained silent, letting her piece together the clues before her and battle the internal curses within, process the two in her own time. And then, hopefully, Live would share the reason for this confrontation, if she had any at all. Not that he cared if she didn't.

"What I mean is… I can sense my memory is foggy. I now recognize there are holes, that there might be a part missing. But it's almost worse, because now I feel incomplete. Like part of me has been eliminated and I can't figure out how to find it."

Liv paused, eyes widening. "Sorry, I must be wasting your time with my troubles. It's just that staring into the sky comforts me, and a couple nights ago I swore it spoke to me and said 'Ollie,' so… I don't know. Or why I'm rambling to you of all people…" She paused before deliberately declaring, "I should go."

"No please, don't stop. Stay." Hayden insisted calmly, although internally he was anything but calm. "It might help."

Liv turned to Hayden, still clinging to the balcony for strength. She was shaking.

Stay quiet. Hayden reminded himself. *If she needs to go, you have to let her.*

"It's stupid. But," she looked up to the sky, smiling, "those stars arranged right there," she lifted her hand to draw out her constellation, "I feel like they're apart of the puzzle. A clue to find my way."

Hayden smiled, genuinely. "A loved one once told me to 'look to the stars for guidance.'" He nodded to the constellation, "That star formation you're referring to is called Ollie."

Liv tensed; Hayden hoped he didn't just royally fuck up the moment. She looked back down to her hands, once again clasped to the balcony, fighting the urge to run.

Shit. Had Hayden gone to far? Tarnished her one piece of solace?

Liv grinded her teeth and stared at the ground, trying to remember. She gulped before softly asking, "Coincidence?"

"No." Hayden admitted.

After a moment of silence, he finally turned away to let her be. Give her more space to process everything from the night.

It was the hardest choice he had made all day.

"Wait." Liv demanded.

Hayden turned back, facing Liv once again. "I don't want to hurt you, Liv."

Liv looked up to the stars. Then back down to the ground. A tear slid down her cheek.

"No, don't call me Liv. Please call me Ollie." She pleaded, forcing herself against her comfort zone, her breaking point. "Like you used to."

A warrior, a stubborn warrior.

Hayden choked with joy. "As long as you wish, Ollie."

LIV

Look to the stars for guidance.

Rei had suggested the same thing, mocking her when she didn't recognize the advice. And yet, it was the first concrete step that helped ease her tortured mind.

Standing so close to Hayden on the balcony proved to push every limit Liv feared. Yet, after Hayden declared he would support her no matter what cost during the meeting, letting those who opposed him leave freely, Liv had convinced herself, it was time to face him. To give him the chance her friends vouched for, to keep the open mind as she had always prided herself in having and try to combat her fear with a clean slate.

In this atmosphere below the stars, and with Tristan watching, Hayden didn't seem evil. He seemed kind, thoughtful and welcoming.

Unless that was his game.

Do you want to play a game, Ollie?

"As long as you wish, Ollie."

Liv turned to Hayden in response, another image flashed across her mind.

Yet, in this particular memory his eyes were blue, not the poisonous green she had known all too well to haunt her visions. Hayden, radiant with his sun-kissed glow and golden locks, dapper in a loose white t-shirt, jeans and a grey wool lapel coat.

Was it déjà vu?

She had seen him before, here.

"Ollie? Are you okay?"

Hayden took a step forward, worry painted across his face.

Liv instinctively took a step back in response.

He froze.

Liv looked back at him, shrugging with apology. She turned to her constellation, seeking comfort again to level her pulsing heart before she returned back to his gaze.

The feeling from her image had evoked so much joy. Pure bliss. Something she had never recalled feeling before.

But she had. Once.

She could still feel it, beneath the layers of fear.

He looked beautiful, forever taking her breath away. She had snapped the image to lock into her memory vault, but wondered if moments like these were limited.

Were they?

"You remember." Hayden stated blankly.

"Does it count as remembering if I can barely piece it together?" Liv whispered, a tear rolling down her cheek. She turned to the sky, desperately pleading to the greater gods in the universe. "I want to feel that joy again. I didn't even know I had lost it… but what if I can't get it back?"

HAYDEN

"…What if I can't get it back?"

Hayden finally broke. Her voice defeated, her body trembling, it was all too much. How could he not try to console her when she was going through such a low?

His tether called to her. He sprung to embrace her, wrapping his arms gently, firmly around his counterpart. Yet, still giving her the choice to exit his safety if she needed.

He soothingly murmured hushes, as Liv wept in his arms, even more confused than before. She was breaking, for better or for worse, but she was breaking free of the curse she had been imprisoned to for too long.

Finally, she tensed.

Hayden immediately let go, wearisome for another terrifying meltdown from his selfishness.

He reminded himself again that she needed space, she needed to heal. That she needed him to back the fuck off.

"Sorry, Ollie. Force of habit." He apologized, shrugging and taking a step back.

Her eyes went wide. She turned to the patio doors, spotting Tristan for security. He signaled to her, soothing her with his presence.

It made Hayden want to crumble, fall to his knees and surrender.

Was he hurting her more by trying to help her?

He almost asked she end his life right then and there, her pain was too much to bear at his expense. He already felt a thousand knives had penetrated his soul tonight. What was one more when it really counted?

Liv turned back to him, eyes on the ground as she admitted, "At first, I liked it."

"At first." Hayden reiterated.

Liv frowned, closing her eyes to focus on that image from a different lifetime.

"I'm sorry. I wish I could remember." She took a deep breath.

"I'm surprised that's what you remember from that night to begin with." Hayden huffed, without thinking.

That caught Liv's attention.

Finally, she studied Hayden, trying to picture him in comparison to her photo memory. "You know which night I'm thinking of?'

Hayden stuck his hands into his slacks' pockets and leaned against the balcony.

"That night, you… expressed a sentiment about capturing a photo of me to memory. I stood still for a moment longer to fulfill the request." He looked around the patio. "It was out here. And you were standing… about there." He pointed to Liv's left. "And I was here." He shrugged, stepping into the spot he described. "It all comes together."

Liv absorbed the information. Taking a step to where Hayden pointed, now standing in the exact spot of her original recollection.

Liv's epiphany of surprise matched a diluted sentiment Hayden could vaguely register.

It was him.

Her voice quivered as she softly requested, "Can you tell me about that night?"

They were so close. Only a foot apart. Hayden felt nervous just from the proximity to her. He could smell her – fresh strawberries and daisies. He gulped, trying to keep his calm composure while he lost all of his senses in her.

He was sure she saw right through him.

"Of course, Ollie."

NINE

TRISTAN

"I still can't believe you are *surprised* that you didn't get attacked by Hayden." Tristan mocked, accompanying Liv back to her dormitory. "Like it's the most shocking thing in the world that our Pure God King didn't assault you among your friends..."

"I never said that." Liv snapped back.

"You didn't have to." Tristan pushed, eyeing his stubborn friend.

After an hour of seeing Liv tense and on edge while outside with Hayden on the balcony, it was a nice change to see her at ease and breathing again. If she had years to give, that meeting easily could have taken a decade off of her life.

He never wanted to see her like that again. If only she knew of the lengths he would go to protect her...

Tristan shook the thought out of his head. He knew that Liv did not return his feelings, they had been down that road before, ending with Liv entirely rejecting the romance both physically and emotionally as possible – catapulting Tristan across the room to distance the two while cementing her loyalty to the opposing Pure God rule.

Needless to say, it wasn't Tristan's finest night.

The most surprising part of it all was that the humiliation changed nothing. Even crazier, Tristan was now a Pure God, having still followed Liv to support her.

He had always despised the light colors, soft fabrications and metallic details – now they surrounded him on a daily basis. Contrasting him even more among his peers as he preferred to keep his Dark wardrobe and physicality.

Yet, he would follow her anywhere, everywhere that she would allow.

So, he accompanied her back to her dorm, ensuring her safety once again and knowing he would spend another restless night as he listened to her breath softly, only 10 feet away. And when a nightmare would hit, he would be there, soothing her to wake, holding her protectively until the demons washed away from her mind.

And he would do it again tomorrow night, and the night after, for as long as she needed.

But if Liv now truly felt only fear with Hayden, that did alter the circumstances from his previous attempt at something more. Had something changed? Could something change?

Yet, deep in his subconscious, a voice challenged with a whisper. *What about Piper?*

"Tristan?" Liv nudged him, "You're certainly out-of-character-ally quiet."

Her piercing blue eyes dazzled with joy and pride at the creation of her clever descriptor.

This was the version of Liv he loved most.

"I like to give my friends the occasional opportunity to fail at outwitting me." Tristan bantered back.

Liv grinned.

"Thank you for this once in a lifetime opportunity. I certainly do hope to disappoint."

"You often do." Tristan organically spat back as they approached her room.

Knowing their unspoken agreement, Liv opened her door and led the way for Tristan to enter.

"Whisky?" Liv hollered from her bar cart as Tristan glided onto the couch, lighting the fireplace with a snap along with a few candles sprinkled throughout the apartment.

"Whatever you're having." He casually replied, summoning textbooks to start working on his school assignments.

A glass sparkled in the candlelight as it floated over to the table in front of him.

"Always one for the dramatics." Tristan smirked as Liv joined him on the couch.

"An ostentatious display for my ostentatious friend. Would I insult you by serving your dram any other way?"

Liv set her glass down and picked up *Simulium Scientia*. "I need a crash course on Greenland since I practically drowned in anticipation of tonight's meeting during Environmental Science today…"

"I applaud your commitment to scholastics, but I'm supposed to be a *bad* influence." Tristan grabbed the book from her hand, "Since you had a long day, are you sure you don't want to do something non-educational – perhaps relax?"

Liv eyed him, reaching for her book. He teasingly pulled it away, until he saw her wince and then felt like a huge dick. Tristan handed the book over immediately after, praying he hadn't caused a cut to reopen.

"What do mortals do to cool off steam?"

"This." Liv lifted her whisky glass in the air with a chuckle.

"Okay, what about pre-alcoholic Liv, then?" Tristan asked again.

"Ouch." Liv set down her glass, grabbing another book from the table. "This."

"You would study?" Tristan laughed, "How pathetic *were* you before I turned you into someone cool?"

"Not study, you conceited asshole. I would read." Liv smiled darkly. "For fun."

"Ugh, that's even *worse.*" Tristan dramatically sunk into the couch, placing his hand against his forehead as he grimaced.

"If I recall, *mister,*" Liv poked her finger in his chest, "I woke up to one Tristan reading leisurely by himself when he had a cabin full of friends to entertain."

"That was clearly pre-alcoholic Tristan." He retorted with a smile.

Liv laughed in surprise. It was a musical sound.

"Well, if I had friends over, we'd watch a movie?" Liv negotiated. "That was a big social activity for pre-alcoholic Liv."

"A movie?" Tristan questioned.

"A movie. And if I'm leading this activity, I highly recommend a comedy or action – you'll definitely cry too much if we go down the romance route."

Liv summoned a blanket to the center of the couch and waved Tristan to join her in the middle. While the kitchen started making countless noises, pots maneuvering around until landing on the stove, his sidekick brought in a projector with some other technologies to assemble.

"What a production this so-called 'relaxing' movie activity is…" Tristan observed, watching Liv study wires before hearing the kitchen teapot start whistling.

"I'm surprised you're complaining, for one doing absolutely nothing." Liv mocked, nudging him in tandem.

That placed her right next to him. Tristan could feel the heat coming from the side of her.

Was she signaling something?

Curiously, Tristan stretched his arm and placed it on the back of the couch, inviting Liv to lean against him.

She didn't exactly move closer, but a moment later, a large bowl of popcorn came floating into her grasp. She placed it on top of Tristan's lap, grabbed a few kernels and plopped them into her mouth.

Then, two large mugs floated in front of them, smelling sweet like cinnamon chocolate and topped with a hearty dollop of whipped cream.

"And for the ultimate experience," Liv smiled as a box flew through her window, "Reeses Pieces to mix with the popcorn, a personal favorite."

She glanced up at Tristan, eyes beaming.

"All in for the experience. Go ahead." Tristan smiled, watching as she dumped the candy into the bowl of popcorn.

Liv quickly blew out all of the candles, but left the fireplace on as the opening credits began playing above the white brick.

And gently, her head leaned against his chest, a welcome weight that inadvertently made Tristan stop breathing. He grabbed more popcorn, trying to distract his focus from her strawberry-smelling hair.

Shit, it was the best tasting thing he had ever snacked on.

But was he chewing too loud?

His palm started growing sweaty.

What did this mean?

Liv chuckled at the movie; Tristan hadn't even heard the joke, but laughed anyways.

Between Liv on his chest, the popcorn in his mouth, the hot chocolate beverage in his hand, his arm on the couch (and now slightly Liv's shoulder) and all of Liv's motives in his head, Tristan needed to figure out a way to focus on the movie, and quickly.

We're just friends. We're just friends. We're just friends.

"Are you warm? I'll turn off the fire." Liv whispered with a quick snap.

It was now completely dark, aside from the glowing scenes projecting against the wall and reflecting against the room.

Her hair smelled so good.

Suddenly, Tristan's lips were against her head – not kissing her head, but smelling her head. But he didn't know what to do. Did she notice?

The door swung open.

"Liv, how'd the meeting-"

Tristan flicked on every flame in the room.

Piper stood in the doorway, her jaw open.

"Tristan!" Piper shrieked with surprise, placing a bottle of wine on the counter. "I didn't realize you two were... oh my gosh, I'm so sorry for intruding..."

"Piper. You're not intruding at all." Liv smiled warmly, getting up from the couch to welcome her friend.

"I can come back tomorrow." Piper squeaked, looking anywhere but toward Tristan.

The look in her eyes – the shock. The pain. The hurt.

He was such an *idiot*.

"Nonsense." Liv waved her off. "We just started *Anchorman* and have enough popcorn to feed an army." She grabbed the bottle of wine, reading the label impressively while summoning a glass to pour Piper.

Tristan scooted over to the edge of the couch, leaving the blanket in the middle for Liv.

"Hey, Piper!" He tried to say kindly, non-chalantly – like he wasn't just debating kissing her best friend. "You've got to try Liv's magical popcorn."

He lifted the bowl and handed it to her, extending an olive branch. She took it with a nod, awkwardly sitting on the opposite side of the couch and as far away from him as possible.

Well, at least that confirmed it looked just as bad to Piper as it felt to him. Liv was oblivious to the growing tension as she dropped to the couch between the two with a relaxed laugh, grabbing a hand of popcorn from the bowl Piper now clutched onto for dear life.

"Are you sure you two don't want to sit closer so we can all share the popcorn?" Liv asked between munches.

"No." Piper and Tristan both replied in unison.

Liv finally clued into the strangeness that was happening, she first turned to Piper, whose eyes were now glued to the movie screen, before switching to Tristan for an explanation.

"I've already had too much popcorn." He whispered with a shrug, realizing how idiotic that excuse sounded as it exited his mouth.

And after a moment of judgment, Liv finally turned back to the screen, unconvinced. Tristan slunk further down into the couch.

Well, shit.

LIV

Apparently, deities *hated* movies.

After Tristan let himself out before the ending credits rolled, Piper was just as quick to leave. She practically had to *bribe* her friend to stay for a nightcap by turning on all the lights, removing the projector and promising to never force her friends to sit through two hours of genius comedy ever again. Instead, she wrapped up the night learning more about Calithya, appreciative for Piper focusing more on the Siren Queen herself instead of Liv and Hayden's involvement with her. Somehow, it didn't feel right hearing about this unknown part of her life from Piper – and was glad her friend understood the unspoken sentiment.

Fortunately for Liv, having sourced all the materials needed for her own personal movie projector, she treated herself to a weekend binge filled with all of her favorite films. *Lord of the Rings, Pride & Prejudice, Animal House, Titanic, La La Land, Enchanted* and *My Best Friend's Wedding*. She had just begun watching *Harry Potter and The Sorcerer's Stone* while simultaneously working on her written assignment about Greenland when there was a soft knock on her door.

Liv paused the movie and strolled over to the entrance, finding Rhys outside with Piper.

"Come on in!" Liv greeted both excitedly, mostly directed toward Piper, who she hadn't seen since she terrified her friend with a comedic film, although she was equally thrilled to see Rhys in hopes of removing or re-adhering her now itchy bandages.

"I hope we're not intruding, I know we're a little early," Rhys apologized, "my meeting with King Hayden wrapped early."

"Not at all." Liv grinned, shaking Rhys's hand before giving Piper a big hug.

Besides silently studying with Kyril, Zayne, Dylan and Tristan in the Galleria Library on Friday, her friend had been nowhere to be seen all weekend. Liv desperately missed her quirky remarks and encyclopedia genius.

That sparked an idea – maybe Piper would prefer a documentary…

Liv shook her head, following Rhys to the sitting area. He automatically sat across from her on the table so he could examine her front bandages.

He lifted up one and murmured, "Okay," before adding ointment and replacing the gauze, continuing on to the next wound with a sigh, saying only "okay," again.

"Rhys, are those good okays or bad okays?" Liv clarified with worry.

Rhys dropped his glasses down his nose as he looked at Liv. "They're neutral 'okays' until I have a final assessment, Miss Olivia."

"Okay." She replied promptly, sitting up straighter.

After thirty more, 'okays,' Rhys finally stood up.

"A week from today, you may take off your bandages to soak in the bath with this medical salt." He handed Liv a jar full of tiny crystals. "It will sting. Do not be alarmed."

Liv's eyes went wide as she accepted the bath salt.

"How much should I use?"

"It will calculate the ratio needed when the bath is full and will only pour the necessary amount. Soak daily, until the bath salt no longer replenishes in the jar."

"That sounds easy enough." Liv noted optimistically.

Rhys then opened a chemistry set from his suitcase, filled with vials, herbs, bandages and measurement droppers.

"I spoke too soon…" Liv countered as she looked into the kit with dread.

"Piper, take notes." Rhys commanded before turning to Liv. "I won't coddle you with false conditions. You are battling a deadly infection with many poisonous wounds, all of which are combatting the healing process. We have to keep a balance between different poisons and deadly powers that are trying to weaken you. So far, my work has shown improvement, but not at the progress I had hoped. We'll need to intensify the treatment with an aggressive dose. Piper has been instructed to help prepare the medicine and reassemble your bandages every day."

He pointed to Liv's arm, "I have color-coated each bandage, so you know what type of ointment to place as a topical or what to boil the gauze in underneath the protected layer."

Piper and Liv nodded.

"Silver means you must boil gauze with this tincture to 102 degrees Celsius." He pointed to a jar with a silver lid before moving on to two blue containers. "Blue means you must mix a 1:1 ratio of these two vials – I recommend 1 teaspoon per bandaged area. Apply it as a topical."

"Got it." Piper confirmed as she vigorously wrote down his recommendation.

"Red means you must light this herb on fire and apply it directly to the wound. Wrap the ashes in a damp cloth and then dry it."

"Red sounds the most painful. We get that one over with first." Liv pointed to Piper, who nodded in agreement.

"Purple means you do Blue's topical with Red's process." Rhys added amusedly.

"Purple is second in our lineup." Liv pointed again, before turning to Rhys, "And that's not funny, sir."

"The last is Gold." Rhys still smiled, a glow in his eye. "You'll need to receive a shot of this antibiotic daily, 2 ML via this syringe, where each gold bandage is adhered. Make sure to sanitize the needle between doses."

Liv's jaw dropped. There had to of been at least twenty gold Band-Aids across her body.

"Is that it?" Piper confirmed, calmly.

"Is that it!?" Liv's eyes were wide.

"This is why I prefer my patients to be unconscious when I treat them." Rhys laughed as he stood up, gently patting Liv on her back. "I'll be back in a few days to check in again."

"A few days?" Piper clarified, looking worried. "Should we be concerned?"

Rhys nodded grimly, "If you feel lightheaded, lethargic, dehydrated or notice any of the wounds getting worse or bruises darkening, summon me immediately."

And with that, the Medicine Elite departed.

"Talk about a mood kill." Liv frowned, leaning into her couch.

"Are you scared?" Piper softly asked, sitting down beside her friend and gently placing a cool hand to her shoulder.

"In your care? Never." Liv smiled, although it didn't reach her eyes. She sighed, running a hand through her hair.

"What can I do?" Piper offered immediately, "Tea? Chocolate Peanut Butter Icecream? Alcohol?"

Liv laughed, "Maybe water? I'll try to prevent the dehydration side effect for a start."

She turned to the projector, seeing the night scene with lampposts on Privet Drive – the beginning of a beautiful adventure.

"Hey Piper, I know you hate movies and all, but would you mind watching one with me?" Liv whined in her best needy voice. Piper could never turn down her needy voice.

"I don't *hate* movies." Piper retorted with her natural, high-pitched tone.

She handed Liv a glass of water and fell back into the couch. "What are we watching?"

Liv smiled, slamming her Environmental Studies textbook and tossing it to the side.

"Prepare to lose your Slythershit over this." Liv hollered, pushing play and immediately feeling warm inside from the nostalgic chimes of the opening score.

By the time the movie concluded, Piper was hooked.

"Hermione is my Vulcan Mirror." Piper praised, turning to Liv immediately. "She actually said aloud the debate I've battled internally for years – what's worse? Death or expulsion." Piper squeezed her pillow with adoration, before turning to Liv, "Can we watch another?"

"Let me accio the next movie, then." Liv smirked, summoning the second film. And secretly wondering if any wizarding spells would activate her powers. Another must-have experiment to test in the future.

Piper smiled, looking outside to notice the sky quickly turning from dusk to night.

"Hey Liv," Piper paused, clearly debating whether expulsion *was* truly worse than death, or something even more conflicting to ask aloud. Finally, she breathed, "Is Tristan going to head over soon?" Before Liv could reply, Piper continued. "I would hate to have to pause the movie mid-way so maybe if he is coming tonight, it's best we hold the marathon to next weekend. Or, you know, let him start the series, watch the first movie alone, catch up to where we are, so we can all watch together, later. In the future…"

Liv's raised eyebrow slowly quieted her friend.

"Just trying… to be considerate." Her mousy voice concluded in a whisper.

"You two have both been weird since I…" Liv, paused coughing the concluding sentiment instead.

Piper nodded, in understanding.

Since she had been kidnapped. Since she had returned. Since her entire world was set upside down.

"I've tried not to make it weird. I know you both will come to me when you're ready to explain." Liv huffed, "But, in all honesty, I don't even know what to *think*. Do you like him? Are you just friends? Sworn Enemies? Did you get into a fight?"

"Just friends." Piper squeaked in reply.

"Okay." Liv accepted her friend's reply, although severely doubting that it encompassed the entire truth. But she trusted her friend's honesty and low tolerance for embarrassment, so dropped the conversation. She had pressed enough for now. And Zeus knew Piper had been even more respectful to Liv's situation.

"If you do ever want to talk, I'm here. You know that, right?" Liv offered, adding jokingly, "I may be Huffle-fucked in the head, but I give a Gryffindamn about you, love."

She walked over and gave Piper a hug, albeit a weak one, because her injuries still hurt like shit after Rhys's prodding.

"You're full of Ravencrap, but I still love you, you Muggle-fucker." Piper sang sweetly in reply. Such foul words did not match the clean mouth in which they emerged.

But that was exactly why Liv loved Piper, too.

PIPER

She had successfully avoided Tristan for the entirety of the weekend.

Not that she wanted to avoid him, exactly. In fact, it was quite the opposite that she wanted to do. Really, Piper wanted to spend every spare moment with Tristan – intoxicated by his warm scent, entranced by his devilish intelligence and melt into those caramel eyes...

Stop it. Stop it. Stop it.

Piper suspiciously looked around to make sure she hadn't walked into a Tristan trap both mentally and physically.

With a sigh, she leaned against a statue of her hero, Hephaestus, catching her breath. The cool marble comforted her heated body.

Ironic since Hephaestus was the previous God of...

Shit.

Piper jumped off of Tristan's ancestor and collided right into the God of Fire himself.

"Woah! Piper! You okay?"

Tristan gently held Piper's arms, ensuring she remained steady.

They were less than a foot away.

Piper inhaled his smell of cinnamon and smoky embers before realizing she hadn't responded. Immediately, she took a step back and coughed.

"I'm fine. Thank you."

Piper turned away, walking toward Warfare & Defense class, praying to Zeus that Tristan wouldn't follow her.

She wasn't ready.

Truthfully, she wasn't sure she would ever be ready to be *only* friends with Tristan.

Exiting the formidable doors containing the warmth within Puerdios, Piper was relieved to meet the crisp, fresh Spring air that late-March brought to campus. She wrapped her boxy grey peacoat closer to her body, covering her velvet, high-waisted, navy trousers and green cropped leather jacket, only exposing her jewel silk scarf tied in a relaxed fashionable bow.

"Hey Piper! Wait up."

Was it faint enough to justify *not* hearing it?

Piper continued on, although cringing with each step.

Tristan hollered from behind again, his voice growing louder until she heard his footsteps approaching.

She knew she couldn't avoid him indefinitely, but she still was hoping for a little bit more time.

Okay. She was hoping for an infinite amount of time. And perhaps her prayer to Trellis *had* been a bit aggressive.

"Hey, Piper!" Tristan finally caught up, walking beside her.

"Oh, Hi Tristan." Piper greeted him. "I didn't realize you were heading this way…"

She regretted the lie the moment the poisonous words left her mouth.

Come on Piper. Use your brain. It is literally all you have been blessed with for powers.

Tristan's face grew serious, ashamed, as he registered the blatant lie his friend so easily delivered. But he didn't call her out on it, which Piper appreciated, hoping the guilt plastered on her uncontrollable face apologized enough.

"Look, I just wanted to apologize about the other night. At Liv's…" His voice drifted off, before he cut back, clearer and crisper than ever, "It wasn't what it looked like. At all."

His eyes were pleading. It broke Piper to see him so hurt.

"There's no need for an apology." Piper replied back with a sigh, but continued to keep her pace as she marched forward.

It was true.

They technically weren't together.

Tristan and Liv were both free to do whatever they wanted. Piper had no claim to Tristan, nor did she want to make one if it would create a weird dynamic (…weirder than the one they currently had). And, if two of her friends got together, she would be happy for them.

Because that was the type of person Piper was; who she wanted to be.

She just wished it didn't hurt so much.

"No. I mean, it's not like that. I wanted to explain, clarify." Tristan continued on, inevitably lifting Piper's spirits.

What if he was trying to relay something bigger, something pertaining to his feelings for her?

"Liv doesn't like me in that way. We're just friends."

Liv.

Liv doesn't like Tristan in *that* way. Not the other way around. Tristan apparently had no reason to declare how he felt in *that* way.

Piper's heart dropped from the top of a building, splattering against the concrete in unison with the relentless, pouring rain that craved to be released from her eyes.

"Noted." Piper nodded, choking on her tears and continued forward.

Tristan gently grabbed her arm, forcing Piper to slow down.

"So, you and I – we're okay?"

His eyes looked hopeful. It made Piper want to scream.

But she was a rational deity, so she thought about the question, rationally.

Technically, they were never *not* okay. Tristan didn't disrupt their existing relationship with anything revolutionary or breakthrough. Nothing had changed, which was precisely the problem.

"This changes nothing." Piper stated, finally meeting Tristan's eyes with honesty. She weakly smiled, her only demanding focus that kept her from collapsing entirely.

Tristan grinned, his liquid amber eyes dazzling with happiness. Piper loved seeing him smile, forcing her mouth to naturally curve upward.

On the contrary, they had approached the East Lawn, receiving a scowl from Rei as he greeted them for class.

She nodded to Tristan conclusively, breaking away from him to begin her warm-ups for Warfare & Defense and closing the discussion for good.

Because the truth was, Liv may not love Tristan, but he still had deeper feelings for her. And he may like Piper in a different way, a more meaningful way than friendship, *that* way, but as long as Liv was around, his feelings would never be able to match and reciprocate how Piper felt about him.

Liv would always be Tristan's first priority; he would always choose her first. She was his Elite, his best friend, his family, his person.

And Piper was exhausted of feeling unworthy.

After a glimpse of what it felt like being someone's only, that-one-of-a-kind-only-eyes-for-you romance, the formation of a bond, a beginning to understand the needs and desires of another and putting those before you, a future had once flashed across her mind of what Tristan and she were capable of having.

Now, it was only coal dust compared to the diamonds.

And Piper had determined she'd never settle for something less again when choosing her eternal partner.

TEN

LIV

As she watched more Puerdios students arrive for Warfare & Defense class, Liv was still pissed she couldn't participate. But, if she were being honest (in her head, never in her silly class journal), Liv also needed to recognize the relief she felt at the idea of being glued to her tree stump for the next two hours.

Rei had not been kind to her this morning. He had been relentless, grasping joy from her screams and pushing her yet again to her ever-growing limits.

Even reaching to grab her pen made her wince; her fingers ached.

Everything ached.

With a sigh, Liv flipped the next page in her notebook, finally determined to try and express her feelings or whatever sappy, or terrifying, shit existed within. Mostly because she couldn't fail Rei's class when the task seemed so reasonable compared to her other never-ending piles of schoolwork.

Plus, after witnessing how Piper's reluctance to share her inner truth was rotting her friend's core the day before, and learning how her own wounds were literally rotting her *own* body's core, Liv was desperate to find any therapeutic solution to help her heal.

I feel...

Liv bit the tip of her pen, hearing laughter and yells from her carefree colleagues. Watching them smile, or if they showed struggle, it was still felt with innocence. Their souls had not been blackened; they still felt *safe*.

Liv no longer felt safe.

The mask of Rei's protection, Peyton's guidance or the Pure God's rule keeping order no longer applied to her. And if she escaped to her mom's for refuge, well then her mom became a target, not her safekeeper. Liv could only protect herself, and that was a pretty terrifying revelation to an eighteen-year-old. In reality, she had no one. And once believing she had protection had been a naïve mistake, almost costing her life. She would not make that mistake again. Feeling safe would be the worst healing mechanism for her, and she needed to accept that. Feeling safe was no longer an option.

She scribbled out her sentence.

I have...

Anger.

Clearly. Liv rolled her eyes. That wasn't a breakthrough emotion. But anger usually stemmed from something deeper. A bigger feeling, like pain.

Liv scribbled out her second attempt and re-wrote her initial thought.

I feel...

She felt a lot of fucking things.

Staring at her neon yellow silk trousers, which matched her cashmere cropped turtleneck, stiletto boots and angora coat, she remembered this morning when she froze at the sight of a newly made olive green gown. Flashbacks returned of the cruel dinner, where she was forced to go head to head with both Arlo and Kronos, plus Cleo *and* Klarya. Where Cleo became the closest thing she had to kindness.

And if it wasn't for Cleo's uncharacteristic compassion, Liv may not have been able to escape.

Olive green had been casted from one of her favorite colors, to one that now tormented her.

Even the outdoors had a conflicting narrative. It once represented freedom and purity, but also exposure and chaos. Now, Liv no longer felt like she had control outside, and seeing that god-damn green hue everywhere made her heart race even more.

On edge.

Liv felt on edge all of the time, like she was wasting borrowed breaths.

Conflicted.

That she should appreciate what she had, but also needed to be skeptical of everything and everyone in order to protect her battered soul.

Terror.

Something felt off. Liv recognized it now. She had felt incomplete, missing a piece of her former self for such a long time that she naturally assumed it was due to the blurry, dark, tortuous moments in the cell, slowly chipping off pieces of her humanity – and she still knew that was the main cause – but recently the hole felt almost self-made, which was scariest of all. Her former self would never return, and it was her own self-sabotage to blame.

It was one thing to place blame on others, but what happened when you were the truest detriment to yourself? Where did you go from there?

Liv shivered, scribbling out the two words again. Instead of ignoring it, she needed to mourn it.

She turned the page. A clean slate.

I feel...

Disconnected.

This weekend, having to explain what such a common thing as a movie was to her friends, Liv had never felt more disconnected to this new world. She could never recall ever feeling so lonely, so lost.

Nobody here understood her, where she came from. What the mortal world truly was like. How were her colleagues supposed to be groomed to lead these people when they knew *nothing* about their culture?

Ugh. If Rei read that, he'd roll his eyes.

She scribbled out the words again.

I want...

She looked up at the sky instinctively, the calm blues counteracting the angry greens from below, bringing a sense of ease that she wished she could carry instead of the constant battle of panic and dread that now felt apart of her core DNA.

Every time a student or faculty member passed by her unexpectedly in the halls, flashes of Kronos controlled her mind, sending her into high alert. Even when they looked *nothing* like him, a moving shadow sent her mind spinning at the frightening possibilities. When she heard her name called, "Olivia," her knuckled clenched with hatred, remembering how Arlo, her own kin, would taunt her by lacing his sweet words with poison. How she had to spend *weeks* locked up, helpless, while she faced the uncle who had murdered her own father. The only question remained, why hadn't her uncle sent Liv to the Underworld when he had the chance?

Her eyebrows furrowed and her mouth pursed in memory.

She scribbled out the words, breaking her pen in the process.

"Shit." She muttered aloud.

Liv sighed, focusing on her breathing to calm herself down.

Ignoring both Rei and Piper's worried glances in her direction, Liv leaned over to grab another pen, cursing again in the process while she held her abdomen to help support her aching, contracting muscles.

I wish...

Everyone would stop treating me like a nutjob.

But even if she wrote that, Rei would shut it down, claiming he didn't. Nobody saw her as crazy. Liv sadly chuckled. He'd probably first need to clarify what a 'nutjob,' meant...

Liv scribbled it out, turning the page once again.

I feel...

Liv bit her pen, continuing to contemplate her spectrum of disastrous emotions. Finally landing on what was expected of her.

I feel fine.

HAYDEN

It felt strange walking across the East Lawn, the first time in months, to a class he was technically enrolled in, and incredibly late to.

Sort of like playing hookie but having a justifiable reason to do so.

It reminded him of when he had been able to stay home during his scheduled 'dentist appointments,' a façade created to keep up the appearance he was a regular mortal student in need of dental cleaning. And although he usually spent the time studying or preparing for his royal duties, there was still a stigma of wrongness to it.

Perhaps the whole façade was the wrong part.

Hayden had offered to stay away from their corresponding class for Liv's benefit, instead taking private lessons with Rei in the evenings when other royal obligations did not conflict.

Hayden had essentially doubled his Security Elite's educational workload while tripling his actual Elite duties for the greater good of Liv's safety. That didn't even take into consideration the additional time spent on alliance opportunities and war strategy.

But, it had been months since he checked in on Puerdios's curriculum, overseen by his Mother, the Candor Elite, which she had so graciously mentioned was stirring buzz with faculty on whether King Hayden *cared* about the future generation (even though he was *apart* of the future generation). So it was time to do his due diligence and appease the educational masses.

At first, he had held off on visiting Liv's classes out of respect for her recovery, but even that started controversy when Professor Deligne cornered him last week asking why he hadn't sat in on her renowned Meteorology lectures yet.

Hayden figured it would be best to trial the uneasy interaction with Rei present, within a group setting and working in the expansive outdoors, instead of creating an intimate classroom space with only Piper and Professor Deligne to ease Liv's post-traumatic-stress.

So, with their minor yet huge breakthrough last week of Liv actually approaching and conversing with him instead of freezing with bloody murder at first glance, Hayden felt okay.

Nervousness still lingered, building in anticipation with each step he took toward the East Lawn. He was always excited for any chance to see Liv, but had grown weary to her heart-clenching and daggering reaction to his presence. He still had to proactively prepare his brain to anticipate suspicion and alarm as opposed to the natural inclination of receiving sparkling eyes and a bright, welcoming smile from his love.

It was a fine line between excitement and torture now.

So, he had kept his distance. But now, royal duty called.

He found Liv immediately in a bright neon ensemble, and his heart skipped a beat. He laughed internally, watching from afar how she stubbornly scribbled against a notebook, knowing the pure hatred she must have felt from Rei's implored class assignment.

She was a warrior, not a writer.

Liv preferred to imagine volleyballs as the faces of her enemies and punch them head-on or spike them to the ground. And although she loved to distract herself with an all-consuming story – whether book or movie marathon – asking her to reflect on her emotions was the exact way to make her shut down even more.

Hayden had, of course, advised Rei as such, but his Security Elite was just as stubborn as his ex-girlfriend.

Ex-soulmate.

Hayden stopped. Reminding himself he could not casually approach Liv from behind. That would terrify her beyond all means. He could already imagine her eyes turning black as tortuous memories flashed across her mind. He needed to loop around so she could see him in the distance and approach her slowly so she could prepare for an interaction.

But only if she welcomed it, of course.

He watched as Liv's pen snapped, her face boiling with anger and frustration before grimacing to grab another. Her concentration remained on the paper, although she didn't write anything.

Did she feel his presence? Was she already scared? What if she was combatting her inner demons already?

Hayden stopped again, looking for Rei. The Security Elite was across the lawn, overseeing part of a simulation that appeared to involve fire. And although both Rei and Piper noticed him immediately, Rei shook his head with a shrug. He couldn't interrupt class simply because one of his students was working on her written assignment in the presence of the king.

That certainly would stir up an abundance of unwanted rumors.

So instead, Hayden carefully paced on. Liv hadn't screamed, stood or insinuated any sense of immediate danger, so perhaps she was welcoming his visit; however challenging it may be.

Ten feet away, she still hadn't looked up. But she did turn the paper, writing briefly for a moment before another pause.

"Hey Ollie." Hayden whispered, keeping his distance.

Her head shot up, eyes wide with terror.

She crawled backward, hitting the tree with abrupt impact. Her hands tensed into claws.

Liv was trembling, yet she hadn't screamed.

It broke Hayden to see her like this, at the cause of his simply *being* there.

He hadn't imagined the silence could be worse than the vocal rage.

But he was wrong.

He had been wrong about too much.

It *was* too much.

He thought he could be stronger, fight through the hurt for her, but instantly his mind doubted her ability to communicate that he needed to leave.

"I'm sorry. I didn't mean to sneak up on you…" Hayden's voice quivered. "I can go… I'm so sorry, Liv."

He turned, clenching his fist in unison with closing his eyes.

It was too soon.

He had been too naïve in hopes of a silver lining.

Perhaps this was their eternal curse, a destiny filled with pain. Soul mates whose bond had been torn and could never become one again.

Perhaps the prophecy was a lie and they were destined to fail.

Just like he had in keeping the most precious thing in his life, safe.

And this was his forever punishment.

LIV

He was walking away.

Liv was sinking further into darkness.

The dirt below her turned into cold stone.

She clung to the earth, trying to keep an anchor to the present.

Why did he have this affect on her?

He wasn't Kronos.

He was walking *away.*

Kronos would have never walked away. He would have never left an open opportunity for torture.

Kronos would have laughed cruelly, grabbed her, confined her…

Liv shook her head out of the evil memory, fighting her mind to stay in the present and not weakly default to the darkness.

She hated him with so much anger it made her cry.

A tear of frustration ran down her cheek.

She was shaking, but from infuriation. From not having been able to do enough before. From not giving that sadistic asshole the wrath that Liv could have designed to make his life a living hell.

Stop thinking about Kronos.

He would have never walked away.

Liv wanted to punch something. She needed to get out this boiling fury within her bones. She needed to feel something, again. Anything.

"I TOLD YOU TO CALL ME OLLIE, GOD DAMNIT!" Liv finally screamed in frustration at the distant figure.

She opened her eyes, her mouth dropped.

The King of Gods stopped, slowly turning around in confusion.

Her first offense of not bowing, or Hades, acknowledging a royal, was politely excused. But Liv was pretty sure a second offense of cursing and commanding the royal directly, without permission, may not be so kindly overlooked.

His piercing blue eyes locked with hers, but they were assuring, peaceful, the same shade of the sky above. They sparkled with a slight amusement Liv was not expecting.

"My apologies, *Ollie*." His stoic face slowly curved upward, revealing a hint of a smile.

When his being didn't torment her inner core, and she was able to see him in his full glory, King Hayden truly was a dazzling specimen. His camel coat accentuated his broad shoulders and as he turned, his thin, grey cashmere sweater revealed a glimpse to what lay a very toned 8-pack beneath. He was young, couldn't be over twenty years old, if immortality wasn't a factor, yet wisdom and responsibility matured him. An old soul in a primed vessel.

Liv's heart started beating faster, but not from terror, a fear stemming from *another* intrigue. She blushed at the thought – there was no way the

King of the Pure Gods would ever have interest in a broken Pillar Elite, one of which continued to lash out negatively at his presence.

He needed an alliance, someone strong and capable to lead his people.

Not her wreckage of a self.

It was a silly notion.

"No, I should apologize." Liv mumbled quietly, growing redder at the impure thoughts she just had about her king. "I don't suppose cursing at the king is the best way to gain favor."

"And why would you be concerned with gaining favor?" He continued, slowly approaching her again, as if asking permission with each step. "You already have it, if that's what worries you."

"I-I barely know you." Liv admitted, staring back down at her notebook for reprieve. But the blank page that faced her just made her more infuriated.

Hayden's footsteps ceased.

Liv looked up, finding a curious flash of hurt expressed on his handsome face before it returned back to neutral.

"Perhaps it's time we change that." He offered softly, taking a couple steps to Liv's side before asking, "May I?"

"Of course, your highness." Liv whispered, scooting over to make room, yet gripping more intensely on her precious notebook.

"Please, Hayden." He corrected her.

"Hayden." Liv tested the name against her tongue. It felt like a breath of fresh air as it emerged from her mouth, certainly more natural than the hardness of stating 'your highness.'

She blushed, softly smiling down at her notebook.

"So, *Ollie*," Hayden emphasized the name lightheartedly, "What are you working on?"

He casually nodded over to her blank notebook, adjusting into his seat beside her by leaning against the trunk, clasping his hands and placing them over his bent left knee.

Ugh, her assignment was so lame. Did she really have to explain this of all things?

"Well, *Hayden,*" Liv retorted with the same name-emphasis, "Mostly just doodling against Rei's will."

"Doodling?" Hayden clarified, "You're really trying to get under Rei's skin, aren't you?"

Liv laughed, rolling her eyes.

"I'm supposed to be... writing about my feelings." Liv explained, trailing off as she turned away.

Out of all the things she could have been tasked to do while interacting with the king... he was going to think she was a weak, pathetic half-god.

"So Rei's trying to get under your skin, as well." Hayden chuckled. "Looks like the two of you are evenly matched."

His laugh was melodic. It gave her butterflies. It brought her back, centered her, vibrated within her.

He thought she was amusing, interesting. *A match for Rei.*

"It's not necessarily... my *thing.*" Liv glared at the notebook, sighing with dread of the inevitable return to her assignment.

Hayden looked back out to the field, where the sane students were throwing flames at one another and extinguishing the fiery threats with water, before returning his gaze back to Liv. With a determined nod, he stood up.

Makes sense.

Truthfully, Liv was surprised his crowned majesty stayed around this long.

She turned the page in her notebook and bit her pen, trying to concentrate again (and failing again) on what to write or draw next, when a hand reached out before her.

Hayden's hand.

An open invitation.

Liv stared at the strong gesture, contemplating if she could touch him – if it would send her overboard, or if it would get her into trouble.

She warily looked up first to Hayden for an explanation.

"I have an idea." Hayden offered, "I think you'll find it more fulfilling than staring at blank paper."

Anything would be more fulfilling than staring at blank paper.

Hayden prodded his hand closer to her, encouraging that she trust him.

What the Hades.

She grabbed it.

An electric shock buzzed through her body upon her skin making contact with his, she gripped his hand, binding their limbs as one. Effortlessly, he lifted her up, so that she stood directly in front of him.

Liv gulped, unsure what to expect. She looked around, trying to decipher a clue.

Slowly, her gaze returned to Hayden's. His look was fierce, almost intimidating, like she were the only one around, and not surrounded by dozens of other students.

He smiled, genuinely, radiating pure joy as the arm behind his back swung around to reveal a volleyball.

Liv almost tripped from her excitement. Grabbing the volleyball immediately, she turned to Hayden, beaming.

"You know how to play volleyball?" She questioned suspiciously.

Frankly, she wasn't sure if she cared.

Liv remembered the unsuccessful attempt of trying to teach Piper the game, but all she accomplished was increasing her friend's contempt for the purpose of sports. Liv laughed internally as she remembered Piper actually asking her if there was a point to hitting a ball repeatedly over the net since she didn't care about winning.

"I've been known to rally every once in a while." He admitted, leading her away from the class simulation to a makeshift volleyball court he created quickly with his powers behind the tree.

"I'm surprised you even know what volleyball is." Liv confessed, realizing he probably thought the same of her. Turning to Hayden as she walked to her side of the court, she explained, "I grew up in the mortal world – so, it's rare when I find a deity who can relate to any fraction of my upbringing."

Then she remembered the zombie explanation.

Perhaps he had spent more time with her mortal kind than he led onto.

"Well, I'm a sports junkie," Hayden declared with a laugh. "Football, basketball, tennis, wakeboarding, snowboarding – I can't get enough of it. My mom used to remove my TV privileges during March Madness because I was glued to the screen." Then he smiled, cupping his mouth to a whisper so only Liv could hear, "Still does, even though I'm king."

Liv burst out in laughter, not expecting that all-too relatable comment, before removing her stiletto boots and tossing them to the side of the court.

Perhaps his screen addiction explained the zombie insight.

She walked back to behind the court line, preparing to serve.

"Ready?" She hollered.

"Born ready." He yelled back.

She looked at the ball, immediately imagining Arlo's face on the surface of it. How'd she'd been *longing* to punch her uncle's jaw.

Well, now she could.

She tossed the ball up in the air with precision and smacked it over the net.

That felt cathartic. Liv hummed as she ran to the center of the court, preparing for Hayden's next move.

With impressive form, he bumped the ball over the net.

Liv dove to dig the ball up into the air, stumbling to stand and prepare to set it up for the inadvertent spike. She lifted the ball back into the air, directing it toward the net.

As Klarya's eyes floated into the sky, Liv evilly smiled.

Time to spike that bitch where she belongs.

She blasted the ball over the net, letting her muscle memory guide her aching limbs.

Hayden dove, bumping the ball into the air effortlessly, setting it up and exchanging a devilish grin in Liv's direction, before spiking it over the net in rebutte.

But Liv was one step ahead of him, already in the air for the block, sending it pounding back to his side and out of his reach.

The ball bounced within inches of the court lines, to Liv's delight.

She felt elated, genuinely in her element, and more importantly, *herself* for the first time in months.

Next up, serving up Kronos's head to his kinder twin.

Liv smiled, walking back to begin the next point.

"1-0."

This was precisely the type of therapy she needed.

HAYDEN

He finally recognized the Ollie he loved return while she demolished him on the volleyball court. Hayden would gladly take the loss many times over if it helped keep her in such peace.

It wasn't like he had ever won against her in the past. Why start now?

She had won the first two sets by a landslide, but had pleaded they continue until Warfare & Defense concluded. He obliged, as if it were even an option.

Hayden was doing better in this set, at least keeping it relatively even. He attributed it to finally discarding his restricting camel coat. Although, it wasn't as if Liv's neon look was any more performance driven to constitute an advantage.

He threw the ball up in the air to serve, when he heard a subtle cough from across the court.

Catching the ball, Hayden caught Liv's change in demeanor first. She now stood upright and her eyes diverted to his right, pointing discretely in the direction as well.

Hayden turned to find a very irritated Security Elite stomping over to their game.

"Liv, your assignment is due by the end of class, or else you get a zero mark for the past two weeks." Rei commanded, pointing back to the tree. "Go. Now."

Liv scurried, running toward the tree, before pausing, turning around and grabbing her shoes, racing even faster for her retrieval amidst Rei's dagger-ish glare.

But Hayden's heart leapt when she mouthed, "thank you," with a genuine smile before crossing the court and returning to her writing arena.

Before, Hayden would have craved more – a hug, a kiss – some acknowledgement to reaffirm his feelings, but in that moment, he realized it wasn't about the expression but the meaning behind it. And in that moment, the secret smile Liv shared meant more than a hundred casual hugs combined. She was safe. She would be okay.

And even if they never got back to being Hayden and Ollie, Hayden had already accepted it – as long as Liv was happy and he could help her remain that way.

Maybe that was growing up, or truly discovering the meaning of love.

"You come to review my class and then I find you've ignored the entire lesson and instead stolen a student to play a mundane sport?" Rei accused, cornering Hayden with amusement. "If you give me anything less than a perfect report to Daphne, I will personally send you to hell. Not the Underworld – something worse by my own design."

Hayden laughed, nodding to Liv who was now vigorously writing by the tree stump.

"You're welcome." He prompted, nodding to the newly studious Liv while following Rei's lead to return to the actual simulation.

"Don't be fooled. She could be drawing another animal or plant." Rei retorted.

"Extra points for being fondly receptive to constructive criticism." Hayden dryly joked, ignoring the statement.

"The class will be wrapping up their simulation shortly. Perhaps you can shift your efforts to get a glimpse of what you actually came to evaluate?" Rei sweetly suggested.

"Of course." Hayden replied, watching as Tristan, Kyril and Zayne jogged over to Liv, being the first students to complete the course. Liv jumped up with excitement and immediately greeted Tristan with a hug.

Such a small maneuver managed to steal all of the joy and accomplishment from today's small triumph, once again emptying Hayden's soul to ground zero.

Rei observed Hayden's gaze, but remained silent.

Hayden looked down at the ground, wishing it didn't sting *so* much.

Liv was happy. That was all that mattered. That's all he wanted.

Finally, Hayden continued his thought in a low whisper, "Even without visiting your class, I'd give you full marks and an excellent review, you know that, right?"

"I do." Rei calmly replied back, no emotion attached.

Hayden took a deep breath, grateful for his friend for understanding, but not speaking with pity or sadness.

"Daphne does, too." Rei added with a smirk, changing the subject. "So, at least make the paperwork appear efficient, for all of our sake?"

Hayden laughed, nodding in agreement. He spotted Piper concluding the course and directed himself to her for 'class reporting intel.' She would be unbiased, at least.

After chatting with Piper for some time, it appeared obvious she was more than happy for someone to talk to during the remainder of class. Hayden followed her eyes as she seemed to finally relax, or grow closer to the term 'relax' as was capable within Piper's abilities, at the sight of Liv and Tristan exiting the course.

He knew it wasn't his place, but Hayden also suspected if it involved Piper's two best friends, she couldn't open up to them directly, so he prompted her with an opportunity. Especially because Piper was now one of his closest friends, too. And he cared for her like a sister.

"If you want to catch up to your friends, please don't stay on my account. I have all I need…"

"It's okay." Piper quickly replied. Her response was polite and short, but her body language and tone revealed layers of depth beneath the words.

"I thought you were attached at the hip between those two." Hayden offered, chuckling lightly. "I would hate to be the cause for an amputation of sorts…"

Piper eyed Hayden curiously, giving him the look that always kept him on his toes. Hayden knew Piper was a keen observer and intuitive as Hades, so as she squinted her eyes, he knew she saw right through his ploy.

"Does it hurt to see Tristan and Liv getting on so well?" She finally asked, her question soft and kind, but a trail of sadness clued Hayden down her intentional, or possibly non-intentional, path.

"That's a loaded question." Hayden admitted.

Piper sadly smiled in understanding.

"I know."

So Hayden stood by his friend in silence, until the neon yellow vision disappeared through the arching stones, before Piper finally said her good-byes to follow the same route, a distant memory living forever as a minute in the past.

He watched Piper cross the lawn, noting to send Peyton to her room that night for some much-needed girl time. It was one thing confessing your love-triangle issues to one's king, so he hoped Peyton could provide some reprieve where he could not.

"Dig up anything noteworthy?" Rei hollered, joining Hayden.

"Other than Piper reporting that your class is pure torture? Nothing new." He retorted with a laugh. "Tonight, I'll be happy to alert my mother that you passed with flying colors."

"Well, I have to admit, whether it be my hard deadline or your creative intervention, we finally got something out of that stubborn blonde of yours." Rei admitted, handing Hayden Liv's notebook.

Hayden stared at the leather-bound book.

Albeit tempting to understand another layer of that intriguing mind, Hayden shook his head. "I shouldn't. It's private."

"Either you read it, or I will." Rei challenged. "She needs a grade. And I think it makes more sense for you to have the insight than me."

Rei prodded the book in front of Hayden; Hayden still resisted from accepting it.

Rei sighed. "You helped her today. You got through to her. Not me. This is *your* work. And I think you need to see this."

Hayden didn't move.

"Or hear it…" Rei sighed, flipping through the pages, beginning to read aloud in an imitation of Liv's voice.

"I am a warrior. I cannot…"

"Give me that." Hayden growled. "Your reading it out loud is even worse. No wonder Piper wants to cancel your class. You're spineless."

He turned his back to Rei, taking a deep sigh before glancing down at her inner thoughts.

I'm a warrior. I cannot be broken.

I feel defeated and angry now, but I will overcome this. There's no other choice, no other path I want to take.

I will find a newer, better version of my life – and it may be different than before, because I'm different than who I was before, but I will not let this chapter in my life define who I am or impact my legacy.

As somebody once told me, "Follow the stars for guidance." And that's exactly what I'll do. I'll keep looking up and never stop finding the sparkling, infinite light among the darkness in this world.

Short and sweet. Hayden was a little relieved to find no mention of Kronos, of *him,* Arlo or Tristan… It didn't seem to cross too far past a boundary, exposing her deepest thoughts or granting access to something he had no permission to know. She spoke of the future, of hope.

Turning back to Rei, he concluded, "Pass," before turning the pages to close the spiral notebook.

He paused, stopping on an exposed page that caught his eye, remembering small insights he had heard throughout the day, clueing together the pieces he was too distraught to recognize in the first place...

"*Don't be fooled. She could be drawing another animal or plant.*"

"*Mostly just doodling against Rei's will... I'm supposed to be writing about my feelings.*"

What if she had been drawing her inner conflict this entire time?

Hayden grazed to the image, his jaw dropping as he absorbed the stunning design. His fingers traced the lines of which he knew all too well.

A flower glowing among the sky above a stellar mountain, taking shape from an intricate constellation in the sky, her constellation, *Ollie*.

Below the mountain on earth, a stag, grazing among the valley.

Crests of two houses, forged as one.

Their crest.

"Oh great. She found time to draw a mountain today." Rei retorted, oblivious to the tear trailing Hayden's cheek. Hayden heard his friend curse under his breath as he walked away. But Hayden didn't care.

She was remembering. In her own way.

And, perhaps she had never truly forgotten.

ELEVEN

PIPER

She slammed another book shut, taking a deep breath and closing her eyes among the silence of her apartment.

Rei had been correct.

This wasn't the end, just another closed road.

Piper took a sip of her chardonnay, soaking in its crisp flavors of honeydew melon, tangerine, orange blossom and sage as it tickled her palette.

Focus on the white nectarine and apricot, not the failure...

She took another sip of the glorious juice before filing the Nordic relic to her 'read pile.' It was growing larger by the day, without any hint of coming closer to completing her royal assignment. Now, it stood as the only evidence of Piper's growing debt to time without producing results.

The King of the Pure Gods had tasked her with one thing: find any clues, any facts, that could lead them to ancient deity civilizations of the past and prove that they were still intact.

Buddhist, Egyptians, Norse or Celtic Gods.

Just one proof of evidence would suffice for today.

With a stubborn sigh, Piper grabbed another tome and plopped it on her white marble kitchen island when she heard a knock at the door.

She sat up straight, not recalling making plans with any of her class-mates tonight. Hesitantly, she approached the door, wearisome of some evil capture awaiting her front entrance. But who would want to capture her? She couldn't even do her basic job of sourcing facts from historical documents – and reporting was her essential duty as a deity.

Piper waited, biting her lip, before finally deciding to call through the locked door.

"Who is it?" She squeaked, shutting her eyes and praying a demonic voice would not answer her question.

"Piper – it's me. Peyton." Her friend hollered from the other side.

Piper let out a deep sigh, unaware she had been holding her breath during the interaction.

"And Dylan." Peyton added honestly, knocking on the door again. "You okay?"

Zeus.

Piper's eyes went wide as she frantically unlocked the barrier and swung it open.

"Sorry about that." She whispered, staring at the ground.

"No problem." Peyton grinned, pulling Piper into an unexpected embrace. "Shit's been weird lately. I'd judge you if you *weren't* concerned."

Piper laughed, awkwardly.

"Hey Piper." Dylan smiled genuinely, looking around the apartment. "Wow, your place is *incredible*."

Piper perked up at the compliment, blushing as she led the two ladies into her loft. She liked her modern space; everything meticulously placed and organized – the minimalism serving as the best source of concentration.

Soft toned linens decorated her couch and cedarwood structured her furniture. Nothing strayed from white, cream, gold, grey and brown, beside accent plants of green. That and the result to the craziest thing she had done to her personal haven, when she turned the cabinets in her kitchen black, the perfect and subtle nod to her time as a Dark God. Yet, it still seamlessly tied into the darker metal furnishings like her ceiling lamp structure and hollow fireplace.

"You're probably wondering why we're here." Peyton offered, summoning two glasses of wine and revealing a bottle of rosé. "You're more than welcome to have some after your white, but we didn't want to come empty handed for girl's night."

Piper coughed. "Girl's night?"

Her eyes trailed Peyton as her friend promptly sat on her cream couch, making herself comfortable instantaneously. Her relaxed olive-green silk gown and robe set was almost too perfect a match for her cozy vibe.

Dylan placed a gentle, warm hand on Piper's shoulder. "We've noticed you've been down on Tristan-"

"Zeus knows why!" Peyton rolled her eyes jokingly.

Dylan smiled, shushing Peyton before returning her calm gaze to Piper. "-Among other things, like the heavy task of researching ancient communities known to be extinct, so we figured we'd come over, help you out and cheer you up."

Unlike Peyton, Dylan was still dressed properly in an argyle cardigan and skirt, paired off with knee-high black boots. The autumnal color palette perfectly brought out her ivory complexion and rich auburn hair.

"And drink profusely while achieving it all!" Piper smirked, raising her glass in the air as she kicked her legs over the couches' armrest. "It's not easy being this fabulous."

"Do you want us to go?" Dylan whispered, ignoring Peyton's ridiculousness with honesty and understanding radiating from her question.

"No, of course not." Piper responded quickly, grabbing her wine glass.

"You want Peyton to go?" Dylan clarified with a grin.

"Hey!" Their friend yelled from the couch. "We're a package duo!"

Piper laughed, genuinely, trying to hold back tears regarding the consideration of her incredible friends. She didn't realize how desperately she needed this.

"Dylan is here for the responsible council, but I'm here to help unleash anger, make bad decisions and encourage you to wake up with regret, obviously," Peyton continued, murmuring 'obviously' to Dylan with a devious smile, before returning to Piper, "But also provide a full recovery from your sadness, no matter what." She lifted her glass again, taking another sip.

"I'm afraid for at least a portion of what I require, you'll need to be moderately sober." Piper mentioned, hating how her mousy voice raised itself an octave when she felt awkward.

"Then let's do that one first." Peyton drawled with a wink.

"You're the God of Discovery. Can you help give me any leads for the Buddhist, Egyptian, Norse or Celtic Gods?"

"My grandmother's cousin's great-aunt, I believe, derives from Celtic descent." Dylan offered. "She emigrated to our society a few centuries ago, but I'll see if I can connect with her for any relevant information?"

It wasn't much, but it was more than Piper had gathered in weeks. All she had been able to find was a 5th century document of a marriage between the first Elemental Elite and Celtic Queen. Yet, after the alliance had been formed, it seemed any reports of the Elite and the Celts dissolved – the Irish deity community in general evaporating into concealment along with them.

"You should come to the Elite Meeting on Thursday. Inform Hayden." Peyton nodded in agreement before warning, "But, ask him first before pursuing. This research is not something we want shared publicly."

Although Peyton remained kosher with her delivery, Piper understood the underlying threat. The research was not something the Pure Gods wanted the Dark Gods to seek.

"Of course." Dylan smiled, taking a sip of her wine.

Point taken.

"So let's start with the first – Buddhism." Peyton relaxed, kicking her right leg up in the air before balancing it across her left knee. "It makes the most sense that whatever temple or place the Buddhist deities – or any deities for that matter – chose to hide their community would be reveled today. So what are the most coveted temples or relics of the religion?"

"Angkor Wat? It's the largest religious monument in the world." Piper chimed back.

"Sounds like the best option to host a secret society in terms of size alone." Dylan agreed.

But Peyton frowned, her eyes scrunching closed as her mind searched her depository of facts that could prove helpful.

"Angkor Wat was originally constructed as a Hindu temple, dedicated to the god Vishnu for the Khmer Empire. It gradually transformed into a Buddhist temple towards the end of the 12th century."

"When the Buddhist Gods chose to isolate their powers from the deity world?" Dylan offered, hopeful.

"That was about when we stopped having our documentation, however sparse it was to begin with..." Piper sighed.

"It feels too risky." Peyton pushed, "Why select to move to a location heavily worshiped by another powerful influence? You want to make sure no harm would come to the area, lest you be trapped in another dimension forever."

"True." Piper agreed, immediately thinking of Hades and whether he would have ever opted to move the Underworld location to Westminster Abbey versus the Parthenon if given the choice. The answer was far too easy to assess.

"Keep it on the list. If we find success with Rei's past relationships with the Norse Gods, Dylan's lead with the Celts and magically discover Egypt's highly envied army as portrayed in hieroglyphics, maybe we'll engage the Hindu deities for shits and giggles." Peyton smiled, sitting up and summoning her bottle of rosé for a refill.

"Wat Arun?" Piper asked, summoning another item from the kitchen, but far from Peyton's choice of liquid knowledge amplification, she grabbed her notebook and pen, immediately reorganizing her notes into a list of notable places.

"Wat Arun Ratchawararam Ratchaworamahawihan." Peyton clarified, "Stunning temple. Definitely a contender. Could be possible if Aruna became Queen before choosing quarantine... keep it on the list."

"Okay." Piper nodded, before adding, "According to our files, we only have documentation of a… Prince Rāhula succeeding his father… Siddhārtha Gautama by 410 BCE."

Piper had always wanted to visit Thailand, and simply speaking the names and locations coveted in their records and mythology sounded so beautiful on the tongue; Piper made a mental note to study the dialect of the Thai culture.

Perhaps after this war.

But, even more concerning was that her more recent research still gapped the present by over two thousand years.

"Rāhula is the only known son of *the* Buddha." Peyton explained, "If he found the path to enlightenment, he could still be ruling today."

Peyton furrowed her brows, taking another sip of her wine.

Piper could only imagine how exhausting searching for these details would wear on her friend. It had taken Piper essentially *months* to get this far, and it drained her daily.

Peyton was essentially an exploding firework to Piper's candleflame when it came to her speedy deliberation. Although more impactful to light up the sky, a firework also burnt out much quicker.

Moving forward, Piper would need to be selective with what she asked Peyton to really dive into. She bit her quill, maneuvering through her notes and organizing them into ranking tiers so her next offer would be the best contender.

And possibly, that meant the *only* contender.

"Wat Phra Kaew?" Piper offered, her voice a higher pitch than ever.

The anxiety and pressure were going to send her voice to another soprano key unheard of to this universe.

"Temple of the Emerald Buddha?" Peyton perked up, before frowning yet again. "But it wasn't built until the 18th century…"

"I've seen the Emerald Buddha. It's a huge symbol to Buddhism." Dylan challenged, "What about that?"

"Not only Buddhism, but to the king." Peyton explained, "The power of the Emerald Buddha gives legitimacy to the king and protection to the nation. The image's significance is built upon its long history and symbolism as an object of power for those who are able to possess it."

Getting the chills from the discovery, Piper anxiously checked her notes. "Historical sources indicate that the statue surfaced in Northern Thailand in 1434."

"The creator is unknown. There's no known creator." Peyton confirmed, beaming. "There's NO KNOWN CREATOR!"

"Okay, Jardin Anglais, slow down on the rosé." Dylan joked, her energy matching Peyton's infectious excitement as she laughed. "Too many roses means an abundance of thorns."

"Holy shit." Peyton breathed, looking to Piper, "This has to be it. Right? Do you feel it?"

"I'll do some supporting research to fact check our thoughts and properly eliminate other contenders, but.... yes," Piper breathed, her mouth slowly curving upward into a smile. "I feel like this is right. My gut feels like this *has to be it.*"

"You… or your chardonnay?" Dylan smirked.

Peyton turned to Dylan, eyes narrowing down on their Dark God friend. "Hey. *I was going to say that.*"

The three girls broke out in simultaneous laughter, before Peyton finally lay back against the couch with a sigh.

"I'm spent. Can we end on the high note and be done with research?"

"You just catapulted my research by 25% within an hour, I'm eternally grateful for what we've already accomplished." Piper agreed, summoning her notebook back to the kitchen among her pile of textbooks, placing it meticulously parallel to them.

"So, to get back to the original reason we came over, then…" Peyton deviously smiled, "Rumor in the hallway is that you have the hots for Tristan?"

Piper's eyes grew wide.

"I don't have '*the hots*' for Tristan." She declined the question, although yet again, her voice had hit an all-time record high pitch. "I don't even know what 'I have' for him, to be honest."

"That's even worse." Peyton moaned.

"What? We're friends. He's nice. We laugh together. That's it." Piper explained, nervously taking another sip of her wine.

She preferred pining for him in solitude, not as a social observation to be conversed about.

"Just, be careful, Piper." Dylan warned. "I hate to break this to you, but Tristan's mind is wrapped around Liv. And he'll say it's not true, that he knows Liv is destined to be with Hayden or that she's too weak right now for it to even be of consideration... but those are just excuses to him."

"Dylan, we're supposed to be making her feel *better*." Peyton muttered, angling her hand to cover her mouth in hopes of being less obvious.

As if Peyton had forgotten, there were only three people sitting on Piper's couch and armchairs that surrounded her square coffee table.

"I know." Dylan sighed apologetically. "And after I clear my conscious of sharing what I've seen – that he hasn't gotten over her – we can forget I said anything." She turned to Piper with a sad smile, "I don't want you to get pulled into an easily avoidable love quadrangle."

"Trust me, I want to steer clear." Piper declared, admitting honestly, "Even Hayden and Liv's *singular* relationship is too complicated for me."

"They're never easy, that's for sure." Peyton chimed in with an assuring nod.

"How do you determine if the challenges are worth the combat for love?" Piper asked curiously, turning to her two girlfriends who were both in relatively steady relationships.

Both took sips of their glasses, before Dylan took the first attempt to drunken philosophy.

"I guess as long as you feel the good outweighs the bad?" She wondered aloud.

"Only you can scale your own happiness." Peyton added, "And your partner should enhance it, not take away from it."

Piper nodded, trying not to compare Tristan with each nugget of advice. She hoped her friends didn't notice her cheeks blushing at the thought of his fiery smile lighting up the darkness of her mind.

"We may be immortal, but that doesn't mean we should take any time for granted. And no matter what, you're the one who has to live with your immortality, so might as well craft a life *you'll* enjoy."

Piper didn't note who continued to speak, instead she focused on her internal thoughts.

Dazzling amber eyes ignited Piper's heart.

If only her eyes did the same to him.

How long was spending *too long* in trying to make the fire burn?

TWELVE

LIV

This time, Liv woke up not entirely dreading the day leading up to their weekly Elite Meeting.

A small but mighty improvement.

It was a relief. With the aches and pain her body continued to endure, giving her mind a break was long overdue.

Liv enjoyed Chemistry, focusing on the element Tungsten to her delight. Liv had recalled how her first tennis racquet marketed having the element in the frame, which made the lesson all the more enjoyable. Even more so, she was impressed to discover Tungsten was more resistant to fracturing than a diamond and harder than steel.

"It's essentially the ultimate under-the-radar element." Tristan claimed, turning his head toward Piper's desk behind him with a grin. "Piper, should I start calling you Tungsten Pipes?"

"What is it with you and nicknames?" Piper retorted back, not even looking up from her notebook, but her cheeks did turn a slight shade of pink.

"They're terms of endearment." Tristan bantered with a grin. "It's supposed to be a compliment."

"I like it." Liv agreed. "Tungsten was my favorite element growing up, and Piper is my favorite Element, now."

Piper finally looked up to Liv, beaming.

"Hey! Am I chopped liver or what?" Tristan twisted entirely in his desk to face Liv head on.

"Well, you're certainly no Tungsten." Liv sadly shook her head, before smirking and returning to their in-class assignment after Professor Ilio had hushed them all.

When they had been dismissed from class, Liv and Piper immediately sought refuge on the sunny patio for lunch. It was a beautiful spring day, gently windy but with the perfect balance of warmth radiating from the sun.

Liv almost wished she wore something more heat appropriate. Although the light cotton fabric in her long-sleeved turtleneck dress was breathable and comfortable, the skin exposed across her core from beaded sections could prove challenging for a base tan she'd combat for the remainder of the season. Unless deities didn't tan to begin with? Liv contemplated the thought until Piper caught her attention.

"Do you need Hayden to create another personal air-conditioned cooling space for you?" Piper joked, removing her off the shoulder olive green pea coat to reveal a safari inspired look beneath. With a black off-the-shoulder long-sleeved onesie paired with a black and matching green color-blocked, high-waisted, trouser short, Piper looked like a streetwear model.

"King Hayden?" Liv questioned with intrigue at her friend's comment, before searching for something relevant to tie the assumption to and coming up blank, "I think you're mistaken."

"Oh, right. He did that for… my other friend." Piper mumbled, immediately taking a bite of her sandwich; however, something – or someone – caught her eye as she waved them over.

Liv turned to spot Dylan's fiery hair entering the grand hall with Hayden, now heading in their direction.

Liv panicked, turning to Piper with a silent "What the Hades!?"

"What, you two are cool now, right?" Piper confirmed against a mouth full of bread, then covered her mouth in embarrassment before choosing to go with a silent charade, acting out serving a volleyball to continue her point.

Liv shook her head, waving Piper to stop.

She turned back to find Hayden whispering something into Dylan's ear. She nodded in agreement to whatever he said.

In relative terms, Liv guessed they were *fine*. But still, it wasn't like they knew each other. Like they were *friends*. It was one thing to see Hayden during class or the Elite meeting and be forced to interact with him for required social obligations, but inviting him to join them for lunch seemed *too* casual, especially when she would now have to elegantly maneuver eating a deli sandwich in his royal presence.

For some reason, Liv figured the King of Gods needed something fancier like caviar, oysters or escargot.

Sandwiches simply did not make the cut for royalty.

This was embarrassing. She was the Elite of the Elements Pillar! She tried to summon something a little more elevated to the table – a charcuterie board in the least, when Dylan greeted them, Hayden trailing behind.

"Hey Liv, Hey Piper." Dylan smiled, hugging both accordingly. "Is it okay if we join you?"

Hayden remained behind, although his gaze was upon Liv to decipher her reaction.

"Of course." Liv obliged, "We have a charcuterie board on its way."

Piper stared at Liv in surprise, before moving her attention to his royal highness.

"Nice to see you, Hayden. Are you here for more evaluations or actual class?"

"Piper!" Liv exclaimed. "I'm so sorry, your highness. Welcome! We're so happy to host you on this fine March day."

Hayden stood speechless, but the hint of an amused smile appeared as he sat at the table, removing his thick grey scarf and beige leather jacket to reveal a nicely fitted white crewneck sweater.

"No apology necessary, Ollie." Hayden smirked, "And please, call me Hayden. Piper has single handedly been helping me pass my classes this year. She can poke fun at my scholastics as much as she desires. It's the least I can take to show my deepest gratitude."

Soon, two plates arrived for Hayden and Dylan; Dylan had opted for a salad, but Hayden had surprisingly ordered a cheeseburger.

"I'm glad we ran into you, Liv," Dylan prompted. "Piper told me about your plan to try and connect with other deities around the world."

"It's just an idea. We're still in the ideation phase." Liv chimed in with a laugh, "More of the 'how the Zeus will we begin searching for communities that haven't been seen or heard of for hundreds of years' phase."

Dylan chuckled in reply, taking a bite of her salad before continuing on, "I have a distant relative who claims to be of Celtic descent. I mentioned it to Piper, Peyton and now Hayden – she may be able to provide information that could help you find them... I could ask?"

"We would be forever grateful for anything you're able to find out." Hayden nodded politely.

Shit. While Liv had been doodling, getting tortured by Rhys and distracting her rotting soul with limitless cinematic distractions, King Hayden and her friends had actually been pursuing her project and moving it forward.

"Come to tonight's Elite meeting with Piper, you both should report on your recent findings." Hayden offered, kindly.

"No guarantees. But I'm happy to inquire." Dylan smiled, before finding Zayne, Kyril and Tristan exiting the castle and flagged them over.

When the remaining elemental male deities sat down at the table, Piper started chatting with Zayne while Dylan hugged Kyril and began prodding Tristan for ditching her the night before, ultimately leaving Hayden and Liv to their own devices.

Liv bit her lip, watching as Hayden took a bite out of his burger.

He even made *that* look effortless.

"Thanks again for helping with my Security & Warfare assignment earlier this week." Liv politely offered, secretly wishing that Hayden would admit some royal duty beckoned and leave her to crawl under the table and never be seen in public again.

Her hands still clasped onto her patio chair, her body's programmed reaction to fend off an attack from Kronos. Alas, even worried about eating her lunch did not serve as a strong enough distraction – she remained anxious, nervous and sweating. And hungry.

It was one thing to dine with the king. It was another when he resembled the face of your worst nightmare.

Liv closed her eyes.

He's not Kronos, she reminded herself.

Liv came to just as Hayden finished his statement.

She hadn't heard a thing.

But he was chuckling, so she laughed in return.

Hayden eyed her in response, clearly taken aback at her reaction.

Apparently she had over compensated the not listening part….

Liv eyed her sandwich. She just wanted to eat her lunch in peace, without any royal presence.

Shit.

Liv looked up at Hayden.

Did she look like she was hungry?

Was it obvious she hadn't touched her plate because she didn't want to shove a sandwich in her mouth in front of the king?

Finally, Hayden sighed before leaning toward Liv and whispering, "You need not be nervous around me."

"Nervous?" Liv questioned, grateful the word came out naturally instead of in a high-pitch or obnoxiously loud tone.

"You haven't touched your lunch since I arrived." Hayden nodded toward her plate.

Shit. He did notice.

Liv glanced at Hayden; he seemed genuinely concerned. Perhaps honesty was the best option.

Well, aside from telling Hayden that he scared the living shit out of her and that Liv was constantly battling an internal desire to attack him because that had to be some kind of royal offense of some sort. Or, the simple idea that he was the *freaking* King. Royalty. All powerful and everything.

She decided to go with the latter reason but delivered more eloquently. He was royalty, after all.

"It's just, you're *the King.*" Liv whispered, not wanting the others at the table to overhear.

Hayden leaned in and matching her tone, inquired quietly, "And you're waiting for me to yell 'off with their heads'?"

He looked at her without a hint of humor.

Liv paused, speechless and impressed with his dry response.

"No." She finally retorted with a laugh. "At least not until you declare the roses must be painted red."

Hayden considered the offer, taking a bite out of his cheeseburger.

And as a slab of ketchup remained on the cusp on his lip, with a straight face he looked Liv straight in the eye and replied, "Unfortunately, red just isn't my color…"

They both challenged to keep the serious bluff for a moment before instantly breaking in unison, and bursting out into laughter.

"Okay, white flag. I'll eat my sandwich." Liv waved her cream napkin in the air before offering it to Hayden with a chuckle. "Has anyone mentioned you're ridiculous?"

"Not today." Hayden grinned, accepting the napkin and finally wiping off the ketchup that now ran down his chin, "But there's still time to meet my daily goal."

Liv took a bite of her sandwich, appreciating how down-to-earth Hayden seemed to be, nothing compared to the 'royal-high-pain-in-my-ass' stereotype she imagined and couldn't wait to tease him with in the future.

If there even was a future.

Could there be?

Could they actually be *friends*?

Liv eyed the King of the Pure Gods, seeing him in an entirely new light. He looked young, not much older than her. Especially if Piper was helping with his curriculum. But Piper was also a genius so that didn't exactly help narrow down the gap.

He was handsome, with a west coast prep style. Tanned skin, a golden glow, surfer hair. But he was polished, toned. His arms alone looked as sculpted as the statue of David.

They certainly didn't groom men like this at her previous school in Oregon...

"A penny for your thoughts?" Hayden finally asked.

"Oh, I was just... thinking about... Oregon." Liv improvised, taking a slight breath before explaining, "I went to the University of Oregon before attending Puerdios."

"Go Ducks." Hayden smiled, flashing an O by raising his burger in the air and looking overly impressed with himself.

"You've heard of Oregon?" Liv inquired, before remembering and pointing to Hayden, "Ahh I forgot ... March Madness junkie."

"They actually play tonight." Hayden stated, before asking shyly, "Would you have interest in watching the game at my loft before the Elite meeting?"

"With you?" Liv almost spit out her bite of sandwich.

The King of Gods just asked her to watch a NCAA basketball game.

What kind of upside-down universe was she living in?

"Well, if you're coming over to my loft. I hope I'm there." Hayden replied with a grin.

Liv smiled. Her heart was racing, but she also couldn't resist those baby blue eyes.

"Okay."

HAYDEN

It had felt strange courting his best friend of seven years as if she were a stranger, especially when over three of those years she had been his girlfriend and even more recently, his soul mate.

But to Ollie, he *was* a stranger to her.

Hayden needed to keep that in mind if this was going to work.

He had been lucky at the coincidence of knowing about Oregon and the timing of March Madness. It was one thing to offer up common mortal knowledge, but if he continued throwing out Ollie knowledge, Liv would start becoming suspicious and creeped out.

And he'd totally understand why.

He had lowered the big screen TV so that it hung above the fireplace mantel, eliminating any trace of the Mark Rothko painting it now covered.

Hayden opened a bottle of pinot noir to let it breathe before returning to the daunting task of cooking Liv an edible meal.

He knew that Liv was a natural chef, but Liv on the other hand, had no inclination to just how inexperienced Hayden was in the kitchen. And he wanted to impress her.

Hayden checked the oven; the chicken and potato roast looked fine. He hovered over the cooking book, eyeing the pre-chopped broccoli lightly garnished with salt, pepper and oil. With 10 degrees left on the clock, it was time to put the broccoli in the oven.

After cautiously placing the tray of vegetables on the bottom of the oven below the chicken, Hayden took a deep breath, opened the refrigerator and relished in the cool breeze for a moment before chugging a bottle of water.

There was a delicate knock on the door.

Hayden closed the refrigerator, walked by the dining room table and toward the entrance, stopping momentarily to make sure he wasn't perspiring like the nervous wreck he felt on the inside. After smoothing out his Oregon crewneck sweatshirt, he opened the door to greet his guest.

She was absolutely radiant.

Liv had changed into a white, thickly beaded gown, adorned with pearls that matched the choker around her neck. Her shoulders and collarbone were entirely exposed; the gown began at the corset and attached to long sleeves that hung off her shoulder. A high slit revealed pearl-strapped stilettos attached to her glowing legs.

He was ridiculously underdressed.

Shit.

Liv mischievously smiled, lifting her right hand which had been hidden behind her waist, revealing a grey Oregon hoodie in its grasp.

"Oh, thank Zeus." Hayden joked, "I wouldn't have been able to let you in, otherwise." He laughed nervously, welcoming her into his loft simultaneously.

"I wasn't sure what attire was appropriate for both a NCAA basketball watch party and power-hungry Elite debate." Liv admitted, throwing on the hoodie over her couture gown.

"As long you don't show up in Michigan gear, you're good."

"Shoot. There goes my halftime outfit change..." Liv retorted back.

And for a moment, it felt natural.

Until the silence took over and Hayden remembered this was a first date.

A first date... with a friend.

A first... friendly date.

A first.... dinner with a friend.

A first for Ollie.

A first for him, too.

"Would you like wine? Beer? Whisky? Hard seltzer?"

Liv glided onto the barstool, nodding to the decanter. "Wine sounds good."

"It's a pinot noir from Willamette Valley." Hayden explained, pouring the deep red substance into a stem-less glass and handing it to Liv.

"I applaud your diligence to thematics." Liv smiled, finally accepting the glass. "And, thank you for having me over for dinner."

"The pleasure is all mine." Hayden lifted his glass and clinked it with hers.

Truer words were never spoken.

"Is something smoking?" Liv sniffed the air, before studying the oven, eyes growing wide.

Simultaneously, they both darted to the back of the kitchen.

When Hayden tilted the oven door back, black smoke emerged from the oven.

"Oh shit…" Hayden muttered, fully opening the door and grabbing oven mitts immediately to pull out the chicken and potato roast.

The broccoli underneath fared worse. They were entirely burnt.

"Well, I guess now is the time to admit I'm a terrible cook…" Hayden sighed, waving the black smoke away with his oven mitts. Yet, when he heard no immediate sarcastic reply, he turned to Liv, but she was no longer by his side.

She was against the wall, clenching the bookshelf, and trembling.

Black smoke. Shit.

"Ollie, it was just the oven." Hayden gestured to the oven, coughing amidst the smoke. "I'm sorry… you're okay. You're safe."

Liv closed her eyes and took a couple deep breaths.

She reached for the shelf, slowly and gently touching books that lined the space within.

"Keep talking." She whispered. "Please."

"I wanted to impress you, so I found this hearty but robust culinary dish. I diced onions and sliced potatoes and…"

Shit what do you call those things of garlic?

"And cracked a-whatever-you-call-it of garlic before chopping it into tiny pieces…"

Liv's mouth curved into a hint of a smile. She opened her eyes, nodding to encourage him to go on.

Hayden eyed his burnt broccoli. The bloody bastard that ruined it all.

"I'm not sure what happened. I put the broccoli in the oven like the recipe said and…"

Liv eyed the oven, her curiosity conquering her fear. She finally pointed to the oven and inquired, "There's only one oven rack?"

"So?" Hayden replied, looking into the oven to see what had caught her so off guard.

"Where did you put the broccoli?" Liv clarified.

"On the bottom of the oven, below the chicken." Hayden confirmed.

Liv's faint smile turned into a blasting grin. She coughed, trying to contain her laughter.

Her amusement was infectious; Hayden was the first to break the ice and started laughing himself.

"I think we found the perpetrator." Liv kindly explained, grabbing an unused oven rack from the top of the refrigerator.

"I took that one out to make room for the chicken roast…" Hayden admitted guiltily.

Liv inspected the charred chicken, "I think it's salvageable…"

Hayden loved her for that kind optimism. But there was no way in Hades he was going to make her eat that, now.

"Do you like spaghetti?"

"I love spaghetti." Liv replied with a smile.

"Great. That, I know how to make." He picked up the recipe book and summoned it back to the bookshelf.

"Can I help?" Liv offered, peaking over Hayden as he grabbed an onion and more garlic cloves from the pantry.

"You mean… supervise?" Hayden joked. "At least you can't overcook pasta. Or can you?"

"I'd be very impressed if you managed that." Liv chuckled, "But to be safe, I'll handle that part."

Hayden grabbed a cutting board from the side of the stove, before remembering Liv didn't know her way around this kitchen. Their kitchen.

"Noodles are in that cupboard over there." He nodded over by the oven, opening one below the stove to grab a large pot.

"Got it."

She joined him by the stove, placing the box against the wall before grabbing the pot to fill it with water. She turned on the stovetop and poked around other cupboards until she found salt, adding a pinch of it to the boiling water.

Liv turned to Hayden, who was now hard at work dicing the onion.

"I'm surprised you don't use your powers to cook." Liv observed, watching as Hayden slowly, painfully chopped up the vegetable into smaller pieces, one slice at a time, his eyes taking the majority of the repercussions from his actions.

She smiled, "Here, let me show you."

Hayden paused, allowing Liv to place her hand over his while he grasped the knife and show him a chopping technique.

Her touch was electric.

She smelled so good, like strawberry and florals.

Hayden prayed Liv didn't hear his heart pounding faster.

"By keeping the tip of the knife touching the cutting board and using this hand," she grabbed his left hand and placed it on the dull back of the knife's blade, "you'll have more control to chop faster."

Hayden picked it up quickly.

"We may just eat before sunrise after all." Liv smirked, moving on to the spaghetti box to begin breaking the pasta noodles in half.

"Oh, strange. You may be eating the burnt chicken after all." Hayden joked back.

Liv chuckled, taking a break from her spaghetti splitting to take a sip of wine.

She turned to Hayden, who was still chopping away but at least now working on the garlic clove.

"Do you want your wine glass?" She asked, eyeing his glass by the kitchen sink.

"Must. Not. Stop. Chopping." Hayden retorted back with a grin.

"Here." Liv smiled, grabbing his glass and raising it to his mouth. "You should keep your nourishment if you want to survive preparing this meal."

"The irony in that statement..." Hayden rolled his eyes, obliging to Liv's gesture, letting her gently tilt the glass into his mouth so he could have a sip.

Liv was so close to him, she had gently placed her hand on his shoulder for balance.

She had not removed her hand yet.

Liv gazed into his eyes, before glancing quickly down at his lips before biting her own.

Hayden recognized that gesture too easily.

He held his breath, commanding himself to stay put. If this was going to happen, Ollie had to initiate it.

Was she starting to lean in?

Beep! Beep! Beep!

Liv pulled away, looking in the direction of the noise.

"The timer." Hayden quickly concluded, "Tip-off is about to start."

"You set the stove timer for *the game*? Well, that explains it all." Liv huffed, taking another sip of wine.

"Ouch." Hayden responded as he mimicked getting stabbed in the heart. "Are you trying to burn me to a similar extent in which I burnt the chicken? That's cruel."

"That's justice." Liv chuckled, throwing the pasta into the now boiling water. "You now know the trauma the chicken dish endured."

She ducked below the stove, easily finding a colander within the compartments underneath.

Hayden summoned the television on, feeling at ease with the static noise of the recognizable sports commentators filling the background. He drizzled olive oil in a pan and slid the chopped onions into it to sauté.

Minutes later, he added the garlic.

Liv continued to stir the pasta and after a couple of moments of comfortable silence, Liv grabbed a piece of pasta from the pot and threw it against the cupboard.

"What on earth?" Hayden looked up in awe to the spaghetti that now decorated his kitchen.

Liv giggled, "It's how you tell if the pasta is ready. Which, surprise! It is."

"Great timing." Hayden opened a can of Tomato sauce, pouring it over his pan.

"And lucky you," Liv held up her wrist as she looked at an imaginary watch, "You still have 190 degrees until sunrise…"

"More importantly, one degree until tip off." Hayden corrected as he handed her a bowl and a ladle.

He tried to deliver his response with a lighthearted scowl, but it was growing harder by the minute to act neutral and mysterious around Liv when on the inside, he was beaming.

LIV

She only had three potentially catastrophic incidents.

Liv was counting.

The first, when the black smoke emerged in the air and Liv had been catapulted back in time, anticipating capture and a forced return to imprisonment with the Dark Gods.

In that moment, she saw red.

The second, when she had almost kissed King Hayden after sustaining his cocktail consumption. His lips were as delectably ruby as the wine.

In that moment, he had not given any inclination of kissing her back.

The third, when Hayden had stood up abruptly at a stolen pass that resulted in an Oregon slam dunk in the first quarter.

In that moment, Liv wanted to attack Hayden and cause him pain.

That was when Liv had started counting her incidents and prayed the number did not grow.

He was her *king*.

And although he adorably burned dinner and his blue-eyed gaze gave Liv butterflies and their conversation had grown into something so natural and effortless, Liv knew he was entirely off-limits.

But damn, was he funny. And pretty perfect, too.

Aside from the whole wanting to accidentally hurt him inclination, of course.

They had eaten their spaghetti on the couch, Hayden offering Liv a cozy blanket to cover her white couture gown as she slurped down the light pasta dish.

Hayden had unknowingly made his spaghetti exactly how she made hers. Exactly how she loved it, in fact, avoiding the common choice of using pre-made spaghetti sauce.

Which is why whenever Hayden made the slightest movement, Liv taught herself to anticipate it. She channeled her anxiety into whatever object she held – the spaghetti bowl, the pillow, the blanket – to ensure she would never cause the king harm.

But every so often, when he told a long story, Liv found herself getting mesmerized with his lips, how they looked so soft and so perfectly accented his chiseled jaw. The ideal balance of strong and delicate, creating a truly beautiful piece of art.

Liv took a gulp of her wine.

She was seriously fucked in every masochistic way.

"Here, let me refill that…" Hayden reached for her now empty glass, considerate and selfless enough to notice the exact moment when his guest's beverage depleted. Unlike most guys, who couldn't tear their gaze away from the precious game even if their female counterpart was prancing around naked, the game always seemed to come secondary to Hayden. Conversation took priority, Liv's comfort took priority, and spending time to get to know her took priority.

And yet, with the unexpected and in hindsight, thoughtful action, Liv's initial reaction was to throw him against the wall.

"It's okay I got it." Liv swatted away his hand, ignoring the red blaring in her mind, as she began to stand up.

But upon impact, she held onto his hand instead, and didn't let go.

She was holding his hand.

And he was holding hers.

And it felt like the most natural thing.

Until Liv realized this *wasn't* a natural thing to do with your crowned king.

And Hayden had just eyed her warily, unsure of what to do.

Liv jumped up. "I'll just bring the decanter over here. That way we can both fill up our wine glasses, individually, whenever we want!"

And with that declaration, she marched to the kitchen, counting in her mind.

She only had four potentially catastrophic incidents…

HAYDEN

Ollie had just held his hand.

Did that mean she was friend-zoning him?

But he couldn't deny the uncanny sexual tension that they both had been combatting since they almost kissed in the kitchen.

And then she held his hand.

It wasn't like Hayden was expecting anything out of the night – he could simply *feel* the lust they both shared for one another – but he also sensed her internal conflict of assessing their relationship between King and Elite. All he truly wanted to do was spend time with Ollie and show her he wasn't this high-strung royal she made him out to be.

He just wasn't expecting *that*.

"Yes!" Liv screamed from behind.

Hayden looked up to the TV, watching the replay as the player Dorsey spun to score a basket for Oregon to take the lead.

"Next time I invite you over for a game, can you make sure it's not such a close one?" Hayden joked, his eyes glued to the TV with only a minute left.

"This is what March Madness is all about, as you should know." Liv joked, pretending to shoot an imaginary basketball into the air.

"And… it bounces off the rim for Hayden to get the rebound!" Hayden jokingly commentated, hand in a fist to serve as a fake microphone.

"I'd like to challenge the call, ref! That was a swish and you know it, mister." Liv pointed at Hayden before playfully shoving him into the couch and colliding beside him.

Anyone else would have succumbed to his rapport simply because he was king.

Zeus, she was *incredible*.

"I'll be ecstatic if Oregon wins, but I do feel like a semi-band wagoner for rooting for them. I practically hated the college while I attended school there." Liv admitted.

"You're allowed to have a change in opinion." He replied, refilling his wine glass with the decanter Liv brought over, trying to ignore her leg touching his. "And it seems to be a rare enough occurrence…"

Liv glared at him, "I'm going to take that as a compliment."

"That's the beauty of an opinion. It can differ between two parties." Hayden smirked.

Liv's jaw dropped in amused surprise.

Oh how he loved shocking her.

"Your royal high-pain-in-my-ass, I think you've had enough to drink, sir." Liv nodded with a grin. "How on earth are you going to lead an Elite meeting in ten degrees?"

Hayden sobered immediately at the nickname, but immediately deflected by responding to Ollie's question.

"Simple. I'll table things I don't want to discuss and ask *you* to report on any agenda items of interest." Hayden grinned.

"You're cruel." Liv shook her head in disappointment.

"As if you wouldn't do the same." Hayden darkly retorted.

"I wouldn't." Liv defended, before considering the reality and continuing on, "...I surely *wouldn't* have warned you of my evil plan in the first place. Rookie mistake."

"You're twisted and I like it."

"Great minds." Liv smirked, lifting her glass to clink it with Hayden's.

When the basketball game came back on with Oregon still in a one-point lead, Hayden and Liv were both literally on the edge of their seats. The timer was running down with the opposing team in possession of the ball. Three... two... the ball bounced off the rim for a missed shot.

"Oregon won!" Liv jumped, turning to Hayden and pulling him into a hug.

They magnetized toward each other.

Suddenly the mood shifted, from frenzied adrenaline to slow-moving tension.

Her arms were around his torso as she looked up again into his eyes. Her glacier blue gems penetrated his own, singing melodies only Aphrodite would know.

She bit her delectable lip, her gaze slowly drifting downward to his mouth.

Hayden knew what that meant, and this time, he wasn't going to lose the opportunity to kiss Ollie.

He leaned in, slowly, to make sure she was open to the gesture.

Liv didn't falter.

Hayden placed his hand on the back of her neck, gently, to steady his path and give into the magnetic pull.

"Go Ducks!"

Hayden and Liv split apart, finding Peyton and Rei entering through the front door.

"I really need to change my password." Hayden muttered to himself, before turning to his friends with a forced smile. "Did you watch the game?"

"Obviously not." Rei retorted, nodding to Peyton. "She searched for the score."

"Unlike you, we don't need to support the collegiate athletics of a mortal school we fake enrolled in for a month."

"Hey! I was actually a student there." Liv hollered as she pulled off her hoodie.

"I just really like basketball." Hayden admitted, also removing his crewneck to reveal a camel crewneck sweater beneath.

"And yet, tomorrow you *won't* be wearing a Badger sweatshirt," Peyton chirped back accusingly.

Peyton donned a long-sleeved, feathered turtleneck and draped baby blue silk taffeta mini skirt; Rei on the other hand wore a more casual geometric print sweater with bronze yarn stitched within, matching the glass of bourbon he currently poured himself.

"Could you imagine Calithya's reaction if I did?" Hayden dryly commented, clicking a button from his television remote to lift the screen back into storage.

"Is she not coming tonight?" Liv clarified.

"Ammiras sent word he would join on behalf of sister, again." Rei growled, taking a sip of his cocktail. "We cannot afford to lose another alliance."

"Precisely why I'm paying Calithya a personal visit this weekend." Hayden sighed, rubbing his eyes. Sometimes he seriously wondered if he was rewarding bad behavior and Calithya would actually hold out on her decision as long as Hayden continued to offer his time persuading her otherwise.

The door opened again, revealing Daphne, Silas and Jocelyn, the latter holding a candle and walking directly to the kitchen.

"It will pair well with smoke." Joss smirked, lighting the candle and placing it on the counter by the oven.

"Smart ass." Hayden retorted, pulling his sister into a hug.

"You're welcome."

Jocelyn went to hug Liv, Rei and Peyton, receiving compliments on her deep cut navy dress and oversized gold chain choker.

In all purple silk tailoring, Daphne greeted her son by kissing both of his cheeks.

"Looks like tonight went well?" She inquired softly, eyes sparkling as she glanced quickly in Liv's direction.

"Please don't..." Hayden groaned, "On all accounts, Mother."

"Okay, okay. Note taken." Daphne beamed, stepping back and letting Silas shake hands with Hayden.

Shortly after, Demetrius and Rhys arrived, followed by Ammiras and Dyoedi. Given the necessary 15 degrees allotted for obligated decorum, everyone soon grabbed a beverage of choice before it was time to begin the meeting.

Hayden stood at the head of the table, acknowledging the Elites and leaders that remained loyal to the Pure God rule. He was grateful for each and every one of them; even those who remained undecided like Rhys and Ammiras. They were here in support for now, and that was enough.

"Silas, what progress have you made with the Soulless?" Hayden nodded, sitting down and giving the floor to his Security Elite.

"That Piper, she is an impressive researcher." Silas complemented first, before shifting in his seat, "But I'm afraid there is minimal resources to work off in our archives."

"Have you found any leads?"

"Some tales and old folklore mention creatures who have risen from the dead – but the descriptions are too generic to know for certain that they describe the Soulless. And even if they did, the story doesn't give hints of how to exonerate them."

Hayden turned to his mother, mentally asking if she had any truths to this unseen specie.

Daphne sighed, her tone already apologetic, "The Candor Records have no mention of this creature, that means it is not one of our world. We are unable to use our powers with that barrier."

"The Soulless are dead. The undead." Peyton thought aloud, her eyes searching within the powers of her mind, connecting the scattered dots together. "They are not from this world."

Liv sunk in her chair, dread growing on her face. With a quiet whisper, she concluded, "The Underworld."

THIRTEEN

LIV

And her week had been going *so well*.

Leave it to Hades to put a damper on her mood.

After the board discussed responsibilities and next steps, it was decided Rei and Peyton would accompany Liv and Piper to the Underworld, so Silas could accompany Hayden to the Siren Seas.

Liv had struck the deal with Hades, so it was her responsibility to figure out what on earth had gone wrong.

Or – what *not* on earth – went wrong.

"You've been enchanted by Lyssa if you think I'm going to let you visit the Underworld without me."

Tristan had confronted Liv first thing on the 6th day, in the morning, regarding her weekend activities. Fortunately, he had brought coffee, which made Liv a bit more tolerating after her first sip.

"What if Hades has joined forces with Kronos and Arlo?" Tristan pressed on. "Have you not wondered where Kronos is getting all of these dead vessels?"

Liv had been ignoring all of his concerns. They had already been thoroughly discussed at the Elite meeting and she really needed to first figure out what to wear for the day.

Perhaps inspired by Calithya, as images of the Siren Queen and Hayden continued to torment her mind while her king visited the tempress, Liv selected a light blue and gold beaded gown, where the sleeves cascaded into a cape that flowed behind.

Liv frowned, internally conflicted if she should be angry or grateful that nightmares of her cell dungeon had been replaced by jealous wonderings.

She slammed her armoire shut.

Nothing had happened between Hayden and her. Nothing *could* happen.

He was the Pure God King and she had to focus on fighting her unexplainable inclinations to *hurt* him.

She barely knew him.

And that's how it needed to remain.

Liv ran to the bathroom, angrily brushing her hair.

Stop. Thinking. About. His. Smile.

She sighed, leaning against the counter, and stared in the mirror.

It was intoxicating. He was intoxicating.

But he would never want her. Liv examined her neck, wishing her bruises would finally disappear. She was sick of the constant reminders of the darkness she endured and continued to fight, the battle raging on beneath her skin and within her soul.

A knock at the door told Liv she needed to hurry the fuck up, so she quickly styled her hair into a messy side braid.

Departing her self-inflicted therapeutic bathroom session, Liv found Piper staring Tristan down, before turning to Liv.

"You didn't mention Tristan was joining?" She asked sweetly, but in a higher pitched voice than usual, laced with tart.

"More like crashing." Liv clarified, taking a sip of her Americano.

"You'll both *thank me* when Hades attacks you all." Tristan defended, before turning to Piper and telling her she looked nice.

Piper blushed, before catching Liv's eye, and darted to the kitchen.

While Liv had chosen a serene outfit reminiscent of the beach, Piper had selected an opposite vibe, sporting a black corset and trousers with a green snakeskin blazer. She practically matched the Fire God's leather jacket, black and white printed sweater, grey wool trousers and green loafers.

"Do you think it's possible Hades has gone Dark?" Piper whispered, as if the God of Death could hear the murmur of his name.

"By force, perhaps." Liv thought about the last encounter she had with Hades, when they had made their mutual pact to seal The Underworld. "I think we would know if his loyalties had shifted – but he was pretty terrified of the idea of his father being released. He had kept Kronos confined for over two million years. It wouldn't make sense for him to go against our pact now."

The door knocked again, to Liv's surprise.

Tristan hopped up. "I may have called in additional reinforcements..."

He ran over to the door and opened it, where Kyril, Zayne and Dylan stood in the doorway.

"Rei is going to kill me." Liv muttered under her breath, although secretly glad to have the support of her friends.

She gave Dylan a long hug, Zayne a quick one, and then punched Kyril in the arm

"Hey! What was that for?" Kyril shouted.

"For the obnoxious thing you're bound to say in the future." Liv grinned. "Promise me you'll be on your best behavior?"

"But what if I want to be spanked by Hades?" Kyril grinned devilishly.

Liv punched him again.

Rei had told Liv to meet Peyton and him at the unofficial back entrance to the Underworld, the path for living deities, confirming that a troop would be at the ready to protect the area upon arrival.

He had planned to take Peyton separately, to give his partner time to grieve her brother, Xavier, who had been sent to the Underworld after a bloodbath caused by Arlo.

Liv shivered at the memory that lurked in the deepest shadows of her mind, of the bloody X's that she discovered upon her last visit to the Hades's kingdom.

It seemed like *years* ago.

Is this what immortality felt like? A blur of distant memories, slowly blending into one dark chaotic mess?

It was what Liv's life was beginning to feel like.

Ignoring the temptation of spiraling down an endless comparison of fear, Liv instead followed the four pairs of black wings that each carried her friends. Tristan's wings looked like they were laced with embers, Dylan's glistened with black and ruby diamonds, Kyril's were in a dramatic, gargoyle shape and Zayne's were matte ink. Piper followed with her silver wings, looking like the brightest target in the sky.

Liv was thankful for her wings that Rei had given her months earlier, the golden tips easily serving as a better camouflage in this moor than bright silver.

Yet, when she and her friends curved the hill and approached the designated meeting spot, Liv let out a breath she did not realize she was holding.

Security guards were in line, in place, in order. Rei and Peyton stood at the corner, waiting for their arrival.

Peyton looked the warrior, ready to fight. She wore a grey cashmere long sleeved dress, bonded in leather armor. Rei, on the otherhand, had on black jeans and a white snow jacket.

They all landed fluidly, Liv running first to Peyton to give her a big hug.

"Thank you." Peyton trembled, squeezing Liv a little tighter, before taking a huge breath and releasing her friend from her grasp.

Rei stepped in and took Peyton's hand.

"You ready?" He stared at Liv, but knew the question was intended for another in the party. She nodded anyways.

It was time to pay a visit with death.

Liv had mentally prepared for games, Hades's manipulated tasks to fuck with their mind and torture them as she returned to the abyss of darkness – yet the biggest mind fuck of it all was the straightforwardness and relative ease in which they ventured to his office.

With every turn, with every step, Liv anticipated something jumping out or being posed with an incomprehensible assignment in order to move through and on to the next challenge. Yet, when she finally saw the twinkling light growing lighter among the darkness, Liv had to admit defeat – perhaps Hades had turned a corner.

She raised her father's white druzy stone from her décolleté and scanned it in front of the sensor.

The door clicked open, welcoming everyone into an empty office.

"Where *is* he?" Liv panicked.

Suddenly, a blast went off in the hallway that connected from across the room.

Instinctively, Liv sprinted after Rei, following the sound.

They found Hades curled over on the floor, coughing blood and shaking.

"Liv!" Tristan shouted.

Liv turned to her left, finding a handful of Soulless deities approaching her, fury raging from their eyes.

Talk about a plot twist.

"Kyril, Zayne – move Hades into his office!" Rei commanded.

Within moments, Tristan, Piper, Rei, Peyton and Dylan were by Liv's side.

"Piper, any ideas for how to finish them off?" Liv asked, eyes growing wide.

The Soulless were moving slowly, as if assessing whether the new visitors posed a threat.

"Can we try containing them?" Piper squeaked.

Rei casted a flaming rope to lasso one against the wall. It shrieked, like an army of nails scratching against the chalkboard.

The other Soulless did not appreciate the action and started crying as they began attacking.

Chaos emerged, each living deity combatting against the dead.

The one Soulless pinned against the wall ripped its hands and legs from the restraints, separating the body parts to escape its binding, before reattaching them after.

Liv screamed at the sight.

"Binding doesn't work!" Liv yelled, blasting a firebolt against a female creature to her right. Could they be burned?

Her opponent did not like the fire; more nails scraped against the chalkboard.

Liv had to cover her ears, the shrieks screaming bloody murder was becoming too much.

"Security bubble?!" Piper hollered from the side, blowing a Soulless back against the far wall.

Distanced from their enemy, it gave everyone more time to think. Or panic.

Liv followed suit, sending a tornado to collect the zombie deities, some burning, some with a time bomb blasting within their corpse, and all hissing so aggressively it was tough for Liv to concentrate on willing any more powers.

"I can't keep this up much longer!" She yelled.

A purple bubble emerged, growing larger as it moved to encompass all of the living. When it passed by Liv, the terrible noise muted. Peyton was maneuvering her hands to expand the bubble, while Rei began forging a metal wall to keep them out.

When the wall fully closed, Liv could no longer cast her tornado spell. The strength between Rei's fortress was too strong to penetrate.

The room grew silent.

Liv turned around, finding Dylan on the ground, clutching her leg.

"Are you okay?" Liv ran over, Piper close behind her.

"One bit into my leg." She breathed, "I think it broke my femur..."

A crunching noise penetrated Rei's wall.

Liv turned slowly back toward the fortress.

The wall shook as another object impacted against it.

And again.

"Dylan, can you get yourself to Hades's office?!" Liv asked, assessing whether there was time to assist her friend. The wall shook again, answering Liv's question for her. "Tell Kyril and Zayne we need them out here!"

Dylan nodded, sliding her body across the floor. Her white silk coat-dress now soiled with dirt and blood.

Beneath the wall pounding, Liv could hear the masked moans of Dylan's agonizing pain with each forced maneuver to drag her broken limb across the battle space quickly.

Another pound against the wall turned Liv's attention back to the enemy.

She spotted an axe blade that finally penetrated through.

They had weaponry.

Piper's squealed, turning to Liv with wide eyes. Rei pulled out his sword, ready to fight. Peyton followed suit, pulling out her own crossbow and stationing herself to shoot.

"Get behind us." Liv commanded Piper, pulling out her own sword.

If magic didn't work against these monsters, perhaps the classic cut to the throat would.

Another pound, revealing a spiked club outlined around the already slim abrasion.

A flame sparked beside Liv. She turned to Tristan, finding him carrying a flail, the impacting ball attached ablaze in fiery glory.

Another hit. The club head fully broke through, revealing blank eyes within the open space now removed.

Peyton shot her arrow, hitting a bullseye between the Soulless's white pupilless gaze.

It flailed back and the shrieking began again.

Another hit.

And another.

More weapons started pounding throughout the wall – a cult growing in numbers with exponential impact.

Liv gulped, trying to calm her jittery muscles by re-setting her war stance.

The Soulless were making traction, and eventually would break down Rei's protective wall. And if they were able to overcome the Security Elite's soundest powers, Liv began concluding that they would be battling to their death – fully recognizing that the already dead could not be killed.

Her heart started beating faster, with every impact against the wall, harder. Her palms grew sweatier; Liv worried her sword would slip when she finally went back into combat.

Focus.

A vision flashed to Hades curled against the ground, exhausted and sick.

Depleted.

And he was the oldest deity of them all.

Aside from Kronos.

Liv gulped. But she refused to believe they had already lost this war.

The entire room was shaking, the wall now about to crumble. She turned back to Dylan, who had almost managed to exit the room and enter Hades's office.

Liv caught Piper's eyes, filled with terror and the same question that raced through Liv's mind.

Who could beat Kronos?

Liv started panicking, willing herself to stay calm.

If she were going to die tonight, she wanted to be at peace. Not scared.

For a final moment, as the wall finally broke, crumbling down to reveal over a dozen fully healed Soulless armored in weaponry, Liv closed her eyes, imagining the starry night sky, begging for solace and strength when she faced her inevitable death.

Just make it quick.

As a tear escaped her lid, Liv reopened her eye, fiercely determined to do the stars justice.

She would fight to the death.

And be reunited with her father.

And he would be proud.

The silver lining in tonight's darkest storm.

Five Soulless began running in slow motion toward them; the remaining held back by Piper's wind. Giving them a sliver of hope in not having to combat them all at once.

The House of Wind had arrived.

The metal of Liv's sword slammed against her opponent's mace, fusing sparks as the metal scraped together in the collision.

And soon, they were dancing against death.

Liv ducked her head below the spiked tip as the Soulless's mace swung above where her neck once existed.

Her opponent shrieked in fury at the missed target.

Liv struck her sword forward, but the offensive maneuver was too quickly blocked by the mace, and from the foolish action where she no longer blocked her core, had allowed the Soulless female to hit her side, knocking Liv to the ground.

She scrambled to stand back up, rushing backward and closer to Piper.

"I can't keep them back much longer." Piper warned, shaking from the immense concentration and forced battle within.

"Liv behind you!" Kyril shouted as he ran through the doorway, war hammer in hand.

Liv turned and swung her sword to block the Soulless's mace in the air.

That would have been her skull.

Liv heard Zayne yell, "shit," from behind her, but her attention was back to the Soulless bitch that was determined to end her life.

Liv blocked another attack, levering the mace downward to the ground with all of her strength. Finding Peyton had switched to swordplay for a close-up opponent as she danced across the floor, swinging her blade in fast-forward mode against another.

The angry shriek brought Liv back to her own problem.

Her sword slammed against the Soulless's weapon yet again, before they too began mimicking Peyton's quick paced swordplay against one another.

She was starting to tire...

The small loss in concentration made Liv lose her balance by overcompensating a reaction to her opponent's swing.

Liv barely leapt out of the mace's motion, rolling onto the floor before jumping back on her feet again.

Even if she killed of this one. Would she be able to fight off a handful more?

She found Rei combatting against *two* Soulless.

Piper's wind powers were starting to dwindle.

Not much longer and her friend would be depleted.

Focus.

Liv returned to her opponent, equal fury raging between the two.

As her opponent prepared to fight again, Liv got into position as well, for her sword to cause bloody murder.

Again, their weapons collided, sparking fuses of glory as they both fought against eachother's strength.

Liv finally fake swung to her opponent's right, anticipating the block, creating the opportunity to strike from the left.

She blew the Soulless into two.

Upon impact, her opponent didn't shriek.

She didn't flinch on the ground. She didn't repair her broken limbs.

Instead, she rotted into ashes. The only evidence of her existence, debris floating in the air. Liv stepped toward the disaster to observe.

She heard another shriek in the distance, the result of Peyton finally slaying her sword through her opponent's chest, before cutting her into two and moving onto the next attacker.

Liv's excitement burst, until her jaw dropped.

Peyton's opponent didn't slink into dust. Her bottom legs crawled toward her sprawling torso, reconnecting together and becoming one again, ready to battle once more.

Liv stared back at her sword.

Holy shit.

But could she stay strong enough, and *alive enough*, to combat each individual, already deceased, deity?

Liv ran toward the newly formed Soulless, screaming as she swiped the deity's head clean from her body, expecting another moment of reprieve while the Soulless repaired her broken body once more.

Instead, her head sizzled, combusting into flames as her body disintegrated into ashes.

"I'm sorry!" Piper cried, grabbing her head as she crashed into the ground. Her friend clenched her stomache as she puked against the dark black marble floor.

Fuck. Fuck. Fuck.

"Pull back! Circle around Piper. Backs together!" Rei commanded jumping across Piper as he blocked a Soulless who had almost penetrated the depleted, living deity with an axe.

Liv sprinted to Piper, slamming her body between Rei and Tristan's.

"I'd really appreciate it if this… fucker actually died, considering I've murdered him at least five bloody times!" Tristan retorted, again wrapping his fiery chain around his opponent to choke him.

"Let me show you how it's done." Liv smirked, slamming her sword into the captured male's torso.

Immediately, it caught flame and finally dissolved into debris.

"What the Hades?" Tristan cursed. "You'll have to explain that later!"

Five more Soulless started heading in their direction.

Liv heard all five of her standing friends curse under their breath, each facing a few Soulless to combat.

They were so royally fucked.

...Even with Liv's magic sword.

Every impact against her opponent made all of her muscles cry in pain. Her clotted cuts so carefully attended to by Rhys were ripping apart slowly with each outstretched arm or sudden movement to avoid a blade to the throat.

Her arms were shaking.

It had been too long since she stopped training with Rei. The recent boot camps had only been a returned hint to the reality of battle.

Desperately, she took a hand from Piper's playbook, blasting their opponents against the wall, pinning them with vines that fully covered their corpses, leaving only a few for her friends to combat for this round.

With the Soulless outnumbered for a minute, she might be able to get to them.

And end them.

But she was shaking. The concentrated power of holding a dozen Soulless against the wall was draining her, and quickly.

Focus.

Liv ran behind Rei's opponent, slicing the Soulless's leg and sighing with relief as it began to burn.

She limped further, swaying as she determinedly progressed forward, to the Soulless that Peyton and Kyril both combatted together.

Liv started seeing black dots.

She couldn't hold out much longer.

Just kill one more...

She swung, half-heartedly, but swiftly enough to let the weight of her blade do the dirtywork. The overly stimulated Soulless easily crashed as the metal sliced through its core.

But Liv fell instantly afterward, trembling as the Soulless finally cut through her vines and broke through her power on the wall.

"Take...my...sword..." Liv whispered, perhaps only within her mind, as nobody clamored to grab the one weapon that could destroy them all.

Slowly. But surely.

Liv took a deep breath, gradually pushing herself upright against her body's cringing protests.

Her head was dizzy.

An unexpected blast of white light emerged from Hades office, causing Liv's consciousness to focus on its source.

All of the Soulless shrieked and cried for Satan, unable to exist in the light.

They floated in the air, screaming as the light blasted them through the Underworld portal.

And when they disappeared, the room returned to its normal lighting.

Liv squinted toward the door, revealing a rushing Hayden heading toward her.

"Are you okay?" He panicked, assessing her weakened state. "Oh god, Ollie."

Green eyes.

Liv recoiled, seeing darkness.

She heard screams.

They were her own.

Ollie...

She was so weak.

"Liv, find the bond. Rely on the bond. That is real and can show you my true intentions, always. If you can't see me right now, if you're scared to hear me, focus on that."

But the words stated after the calm instruction peaked Liv's interest the most.

"Find your soul. Find me."

She focused on her soul, what she knew of her strength, her intentions. Her judgment.

The room came back into focus.

Hayden leaned over worriedly.

Blue eyes.

He had extinguished the Soulless.

"Hayden…" Liv whispered, "How did you…"

She looked around, finding Tristan hovered over Piper, lifting her into his arms.

"Liv, is it okay if I pick you up and take you into Hades's office?"

Liv snapped her head back toward Hayden.

His voice sounded like the beginning tune of her favorite song. Sipping salted caramel hot chocolate before a crackling fire. Taking a warm shower after being stuck outside in the cold. It sounded… like home.

"If you call me Ollie, I'll consider it." Liv retorted, yawning in exhaustion.

She heard him quietly laugh.

"You did good, Ollie." He whispered, gently placing his hand beneath her back, pausing for a moment, before scooping his arm below her legs and swiftly standing up in a seamless move.

Liv finally closed her eyes, feeling as if she was floating on clouds.

PIPER

Her entire body hurt.

Piper groaned as she finally opened her eyes, revealing a room full of equally destroyed deities.

Liv slept curled in Hayden's arms, who sat against the wall near the fireplace. Rhys stood over Dylan, wrapping her leg in a cast while Kyril iced his torso beside her.

Peyton and Rei both lay on the floor, with random bandages, heating pads and ice packs placed strategically across their bodies to combat their wounds. They clearly weren't sleeping but both had their eyes determinedly shut.

Hades was awake, but looking frail as Zayne fed him a dose of medication. Zayne was working one-handed, as his other arm was pressed against his side in a sling.

Where was Tristan?

With the realization, Piper instinctively started rising, worry blinding her body's immediate protest. But she didn't get far as her muscles truly owned the outcome of the physical battle.

"Take it easy..." A melodic voice hushed, gently smoothing her hair away from her eyes.

Piper breathed and her heart began pounding less, and more, at the same time but for different reasons.

Tristan.

She slowly turned her body to gaze behind her, finding Tristan sitting in a chair and leaning his body against the couch's armrest in which she lay.

He was there.

"What happened?" Piper whispered, her voice raspy.

Tristan handed her a glass of water, gently helping her tilt the liquid into her mouth.

"Hayden summoned the Soulless back into the Underworld." Tristan sighed, placing the glass of water on the table. "Are you feeling alright?"

"I've been better." Piper stated truthfully, trying to sit herself up.

"Here, let me help."

Tristan got up from his chair and limped around the couch, crouching slowly so he was eye level with Piper, before placing his hand below her back and lifting her upward.

Piper watched Tristan nod to Hayden, inviting him to sit next to Piper, now that she was upright. Hayden gratefully obliged, his joints cracking as he stood with Liv in his arms.

"Be careful, your majesty." Rhys warned from across the room. "You're close to depletion – don't exhaust yourself at the expense of Liv."

Hayden ignored Rhys, sitting beside Piper with his prized possession in tow.

Liv stirred at the motion, finally blinking her eyes.

"What happened…?" Her friend choked, slowly looking around the room and assessing everyone's current state.

"You're safe." Hayden confirmed, relaxing his hold on her and giving Liv the opportunity to crawl onto the couch between him and her friend.

Yet, she remained.

"I feel like death." Peyton muttered dryly from the floor.

"You *look* like death." Kyril retorted instantaneously.

"You're as relentless as the Soulless." Dylan spat.

"At least we *have* souls." Liv countered, her voice quiet and low.

"But do we?" Tristan joked, breaking the tension.

"Jury is still out on you…" Rei smirked, eyes still closed.

And after a moment of silence, all the wounded finally broke out into a quiet laughter. Piper chuckled in unison with the others, then winced from the resulting pain in her abs, also in unison with the others.

"Speaking of no souls… what happened, Hades?" Liv finally asked. "Why didn't you summon for help, sooner?"

Hades remained quiet.

"We'll add additional stations in your office, if desired." Hayden offered amidst the silence.

"Clearly." Hades rolled his eyes. "Then I can at least *send* someone for reinforcements. Instead of single-handedly combatting an army of monsters until I shrivel into nothing again."

His tone was curt.

Hades did not like to be bested in his own home. But could he be trusted?

"When?" Rei clarified, cutting straight to the facts and ignoring his tone.

"Two days ago." Hades drawled, "Apparently they can travel through the diseased's path, like smoke in the wind."

"Undetected by our guards." Rei nodded, mentally noting the necessary shifts to be shared with his troops. "Any theories why?"

"The seal has grown weaker, it no longer withstands Kronos's power."

Piper gulped. Liv and Hayden's bond had been tarnished; therefore their combined powers were no longer connected, and now as separate entities, vulnerable against Kronos's absolute control.

"How?" Liv accused defensively.

Awkward silence hovered over her friends as they finally pieced together the Dark God's activities against Liv over the past month. Piper sunk lower against the couch.

Was someone going to break the news to Liv? She was weaker because she despised Hayden, her soul mate?

But as Piper noticed Liv sitting close to Hayden, her body magnetizing to him against the corner of the couch, she wondered if the hatred was transforming into trust.

"This is dark manipulation at play." Hades continued, ignoring the tension in the room. "The Soulless are able to pull bodies from the Underworld, but their souls must remain. Only the most desperate are willing to challenge the balance of a promised immortal afterlife."

"I was able to send them back." Hayden offered, although quietly.

"Once. In close proximity to the portal. For a couple dozen. And it nearly destroyed you." Rei evaluated, sounding as if he was debating between scolding Hayden and applauding him.

"There are more." Liv whispered, summoning her sword from the fireplace into her hands and turning to Rei. "Why did my sword, *only* my sword, succeed in eliminating them?"

"Norse metal has special properties." Rei offered curiously. "The Norse Gods blessed their weaponry with powers far more specialized than our Security and Warfare pillar could dream of."

"Your sword is of Norse descent, too." Liv countered, "It didn't have the same effect."

"Every weapon has a different history." Rei sighed.

"What do you mean?" Liv tilted her head, before studying her sword once more.

"Norse metal is special because it's crafted to absorb elements it comes in contact with." Rei explained.

"Liv killed Kerberos." Hades spat, standing up slowly. "He alone had different poisons in every tooth, tailored to defeat any magical creature or monster – the ultimate kill unique to every pending bite."

"I didn't use the sword then." Liv sighed, clearly still annoyed by the entire encounter, before her eyes lifted. "I stabbed Ophion, though."

"Ophion?" Hayden eyes went wide, cursing under his breath.

"The snake's blood can burn victims. His eyes curse those he hypnotizes with deadly diseases. Sometimes with incurable implications." Rhys explained somberly.

No wonder he had so many strategies with combatting Liv's recovery.

Piper sunk further in her chair, realizing she would be put to the test the following day, trying to piece all of this enlightenment together.

"Can we forge another weapon from this one?" Liv turned to Tristan, holding out the sword in his direction, it's blade only inches from Piper's throat. "So Hades can protect the Underworld properly?"

"I'm not a blacksmith!" Tristan huffed indignantly, guiding the blade away from Piper.

Piper sighed in relief.

"You would gift me with part of your protection?" Hades clarified, curiously studying Liv.

"Well, it's the least I can do." Liv mumbled, "I killed your dog."

Hades limped slowly to the couch, making his injury still look elegant as he relied on a sleek mahogany cane and gripped its ruby handle. He prompted for the sword, which Liv handed over willingly, and began inspecting it.

With a nod, Hades finally concluded, "Hephaestus can advise on the metal's magical properties and forge another weapon without fully hindering the original sword."

"Hephaestus?" Hayden questioned speculatively.

"It's okay." Liv whispered, "The sword is a bit heavy for my liking. No offense Rei," she added apologetically before nodding to Hayden, "Can you summon him?"

"I cannot." Hayden admitted with an edge, turning to Hades. "He's in the Underworld."

A flash of realization crossed Liv's mind as her mouth dropped.

"Why not just summon Kerberos, then?" She pressed.

"Once you pass onto the Underworld, you forever remain bonded to that world." Hayden explained softly. "When you pass the threshold into our world, it's like stretching a rubber band, forever wanting to pull you back into the static position. You wither away if you fight it for too long, so you must always return, even with Hades's blessing."

"Kerberos would only remain strong enough for a week, two at most before needing to return for an equal amount of time, or more to recover." Hades explained, "Plus, as the Underworld's keeper, it wears on me just as much. It's hasn't been worth it since Persephone. Until now."

Hades eyed the sword, once again asking Liv permission to proceed.

She nodded.

Piper internally couldn't believe she was about to meet Hephaestus, the master blacksmith, Tristan's ancestor and the original God of Fire. He was a direct descendant of Zeus and Hera, and it was rumored that the weapons he forged contained mystical elements to the benefit of the beholder, traces of magic with work he left behind still being discovered today. He was a legend, the first cripple, or *different* deity, to be recognized and martyred for his value.

He was like Piper.

She had spent countless nights reading about his life and had memorized all of his adventures, although blocked out most of his arranged marriage with Aphrodite, instead dreaming of what it would be like for the day they could finally meet in the Underworld. Wondering what she would say, fantasizing on whether he would notice her. She had once romanticized her afterlife because of him.

Piper blushed at the memories, turning shyly to her living, breathing Fire God.

It was funny, she hadn't thought about Hephaestus in any capacity since she had met Tristan.

In fact, now she dreaded the idea of departing this world with so much unsaid.

But she still took a look at her clothes, dirty and torn. She quickly tried to tame her midnight bob, combing her fingers through it and attempting to create a new part by throwing half of her hair over to the other side of her skull.

As Hades departed his office and entered the hallway with dread, even with Rei behind him, Piper quickly used a fraction of her powers to air dry her clothes, blasting away any dirt particles to at least clean up her appearance for her childhood hero.

Thank Zeus she wore black today. The subtle rips in her trouser and corset added an adequate grundge vibe tolerable for her snakeskin blazer. She crossed her legs, purposely hiding the biggest tear on her thigh.

"Are you nervous, Piper?" Tristan whispered, aghast.

"Of course not." She replied, too quickly. "I don't even *know* Hephaestus."

"But you clearly want to make a good impression." Tristan observed with a smirk before leaning in and taunting her further, "Meeting the fam… it *is* a big deal."

Piper glared at his amused smile.

"Shut up."

She turned back to her shoes, cringing as she saw dried blood on her skin. But she could feel Tristan's gaze on her, so she didn't *dare* try to remove it.

Piper just hoped it was her own blood.

To avoid gagging, she desperately looked for a distraction.

Liv and Hayden were in deep conversation, but she noticed that Liv looked tense, as if fighting against her natural instincts to recoil into distrust of their king. Hayden looked exhausted, worried and happier than she had seen him in months. He whispered something with a playful smile, which made Liv laugh. And although Piper couldn't see Liv's face anymore, as soon as the chuckle vibrated from her body, Hayden laughed in response, pride radiating from his demeanor with the knowledge he had made *her* laugh.

Piper smiled at the notion. They were too adorable. Even among the pain and torture they endured, Liv and Hayden still managed to enjoy the small things with each other and continued to find their way back to one another. They found the beauty in the landscape beneath a harrowing mass of clouds.

Hades appeared yet again, causing everyone to lose their relaxed demeanor and sit up straight, holding their breaths to be introduced to a legend.

The God of the Death stepped aside, revealing a path for Hephaestus to enter.

He moved slowly, his limp more prominent than Hades's graceful injury. Hephaestus favored neither of his feet, which were rumored to have suffered from bilateral congenital clubfoot.

He wore the pain on his sleeve with pride, refusing a cane or any device to ease his condition.

Piper beamed.

He was absolutely stunning.

Hephaestus was rough on the edges, but underneath his hardened exterior were bright green eyes and a smooth complexion. He had strong cheekbones and a slender face with symmetrical features coveted by a model. His sandy hair was wavy, tousled to perfection.

"If you stare any longer, you may start drooling." Tristan whispered in Piper's ear.

She gently put her hand against his forehead and pushed him away.

Piper wanted to say something, but alas she was rendered speechless.

"The weapon?" Hephaestus asked Hades, finally speaking.

His voice was coarse, like a soothing vibration of a car running on a freshly paved highway.

Rei summoned the sword, handing it to Hephaestus within moments.

Had he been behind Hephaestus the entire time?

Truly, Piper didn't really care. She sighed and leaned further into her palm, smiling at the sight.

Tristan furrowed his eyebrows, motioning his hand in front of Piper's infatuated gaze.

"Did you hit your head earlier?"

Piper glared before she swatted his hand away.

Tristan tilted his head in observation of his ancestor, who now compared the Viking sword to Hades's rapier with deep consideration.

"I don't see it." Tristan dryly commented.

Piper rolled her eyes, finally turning to Tristan, and snapped.

"Oh, so because the attention is not on you for once, you're suddenly a dog begging to be pet?"

Her outburst made her blush, even more so when Tristan chuckled, leaning back in his chair smugly.

"Who does this weapon belong to?" Hephaestus inquired, searching the room.

Liv stood and whispered hoarsely, "Mc. Olivia."

The ancient deity locked eyes with her and nodded. "You're Liam's daughter." He studied her, sizing her up as he continued his assessment. "… The Elite of the Elements Pillar."

"Correct." Liv lifted her chin dignifiedly, wearing her tarnished gown and cuts with pride.

"And do you give me permission to proceed?" Hephaestus confirmed, with an undertone of irony.

"Correct." Liv replied sternly. "It is my duty to protect the Underworld."

"I've never seen an Element Elite so concerned with the deceased." Hephaestus retorted boldly, beginning to melt the tip of the enchanted weapon. "Usually that is the shared concern of royalty."

"It is." Hayden stood defiantly.

Hephaestus paused, finally acknowledging the king.

"I misspoke. I did not realize Rowan's son was present." He looked between the two, standing together in unison, yet still divided. "Both of your fathers will be happy to hear I saw you, together."

His gaze slowly turned back to his project, before catching Piper's eyes still intensely staring in disbelief, and then finding his own kin sitting beside her.

"Yours, too." Hephaestus nodded sternly to Tristan, before fully returning to his duty.

Liv turned back toward Tristan with sad, understanding eyes.

Piper instinctively grabbed Tristan's hand in support.

She didn't dare look at him, but if Liv's demeanor were any clue, Tristan was hurting.

He may have been a dog, but he was hers to pet.

And she would forever remember the moment Hephaestus actually looked into her soul before showing compassion for the love of her life.

HAYDEN

She looked so stunning, but she always looked stunning.

And he beamed with pride that she chose to stand beside him.

That she let him stand beside her.

She still looked at him with trepidation. Hayden understood that she still battled inner demons, but it would forever pain him to know he was the cause of her unease.

And yet, he didn't want the night to end with her.

He dreaded returning to the Siren Court, knowing that inevitably his duty would call, and he would need to depart shortly to continue strengthening the alliance. Fortunately, being able to report that they defeated the Soulless tonight could help sway Calithya, especially now knowing Hades fully supported the Pure God rule, at least enough to eliminate threat against his stronghold.

Now his only concern resided with the hope that his sister Jocelyn didn't deter Demetrius away from the fight.

Hayden sighed, running his hand through his hair as he returned to the present, the controllable, and watched Hephaestus finish welding the melted Viking metal atop Hades's personal sword.

Small victories.

Liv turned to Hayden, her eyes shyly meeting his.

He caught her gaze lower to his lips, biting her own in response before immediately returning to his blue eyes.

She had told him his eyes were the key distinguisher between her king and her tormenter.

And yet, he still yearned to be so much more than her king.

He wanted to be her *everything* again.

Signaling his intent before initiating and waiting for her approval, Hayden leaned closer to Liv, understanding that she still fought against the instinct to recoil in his presence.

"Today has been rather… aggressive." He offered, eyes sparkling as she huffed at his simple description for their predicament, "Would you be up for having everyone over to my loft for pizza and boardgames tonight?"

Liv tilted her head in consideration, eyeing him deviously as she considered his proposal. "You certainly don't need *my* permission to hang out with your friends, your high-pain-in-my-ass."

"Thank Zeus." Hayden breathed sarcastically. "And here I thought I was incapable of making my own choices."

Liv smirked, still trepidly staring at Hephaestus and Hades.

Hayden watched as she gulped, still fighting against the short distance that almost disappeared between them. He could feel her heat radiating beside him.

"The thing is, Ollie." Hayden continued, tilting his head slowly closer so he could whisper, "The only person I truly want to spend time with is you."

Liv turned to Hayden, her jaw dropped. Her gaze lowered to his lips once again before returning back to his eyes.

Hayden waited for her to respond. To say *anything*.

Yet she remained silent, trying to process the statement.

Don't give her time to deflect.

Against his will, Hayden took a step back, adding what he hoped sounded nonchalant, "I mean, if you're not interested in defeating me in Catan, then might as well call the whole night off and save the carb overload."

He shrugged, smirking before he turned his gaze back to Hades, who inspected his new weapon, now blessed by the gods to defeat the Soulless.

Liv shifted, taking a step in his direction so she once again closed the gap between the two.

"It depends," Liv contemplated, "How many sheep will I need to trade for a slice of pizza?" She looked up mischievously in his direction.

"Three trees at minimum." Hayden countered.

"Oh, so you can set the kitchen on fire again?" Liv chuckled.

Zeus, he loved her laugh.

Even when she taunted him.

"Well, with that attitude, you'll find no trading alliances with me." Hayden retorted, watching her reaction while he walked toward Hephaestus to offer his gratitude for his service.

She had him wrapped around her finger. And he was happy and obliged to be there, so long as she wanted him. If she had asked him in that moment to leave now, he would have simply asked her, "Where to?"

But she let him conduct his duty, although Hayden could feel Ollie's gaze intensely staring him down, filled with curiosity, intrigue and worry.

But less worry than the time before. Which was less than the time before that.

Kronos may have cursed them, Arlo may have tried to tarnish their memories, the Dark Gods may have tried to destroy their connection. But slowly and surely their bond was bringing them back together, forging back as one just as Hephaestus had welded another weapon from an original source, allowing two to become one and strengthening their cause for the better. Greater gods blessed their relationship, even if darker ones tried to break them apart.

"Thank you for your expertise, Hephaestus." Hayden nodded respectfully. "We are fortunate to have our ancestors on our side during this divide."

Handing over Liv's leaner sword, along with a block of metal, Hephaestus explained that other Viking-made weaponry should also absorb the block of power containing Ophion's destructive elements.

"I could not imagine coming back into this world without my soul." Hephaestus shook his head grimly, eliminating his tools from his makeshift workstation. "It's bad enough coming back with Hades's permission."

"I wholeheartedly agree." Hades drawled, eyeing his nephew Hephaestus, looking worse for the wear. He turned to Hayden, "Don't expect this to happen again anytime soon."

"Never crossed my mind." He admitted. "We'll let you rest. Rhys and Silas will check in on you tomorrow. Thank you, both." He added, curtly, before turning back to his friends, to Liv.

"I've summoned two carriages to transport everyone back to Puerdios University, if desired?"

He didn't mention that the ask almost deplenished his powers once more. That the amount of strength it took to overcome Kronos's pawns terrified him to his core.

Focus on the small victory.

Like when they emerged, and Liv spotted Pegasus glowing on the cliff and beamed brightly enough to light up the entire night sky.

"Where have you been, my pretty girl?" Liv pet the white horse, nuzzling her head against her pet's neck.

Pegasus neighed as Hayden approached.

"We had her at the palace." He smiled, scratching behind her ear.

The horse closed her eyes and leaned happily into Hayden's hand.

"She likes you." Liv observed, eyeing Hayden. "Everyone likes you."

Ollie said it playfully, but there was a questionable truth laced beneath her tone.

Hayden furrowed his brows, trying to assess what she needed.

It was so hard to stay away.

She turned toward Pegasus, smiling naturally once again, but her mind was clouded with doubt and speculation. Demons that continued to haunt her present.

He determined it was best to give her space.

"I'll let you reacquaint yourself." Hayden concluded, swiftly brushing Pegasus once more before turning back toward the carriages.

"Wait."

Hayden spun around, as if on command, cursing himself for his blind obedience.

Not because he cared about Liv's influence over him, but more because it was obvious the Dark Gods knew Liv was clearly the vessel to penetrate his soul.

She didn't make eye contact with him. Instead, Liv determinedly continued to brush Pegasus with her hand, a therapeutic, calming maneuver as she sorted through her thoughts.

Finally, Liv turned to Hayden, distress wavering on her face.

Her lips began quivering.

Hayden's soul was crushed. It would be easier for him to walk away. Leave her be. Let her find peace. And yet, he stayed. He would always stay. Even if it destroyed him.

"I don't know what to do." She admitted sadly, finally finding his gaze. She looked up into the night sky, before turning back to him, then looking behind him to her friends, who all waited in their carriages for departure. Fidgeting, she leaned her face against Pegasus's neck.

"All of the evidence tells a different story than what's imprinted in my head." Liv admitted, closing her eyes. A tear emerged from her lid. She looked up to Hayden, pleading, "I'm starting to think I'm crazy. That I belong in a mental institution."

"Ollie, no…" Hayden instinctively reached out to her.

Liv jumped back, recoiling from the action.

Further proving her point.

She cringed, looking up toward the stars again. Summoning him unintentionally, again.

"I have beliefs that conspire against my king." She sighed, biting her lips as she hesitantly looked toward Hayden. "You know I do. Don't deny it. And yet, you don't imprison me. You make an exception."

"Ollie, you're recovering…"

"You think I'm confused." Liv admitted, shaking her head in embarrassment. "But my thoughts and actions are still an executional offense. And I don't understand why you choose instead to be kind to me. You owe me nothing."

She shifted her weight on her feet, biting her lip.

"Am I going crazy?" Liv finally asked, her voice cracking, as she broke down, finally removing the strong façade and leaving only her vulnerable and scarred remains.

"No. You're not going crazy." Hayden stated, with as much distinction and assurance as he could deliver with five words. "Kronos and Arlo manipulated your memory, tortured your mind and are who to blame for your conspiracy theories."

Liv processed his words, challenging whether to believe them or not. Finally, she looked to him.

"What if I forget more? What if this is only the beginning?"

Hayden shook his head, refusing to believe it possible.

"The fact that you are even asking me these questions, makes me optimistic that this is the end of your demise, the beginning of a better chapter. Nothing more will come between us. And if we stay the same as we are now, I will be forever thankful that you're in my life."

Liv nodded, staring at the ground, as if convincing herself his words were true.

"But, if you do forget more, I'll still remain by your side. And I can remind you of our past, as long as you'll let me." He added, slowly reaching out his hand.

She glanced over at it, grasping Pegasus tighter at first, before returning her gaze to Hayden.

"Will you ride with me back to Puerdios?" Liv took a deep breath, pausing before adding quietly, "And tell me about our past?"

Her gaze returned to his hand, debating if her actions could truly follow through with her words.

"It would be an honor." Hayden smiled, continuing to hold his hand out.

At her pace. He needed to wait for her.

Determinedly, Liv nodded, finally locking her hand with his.

Electricity fueled the contact, brightening the stars in the sky above.

She looked up immediately, feeling the connected power upon impact.

Ollie smiled, beaming as she looked over to Hayden, nodding toward Pegasus as she led him over to her horse's saddle.

He could tell she was still nervous, but she prompted him to hop on the mystical beast first.

After he had mounted Pegasus, he held out his hand to her once again.

It still took only a moment of uncertainty before she grabbed it and propped herself up behind him.

Small victories.

She had chosen to *trust* him – as they soared into the starry sky – wrapping her body against his, alone. And the foundation of trust was a beautiful thing.

"So, I suspect there's a larger explanation to zombie intel and ESPN addiction?" She purred inquisitively.

Hayden chuckled, looking back in her direction briefly.

Where could he *begin?*

Her strawberry scent lingered as she set her chin softly on his shoulder. The perfect weight, a soothing pressure that couldn't have been wanted more.

"Before I was king, I attended school in the mortal world." Hayden started, "It wasn't necessary, but a request by my mother to prepare for my eventual responsibility of governing over the deities and therefore, the human race."

He felt Liv's mouth curve upward, the best encouragement to continue.

"I remained because I befriended a girl. A special girl. A girl who single-handedly changed my life."

Liv stiffened behind him.

Too much. Hayden noted to stay neutral. Tonight was not the night for a romance retelling.

"Well, to say the least, she became my best friend."

Liv nodded as she whispered to confirm, "Ollie?"

"Er, this is awkward…" Hayden teased.

"No?" Liv asked, mortified.

"Nah, joking. You're correct." Hayden chuckled, amused.

Liv playfully hit him from behind, before settling atop his shoulder again.

But he could feel her relax behind him, exactly what he wanted to achieve.

"More importantly, her mother adored him." Hayden added with a grin.

"Stop." Liv retorted, her smile spreading wider. "There's no way. You don't know my mom. My mom cannot know the King of the Pure Gods. That's insane."

"Julia? Sure do. In fact, I like to believe I'm the son she's never had…" Hayden replied cockily. "She and Charles invited me to go fishing next month."

Liv laughed, mortified. "No, they did not."

"Were you not invited? Makes sense…" Hayden spat back with a grin.

Liv couldn't contain herself. Finally, she calmed down.

"I know Lace, too." Hayden admitted.

Liv sighed, "I miss them, a lot."

He knew. He did, too. But they couldn't dwell on a world they could never organically be apart of. It was time to change the subject.

"What else do you want to know? I'm at your disposal." He offered, genuinely.

Liv adjusted her grip around his waist, contemplating her next question.

"Pizza or tacos?" She asked smugly, a smile growing against his shoulder.

"Both." Hayden retorted, "Taco pizza."

"Spoken like a true politician." Liv called out.

"But if I had to choose," Hayden continued, "Pizza… because that still counts taco pizza, right?"

"You're the king. You make the decree." She hollered back.

"Then no question, it counts. What about you?" He lobbeyed back effortlessly.

"I would say tacos." Liv breathed against his neck, sending chills down his spine. "Street-cart style tacos, obviously. But taco pizza is making me re-evaluate my question…"

"Taco pizza makes me re-evaluate everything."

"Everything?" Liv purred.

"Like, my morals, for one. Exactly what would I do to get taco pizza? That could potentially go down a dark path I do not wish to tempt…" Hayden joked.

"Calm down, sir. I'll get you your damn taco pizza tonight. But that'll cost you two oars." Liv teased.

Hayden felt her flip her long blonde hair to the other side of her head as her luscious locks bounced off his back, sending another whiff of her intoxicating smell in his direction.

After a moment of fighting against the urge to turn around and kiss her, Hayden was granted sad relief when Liv spoke again.

"What is it like knowing that you're the top god, yet I'm the true badass of this duo?"

Hayden coughed, certainly not expecting *that* question.

"I'm glad your humility will forever keep me grounded." He retorted back.

Liv seemed pleased with that response, leaning further into him as she stared up at the sky.

"You can almost see every star from here." She muttered in awe.

He looked into the sky, for the first time noticing the beauty of sparkling diamonds in thousands surrounding them. It was truly a sight to appreciate. Yet, Liv still shined brightest.

But he couldn't tell her *that* tonight.

"Favorite childhood memory?"

This one would be more challenging to answer. Hayden knew he was walking a fine line between connecting with Liv to put her mind at ease and freaking her-the-fuck-out from how much he actually knew about her personal life.

"I had two very separate lives growing up and both were equally great." Hayden began, "But I always felt a part of me was missing between the two. When I was with my mortal friends at school, there was a constant guilt hidden behind revealing my true identity. When I was with my kind, they didn't understand the beauty of the mortal world – so there was always this disconnect."

"This doesn't sound like a great memory." Liv stated, not judgmental, just curious.

"It gets better – just giving you context, impatient one." Hayden chuckled, continuing. "My favorite place in the world is my family's cabin. It's nestled by a lake, surrounded by stunning mountains and has no essence of royalty. It's where I would go to find the balanced in-between for my very radical childhoods. It's where I go now to find some normalcy among this intense society."

"It sounds like a wonderful place." Liv whispered.

Hayden pressed on, "I would invite my high school friends to come all the time, and occasionaly my deity friends, too – separately of course," Hayden grinned at the thought of introducing Rei and Peyton to Lace and his football team mates, "Because it was my own secret way of blending my two identities in the most approachable way possible. So my *favorite* memory was the last time my friends all gathered there during the fall of my senior year in highschool. It was bittersweet, knowing I would have to say goodbye, but I'll forever cherish the last time I had all of them in one place, even if it was the conclusion of my mortal chapter."

Liv didn't roll a sarcastic comment off her tongue, but instead hugged him tighter.

She of all people understood the beauty of growing up in the mortal world, the gift of childhood innocence from existing outside of the powerful and dangerous deity society. The responsibility they held to maintain balance in the world. They had been safe as mortals, living in a bubble and surrounded with relatively small concerns like winning a football game or getting into college. Hayden had been given a chance to live with less responsibility, less weight in comparison to his life now.

Being in charge of the fate to humanity was no small burden.

"I was at the cabin, wasn't I?" Liv admitted sadly.

That part of her had been taken. Pieces of her childhood innocence stolen, memories that Hayden heavily relied on to get through the darkness, removed from her archive of light.

"You were." Hayden gulped.

He would destroy Kronos.

"Can you tell me more about the trip? Our friends?" Liv sighed, longing for reassurance.

Hayden closed his eyes with gratitude and anger. He had lost his rock, but he had known what they were and used that as his saving grace, but that luxury had been eliminated from Liv. She missed her past life, yet had no one to reminiscence with, secluding her further into the darkness. But, he was so grateful that she was fighting for it back.

"It was your seventeenth birthday weekend celebration. Lace was adamant about getting you a birthday cake in the shape of a coffee-filled mug."

"I remember that." Liv laughed, lifting her head from Hayden's shoulder, "She was pissed when she opened it to find only a coffee cake instead."

Liv even mimicked how Lace said pissed, emphasizing the 'eh' by drawing out the sound, but her laugh grew silent.

"It's strange to remember parts of that weekend, but not fully." She admitted sadly, turning her head sideways and resting her cheek against Hayden's back. "I remember the cabin and Lace, plus Rob and Malcolm, and Courtney and Emilie being there, but I guess I hadn't thought about not knowing *whose* cabin we were at. There's a distinctive blank part of that memory that I can't seem to draw out…"

"It's okay." Hayden offered, although his delivery was not as wholehearted as he would have liked.

"How can I remember something, but only parts of it?" Liv shook her head in disbelief.

"Mnemosyne. She's the god of memory and although a part of the Candor pillar, I continue to question their loyalty to the Pure God rule."

"But, your mother and sister are the pillar Elites?" Liv inquired, no longer aware of her personal history with them, relative to Hayden.

"I find they use the 'fate of the future' excuse when convenient." Hayden shook his head, reminding himself he wasn't speaking with his Ollie, but a stranger to his family dynamics. "But, it's not worth spending the time debating the possibilities. The truth will come out eventually."

"When is that?"

"When either the Dark Gods or Pure Gods triumph in the end."

FOURTEEN

LIV

As long as she didn't move, she was okay.

Liv gripped onto Hayden's toned torso, her hands clasped to his cashmere sweater, a thin layer that revealed his six-pack all too well underneath. And Zeus, it felt like solid rock against her grasp.

And his broad, strong shoulders were very welcoming for her face to rest against. She stared at his sculpted arm, imagining the muscles underneath the camel coat.

She loved feeling his body vibrate when he chuckled, a light, melodic tune that sent butterflies sparkling down her core.

And he told her of playing soccer and barbecuing, and helping her mom with groceries or fixing their plumbing before she had met Charles.

The King of Gods knew what groceries were and how to unclog a toilet.

And he even made those topics sound sexy.

All was fantastic and there was no avoiding the inevitable – that she would begin to fantasize about a future with this seemingly perfect specimen.

Liv was in heaven, until she was in hell.

When Hayden would kindly look back in her direction, a whiff of his scent would breeze past her nose – verveina, cedarwood, cardamom and leather. And Liv would freeze, fighting every instinct to rip his throat apart.

As long as she *didn't move,* she was okay.

Focus on the stories, the good. She would remind herself.

And yet, without her personal memory connected to these experiences, they began falling flat, just words and promises without merit.

And Liv would begin spiraling again. Staring off into the stars to pacify her rapidly beating heart, her warming skin and her surfacing anger.

As long as she *didn't move,* she was okay.

As long as she didn't *murder* the king, she was okay.

And slowly, she began tuning out Hayden's excited words, only capable of repeating the necessary thoughts to survive the ride back to Puerdios.

As long as she *didn't move,* she was okay.

It had all sounded so nice. Like a world she had wanted to be a part of.

As long as she *didn't move,* she was okay.

A tear slowly emerged from her eye, but she didn't dare wipe it away.

As long as she *didn't move,* she was okay.

REI

This game was stupid.

Of course he could successfully build a settlement, but the fact that he was neck in neck with Peyton for largest army was an absolute joke.

If this were a real scenario, they would ally together and combine their forces as one, splitting the victory points between the two. Yet, when he explained this reasoning to his girlfriend, she simply chuckled and proudly declined his proposed trade with the use of subtle curse words and taunting insults.

He hated boardgames. It brought out the worst in people, encouraged selfish competition and hindered the greater good. And it was a waste of time, focusing energy and resources on a make-believe world.

"Does anyone need hay?" Liv inquired.

"Hay girl hay." Hayden retorted, deviously eyeing her from across the table "What do you want in return?"

Well, his royal highness was certainly in a good mood. Even when he continued to rename wheat and basically rewrite the rules of the game because of a certain love interest.

Rei rolled his eyes.

Trades shouldn't be based on pleasing your opponent, but instead discussing what you need and finding others who can mutually benefit from the exchange.

Hayden was so whipped.

"Oar?" Liv asked, biting her lip.

She was just as desperate as Hayden. At least she called Oar by the right name.

"Deal." Hayden nodded, handing her his Oar card in exchange for her Wheat.

Liv flinched when their fingers touched in the trade, Hayden frowned for a moment but covered it up quickly by standing up and walking to the kitchen for more taco pizza.

Rei took a sip of his whisky, wondering if he shouldn't be so mentally hard on the both of them.

"Building a city." Liv handed her cards to Piper, the banker.

Or maybe he should. His hands tensed at the announcement.

"Another?!" Peyton spat, turning to Hayden, "I told you to stop trading with her! You're going to cost us the game. She has eight points!"

"You do, too!" Liv pointed out smugly.

"But Rei is on my tail, he's going after Largest Army and if he gets it then I'm back to six points!" Peyton argued her case for the whole table to hear.

Another stupid tactic – obviously all should be kept confidential. Peyton *knew* that.

"And we care because…?" Tristan retorted, rolling the dice.

Rei chuckled in complete agreement. It was late and with six teams playing – Dylan and Liv, Piper and Hayden, and Tristan and Kyril had partnered together – this game had dragged on much too long. Fortunately, he had a victory point, so if he *did* get Peyton's Largest Army, he'd officially be back in the lead with nine points.

To hide his strategic glory, Rei took a sip of his yet-again-almost-empty whisky glass.

"Seven. Damn." Hayden sighed, counting his cards.

"Thank Zeus." Zayne had muttered, who had been blocked from receiving his four Wood cards whenever an eight had been rolled.

"Well, easy choice to place it here and shut most of you up." Kyril smirked, moving the robber onto the six where Zayne, Peyton and Liv and Dylan's cities bordered.

"Cruel." Liv furrowed her brows, turning back to her cards and trying to determine a new strategy. "At least I don't have seven cards like Rei."

He fucking hated this game.

"A new whisky to help drown your sorrows?" Hayden offered a full glass with a forced smile.

Hayden *knew* Rei hated this game.

Rei discarded his Wood and Brick cards angrily, taking a sip of his new whisky glass.

Zayne rolled next with a five.

Piper handed two Wood cards out accordingly to Tristan and Kyril, and then two to herself and Hayden.

"I can't do anything." Zayne said calmly, passing the dice to Piper, who handed it to Hayden.

The king rolled the dice next, thrilled when a five and a three appeared on the table.

Piper looked at Hayden, her jaw dropping, staring back at the board before going back to her partner to confirm. She collected four Brick cards and two Oar, passing them to Hayden with a giddy nod as she then handed out everyone else's cards dutifully.

"We'll build two roads." Hayden handed four cards to Piper, "Letting us take back Longest Road." He grabbed it from Tristan's display of victory points and development cards.

"And we have two victory points!" Piper squealed, turning over their development cards before clapping. "We win!"

"Cheers to that." Rei smirked, lifting his glass.

"Good game you guys." Liv grinned, looking up to Hayden. "Rest assured, knowing our king is fully capable of building the most successful settlement in a fantasy board game."

"You were just on the edge of your seat *waiting* to say that, weren't you?" Hayden glared, although he was grinning, clearly amused.

"It was truly the only reason I suggested playing this game in the first place. Who knew my plans would be so tastefully executed?" Liv grinned, summoning the pieces to return from the boardgame and filing the container in its place on Hayden's bookshelf within seconds.

"What a day." Dylan commented, slowly getting up and using Kyril as a personal crutch while her leg still healed.

Kyril kissed her cheek, before lifting her up into his arms with a swift movement.

"We'll catch you all on in a couple days – except your highness and Peyton of course, safe travels and good luck with the sassy sirens." Kyril grinned, nodding goodbye to everyone before departing with his red-headed hostage.

Zayne managed to politely hug or shake hands before saying his good-bye, but followed behind his two friends.

"I need to go work on Professor Deligne's assignment tonight, unfortunately." Piper admitted with a yawn.

"Piper, you should rest. Today was insane. Professor Deligne will understand." Liv implored.

"I'm not tired." She spat back.

"Ah, and the first part of that declaration was just to make sure your mouth still worked?" Tristan smirked.

Piper scowled, ignoring him, and instead grabbed her snakeskin blazer before pointing to Liv, "I'll see you tomorrow?"

"Can't wait." Liv saluted her friend.

Piper made her rounds, with Tristan close behind, before departing Hayden's loft along with the Fire God.

"And then there were the fabulous four." Peyton grinned, continuing, "The originals. The OGs. The OG-Oregon alumni." Then she paused, "Can you actually call yourself an alum if you only attended classes for a month? Or what if you just pretended you were going to attend classes but never showed?" She smirked, elbowing Hayden before groaning and grabbing her side. "Ugh, I forgot I broke that rib today."

Rei finally cracked. His girlfriend was absolutely ridiculous. He couldn't help but laugh with her.

"I think that mess is our queue to go." He dryly observed.

"Stay a little longer." Hayden quietly requested to the general group, but Rei noticed his gaze was directed toward Liv.

There was no way he wanted to get involved with *that* fiasco.

So, Rei remained silent and held Peyton back, gently, but with enough emphasis for warning. His girlfriend eyed him angrily in protest before quickly catching on to his meaning.

Liv turned back to Hayden, at a loss for words.

Rei could see she wanted to stay, she longed to stay, but her mind blocked her desire. She cleared her throat, shyly grabbing some glasses from the table, oblivious to Peyton and Rei still in the room.

"It's been a long day." She finally stated, walking back to the kitchen. Liv set the glasses on the kitchen, easing the blow, "And you have to travel to the Siren Court tomorrow. We should all get some rest."

Even if Rei and Peyton had wanted to stay, Liv still wasn't comfortable enough for the next step Hayden longed for.

"Of course." Hayden cut in quickly, although not genuinely.

Liv smiled shyly, before walking over to Peyton to hug her friend goodbye. She turned to Hayden, not initiating contact, but formal gratitude. "Thank you for having us over tonight. I think we needed this, as much as Rei hates Catan."

Liv smirked at Rei after her callout; he glared sternly in her direction, communicating that the Element Elite *would* pay for her betrayal.

Soon, her light blue gown disappeared behind the large mahogany doors before they slammed shut.

Peyton cautiously glanced over at Hayden, assessing the vibe. The king still stared sternly at the door.

"She's coming around." Peyton commented optimistically, but still unsure to Hayden's reaction.

"I assure you the notion does not lessen the blow." Hayden finally stated quietly. He bowed his head, before heading toward the stairs and summoning the rest of the night's evidence back into its rightful place.

"We should go." Rei commanded softly, reaching out his hand to Peyton as he joined her by the large table's corner and guided her out of the king's loft.

They decided to crash at Peyton's on-campus apartment, since she needed to repack for her upcoming and dreaded return to the Siren Court.

"I just don't understand why we can't tell her about her life, the prophecy, her undying love for the man she thinks she hates?" Peyton rolled her eyes frusteratingly, unbuckling her leather dress contraption and throwing it on the cream armchair.

She followed a similar fashion in her loose cashmere grey sweaterdress, falling onto her matching couch cushioned with cinnamon rose pillows. Peyton lit the five staggered candles in the middle of her large coffee table, sinking further into the depths of her comforting furniture.

Rei knew to let her fully exert her anger, speak her words and let her truly feel the extent of her emotion before cutting in. He wouldn't hear the end of it, otherwise.

Peyton pointed at Rei determinedly, "If the fate of our world ever falls on my shoulders, you better promise you will keep it straight with me? No matter what circumstance?"

He sighed. Usually her monologues involved dramatic speeches and rhetoric questions, never a pointed question that required a response.

Rei sat down next to Peyton patiently, extending his arm around her so she could lean against his chest. She smelled of amber and peonies, a perfect reflection to the calming, bohemian aroma that decorated her apartment on the Puerdios campus.

"It's never that easy, Peyton." Rei replied honestly.

"And it's easier seeing both of them hurt?" She challenged, summoning two glasses of pinot noir, perfectly matching the darker tones of her decorations sprinkled around the candle-lit space.

"Whatever we're feeling, they're experiencing it ten-fold." Rei challenged, taking a sip of his beverage.

"Exactly my point." Peyton huffed. "Last time, the pressure of the prophecy almost broke them, and I know that we run the risk of the same happening if Liv is not able to discover her natural feelings toward Hayden on her own, but *we're running out of time*."

Rei couldn't disagree; even he was beginning to worry about the growing threats that posed against them.

"He created *a new monster*." Peyton trembled, emphasizing the encounter with the Soulless. Rei hugged her tighter. "As Hayden waits for Liv to come around, Kronos grows more powerful. His armies build, his forces strengthen, and what do we have? A hope for a damn prophecy to come true?"

She turned to him, her bright hazel eyes raw and exposed. "It's not enough."

Rei had expected this. Regret, remorse and desperation as the death of her brother, Xander, resurfaced to Peyton's consciousness after returning to his slaughter scene. This, he felt he could handle.

"I could say something inspirational and lame, like 'The moment you give up is the moment Kronos wins' or some bullshit of the sort, but we both know this conversation is not what's really troubling your mind."

Peyton looked surprised, but didn't challenge his intuition.

He gently swept her hair away from her face, revealing the beautiful freckled face he adored so much.

"Deities are going to die, Peyton." Rei took a deep breath, inhaling her sweet English rose scent. "We're in a war, and the Underworld will collect soldiers no matter what side they fight for. But, if we choose to fight for love, freedom and life – we honor Xander and what he valued. And just like your brother, I would rather die trying to keep those values alive than choose cowardice and survival. His death will never be in vain, no matter what comes with the prophecy."

Peyton remained silent, her head resting against Rei's white jacket. He rubbed her back gently, hearing a quietly contained sniffle as she remained still in his arms.

LIV

"You ready?" Piper glanced over to Liv, delicately shutting her textbook.

They had been postponing the inevitable changing of the gauze, both choosing to focus studiously on their curriculum rather than ripping off the band-aid, *literally*, and begin the tortuous process Rhys had set the week before.

It *was* getting late. And poor Piper, who wanted nothing less than to intentionally hurt her friend, having been dragged into this mess, and now patiently waited for the convenience of her patient.

Liv knew the same thoughts that haunted her mind crashed into her friend's as well.

What if the bruises had gotten worse? What if they didn't treat her wounds properly tonight? What if the pain was so intolerable that they both would not be able to fulfill what Rhys required of them?

"More than I'll ever be." Liv finally admitted, running her hand through her hair.

"What if we just focus on one thing at a time." Piper offered, "Removing your bandages and soaking in a bath doesn't seem so terrible?"

"Your right." Liv nodded, slowly getting herself off the couch, grimacing as her tightened muscles protested the activity. Although her mind enjoyed playing volleyball with Rei earlier in the day, her body had not appreciated the additional curricular activity following her already strenuous private training with Rei. Not to mention the unexpected recovery inflicted upon her visit to the Underworld the day before. Once she was fully upright and recovered, Liv pointed toward the bathroom. "I'll holler when I'm done."

"Take your time." Piper replied kindly, cozying up with another book in the corner of the couch.

Liv marched to the bathroom and flicked on the lights, facing a stranger in the mirror.

She had tried her best to avoid gazing into the reflection since she returned.

Once, her likeliness had terrified her in the dark, black eyes and dark hair, shocking her into thinking a demon mirrored her existence. Now, her recognizable features taunted her in the light – blue eyes and ice blonde hair – yet no life radiated from her soul anymore.

Liv had hollowed cheeks and tired eyes, scrapes and bruises discoloring her usually glowing, golden skin to a dull complexion. She looked better than before, but she still didn't look like herself. Perhaps she never would.

She sighed, focusing instead on the task at hand. Liv turned the hot water faucet so the bath soon steamed with warm water and observed the jar Rhys had left for her soak in – she unscrewed the top and tipped the bottle upside down to release the medical salt. And as the Medicine Elite had advised, only a fraction of the jar released into the tub.

Liv sighed, placing the jar on the counter and moving back to focus on her body. She gently removed her gray turtleneck and slid down her black, silk trousers, exposing her bare body. As planned, Liv grabbed her Polaroid and snapped photos of her bandaged limbs to help guide Piper and herself with the color-coordination later.

Liv observed her chest and arms, the white scarred tissue a sad existence beneath the layers of gold band-aids and bandages. Tristan would cringe to see her capturing his desecrated art in this ruined circumstance.

To add some life to her pale skin, she flashed some flames within to warm up her naked body in the cold space but to also give some integrity to the tattoo as it was intentionally imagined to be.

Behind her, Liv noticed a flicker against the back wall.

She remembered her tattoos on her chest and arms… but had forgotten the one she commissioned for her backside.

Intrigued, Liv shut off the bathroom lights, illuminating her back tattoo against the wall so she could see it clearly.

A stag. A mountain. And a constellation.

Liv's eyes grew wide, she had unknowingly drawn the same artwork over the course of weeks in her Security & Warfare class.

The stars sparkled against the wall and a whisper echoed in her mind.

Ollie…

Liv dropped the camera. Like the processing of her memory, it moved slowly down through the air, until it crashed against the tile upon impact.

She couldn't get the image out of her head. In the sky, in her notebook, in her mind, in her world. It was as if the memory was crawling back to her, fighting against every roadblock and pounding against any barriers to break through every dark hole and find the light.

She remembered.

Liv grabbed her sweater, throwing it atop her head as she jumped out of the bathroom, slamming the door open while trying to simultaneously get her legs through the silk pant holes.

"What the Hades, Liv?!" Piper stood up and squeaked.

"I have to find Hayden." Liv explained, running to her armoire for shoes.

"He's not here." Piper explained, curling around the couch to meet her friend head on. "And you have to soak!" She eyed the bathroom, relieved to find the tub still full of steaming water.

"I can soak later." Liv combatted, summoning her wings.

"No you cannot!" Piper yelled.

Liv finally stopped, one shoe on her foot, the other in her hand. Mostly in shock from hearing Piper's commanding voice. Zeus, it was intimidating.

"Twenty minutes." Piper counseled, lowering her voice. "I only need twenty minutes. Then you can go get yourself kidnapped in the middle of the night, but I will have a guilt-free conscience because your bloody bandages will be cleaned and reset."

Liv gulped, still in shock from the outburst.

"Bathroom. Now." Piper commanded.

Liv slowly sauntered back into the small room, unsure of what the Hades had just transpired. She turned back to her friend from the doorway, hoping she may have changed her mind.

"Twenty minutes." Piper repeated, arms crossed.

"Twenty minutes." Liv agreed, stepping backward through the threshold.

And without touching the door, Piper had slammed it shut on Liv's behalf.

The peaceful soak was anything but that. It stung. Liv felt anxious. The time moved too slowly. When she had finally counted to 300, Liv burst from the water, relieved for that paused torment to conclude.

She grabbed her towel and raced to the couch, bringing the now developed photographs to Piper's attention.

Liv counted to 300 again, trying to make the time go by quicker as her friend diligently studied the photos, her notes and then the peculiar bruise or stitched cut for the right course of action.

Her leg was tapping; Piper gently held it down for a moment.

"If you try to hold still, I may be able to work faster." Piper commented softly, her nose an inch away from Liv's scraped arm as she wrapped boiled silver gauze around it. "After I complete your arms, you can help apply the directed blue topical and purple's prep to your legs while I continue on your back."

"I love your thinking. But disclaimer, there is no way I will be able to burn myself when we get to the red phases." Liv shuddered at the thought.

Piper placed her hand on Liv's thigh again to stop it from bouncing, she glared at Liv before continuing on.

"I'll handle the burning red. Can you at least give yourself the gold shots?" Piper finally asked, handing Liv a needle filled with the necessary antibiotic.

"Sure." Liv winced as Piper set a flame to her forearm. She found the bruise a little higher above and stuck in the needle accordingly.

That stopped her involuntary leg tapping immediately.

Quickly, painfully and anxiously, but fortunately without ripping out one another's throats, Piper and Liv successfully reset all of Liv's bandages and administered her topical and internal medications. With a final approving nod from Piper releasing Liv from her nurse's restraints, Liv sprinted to her armoire and pulled out a clean, chunky, dark grey turtleneck sweater, cursing at every shot that furiously protested her arms lifting above heart level.

She fought against the pain. Her heart was racing.

Liv grabbed a soft plaid flannel skirt that draped like a kilt in the front, unsure her legs would succumb to jeans, and finished the look by grabbing knee-high cashmere socks to peak out above her lace-up combat boots.

Liv was ready for him, but how would he react after what she had put him through?

For a brief moment, she considered throwing her need away and crawling deep into the protection of her heavy comforter to ease her aching body, until she was reminded of the night sky with the stars twinkling loud for her to hear. And although Liv was tired, weak and exhausted, she marched over to her makeshift rooftop balcony, a spike of adrenaline pulsing through her veins as she hopped onto her desk and out through the window, looking up into the night sky, at her constellation, *Ollie*, and deliberately, *desperately*, summoned Hayden, wherever he may be, and pleaded with the gods that he may come.

She could feel him. Liv could finally feel something through their bond. The summoning raced down the chord, pulsating life back into the connection. It struck the other end, revitalizing it to a new energetic source.

She finally felt complete.

He was coming, unintentionally signaling to her that he would land in the courtyard. Instead of entering through his usual route, Hayden's weariness of Liv's current condition informed her that he would take the more formal path.

Had she driven him *that* far away that casualties were no longer an option?

After hours of endless anticipation and mind stirring anxiety, Liv felt him approaching the security border of Puerdios. He was near, and she couldn't wait any longer. Impulsively, she leapt from the rooftop back through the room, sprinting across it to the door.

She heard Piper faintly in the background, but Liv's only focus was on the bond, guiding her to magnetize toward his arrival, to him. She ran down the hallway, feeling free for the first time in weeks.

And even combatting the strain her fatigued muscles endured with every step, the pulsing of her veins screaming against their willpower, she no longer felt caged or weak.

She had been liberated.

Liv swung the castle's formidable stone doors open to the courtyard and spotted him immediately in the sky, near the tree line, descending.

Her heart was anxiously beating louder than ever.

A huge smile broke onto her face at the sight. She jumped down the stairs and ignored the pain throbbing through her body as she continued, desperately, rushing toward her reconciliation target.

As soon as his foot hit the ground, Liv jumped into his arms, clinging onto him for dear life, her lifeline.

"I'm so sorry Hayden." Liv cried against his shoulder. "I remember it all. I remember you. I remember us." She pulled back, grabbing his face, and looked into his eyes – his kind, glacier eyes – and sniffled with joy before whispering, "I love you."

"I love you, too." Hayden smiled, pulling her back into an embrace.

Liv froze. His voice triggered something unexpected, something angry from within. She *hated* him.

Liv pushed Hayden away, forcibly creating distance between the two before she realized what she had done.

Her jaw fell open. Liv stared blankly in horror at her target, before she came crashing to the ground.

"I-I'm… sorry…" She cried, dropping her head into her hands.

What had just happened?

Panicking, trembling, Liv prayed she didn't set off an angry flame.

She couldn't have Hayden turn into Kronos. Not now.

He kept his distance and remained silenced, the scariest reaction of them all.

Was this her curse? To create new ways to torture her loved one, and inevitably herself, forever? She had remembered. Wasn't that enough?

After a minute of silence, or trying to process her thoughts, Liv finally gathered the courage to look up at him, and with tears streaming from her eyes, finally whispered. "You sound just like him."

"But you remember?" Hayden clarified, hopeful.

"Everything." Liv sighed, brushing her hand through her thick blonde locks. She wanted to smile and she wanted to frown. "I think my subconscious has been piecing it together over the past weeks." She took a deep breath, before staring at the ground, "I started staring at Ollie, and as that constellation holds our history, I felt comforted." Liv furrowed her brows, attempting to piece together parts of her memory that had resurfaced, the old with the new. "I didn't realize the constellation was a piece of me, tattooed on my back, until I removed my bandages and cleaned my body this evening. I dared to ignite my power so I could see it refleced on the wall and… something sparked. The blurry images became clear, the chaotic map turned into a simple path, and all of the images and memories finally connected together." She looked back up to Hayden, a smile slowly forming on her ever-tormented mind, "It brought me back to you, and a part of me came back to life."

She started seeing spots. Liv swayed, trying to combat her body's trembling into exhaustion.

"Then, that's enough, for now." Hayden nodded.

Liv tried to ignore the worry in his eyes. He could tell she was dizzy, that the run and activity exhausted her. But he could only do so much when she recoiled at his touch.

"I'll walk you back to you room, make sure you get back safely." He declared, putting both hands deliberately in his pockets as he waited patiently for her to make the first move.

Liv turned back toward the pavilion but cautiously tipped her head back to watch Hayden trail behind her.

It was the strangest mix of comfort and fear.

Of desire and hate.

Of history and the unknown.

When they finally returned to her loft, they both paused, each standing on the respective ends of the door between.

Liv smiled shyly, finally reaching for the door.

"Goodnight, Ollie." Hayden beckoned, taking a step back from the residence's entrance.

"Stay." Liv whispered, hesitantly.

She looked up at Hayden, eyes wide. Her mouth had instinctively spoken quicker than her brain could process.

Not that her brain was angry about it.

HAYDEN

She spoke so quietly; he thought he had imagined the request.

But that was exactly it, she wasn't confident around him. She didn't trust him.

If he obliged her needs, would he destroy her recovery?

He looked up at Liv, making sure he had heard her correctly. Bright glacier eyes met his gaze, demanding a response.

"I don't think it's a good idea," Hayden contemplated aloud. "You're still healing."

Mentally and physically.

He hoped his tone still reiterated just how much he cared for her. That if she truly wanted him, he would drop at her knees.

"Please." She asked softly, biting her lip as she opened the door wide, motioning him to enter.

And even though he followed her request, walking through the threshold and into her loft, he still reiterated his worry.

"I don't want to overwhelm you, Ollie."

"You won't." She nodded stubbornly, gulping as she sat down on the edge of the purple velvet couch. "Or, at least no more than you already do."

Hayden chuckled, following suit as he sat across from her on the opposite end.

Liv smiled; clearly glad her dry comment was taken into appreciation instead of disdain. She turned to the fireplace, igniting it with a flick of her fingers.

A comforting silence took over as they both watched the fire spark to life.

"Yesterday, I was terrified of you. Today, it feels strange to have this weird space between us. Yet, I'm still weary of closing the distance."

Hayden turned his gaze from the bright fire to the illuminated face of his soul mate.

"That's okay, Ollie." Hayden assured her, "I feel that same way."

Progress. Today was progress. Focus on that.

"Is it?" She challenged with a cry. "I'm damaged, Hayden. What if we can't get back to us? What happens to our souls?" Liv looked worried, so fragile.

Hayden lifted his finger in the air for a moment, simultaneously summoning two glasses of whiskey. He placed one in front of Liv on the table and grabbed the second in his hand.

Liv breathed in agreement, smirking appreciatively as she grabbed her own dram, taking a sip almost instantly.

Hayden had to catch his breath at the sight. Her hair glowed against the sparkling fire. Her skin looked soft and kissable, her collarbones accentuated with the shadows of the dim lighting – she was absolutely stunning.

"A soul can repair, regenerate, if one rejects the connection." Hayden took a sip of his own cocktail, turning his gaze back to the intoxicating fire in an effort to avoid staring at the vixen who controlled his heart. "It's possible to survive, although, painful. You have to find something else big enough, worthwhile to fight for, so you can get through it."

"Like, the responsibility of ruling a kingdom." Liv retorted, sadly. "The moment Tristan kissed me was when you finally let the connection start diluting itself away."

"I thought it was what you wanted." Hayden's jaw tensed, not ready to ask what needed to be addressed. Hesitantly, he added, "Is that what you want now?"

"No." Liv immediately replied, to Hayden's surprise.

He stood up, noticing her automatic flinch at the quick movement. He needed to remember to move slowly, more calmly around her... until she felt comfortable again. He paused, waiting for her to make the next move.

Liv sighed, almost in annoyance at her new developed reaction. She gripped her glass between her hands, as if channeling all of her energy into the pressure point of holding the object between opposing forces.

"The connection is the only thing that makes me feel, like me. Like I can get through this." Liv admitted with a shrug.

She didn't motion for Hayden to proceed forward, so he remained still.

"When I was in the cell, the bond was the only comfort that gave me strength, reminded me that I had something, *someone*, worth fighting for." Liv weakly admitted with sorrow and clenched her jaw, "The fact that it's tarnished now, destroys me."

It took everything Hayden had to not run toward her, embrace her and whisper reassuring sentiments in her adorable ear.

Liv stood up, facing him head on.

She looked taller than she had in a while, all five feet and eight inches holding its own against his six-foot-three frame.

"I know I'm messed up, and I'm not acting like your other half, but you, and that connection, are *my other half*. Mine. The one I want to find again. That's the something I want to fight for." Liv slowly shook her head, whispering with a chill, "My only link to *me*."

She looked up to her other half, pleading. "I need you Hayden. Even if I can't show it right now." She bowed her head low, in disgrace. "I'm always asking the world of you and never giving anything in return. I'm sorry. I'm like, the shittiest soul mate ever."

There was no such thing.

Hayden smirked, remembering when he once felt the same way.

"I was once the shitty soul mate." Hayden nodded in reassurance, relieved.

She still wanted him.

"I guess we deserve eachother then." Liv huffed, and then shook her head before looking out to the window, almost speaking to herself as she murmured. "No, it's not enough –f you deserve better than this. I'm not enough for you, Hayden."

Now, Hayden was panicking. Although he refused to let it show on his exterior.

"Never think that, Liv. Never think that you are less than my entire universe, because you're more. You're my everything, my soul. And I love you, Ollie. I will always love you."

She sighed weakly, trembling, but managed to smile sadly.

It broke his heart.

"You need rest, Ollie." Hayden finally determined. "With peace. Not constantly wondering where I am in the room or what my next move will be."

Liv began to protest, but Hayden took one step forward and she flinched, losing her balance, and collided into the couch. To Hayden's dark humor, he appreciated Liv's immediate attempt to dignify the maneuver with a slick recovery out of stubbornness. But even Liv knew she had proven Hayden's point with impeccable timing.

"I'll come back tomorrow." Hayden promised, "If you'll allow me?"

"Yes." Liv breathed, curling her feet behind her to find a 'relaxed'-looking position on the couch. But her eyes told a different, pleading story when they locked with Hayden's.

"You gave me all that I needed for today, Ollie." He assured her.

If only he could walk over and hug the soul that he shared with his own.

"I wish we weren't leaving on such strange terms." Liv admitted, clearly conflicted with her past memories and present instincts.

"If we didn't have strange every once in a while, then things would get boring." Hayden retorted with a devious grin. "You don't have to worry, Ollie. We can pick up the strange again tomorrow. To be continued."

Liv smiled, the first genuine, innocent smile he had seen since her memory's return.

"To be continued, Hayden."

"Well, you certainly look like fresh shit, your highness."

Hayden groaned.

It couldn't be morning. Not already.

He had spent the entire night wishing the sun would return and now that it had, he dreaded facing the day head on.

He squinted an eye open, finding Peyton dazzling in a casual grey jumpsuit and holding out a cup of coffee.

"Thanks." Hayden mumbled, taking the caffeinated gift graciously and sinking further onto the stone foor.

"Please don't rate 'Hotel Puerdios University' poorly based on your stay tonight, because sir – we *do* have beds…" Peyton mocked, holding out her hand to help Hayden stand.

Everything ached.

Hayden wanted to retort back with a dry comment, but alas, he was too fatigued to care.

Taking a sip of his caffeinated savior in one hand, Hayden massaged his neck with the other, cracking the kinks and knots his body had accumulated from his unofficial overnight stay outside of Liv's loft.

Using marble as a bedrest and stone as a mattress was not one of his smartest ideas.

Hayden sighed, eyeing his makeshift accommodation for the night with disdain. And although he had anything but a peaceful night's rest, Hayden felt confident Liv finally had a peaceful, calm slumber.

"Here." Peyton pushed a coffee tray filled with another cup – an Americano, Hayden presumed – and a chocolate croissant and blueberry muffin, paired with a condescending look that screamed, 'you-look-like-shit-how-on-earth-are-you-going-to-win-her-heart-living-like-a-homeless-man,' before turning away.

"Thanks, Peyton." Hayden hollered, "But to clarify, I *was* originally planning to shower before I brought her coffee!"

Peyton waved him off by flipping him the bird, already turning the corner back toward her own apartment.

Hayden set down the coffee tray, flying to his apartment in a flash to shower and change clothes, before returning only moments later to the outside of Liv's loft.

Still exhausted, Hayden felt relatively like a new man. Or at least a clean one. Rejuvenated, like life once again pulsed through his immortal veins. His white hoodie felt soft, fresh against his buttermilk skin. His olive bomber jacket felt crisper. When he breathed, it finally felt like the oxygen was turning into CO_2 and nourishing his body more than the past months worth of nutrition could provide.

Ollie remembered him. She remembered *them*.

He picked up the coffee tray and with a final breath, knocked on the door.

Hayden could already imagine Liv a sleeping monster, squinting at the sunlight and moaning at the unexpected alarm from her door. Hopefully the

Americano would appease his promptness, as he imagined Liv turning over into another pillow to ignore the morning responsibility of the day to come. *Be patient.* He reminded himself, holding his hand from gently tapping the door again.

In his mind, he saw a zombie-esq teenager stomping slowly across the apartment, quickly taking a mop of long blonde hair out of her eyes and tossing it into a messy bun atop her head. Sight still unavailable as she combatted the morning rays with her stubborn desire to keep her eyes closed.

But as she neared the kitchen, Liv would finally smell the fresh brewed coffee seeping through the doorway from the other side. Her eyes would spark open and she would finally unlatch the door.

On queue, the handle's knob turned, and the large stone door swung open. Messy bun atop her head, Liv's eyes opened wide in surprise at who stood before her.

"Hi!" She beamed, before looking down at her attire. Flannel pajamas and a grey v-neck cotton tee. Her cheeks colored, "Er, sorry… I didn't know… I wasn't… expecting you…"

Hayden waited, remembering the way she flinched the night before, so stood paused in front of the doorway as to not intrude or bombard the sleeping beauty.

Liv bit her lip, looking back up as she awkwardly pulled a piece of hair from her face and tucked it behind her ear. When she caught his eyes again, Liv smiled.

Full of joy, life and happiness.

"Americano?" Hayden held out the coffee designated for her.

Her eyes lit up. "You speak my language."

"I've learned caffeine is a universal one." He smirked, handing her the cup.

Their fingers touched briefly. It sent sparks down his arm.

Liv's too, as he noticed she swiftly grabbed her elbow of the arm holding her coffee and tried to cover it up by taking a sip from the cup.

Don't pressure her. He reminded himself.

Of course he wanted more. More time, more of her, more of her faint giggle that briefly emerged when she was amused. But he knew this would be a slow progression and he was willing to wait.

"I should go." He offered, beginning to turn before remembering the breakfast pastries. "Oh, I forgot – here's a muffin and croissant for you."

Liv hesitantly grabbed the two pastry bags, looking into her apartment before biting her lip and turning back to him.

"Do you want to come in?" She offered shyly. "I mean, you did bring breakfast…"

"Technically, Peyton brought breakfast." Hayden clarified with a grin, "But sure. If that's okay with you?"

"I already asked you, didn't I?" Liv smirked, nodding him into her loft.

She headed straight for the kitchen, grabbing plates to put the blueberry muffin and chocolate croissant on, cutting both in halves so they could split the two options. Hayden sat down on the couch closest to the door, letting Liv decide exactly how close she would want to be in proximity to him.

"Good news, I still seem to have a caffeine and chocolate addiction." Liv smiled bleakly in appreciation, handing Hayden a plate before sitting perpendicular to him and taking a bite of the croissant.

Closer than he would have anticipated.

He took a sip of his coffee, gulping the hot beverage down immediately.

Hayden smiled, wanting so badly to tuck away the loose strand of hair behind her ear, but held back, knowing unexpected contact would not go over well.

Yet, even in her pajamas and fresh out of bed, Liv still managed to glow with natural beauty.

Stop thinking about that. Hayden shut his brain down, going for the blueberry muffin instead.

Blueberry muffins were neutral, with zero sex appeal.

Focus on that, you idiot.

Liv finally set the coffee cup down.

"Hayden, I've been thinking."

Oh god, Hayden tensed up. She can't do this.

"The Dark Gods want to break this connection between us. That means they're scared of it. It means that together, we may actually be able to beat them and their armies." Liv looked up, determined and strong as she stared into Hayden's eyes, longingly, almost as if she had no fear of him once again. She clenched her teeth with resolve, "I won't let them win."

The look she gave him broke all restraints.

She was still in there.

Relief overtook him. Hayden instinctively kissed Liv in reassurance, a natural reaction before thinking, but found air where her head was supposed to be. He opened his eyes, to find Liv curled up on her side, head hidden beneath two arms, shaking.

"Zeus, Ollie, I'm sorry! What was I thinking?" Hayden spun, grabbing his hair at his stupidity, trying to keep the fire within him from raging for her sake.

Liv trembled, still curled up in a ball.

"It's okay." Her voice quivered.

The sight broke him. She must have *hated* him. He didn't think for a second and look how much he hurt her, when all he wanted to ever do was bring her happiness.

"No. It's not." He scolded to himself. "You can't stand to be touched, and without thinking I just..." His voice cracked in pain. "God, I'm sorry, Ollie. That was a mistake."

If only he could be the reason of her joy and not the source of her pain.

Finally, fighting every bone in his body, Hayden concluded, "Maybe I shouldn't be near you, for now."

Watching her tremble, curled like a scared child lost in the dead of night, would be his undoing.

What did *he* do to her? To *them*?

He was going to murder Kronos. And then use his ancestor's corpse to suffocate Arlo and send both unworthy deities to the Underworld for a punishment crueler than Pandora's.

"No."

Once again, Liv fought back with an unexpected response, making Hayden turn questioningly to the source of the voice he had heard.

Arctic blue eyes challenged him from the ground.

"I know you slept outside my door, and it's comforting." Liv explained, her voice growing less stern as she continued on. "It helped me get through the night. I didn't have nightmares – it was the first night I didn't have nightmares. So, I think I need you here."

She paused again, before clarifying, "I *want* you here."

Hayden eyed her curiously, but sat back down on the couch.

Giving her an inch, to let her know he would stay for as long as she asked.

Liv nodded, looking down at her hands shyly.

"I can stay and sleep outside your apartment for as long as you want me to." Hayden confirmed, not in mockery, but in assessment. For her, anything she needed.

"No, I don't want that either." Liv sighed, uncurling herself, forcefully. She took a sip of her hot beverage, clearly using the focus of coffee to help with the movements of sitting up.

It was a universal language, afterall. And spoke comforting words when sipped.

Hayden drank his own beverage as well, summoning courage to continue.

"You flinch when I approach you." Hayden countered, after gulping his coffee.

Liv froze at the accusation, closing her eyes in concentration before opening them again and facing him head on.

"Let me try approaching you, instead." Liv suggested, so sternly holding her cup, the container itself was fit to burst.

She walked over to the kitchen, slowly setting down her coffee, her binky, onto the kitchen counter, with a final conclusive nod.

Liv turned around, stepping into the light that now infiltrated her loft from the sunrise's glorious rays, revealing contrasting bruises that accentuated the bandges and scrapes angrily lashed across her skin.

He couldn't even *imagine* what her back might look like, what pain she must have been enduring.

Hell wrath fury on Kronos and Arlo, when Hayden got the chance to avenge his soul mate…

"God, Liv." Hayden took a step forward, reaching out to her.

"Don't." Liv commanded, stopping Hayden instantaneously. "I need to be in control and I promise, it's not as bad as it looks." Liv added bleakly.

Not as bad on the outside compared to the inside, Hayden thought sadly. He respected her for being able to go on this long, battling demons he could only imagine from within.

"I carried you here that night. I have a pretty vivid and accurate assessment in my mind." Hayden retorted, but remained still.

It had been weeks, and she still had bandages.

He would ask Rhys to check on her again today, even if the Medicine Elite had set Piper on a healing regime.

Liv just shrugged. Then took a step forward, looking up at Hayden.

"Just focus on the connection, Ollie." Hayden encouraged.

Liv nodded, taking another step. After what felt like forever, but only two more steps, Liv was standing directly in front of Hayden. Her eyes filled with rage, flashing red as she contemplated murdering the king once again.

He hadn't realized just *how* bad it had been for her. His heart was beating. Hayden was sure it would leap out of his chest.

… If Liv didn't stab it with a knife herself.

FIFTEEN

LIV

"Kronos had different eyes than you. His were icy – a cruel emerald that cut to your core. Your eyes are…you. Or at least, the eyes that I love." Liv looked down at his hand, feeling the unconditional devotion penetrating through their bond, calling to her to gently touch it.

She stared at the first step, yearning to make contact, but unsure she could handle it. Liv fought against the instinct to hurt him, instead focusing on his eyes – what made Hayden, *hers* – until finally desire overtook reason and she succumbed to the temptation and softly grabbed his hand.

Her first cognizant contact since capture.

"Ollie."

Liv reactively tensed at the name.

Hayden sounded so much like Kronos.

She shut her eyes, rewiring her thought process.

No.

Kronos sounded so much like *Hayden.*

Focus on the bond, Liv. She reminded herself. *Focus on Hayden.*

Taking a breath, Liv turned her head upward, to gaze into the eyes she adored so much.

Concern. Love. Hope.

Bright with optimism as blue and clear as the sky above from a morning awaiting possibility.

Instinctively, Liv stood on her toes, moving closer to the enchanting gaze, before becoming eye level with his lips. The action had never felt more right.

She had never felt more right.

Liv sensed Hayden's smile, his heat radiating off of his body.

He was being *so* patient with her. Liv appreciated how Hayden hadn't moved his other arm, or his body, but remained a stone to let her lead the way. A true soul mate, anticipating her every move.

And although trembling, Liv pushed forward, her lips finally pressing against his as she grabbed his neck and pulled him closer.

Home.

For a moment they stood together, their lips uniting them as one. Liv explored the ecstacy, wanting more, craving him like a drug. All the while her body began to kick into place, pushing her mental comfort. So, she knew she needed to pull away, lest she allow her mind and body duke it out and wound her even further.

Lightheaded and dazed, Liv sighed dreamily and leaned against his chest.

Hayden still hadn't moved, but instead assured Liv by murmuring, "I'm right here."

Liv smiled, appreciating the calming heat on her cheek. Until the calming heat turned into a flaming fire.

He had finished his phrase with "Ollie" and an arm movement, a mistake.

Liv ripped her hand from his before he could register what he did to send such a trigger. Before he knew it, Hayden was shoved across the room and blasted against the wall.

Injured Liv may have been, but weak she was not.

In horror, Liv clasped her mouth.

"I'm so sorry!" She cried, sliding her body into a crouching position, hand clasped over her mouth. "I'm so sorry. I don't know what came over me..."

Hayden peeled himself back up, immediately switching to defense, but as soon as he saw the terror in Liv's eyes, he retracted. Instinct kicked in, and he understood what she needed.

"I should go." Hayden tersely stated, heading for the door.

"No! Please. No..." Liv begged, her voice choppy, desperate.

"What do you need, Liv?" Hayden pressed, "What do you need me to do? I'll do it. Just ask." He crashed to the ground, his voice cracking with agony.

He only heard her tears, each liquid drop chipping away his restraint.

"I hate him." Liv finally sneered, sniffling between words.

Hayden groaned with dread, turning to Liv with a revelation. "You need to be able to feel dominance over me. Is that it? To get back at Kronos? Am I the vessel?"

Liv shook her head, tears streaming down her face, feeling tortured by the request.

There had to be another way.

But she couldn't endure seeing him so heartbroken, after all of the pain she had made him suffer through for her own selfish recovery. She could never intentionally hurt him...

Yet, Hayden's mind was already made up.

He stood up, sneering. Gone was the kind, gentlehearted Pure God King and in return stood a vindictive, evil deity. Kronos reincarnated.

"Then do your worst, *Ollie*." Hayden emphasized her nickname with a hiss. "I'll take it. Just let that rage, that violent retribution out. I'm yours, a punching bag to hit, if it'll make you feel better, and maybe then your subconscious will remember that I would never hurt you. That I will never hurt you. No matter what you do to me."

Then suddenly, Hayden fell on his needs, arms spread out. Defenseless.

Back was the caring, gentle man she had fallen in love with and given her soul to.

And yet, Liv remained in shock.

Shocked at how she had just attacked him, why he would give himself to her in the cruelest way, and even still after that, what he would endure on her behalf, even without the assurance that it would guarantee her return to him.

Another trial at his expense to help her heal.

"Hayden, I-I don't want to hurt you." She ran over and fell to her knees in front of him, still crying. "I can't. I'm sorry. I can't…"

She was breathing rapidly, her heart was pounding.

"I give you permission. Let it out." Hayden assured her, words kind. "You're terrified of me. Show yourself you needn't be."

"No. Never." Liv cried.

And then, the connection blossomed, sparks flying once again as Liv launched herself into his embrace.

"Liv, you're shaking." Hayden started loosening his hold on her, but she only held on tighter.

"I can't let go, Hayden." Liv sobbed. "I won't let go."

HAYDEN

Hayden held her for a little while longer, softly stroking her hair as he whispered soothing sentiments into her ear, calming her down into a quiet slumber.

Finally, he carried Liv to the bed, gently resting her on her side; he started standing up to leave her, when he realized she still had a death grip on his neck. She wasn't letting go.

Hayden tried to unlock her hands from his neck, but instead found her hand had attached onto him as a new latch. Liv's eyes fluttered open at the movement and murmured with command, "Stay."

As much as he wanted to, he couldn't push her.

"I'll just be outside, you're safe."

"You look like an insomniac." She countered, her free hand shyly patting next to her on the bed.

Hayden chuckled. Between Liv and Peyton, he would never go unrested or unfed, or have his head swell.

He tried to go around the bed like a gentleman, but Liv's grip wouldn't budge.

"I see your stubbornness hasn't changed, either."

Liv rolled her eyes in response. Her lips ended with a slight curve upward, making Hayden's soul explode with joy.

"Is it okay if I crawl over you?" He asked, shyly.

Liv nodded, with a grin. "If you need to take a break on top of me, that's okay too."

"Someone's greedy." Hayden retorted, maneuvering himself carefully over Liv after she let go of his neck.

She was trying act calm, but he could feel her anxiety boiling underneath her skin.

He noticed Liv tensed, but her subtle smile remained, even if strained, so he considered it a win. He slid to the other side of the bed and she followed, rolling herself to face him and scooting her body to lay beside his, hands wrapped on his arm and head placed perfectly atop his shoulder. She was still shaking, but quiet. He had to commend her stubbornness; it might be the very thing that won this cursed battle between her mind and heart.

"I am all powerful, Liv – and yet, you're in pain and there is *nothing* I can do about it." Hayden stated.

"Just do exactly what you're doing. Exactly this." Liv sighed, shutting her eyes slowly while pacing her breath into a soft rhythm.

And for the first time since Liv's capture months ago, Hayden felt at peace. Liv's breath tickled his neck, her hands gently calmed his body, and so his eyes finally grew heavy in the cozy bed. They were going to be all right.

Finally, he dozed off next to the one he loved. A sweet dream he looked forward waking up to.

LIV

Liv stirred, smiling in a daze before she froze, quickly opened her eyes and shot out of bed.

Hayden reacted immediately and followed suit, now standing across from her, the bed's fortress between their two bodies.

"What's wrong?" He asked, sword out and already ready for combat.

Unbeknowest to Hayden, he mimicked Liv's defensive position, as she partook in her morning ritual of waking up terrified before assessing where she was and confirming she was safe.

"Sorry." Liv shook her head, "Habit."

Hayden tilted his head, observing her body language as it shifted from resistance to comfort. Finally, he chuckled in disbelief, nodding to the bed as he tucked away his weapon.

"You were so peaceful moments ago."

Liv blushed. She wasn't used to sharing a bed with a male, especially one so drop-dead gorgeous, even if only for a moment before rolling out of bed, literally. The memories of mornings woken beside his side seemed like a distant life, one she hadn't lived in for quite some time. A strange blend of her knowledge of their history mixed with the recent shyness and insecurity of being with the king of late. Liv knew him, but was still nervous and unsure.

"I hope I didn't keep you up." Liv gauged Hayden's sleepless eyes and retracted, admitting with a mumble, "Piper says I make noises."

The sun hit his creamy skin, it dazzled in the sublime light.

"I'd like to hug you." Hayden requested calmly.

Liv gulped, her body frozen, but she nodded in approval. She yearned for his touch, yet feared what it may do to her – in any and all circumstances. She knew he had her soul and he hers, but worried what would become of them if their bond could not be reforged.

But Liv knew she need not run away from her trepidation and wanted to face it head on. It had taken her too long to become his equal, she did not want to mark today as the day she became his lesser half.

So as Hayden took a step toward Liv, she matched his step equivalently.

She was trembling. Frightened with anticipation of each step as they pulled their strengthening magnetic force into one. But she would not give up on them.

Not knowing how she could calmly seek refuge in his arms terrified her most, but she knew one thing – Hayden was her world, her galaxy, her beginning, middle and end, and everything in between. And together, they could conquer it all.

Finally, and not soon enough, her arms finally encircled around his steel core, trim and no longer with a hint of a youthful softness, because Hayden was no longer a boy. He was a man, he was the king, and he was her soul mate.

His strong arms gently encapsulated her tiny body, managing to avoid all of her cuts and bruises that stung her back and shoulders.

She hoped he wouldn't feel her shaking, but deep down Liv knew Hayden could see through her body, heart, mind and soul. She dug her cheek further against his broad chest, reveling in the heated muscle that provided comfort and fit to her cheek like a glove.

"The moment you say stop Ollie, I'll retract." Hayden whispered, sending chills down Liv's spine. "I need you to know that I would never hurt you. Anytime you say stop, or even think it, I'll respect the request and move away."

Liv heard his meaning, she understood where his heart stood – Liv consciously knew Hayden would *never* hurt her intentionally. Yet, the thoughts wandering through her mind scared her more than the knowledge of what he wouldn't do. Because she knew what he *could* do, and it sent fireworks through her body, whether she was prepared for the explosive show or not.

Slowly turning her head upward, she breathed, "I don't want you to stop."

Hayden's dazzling arctic eyes peered down, latching onto hers with intrigue.

Liv's heart was pounding, her breath growing shorter by each impure thought that clipped through her mind. Her desire growing ravenous by his touch.

She slowly unlocked her arms around his core, gliding them softly along his chiseled arms and trailing the curves of his muscles until she reached his neck.

Liv bit her lip, looking up to Hayden once more before standing on her tip toes and lifting her mouth to his.

Her hands continued their journey, grabbing onto his jacket lapel and pulling him closer once again, before shedding the bomber off of his body. Their lips didn't leave another, acting as the lifeline to the bond that so weakly connected them.

Liv tossed the jacket onto the purple velvet couch, ravenously debating for a split second if she wanted to take him on it, or have him take her, before returning to her bait.

She began lifting his white hoodie above his torso, revealing the trim six-pack she had slept against throughout the morning. That she had imagined in her darkened sleep for weeks, causing her to drool on her pillow then and figuratively, even more now.

"Liv, are you sure you want to do this?" Hayden breathed between kisses, stroking the back of her neck gently.

"Don't stop." She whispered, too distracted by his sexy physique to seek reason.

Hayden began kissing her neck, his soft stubble of a five o' clock shadow tickling her neck and sending her *all the feels* down her body. She no longer trembled, she *craved.*

Quickly unbuckling his pants, Liv moaned, relishing in the rough mixed with the delicate – the soft touch of his lips with the hoarse stubble on his jaw – as he continued working pure magic on her neck before moving down to her chest.

He paused only for a moment to rip off the sweatshirt over his head and let Liv revel in the sight before her.

The months had not been kind to Hayden, Liv knew that, and yet he looked more glorious than she had ever seen him. No longer a cute teenager, the changes had turned him into a ruggedly handsome man. Hayden had grown out of his innocent demeanor and into a reckoning force.

His shoulders were broader, his arms more muscular, his abdomen toned.

Yet, the light still radiated off his golden skin. He was still marvelously and in all his glory, her Hayden.

Liv blushed, finally realizing just how far her mindless desire had led them both. She eyed her plaid flannel pajama bottoms on the floor and quickly crossed her bruised arms to cover her bandaged skin.

How could such a beautiful specimen find her remains of a body attractive?

"Ollie," Hayden whispered, reaching out to her slowly as he immediately caught on to her shift in demeanor.

Liv looked hesitantly up to his intoxicating charm, awkwardly chuckling at her shyness. This was Hayden, her best friend of eight years. Her soul mate. Her eternal partner.

"Do you honestly want me?" She retorted. "Bruised and battered? Like this?" With a deathly, introspective whisper and her eyes dark and distant, she concluded, "I'm ruined."

His hand reached her cheek; she leaned into the touch, into the warmth.

Her entire body began to naturally gravitate toward his once more. Like it once had, like she wanted it to.

"Ollie, I want you in any way I can have you." Hayden murmured, his deep vibrations melting Liv's core into lust.

"Unwhole?" She whimpered, longing for more of his touch, but resisting the desire from her present self-consciousness.

But instead of recoiling, she grabbed his other hand, taking a step toward him, signaling to him that she was okay.

"Have you not realized?" Hayden asked with a smile, before stating, "We are only whole, together."

He gently tugged her hand, pulling her into him and passionately kissed her again. Giving her parts of him that she craved and absorbing what he needed that she could give.

Touching his bare skin sent evocative chills throughout her body. Hayden gently lifted her grey shirt, revealing her exposed chest, but she no longer cared. His gaze in itself healed her cuts, erasing them from Liv's mind and soothing the pain with every kiss.

"Awaken my soul, Hayden." She demanded.

Instantly, Hayden locked his lips with hers, lifting Liv simultaneously back onto the bed, and setting her tenderly onto the mattress and pillows before hovering over her.

Liv reached for Hayden as they kissed again, wiggling her lower half to help Hayden remove the remains of her lingerie.

She looked up into the blue eyes that only promised her prosperity, hope and adoration. How she could have ever found him to be her enemy was only a testament to the cruelty and dark powers Kronos possessed. And yet, they were finding the light, eventually returning to a world worth fighting for.

They would always find the light.

"I love you, Hayden." Liv whispered, holding his head in place with her hands.

She saw, she felt, the muscles in his chiseled face draw upward. The tortured wanderer returning to his beloved partner.

"I love you, too." He smiled, before planting her with another kiss.

Liv stretched her legs open, pressing against his body in between them. Demanding more of him, urging him to fully complete her.

"You sure?" He asked hesitantly, again.

She loved him for caring, but Zeus she hated him for making her beg.

Actually, she *loved* him for making her beg.

She smiled darkly, pinning him to the side and rolling on top of him.

"You want me anyway you'll have me." She teased.

He had been so gentle and considerate with her healing body, Liv knew they would get no where near the satisfaction she craved, the ecstacy she knew Hayden could deliver, if she let him remain in control.

She pressed against his body from the top, rubbing her breasts along his breathtaking chest, trailing her fingers down his abs before following with a trail of kisses.

Liv heard Hayden groan, so she bit his shoulder deviously before massaging the growing friction below. He was more than ready, craving her just as she craved him.

Guiding him, Liv cried with release as soon as he had fully entered her.

"Oh god…" Liv moaned, beginning to drive her body up and down.

Feeling him inside her set off unimaginable fireworks, full and explosive within her body, but his touch on her breast, her backside, her back, sent arousing vibrations to every muscle, sensory nerve and tissue deep into her soul. He ravished her, making her feel like the goddesss she was, worshipping her every curve.

He kept going, flipping her back below him, pounding against her until she started crying his name with pleasure. They were soaring above the clouds, climaxing to the peak before they both screamed each other's name in unison and crashed back down to earth, together.

"Holy shit." Liv panted, rolling onto Hayden with a grin that spread from ear to ear. She kissed his shoulder tenderly. "I've missed that."

Hayden extended his arm around her, pulling her into an embrace and kissing the top of her forehead.

"Holy shit is accurate." He murmured with a chuckle, before groaning, "Olivia Monaco, you're going to be the end of me."

"You're the one who said it was always going to be us in the end." Liv teased. "You basically set yourself up for this."

"Touché. Why do I always have to be so damn accurate?" Hayden grinned, his eyes still closed in bliss.

"Someone's gotta be worthy of the 'Holy Shits.'" Liv sighed playfully, shrugging against his body. "Might as well be the king."

Liv paused, realizing what she had just said aloud. She closed her eyes and laughed.

"Eloquent, as always, Ollie." Hayden retorted with a laugh. "Should that be our reign's mantra? 'Someone's gotta be worthy of the holy shits'..."

Before he could continue mocking her, Liv sat up and smacked his adorable, shitty face with a pillow. He tried to tickle her to combat the playful madness.

"High-pain-in-my-ass, King of the Holy Shits..." She hollered, barely able to say the nicknames aloud because she was laughing so hard.

Finally, he had his body wrapped around her, cocooning her with his naked skin.

"You realize that now it's the two of us. So that makes *you* an equal high-pain-in-my-ass, Queen of the Holy Shits, Ruler of Profanity and Majesty to Inmature Humor..."

Liv finally retorted with a laugh, "Well, so long as we're on the same maturity level, then."

When Hayden could no longer delay his inevitable departure to the Siren Court, he finally rolled out of bed. After a full morning of intimacy, Liv gathered it was 360° SS when she located the sun's orbit.

"The true question will be the response I get from Calithya after departing so suddenly and arriving so late to our scheduled meeting." Hayden pondered aloud, throwing on his white cotton hoodie, to Liv's disappointment.

She still hadn't secured a comfortable handle to their interactions, but it didn't mean she didn't like to *stare* at him from afar. A glorious physique like that deserved to be seen, praised, and magnificently fucked.

Liv shoved her mind out of the gutter, or else they'd *never* leave this apartment.

"Same curiosity I have regarding Rei and my no-show for training *and* his beloved class." Liv sighed, boiling water for her French press. "Want to trade places?"

"Calithya for Rei? In a heartbeat." Hayden retorted with a grin, sliding his olive jacket over his hoodie. "You want to reconsider that bargain?"

"For a moment, my blissful oblivion caused me to forget that your dreadful encounter has a spiteful vendetta against me, too." Liv rolled her eyes, laughing as she poured the scorching water into her metal contraption to begin brewing the coffee.

"Did your blissful oblivion also cause you to remiss that it's noon?" Hayden teased, eyeing the coffee.

"Force of habit. Who cares? It's brew o'clock somewhere. I can't have wine yet. Caffeine is a universal language." Liv rolled off as many responses that could be applicable to the redundant question, smirking her way through each retort. "Shall I go on?"

"And to think, all of that was *before* you drank the coffee." Hayden's eyebrows bounced up jokingly. "Perhaps after, you can do me a solid, by taking on both Rei and Calithya?"

Liv ignored Hayden, still smiling as she held up the French press. "Want some?"

"Obviously. Is that even a question?" Hayden grinned.

Liv rolled her eyes, but poured him a cup, obligingly.

"Oh, I thought you were offering up yourself?" Hayden asked smugly, before gratefully taking the mug Liv slid in his direction.

"Funny." Liv laughed, shimmying her body as she poured her own cup, but then sighed. When she joined Hayden at the counter, reality set in. "When will I see you next?"

She stared at his hand and then his knee, wanting to touch him, but unsure if she could command her body to make the first move. It almost felt *more* intimate of a maneuver to the lustful, wild reunion they had experienced in her bed only minutes before.

He's your soul mate. Just fucking touch him. She yelled in her mind.

Liv grabbed his knee.

It did not feel natural.

It certainly did not look natural.

Hayden turned to catch her eye questioningly, pure oceanic mist connecting with her own frozen glaciers.

She laughed shyly, loosening up her grip, thankful when Hayden joined her with amusement.

He gently grabbed her hand, squeezing it atop of his leg. He was so suave and she was such an idiot.

"I'll be back for the Elite Meeting, Thursday."

Four days.

Liv could survive four days.

She nodded.

"I'll try to come back sooner, please know that." Hayden reiterated, his gaze growing stern and full of concern.

"What if something happens and I forget again?" Liv asked quietly, looking at her hand entwined in his. She never wanted to let go of him again.

"I won't let you forget again." Hayden challenged with a sweet smile. "I'll never let you forget. Besides, it didn't work this time, did it?"

Liv sadly smiled, pressing her forehead against his shoulder and gently kissed it. "It didn't." She admitted, "But we lost time. And we have to rebuild what we lost…"

The bond. Their power.

Hayden gently lifted Liv's chin upward, locking eyes once again.

"We have lost nothing, as long as we are *both* here."

His eyes asked to kiss her, so Liv leaned toward their soft touch.

Fireworks sparked within her soul once again. She hoped Hayden felt the same way, too. And that one day, they could both feel the same, as one, again.

"I love you, Hayden." Liv reiterated, pulling away for a quick breath as her forehead rested against his. Saying goodbye would always be the hardest part, yet she longed and already looked forward to his sweet return.

"I know." Hayden replied, kissing her forehead. "I love you too, Ollie."

Four days. Liv reminded herself, willing her soul the courage and strength for the impending goodbye.

Hayden stood up, still holding her hand. He wrapped his arms around her from behind, enclosing her in one last embrace as he kissed her cheek playfully.

"So, will you play hooky for the remainder of the day?" Hayden asked inquisitively, still hugging her.

She didn't want to let him go.

"Honestly, I think I'll head to the library and try to help Piper with our international diplomacy research efforts." Liv stated blankly.

Suddenly, the Siren Court, with Hayden, didn't sound *half so bad*. Beautiful beaches, tropical weather, new culture to explore...

But again, anything was preferential when it involved Hayden.

"On that note, I can't wait to hear what you have to report by Thursday. For now, even the Buddhist lead is a great update. Don't push yourself too hard."

Hayden squeezed Liv one last time, before she turned and grabbed his face. Her palms pressed against his cheeks, and she challenged her comfort zone once again by bringing his lips to hers and pressing them against one another as if he was oxygen and she needed him to breathe.

"Well look who decided to grace us with her presence for Study Hall." Tristan drawled, sliding into a chair across from Liv and sporting an all-black suited look, paired with leopard printed Chelsea boots. Piper, Dylan, Zayne and Kyril followed, filing into chairs accordingly for their six-person table.

Liv rolled her eyes with a grin.

"You seem chipper?" Tristan observed curiously. "I'm sensing you're no longer channeling your child of darkness vibes?"

"Child of darkness vibes?" Liv laughed, swapping out her textbook for another ancient Egyptian history tome after inspecting her navy long-sleeved cropped shirt and mini skirt set. Sure, she was wearing thigh-high leather boots, but nothing yelled extreme gothic or pop princess. "What do you mean?"

"You're laughing a lot." Kyril chimed in. "And smiling. It's weird."

"Am I not allowed to smile?" Liv asked, shocked.

"I thought we discussed this," Dylan chimed in, tsking, "None of us are allowed to be happy. Ever."

"Clearly." Liv grinned, before turning to Piper and sliding a book toward her friend. "I think I have leads for Egypt."

"I'm all ears." Piper sighed gratefully, crossing her bare legs exposed by a shirt dress and layered with a navy sweater adorned with gems.

"The only Seven Wonders of the Ancient World that exist today are the Pyramids of Giza." Liv offered, flipping open a textbook that went into grave detail about the monumental tombs and relics of Egypt's Old Kingdom Era.

"To the mortal world." Piper clarified with a grin, subtly referencing to the Wonders their own kind had claimed over the past centuries.

"Okay, sure. But, they're over 4,600 years old and the whole complex is numerously noted as being shrouded in mystery." Liv pointed to a section, "And here they're recorded as being built to *endure* an eternity."

"That certainly would provide opportunity for immortal gods." Piper agreed, pulling the textbook closer to her to peruse. "May I?"

"My pleasure." Liv smiled, moving onto the next culture for identification: The Norse Gods.

She had hoped Rei would have proven more fruitful with his personal history among this group, yet Rei had not yet offered his insights or services yet. He was stubborn as shit, so Liv also knew that unless he came forward, it would be an entirely different battle to get him to agree to helping their committee.

Plotting ways to conspire against him with Hayden or Peyton, Liv opened the first historical text on Norway, surprised to find blank spots where text had clearly once resided.

"Piper?" Liv whispered, turning more pages to confirm her speculation.

Her friend pulled her nose out of the Egyptian textbook and refocused on Liv.

"These books, they're missing information?" Liv asked aloud, moving so that her friend could get a better look. "Have they been tampered with?"

Piper looked at the textbook, unconcerned. "They look fine to me?"

"Right here. It's entirely blank!" Liv pointed to an obvious spot.

Piper furrowed her brows, glancing back at Liv with a concerned expression. "I'm not sure what you're talking about. It says, right there, '*The God of Thunder and Lightning, Myrko, son of Odin and Fjörgyn, ruled the Norse Gods from Reine until the Ragnarök in 1384*'."

Liv bent over the invisible space, wishing she could visualize what Piper supposedly read.

"Piper, can you write out what this section says?" She asked eagerly, trying to remember what knowledge she had of Norse mythology.

"Sure." Piper replied questioningly, grabbing her ink quill and copying word for word what Liv could not see, pushing her notebook over for Liv to study, separately from the textbook.

The God of Thunder and Lightning, Myrko, son of Odin and Fjörgyn, ruled the Norse Gods from Reine until the Ragnarök in 1384. The final battle between the Aesir and Giants on Vigrid marked the end of Norse Gods and Goddesses.

"Piper, none of this is accurate." Liv focused in on her friend's written words. "First, Thor was the God of Thunder and Lighting."

Piper looked quizzically at her friend. "What do you mean? Could this be another example of mortal falsities compared to the deity records?"

Liv contemplated the reasoning but shook her head. Something didn't feel right about this book. She went to grab another textbook, finding the same blank patterns throughout the pages.

"Call it intuition, but with the previous corrections, I believe my knowledge as true, maybe because Thor and I share a powerful connection with the Elements. But I know that whatever you're able to see, I cannot. So, these records have been tampered with."

Liv grabbed a third book, proving her point once again.

"They ruled in Asgard, not from Reine..." Liv muttered, shaking her head. She turned to her research companion, "Piper, you cannot use any of these books for records. For whatever reason, where information is supposed to exist, nothing appears for me, but false information appears for you. That cannot be normal."

Piper cautiously grabbed a text, further examining it.

"You've never experienced something of the sort before?" She confirmed, lifting a page up in the air and inspecting it from the edge.

"Only with these books. The only commonality I can conclude is Norse-related documents."

Liv sighed, pressing her hand between her hands.

Well fuck.

In pursuit of moving forward, they had officially taken 1,000 steps back.

And even if her gut knew they were located in Asgard, her memory vaguely recalled the city existing in the sky – she believed it to be in another realm, at least somewhere inaccessible to the world they currently existed in.

"Thank Zeus. Child of Darkness has returned." Kyril spat.

Liv looked up, channeling her inner demons to thwart her obnoxious friend.

"I don't know about you all, but I'm ready for a dram." Tristan sighed, instantly neutralizing the tension between Heaven-and-Hell-rollercoaster Liv and dumbass Kyril who-chose-to-ignore-all-social-cues-for-the-benefit-of-his-own-devilish-amusement.

"Please." Dylan concurred, quickly throwing her scrolls into her spiked purse, and flipped the bag behind her red and navy leather mini-dress.

Liv gathered her useless Norse mythology records and summoned them back in place within Puerdios's expansive library. She'd combat that falsehood once she could prove she indeed, was not going insane.

Again.

"I'm in." Liv confirmed as she stood up, eyeing Kyril with a devilish smile. "So long as Kyril takes a shot of Fireball for being a dick."

Kyril threw on his embellished white coat over his lime green silk blouse, pausing mid-way to dramatize his consideration.

Zayne simply chuckled, always unfazed by his friend's theatrics. It was a wonder that someone as sincere, quiet and considerate as Zayne could put up with Kyril's constant need to push boundaries at every opportunity.

"Deal." Kyril grinned mischievously, winking at Liv before following Tristan out of the Great Hall, Dylan and Zayne not far behind.

"You coming?" Liv asked Piper, noticing her friend still had all of her Egypt textbooks scattered on the table.

"I should probably do more research…" Piper explained, quietly.

If Liv was the child of darkness, Piper was the princess of self-destruction.

"As your Pillar Elite, I command you attend this very important Elements meeting." Liv teased, hoping her request would encourage Piper to reconsider.

Piper stayed silent.

"Come on, we've already narrowed down Egypt and Thailand. We can't make any progress until I order Norse texts from anywhere but this tampered library, and there's no point in researching Celtic Mythology until we meet with Dylan's distant relative tomorrow night. You deserve a break, my loyal, selfless, beautiful and kind friend."

"You really think so?" Piper asked softly, "I feel like I deserve nothing."

Liv sat back down next to Piper, grabbing her hand and squeezing it, staring deeply in the pure crystal eyes that pierced her heart. "Piper, you deserve *everything*."

Piper's jaw dropped, as Liv expected. So, Liv used the shock to her advantage by slowly grouping the useful textbooks and summoning them back to Piper's apartment, before lifting her friend and wrapping her arm around her shoulder, guiding her to Tristan's apartment for some much-deserved downtime.

Too long had Liv been so focused on herself, she was unable to take care of her friends and give back what they had so selflessly invested in her these past weeks.

Between the hell she had returned from and Piper's continuous self-pressure, they both deserved a break. They both deserved it all.

So as Piper finally sighed in surrender, causing a strong wind to slam the door to the Grand Hall's close after their exit, Liv smiled, knowing that the well-deserved 'having it all' may just become an attainable goal someday.

Not just may, it *must*.

For both of them.

PIPER

How she allowed Liv to convince her to walk into the lion's den was beyond her. Sure, things with her and Tristan had been *fine*, but she had been strictly avoiding him outside any public obligations, and now all of that went to *shit* knowing she was about to be in close proximity to his bedroom.

Where he sleeps.

Deep breaths, Piper reminded herself, not wanting to be rude to her friends but also wishing she could have proceeded with her day as planned – studying for another hour, going home, opening a bottle of chardonnay, organizing thoughts on Liv's newest revelation for Egypt, working on her Advanced Meteorology assignment and then falling asleep – *not* dreaming about fire, or anything related to the element for that matter.

But now all that went to *shit*.

Following Liv down the hall, every step felt like another burden toward her impending doom. The caramel eyes, the smug grin. Piper hated what Tristan had done to her conscience in a matter of months. She should be focusing on her studies, not studying the Fire God.

Finally, they approached his apartment, standing once again outside a large, foreboding door, but instead of waiting patiently to enter, it swung open immediately, allowing the warm, inviting glow to burst into the Puerdios marble hallway, beckoning Piper to enter, tempting her, if she dare.

"Took you long enough." Tristan smirked, welcoming them inside instantaneously.

Piper tucked a mass of her midnight bob behind her ears, lifting her brows in rebellion to the comment as she ran indoors to speak with anyone else but him.

"Tonight, we determined margaritas were the happy hour specialty." Dylan explained, pouring a pale mint green mixture from a blender into festive glasses and handing them out accordingly.

"Well, we do say that tequila is like coffee for adults." Liv grinned, grabbing a glass and taking a sip immediately. She jokingly smacked her lips together at the tartness with a giggle. "Are you trying to get all of us on the floor with these? Damn."

Piper hesitantly tasted her beverage, expecting it to be essentially straight tequila, but was pleased to find a sufficient amount of lime juice and orange liqueur balanced the blended beverage.

She sat herself on a barstool next to Zayne, the only sane one in the group among these maniacs.

"Cheers to drinking on 1… we're officially alcoholics." He joked quietly, clinking his glass against Piper's.

"How have you kept up with these wild ones for so long?" Piper asked incredulously, watching Kyril take a shot of tequila and then chase it with his margarita.

"The key is adding water to your beverage when nobody's looking. Drink gets diluted and lasts longer without anyone noticing." Zayne grinned. "Your hangover will thank me tomorrow."

Piper appreciated the advice, noting to exit to the bathroom mid-way through her drink to dilute as Zayne advised.

"Why don't we play a drinking game?" Kyril asked, pulling Dylan to the couch area and waving everyone else to follow suit.

Piper slid off her barstool and magnetized to Zayne, ensuring she sat as far away from Tristan as possible. Where tequila was concerned, she doubted she would be able to keep her act together long enough if Tristan's presence and intoxicating scent of smoky embers and cinnamon loomed over her soon-to-become-foggy-mind. She already dreaded the possibilities.

"What game?" Zayne asked, sitting down next to Piper.

Mission accomplished.

Except caramel eyes locked directly across from her. It would be tough to miss his gaze with Liv sitting on the end of the couch next to him. He was centered just enough to catch eye contact between her best friend and Dylan and Kyril.

Zeus help her.

"Take Your Best Guess?" Kyril proposed.

"What's that?" Liv spat.

"Everyone writes questions, like '*Who do you think the most attractive person is in the group?*' me obviously, but then we pair with a direction, '*person on your right, left, two to the right,*' etc. And you have to guess the answer to the question for the according person. If you're right – they drink, wrong – you both drink."

"This sounds like a way to just get all of us drunk." Liv retorted back, but clearly down to play as she summoned a notepad of paper with accompanying pens for everyone.

"If they're wrong, does the delegated person need to provide the correct answer?" Piper finally asked, nervous for what debacle this game could get her into.

"That's the beauty of it, if guessed incorrectly about you, you can either drink and take the true answer to the grave or reveal the truth and not have to drink."

"Okay, I'm in." Piper confirmed, grabbing her piece of paper. "How many questions?"

"Let's start with three." Kyril proposed, scribbling away on his notebook immediately.

Piper sank back further in her chair. Zeus, what had she just gotten herself into?

After everyone had folded and contributed their questions to the center table, Kyril eagerly shuffled the pile together, confirming that he'd start.

He pulled a scrap of paper from each pile, and mischievously grinned before reading. "Question: Who's your hallpass?" Kyril wiggled his eyebrows, soaking in the glory of all the attention focused on him, "Two from my left: Zayne."

Kyril studied Zayne dramatically, before nonchalantly guessing with a knowing tone, "Easy. Ammiras."

Zayne grinned, cursing as his eyes narrowed on Kyril, before taking a sip of his margarita.

"Nailed it." Kyril grinned, turning to Dylan. "Your turn, queen."

Dylan's eyes went wide with a smile as she leaned toward the table and grabbed two slips of paper, coughing before she spoke aloud. "Question: What's your biggest turn on? One from my right: Kyril."

The auburn-headed vixen casually turned her gaze to her boyfriend, studying him curiously in a mocking way. Finally, she kissed his cheek, leaving a burgundy mark from her lips before she whispered loudly in his ear for the room to hear, "Anything that has to do with the color red."

Kyril turned to Dylan, his mouth agape and already distracted.

Piper blushed as she tried to hide behind Zayne.

Yet again, she caught those caramel eyes, smirking at her innocence.

"Clearly Kyril needs to drink." Zayne smiled, going into the pile.

"Question: When was the last time you had sex?"

The room focused in on Zayne.

Piper prayed for dear Zeus they didn't call on her. The last time she had sex was never. And she was nineteen. The oldest one out of this entire group and yet the least experienced.

"To my left, two over." Zayne grinned, staring at Liv curiously. "Before you were captured by Kronos?"

Liv blushed, slowly shaking her head as she took a sip from her marg and then put the pressure back on Zayne to drink, as well.

"Damn. But you go, girl." Zayne raised his glass to Liv in applause.

It was small, and perhaps nobody noticed it but Piper, but she silently watched as Tristan's head had snapped toward Liv, his jaw dropping in pain when he interpreted her signal.

Did that mean Liv and Hayden had gotten back together? Or had Tristan fulfilled a lustful need and not expected Liv to reveal their secret truth?

Piper felt like she was going to be sick.

But it was her turn.

Grateful for an action to distract her, she grabbed the questioned paper, unfolding it and reading, "Question: Out of everyone here, who's the first person you think of?"

Damn, if only she had pulled her own.

She reached for the second file, cursing the gods at the irony of the outcome. "Two from my left."

Piper finally met those caramel eyes straight on. She hoped her crystalized gaze looked like a pool of ice. Deadly and death in itself.

"Easy. Liv." Piper whispered, nodding to Tristan to take a drink. She tossed the papers back into the discard pile, refusing to return her gaze back to his.

She couldn't let his fire melt her ice into pools of teary water. Not tonight.

"That would be incorrect, Piper." Tristan countered, his voice smooth as the caramel in his eyes. "Drink."

"Miss Know-It-All indeed does not, *know it all!*" Kyril yelled excitedly, clapping. "I think we should *all* drink to that."

Piper ignored Kyril, her eyes once again meeting Tristan's, curiosity taking over her mind of the possibilities. She sipped her margarita, slowly, all the while not leaving his gaze. He gave her no inclination as to what the Hades his response meant, dull and lifeless in his critique.

"I'll drink to that!" Liv smiled, leaning toward the table to grab her question and corresponding victim. "Question: What's your biggest fear. Oooh…." She wiggled her eyes, staring down each player in the room dramatically, before coughing with a smirk and unfolding her next target. "Two from my left… Kyril!"

Liv focused in on Kyril, jokingly adding the pressure to his own crafted game.

Of course, Liv got to pick Piper's less scandalous question.

"Okay, seriously why are you so… glass-half full tonight?" Tristan chided, a subtle snarl to his tone.

Clearly the God of Whisky was no longer having a smokin' time.

Piper rolled her eyes.

"Obviously because Miss Positive Princess got laid!" Kyril hollered. "Did you not pay attention to Zayne's round?"

Liv blushed, biting her lip as she awkwardly laughed and changed the subject quickly. "Kyril, we're discussing your fears. Not my personal life…"

"She's not denying it." Kyril grinned.

Liv glared at Kyril, shaking her head slowly. "Well, your biggest fear is Kronos."

"And why do you say that?" Kyril asked tersely. He sat up straight, no longer the laid-back jokester mocking his friends.

Okay, maybe Piper was glad she didn't draw her own question.

Liv shrugged, "If he's not, then I would consider you an idiot or an enemy."

Kyril studied Liv intensely, perhaps in a more serious tone than Piper had ever witnessed. Dylan eyed Kyril curiously, a poker face remaining on his girlfriend's face.

Finally, Kyril chuckled, breaking the tension as he took a sip.

Piper exhaled, finally noticing she had been holding her breath.

"I'll take a sip, but in all honesty, I think you should, too." Kyril raised his glass, "In fact, we all should. To remind ourselves that we face not one, but two enemies with the Dark Gods. Kronos may be terrifying, all-powerful and cruel, but lest we forget Arlo – cunning, malicious and equally an opposing threat. In terms of the Radical Dark Gods, I fear them *all*, and you should too."

Piper gulped, staring silently around at the others, before taking a sip of her margarita.

"Famous last words." Tristan drawled, leaning in toward the table to continue the game.

"And, of course." Tristan stated with a sigh, sarcasm driving his tone. "On the record Kyril, I fucking *hate* this game." He turned to the other card, his expression shifting even darker.

He looked up at everyone, then Piper, before returning his gaze to the group. "I'm not doing this. Sorry. Not asking this question." In an instant, the paper burst into flames, quickly turning to debris on his coffee table.

"Oh come on!" Kyril groaned. "Don't be lame. You have to ask the question. Game rules."

"Game over." Tristan shrugged, burning all the papers that remained on the table. "I'm not doing it. If that makes me lame, then so be it."

"Was it another one about Liv and her 'personal life'?" Kyril smirked, taking a sip of his margarita.

"Okay. Symposium over." Tristan concluded, standing up. "Or, you can stay. I'll go."

And with that, he stormed out of the room.

"Who lit his wick?" Kyril asked in shock.

"In this case, it might be more about who *hasn't* lit his wick..." Dylan observed quietly. First looking at Liv, before meeting Piper's gaze.

Did that mean Liv and Tristan *hadn't* been intimate?

Oh Zeus, this was too much. And ultimately impossible to find out, unless Piper wanted to outright ask her best friend who she slept with in the past days... which of course, was *never* going to be an option.

"Come on. Let's go. Perhaps bartender Dylan made our margaritas a bit too strong for tonight's festivities." Zayne proposed calmly, standing up and offering Piper his hand for support.

Dylan stood up immediately, "How am I to blame for this?!"

Surprisingly enough, Liv remained in the room with their friends and had not run after Tristan to check on him.

That was typically her queue.

Piper debated whether *she* should go and check on him, and make sure he was okay. Although she dreaded the possibility of opening a dam of Liv-flavored water rushing into their stream. She wasn't sure she could bear it; however, as she contemplated her next maneuver, she noticed her friends were already exiting his loft.

And like the coward she felt she would always be, Piper followed them mechanically, gazing down the dark, empty hallway for a moment too soon, before walking through the threshold's exit and closing the mahogany door.

SIXTEEN

DYLAN

She would be lying to herself if she admitted she wasn't nervous.

Dylan took a look at herself in the mirror, hoping her appearance would insinuate a continued loyalty to the Dark Gods. She and her family had not been on the *best* of terms since she had chosen to follow Liv as her true pillar Elite. And *best of terms* was describing it delicately.

Her family had been prestigious members of the Houses of Water and Wind, Dylan a gem when she inherited powers from both. She had grown up in a world stripped of choices and opportunity, continually yearning for the independence she craved since she had boycotted an orange-colored dress her mother had once insisted she wear for a family dinner as a young girl. Dylan had soaked it in bleach and added a black belt before her mother caught her in the new fashion and discarded the dress immediately into the fire, letting the flames churn it back to its intended color and inevitably burn it to ash.

Dylan cringed at the memory of screaming bloody murder in protest to wearing something she believed would turn her more orange, at the time disgusted to why she was the only Element darling who had red hair.

Now, Dylan stared at her silky auburn mane, coveted by the imprisoned Element Pillar deities as it was a tough decipherer for where loyalties lay between Dark and Pure. A small gift that hid her true loyalty to the Pure

Element Elite, Liam, all this time. Now, it served as a warning to her kin, wary if the auburn hair meant what it once had.

Just like her family now, it was precisely why she had always remained equally as suspicious to Matthias, many times questioning Tristan's amber eyes matching her own, and had wished to express her concern to whether Matthias could truly be trusted or debating if Tristan should become a closer confidante.

Dylan finished curling her hair, now braided intricately into a low ponytail, the remainder of her flowing thick locks looking as captivating as ever against the stark contrast of her black, geometric cut-out, velvet long-sleeved dress. She painted her lips with a deep ruby hue and added another layer of mascara to thicken her lashes and accentuate her winged eyeliner, hoping that with the addition of her fur coat, she would look like the princess of blood darkness she had always been bred to be.

Realistically, Dylan knew it wouldn't help. Her family had already disowned her, cast her aside as a rebel and stuck up their noses when she had initially reached out in attempt to trace her distant Irish heritage. Claiming it to be for a school project, Dylan finally got her youngest aunt to concede. Although all she had received was a name and address. No greeting, no well wishes or any salutations of the sort.

But it was better than nothing.

For example, no responses from her inquiry had been sent by her parents. And typically, her mother, Thalia, could never shut up.

But fortunately, her mother's youngest sister, Aislynn, had been close to her grandmother and the kindest of her relatives. Or, more accurately, the least likely to murder Dylan if she were granted a visit. Perhaps it was because she was also the most affected by the Dark God's slaughter, when Dylan's grandmother, Aislynn's mother, had been unjustly murdered simply from having strong powers affiliated with being a member of the House of Wind, only to make Kai's ascension to the Pillar Elite all the less earned. Unlike Dylan's mother, already a century in age, Aislynn was only a teenager and had not inherited her own powers, so protested the notion while the entirety of Dylan's family had supported it.

It was for the glory of their house and they would not allow their mother to soil it.

All to keep getting invited to the prestigious Element Elite dinners and be Kai's personal lapdogs.

Dylan shuttered, throwing on her fur coat and praying to Zeus this distant aunt took more after their Irish ancestors in terms of what the definition of glory meant. She refused to enter this meeting optimistically, but at least that would explain why she had never met this distant relative before.

Well that and the fact that Dylan was her grandniece, twice removed. If that even was a term that could be used to describe her familial relationship with Great Aunt Danu.

Dylan didn't even know what her Irish elder's specialty powers included, ashamed she could be leading her friends into Zeus knew what. If Danu were the ancient goddess of death, war or anything of the sort, their powers would be no match.

Liv and Rei were already aware of the dangers involved with pursuing an unknown deity, but insisted they accompany Dylan for safety in numbers. Although Dylan fully understood Rei was only promising his protection because Liv was insistent on offering hers.

They planned to wait outside, but at least would be in close enough proximity if the conversation went to Hades. Piper wasn't entirely on board, but her shy stubbornness prevented her from being eliminated from the dangerous equation. And when Dylan refused to lie to her boyfriend about the whole ordeal, Kyril was adamant he join the crusade, at least as ammunition to support their Dark God storyline.

To each their own, Dylan had warned. She walked toward the door, turning off all of the lights in her dark, pagan-inspired room with one nod. The already shaded room, painted with navy walls and crystals, plants and symbolic decorations nodding to witch practice – moon phases, skulls, candles and incents – turned darker.

Dylan sighed, taking a final snapshot of her personal apothecary, and hoped she'd return without needing medical attention from it.

While the sun twinkled above the horizon and after Dylan approached her friends in the courtyard, Liv immediately handed her a coffee cup.

As requested, her caffeinated friend reverted back to her Dark God disguise, chocolate hair paired with brown contacts, perfectly suiting her burgundy corseted velvet gown.

Rei had followed suit, dawning an all black ensemble, black leather boots and a black trench. And although he wasn't able to accommodate trickery with his eyes, fortunately the sun provided a reason for him to sport black wayfarer sunglasses with a leather trim.

She kissed Kyril to greet him good morning, grateful that he cared so much for her well-being that he was willing to put himself at risk, and appreciated the camo-colored snakeskin blazer he layered over a black cardigan.

Finally, she approached Piper, giving her a friendly hug. For everything Piper lacked in confidence, she more than made up with heart. Her bright blue eyes had been once again darkened with another pair of contacts, bringing her own dark fashion flair with black leather buttoned-harem pants and a black and grey tweed jacket.

"To Ireland." Dylan finally nodded, taking a deep breath and running for takeoff, her heart pounding with dreaded anticipation.

They sooner they left, the sooner they would arrive and the sooner they could put this encounter in the past.

If they survived, at least.

She took a heavy sip of her hot coffee, letting the scalding liquid burn her throat against the rising sun. At this point, anything was a better distraction to her dooming imaginations, and Dylan might as well caffeinate while processing her potential demise.

It had been a long flight, peaceful in theory, but a war raged within Dylan's mind. Waging the challenge between wanting to be helpful and pulling her friends into uncertainty because of it.

They finally landed in the fields ten miles north of Kilkenny, approaching the Dunmore Cave in which her aunt had advised they could locate Danu.

Dylan had researched the historical site before dragging her friends into the unknown. So, although she could not find much information about Danu the goddess, she had learned about Dunmore the cave. Yet, what she discovered did not soothe her conscience but dug it further into chaos. For instance, the geological cave served up a Viking massacre in 928 A.D and not only did it provide shelter to those looking to disappear in its natural darkness, but it also had evidence of individuals being burned alive within. As suspected, supernatural stories had been associated with the site, from mythological monsters living within to a 'fairy floor' suspected to connect to the fairy world and rumored to be where the fairies dance when they visited the realm.

One thing Dylan's research had proved was that once she entered the cave, there was only one direct route out. So, if she was blocked from leaving in any capacity, that was it. There would be no other escape and she would be trapped. And with caves being the gateways to the Underworld for some cultures, Dylan had an impending dread that her fate would most likely join one of the more morbid stories from her research.

The surroundings of the cave looked like an Irish jungle. Inviting, with luscious green plants, trees and wildlife surrounding the steep 350 steps atop an aggressive decline. It was as if green eyes observed her from afar, assessing her next move on this ancient land.

"If we succeed today, I propose we at least stop by the Guinness Storehouse in Dublin and get a pint?" Liv offered, wiggling her eyebrows to Kyril to lighten the mood.

Dylan was too nervous to plan. Planning created hope, and she didn't want to misguide her mind.

She took a deep breath, beginning her descent. She heard a light wind in the trees, causing the branches to rumble against one another and leaves to turn as if one was walking above ground through the forest.

"We'll follow you to the first platform. I don't want to be 200 steps away from you." Kyril insisted, following behind her.

"Are you sure?" Dylan asked, still descending. If she stopped moving downward, she would not be able to force her trembling limbs to continue forward. She looked down at the ominous darkness ahead, as if shadows were dancing, beckoning her. "It might be better to split into groups?"

"I'll go with Kyril." Liv agreed, beginning her pursuit downward.

Dylan heard Rei curse under his breath, forcing a slight curl to her mouth. Leave it to Liv to always find a way to push Rei's buttons, no matter the circumstance.

"Rei, we'll remain in sight, just to that first ledge." Liv nodded. "We'll still be in the light. Just closer to the Dylan and the darkness."

Dylan could feel her friends' eyes shift warily to her back.

"Fine." Rei growled. "We'll keep watch. If you hear me whistle, you better fly up here faster than I can curse your name."

The distanced threat echoed quietly through the wide entrance of the cave.

Dylan continued slowly, each step moving her closer to the pit.

Barring any other circumstance, the Dunmore Cave would have been a fascinating visit, with some of the finest calcite formations found in all of Ireland. Yet, as Dylan migrated downward, the pressure built in her ears, in her chest. Until finally she reached the lit platform and stared into blackness from then on. She followed the trail, refusing to turn back or pause for a goodbye.

Turning a corner, she could no longer see. Dylan casted light from her fingertips, revealing a rocky path that worked itself deeper into the burrowing cave. Wet and murky, Dylan caught a chill with the drastic change in temperature as she moved further down in elevation. She heard droplets of water plopping against limestone. The only noise among the standstill silence.

Finally, she approached the Market Cross, one of the largest calcite formations known to man. Dylan was officially at the bottom of the cave, and exactly where creatures of the past had hidden, burned or died.

She thought about walking over to the Market Cross to inspect the worldly geological landmark but refrained from leaving the path – she was in no mood to trip over a skeleton at this moment in time.

"You're late."

Dylan jumped, turning around in the darkness to try and make out a shape, or any *evidence* for where the stark voice came from.

"Great Aunt Danu? Is that you?" Dylan called out to nobody in particular, turning around and trying to direct her fingers to every hidden crevice of the cave. "I apologize for my tardiness, I flew from Puerdios University this morning."

Nothing. Only the occasional water droplet.

Had she imagined the declaration?

"Great Aunt Danu?" Dylan asked again, much more unsure this time.

"You're late and you *lie*."

Suddenly, an orchestra of lights blasted from the darkness, revealing the Market Cross in all its glory.

"Not intentionally, Great Aunt." Dylan explained, hoping if she reiterated their blood relationship, it would defer her relative's already growing irritation. Not that it would have worked with her own parents. "I misspoke. My friends accompanied me here, of course, but they remain in the light, so we could still meet in privacy here."

She didn't see any shadows revealed from the new glowing lights, only those that naturally occurred from the geological landmarks in the eerie atmosphere.

"You're Thalia's daughter?" The voice asked speculatively.

"Correct." Dylan nodded eagerly, gulping after.

"Very well." The voice stated blankly.

A moment later, a figure emerged directly from the Market Cross. Dylan's eyes went wide, not expecting the transformation to come from calcite and reveal a stunning red-haired goddess wrapped in an emerald cloak that matched her bright green eyes.

"How did you...?" Dylan asked inquisitively. Now that she could put a face to the voice, a target to the potential threat, she felt more at ease and hoped casual conversation could serve as a natural transition to the true inquiry at hand.

"Dear child, among many things, I am the goddess of the earth. Celtic life flows through me." She nodded to the large Calcite formation, before turning back to Dylan with a proud smirk. "I also reside with the fairies in their realm."

"The cave is a portal." Dylan nodded her head, admiring the hidden truths and secrets the Calcite and Stalactites contained. The fairies may have danced on the fairy floor, but the immortals used other means to connect their world to the living mortal's.

"So, as the Goddess of wisdom, I am aware you seek information?" Danu casually cut to the chase, her voice remaining calm and monotone through the drastic change from small talk to purposeful conversation.

Dylan gulped, absorbing the warning not to lie again. Why couldn't her relation be the goddess of love and friendship? She immediately tossed the scholastic angle that had worked so seamlessly on her aunt.

"I want to find the lost Celtic Gods." Dylan stated bluntly, hoping Danu would conjure her own reason as to why.

"To offer refuge? To create an alliance? To use as weaponry and discard the moment they no longer serve *your* personal agenda?" Danu accused, observing Dylan directly and smirking, "You're no queen. Why would I share the Celts greatest secret with *you*?"

"She's no queen. But I am."

Shit. Liv's husky voice echoed in the impending darkness.

Danu smiled slyly. "Olivia Monaco, daughter of Liam. Demi-goddess and Elite of the Elements Pillar. Impressive." She cocked her head slightly, eyes narrowing down to the shadowed shape forming into the light. "What an honor it is to make your acquaintance… but you're no queen." She smirked, tossing her thick hair behind in satisfaction.

"Soul mate to King Hayden and recognized by his majesty as an equal partner to rule." Liv challenged back, coming into the light. "As the Goddess of Knowledge, you can confirm the truth in my current and future royal influence."

Dylan's eyes went wide. Well, timing for Liv to remember her history with Hayden couldn't have surfaced at a better time…

Danu paused, studying Liv as she joined Dylan and stood impressively by her side.

Liv radiated power, royalty and importance.

The queen, indeed, had returned.

"I'll accept it." Danu nodded affirmatively. "The remaining Celtic deities, known as Tuatha de Danaan, reside in the fairy realm." Danu looked back to the Market Cross approvingly.

"That's it?" Liv blurted, before tilting her head accusingly to Danu. "Why did you tell us so easily?"

At first, the Celtic Goddess looked caught off guard, finally meeting her match in dominance, but the surprised expression quickly turned to a knowing look as she smirked and looked behind them, toward the exit.

Danu walked back toward the Market Cross, placing her hand gently on the crystal. "It's simple, really. You will not be escaping today. Get ready to meet your demise."

And with that, she laughed, merging back into the cave as all of the lights went dark.

An instant after, a blast erupted in the distance.

From the *light*.

LIV

What hot mess had they gotten into this time?

"Upstairs. Now." Dylan commanded, grabbing Liv's hand and yanking her up the slick path. Only Dylan's free hand provided a dim light around the blackness.

Liv used her free hand to help guide their path ahead, spotting only Dylan's red ponytail bopping among what looked like obsidian walls.

"Dylan! Liv!" Kyril's voice echoed faintly among the growing pellets smashing against the rocky surfaces.

"Coming!" Dylan screamed frantically.

But, when Dylan pulled Liv, she accidentally resisted, causing her friend's balance to falter and consequently smash into the ground.

"Shit." Dylan breathed, scrambling up, but her leg gave out and she went crashing down again.

"Here." Liv blindly tried to find her friend's body, accidentally touching her breast before finding her arm socket and sliding her hand beneath it for support. Dylan's leg clearly still hadn't healed from their last ambush near the Underworld.

An explosion lit up the cave into tiny red and orange fractions, before going dark again.

The resemblance to their current predicament and the Underworld hit too close to home.

"If she manages to close the entrance, we're fucked." Dylan panted.

They hobbled slowly up the pathway, finally curving to a glimmer of light. A little further and they could move faster with the gift of sight returned.

The cave shook, causing them both to lose balance again and crash down against the wall. Dylan slammed into Liv, before they collided against the ragged stone yet again.

Liv stood up, ignoring the pain of her bones screaming internally on her behalf. She reached out her hand to Dylan yet again, pulling her friend up with pure stubbornness than physical capability.

Rocks started raining down from above; Liv tried to shield nature's self-made bullets, using wind to blow them back upward toward the light.

"Dylan!?" Kyril hollered again, struggle laced in his call.

"COMING!" Dylan screamed again.

They turned another corner, relief flooding Liv for only an instant until she saw Kyril on the Fairy Pool viewing platform. The rocks had nearly infiltrated the light, half of the entrance now barricade by outside materials. One more explosion and they'd be left to rot with the skeletons of the past.

Liv focused all of her powers to the entrance, gusting wind outward to block any additional materials downward.

"Olivia Monaco…" A silky voice hissed from afar, slithering its way via echo through the acoustics of the cave.

Liv saw green immediately.

No…

"Kronos is here." Liv cried, her body trembling.

"We'll deal with him once we're at ground-level." Kyril said. "Can you both fly?"

The rocks began infiltrating the cave once again.

But Liv only saw Kronos, with his darkness blurring her vision. Her thoughts moved slowly.

"LIV!" Dylan shook her friend.

Bright red hair took over her sight, amber eyes penetrated her soul.

Snapping out of her cursed trance, Liv regathered her composure.

"Right." Liv shook her head, trying to clear her foggy head. "Yes."

She again willed the wind to blow upward and summoned her wings to reattach simultaneously, blasting toward the light in line with Dylan and Kyril.

At one point they had to fly in a single file, curving along the path before returning to the Irish jungle. She spotted Rei and Piper at the forefront of the stairs, Rei sending off his own offensive attacks while Piper executed what seemed to be a protective windshield.

"About damn time!" Rei yelled, turning back for only a moment to confirm they had made it out of the cave.

"I can't hold them off much longer!" Piper squeaked, sweat beading down her face and soaking through her shaking black ensemble.

Liv joined Piper to help manage the wind shield, her eyes growing wide as her recent psychiatric breakdown proved to be a dark foreshadowing to what they stood against.

No shit Piper was turning into a lake.

Arlo and Kronos both stood at the forefront, Klarya smirking beside them alongside a group of redheaded individuals, one particular auburn-haired woman having a striking resemblance to Dylan.

"On three…" Rei panted, "You fly for your god-damned lives."

Liv nodded, glancing at a silent Dylan. Her friend stared dumbfounded at the group before them.

"One. Two. Three!" Rei then screamed, "SPHAERA TUTELAE MAXIMUS!"

A blasting blue bulb blasted outward, expanding infinitely away and across the lush forest, but Liv didn't stay long enough to see how it reacted upon passing through the Dark God fortress. She jumped in the air, flying in the opposite direction immediately behind Piper.

Within flight, Liv casted her own protection bubble, only taking a moment to look back and spot Dylan and Kyril directly behind her.

She didn't see Rei. *Where was he?*

Her heart began racing, as she forced herself to continue on, accepting the fate of one Pure against an army of Dark. To go back would be suicide, Kronos and Arlo again victorious in her capture. A tear trickled down her cheek as she remembered the conversation she once had with her solitude reader, repeating it in her head to distract her flight and remain true to her decision.

"It will be an honor to die in the effort to keep you safe, but a tragedy if I do not succeed in keeping you alive in the process…"

So, Liv flew, fought against every desire to turn back and help her friend, and continued to flap her wings onward. It was the only way she could go, the only thing she could do to honor her protector's legacy.

But soon she lost control, keeping her focus solely on pushing her resistant body toward sanctuary. Nothing else mattered. She had no boundaries with her powers, they blurred together with her being, her emotion, her sadness.

The sky clouded around her, covering the sun, and within moments rain raised fury as it pounded against the green fields of Ireland and washed away tears of her very own.

SEVENTEEN

LIV

When they landed at Puerdios University, all four remained silent.

Even Kyril.

They all wandered, to no particular destination. But as her body took steps by memory, Liv found herself standing before Hayden's loft. And apparently Dylan, Kyril and Piper had ended up following her to Liv's magnetized destination in a similar trance as they crowded behind her.

No longer needing to speak a password, *no longer able to speak*, Liv weakly flashed her crest toward the door, unlocking the hinges immediately.

She dragged her feet through the empty apartment, unsure if coming here was even the right move to begin with. The silence of Hayden's place, no longer belonging to her, taunted her sadness and provided no comfort. Yet, she couldn't fathom being anywhere else.

Liv plopped onto the leather couch, summoning a blanket to cover her numb body.

Kyril, Piper and Dylan followed suit, as if playing a grotesque game of mimick the leader.

If she had only been stronger, he wouldn't have had to *babysit* her. He wouldn't have been there.

Liv didn't even get to say goodbye, to thank him for being the biggest and best pain in her ass. That she'd never forget him.

She closed her eyes, refusing her mind to go there. Not yet.

"Shit." Kyril finally breathed, "I need a drink."

He mustered four glasses to the table, bringing a bottle of whiskey to join their unofficial mourning. As Liv took a sip of her glass, she reveled in the warmth of the substance scratching her throat as it went down and scorned that her own friends had seemingly dressed for the occasion preemptively.

"What do we tell Peyton?" Piper whispered, staring blankly ahead into the empty fireplace.

"How do we tell *anyone*?" Liv took another gulp of the liquid reprieve, addicted to what the alcoholic beverage made her feel, or *stopped* her from feeling. As soon as it disappeared into her vessel, she was numb yet again. She ran her hands through her hair, grasping her skull before taking a deep breath. This was bigger than her. "We have to send troops back. We can't leave him to perish…"

"We should summon Silas." Piper offered.

"No." Liv clenched her jaw. "I refuse to give any father the inclination that his son is gone unless we are one hundred percent in belief that it's true." It was the most she had spoken since they escaped the damned cave.

Liv dragged herself from the couch, determination and obligation driving her brain to command her functioning body parts. In a daze, she walked to the balcony, finding her constellation across the world in moments, and summoned the only other person with the power to send an army to Ireland.

The oversized, industrial-styled oak doors burst open and slammed against the wall, the impact reverberating throughout the loft.

Kyril's eyes flashed to the door, instantly maneuvering from protective to passive, taking a calming breath and retreating back to his silent state.

The four who survived hadn't spoken a word since the immediate action had been determined. There had been nothing else to discuss.

A blend of heat and strength embraced Liv, a gentle hand guiding Liv's head to his chest. She collapsed into his arms, shivering against his warmth.

He rocked her, looking up to Kyril for guidance.

"What happened?" Hayden asked bleakly.

Liv followed Kyril's gaze toward the door, when she heard lighter, slower steps approaching. In the corner of her peripheral vision, she spotted sun kissed, wavy hair gliding like a ghost through the air.

"Did you send investigators to Ireland?" Dylan countered, her voice wavering and demanding.

"Yes. As soon as Ollie requested. But *why*?"

He looked around, continuing to slowly rock Liv, but nobody spoke.

Among the silence, Liv's crying amplified.

Then, Hayden stopped rocking Liv and instead held onto her tighter. As if now she was the rock to soothe him.

"Where's Rei?" Peyton whispered.

Liv broke, shaking her head but refusing to say the words aloud. She grabbed onto Hayden's arm, clinging to it like a lifeline. She started breathing heavily, no longer able to control the tears in which she had been certain had long dried up during the return flight. But it was a ridiculous notion, thinking she had run out of what she could give. For Rei, it was limitless, because he was exactly the person who had taught her that. That she always had *more* to give.

And yet, when it mattered most, she didn't have enough to give to him.

Peyton dropped to the ground, unable to breathe or cry, but slowly her mouth closed and she began shaking. She punched her fist against the back of the couch, moving the furniture forward despite the bodies atop it, before finally collapsing against it. Peyton closed her eyes, increasing tears and rapid breaths no longer contained by her body's grief.

"Peyton..." Dylan ran to her friend, sliding against the wooden floor to pull her into a hug.

First Xander, then Rei...

Liv's throat tightened; gut-wrenching sobs tore through her chest.

And she must have been experiencing only a fraction of what Peyton was going through.

What was a year compared to centuries?

Liv pulled herself together enough at the thought, finally pulling away from Hayden to check in on how he was doing. Rei was his best friend.

Upon sight, Kronos's smug face maliciously flashed in memory.

Liv closed her eyes.

Blue eyes. Remember the blue eyes. Remember the bond.

Prepared this time, Liv opened her eyes, locking with Hayden's.

Not only were they blue, but they were red, his bloodshot eyes intensifying the pureness of them.

Liv frowned, pulling Hayden into her arms and letting him be comforted this time. He had already been strong enough for the two of them; it was her turn to give him the time to properly mourn.

She saw Peyton crash into Dylan's arms, both weakly leaning against the couch. She saw Piper curled up into a ball, her face hidden beneath her arms against her knees. She saw Kyril staring blankly into the fire, unsure as to when it had been lit.

She felt Hayden tremble, trying to contain his own grief.

Liv heard the door creak open slowly, yet again. She dreaded looking to the entrance and finding another in need of comfort.

"Well, this is the most fucking depressing symposium I've ever seen."

Liv's head shot up.

A blubbering Peyton had already collided against him, crushing against the Elite's chest.

"Aren't you supposed to be with the Sirens?" Rei observed dryly, still entertaining his girlfriend's desires by pulling her into a questionable hug. "What's wrong?"

"Where the *Hades* have you been!?" Peyton asked between clenched teeth, before pulling back and shoving him away.

Liv was still trying to process the rollercoaster. Hayden looked just as dazed as she.

"I brought Guinness?" Rei stated inquisitively, holding up a six-pack of the Irish beer.

"We thought you were captured! Worse, sent to the Underworld! And you were getting fucking beer!?" Peyton cried, shoving him again.

"Whoa!" Rei jumped back, putting down the beer immediately and going on offense. "Am I supposed to be thrilled you cared so much? Because honestly I'm a little pissed that you think so low of my capabilities to survive."

"You don't get to be pissed!" Peyton yelled again, tears streaming down her cheeks. "You don't get to be… anything…" She breathed heavily, trailing off, catching her breath as she slowed down her sobbing. "Oh, to hell with it. Give me a beer." She summoned a bottle, cracked it open with her teeth and stubbornly took a sip. She shoved Rei again, but a little lighter, before finally calming to fall gracefully into his embrace.

"If you want to blame someone. Blame Liv. It was her goddamned idea to celebrate with a pint of Guinness after our adventure." Rei smirked, catching Liv's eye before summoning the remaining beers and guiding Peyton over to the couch, his arm wrapped around her shoulder as she clung to it.

Liv rolled her eyes but was speechless, still comprehending what the Hades had happened while being simply thankful for Rei's sarcastic view on life to still be among the living. She shook her head and squinted in judgment, but grabbed a bottle from his carrier and broke it off using her powers, taking a sip without pause.

All of this, for an Irish beer.

She handed the bottle to Hayden so they could share, he also shook his head in disbelief, before taking an immediate swig himself.

"Oh, so you two are back to a sharing basis?" Rei inquired.

"Okay, we still need to get over the fact that you are *not dead* before we change the subject." Peyton hissed back, but looking more content within his arms.

Liv sighed in relief, glad to have dodged a bullet for the time being.

"But don't you dare think we won't talk about you two later." Peyton demanded after she took another sip of her Guinness.

Liv grinned, turning to Hayden, whose emotion reflected the same as hers.

But the moment was broken by Piper, who finally asked Rei, "How *did* you escape?"

Liv turned, along with everyone else, curious to hear this particular story.

Rei sighed, leaning further into the couch.

"I cast a protective spell, holding it long enough to ensure you had enough distance between The Dark Gods to safely return. And fortunately, I was able to hold out long enough to fly north, toward Dublin." He weakly grinned, "They did not anticipate my route could take me somewhere *other* than directly back to Puerdios." He raised his bottle toward Liv, "Your insane request for a celebratory beer may have saved my life."

"That still doesn't make up for the fact that you were ambushed." Peyton scowled.

Dylan's face heated as she hid it behind a Guinness.

"I don't believe Danu was apart of it." Liv offered, "But her information gives us a lot of leads to research for Thursday's Elite Meeting."

"But if she's in league with the Dark Gods already?" Peyton pushed, "Is it even worth risking?"

"She's not."

All eyes turned to Dylan, who had remained silent and in a dreaded daze since their return to Hayden's apartment. She spoke with no emotion, eyes still staring at her Guinness.

After a deep sigh, she continued, "To schedule the formal introduction, I reached out to my family. I should have known they would have chosen the Dark God cause over me, that they would have tossed me off the cliff at the first chance." She stood up, finishing her Guinness before confronting all. "I lead us into that trap blindly from my naïve and blind trust. I'm sorry."

Dylan stood up, conflict and guilt painted on her face, before she turned and marched toward the kitchen.

"No apology needed." Liv offered genuinely, following her friend once she realized Dylan was instead walking toward the door. "Dylan!"

The stunning red head paused, turning to her Pillar Elite, revealing watery eyes.

Liv immediately pulled her friend into a tight hug and whispered in her ear, "We're your family now," and let the shaking Dylan lean further into her embrace.

Piper was the first to leave, Dylan and Kyril not too far behind. By the time Peyton and Rei dragged themselves toward the door, Hayden smirked as he grabbed a now-empty bottle of pinot noir from the table.

Liv grinned, cleaning up the empty Guinness bottles that remained, mirroring Hayden from behind as she walked over to the recycling bin and discarded the evidence of their very weird and long week. Had she really been in Ireland the day before? The thought made her yawn instinctively, exhaustion finally taking over, crashing hard and quickly, now that she had a moment to breathe. She rubbed her eyes, leaning against the kitchen counter.

Liv wanted to sleep, but she also didn't want to leave.

"You planning to stay up much longer?" Liv asked, letting Hayden set the tone for how much longer she could stay.

Hayden shut the recycling cabinet door, eyeing Liv speculatively. "I could stay up for a bit."

Liv nodded, adding softly, "Would you like some company?"

Hayden beamed, "Of course. With you, always."

Liv smiled, taking a deep sigh before heading back toward the couch. She collapsed into the leather clouds, relief lifting and soothing her soul as the promise she sought fueled her present: she had a couple more hours with him.

HAYDEN

By the time he had finished cleaning up the kitchen, Hayden heard snoring from the couch.

Peaking over the furniture, Hayden had to contain himself from letting out an amused chuckle at the sight of his sleeping beauty.

Mouth open and drooling, Liv was sprawled out and in a deep slumber, purring as she breathed.

Hayden hovered behind the couch's ledge, grinning at his snoozing soul mate, and summoned a blanket to pull over her delicately.

Well, her company certainly provided amusement tonight, even if it was unintentionally so.

He summoned his paperwork full of proposals to review, gently sitting himself beside his snoring partner, finding peace in the rhythmic beats of her breathing.

A couple hours later, she finally stirred.

Liv froze mid-blink, looking up to Hayden with one eye to assess her surroundings.

"What happened?"

"Well, you have been sleeping quite peacefully while yours truly worked his very-toned ass off." Hayden replied, looking over his stack of papers.

"I should go home..." Liv lifted herself up, her voice trailing as she looked around, pausing in movement, almost as if her body combatted her brain's choice, before returning to Hayden in question.

He noticed that she hadn't yet lifted the cashmere blanket that covered her body, hadn't fully committed to her polite declaration.

"It's late, Ollie. Stay." Hayden insisted, nodding up to the bedroom. "Most of your stuff is still here – toiletries, pajamas, gowns."

"Are you sure?" Liv bit her lip sheepishly. "I know things are still... new between us. I don't want to intrude. Or assume."

Hayden laughed as Ollie's eyes grew wide with stating the last word, clearly inferring the 'ass out of u and me' notion.

His girlfriend of four years and recently declared 'soul mate' now all of the sudden wanted to take things slow. After having already snored on his couch for hours.

"I insist." Hayden grinned, trying not to embarrass the delicate deity in already knowing what she truly desired.

Liv relaxed, her sleepy smile spreading symmetrically to both sides of her face.

"Okay."

She lowered herself back down, readjusting the pillow so that it lay across Hayden's lap, snuggling against him properly.

He naturally set his hand against her back, feeling her stiffen at the touch, but soon breathe through the tension as he began to rub her back, trailing his thumbs in circles across it.

"Can I help you with your work?" Liv asked politely, turning back to gaze up at her boyfriend.

Boyfriend. If that's what she considered him to be again. Hopefully.

"The words were beginning to blur together, anyways." Hayden sighed. "It was time to call it a night."

Liv turned forward again, trailing her hands lightly across his knees, sending shivers up his spine.

He pulled her hair back softly, kissing her temple for a warm welcome.

"I'm glad you're here, Ollie."

Liv sighed, turning back up to him, her eyes glowing. "Really?"

"Of course." Hayden grabbed her hand, pulling it close to her chest so he could guide her in the action to wrap his arm around her body. "You're always welcome here."

Liv nodded, kissing his hand.

"Sometimes, I feel like a burden." She shrugged.

"A burden?" Hayden retorted in shock. "I hope not because of anything I've done or said…"

"No. Of course not." Liv lifted herself up, facing him directly. "If there is anyone at fault for this feeling, you are far from the reason. You make me feel whole, complete, loved, capable…"

Liv looked around, the loft that once was her home. To which Hayden hoped she would find comfort in again, which is why he would extend it graciously and with opens arms to her, infinitely. For as long as it was an option to give.

"I've been a wreck the majority of the time we've spent together since graduation." She laughed darkly at the observation, "Hell, I'm still a wreck."

"Ollie." Hayden stated, cupping his hand against her cheek. "You're my wreck and I would not have it any other way."

"But I hate this tip-toeing around eachother nonsense…" She started, but Hayden cut her off, needing to affirm all that he thought she already knew. Thought she still knew.

"You love passionately, fight stubbornly and crash with a blazing fire… until you're off fighting the next daring battle because you believe in it wholeheartedly. I didn't sign up for a subdued half-love, and I'll be damned if I ever want one. I signed up for all of it, all of you, because I want the good, the bad, the ugly and the best, and nothing less."

Liv's eyes sparkled, the water glistening as it welled up against her bright blue eyes. She nodded, grabbed his hand on her cheek and kissed his palm in agreement.

"I want to spend the night." Liv stated blankly.

Hayden tilted his head, his smile growing simultaneously with his furrowing eyebrows.

"Before, I didn't want to intrude. So, I was trying to respect your space…"

Hayden laughed, pulling her into his arms, "Stubborn battle, Exhibit A."

"I felt guilty coming here, having everyone over, it's *your* loft. Your space." Liv continued, all feelings exploding out of her soul like a firework in the sky.

"It's *our* space, Ollie. And everything that comes with it. Even when you refuse to believe it. All that is mine, will forever be yours. I will forever be yours."

"Our space…" Liv smiled, finally relaxing into Hayden's arms comfortably. She looked around the loft again, her eyes twinkling. She snuggled further against him, her head a heavy weight against his chest, her arms delicately finding their place around his waist.

She looked up at him questioningly, "Do you want to share my apartment, too?"

"Honestly?" Hayden smirked, "I want to burn that loft down so you never return to it again."

Liv laughed, cozying up against the beating of his heart, steady and strong.

"Come on. Let's go to bed." Hayden cupped his arms around her shoulders and legs, standing up with Liv in his grasp. "*Our* bed," He clarified.

"Point made." Liv rolled her eyes, grinning. "But I still like the sound of it."

"*Our* stairs." Hayden purred, carrying her up them after pausing for emphasis on the base steps that they had already christened.

"*Our* lips." He continued, touching his gently against hers.

"*Your* bathroom." He joked, nodding to all the product that filled the drawers, contacts of varying colors, hair products and dyes, cleansers and toners and facemasks for her skin regime…

Liv nudged him jokingly with her free arm as he turned through the doorway and into their room.

"*Our* constellation." He twirled her in front of the framed graffiti Galileo artwork, before gently placing her on the bed. "*Our* love."

He leaned over her naturally, pausing to intake the amused and stunningly beautiful face glowing back at him.

She was truly a sight to behold. He would forever be grateful for any moment, all of the moments, that granted her in his sight.

"*Our* love." She repeated, placing both hands around his neck.

Gone was the amused smile, and instead her mouth opened softly, her tongue lingering behind her teeth as she stared warmly into his eyes, pulling him closer to kiss her once again.

He felt every curve against his upper half, the pressure of her breasts against his chest, the flatness of her torso that so delicately rounded inward at her waist. He tried to keep his breathing under control, but his heart was pounding in anticipation.

"*Our* bond." She breathed, pulling him fully on top of her, vertical now and in between her silky legs. A warmth triggered within his core, pulling her closer together, until tightening and locking into one.

Suddenly, a swarm of emotions struck him like the lightning she could so powerfully cast.

Desire, lust, comfort, impatience…

He grabbed her neck, pulling her toward him so he could connect in the physical as strongly as their souls had rebound as one. Liv slid her arms down his side, sending chills of lust throughout his body, before she grabbed his ass and pulled him down on her.

"I need you…" She whispered, "Now…"

"Ollie…" Hayden nuzzled her neck, kissing a trail up to her ear before softly biting it.

"Hayden…" She whimpered desperately as she began rubbing herself against his hardening bulge below.

Hayden tore off his shirt, returning swiftly to run his hands through her hair and lift her neck to kiss her once again. His other hand slid behind her and began unzipping the gown, peeling it off with her eager support.

She went for his pants, unbuttoning his jeans and pushing them away, before sliding his boxers in the same direction immediately after.

Liv rolled Hayden over, snapping her fingers to rip his bottoms off in one slick movement. She bundled her dress up before swiftly sliding it over her head and tossing it to the ground.

Hayden sat himself up, carrying Liv on his hips, before he began massaging her exposed breast, reveling in the soft noises she made in response. He lowered his head, licking her nipple and grew more aroused as it hardened instantaneously. He sucked the other one, teasing Liv until she sighed with a hungry smile, grabbing his dick in response.

"Ollie… wait…" Hayden pleaded, pulsating a finger into her and becoming even firmer at how wet she felt inside, how much she physically demanded him.

"*Our* sexual experience." She challenged, quivering at the movements he prompted within her, before grabbing his hand and pinning it against the wall.

She stuck herself on top of him, encompassing him completely. She moaned in pleasure, mirroring Hayden's own aroused sentiment. He groaned; his mind, body and soul on drugs, tightening his grip on her ass as she began pulsing up and down.

He spun her over, penetrating her deeper, causing Liv to cry his name. The way his name left her tongue sent him over the edge.

Her nails clawed his back, but Liv tilted her head back, smiling in pure ecstasy as she moaned louder and louder with each thrust. Her neck exposed, Hayden dove toward the delicate skin, kissing, licking and biting his way down to her shoulder before returning back to her plush lips.

All the while, Hayden was feeling it to, the rising, the elation, the dizziness in his head…

Together, they erupted. Shaking as they combatted the vibrating high.

With a final deep breath, Hayden collapsed next to his love, wrapping her in his embrace and pulling her close; yet he couldn't help himself when he concluded, "Our climax."

Liv turned her head to him, smirked, and jokingly hit his chest with a concluding, iconic eyeroll.

LIV

Waking up to Hayden had set a blaze in her soul that she had forgotten existed. She had been fueled by the need to survive, to protect her friends, her pillar's subjects, but she had forgotten what it meant to live, and to believe in something bigger than herself. To have hope. And oh, it was a spectacular reminder.

She borrowed one of Hayden's chunky black, woolen cashmere knit sweaters, wanting to be intoxicated by his smell while she attended classes for the day. Now that she had started getting used to the triggered reminder of the darkness, Liv sought to train her personal comfort by immersing herself with his scent. As she had resided within his loft for the past two days, his scent had started morphing with her sense of normalcy. No longer separate from her own floral scent, Hayden's distinguished scent stopped flashing green, but Liv worried being separated from it, even for the eight hours, would retract her progress.

She paired the thick sweater with a gold sequined A-line skirt and her staple messy braid. Staring in the mirror, Liv took a mental snapshot of the outfit, of the feeling of normalcy, of a routine – for a quiet part in her brain lingered, knowing what was to be discussed at tonight's Elite meeting. Liv had a wearisome inclination that today marked the last day of her studies as she knew it for the near future.

Liv walked downstairs, finding Hayden in the kitchen, clad in gym clothes and scrambling eggs on the stove.

He wasn't the best cook, but he had fortunately learned his way around eggs, toast and potatoes for the morning, attempting to make dishes by hand before heavily relying on his powers to dish up the later meals of the day. But he was an incredible sous chef and dishwasher. And sexy as hell.

A balance of normalcy, he had promised her once. A balance between their previous life and the current. A promise made so long ago its relevance and importance barely stood for Liv in comparison to everything else, but she appreciated it all the same.

It was simply one of the many reasons she had fallen in love with Hayden in the first place.

Another, how he had so diligently woken up an hour before, proof of his morning activity making Liv bite her lip in lustful observation as she studied the remnants from his workout. How his strong shoulders sculpted into toned biceps and how the light, breathable fabric gave no reprieve to showing off every inch of his sculpted body.

She wanted to lick off the salty sweat from his body and use it as seasoning on her breakfast. Zeus, she wanted *him* to be her breakfast.

Curling her toes and finally joining Hayden by the oven, she wrapped her arms around him smugly.

"Good morning." She hummed from behind.

"It's shocking how much quieter you are when you're awake." Hayden teased, playfully hitting her backside with his arm.

Liv blushed, cursing her mom for inheriting her mortal snoring genes. For still being reliant on sleep for any form of functionality the following day.

But, there was always coffee. Liv smiled, seeing a mug float over in her direction, courtesy of her king. She let go of Hayden, grabbed it with her hands and playfully bumped his hip with her own.

"Fortunately for me, my soul mate will survive being kept awake at night." She winked, walking herself to the kitchen counter and setting herself upon a barstool, grabbing a copy of *In Diurnus* and perusing the front page of the deities' daily newspaper. She spotted an article written by Jocelyn and began reading her report on the Dunmore Cave attack.

"Fortunately for you, your soul mate *enjoys* being kept awake at night." Hayden challenged, his eyes dark with lust. "Particularly when his soul mate does that thing with her tongue…"

Liv grinned, remembering that distinct moment, crossing her legs as she started feeling hot and heavy within. Yet, she couldn't help herself as she added, "Must be why his royal pain-in-my-ass demands to 'awaken his soul' every time he gets greedy."

"Whatever pompous requirements I demand, I make up in pure obedience." Hayden grinned, sliding a plate over in her direction, while refilling her coffee. "Breakfast is served, or otherwise known as my gratitude for your humble service to the crown."

Liv choked on her coffee. Both in shock, lust and from that goddamned knowingly desirous look in Hayden's eyes. She wanted to toss the culinary offering to the ground and lunge over the counter toward him in need, to reunite his lips with hers.

She could feel his amusement shift to the same immoral thoughts, his breathing growing deeper with each passing moment of their eternal stare. Liv could see through his eyes, into his soul, the fiery blaze at the other end of her own-mirrored flame.

Hayden took a step closer to her, magnetizing toward the bond.

The door chimed, breaking their pull instantaneously.

"Don't answer it." Hayden growled, stepping closer again.

He pulled her into a passionate embrace before kissing her deeply.

Liv fell dreamily into his strong arms, but another momentary interruption from the door demanding attention snapped her conscience to the present – to her reality, to his, filled with responsibilities and obligations. It also forced her to capture the sun and realize she was five degrees away from being late to her last day of normalcy.

Liv smirked as she pulled away, sensing the king's yearning for more, before she ran to the door and greeted Piper.

"Give me one degree." Liv requested, holding up one finger, its nail painted black with a minimal gold trim, before jogging back into the loft to summon her notebook and reading materials for the day.

"Good morning, your majesty." Piper squeaked, waving from the doorway.

"Good morning, subject." Hayden retorted with a grin, jogging over to give his friend a proper hug. "And please, Hayden. For the infinite time."

"Or my preference, block head." Liv grinned, kissing Hayden on the cheek before grabbing Piper's hand and leading her out the door.

Within moments, Liv caught on to Piper's fidgeting fingers as they walked their way toward Advanced Chemistry in the South Tower. As if walking into an interview, not a first-year class, Piper continued to straighten out her navy, leopard-printed blouse dress, adjust her deep blue satin blazer, and run her delicate hands through her spiky midnight bob.

"Piper, what's on your mind?" Liv asked instinctively, wholeheartedly expecting her best friend to reply with, "*Everything*."

Instead, Piper eyed Liv curiously, her mousiness intensifying with her uncertainty, before looking up at the ceiling and finally admitting, "You mentioned your friends celebrated your birthday once – went to a cabin and had coffee cake and made a trip of it."

"We did do that." Liv grinned, "Not to say that summary is what you would call a typical birthday celebration…"

"Of course, of course. Totally." Piper agreed immediately, before returning to her inquisitive tone. "Would you consider 'birthday celebrations' as something you would still have interest in doing?"

Shit. When was Piper's birthday? With all of the madness and memory loss, had Liv royally fucked up and forgot her best friend's birthday? Was it today?

"I mean, who actually wants to celebrate getting older. Am I right?" Piper recovered, apparently seeing Liv's unmasked dread, not realizing that in their world, there wasn't actually a true concept as 'growing older.' "It was a silly thought to bring up. Forget that I said anything…"

"Piper, when is your birthday?" Liv tilted her head inquisitively. Whether Piper wanted to celebrate it or not, Liv wanted to celebrate her friend's birthday properly. Even if it had recently passed.

"Oh, I was born a Gemini. I'll be twenty after we cycle through Taurus."

"You're almost twenty?" Liv asked, surprised. Still being eighteen, yet young for her grade, she hadn't realized Piper was considered old for her class. "I thought you would be turning nineteen, like Hayden next month."

Piper blushed, "My parents held me back, hoping I would have more time to absorb my powers before enrolling."

Liv nodded in understanding. If only her parents knew now their daughter was blessed by the elemental gods and still absorbing wind powers of unthinkable strength.

"Well, I for one, want to celebrate 20 years of this world being blessed by your existence." Liv circled back to Piper's original and sufficiently awkwardly-phrased ask. "I'll plan a party for you, of course. Is there anything in particular you would want for the celebration?"

Piper's eyes went wide, "You do not have to plan something like that for me! You'll be busy with Hayden's birthday festivities…"

Liv rolled her eyes, waving her off. "I'm sure the Royal Events Committee will pull together a celebration for Hayden in which I could never compete, but for you, Piper, I want to give you the world."

Piper smiled shyly, "I've never had a birthday celebration before. But, truthfully, the coffee cake and trip to Hayden's cabin sounds like such a special way to celebrate. But the trip is totally optional, of course. A party at Puerdios with coffee cake would be incredible, too."

Liv grinned, not wanting to spoil Piper's dreams of receiving her very own coffee cake for her birthday… but couldn't wait to tell Lace how she had unintentionally started a strange trend at college for birthday celebrations.

She paused, realizing she may never be able to tell Lace about her influence. Or at least, never tell her best friend the full truth.

"We don't need coffee cake, if that's too much." Piper offered, once again chipping off her value until she felt it matched her worth, too low for Liv to ever accept.

"We need *twenty* coffee cakes, if we're going to do this correctly." Liv grinned, pausing to share what was on her mind. "The memory just reminded me of my mortal friends, and that that's all they'll ever be, a memory of good times from my past."

Piper's bright blue eyes watered, understanding Liv's pain. "I can't really relate because I never had any good memories with any friends – or any deities, period… until I met you." She sniffled, wrapping her arm around Liv and squeezing her shoulder before continuing, "But, maybe for us it's accepting the end of our past years around the sun, however painful they may be to us now, but also celebrating the unknown to come. To look forward to those *good* memories that have yet to be made."

When Liv returned to Hayden's loft – *their* loft – she corrected herself with a smile, and found him no longer in casual work out gear but instead working at his desk and sporting a sleek navy suit.

"Hey Ollie." He hollered, turning in his chair and standing up to hug her. He kissed her temple, sending comforting chills down her spine.

"Hungry?" Liv asked, eyeing the dial-clock to determine whether she had time to make something before the Elite Meeting. She and Piper had stayed an hour longer at the Galleria Library to prepare for their alliance updates.

"There's pork chops and brussel sprouts in the oven, if you're interested in having that for dinner." He offered, turning to his bar to pull out a bottle of wine. "A pinot noir from Newberg, Oregon, if you're interested in pairing that with dinner, too."

"Did you…?" Liv looked speculatively toward the kitchen.

"Oh, Zeus no." Hayden admitted, shaking his head immediately. "Agnys from the Royal Castle prepares lunch and dinner here when I request it."

"For the super busy kingling?" Liv mocked, pulling open the oven and smelling the dish with impress. "Well, here to report that Agnys is a magician, it smells incredible."

"It may seem a surprise, but there are *some* perks to being king." Hayden laughed, pulling out the cork from the bottle and setting both on the table.

"Not many, but I'll take what I can get." Liv retorted, grabbing two wine glasses and filling both with pinot noir. "If you need to work, I can handle the kitchen for the time being. Another perk, you could say." She wiggled her eyebrows, leaning in for a kiss before beckoning him away.

"Being pulled away from you is certainly never a perk." Hayden challenged, but grabbed his wine diligently and whispered, "Thank you," before returning to his desk.

Piper and Tristan arrived early, the latter to share updates from his visit to the Elements Pillar the night before. Hayden remained at his desk, hovered over reports, but not until after he greeted their friends and offered dinner and wine, courtesy of Agnys.

"You're a godsend." Tristan stated gratefully, "I essentially flew directly here after a full evening of back-to-back meetings."

But then he added some bite to his seemingly sweet appraisal, taunting with a finite revelation and baiting Liv for gratitude, "Oh, and after a long day of classes, too..."

"Thank you again for handling today's visit." Liv sighed, appreciative for all that Tristan had sacrificed for her, for all that she could not return in what he seeked from it. She knew she needed to have that conversation sooner than later, and only hoped he already accepted her fate, her choice, and valued their relationship as friends. Liv couldn't fathom any other alternatives. Now that she had her memory back, she needed to clarify her non-memory time didn't send any wrong signals.

Still, it was strange to imagine a conversation set up to explicitly reconfirm what had already been discussed and agreed upon before.

But, watching Hayden still reviewing correspondence, knowing exactly how much he worked to keep up with the responsibilities of ruling this world, even with the support of the royal family, Liv began to wonder how she could alleviate the workload once she joined rank as Queen. More importantly, what that meant for the Elements Pillar.

The one thing of which she was certain, was that her loyal friend Tristan was more than capable and trustworthy to step into her shoes. He had always been the true leader her pillar needed and had earned the position as opposed to being born into it, like the privilege she had. And as she watched Piper giggle admiringly at her male of interest, a distant spark formulated in her head. The House of Fire and the House of Wind. With his political knowledge and her brilliance, if their houses merged, she truly could not think of a better duo to come together and be the future of the Elements Pillar.

An opportunity to enact the world she had envisioned for her people since accepting the position of Pillar Elite.

Liv would fight for her people, for a better world and all that they deserved, even if it meant it did not include her in it.

"Penny for your thoughts?" Hayden whispered, refilling Liv's wine glass.

"Just planning. Theorizing, really." She smiled softly back, staring up at the bright blue eyes that always guided her home. How she would kill for a moment to return back to Hayden's cabin with him, to openly discuss all these thoughts entirely and conspire together.

"Hey, your birthday is coming up." Liv stated, remembering Piper's request earlier that day. "Anything in particular you want to do to celebrate?"

Hayden sighed, dreadfully. "Don't remind me."

Liv furrowed her brows, tilting her head inquisitively. "*That* anxious about turning nineteen?"

Yet as the words escaped her mouth, she studied Hayden, knowing he had already matured to his immortality, now looking much more like an adult than a teenager. For them, age no longer mattered. She wondered if she looked older, too – having aged to a frozen twenty-five in comparison to what her eighteen-year-old self would have looked like if aging against a mortal timeline.

Hayden grinned, chuckling. "More about the fuss that goes behind the royal celebration." He shook his head, "Truthfully, I'd be content just spending the day with you. But it's protocol to have an official symposium, with every deity of note and their entourage in tow." He rolled his eyes at the nonsense. "You remember my father's circus last fall."

"Now I'm trying to gauge if the better gift is to offer taking over the party planning…" Liv smirked.

"The one consolation is that my birthday symposium will take place on the first day of the Taurus cycle, not the date we've traditionally celebrated in the mortal world."

"Well, what do you say to properly celebrating your birthday at the cabin?" Liv asked, pausing before realizing how perfect the zodiac calendar was aligning for her. "If you don't mind extending the celebration to the Gemini cycle on May 20th, for Piper's 20th birthday?"

"Already you're a more competent party planner than my paid staff." Hayden smiled, kissing Liv's cheek in approval.

Usually a simple touch from Hayden casted Liv fully under his spell, but she caught Tristan watching out of the corner of her eye, and determined it was time to fully rip off the band-aid. At this point, she wasn't really protecting anybody by not addressing it.

Tristan met her halfway, leaving Piper to her books and pork chop dish at the table. Liv nodded to the couches, taking a deep breath and grabbing her pinot for support.

TRISTAN

He knew it was coming, eventually.

Hades, he even *supported* their reunion.

Tristan had accepted the inevitable. Or at least, his head did.

His heart was still coming to terms with the fact that it was impossible to compete with a soul mate.

Yet, seeing Liv's eyes sparkle in delight at someone else…

She used to save those adorably amused glances for him.

He used to *earn* them. And look forward to procuring the next.

Tristan just thought he had more time, more days to process, more moments to soak her in before he lost her forever to him, again. It was strange, in hindsight of already anticipating the inevitable, he had the cunning to make him cherish the small moments and appreciate this mini chapter even more. He knew he was the rusted squire, the backup in this medieval tale, but he also knew that they hadn't fully returned to their own once-in-a-lifetime golden friendship. Especially since the last weeks proved there were better moments to come, that they were approaching those idyllic memories once again to implant into their minds for eternity. Those quintessential moments that would define and solidify their friendship as the greatness that it was. He had just hoped Liv would have been Liv for a bit, before she returned to her knight in shining armor.

"You and his royal 'pretty boy' highness seem to be doing better." Tristan observed, sitting down beside Liv, already dreading the impending news.

"We are." Liv nodded shyly, biting her lip. She tapped her foot against the ground before sighing and blurting out, "I'll just say it. We're back together. I've remembered everything about Hayden, about us. I'm moving back in. I'm not sure when. After tonight, who knows if I'll remain at Puerdios, but it's weird telling you this so I'm changing the subject. Piper's a Gemini and we're celebrating her birthday the weekend the Gemini cycle begins at Hayden's cabin and you're invited and should be there."

"I will be there." Tristan stated, appreciating the topic switch and ignoring addressing anything said before Piper's birthday.

"Good. You should be," Liv repeated. "Like I said."

"And like *I* said, I will be." Tristan challenged. "But I want to host her birthday party. So, it's going to be at *my* cabin."

"Okay." Liv replied quickly, "We'll have it at your place. I appreciate the offer. Thank you." Her tone was short.

"You're welcome." Tristan replied equally as sharp.

There was a pause.

"Are we fighting?" Tristan broke the silence.

"I hope not." Liv said.

"Okay good. Me either." Tristan responded, although he knew something already felt off between them, before catching Hayden's gaze, knowing his royal highness probably heard everything. There was another break in their battling conversation, until he sighed, finally whispering, "I'm happy everything worked out with you and Hayden."

He said it so quietly, he wasn't sure Liv heard him.

She turned toward Piper, still diligently studying a textbook. He followed her gaze, smiling at the sight of Piper's relentless loyalty, goodness, and hoped for dear Zeus she hadn't overheard this balderdash exchange unlike their king.

When he turned back to Liv, she was already looking at him, a subtle, knowing grin growing on her warm complexion.

"I hope everything works out with you, too." Liv grabbed his hand, squeezing it in assurance. "Eventually."

Tristan nodded, but knew for the foreseeable future, there would be a necessary distance between his best friend and him. And he wasn't sure if that void would ever return back to normal. He just wasn't sure he could accept that fact just yet. So, for now, he relished in her consoling touch.

Finally, the moment was interrupted by the dowager queen and princess's arrival.

"Does Piper know about the party or is it a surprise?" Tristan clarified.

Liv stood in preparation to greet Daphne and Jocelyn, her future in-laws. "I think you should be the one to tell her." She offered, shrugging before she turned and began walking toward the royal family, calling Joss's name before pulling her into an embrace.

Tristan took the opportunity to return to the kitchen table and finish his dinner before more games were dealt during the upcoming meeting.

"Your pork chop is cold." Piper stated blankly, barely tipping her head up to stare over her adorable, mousy nose in judgment.

"Perfect, just how I like it." Tristan smiled, even though he knew it felt forced, an act, when he smugly added, "Matches my soul."

Piper fought against her amusement, only revealing a slim smile as she subtly shook her head over the textbook.

"I also hear we have a birthday coming up." Tristan observed casually, taking a bite from his plate.

That caught Piper's full attention, as he had fully intended it to. She wouldn't have moved faster even if he had told her she failed her midterm exam.

For a moment, Tristan considered taunting her with a mischievous prank, but held back since Piper already looked like she was turning blue.

If only he could chew faster... damn it. He didn't want her to suffer from anticipation.

"Piper," He almost choked on the meat that he forced down his throat too quickly. "I'd love to celebrate your birthday by having everyone at my cabin for the weekend. How does that sound?"

"My birthday?" Piper clarified. "What about your birthday?"

"My birthday?" Tristan raised an eyebrow, "I'm a Leo. We have time to plan that later..."

"Right." Piper nodded, scribbling something in her notebook.

Tristan let her process the request, anticipating the slow turn of her head, now prepared to discuss.

"Why would you want to do something so nice for me?" She asked shyly, unable to meet his gaze.

The honesty in her voice gutted his soul, as if she had pulled out his heart and dropped it in the Arctic Ocean to freeze for eternity and never be felt again. But the belief that she wasn't worthy of a kind gesture only made him want to fight harder to emerge from the expansive seas victorious.

No matter what she did with his heart, Tristan would willingly give it back for safekeeping.

"Well for one, you're my friend." Tristan began, surprised he had to remind her, and felt more sympathetic for what factual delivery Liv just addressed with him minutes before. "Two, you deserve to be celebrated..." She slowly turned toward him, catching him off-guard with her mesmerizing, piercing blue eyes. When Piper looked at someone fiercely, it was unhinging. Tristan composed himself before continuing. "And three... just let me throw you a party because I want to and refuse to be told no."

Okay, so his third point wasn't the strongest, but he didn't care.

Piper laughed, a sound so rare but melodic and hypnotizing when done with amusement, not discomfort. "Well, by all means, *throw me a party, then.*"

Just for another dose of that reaction, Tristan would have offered a thousand parties and more absurd reasons for the cause.

LIV

Even though Hayden had warned her, her stomach still dropped at the sight of Calithya entering the loft. Not only was the Queen of the Sirens a constant reminder that she almost lost Hayden from her stubborn independence campaign (although Hayden continued to defend that was never the case), but tonight it was almost as if Calithya was on a mission to show Hayden exactly what he had missed.

Clad in skin-toned beaded fabric shreds, there was more skin on display than gown in terms of body to coverage ratio.

Liv sunk into Hayden's sweater, reminding herself she had nothing to worry about, even if the siren still managed to terrify her.

Ammiras followed behind his sister, smiling deviously in Liv's direction. She immediately thought of Zayne and wondered if the Siren prince had alternative reasons for never missing the Elite alliance meetings each week.

Hayden slid into the chair on Liv's right, at the head of the table, after excusing himself from Dyoedi's conversation with Silas, and called the meeting to order.

Under the table, his hand found her knee, the warm weight that rested in her lap comforting her immediately and erasing all thoughts of Calithya's vixen-like ways.

To Liv's surprise, Joss chose to sit across from her, but apparently as far away from Demetrius as possible. Liv thought they had resolved their issues once and for all, with Jocelyn's gold, geometric gown with beaded sleeves perfectly matching his all-over check printed suit. Per usual, Demetrius's outfit selection was definitely 'a look,' but if it was to match his love in adoration, then she thought it was cute. Although, she didn't put it past Demetrius to still want to color-coordinate, even if it made the whole sentiment all the more obnoxious.

"Silas, I reviewed your bill to increase militia supplies and approved it. You should expect three thousand mercurius to be added to your budget this week." Hayden began walking through all the proposed pillar bills, as usual, to kick off the meeting.

"Daphne, I support your campaign to grant education for all, but I think we need to set up a neutral learning facility unassociated with the royal family. Can we enlist Professor Ellasie or Professor Claredon to head the committee under a Puerdios University decree?"

"Of course. As long as it gives the best chance for young Dark Gods to still receive a well-rounded education." Daphne smiled in agreement.

After a few more proposals, it became Liv and Piper's time to share updates with their recent global deity research. Hayden nodded to Liv, giving her the floor.

"We have made great progress in narrowing down our search for finding where the lost deity communities around the world may exist." She shifted through her notes, coughing to clear her throat. "We have strong reason to believe the Egyptian Gods live hidden within the Pyramids of Giza."

"The only remaining Seven Wonders of the World?" Calithya retorted, "Seems a little too obvious?"

"Let me explain." Liv demanded sweetly, "It's where many of Egypt's pharaohs are buried for the afterlife. In Egyptian culture, these pharaohs were expected to become gods after death. So, to prepare for the next world, they erected temples to the gods and massive pyramid tombs for themselves – filled with all the things each ruler would need to guide and sustain him or herself in the next world. It literally tells us that this is how to enter the afterlife and find Egypt's deities, where the community has resided since the pyramids were built over four thousand years ago."

Calithya remained quiet and without another comment, to Liv's satisfaction.

"There was a time when the Greek Gods had an alliance with the Egyptians, a little more than two thousand years ago." Jocelyn cut in, "I can send through any relevant excerpts from journals during that time – according to our records, I believe Dionysis spent time with the ancient Egyptians in Alexandria during the Ptolemaic period."

"You have access to Dionysis's journals?" Piper exclaimed, before reigning it in and commenting quickly, "I mean, of course they would be beneficial to our research. Would love to see them…"

Liv smiled, continuing on.

"The next community is the Celtic Gods. We visited Dunmore Cave to meet with Dylan's distant Irish relative, Danu, who insinuated that the Tuatha de Danaan, the remaining Celtic Tribe, reside in the fairy realm, accessed through the Market Cross."

"Before they were *ambushed* by the Dark Gods as Joss reported in *In Diurnus!*" Peyton interrupted. "How do we know Danu can be trusted?"

Immediately, the table's gaze shifted from Peyton to Daphne, to Jocelyn. Their heads a domino affect cascading in a synchronized fashion.

"I'm unable to see the future around these deities, in fact, all of them. My powers must be shielded from seeing into protected sanctuaries." Joss admitted, her voice strained as she concentrated within her mind. "Even the cave is hazy, the realm entirely inaccessible, location unconfirmed." Jocelyn breathed, turning to her mother for guidance.

"Same applies with me." Daphne offered sadly, turning to her son. "I'm sorry."

But Liv knew the look Hayden responded with, furrowed brows and speculative observation; he may have believed Jocelyn's feedback but Daphne's verdict remained up in the air.

Liv continued. "We believe the Buddhist Gods must be connected to the Emerald Buddha, located in Bangkok, Thailand."

"By believe, she mean's we're like 100% positive." Peyton interjected again, immediately raising her hands in the air in surrender. "I know Liv isn't allowed to say it because 'politics,' but I'm saying it on her behalf we're 100% positive. And if we're wrong, I'll go down on the sword for it." And with that, she assuredly took a final sip of her wine.

Liv rolled her eyes, but appreciated the interrupted break so she could catch her breath again before proceeding.

"The Norse Gods have proved trickier to collect and compile valid research. It seems the documents we have on file have been tampered with."

"Tampered with?" Rei asked, grabbing Peyton's empty wine glass to refill it in the kitchen.

"It seems the records have been rewritten somehow, erasing the original details." Liv sighed, turning to Peyton. "Can you work on sourcing reliable facts and reporting back?"

"Of course." Peyton smiled, turning to grab the now full glass of wine Rei offered from behind. "Will work for wine!"

"It might make more sense for Peyton and I to research the Norse Gods together." Rei offered, sitting down beside his partner in crime. "With my knowledge of the territory and history with their kind paired with Peyton's discovery powers, we may be able to do you one better and meet with them directly."

"Case assigned. Thank you." Hayden nodded.

Liv gulped, now was the moment she had been anxiously waiting for, the time that would define her future.

"Joss, I ask you explore Dunmore Cave and see if you can pick up any clues as to Danu's truth. Being the Goddess of Knowledge, she may be able to relate to you on an inaccessible level to others."

"I'll go with Jocelyn." Demetrius stated. Not a request, a demand.

And laced beneath it, delivered with his powerful eyes, hinted that Hayden's response would determine whether the Pure God King would still have an alliance with the God of the Solar System.

Jocelyn's look told another story, that she would torment her brother for eternity if he gave into Demetrius's request.

But apparently an alliance held out over his sister's love.

"Done." Hayden nodded, moving on. He didn't dare look up to witness Jocelyn's shaking body and clenched jaw, knowing all too well at the moment his sister saw red.

Liv looked around, assessing who else could be assigned this delicate case. Silas was overseeing the militia, Calithya and Ammiras were too slimy to be trusted (both figuratively and literally), Dyoedi would never pursue such an open-ended request, and Daphne had been so bland during this entire war, Liv knew Hayden would never consider enlisting her to actually choose a side and do something for once.

That left Tristan, Piper, Hayden and herself. And she'd be damned if Hayden sent himself anywhere alone.

"Tristan and Piper, would you be comfortable exploring Thailand for the Buddhist Gods?" Liv asked politely.

"Of course." Tristan nodded immediately, turning hesitantly to Piper.

"Chi." Piper smiled, then beamed when Tristan's jaw dropped before proudly explaining, "I may have been practicing Thai for a future dream vacation inspired by my research."

"Well, you more than convinced me." Liv laughed, turning to Hayden for confirmation. "Your highness?"

"Chi." Hayden repeated. "Well, Monaco, I guess that leaves the Egyptian Gods to you and me."

"Us." Liv clarified.

And like a deadbolt finally locking into place, the course of Liv's future had been set, flashes of images she had dreamt up during the week becoming clearer and more focused in her mind, her future reality concreted.

PART TWO

EIGHTEEN

LIV

Saying goodbye to Puerdios University seemed surreal. She and her friends had planned to depart the following night after the Elite meeting, providing sufficient time to pack up and organize their life separate from the campus.

Only one day to prepare departure from the scholastic safehaven and enter into the unknown.

Liv never thought she would be one to turn around in longing, but as she flew with Hayden over the mountains that radiated against the backdrop of a setting sun, Liv looked back. The castle glistened, the warm candles shining through the hallway windows, as if emitting a farewell glow.

Yet, the hollow darkness from the far west tower lingered in her final snapshot of the beloved school. The now deserted loft forever living in her memory archive. Even if Liv returned to her scholastics, who knew if the loft would still be her home. Hayden had been existing there as a courtesy to her recovery, and the only true inclination she knew was that her royal and Elite duties would continue to grow, a larger branch slowly pulling her obligations further from the Puerdios trunk.

Flashes of each friend pulsed in her mind. A blotchy-faced Piper pulling her into a delicate, yet tight embrace. Peyton smirking, making inappropriate comments that bordered along the lines of cruel insults. Rei's no-nonsense attitude, arms crossed and silent as he judged everyone's ridiculous farewells. Tristan's uncertainty, still torn between leaving his Elite or following through with his assigned royal duty while conflicted with how they had left everything the night before; Liv had felt the uncomfortable weight twofold. Zayne's calm demeanor and genuine concern for everyone's safe return, marking his goodbye as the kindest and most natural of the group. And in contrast, Kyril's excitement to 'hold down the fort,' only amplified the quiet tear of Dylan, trying to quietly process being left behind.

Once all six friends had received their warnings to be alert while in flight (and any time there after), they departed the loft and headed their separate ways. Liv already felt emotionally drained, her mind heavy and ready to crash into bed. But she had trained to be stronger than that, and instead, focused on Hayden, concentrating on her gratitude for eliminating what would have been the most heartwrenching goodbye of them all.

Now, flying over the Mediterranean Sea, Liv appreciated the brisk calmness the view provided. The dark body of water was clear and perfectly mirrored the sparkling sky, making it seem as if she were flying through a dazzling galaxy, with diamonds encompassing her every turn. Hayden turned back, catching her eye, his own body like a shooting star blasting through the sky.

Another chapter closed; a turned page to begin the next.

PEYTON

They had made it to Norway in a matter of hours. Rei had elected they start in Ålesund, where a statue of Rollo remained in the Town Park in the west side of Mount Aksla.

It was cold and rainy in the mountainous terrain, bordering the thousands of harbors barricading the Norwegian Sea. Peyton had immediately requested they find boarding to serve as a dry place to gather their notes and strategize; there was no way she would ever be able to think clearly in this downpour, the fog directly correlating with the clarity in her mind.

Truly, it was a ploy to remove herself from the direct contact of a seemingly cursed land. For when her foot had finally hit soil in the darkness of the Norwegian woods, something didn't feel right. She had hoped it was because they were so distant from the town, but nevertheless, an ominous feeling overtook her.

With no targeted locations or leads, and Norway expanding almost fifteen hundred miles, both she and Rei had their work cut out for them.

"After we check in, you want to grab something to eat?" Rei offered, stomping through the muddy grass across the field, toward the twinkling lights of civilization.

Peyton gazed around, a foreboding dread pressed against her conscience. As if they were not welcome on these lands, outlanders imposing upon enemy territory. Spirits of ancient pasts howled through the winds, a symphony of warnings amidst hidden screams.

"Peyton, are you okay?" Rei reiterated, studying the glazed over eyes of his girlfriend. He reached his arm out to her.

Upon touch, Peyton jumped. She took a deep breath, before wrapping her arms around her, studying the unknown through the mist surrounding them. For an instant, she thought she had seen gold eyes flash deep from within the woods, but when she fully turned, alert and defensive, they had disappeared.

The lack of sight prickled her skin further, sending shivers along her bodily surface.

"Let's just stay in, tonight." Peyton whispered.

And as they walked toward the glimmering town, the gold eyes flashed in her mind, a stern gaze, demanding to deliver one message: do not search for more.

PIPER

Most of the flight incurred Piper pinching herself to make sure she wasn't dreaming. Not only was she in route to *freaking* Bangkok, Thailand – one of the coolest cities in which she had wanted to visit since she could remember – but she was flying there with *Tristan*.

For how Piper felt about the matter, truthfully speaking, the latter half of the scenario was still up in the air. On one hand, she was so enthused to visit Thailand, even under the desperate circumstances, but on the other hand Tristan only recently become a relatively good friend of hers. She just wasn't entirely sure *how good* of friends that entailed and that itself both excited her and terrified her simultaneously.

Fortunately, the long transit through the sparkling night sky both provided time for Piper to think, but unfortunately the long transit through the sparkling night sky provided time for Piper to *overthink*.

He was still so hung up over Liv, her best friend. And even if that weren't the burden of terrible and awkward circumstances, Tristan was also the Elemental Elite's advisor, again precluding a heavy loyalty to Liv. He was so rooted and connected to Piper's best friend, it felt silly to consider branching into the unknown to explore what might be there between the two. Not that she even considered he'd be interested in her. And *to think* of the awkwardness if it didn't work out...

That was definitely the necessary starting point.

And clearly with no existence of a start, there was no way an exploratory path could develop.

Piper finally nodded at the conclusion.

It was a no-go, off-limits, outside of the territory zone, kind of thing.

Nothing at all between the two.

Nope...

"Piper! Look!" Tristan yelled, his voice crisp and refreshing across the silence of the stars and the obnoxious sound of her own internal soliloquy.

The glimmer of Bangkok's bright and dazzling cityscape came into view ahead, but Piper was fixated on the golden sparkle blazing from Tristan's eyes instead. And his genuine grin, truly ecstactic to be with Piper when she saw the city for the first time.

Piper shook her head, contemplating why Liv always told her to look for the stars for guidance. The stars were terrible listeners. And they gave terrible advice.

Tristan slowed down, grabbing Piper's hand to stop her as she began flying by.

Heat radiated from his palm, electrifying her own body among the cool breeze.

Piper felt heavy – not just from the social predicament at hand, but physically with the additional weight of an axe Rei had gifted her before departure, with the sound advice to 'keep on surviving.' And here she was, simply trying to survive *Tristan*.

"Is it everything you thought it would be?" He asked, although unable to deliver his usual smirk, and instead grinned with pure joy.

Piper smiled, unable to compete against his own contagious excitement.

Could it be? Was Tristan more elated for her happiness of finally seeing Bangkok than she felt of fulfilling a dream?

Only for a moment, Piper quickly realized she hadn't spoken yet. She turned to Tristan, her heart racing to find the right words to say, when she found him not focused on her, but the view ahead.

It calmed her for an instant, until he began turning back her way.

Quicker than the speed of light, Piper swapped her gaze back to Bangkok, forcing herself to fully soak it in. Yet, she remained calm. He hadn't commented on her silence but was letting her experience it for the first time, at her own pace.

"It's spectacular." Piper whispered in awe.

Little did he know, she was considering both him *and* Bangkok.

The farthest Piper had ever ventured before Puerdios, before meeting Liv and before having her world turned upside down, had been the distance only from her childhood home to the Elements Pillar.

Now, she flew over another continent, staring at the edge of a neon globe, a city glowing with lasers as if it were destined to become apart of a futuristic game.

It sparkled. It hummed. It was electrifying.

And, if it indeed housed ancient deities, Bangkok was certainly bigger than itself.

"We should probably locate a hotel to set up a basecamp for the night." Tristan offered, scanning the city with laser focus.

Piper's eyes went wide.

There was no way in Hades she was going to share a bedroom with Tristan.

"I think we should stick to the plan, go straight to Wat Phra Kaew." She countered, wishing she hadn't blurted out the proposal at such a high intensity.

"Oh, come on, Pipes – you cannot tell me you're going to visit Bangkok and not even have a little fun?" Tristan objected, but was met with silence. "Seriously, all work and no play?"

"We can... come back when Kronos is dealt with." She offered weakly but added an ending nod to solidify the claim.

"Okay, I'll go on one condition." Tristan offered.

"Which is?" Piper asked, her arms now crossed.

"If we stop by a rooftop bar on our way." He proposed.

Piper stared at him, speechless.

"Come on, live a little, Piper!" Tristan pleaded with mockery.

"You're telling me that while we're tasked to gain an alliance as quickly as possible, you find it perfectly acceptable to spend time to go drink whiskey?"

"I find it perfectly acceptable to go drink whiskey at *any* time. If you'd allow me – the Mahanakhon Sky Bar is where I want to take you, but then there's the Lebua Sky Bar, Maggie Choo's the speakeasy, Saawaan... which is technically where I would take you for dinner, but rest assured I'm sure I could secure whiskey there too..."

"Okay, fine!" Piper interrupted, laughing and sighing and shaking her head all at once. "Zeus, you could talk for hours, even to a wall, if someone set you up to it." She contemplated his many proposals, before concluding, "We can go to one of the Sky Bars before we visit the Emerald Buddha."

"Seriously Pipes? We're supposed to stay focused on this mission and all you want to do is drink and play tourist?"

Piper looked at Tristan, confounded before she spotted the trace of Tristan's grin emerge.

"Race you!" Tristan yelled, blasting off toward the glowing lights, and before Piper could smack him behind his head, he called out, "Loser buys the first round of drinks!"

"You're the worst, ember… jerk!" Piper scowled from behind, then scolded herself for being unable to come up with a better insult.

"You'll have to come up with worse to offend me!" Tristan hollered with a laugh, clearly amused, racing ahead.

"I know, I literally just thought that to myself." Piper mumbled quietly, her teeth gritted, before she realized she was already set up to lose. "Hey! I don't even know where this bar is located!?"

Tristan slowed down, only enough to reply sweetly, "Looks like you're in deep shit, then." And then blasted forward once more.

Piper furrowed her brows, concentrating on her flight speed, determined to figure out some way to beat him. She could feel the wind pulsing her direction and curiously took grasp of the air to blow to her advantage, accelerating her speed by pushing herself toward Tristan.

She looked around, hoping for a clue to which building they were visiting. Alas, Bangkok was filled with too many domineering skyscrapers, all to be equipped with a Sky Bar of their own. Then, she saw Tristan mark his landing, lowering down to the ground near a gigantic building with a grand entrance.

Yet, while Tristan looked down, Piper looked up, and grinned.

Chasing Tristan toward the same building, but remaining at a safe distance above, she waited until his feet gently grazed the ground near a dark, vacant alley.

Sadly, but oh so sweet – arrogant ember jerk did not understand just how slow elevators worked.

When he finally noticed Piper was no longer directly behind his tracks, he looked up, seeing her silver wings sparkle as they cascaded into the sky and directly landed atop the building.

Adrenaline building from her upcoming victory, Piper gently sent a gust of wind to push bar visitors in the direction opposite of her landing.

Her heart was pounding as she glided into the bar, grinning from ear to ear before the chaos ensued of individuals regaining their footing, looking around incrediously for the invisible reason they had all almost fallen, before murmurs and chatter slowly consumed weather talk to normal happenings, next rounds of drink orders and inevitably back to the incredible view.

And wow, the view. Piper's jaw dropped yet again, magnetizing toward the edge.

When she watched the city from what felt like afar in the sky, she could sense the buzz that now pulsed around her, consumed her. She had been an outsider, simply studying the city from her books like she had so ardently, desperately read about before. Wishing she could visit the intoxicating acceptance and welcoming beauty of the other infinite places she had fantasized about as a child. But now, she was in it – living it and becoming it.

When she didn't hear her normal tongue, it felt strange to see others communicate in languages she had only read about. It was breathtaking, inspiring and all she wanted to do was stay here forever.

The best part – she could be *anyone* here.

"You haven't even discovered the best part."

Piper grinned, recognizing the sweet melodic tone of the voice behind her, unsure he could top her current ecstacy. She turned swiftly, finding Tristan amusedly holding out a peace offering: a glass of champagne.

Yet, her grin turned to adoration as she fully absorbed his incredible glory. He stood before her in his black suit, crisp shirt effortlessly unbuttoned for a casually chic look, showing the edges of his toned pectorals, paired with grey canvas sneakers. Instead of drooling, Piper grabbed her prize, avoiding the smoldering gaze that so directly penetrated her core, more than ready to hypnotize her already intoxicated soul.

Yet, Tristan, trained in this game, was so effortlessly able to control her next move with his following words.

"Congratulations, Piper. You bested me, in which I am by no means surprised." He raised his glass, summoning her back into his territory, unaware of the spell he so easily cast over her.

They clinked their glasses in celebration; Piper sipped hers immediately.

Changing the subject, even if Tristan hadn't realized *he* was the subject in her mind, Piper turned toward the view, "I can't imagine something better than this?"

Why was her voice a whisper? It was like every word came out as another breath, her body's natural response to slow down her racing heartbeat.

Tristan raised a brow, smiling with the challenge.

"Come with me."

He extended his hand, which she so gladly obliged by taking it. Piper prayed to Zeus that her hands weren't clammy and immediately chilled them against his heated skin, just in case.

As they walked through the buzzing tables and standing guests of the more formal restaurant, Piper noticed how every mortal of the fairer sex's eyes peaked up and stared at the sight of Tristan before her. She ducked her head, not wanting to be the afterthought in speculation as to how *she* managed to end up holding *his* hand at this trendy bar.

Even the mortals here who had dark hair were blessed by the gods with brown eyes to match. And although rare in this room, the few blondes she spotted stared back with bright blue or green glares.

Perhaps she actually couldn't be *anybody* here afterall. Only Piper, forevermore.

She breathed in relief when they finally exited the dining space and found an enlarged concrete staircase completely exposed without any walls, she was so mesmerized by the fixture and potential view, she snapped toward Tristan when he guided her away from the fixture and toward the edge.

"How is this any different than the previous view?" Piper questioned.

Tristan smirked, "Look down."

Her head dropped, and her body jumped.

"Oh!" Piper's eyes went wide as her hand clasped her chest for comfort.

The floor beneath her was nearly infinite, a concrete jungle able to be clearly seen from directly above where her feet stood planted on the endless ground. She was flying and standing still. She was infinite.

After she caught her breath and stabilized the electrifying beauty beneath her, Piper lifted her head up in amusement. She directly met Tristan's flaming eyes against her glaciered own.

But in time, something shifted in the air; she was no longer laughing, and neither was he. His gaze slowly drifted from her eyes downward toward her lips.

The breath she had just stabilized froze as her heartbeat picked up, she mirrored his own eyes and lowered hers to his pout. Gone was the smirk that she had grown so accustomed to fighting off and in its place a seemingly incomprehensible desire, shifting his face from a hardened façade to a vulnerable, raw need.

He took a step forward, leaning into her, before glancing up one more time to assure her approval with taking the next step.

She was ready to leap, instinctively gulping with terror from the anticipation.

"Can you take our photo?"

The magnetic chord snapped; Piper took an immediate step back, nearly tripping over her mustard yellow fringe and pleated dress.

Two young ladies handed over a camera insistently, Piper grabbed it, not entirely sure how to maneuver the contraption. She had read about them, of course, but there was certainly a difference between learning about the uses of a device than actually navigating one in the flesh, and under pressure.

"Sure." Tristan confirmed, steadily grabbing the camera from her shaking hands.

Now out of the moment, Piper took a step back, numbly hearing Tristan's flirtacious grin as he commanded, "Smile!" to the tourists and in return, their infatuated giggles rose as the two women sat, stood and silently demanded multiple shots be taken in the city landmark. Piper was still trying to process the blur, her hands still holding an invisible device.

What the Hades just happened?

Her body was molasses, moving slowly and unsurely – but her brain was on fire *about fire*, shooting rapid thoughts of grief, anxiety and curiosity. She felt cold, wishing she had worn boots instead of strappy heeled-sandals, or brought a coat, jacket, *anything more* than just a silk brown t-shirt layered beneath her summer dress. She felt entirely too exposed.

The heat of Tristan's hand beneath the small of her back brought her back to the current flame. Piper snapped in his direction, her face shocked and demanding answers.

"Jenna and Sydney offered to take our photo in return." He explained, clearly amused. He pointed to the dark-haired girl, more specifically to the bright yellow technical device she now held. "Smile." He insisted, bringing Piper even closer to his body.

Piper relished in his heat, seeming to relax with joy. She wasn't sure she smiled, but she felt her face was already beaming at the surface.

The device flashed and spit out a white sheet of paper.

"Another?" Jenna or Sydney insisted, flapping their hands slowly to the ground. "Sit!"

Piper's jaw dropped and she turned again to Tristan for instruction on how to navigate this awkward social debacle.

These two mortal strangers actually expected them to *sit* on the floor in which so many feet had trampled on before? To practically bow to *them*?

"It's for the memory, Pipes." Tristan shrugged, grabbing her hand as he lowered to the ground, helping her simultaneously sit beside him.

She sat up straight, unsure where to go from here. She hoped her face didn't grimace like her insides were, but apparently the two young women caught onto her intensely yet unintentional awkward queues.

"Put your arm around her, come on, act like you like eachother!" The other blonde girl insisted with a joking giggle; prodding Tristan to oblige by nudging him to get closer.

Tristan obediently did as he was told. Piper was shocked when she felt his arm curl around her waist and slide her closer. She turned to him with surprise when a flash went off.

"You two are so adorable!" The blonde girl swooned. "Kiss her!"

Oh Hades... Piper tensed.

Why did these women insist in dragging out this torture?

He wouldn't.

A soft wet pressure collided against her cheek, causing her to laugh in surprise when another flash bolted in the distance behind her closed eyes.

"Thank you, both." She heard Tristan sweetly say as he pulled away from her. She came back to the present, watching him simultaneously grab the camera from the photography-duo and hold out his hand to help her up.

She took it, stubbornly scowling at him as he grinned, clearly amused from having his fun in torturing her.

"We hope you two enjoy the rest of your night!" The girls giggled, swooning even more as Tristan responded with similar sentiments, before departing toward the bar.

When the coast was clear, Piper finally nodded to the device and whispered, "Where'd you get that?"

Tristan observed the camera, flipping it over. "Summoned it. I guess it creates mini polaroids? This must be what mortals consider a 'cheap camera' these days."

"Polaroids?" Piper inquired.

"Here." Tristan fanned out the three white strips, displaying the variety of poses they had just documented. Looking at the photos, then slowly caressing his gaze up to Piper, he whispered, "You look beautiful tonight."

"Thanks." She deflected the compliment and shifted back to the photos, immediately regretting it, "Oh, wow." Her eyes casted to the one of Tristan kissing her cheek.

Their first kiss.

Their only kiss.

With her cheeks heated, the Fire God's mark remained. Piper diverted to another photo, the one where the traveling ladies caught them off guard, sitting on the translucent floor and laughing at eachother. Piper's eyes inflated and she grabbed the photo instantly.

"Can I keep this one?" She squeaked.

Tristan looked taken aback, but ultimately chuckled at her dedication after a brisk pause. "Of course. Do you want any of the others?"

Without answering, she minimized the polaroid to a speck and attached it to her ocean blue-stoned ring, where she kept all things of importance.

She only hoped Tristan hadn't yet seen how she looked so adoringly at him in the snapshot of time, how she had infatuation and desire plastered across her forehead, screaming to be met with the same level of intimacy.

"Memories." She shrugged, repeating his own justification for the nonsense while placing her thumb and middle finger atop the wings that framed the ring's stone that she wore. She began fidgeting with the ring, twisting it around her finger in effort to calm her nerves.

"Well, I wanted this one, anyways." Tristan fanned the photo of him kissing her, tucking it away in his pocket.

To destroy the evidence, most likely. Piper hummed darkly to herself.

"Are you sure you don't want this one?" Tristan held up the remaining photo, the one they took first, taunting her with it.

"Sure." Piper snapped it from his grasp without looking, wanting to get this entire ordeal over with. As quickly as she compacted the first photo, the second followed suit and she locked it away in her personal safe, hoping to never be reminded of the incident again.

Tristan stared at her, his jaw dropped in surprise. He ran his hand through his hair as he looked out at the dazzling skyline.

"We should get going." Piper concluded.

She folded her arms across her chest, hoping he would agree. Yet, she couldn't help but sneak a peak at him absorbing the city skyline view before them.

He was truly breathtaking.

"As you wish." He whispered, turning his gaze to look down to the pulsing city below.

LIV

Cairo was certainly a sight Liv never thought she would see. But alas there she was, nonetheless with Hayden, in a foreign land she had only studied via middle school history. Whether what she had learned was fact or fiction, Liv still only recalled a blurry topline version of it all – Ra the Sun God, Cleopatra the very last Pharoah of Egypt, Anubis the god of death, and sadly not much more than that.

The irony of it all was she did recall a school project, having to create a journal as if living during the Egyptian time, choosing to voluntarily work with a classmate and become undercover spies, together, for their project narrative. Now, Liv felt as if she were living her sixth-grade diary in real life, simply with Lace being replaced by Hayden as her partner-in-'ancient-civilization'-crime.

Liv had once been *fascinated* by the Egyptians, begging her mother to walk through the Egypt Art curation at the Metropolitan Museum of Art when she had visited as a young teen, and still kicked herself for being so emotionally out of tune to have forgotten to ask Peyton for a quick walk through the collection during her last visit. Now, she poised a blend of excited intrigue and terror – she would be lying if she weren't a bit *terrified* of the potential deities and real artifacts they could eventually find.

And she would be lying if she still weren't a bit *terrified* of the deity who accompanied her now.

Returning to the present, to their stunning hotel room where they had selected to set up camp upon arrival, Liv shook the thought out of her head. Instead, she smiled at Hayden as he pulled out another ancient textbook. One of which Piper had so diligently tabbed and color-coordinated for them, along with including a corresponding journal with her appendixed notes. He looked absolutely mesmerizing in the white cashmere crewneck sweater and khaki pants he sported. She knew who he was, of course. Liv remembered all that they had been through. Yet, there were still times when he would laugh darkly at an improper joke, or turn too quickly, when Liv remembered precisely who he descended from and exactly what Hayden was capable of. She had never invited Kronos to be apart of their fated love, but alas the evil asshole figured out a way to wedge himself between them, their saving prophecy.

In addition to finding an alliance, Liv hoped this time alone with Hayden would also strengthen their romantic relationship and eternal partnership. No immediate distractons, only shared obligation.

"Sometimes I laugh at the idea that nearly a year ago, we were both in tuxedos and gowns getting ready for prom." Hayden murmured, his voice low and velvet. "The thought that we'd be here, a year later, in Cairo of all places, never entered even my wildest dreams."

Liv smiled at the memory. Her long navy gown subtly adorned with a string of crystals for the straps would have never survived a night on the Puerdios runway, but she loved that dress dearly and the night it represented even more.

"I should have known then, when you were crowned 'Prom King,' that it was merely a stepping stone for your potential greatness." Liv smirked, remembering how Lace had won 'Prom Queen' but insisted the nominated Liv still dance with her prince, how she had straightened his tilted crown before swaying to the royal court's dedicated melody. "Jokes on us if Lace turns out to be the Queen of the Norse or Celtic Gods..."

"The joke would indeed be on Kronos." Hayden nodded deviously in agreement, his mouth twitching upward in alignment with his raised brow, before sighing deeply and grabbing another textbook. "We've been at this for hours. I feel drunk from simply reading Dionysus's incomprehensible excerpts. All Joss sent was his repeated depictions of the burial process and preparation for entering the afterlife. And all conclude with placing the mummified body into the sarcophagus." Without pause, he continued, "And mind you, we're in the center of Egyptian culture. Why don't we take a break, grab dinner and ask the people about the gods who govern them? Let's live history, instead of speculating it from a written glance."

"Tell me how you *really* feel." Liv joked.

Her eyes left Piper's delicate handwriting, meeting Hayden's challenge before gazing out into the city. From a distance, the pyramids shone, the true epicenter of the city, built to surround the borders of its sacred tombs.

"We can go on a coffee crawl..." Hayden hummed, bribing Liv with her own personal kryptonite.

"Solid suggestion and smart idea to caffeinate before a full night of studying." Liv obliged, standing up and grabbing her burnt orange button-down shirt, buttoning it over her cream tank top and tucking it into her lighter shade of burnt orange trousers.

They walked along the Nile River, the sun turning the city's buildings into gold as it set behind Giza's horizon across the body of water. Slowly, they turned inward from the river and further dived into Cairo, enjoying views of yachts parked along the Nile to crowded streets and cars speeding in a flurry through the many cross streets, with sometimes up to six different roads intersecting into one.

Cars honked and different languages buzzed around Liv as they walked through the chaotic streets, until finally they turned right and found a quaint restaurant nestled in the alleyway between two buildings. Stepping into the building's façade, Liv felt transported into a woodland of the Egyptian fairies. Tree branches made the ceiling, with ornate glass lanterns hanging from the panels. Rich green and deep blues created an impressive atmosphere in contrast with the wooden structures and natural décor, like pebbles creating booths and stones breaking up the walls, all between tree stumps which served as pillars to keep the covering upright.

A waitress nodded kindly, leading Liv and Hayden past a water fountain centered in the middle of the restaurant and to an intimate table for two, pulling out the pale green chair for Liv to sit.

"Beverage?" The waitress asked.

"Turkish Coffee?" Hayden replied.

She nodded, leaving the two to soak in the mesmerizing atmosphere.

"I'm impressed we're marking our first coffee crawl destination in *Cairo* for your map." Liv observed with a grin. "Certainly setting our standards high."

Hayden chuckled, before adding, "And with Turkish coffee, nonetheless."

"I didn't even realize Turkish coffee was a *thing*." Liv admitted shyly.

"It's sort of like an intense, giant shot of espresso. From what I read, they heat one-part finely ground coffee beans with one-part sugar and water. It froths a bit, but should be pretty refreshing."

As if on queue, the waitress brought two mini coffee mugs their way, along with a copper ibrik which Liv assumed contained their caffeinated beverage. Upon placing the clear, oversized espresso cups on their table, Liv noticed a dollop of foam already within her matching copper cup. The waitress poured the remaining coffee within both their vessels, smiled and walked away.

"Cheers." Hayden smiled, raising his mug.

Liv clinked hers against his, taking a sip immediately after.

The smooth, rich beverage slithered down her throat. Warm, comforting and crisp. It was absolutely delightful, if not a bit sweet.

She beamed, watching Hayden try his first sip as well. This is what the two of them needed – new experiences, together. Sharing something new and uniquely theirs to bring them closer against the world.

"Perhaps we purchase an ibrik and Turkish coffee beans as our souvenir?" Hayden offered, taking another sip of his coffee.

"Do deities typically collect souvenirs?" Liv pondered, considering the ask. "It would be nice to build a coffee collection, even if it expands across our three residences."

"Turkish coffee at Puerdios, French press at the Elements Pillar, espresso machine at the Royal Palace…. we certainly would never get bored."

"And what happens when we go to Greece?" Liv challenged.

"Greek Coffee at the cabin, then." Hayden rolled his eyes playfully.

"Drip coffee…" Liv listed off.

"Dalgona coffee…" Hayden added.

"Dalgona coffee?"

"A South Korean home-style coffee, but more like a frappe coffee dessert." Hayden explained smugly.

"Thai coffee." Liv bounced back in a heartbeat. "Also known as Oliang."

"Arabian Coffee." Hayden nodded.

"Next stop on the coffee crawl, I believe?" Liv batted her eyelashes, taking another sip of her strong brew.

"Correct. Ten points for Monaco." Hayden grinned, turning to the menu. "I'll let you win this round, simply because all this talk of coffee is giving me the shakes, and I'm starving."

"I truly have no idea what to order." Liv admitted, staring at the menu. "I like babaganoush and falafel, but don't know much more than that."

"Then we'll start there and take any additional recommendations." Hayden offered, smiling kindly as the waitress returned.

Liv watched them both speak a blur of Arabic and English, to her amazement that Hayden had so quickly picked up the local dialect.

"She recommended Shorbet Ads – which is a lentil soup blended with other vegetables – and Bessara – a fava bean dip." Hayden explained, after handing the waitress both of their menus and wrapping up their order by saying, "Shukraan jazilaan."

"And lots of pita bread?"

"To pair with every item we ordered, of course." Hayden laughed. "It's a relative standard for Egyptian dishes."

"Then we shall feast!" Liv nodded, taking a final sip of her Turkish coffee.

After they enjoyed a delicious bread, fava bean, lentil, and eggplant-centric meal, Liv and Hayden departed the bohemian restaurant and ventured to the next stop on the coffee crawl.

He grabbed her hand, the warmth first catching Liv by surprise, but slowly its gentle heat powered through her veins. Since her memory returned, they had ventured between two extremes: best friends and passionate lovers. It was nice to do something casual and find the balance of the in-between, like holding hands, or laughing about the possibility of getting overly caffeinated, instead of constantly focusing on the never-ending burdens like saving the world or working through traumatic repercussions. It still lingered, of course, and would most likely never fully go away, but for the first time in a while, Liv felt like a teenager, who simply liked a boy and was enjoying a date. It was exactly the medicine she needed.

And inevitably when they returned to their hotel room, they could return to reality. Although, Liv secretly dreaded it because even though she certainly appreciated Hayden's diligent notes and attention to detail when learning Rhys's intricate healing regime from Piper before departing for Cairo, the process ahead would not be enjoyable – no matter how sexy her doctor taking care of her would be. So for now, she'd enjoy being an eighteen-year-old tourist with her deliciously handsome boyfriend.

They had been walking through the city, now fully glowing against the dark sky, a city of gold sparkling in unison with the twinkling stars overhead.

When they passed a stunning Mosque and Hayden noted the hallowed structure of Al-Hussein was believed to be the burial site of the head of the prophet Muhammad's grandson, a chill ran through Liv's body. For a moment, she had forgotten their true reason for exploring Cairo. Liv had left the land of myth and prophecy before being roped right back into it. Once again, she no longer felt completely protected next to the King of Gods.

"Hayden, do you think we'll encounter any Egyptian Gods here?" She whispered, magnetizing closer to his bodily form and wrapping her arm around his.

He sighed, both raising his head to look up at the enchanting building, conditioned to prestige in comparison to the previously run down and exhausted buildings they passed throughout the evening, and wrapped his arm around Liv wholly. She wondered if he felt the same impending dread as she. Liv relinquished his hand for only a moment, before grabbing the other with her right hand and after sliding her left arm around his slim, yet stone, waist.

Suddenly, she felt his apprehension.

The possibility weighed on him too, the unpreparedness of it all. The reality that even if they tried to act like a typical couple, their burdening responsibilities would always crash the innocent fun.

But he combatted the inevitable.

"Well, if we find them at our next stop, worst case scenario would be learning they don't drink coffee." Hayden joked, lightening the mood as he guided Liv across the plaza and to the bazaar next store.

"Oh goodness, a true travesty. Potentially a crime." Liv jumped aboard, happy to sail on the idyllic sea for a little while longer, even against the crashing waves that continued to steer the ship.

"Do you think they'll have a God of Coffee?" Hayden pondered aloud, catching Liv's attention immediately as they entered the bustling café.

"Do *we* have a God of Coffee?!" Liv's heart raced with excitement. If so, she needed a formal introduction like, yesterday.

Small gold circular tables stood centered between chairs on the right and against velvet couches bordering the left wall. Hayden spotted an open table and guided Liv to the velvet seat, sitting next to her so they could truly enjoy the full ambiance of the cultural socialization taking place. The electric buzz of the city's liveliest habitants.

"Is that even a question? If anyone was the God of Coffee, it would be you, Ollie." Hayden smirked.

"*Can* I be the God of Coffee?" Liv pressed.

"Sure." Hayden smiled, signaling a waiter over to their table. "Elemental Elite, Future Queen, God of Coffee. Really rounds out the resume, no?"

"So, now this coffee crawl officially becomes work, apart of my humble duties to serve the greater community." Liv beamed, she couldn't contain her excitement. Whether it was real or not. But for the record, she was whole-heartedly counting it as an official title.

"Precisely why we need to build our coffee collection across all our real estate." Hayden dignified, shaking his head in mocking disappointment, "Always one step ahead of you…"

The waiter had arrived by the time Liv shoved Hayden playfully, giving the two a sassy judgmental look before agreeing to return with two Arabic coffees.

Liv's eyes narrowed, "I still can't tell if you're joking, but I'm taking this gift as fact either way."

Hayden laughed, "My only desire in life is to make you happy – Hades, if I had known you'd be this excited, I would have bestowed the honor as soon as we had discovered your powers."

Liv contemplated it, flashing back to Hayden sacrificing his life for her, for *their* love, enduring social humiliation and royal scrutiny before the fiery lash that almost struck his back ignited a blaze within her that revealed her powers, her true self. It was because of him, for him, always him, that her being had strengthened and improved for good.

She rolled her eyes anyway, not wanting to get emotional and instead retorted, "Sure would have helped with the whole hiding my Elite powers from everybody with a solid alibi. If only you had been one step ahead of me, *then…*"

Liv smirked; Hayden's eyes blazed with impress and lust. She knew immediately he wanted to kiss her, touch her in ways deemed socially inappropriate in this culture. Instead, he grabbed her hand, letting the heat nestle and shoot to her own core, inviting her to imagine all of the things he'd do for her when they returned back to the privacy of their hotel suite.

The waiter returned, sending side-eye glares to their intense gaze before presenting the liquid gold, literal gold, in front of them.

Liv snapped out of Hayden's lustful, beautiful eyes, shocked to find their coffee almost looked like *tea*. She returned to Hayden, in a silent frenzy, demanding he confirm this was correct.

Hayden grinned again, the mood shifting once again from passion to humor.

"Do you think I would actually be idiotic enough to promise you coffee and then serve you tea?!" Hayden asked blankly, before adding with his charming, grin. "Hell hath no fury like a decaffeinated Ollie."

"I've taught you well." Liv smiled, masking her flinch at the endearing name by grabbing her coffee and taking a skeptical sip, but her unconvinced façade quickly shifted to pure delight. "Oh this is wonderful! It's spicier than I imagined?"

"These beans are from the Peninsula and are lightly roasted; it should also include notes of cardamom, saffron, cloves and cinnamon, which it seems you're tasting."

Liv took another sip, humming with delight at the whole experience. She felt like she was in a different universe, surrounded by so many unknown possibilities. Liv hadn't necessarily appreciated all that this new world could offer her, the beauty of it all, having been stuck in the darkness of change and torment for too long. But now, she felt like she had emerged from the darkness and into the golden light.

"Wow. We're really in Cairo, huh." Liv observed aloud, nodding her head as she took a snapshot of the café and tried to absorb everything in sight. She took another sip, before shyly turning her gaze to the most beautiful spectacle in Cairo.

But he, too, was taking in the café scenery. She caught his awe before he noticed her gaze and returned it with equal electricity.

"We really are." Hayden whispered, his eyes full of wonder and possibility.

And for a quick moment, Liv saw the innocent, playful boy she had fallen in love with appear on a relaxed, inspired version of the man he had become. She grinned, snapping the image in her mind, forever reminding her that the teenager she loved would always be there. Even if now they both entered into a new phase of eternal adulthood.

PIPER

Did they have a moment? *Was* that a moment?

Piper could still feel the kiss on her cheek, like a ghost haunting her from the grave.

Now in flight and away from Tristan's delicious cinnamon and burnt ember scent, she felt like she could finally analyze all that happened on that cursed rooftop – figure out what his intention was, what her next step should be and specifically how she needed to react to it all.

No, snap out of it. He is a player – and you have no experience in this game.

There could be no considerations, no opportunties to explore more. They were friends. He was a flirt. That *was* how it was and would *be* exactly how it would be.

Conversation closed. Debate over.

Feeling much more level-headed, Piper nodded to the roof across from the approaching Grand Palace – Silpakorn University. From there, they would need to disappear into the shadows – no being or thing could suspect entry into the sacred Grand Palace that stood beside the historical religious complex. Between guards standing near every entrance and security cameras monitoring all of the grounds, any detected motion would set off a fury of alerted activity, eliminating any chance of discovering the Emerald Buddha.

She landed like a feather, Tristan only a few light steps behind. The two both crouched behind the tallest part of the triangle roof, essentially hanging at a diagonal as they took their planned routes into reality – assessing what still served as the best covering and safest stopping points. To their left, a tiny triangular garden with trees that surrounded a fountain served as the first location. Although delicate and small during the day, in the darkest part of the night, the leaves would serve as the perfect shadowed covering directly across from the Temple of the Emerald Buddha and between the Gate of Mani Nopparat and the Khan Kuenphet Fort.

Seventeen forts bordered the walls of the Grand Palace. All armed with security.

"So, we pass over through the plaza, west of the temple..." Tristan continued.

"Before all Hades breaks loose and we cross over the sacred border and fly like lightning toward Wat Phra Kaew's entrance." Piper sighed, already dreading the upcoming task at hand. If only they had more time to plan properly, research and develop something more concrete... and less along the lines of simply 'winging it.'

"Barricade the door immediately." Tristan turned to Piper, "That's going to be on you."

Piper sighed, embarrassed in having to bring this same point up repetitively. "Tristan, we talked about this. You're stronger. I can't."

"Piper, I'm stronger in fire but we both know you're stronger in wind." He combatted again. "If you want what you've never had, you must do what you've never done. I believe in you."

She hated how she instantaneously believed his words, how he made her feel capable and *want* to believe in herself, too.

"Just promise if something happens, you'll safely guard us with a ring of fire?" She asked quietly.

"I won't need to, but sure." Tristan confirmed. "I've always got your back, Pipes."

"The only thing left to do now is... go." She concluded, her voice shaky.

Piper turned slowly to Tristan, waiting for him to instigate action. There was no way in Hades she was going to be the one who jumped first.

"Follow me." Tristan commanded, looking her directly in the eye.

Anywhere.

Piper nodded instead.

He jumped from the roof and shot through the air, she followed suit, using all her strength to magnetize to the garden's tree branches as swiftly as possible.

"The bushes across the street." Tristan mouthed, pointing to the smaller plants that cornered a grassy plaza behind the Khan Kuenphet Fort.

Piper nodded, appreciative for more shadows to linger in before there was absolutely no turning back.

Tristan jumped again, curving around the road to pass over the wall between the two security gates and without thinking, Piper obediently followed after him while, admittedly, clasping her eyes shut as she passed over the white fortress. She pranced on the ground, delicately lunging behind the shadow of the nearest bush.

Her heart was racing.

Once, she remembered her parents made her play a game of hide 'n seek. Her mom helped her find the best hiding spot in a small cupboard above the wine cellar in the closet. And although she knew she was hiding from her father, she still instinctively recalled the excited fear of being found, the adrenaline that encompassed covering her mouth to ensure she didn't make a sound, as instructed by her mother. The door creaking open as a low voice asked, "Are you sure you do not have a daughter in this house?" Clearly, her father playing along with the game. Her mother too, replied in character, innocently stating, "No, sir it's just the two of us. You won't find any cherubic goddess here."

Her father crept around the room, commanding light as it began shining through the cupboard's edges. Piper had closed her eyes and remembered her mom's instruction, "This is a game, but you must not giggle. For if your father finds you, you will be in grave danger."

Her mother's words had been kind, lighthearted, but Piper had always wondered what caused the fear to glow from behind her eyes.

The flashback, the feeling, both precisely matched Piper's interior emotions at present. Excitement and terror all mixed together.

She finally opened her eyes, just like she had as a child in the cupboard, now prepared to face whatever would find her.

"We're about 300 feet from the entrance." Tristan whispered before lifting his gaze up to the sky, "Please Hermes, grace us with your speed."

Piper studied him curiously, appreciative for the prayer.

He turned to Piper when he finished, nothing more to be said than, "Let's go."

With a deep breath, Piper flashed through the sky, over the brick red and white walls once again, before she leapt onto the ground and began sprinting up the stairs to the temple's entrance.

"Patentibus!" She commanded under her breath, blasting the locked doors apart.

Her eyes grew wide, she reached for Tristan and pulled him back.

"Your shoes!" Piper exasperated, throwing hers off as a courtesy to the religious space. Tristan followed suit and as soon as his sneaker bounced off the ground, he had reversed the withholding touch by pulling her into the temple instantly.

His following command, "Prope!" echoed within the walls of the ancient space, closing the two fixtures once they were both safely inside.

Piper took a moment to summon her wind powers to push them against the doors, pressuring them to remain closed no matter what resistance met their end.

And then there was silence.

She turned to Tristan, questioningly. His gaze connected with hers, before they slowly turned behind them to find the Emerald Buddha in all of its glory.

It radiated in the darkness, casting a green light that echoed against the shadows, pulling them closer.

Piper took a step forwad, instinctively.

A blast of green light penetrated her skull.

And then everything went black.

NINETEEN

PEYTON

She hadn't slept that night.

Every tree branch that scratched against the quaint cottage inn felt like a dagger slicing her throat. Anytime the wood board groaned in the aging shift of the old bedroom sounded like the cracking of a bone. The shadows crossing the room from the pearly full moon sneaking through wailing trees appeared as ghosts, each dancing their own warning to leave the land of the unwanted.

When the crisp sun rose behind a thick layer of clouds, Peyton nearly jumped out of her bed, before realizing if her refuge felt like this, she may not want to encounter what the outside might bring.

"Let's grab a coffee before we head to the park." Peyton proposed, fighting against her instincts and pulling on her corduroy olive-green jacket – the only jacket she packed, let alone outfit – for this impending doom. Yet, with a monochrome look, including olive green snakeskin loafers and a matching cross body bag, she morbidly thought it may help her camoflauge in the forest. But then the golden eyes flashed in her mind, and she took her internal trying-to-lighten-the-mood-in-her-mind-comment back.

Rei, unfazed to her tense stance, rolled out of bed without a care in the world. But of course the demons of Norway weren't targeting him, because Zeus hadn't blessed him with the powers of discovery – he was simply a

Security Elite. She rolled her eyes at the irony. With a yawn, he put on his beige cashmere poloshirt under his grey silk suit.

After leaving the coffee shop, the friendly barista and the light, fruity Norwegian roast almost made the morning a delightful venture. They cascaded up four hundred steps through the Town Park, before seeing the beautiful view of the port town from the hills. White buildings with grey roofs created a mystical abyss against the lush greenery and salty sea.

It was breathtaking. It was blinding. It was simply brilliant.

Peyton smiled, turning to Rei, who caught her own gaze with a matching grin. This moment, with Rei, was the kind of experience she had been chasing for centuries.

And then she attacked him with her lips.

Because she still hadn't hit him hard enough for the grief he mistakenly gave her earlier that week, the pain that hollowed out her soul momentarily and finally made her realize how distraught she would ever be if he didn't exist in this world.

He bit into her shoulder playfully after, before walking across the path and deeper into the park, where the ancient Viking stood himself.

Rollo.

Holding the hilt of a sword in one hand and pointing down with the other, the sea green statue depicted the conqueror in all of his glory. *Including an aggressive hearty mustache*, Peyton dryly observed, deciding it must be compensating for a lack of other manly features. She scoffed at the statue as she approached.

Yet, once she stepped on the grass, a force penetrated her body, blocking her passage any further.

"They're not here." Peyton declared in a trance until she finally turned to Rei, defeated.

Rei looked confused, "Are you sure?" He walked closer to the statue, touching Rollo's foot that stood at eye level.

Peyton turned behind her, the same prickling feeling crawling across her back.

"Rei, it doesn't feel right..." She admitted, less confidently this time.

Peyton slowly trailed her eyes to the sky, hearing the imploring thunder roar from the ashes within the clouds.

A storm was approaching, but Peyton was unsure if it was to balance the natural ecosystem or to wash them away. Either way, she knew it was the work of gods. And she suspected Liv would have combatted any nuisance weather if they were on her lands.

Peyton gulped, turning desperately to Rei.

"Okay, we'll go." Rei nodded, looking up to the foreboding, darkening sky with an understanding look. He wrapped his arm around Peyton and they rushed back to the confines of their cottage.

JOCELYN

They had remained quiet for the majority of the flight. Hades, they had been quiet for the majority of the *year*. They certainly hadn't spoken in weeks.

And why Demetrius thought throwing in some dangerous adventure to the mix could improve their relationship... Joss was at a complete loss.

But she refused to use her sight to figure out his mind. That mad path only left her in tears, shaking and distraught to the inevitable.

Joss begged her subconscious.

Think about anything else. Please.

She started retelling her favorite bedtime story, hearing her father's voice echo in her mind as she learned about the Amazons, the most incredible and powerful women ever known. Joss smiled, remembering the not-so-subtle encouragement of how the strong females set themselves up in opposition to a male-dominated society, establishing these women who lived in isolation and resisted men in all that they did as the heroes, *her heroes*.

The expansive midnight ocean blurred in her eyes. *Oh, how she wished her father were still here today.* Her mother had pleaded there had been no other way, but Jocelyn knew if she had the sight then, she would have done everything in her power to keep him alive.

He had always been kind, humorous. Where her mother stood like a trained statue, repeating phrases and responses engrained into her warped mind, limited to protocol and reason, Rowan, her dad, had understood and appreciated Jocelyn's unconventional approach to the world.

And although her mother reiterated that prophesizing, or sharing her sight with Demetrius was unacceptable, a part of Jocelyn wished she could have asked her father whether it was a mad idea to share her fear with the man she cared for most.

Where Hayden mirrored his mother, Jocelyn was uniquely and proudly her dad.

Jocelyn believed Rowan would tell her to follow her heart, to forge her own path and take responsibility for the consequences. But her mother's echoes of restraint pressed against her conscience.

His voice was weakening in Joss's memory, her mother's advice loud and alive, growing stronger each day.

And ultimately, *he* wasn't there anymore.

LIV

She was drinking Arabian coffee, enjoying the spicy taste and delicious smell as she sat down across the Pyramids of Giza.

The hot beverage in her hands seem to intensify the beauty of the ancient tombs. Cloves, cinnamon… cardamom.

Liv tensed at smelling the distinguished note. Wanting to scream but unable to find her voice.

Cardamom, verveina, cedarwood and leather.

He was here.

Liv dropped her mug, the golden liquid exploding upon impact with the sandy ground.

Yet the liquid wasn't golden, it was blood.

Liv shook in her bed, escaping from the world of dreams, and returned to the conscious. Yet, the nightmare followed her.

She scrunched her eyes tight, still smelling Kronos's scent clinging to the bed. Liv froze, holding her breath and begging to be released from her own personal imprisoned hell.

Was she still dreaming? Could Kronos's power infiltrate her dreams to discover her in the present?

A warm hand barricaded her, sliding across her torso.

Only moments resided between Liv's freedom and capture. She refused to return, refused to relinquish her control against his will without any means of escape. At least not without a fight.

Liv jumped out of bed, casting fiery cuffs to capture her attacker.

"Liv!" Hayden yelled, his innocence penetrating the clouded veil, now bound on the bed with burning flames.

Liv crumbled, hand over her mouth, releasing him at once.

"Oh my god, Hayden." Liv cried, crashing to the ground. "I'm so sorry. I'm so sorry... I thought you were him..."

Hayden jumped off the opposite side of the bed, calmly shushing Liv from afar.

She was shaking, rocking herself back and forth instinctively as a self-healing mechanism.

"It's okay, Liv." He consoled, slowly tiptoeing in her direction, pausing before each additional step so she could give consent as he approached.

When he was close enough, he gulped, whispering, "Can I touch you, now?"

Liv nodded quietly, her eyes closed, but she felt a tear sliding down her cheek, already betraying her instability.

Warm, strong arms pulled her into his lap. Hayden took over the rocking, gently brushing her hair from her face as he kissed her on the head.

"I will destroy him, Ollie." Hayden promised, "And cast him to a confinement crueler than Pandora, so you never have to worry about him haunting you or your loved ones again."

Liv nodded, albeit halfheartedly. She wished she could wake up in her soulmate's arms, calm, happy, safe and not cursed by another's whispering presence.

She turned toward him, wrapping her legs around his waist while cupping his face, bringing him to her so their lips could meet. So, she could show him how much he meant to her.

Her lips grew eager, now cognizant and able to feel him entirely, she wanted all of him.

"Liv, we don't have to…" Hayden panted, between breaths of longing.

This time, Liv shushed Hayden, placing her fingers gently on his lips.

His eyes dazzled in the sunlight.

She grabbed his hand, placing it on her breast, before moving back in to kiss his soft lips, now relaxed and open with pleasure. She reached within his boxers, delicately grabbing him before massaging the mass, feeling him breathe heavily, completely wrapped around her finger and her fingers completely wrapped around him.

Hayden moaned softly, kissing her chest in gratitude before he lifted himself up and fully removed his boxers, allowing Liv to slowly slide atop him and intensify her movements before resuming in his lap.

As he entered into her, she felt full, complete, and her cathartic groans only encouraged his manhood to work more magic, however impossible it seemed.

And soon, she was shaking, convulsing, feeling chills everywhere he touched, until she shouted his name in ecstasy, needing every last drop of him.

She fell into his lap, kissing his neck and continued building more friction between him and her, inviting him to come on her adventure and finish together. Rugged, raw and entirely mind consuming, Hayden plunged into her, deeper and more intensely than before, each time more significant and demanding, causing her to gasp in gratification. His own desired hum following after breathing her name and holding her as they finally and finitely collapsed against the wall.

Liv felt lightheaded, giddy. The way she was supposed to feel when she woke up next her soul mate.

It was how this morning should have started, and she had claimed it back.

HAYDEN

The God of Coffee handed him his morning beverage, today opting for a classic medium roast. And even without sugar or spice, it somehow tasted sweeter when topped off with Ollie's smile, sliced in half by her own cup of coffee.

It was much better to focus on how he could make her smile than the potential terror he could accidentally instill in her. Just from his *being*.

He knew the only way to truly get rid of her nightmares would be to eliminate the males who caused them in the first place, which was precisely why they needed to find and ally with the Egyptians.

They hailed a taxi to drive them out west toward the land of the dead, the sacred burial ground built to prepare pharaohs for the afterlife, where they too, became gods. Today, they planned to explore the three famous Pyramids of Giza, hoping that Pharaoh Khafre, Pharaoh Menkaure or Pharaoh Khufu's mausoleums would show promise for a way to find the hidden world the Egyptian Gods now currently inhabited.

They had selected to first visit during operating hours, wanting to cover as much ground as possible while the God Ra blessed them with natural light. Once they got the lay of the land, selected a location and memorized the precise route to avoid any accidental desecration, Hayden and Liv would return in the night, out of sight from any bi-standers, especially guards who would question the visitor count not matching the end of day departures. They had both agreed that the least amount of impact would be best, wanting to remain respectful to the sacred site and keep as much as possible untouched. The less of a trail they left, the better likelihood they would remain unharmed.

"You know, studying ancient Egypt was my favorite educational topic, aside from the Titanic, growing up." Liv boasted as they walked through the entrance and onto the historical site. She looked back to Hayden, shining brighter than the sun.

"Is that the true reason you volunteered so enthusiastically to accompany me?" Hayden teased.

"Hey, I didn't spend my sixth-grade weekends watching documentaries for nothing – I simply couldn't let this knowledge go to waste." Liv turned around to face Hayden straight on, while pointing to her head, before twirling to complete a full circle and continue on.

"I would be obliged if you shared that impressive knowledge." Hayden prompted, fanning out to walk alongside her.

"I forgot most of it." Liv admitted, "But, my more recent studies rekindled past insights."

"Knowledge is knowledge. Strange how some memories never truly leave us. So, tell me what you've got, Monaco."

There was more to Hayden's observation, Liv knew it. But now was not the time nor place to discuss the wounds, so instead she readjusted her thoughts and went full steam encyclopedia.

"They were the first known people to create a written language – ironically the hieroglyphics were formed not to tell stories but for commerce purposes. My favorite fact is that nobles actually cleaned their teeth! Sure, it was more so to cleanse their words for the gods they worshipped, but it had to have helped dental hygiene, right? *And* it was a practice other civilizations didn't concept until the 19th century."

"I would have been impressed and glad of the act itself, whether or not it was in my honor." Hayden agreed with a soft chuckle.

Liv's informative rapid fire lasted through the formal ticketed entryway. Now standing among the three large pyramids before them, Liv went silent, taking in the view for all of its glory.

Hayden smiled, watching her appreciate the sight; this was all he wanted to provide her – sought after experiences that were worthy of eternal memory.

"Hayden, when someone does pray to you, what does it feel like?" Liv asked softly, her eyes still glued to the intimidating, ancient pyramid structures.

He considered the question, since it happened so rarely. Many mortals didn't believe in gods and nobody knew of his name to specifically plead or give gratitude.

"It feels like a tug, or a pull, or being thwarted out of your seat, depending on the scale and urgency of the prayer. Mostly, I suspect it's similar to how our bond feels when we communicate with one another."

He didn't specify whether he meant at its height, when they had declared their commitment to one another, or now, a mending vessel longing for its former glory. The scale in itself pretty accurately described the range of the pull.

"If we prayed to these Pharoahs – Khafre, Menkaure or Khufu, who were believed to have joined the gods and become one in the afterlife – do you think they could hear us?" She whispered, only a breath that Hayden had to lower his head to hear properly. "They may not be able to do anything, but we could at least try and communicate that we're hoping to visit?"

It wasn't a bad idea. To hell if they knew how to open and travel through a portal. Or what language Egyptian deities spoke after being hidden from the modern world for thousands of years.

Don't overthink. Just small steps.

Hayden breathed, focusing on the tangible to avoid spiraling.

"Yes, let's pray in each mausoleum and find a scribe tonight." Hayden agreed, turning sharply left to find the official entrance to the religious site. The authentic entrance built to protect the sacred grounds by the ancient Egyptians thousands of years ago.

Liv looked up, observing the limestone sphinx and commenting dryly, "Feels strange not having it chase me through the grounds..."

"Oh, no worries, I'm happy to fix that." Hayden joked; raising his hand in the air.

Liv's eyes grew wide, turning quickly to Hayden and clearly preparing to yell, 'No!' before finding an amused grin growing on his face.

"You little asshole." Liv chided, her eyes narrowing into slivers.

"I figured you hosing it with a surge of water would probably not bode well with security." Hayden considered aloud.

"Or more importantly, the deities it was built to protect…" Liv added contemplatively. "Leaving zero trails is truly no fun…"

Yet, she still returned her gaze to further study the figure, preparing for the likelihood of it indeed sparking to life and chasing them both away.

But admittedly, Hayden also felt on edge as soon as they passed through the threshold, instantaneously throwing a protective shield around both Liv and him, and instinctively pulling her closer.

Chills crept down his neck, as if an invisible presence hovered behind him.

It felt very clear that they had departed the land of the living and now resided among the land of the dead.

TWENTY

PIPER

Zeus, she was like a tectonic plate that just endured an earthquake. Her limbs felt as if they had been pulled apart and then contracted back together.

Piper stirred, trying to remember what she had seen last. Yet, all she saw was Tristan and green, and then darkness.

She squinted an eye open, finding many people whispering and humming around her, buzzing even more in speculation as she slowly lifted herself up into a sitting position.

Tristan was still knocked out cold, face down on the ground and possibly drooling. Piper kicked him, hoping it would encourage consciousness, for she could really use an ally against the unknown crowd encircling them.

They all dressed in fine silk and a stunning curation of Japanese, Chinese and Thai-inspired clothing. Rich colors ranging from navy, burgundy and gold shone in modern interpretations of the traditional Kimono, Hanfu, Qipao, Changshan, Hanbok, Áo Dài, Cheongsam and Sompot Chong Kben influenced styles.

One tall and incredibly handsome man stepped forward, his arm linked around another which belonged to a beautiful woman.

"Who are you?" He inquired sternly.

His voice carried throughout the mesmerising red and gold room, decorated with soft velvet and elaborate sculptures that led up to a grand staircase.

"I'm Piper of the Pure Gods." She squeaked.

She nudged Tristan again, thinking that now would be a very good time for him to wake up. The man's gaze moved toward the lump of flesh that lay before him.

"This is Tristan, Pure God, Head of the House of Fire." She explained, managing to kick the declared deity significantly harder without causing a scene.

That apparently did the trick. His eyes went wide, before recognizing the amount of feet that he could see standing on his level from the ground. He caught eyes with Piper and calmed down with an immediate exhale.

Still determining composure, Tristan first slowly lifted himself up, before lightly jumping to a standing position. Not missing a beat, he held out his hand to Piper to help her up as well.

The movement made her head pound and she began to feel dizzy, black flecks speckled across her vision as she clung onto Tristan through the light-headedness. She pondered how he had been able to stand upright and appear so sturdy, filling her with impress and admiration.

"We apologize for any disturbances." He smoothly offered, his grin dazzling. "Piper and I come to represent the King of the Pure Gods in search of an alliance with your deities."

Tristan bowed, pulling Piper down with him.

After the custom formalities had been addressed, Tristan continued on, "I believe we haven't been properly introduced …?"

The man in which Tristan addressed smiled, beckoning his partner to step forward.

"I am King Rāhula and this is my wife, Queen Chanthira."

Unlike the other men, King Rāhula wore a traditional suit, its deep emerald silk perfectly complementing his beige complexion. Queen Chanthira on the otherhand, had a delicate face with a complexion like a sandy beach sprinkled with pink rose petals.

"You have traveled far to reach us." Queen Chanthira spoke softly, nudging her partner's side.

"Of course, you must join us for dinner." King Rāhula stiffly offered, but a glimmer of amusement sparkled once he swiftly acknowledged his wife.

Piper was too busy staring at Queen Chanthira's stunning yellow and navy high neck gown, her sleeves trimmed with a pale lavendar fur and fabric intricately embroidered. More enchanting, Chanthira wore a gold headress and statement earrings that practically made Piper drool.

Without waiting for a reply, King Rāhula spun around and began walking toward the grand staircase.

Tristan looked to Piper, then looped this arm around hers to respectfully follow the royal duo toward what she assumed to be the grand dining hall.

He leaned into her with a whisper, "We're definitely ahead of schedule."

Piper turned to him in surprise.

"I'm just saying, we totally could have explored today in Bangkok, had another whiskey, and still would have made *great* time." He shrugged, but the mischevious sarcasm still dazzled from behind his eyes.

"Well, hopefully we have cause for celebration when we return." Piper retorted, rolling her eyes before dropping her own voice lower. "Thoughts on our current predicament?"

"They need something." Tristan dropped his voice to only a breath, sending chills down Piper's neck. "And we need to figure it out tonight. Remember, we have the advantage."

"Do we?" She questioned, eyeing the elaborate façade the ancient deities presented, even if only for show. Even from behind, the onyx heads that they followed both radiated power.

"Patience, Piper." Tristan purred. "All will be revealed in time."

The only issue was, Piper had never been very patient.

PEYTON

"Where to, next?" Peyton asked, plopping down on the bed and sprawling her arms and legs across it.

"Shouldn't you tell me, God of Discovery?" Rei challenged back with a smirk.

Peyton sighed, staring up blankly at the ceiling. The heavy weight against her conscience kept leading her astray from her true inclinations. She sat up, determining that she needed to be honest with Rei. "The only feeling I have is that we shouldn't be here."

Rei paused, studying Peyton curiously. "Do you want to leave?"

"No." Peyton sighed again, falling back to the comfort of the mattress. "It could just be this city, or a bad interpretation of some greater power trying to push us to another location…" Realistically, she didn't believe it was either of the proposed notions. "And even if we aren't welcome on Norway soil, I, at the very least, want to confront the reason for it."

Rei chuckled darkly. "Only Peyton. A greater power tells you 'no,' and you say 'not without a valid reason.' Certainly a fighter, tried and true."

"Security Pillar, tried and true." Peyton grinned, pointing to herself proudly. Her lighthearted demeanor turned dark again as she tried to piece the reasoning together. "I just don't understand why we wouldn't be welcome? I haven't visited Norway in centuries and you used to be friendly with their kind. Do you have any reason to believe we'd be unwelcome? Any past conflict not documented in our histories? Liv did mention our records had been tampered with…"

Rei bit his lip, contemplating the facts and his histories. "To my knowledge, we've always been cordial with the Norse Gods. Perhaps it aligns with the reason they isolated their community so long ago?"

Peyton contemplated his response, equally acknowledging and ignoring Rei's daggering stare, pleading that his response might light a trigger to connect the dots and discover a lead. But alas, the Norse Gods remained a mystery, protected against her arsenal of powers.

"I guess the next step is identifying any religious monuments or dedications to the ancient Norse Gods?" She offered contemplatively, "We can visit the more popular ones and see if we find any clues…" Peyton stood up, dread filling her face as she realized the reality of their circumstance without any trails to follow. "The Norse Gods ruled in nine different worlds, Rei. How are we supposed to find and enter nine different realms in hopes of discovering a clue to a potentially extinct civilization? What if we become extinct in the process?"

She started pacing the room, mumbling, "Niflheim, Muspelheim, Asgard, Midgard, Jotunheim, Vanaheim, Alfheim, Svartálfar, Helheim…" Before Rei grabbed her and held her still.

"One step at a time." He growled through his teeth, bringing her back down to earth – or *Midgard,* as the Norse would say it.

Either way, she nodded her head. Even if it were still spinning.

"According to legend, Asgard is where the deities exist. Why should that change?"

"Ragnarök." Peyton muttered, unconvinced.

"Okay, let's stop theorizing about myth. As we learned with Liv, true facts and myth does not always prove to be synergetic in accuracy." Rei pressed, adding, "I remember once before war, our men went to pray before a carved wood statue of Odin. Perhaps we check that out next? See if it triggers anything?"

"Røssvatnet?" Peyton asked, uncertain. "Six hours north of here, but worth a shot."

Anything to get away from this haunted town, this feeling.

So with the beginning of a nod from her partner, Peyton had already run out of the room, proceeding to travel north as quickly as possible.

REI

Peyton had looked weary since they landed on Norway land. Her natural inclination was not wrong. Every uncertain glance or quick turn behind her shoulder mimicked the mental war Rei fought within his own mind.

While his girlfriend battled with the external; Rei fought against the internal.

The knowledge. The purpose. The duty.

He looked forward to the next flight, time to clear his mind and assess what needed to be done. To keep both promises. And remain loyal to those he loved.

The sharp mountains below, paired with lakes and lagoons, brought him back to the time he had spent among the Vikings so long ago. In a world where gods could still walk among the mortals, albeit hiding all their powerful glory.

They were the ones who had remained pure, who respected the civilization they domineered over. It felt like a more complicated time, yet simpler all the same.

Now the simplicity had been completely eliminated.

As they headed toward Odin's tribute, a wooden-carved statue depicting the All-Father of the Nordic Gods, the pressure continued to build as they ventured north.

Similar to Peyton, Rei knew they weren't welcome. He was glad she finally admitted it. For he knew this journey would pull them apart and test the years they had built, together. And her honesty had united them again, against the unknown.

Yet, similarily if they did not ally now, Kronos's forces would only grow stronger, until they were entirely outnumbered to the Dark.

He prayed for Odin's kin to understand there was a bigger, justifiable reason for seeking out their kind, that he came in peace and most of all, to recognize that he was never one to break a promise.

Rei knew he would fight for that last trait until the very end. It was how he defined himself. His character. His worth. Even if it left Peyton wishing he indeed had found his afterlife in Ireland once and for all.

As soon as they flew over the tiny village of Hattfjelldal, Rei spotted the large water mass ahead with the ominous island almost welcoming them into its trap.

Røssvassholmen.

He hadn't been able to fly across the body of water, Røssvassnet, the last time he had appeared in front of the almighty deity, asking for his blessing and guidance for the upcoming battles to conquer Normandy. Imposter's Syndrome at its finest, he followed Rollo's order and prayed to the gods in whose power he did not need; whose loyalty he had not earned.

Whose loyalty he did not wish to give.

Flashes of soldiers past stomped across the sacred grounds, ghosts anxious and excited to get to battle, now wallowing in self-despair. He blurred all the lost souls together, yet he could see every face. A stampede of men all individually unique.

Peyton flew ahead of him, the landing target now certain.

Would he falsely pray again? If so, what would he ask for? Forgiveness?

Swiftly, he leaped onto the ground, jumping lightly across the rocky terrain as he slowed from a sprint into a delicate jog. He didn't dare destruct the Nordic lands with careless concerns, making every move, every word, intricately planned for the benefit of their own good.

"I fear we're running out of time." Peyton observed, shivering among the darkening clouds above, acting like concrete cementing itself into a whole fervent being. If they weren't careful, they would be suffocated beneath it.

Rei nodded sternly in agreement, careful not to verbally agree to her increasing trepidation. There was no point in adding to an already escalading fear, igniting the fire already ablaze for it to burn down the entire forest.

"Perhaps our next stop, if this does not work out, can be exploring the Rök runestone in Sweden." Rei proposed, following Peyton as she marched stubbornly toward the water.

"Perhaps..." Peyton considered, her voice trailing off as she approached the wooden figure.

As suspected, her eyebrows furrowed. She turned wearily behind, looking up into the sky, as if assessing her limits before all Hades broke loose. Ultimately, she took another step forward into the lakeshore; Rei followed suit.

She was the God of Discovery – all he could do is follow her, into any and all circumstances that presented itself from her pursuit, *her hunt*, and hope to protect her from whatever she found.

Both breathed out a unanimous sigh when the body of water remained tranquil. Perhaps, a little *too loudly* for comfort between the two.

These were your friends, once. Rei reminded himself, braving up for the inevitable.

Peyton took another step, plunging her foot deeper into the lake. The icy body of water now stained her olive green trouser up to her knee. One more step and she'd be halfway submerged. Another and she'd be in reaching distance of the holy landmark.

The winds started picking up with her next step, a silent warning. But Peyton, be damned – there was no way they'd come this far without confirming or eliminating the tribute on their list.

Another step, and thunder rumbled in the distance. The wind lifted the lake into a mist, pairing eerily with the light rainfall, almost snow that began drizzling above, effortlessly soaking them from top to bottom. What minutes before was a flawless crisp and clear landscape, now stood fjords that could no longer be seen across the lake because of the fog. But they pioneered on.

Instead of succumbing partially to Odin, they were both now surrounded by water, fully vulnerable to do the bidding of whatever the ancient God desired.

Dread began filling Rei's core. The water grew chillier, the winds crisper. The warning accelerating.

With her usually golden locks now plastered against her skull, Peyton turned back warily one last time, as if asking permission. Finally.

Rei shook his head, but it was too late.

She reached.

And when her cream skin collided with the wooden surface, a wave rose from behind and catapulted over them, drowning them both in a sea of water and wind.

"*Never Tell….*" The body of water wailed within the waves.

Rei only hoped Peyton couldn't hear the warning.

When the water subsided, Peyton had been thwarted back to Rei near the shore.

She collided on the ground, coughing water from her lungs. "Nope." Peyton stated bleakly, trying to catch her breath before looking back to the ominous statue.

"Did you hear?" She whispered silently, before her question was interrupted with more coughs, but Rei understood her intention.

Standing above her with no indication he had been in the same near catastrophe, he nodded silently, matching her gaze back toward Odin, toward the warning he understood all too clearly.

Peyton's gaze had penetrated back to him, speculation radiating as she tilted her head in observation.

And with that, Rei's impending dread thickened within. Still staring out to the misty abyss, he had a revelation of his own.

Rei couldn't lead her astray much longer.

TWENTY-ONE

JOCELYN

As soon as her foot touched the damp, luscious grounds surrounded by the emerald fields of Ireland, a flash of celtic green eyes swept past an emblazoned gold backdrop.

No.

Joss squeezed her eyes shut, forcing her mind out of the vision and to the present.

She was tired of living in the conditional unknown.

"Are you seriously not going to say anything to me during this entire trip?" Demetrius finally huffed, staring exasperatedly as he circled the vast field they had sculpted into their runway.

Trees bristled from a distance; Jocelyn snapped her head in its direction, studying the shadows of the bright forest leaves for any indication of gold.

"We're being watched." She humbly concluded, before picking up her silk and chiffon cyan gown, fighting against the metal accents that appeared like armor, and stomped through the marshes toward the cave's entrance.

Whether a warning or welcome, Joss no longer wanted to deliberate on possibility, but instead live in the moment.

On fact, truth, and in the now.

That was her power and she would be damned if she let it capture her soul.

"Excuse me, we're being *watched?*" Demetrius clarified, chasing behind her.

At least Demetrius hadn't complained about the mud on his plaid suit. Yet.

"It's none of your concern." Joss replied tartly, marching on.

And since he was used to hearing that retort, Demetrius remained silent.

It had cost a few days of Jocelyn playing out all of the possible scenarios and outcomes before she committed to leaving the Royal Palace and helping with the alliance cause. And she had only selected to pursue the quest after determining her involvement with seeking the Celtic deities would truly be entering with blindness and no control. It was the first-time unpredictability had opened a door, and although her powers still haunted her in their world, Jocelyn couldn't ignore the part of her that was exhilarated to enter the uncharted territory and get high off the blind unknown, with no stakes in the game. It was terrifying and incredible.

As Dylan had advised, the cave's entrance would be challenging to spot, but a large parking lot and tourism office would help direct their path. The destination wasn't too hard to find from the field, but the sun's glow still dominating behind the mountains as it rose to announce the day made finding a darkened cave with five hundred descending steps a harder challenge to manage.

And as Joss had foreseen, her armoured gown encouraged her bad temper, so on queue, she spun into another outfit. As planned, Joss now wore a long-sleeved beige gown adorned with a navy trench.

"This way," Joss commanded in a whisper. She hated how her voice came off monotone, as if she didn't care.

As if her actions had not all been laid out before her.

The reality was she was constantly trying *not* to see visions, so she overcompensated in order to avoid sounding like she was certain with knowledge.

"Joss, you know if you ever wanted to talk…" Demetrius began, softly.

"Not now." She cut him off, curt and sharp, like chopping off an unwanted branch from the tree.

They began descending the steps of Dunmore Cave and when their ceiling turned from air to rock, Joss saw a shadowed figure dance across the stone.

She froze, closing her eyes again, until Demetrius collided into her and they almost rolled down through the cave's entrance, entangled in eachother's arms, magnets pulling together while trying to desperately separate.

Joss snapped her eyes open, taking a step forward just in time, before Demetrius had the chance to run into her like her vision had offered.

She gulped. It was as if with every step deeper into the cave, her instinct for knowledge beckoned her further, enticing her to give in to her powers for the pursuit of truth.

Focus.

With the sharp *clip* of her heels hitting the stone steps combined with Demetrius's soft *plump* of his leather loafer, they finally reached a flat surface.

To the right, a balcony overlooked what seemed to be a fairy pool and to the left, a trail to dive deeper into the cave's abyss.

Per Dylan's instructions, Joss headed directly toward the darkness. Her no-nonsense attitude refraining from exploring any unnecessary attraction. But, another shadow erupted from the trail, gliding her sight from the path and directing her eyes back toward the fairy pool.

It dived into the water, disappearing entirely once it broke through the liquid surface.

Although Jocelyn hated to admit it, she knew two things. The first, that she could trust this shadowed friend; which led to the second – they needed to take an alternative route to find their final destination.

"Come with me." Jocelyn proposed, diverting off the planned path and spinning around Demetrius, back to the fairy pool.

"Dylan said…" Demetrius questioned, not necessary challenging her – he knew better than that and trusted her powers – but instead, prompting her for an updated explanation, a chance to let him in.

"I know." Joss agreed, wishing she didn't come off so agitated. "I have another lead."

The terrible curse of her powers was that it was also extremely difficult to lie. For years, she had practiced ways to play the English language, crafting ambigious phrases that both stretched the truth and delivered the statements her peers desired. It was one of the earlier lessons the Candor Pillar had bestowed upon her. One in which her mother excelled.

By the time she had 'explained,' they both hovered over the railing, looking deep into the cave's heart through a sheen of water.

"We must jump." Jocelyn concluded, quickly playing out the effort in her mind, when a flash of an outdoor, rocky terrain plastered the interior of her thoughts.

"Jump?" Demetrious questioned; his voice higher than its usual silk.

"Jump." Jocelyn repeated with a nodd.

"Okay. We jump." Demetrious accepted, eyeing Jocelyn suspiciously. "Together? Holding hands? One after the other? On the count of three? Synchronized diving…?"

Jocelyn huffed, unable to contain the smile appearing as she covered up her laughter with forced indifference.

"Together." She chuckled, shaking her head.

Some parts of her fought to remain authentic.

"Wonderful. If we get knocked out, at least we'll be unconscious together, then?" Demetrius teased, extending his hand.

Jocelyn tenderly grasped it, ignoring the melody that played as their skin made contact. His large, leather hand against her dainty silk one.

It always felt so nice to touch him; her mind immediately calmed – an empty, silent space.

Joss closed her eyes, momentarily reveling in the reprieve.

It was marvelous.

The countdown prepared her quickly for the next needed action.

"Three, two, one!" Demetrius offered, leaping into the damp air with Jocelyn by his side.

Soon they were descending, pencil diving toward the rocky pool, slipping through a veil of darkness before dropping into another world.

Another world with an endless rocky terrain and cotton candy skies.

LIV

Walking up to the Pyramid was exponentially more intimidating than she had expected – the blocks used to create its triangular form were almost as tall as her, making Hayden and her seem disposable in the vast grandness of it all.

"A wonder of the world, indeed." Hayden observed, placing his hand on the second-tier stone and looking directly up to the tip of the structure, his face perpendicular to his neck so his view could ascend as if to the eternal sky.

The sight itself proved considerable. It was precisely the exact reason the ancient Egyptians chose this architecture in the first place, finding ways to continue eternal rest.

The thought had been slowly creeping from the back of Liv's head to the center of it, the whole notion of the pyramids being a grand transportation to the afterlife, where Pharoahs became gods and lived among them. As time passed and they discovered more, and now being here on the holy grounds in flesh, the inkling that their potential allies lived in a completely different world, one made for rest, increasingly concerned Liv. What if they did not wish to reawaken?

Simply from Hayden's observation, she believed he worried about the same discovery, but Liv refused to state it aloud. Agreeing on the notion together would only make it feel all the more plausible.

Instead, she grabbed Hayden's hand atop the rock, squeezing it. Reminding him that even with the pyramids, life remained. Hope remained. Possibility remained. They remained.

He weakly smiled, pulling both of their hands back.

Thank you.

Liv naturally shrugged.

It's a somber site. The least I can do.

Hayden tilted his head, his eyes growing wide. "Did I just hear…?"

Liv's head snapped up, locking directly to his eyes, a sight she'd always magnetize to, but this time it meant so much more.

"I heard you, too!" She beamed.

Holy shit. Perhaps among dead, there indeed could be life. Renewal. Growth.

Well, this will certainly help communicate honestly among strangers and mortals in the future. Hayden commented within her mind, his voice sharper than usual, a velvet alto with words pacing quicker than his typical beat.

And more importantly, fucking around with Rei when we return to Puerdios.

Liv grinned; Hayden rolled his eyes.

"Okay, Monaco. Which pyramid first?" Hayden asked, already walking away.

"The great one. Obviously." Liv hollered, "Go big or go home!"

But, she knew he already anticipated that response, her inclination proven correct when he had already begun guiding her toward the desired pyramid's entrance.

They started walking through the Grand Gallery, a steep incline between two narrow walls that rose 28 ft. high, and slowly merged inward as they continued ascending. Near the top, Liv began feeling claustrophobic, dealing with a width only a little more than 3 ft. She could only imagine if she or Hayden were to upset an Egyptian God within this mausoleum, their wrath would come twofold as the walls crushed together during the escape. Her chest grew heavier with the thought, but she perservered on.

"Watch your head, Ollie." Hayden tapped his hand on their new, smaller parameters for a room, signaling the newest addition to Liv's growing phobia.

The sight of Hayden almost crawling through the next section, the roof's height nearly half his six-foot-three frame, brought Liv reprieve through sadistic joy, even though she too needed to squat in order to avoid hitting her head against the stone.

Karma was certainly a bitch.

But after they emerged from the small tunnel and into a larger (but certainly bare) room composed of granite blocks, Liv and Hayden located the sarcophagus that Pharaoh Khufu was suspected to have been buried in, before pillaging and thievery over the past centuries left only a broken stone casket in its remains. The King's Chamber looked like a dying shadow of its former glory. A sobering sight that still crawled eerily against her skin.

Looking around at the emptiness of the space, Liv eyed Hayden, the growing silence intimidating her pounding heart. In the distance, she heard the sound of sand blowing in the wind, accompanied by faint melodic whispers humming within it.

"Do you hear that?" Liv asked, her voice vibrating against the acoustics of the room.

Hayden nodded, walking closer to the desolate sarcophagus; Liv followed, noting the buzzing noise strengthened with every step. The soft echoes of a melancholy tune sent chills down Liv's spine.

"Don't touch it." Hayden warned, his voice, too, echoed in the confines of the room.

Liv gulped, before turning away to search the bare walls, hoping to find any other clues near the surrounding space to allude to what the structure symbolized. In reality, she *needed* to turn away.

Something about the sarcophagus scared her – whether the unknown it represented or the foreboding power it instilled. The possibility of it being both terrified her even more.

Another group of three young females entered the chamber, 'ooh-ing' and 'ahh-ing' as they whispered and giggled from behind. The sandy winds stopped abruptly; the secrets of the dead resting once again. As soon as the living's naivity penetrated the space, it was as if an electric plug had been pulled from its energy source.

Hayden bowed his head toward the exit and signaled Liv to join, ignoring the playful stares and drooling eyes of their new friends who swooned over his chiseled body and golden features. Refusing to give into the inappropriateness of the entire situation, instead he let the new guests enjoy their time with history's prized possession in private by removing his taunting appeal, allowing the ancient artifacts to refocus the ladies' attention once again.

To ensure they could crystallize their strategy, Hayden and Liv ventured through the additional two pyramids, approaching every nook and cranny allowed during the public tours. Neither experienced a similar enchantment like the first.

Liv had even made Hayden approach the three traveling friends who had not-so-swiftly remained close behind during the entire exploration, exiting after them at the last pyramid and eagerly obliged to make conversation with Hayden; however, she could barely contain her amusement when Hayden eventually asked the young women if they had heard any sand blowing or faint acapella singing in the Great Pyramid's King's Chamber. Their immediate reactions tattled on their obvious shock, before eventually agreeing with Hayden that they, too, heard the noises he inquired about. One girl even had the audacity to put her hand on Hayden's arm; her eyes growing wide as her hand gently grasped the strength of his bicep.

Liv smirked, crossing her arms and turning back toward the pyramid; anything was less painful to watch than the desperation of Hayden's fan club, when she noticed a faint set of symbols carved on a stone.

Her eyes studied the ancient runes, before her curiosity compelled her to lower her head closer, observing the set of hieroglyphics and feeling another pull. All of the other surrounding blocks were blank.

Liv took out a notebook and tried her best to mimic the faint symbols as she transcribed the ancient carving onto college-ruled paper with a ballpoint pen.

When she finished the last hieroglyphic, a gust of wind blew against her burnt orange ensemble, the light breeze giving much reprieve to her sticky skin, but when Liv looked back to the stone, the symbols were gone.

TRISTAN

Their visit had caused quite the stir in the castle; however, Tristan wasn't entirely sure what he *had* expected with meeting the Buddhist Gods. Now, holding Piper and possibly getting led straight into the lion's den, he thought of two things. The first, making sure he kept the current Pure deity on his arm safe at all costs, and second, making sure they both left the upcoming dinner getting exactly what they wanted. But, if it came down to a choice, his resolution would be easy – the first would take priority. There was no other way.

He knew she was nervous. Piper's innocence was exactly what made him worry about whatever would be dealt in their future cards. Not that he had any advantage over this predicament – he just thought darkly enough to already be mentally preparing for how to avoid the worst – whether falling into any preconceived traps or doing whatever needed to get done to ensure her escape.

He had killed before and would kill again, in a heartbeat, to preserve her pureness.

Zeus knew they all needed more like her in this world.

Large gilded doors swung open, creating a thunderous *boom!* as they locked into place, revealing a stunning dining table at the center of the room, levitated higher and above hundreds of tables that encircled it.

King Rāhula and Queen Chanthira glided up the stairs, pausing to acknowledge their guests again as they beckoned Piper and Tristan to join from above.

Tristan felt Piper's grip on his arm tense. He took his right hand and placed it above hers, squeezing it in return, feeling fulfilled when she exerted a calming breath after his assuring gesture.

He wanted to say so many things to her, yet somehow always managed to choke on his words as soon as her piercing eyes intoxicated him to stare in mesmerization or her smile caused him to stutter. The worst was when both penetrated him at once and he was forced to combat his setbacks against even more demanding chills. For instance, right now he wanted to tell her that she looked absolutely regal in her mustard dress, that her midnight sky hair shone like it had stars in it, or that most of all, he wished he was holding her hand instead of politely escorting her. She made him want to be a gentleman while also do un-gentleman-like things to her, all at once.

Most of all, he wanted to be worthy of her. Because she deserved nothing but the absolute best. Tristan knew perfection would never be enough. And that's what sent his mind spiraling into dark despair.

Soon, Piper and Tristan had successfully escalated up the stairs, forcing Tristan to pivot from thinking about Piper's soft, porcelain skin and back to the task at hand.

"Thank you for the honor of dining with you, your majesty." Tristan bowed, gently pulling Piper down with him.

"It is us who have the honor." King Rāhula smiled, pulling out a chair for his queen to sit before following suit.

Tristan mirrored his hosts' maneuvers before seating himself, too.

"We shall discuss everything openly and let truth be the basis of our words. We converse as friends. As equals." The King proposed, finally adding, "Please call me Rāhula."

"I will remain as Queen Chanthira." Her majesty stated, before a smile broke and she finally giggled. "I am joking, please call me Thira."

Piper laughed, the sound pure gold against a colorless canvas.

"I must ask, how did you two find us?" Rāhula asked loudly, his voice echoing through the grand ballroom.

"We're not entirely sure." Piper admitted. "We were searching for your kind, of course, but simply walked through the temple of the Emerald Buddha and…"

"Got pulled through the portal to this realm." Tristan finished. "Where exactly, *are we?*"

"The prison of Shiva." Chanthira replied, her voice crisp and stern.

"Prison?" Piper gulped, her voice raising back up to its normal octave. He saw her flinch out of the corner of his eye, wanting to turn to him, but instead held steady, maintaining the gaze of their guests.

He grabbed her hand subtly beneath the table and squeezed. He hoped she didn't feel his heart pounding through the throbbing of his wrist's veins.

"Seven hundred and forty years ago, Shiva, the Hindu God of Destruction, believed our power was growing too large to properly control. He did not like that so many prayed to Rāhula, me and our pantheon." Chanthira explained softly, yet her voice carried to ensure all within the room could hear the discussion openly.

"Sadly, we fell for his cruelty, an ambush disguised as a treaty to unite our mortal subjects." Rāhula continued, his face burning as he recalled the humility. "We were cursed and imprisoned within this crafted world, forever constricted within this faux green jewel that Shiva replaced and indefinitely unable to escape unless the rightful emerald Buddha is restored."

"I am terribly sorry for your misfortunes." Tristan began, taking a deep breath. Only the coolness of Piper's hand kept his composure. "May I ask if it is at all possible to escape this green confine?" He twirled his hand in a circular motion.

"A few have tried, years ago of course… only one returned." Chanthira offered, her face scrunching into queasiness.

"And?" Tristan pressed, growing desperate.

"Klahan was only green dust, not even a spirit when he returned. He… evaporated." Rāhula stated blankly, his eyes distant.

TWENTY-TWO

PIPER

Queen Chanthira grabbed Rāhula's hand on the table, pausing briefly to lock eyes with the King.

Piper was shaking.

They were going to turn green and evaporate if they left this prison.

She hadn't said goodbye to her parents properly. How woud Liv *not* fail out of Puerdios without Piper's help? She hadn't even kissed Tristan yet. She was only nineteen and was supposed to have infinite years to live. Piper was going to have her first-ever birthday party with actual friends – it was a cruel fate to taunt her with such an awaited experience, to only pull it out and burn the possibility. She hadn't even passed Deity Power II – she hadn't even completed her first academic year at university. Only Satyrs didn't complete their first year at Puerdios, usually flunking out from being in a constant state of drunkenness. She had been destined to graduate at the top of her class and now she would be remembered as one among the Satyrs!?

"Hey. We're not cursed, we may have an advantage." Tristan squeezed her hand, touching her cheek with this other, forcing her to come back to the present from her spiral.

Piper nodded, although over enthusiastically and with a loud gulp.

At least she could still cross off kissing Tristan from her bucket-list if the worst-case scenario presented itself. Even if he didn't exactly kiss her back. She'd count it.

Piper nodded to herself in assurance, before groaning internally.

They weren't even imprisoned in a real ancient jewel. Just her freakin' luck.

"That is true."

King Rāhula's optimistic reply to Tristan's consolation peaked Piper's interest.

"If we're able to find and restore the original jewel to grant your freedom, would you enter into an alliance with the Pure Gods, in return?"

Tristan was already a step ahead of Piper, willing to negotiate dangerously for their people. Dangerously for themselves.

Rāhula paused, taking a deep breath of consideration to the proposal. "I am not sure I can ask such a request of you two. You would risk your life so willingly for our kind?"

"For your alliance." Tristan clarified, his eyes dazzling.

Piper was still deliberating if this meant everyone at present actually believed they could escape safely...

Chanthira cut in, her whole demeanor much lighter than moments before. "It is worth a shot, Rāhula." She turned to Piper and Tristan, and explained, "Our kind is not strong enough to fight Shiva's curse without the power of the Emerald Buddha; however, your source of power is not connected to it..." Chanthira turned back to the King. "They may be our only hope."

"Hope is a dangerous thing to have, Thira."

"Passing up your only hope in seven hundred and forty years is a dangerous thing, as well." Tristan challenged.

"You seek an alliance, but have you not considered that gaining our freedom and support ensures you make an enemy of Shiva and his dynasty?" Rāhula argued.

So, remain imprisoned for eternity, maybe kiss Tristan, or seek an alliance, gain more enemies, get a birthday party and maybe still kiss Tristan?

Piper's head hurt from all the 'what ifs,' desperately wishing Joss was here to just tell her what was going to happen. The uncertainty in itself would surely be the end of Piper.

"We seek to do what's right, and if that means fighting against those who are so daft to choose destruction and darkness, then so be it." Tristan shrugged.

Piper wasn't sure what took over her, but she finally spoke. "Now that we know you're trapped in here, we couldn't conscientiously go on with our lives without helping or trying to help… but we can't guarantee anything."

Her voice was quiet, high pitched and uncertain. But her words rang true. Piper would simply have to learn how to live with discomfort, for she knew it wouldn't be lifted until she knew these two caring souls and their people were vindicated.

Rāhula and Chanthira smiled, seemingly convinced as they nodded.

Piper breathed, possibly the first time since they had sat down for dinner.

"Okay. Then, it's decided." She nodded in agreement as well, needing to confirm it aloud and make sure nothing unspoken remained in the air.

"It is." Rāhula grinned, lifting his glass to toast. "And now we shall feast, celebrate and begin the foundation of this alliance."

Food began appearing magically on the table, a colorful array of Tom Kha Kai, Gaeng Panang Gai, Som Tum and Pla Nueng Manow, with every item tasting better than the last.

As Piper enjoyed the subtle spice of her Gaeng Panang Gai, she finally attempted to source starting points for her inevitable research.

"Is there anything you may be able to tell us about the curse? Any clues for where we should begin?" Piper inquired politely after chewing and swallowing her last bite on the plate.

Chanthira frowned.

"I apologize if this is not the time to pry." Piper replied quickly, folding her napkin crisply and setting it on the table. Her dish disappeared as elegantly as it had surfaced.

"No, it is us who must apologize." Chanthira explained. "The abduction was unexpected, the curse uncontrollable, and we've only been able to interact within our community, each subject as blinded as we were."

Rāhula nodded sadly in agreement. His eyes furrowed, as if trying to remember something. "The only thing we know is that when Shiva cursed us, he said, 'Nagas would make sure the jewel would never be found.' He said that, right my love?"

He turned to Chanthira, who nodded in agreement, but had nothing more to provide.

Piper sunk back into her chair, unsure if she was glad to only have one direction to begin with or terrified of it. She watched as another smaller plate magically appeared in front of her, filled with Banana Roti.

At least if she were to evaporate into green dust tomorrow, she would do so happy and well-fed.

PEYTON

They crossed over the border almost immediately.

Relief swarmed her core as soon as they left the cursed land of the Norse, but she would be lying if she said that the feeling was a good one. Yet, she also wouldn't be entirely telling the truth if she said she wasn't looking forward to the slight reprieve. She needed a break from the weighted warning.

Toward the end, it had felt like the golden eyes penetrated her back at every turn. The disappearance of that alone turned Sweden's greeting into a welcome one.

Which was precisely why Peyton knew in her gut they were now traveling the *wrong* way and was certain Rei was of the same opinion.

Yet, she couldn't figure out why he hadn't vocalized his point of view, why he had remained silent for the duration of this quest. Yes, she was the God of Discovery, but even this level of silence was unusual for Rei.

But now with the clarity of the removed target from her back and the sunshine of Sweden's peaceful lands allowing her to see the Norwegian Sea on her right from high above, a vision catapulted into her mind. Two large cliffs surrounding a large body of water, a powerful river, directing her into the unknown...

"Peyton!" Rei shouted from her left, nodding her toward the opposite direction.

She had begun separating from her partner, heading back to the Norwegian lands.

To the cursed fjord.

Peyton was now 100 yards west of Rei, who still headed south toward Rök. She would appease him, if anything – to mark another idea from the list, and ignore the growing regret that now poisoned her bones.

As she dutifully followed behind her pillar Elite, Peyton couldn't help but focus on the sparkling waters between the foreboding cliffs in her mind, and wonder if perhaps Norway wasn't as terrible as it made itself appear to be.

"The stone should be beside the church." Rei nodded tersely, quickly discarding his metallic blue wings from their tarmac of choice, a gathering of bright green Oak trees in full bloom amidst the deserted farmland of Rök. She could too easily spot the tall white cross contrasting against the bright blue sky; the landmark felt too obvious for the vast expanse of their search.

"Shall we prepare our confession, then?" She retorted, clasping her own crystallized wings to a necklace beneath her olive-green turtleneck.

Rei rolled his eyes, leading the way.

She spotted the stone almost immediately – on display within its own gazebo before the entrance to the actual church – most likely to deter the quantity of tourists from crossing over to the kirkyard, the holy ground beyond.

It was taller than she suspected, growing larger with each step toward the standing stone, carved intricately to depict stories of the lands' mythological past. It almost doubled her in height yet felt much less foreboding than any step she had taken during the past two days.

Peyton studied the carvings as she pressed on, each symbol contradicting the previous. She instinctively touched the stone structure as soon as her arm's length would allow contact and confirmed what she already knew.

"It's wrong." Peyton sighed, disappointed.

Some small part of her had hoped the Norse had been clever enough to combat her inclinations for discovery; a sliver of her hoped it could still be the case.

But ultimately, she knew exactly where they needed to venture.

Peyton spun around to return to the gathering of trees, to prepare for their travels back to Norway, dreading the exploration of the fjords until they found the one that taunted her mind.

"Wait." Rei commanded, quietly.

She twisted her neck only for her eyes to catch his eye, finding a fight between duty and love stern within his gaze.

"A… friend is buried here." He coughed, struggling to get out the explanation. "I wish to see him."

Peyton nodded in tolerance, not agreement. Although, her curiosity was certainly killing her desired cat persona.

So, she kept her distance, following Rei once again from behind as they crossed through the trimmed bush threshold.

She knew that the church had originally been built in the 12th century, but had been demolished and rebuilt in the 19th century, which matched the gravestones that depicted those buried on these grounds.

He dropped against a rock that had the word, "*MINNESLUND*," carved into it.

Memorial.

Perhaps all of the energies of the diseased souls, no longer attributed with modern tombstones, existed here, in this very one.

Rei started speaking in Norwegian, a tongue Peyton had never heard leave her boyfriend's lips in all the centuries she knew him.

She tried to remember phrases that he spoke, translating them as best she could within her database, but the tongue was too complex for her to remember the specifics.

Fenrir, my lost friend, I beg you… we come in peace… please tell Hel to inform Odin we mean no harm…

She cursed, unable to keep up with the pace he spoke.

"Areh mete lofte…"

Honor my promise.

Rei pressed his hand against the rock, the pressure and desperation building in his words as he continued asking for the support of a friend he had not seen for almost a thousand years.

It broke Peyton's heart.

She knew they both had their own share of secrets; it was impossible to possess full transparency when you lived and wanted to live for as long as they had.

But if her powerful Elite was resorting to begging a deceased deity to help them maneuver through the dark Norwegian lands, Peyton understood they were pursuing something more dangerous than she had initially imagined.

And she had already imagined the worst.

Suddenly, the golden eyes returned, bright and cruel, as if mocking her lost predicament with a gruesome smile.

Peyton got chills, forcing herself to focus on the sunlight, pursuing what made her feel positive.

Rei.

She returned back to the present, finding Rei now bowing his head down silently to the memorial, as if afraid to let go.

She understood. As soon as he removed his hand, he would say a final goodbye to his friend. It was evidence that Rei had not returned to these cursed lands for centuries, most likely since the bloodshed first dampened these farming fields years ago.

And if he had made some form of promise to these deities, it most likely revolved around staying away. Peyton felt their unwelcome from the beginning.

He would not return again.

Finally, Rei removed his hand, placing it on his knee for a final breath, before standing fully upright.

"You realize confession usually takes place inside..." Peyton joked, pointing delicately toward the bright white church. "But I suppose a rock can serve as a priest, too..."

Rei ignored her, but she noted a slight upward tilt with his mouth and a sparkle in his eye in reply to her nonsense.

He walked back toward the entrance to the church, almost in understanding of exactly where Peyton needed to lead them next.

Vanaheim.

TWENTY-THREE

LIV

"If only your fan club were fluent in hieroglyphics and not studying backsides…" Liv sighed, massaging Hayden's shoulders as he hovered over her terrible improvisation for hieroglyphics. "We could have asked them to help, or perhaps oogle at you some more…"

She had been teasing him about his 'fan club' all day, with no less than five hundred more taunting comments to go.

Hayden rolled his eyes and retorted, "If only you knew how to work a pen instead of working that outfit… so damn well…" He lifted his hand to squeeze Liv's butt cheeks playfully.

Liv slapped his arm back, nodding to the table of scattered notes and papers with a smile. "You study booties with your fan club and hieroglyphics with me. We've been over this!"

Hayden laughed, before scrunching his face and lifting up Liv's notebook. "Seriously, Monaco – is that a bird or a weapon?"

"A bird." Liv rolled her eyes, blaming Puerdios University for not enrolling her in *art* class if drawing was apparently of such importance to deities. Then again, it might have been Art Pillar curriculum… "And before you ask, the next I think is Anubis, typically represented as having a head and tail of a jackal."

"The god of mummification and the dead." Hayden sighed in observation.

"Sitting atop what seems to be an entrance to a crypt." Liv pointed out.

"Oh, I thought that was just a terrible attempt at legs." Hayden stated blankly.

"Maybe *you* should take a course in contemporary art interpretation." Liv huffed, crossing her arms.

"If I stop criticizing your drawings and obediently pretend to keep studying the hieroglyphics, will you begin massaging my shoulders again?" Hayden asked sweetly.

Liv chuckled, unable to resist his suave plea. "You're intolerable, you know that?"

"Love you, too, Ollie." Hayden grinned.

By the time the sun started leaving its shadow upon the lands, Hayden and Liv hadn't made too much progress with additional translations.

"Do we need to visit the British Museum to study the Rosetta Stone?" Liv asked apprehensively.

They had felt so close to another world earlier that day, but needing to make sure it wasn't a trap made her impatience heavily conflict with her conscience.

"I studied it as a child, but the chances of these three images coincidentally appearing out of my memory and on the stone seem slim; I would suspect the creators would have tried to make unwanted translations as difficult as possible." Hayden retorted, sighing as he ran his hand through his wavy golden hair.

"And if we're the unwanted translators?" Liv speculated aloud, standing from the table and walking over to the bed, hoping the change in scenery would spark some new thinking. "We know that the message mentions the afterlife, whether it be a warning or a welcome, so I think we need to stick to the plan and return where we both felt the most activity from a higher being."

"I can't risk putting you into unknown danger." Hayden debated aloud, almost as if in combat with himself. "I'll go first, to ensure it's safe."

"Hayden, please." Liv noticed how much weight he carried, struggling between the balance of power and loss, so jumped from the bed, walking back toward him and sitting herself in his lap. "I'm the disposable one."

"Ollie, don't say that." Hayden naturally rested his forehead against hers. "You know I can't live-"

"In a world in which you don't exist." Liv smiled, cutting him off. "And I, you. We go together or not at all."

Hayden wrapped his arms around Liv, holding her tight. She could smell the faint linger of salt against his typically sweet scent. It felt older, safer – a mature aging of her favorite wine.

Liv didn't mind it.

"I can't promise you safety. I can't promise you life. I can't promise anything if we do this." Hayden admitted.

Liv brought her lips to his, embracing this final moment of connection. A tender moment, before entering the intimidating unknown. When she pulled away, she swiftly replied in a murmur.

"I'll let it slide this one time."

PIPER

The truer travesty was that the enchanted prison didn't have a library, creating the ultimate version of Piper's personal hell.

A world without books and written knowledge was a catastrophic one, making Piper infinitely debate if she actually *was* a part of the curse.

So alas, she had to toss and turn alone in her beautifully tormented guestroom, filled with deep silks layered on the floor, plush pillows, blankets and drapes, all in saturated hues that should have calmed her anxious demeanor, yet inadvertantly intensified it.

Instead, all she could do was peruse her own collection of textbooks she had preemptively packed for their journey, while trying to extinguish the blazoning image of Tristan's pouty, yet smirking lips from her mind. How he had managed to combine the two into the perfectly enticing kiss would be a never-ending question she had no time to debate.

She was fifty pages into her third book, finding once again that she was unprepared for the subject matter at hand – Piper needed to learn more about Hinduism and India-related histories rather than her curation of Buddhist and Thailand textbooks she had carried this entire way and for nothing – when the door burst open.

"Good morning, Piper." Chanthira bolted through the room, gliding straight to the curtains and casting them aside to let the blazing daylight glitter through the room. She twirled, her decadent red gown flowing in step before she smiled, "Tea?"

"It's morning already?" Piper squinted, sighing at her useless books. She commanded them to clasp behind her ring and quickly discovered a ceramic cup filled with caramel liquid appeared in their place.

"Tristan is downstairs. We were worried about you when you skipped breakfast." Chanthira continued, ignoring Piper's lethargic energy. She floated toward the armoire, pulling out a stunning navy qipao with an intricate gold bodice that clasped around it, as if it served as an artistic corset.

"I didn't realize the time. My apologies." Piper grimaced, taking a sip of her morning tea.

"No need to apologize. Get dressed. We will see you downstairs." Chanthira smiled, setting a pair of gold-heeled silk slippers below the gown that now cascaded off the bed.

In a flash, Piper only saw the back of Chanthira's equally stunning bold red ruffled dress, before the doors shook the walls as they slammed shut. Piper eyed the gold slippers with relief, happy to know that if she did make it to India, at least she wouldn't be barefoot. That followed with another self-scolding, for not having remembered to pack her shoes amidst the chaos of the temple break-in. Next time, she'd be more prepared.

After getting dressed, Piper packed her original clothes again by attachment to her ring, feeling the decorative piece grow heavier with the additional items it now carried.

"Soon, we'll both feel light again." Piper whispered, more to herself than her ring.

She scurried down the main ruby and gold staircase, back into the room in which she had woken up after entering this cursed realm, immediately finding Tristan with Chanthira and Rāhula centered around the typical pantheon of deities that continued to surround them. After dinner, the large amount of focus her new acquaintances put on her no longer bothered Piper, she had grown to already consider them friends and tried to remain optimistic for a successful alliance in the near future.

Tristan caught sight of her first, excusing himself politely to meet her half-way.

"Are you okay?" He whispered, assessing her state.

"I'm fine. Just got lost in a book." She shrugged.

Tristan sighed, clearly a weighted worry now lifted. A sparkle returned to his previously dark eyes.

"How you managed to read this morning will perplex me for eternity." He joked, pulling her into a hug.

Yet, it felt like he needed it more than she did this time.

He guided her through the surrounding bystanders and into the center of the circle where the King and Queen awaited.

"Good morning, Piper." King Rāhula greeted, bowing formally in front of her. She mimicked the gesture wholeheartedly.

"We were explaining to Tristan how previous members of our community attempted escape, in hopes that it may help with your journey." Queen Chanthira offered to segue into the task at hand.

Already, Piper felt heavier than before.

"Essentially, just do exactly what they didn't." Tristan smirked, receiving dark humoured smiles from their hosts.

Piper appreciated Tristan's attempt at lightening the situation, but she still clasped onto his arm for dear life. She noticed his black silk sherwani had a beautiful emerald brocade stitched into the trim and followed its artistic trail longingly down his sculpted, strong arm, until she heard Rāhula's first directions and coughed out of the mesmerizing trance.

"Do not look above at the ceiling until you are ready." He began, "You will see a bright green light at its center: that is the power that will guide you to your realm."

Piper's head snapped up, noting the King's strategic use of words.

Not return, not transport – nothing finite.

With his advice, King Rāhula made it clear he only offered a best attempt back with no guarantee implied.

She bowed her head once again, worry taking over her decorum, and as Piper stared deeper toward Tristan's top, she understood why he had selected these particular colors – a mockery of the stake at hand – his own personal reminder that they still had control over their fate, whatever capacity that may be.

"Think of home – or someone important there." She blurted out, remembering Liv once mentioning a historical fantasy about a time traveler who believed bigger powers pulled the traveler to a destination's time because of a destined person existing there, or *then*. "Think of Liv." She commanded. "It may help us get to our world and stay there, permanently."

She wouldn't dare cite her sources for this particular piece of advice; Scottish folklore and fictional time travel as reasoning would probably cause her more embarassment among these deities. But justified or not, it also couldn't hurt to try to leverage the mortal insight, no matter how fantastical it may be.

"Okay, noted." Tristan agreed. "Are you ready?"

King Rāhula and Queen Chanthira stepped back.

"Wait. How will you know we made it?" Piper inquired, still holding onto Tristan – now both hands clasped across his singular arm, and turned to the royal duo for an answer.

She was not panicking. Her heart would not beat through her skin. The room was *not* spinning.

Piper was fine.

Just focus on his touch. She implored internally to herself, sliding her hands down his arm and folding them into his own, and grasping it intensely.

Instead, Tristan responded with another clarification. "How long did it take for the longest survivor to evaporate?"

His steady voice subdued her nerves. He had not let go of her hand, and instead squeezed it assuringly.

"Fives minutes, at most." Queen Chanthira replied sadly.

Tristan gulped, but his voice remained calm, "Okay." He took a breath before continuing, "If we survive – after five minutes, we'll send my shoe back through the portal."

He lifted his silk emerald slipper in the air, almost as if preparing Piper for the view up ahead.

"You can do that?" King Rāhula asked.

"I have an idea – we'll… see if it works." Tristan vaguely replied.

Another pause burdened the room, Piper squeezed Tristan's hands even harder.

He stepped closer to her; she could feel his breath atop her head as she stared blankly into his black, emerald-crested chest.

"You ready?" He asked softly.

"Wait." Piper breathed, looking up to Tristan unexpectantly.

Determinedly, she took a step forward, turning to face him straight on. Her eyes grazed his lips. If she was going to die, she was going to mark this off her bucket list now.

She leaned in, closing her eyes to cover the terror in what she was about to do.

Instead, she felt a gentle hand on her shoulder and a breath near her neck.

"Not here." Tristan whispered, his voice calm and melodic, amused yet smoldering. "I refuse to have our first kiss be a goodbye kiss, surrounded by strangers who are gaping at us already."

Piper stepped back, kicking herself internally for having actually puckered her lips. How could she be so obvious? It was supposed to be *spontaneous*.

"Of course," she shook her head, her cheeks burning, "I'm sorry…"

"Do not apologize, Piper." Tristan sternly stated, his command the opposite of his gentle touch as he pulled her midnight hair behind her ear. "I need you to have something to look forward to, to fight for on the otherside. I refuse to turn into green dust without exploring your lips and more, on our own terms and at our own leisure."

Oh Zeus.

Piper almost fainted at the words. At his touch.

She swayed, but Tristan's hold kept her upright.

When Piper finally gained her composure, she spoke without thinking.

"I'll hold you to that promise, Tristan."

Tristan smiled; Piper's eyes went wide.

Stuttering, she mumbled, "I mean, if we make it, of course. And only if the moment feels right, again." As she overcompensated, Piper nodded, wishing her pitch had remained calm, hating the squeaky sound her voice made. "No pressure and no expectations."

"No pressure and no expectations." Tristan repeated, grabbing her empty hand once again. "On the count of three."

Piper nodded, inhaling a deep breath of air.

"One, two, three."

She looked up and saw green.

PEYTON

They had selected to stay one night in Oslo before departing for the fjords.

Again, the pressure returned to Peyton's conscience as they returned northwest. The continual warning to leave while there was still peace.

The gold eyes stared back at her every time she blinked. A feral lion, the king, exerting its cunning power over the jungle of Peyton's mind.

Rei had finally explained that he and Fenrir had fought together in a battle long ago, in the Ragnarök. It led to the destruction of Asgard, the home and fortress of the Aesir.

It leveled up to Peyton's inclination of pursuing the remaining Vanir lands that once belonged to the second Norse Gods, in hopes that they had welcomed the Aesir Gods to Vanaheim, which Peyton strongly believed would be accessible through the fjord.

… If she could find the right fjord.

The golden eyes challenged her, *daring* her to test out her theory, making her want to pursue it all the more.

Instead of being nervous about the gilded stare, Peyton was starting to become fucking annoyed by it.

She came in peace. *They* came in peace. What was this intimidation nonsense for?

Her blood started boiling. Instead of kicking the bedframe, Peyton stomped into the bathroom. She tossed her grimy olive-green uniform into the tub, adding bath soap and water to the mix and swirling all around like a hurricane, getting out her fury in the tidal waves of aquatic liquid she controlled in her makeshift washer.

When the clothes and her frustration had been fairly spun, Peyton hung her outfit carefully and hopped into the shower herself, taking refuge in the steaming water prickling her chilled skin.

As the steam blurred her surroundings in the foggy room, her mind inversely cleared. The repetition of the running water served as a calm anchor within the raging storm.

Peyton finally exhaled, taking a deep breath and letting go all of the aggravation within it.

Her mind calmed. The choppy water stilled. The glacier melted, opening the path for discovery.

Peyton closed her eyes and focused on her calm breaths, not the golden eyes, as she finally left the lion's jungle and persevered into the unknown Norwegian fjord.

1, 190 fjords in Norway.

Peyton shrunk; her head already ached at what she knew she must do. She slowly slid down to the floor of the shower and rested her forehead atop her two palms, leaning into the soothing massage of the showerhead atop her skull.

Adventfjorden... a mining camp, named for Adventure Bay.

She tossed that fjord aside and continued on.

Altafjorden... with prehistoric rock carvings dating from 4200 BC to 500 BC.

A contender. Peyton filed it to another compartment within in her mind.

Arasvikfjord... known for its fishery of cod, coalfish and several types of flatfish. Some famous whale Keiko from the movie Free Willy ended his days there. Intrigued, Peyton began searching for film clips before shaking her head and demanding she not get distracted.

It wasn't relevant.

Astafjorden... named after Queen Asta, mother of King Hellige Olav in the 11th century who allegedly brought Christianity to Norway.

Maybe if the king had supported paganism... either way, Peyton passed.

Fifteen degrees had too quickly flown by when Rei finally swung the door open.

"Peyton!?" He yelled anxiously.

"I'm fine." She called back through the steam, immediately leaving the stunning sunny landscape of Eidsfjorden, another dead route, and returned to the suffocating fog. "Just thinking."

Peyton didn't wait for Rei to comment or ask *what* she was thinking about before diving into her next imagined destination, Ekmanfjorden.

Hundreds of degrees later... the water continued pouring. Her skin was burning red, fingers the texture of dates and her lungs stung from the steam. Her head felt as if it contained of helium.

Only seventy left, she reminded herself, forcing herself to continue on. Peyton at least gave her body reprieve by turning off the shower. It was the least she could do. Sliding back against the shower's cool tile and fully lying down, she dove back in.

Saudafjord... no. She removed it from the list.

Only three fjords had been contenders so far. Peyton still had decided if that was a good or terrible thing.

Selbørnsfjorden... no.

Skjerstadfjorden... no.

Skjoldafjord... no.

Peyton moaned. Over 1,000 possibilities... how could *none* of these be a solid option? Even those she had filed as potentials were a stretch.

Skudenesfjord... no.

Skånevikfjorden... no.

Snigsfjorden... no.

Snillfjorden... no.

Sognefjord...

Peyton opened her eyes.

The King of the Fjords.

The largest and deepest fjord in Norway.

During the middle ages, 'sogn' was the name of the fjord itself.

And if her own mind snapping the particles together as her powers naturally started fitting pieces to the puzzle hadn't convinced her of their next destination entirely, the growing golden anger that penetrated her mind cemented her inclination even more.

With an arrogant smirk, Peyton emerged from the bathtub and prepared for slumber. All the well knowing the lion would indeed *not* be sleeping tonight.

TWENTY-FOUR

PEYTON

When she emerged from the bathroom, Rei gave her a condescending eyebrow lift in question but didn't say a word. Instead he returned to reading an ancient journal.

"I had a lot of research to do." Peyton quickly explained with a shrug.

But she knew he already knew that. Rei had never understood why she insisted on running the water when she could instead play an audio track and sit in a tub without wasting such a high quantity of resources. But, until Liv or the House of Water scolded her, Peyton considered to be in the clear.

"So, where's our next destinational victim?"

Peyton held her breath; his reaction was key.

"Sognefjord."

Rei's eyebrows furrowed. "That's the largest fjord in Norway... it's over 100 miles long."

"I know. I'm still working on the specifics." Peyton admitted, sitting down on the large bed structured by large shaved logs, and continued studying Rei further. "But you're familiar with it?"

He paused, gently closing the diary he perused. "My mortal friends told tales of the treacherous fjord – mostly folklore and gossip. Safe passage through the mouth proved worthiness and valor. It became a superstitious moral compass. Now, no more than a simple and obvious understanding of geology."

"Totally." Peyton immediately agreed, although not wholeheartedly, and fell on her back to think about Rei's experience.

She *hated* that she questioned his diminishment of the fjord's supernatural influence. Peyton despised it even more because it further convinced her the fjord's mouth was most likely where they'd find the path toward the Norse Gods.

And she hated most that she felt alone in this quest.

It was a polarizing feeling to have against her Security Elite, whatever his personal motives may have been. Peyton needed to be careful, for if she revealed too much, he could command her to not pursue, and she would have no control but to obey.

Or worse, be prevented from sharing her discoveries with others.

She scooted further into the bed, pulling herself under the comforter.

It was too late to craft an excuse to secretly send a note out tonight without suspicion. Instead, Peyton would need to send a letter to Dylan in the morning, to pursue her inclination discretely if something went awry. Puerdios was accessible and safe – because Zeus, who on earth knew where Hayden and Liv and Tristan and Piper existed at this point.

Peyton woke up early, despite a night of tossing and turning in bed. Nightmares filled of drifting down a strong tided fjord and getting swallowed in a physical mouth between the mountains terrorized her slumber until she gasped awake at the final demise of her very soul.

The sun's glow had only faintly begun to bless the lands, but fortunately her counterpart was still snoring softly on the opposite side of the bed. Sneaking across the room and slipping through the door, Peyton silently summoned her olive crocodile cross body bag and slithered outside.

Quickly scribbling down her historical facts with general knowledge and inclinations for next steps, Peyton folded up the note and dispatched it to Puerdios University immediately, staying in the nearby park to focus specifically on its direct delivery to Dylan. Meanwhile, she reminded herself that she was not disobeying her Elite, for this was the plan they had all agreed to.

She found a bench across from a stunning pond, a mini dam serving as a waterfall. And in the morning with the birds chirping, the flowers blooming and a silent buzz creating a new crisp day, Norway almost seemed peaceful, welcoming.

Almost.

If it weren't for the constant fear of getting stabbed from behind, Peyton would have enjoyed her visit to the Viking lands. Even with the tranquil surroundings of nature, an all-too calculating spy traced her steps with four paws and probably pushed its boundaries to see what she wrote in correspondence.

For a brief moment, Peyton wished she had the comfort of a warm coffee to sip on, but fortunately shortly after, Peyton confirmed her friend had received the letter.

So, she walked off. Her next mission to visit the quaint coffee shop with the exposed interior for two cortados and an alibi for her outing.

DYLAN

She wasn't expecting a parcel to arrive this soon.

After unloading her books from the day's classes, Dylan ran to the window and grabbed the folded paper clinging to the clear glass. Not worried about Kyril's curious gaze as he approached her, she frantically ripped the note open.

Against her internal desires, everyone had determined it would be best for Dylan, Zayne and Kyril to stay at Puerdios – one secure place to report findings, progress and insights. So that the group would have an inclination to what happened if a team did not return.

At first the idea made sense, but as Dylan quickly matched Peyton's handwriting with her inventory of writing samples, a feeling of sick dread took over her body.

Peyton wrote to Dylan because she did not think she would return. Filling her in on her discoveries and intel as vaguely as possible in case the note were intercepted, she wrapped up the correspondence requesting Dylan continue her journey if she did not hear back from them in a week's time.

Yet, the most concerning of it all was the final sentence:

The person I'm with knows something that he's not revealing. Please take this into consideration if I do not return. Sognefjord.

"What is it?" Kyril finally whispered.

Dylan shut her eyes, handing the paper to her boyfriend.

"Why did I offer to be the person to stay here, receive cryptic letters and worry about my friends while I sit around and do *nothing?*" She rhetorically asked while marching over to her bar, and then uncorked a bottle of Cabernet Sauvignon.

Kyril focused on the letter, too entranced with the written update to partake in an easy retort.

Dylan had practically set him up for a punchline.

She took a sip of her wine indignantly before peeling off her black and grey fur coat and tossing it aside.

"Do you really think Rei would betray Peyton like that?" Kyril contemplated aloud, throwing the letter back at Dylan to discard in the fire radiating beside her. "I thought Pure Gods were supposed to have 'honor' and all that pretentious stuff."

Dylan shrugged, tossing the paper into the flames, and then watched it burn slowly. "After living for a thousand years, everyone accumulates secrets of some sort."

She stood up, taking another sip of wine.

Dylan needed something to *do.*

"Where's Zayne?" She asked Kyril, demandingly.

"Visiting the sirens." Kyril replied, unenthusiastically.

Silence re-entered the questioning, stressful space. It was harder standing still when you wanted to run.

Finally, Kyril stomped over to Dylan's makeshift bar – pouring himself a glass of tequila and adding lime juice, grand marnier and ice.

Unlike them, even Zayne had an actionable responsibility. As the group's peacemaker, he had been tasked to work his infectious charm on Calithya and Ammiras to maintain the siren alliance.

A knock at the door started Dylan, her wine glass slipping from her fingers momentarily before she reclung to it with a firm grip.

Dylan turned to Kyril, questioning him if he had any inclination as to who visited their abode. He shook his head with equal astonishment.

Carefully setting down her wine, Dylan glided over to the black, wooden door and opened it, surprised to find the least likely candidate standing before her.

"Mother?" Dylan speculated, opening the door immediately and hesitantly welcoming her in.

Flashes of betrayal cursed red in her mind. She would never forget seeing her mother working to entrap her for eternity with Danu. Against her.

It was one thing that her family had essentially disowned her as soon as they heard she had not only befriended the Elemental Elite who overthrew Kai but also remained friends with her. But silence was much more tolerable than active opposition.

"Oh, hello Kyril." Thalia greeted Dylan's boyfriend with a smile. She ran over to him with open arms, pulling him into an embrace as she continued, "How have you been?"

Dylan rolled her eyes.

Her mother was the queen of games, ignoring Dylan so that she would feel guilty or lesser, while adoring Kyril, who in her eyes had done no wrong except support her confused daughter.

"Mother, why are you here?" Dylan chimed in from behind.

Thalia gracefully turned, exposing a gold silk sheen beneath her black, one-sleeved gown, a hue that dazzled against her ruby curled hair.

"Well, *daughter*," Thalia hissed at the familiar endearment, "I came to fulfill my motherly duty and warn you."

Dylan rolled her eyes again. Her mother could be so thick. But, curious to what her mother had to say and comforted by safety in numbers on Pure God territory, Dylan shot back her wine and chose to ride this unforeseeable journey.

"Warn me?" Dylan clarified, taking a step toward her mother. "Am I in more danger than our *last* encounter?"

"Oh Dylan, stop with the dramatics." Thalia rolled her eyes, the tree in which the apple fell. She helped herself to a glass of cabernet, pouring it without Dylan's permission. "You would have been perfectly safe with our family once we told Kronos that you are clearly confused but in our care!"

"In your care?" Dylan huffed, crossing her arms.

"You are certainly in more danger now." Thalia confirmed without a hint of speculation, raising her nose at her own daughter.

Her mother was insane. There was no use in fighting with a deranged opinion. At best, she could try to understand it. Rebuild the peace.

"Okay, so I am in danger now..." Dylan played along.

"Precisely." Thalia pointed her finger with a cruel smile. "Unless, however, you deem to realign your loyalties to where they should lie."

Would she never stop?

"Mother, we've been over this..." Dylan sighed.

Between Peyton's cryptic message and her already anxious demeanor, Dylan simply didn't have the energy to once again combat her mother in clearly what was a repetitive, losing battle.

"Dylan, listen to me." Thalia pleaded, half-heartedly.

Dylan paused, only to hear the next fantastical reasoning her mother had concocted inside her head to drag her daughter back to proud territory of the Dark. After weeks of hearing the same disappointment and ruin her decisions had caused her family, Dylan realized none of her blood relatives truly cared for her, but only how her actions reflected upon the family as a whole and in Arlos's eyes. Dylan was simply a transaction to her family and no longer a member of it.

After looking out the dark window, Thalia creeped closer to Kyril and Dylan, until she was finally only an arm's distance away.

With blackened eyes, Thalia whispered, "War is coming."

It was almost as if a breath had been released, the air containing the message for only as long as it floated through the air for Dylan to inhale, and then it disappeared without a trace.

Perhaps that's how Thalia desired her presence to be in Dylan's life. A flicker of importance without a permanent mark, where the influence truly mattered.

Dylan watched as her mother recovered, pretending she had said nothing at all as she quickly turned and grabbed an olive-green velvet pillow, flufflng it for no reason.

"What do you mean?" Kyril interjected, his eyes scrutinized on Dylan's blood relation.

Thalia twirled again with a melodic laugh, "Of course, Kyril, I don't blame you. In fact, I applaud you for putting up with my daughter's rebellious phase for this long." Thalia turned back to Dylan, her voice now piercing cold. "I implore you to recognize this is temporary, daughter. Whether you accept it or not, Dylan, you will be a Dark God once again."

"Mother..."

"Your father refuses to speak your name. He refuses to say it in our household." Thalia's jab cut deep like a knife. "How do you like being the cause of our family's *destruction*?"

But if there was one thing Dylan had learned from the Pure Gods, it was that true loved ones didn't try to guilt another as a tool for persuasion.

"Mother, I don't have malintent nor mean to cause hard-feelings..." Dylan tried to explain for the one hundredth time. "You are always welcome here, and I hope one day it can be reciprocated with what I once called home."

Kyril had stepped toward her, stealthily placing an arm around her waist, unified.

Thalia looked at her daughter, as if Dylan were cursing the ground she walked on, forced to hear the words she refused to acknowledge in her fantasy.

"If that's the case," Thalia stuck her nose in the air so she could look down on her daughter, clearly for dramatics, "if you choose to remain with the lesser deities, just know this, *daughter*, soon you will not be welcome in both places you consider *home*."

Dylan furrowed her brows, trying to process the coded warning.

"What do you mean?"

Dylan tried to ask, but Thalia had already twirled once more, seeing herself to the door, and slammed it behind her.

HAYDEN

Images of his father had commanded more presence in his mind since they had crossed into Egyptian lands. Whether for nostalgia, lingering curiosity of how his predecessor would have handled this war or a foreboding warning from the beyond, a desperate ache penetrated his core every time he saw the condescending stare of King Rowan infiltrate his thoughts.

Were they crazy for seeking the Egyptian afterlife? Was it merely a lost trail convinced as a worthy lead, solely because of desperation and false hope? Had others ventured on the same quest, only to find the Holy Grail indeed was a weapon to ensure the end of life and not the eternity of it?

They could be sipping poison and been none the wiser.

"You ready?" Liv whispered, squeezing his shoulder softly.

After their discussion addressing the true realities they faced, both Liv and Hayden had made a proactive effort to continue touching one another. Even now, heading to war among the crypts, Liv's fingers traced a trail down Hayden's arm until her hands grasped his in solidarity.

Sink or swim, they would float beside one another or they would drown together.

Hayden nodded, grabbing the notebook and pen from their makeshift study – a coffee table with two chairs – in case the hieroglyphics served as runes to some extent, an Egyptian spin on Norse magic symbols that kept hidden secrets.

He had finished sending off a vague update to Dylan, hidden with their theories and intentions. It gave him a cruel comfort that if anything went awry, they could expect an army of Pure raging war within the week. And with that thought, he summoned the hieroglyphic texts in case they would need to formulate a new rune. It was a long shot, but he'd be damned if the one-billionth potential scenario presented itself and he didn't have the necessities at hand.

"With a lasso and hat, I could call you Indiana Jones." Liv teased, but the comment didn't deliver with the lighthearted tone she intended. It pained Hayden to witness her smirk not resonating with her typically intolerable swag. But they had decided together to fight against the terror as one. He reminded himself of their choice, Liv's *explicit request*, and so continued to challenge his inclination to protect her, to offer her the opportunity to stay back.

Instead, Hayden took in his outfit, khaki trousers and a white cashmere sweater, sporting the same pieces he wore since they departed Puerdios University a couple days before. He laughed, although not as genuinely a reflection to what typically would have been an impressed noise. It was mechanical, masking his insecurities. He too, wasn't feeling invincible in that very moment, the lingering task ahead clouding his mind and taking away from his true appreciation for the golden light who held his hand.

"Let's go." Hayden commanded, leading Liv out of the room, then the lobby and then finally, the hotel. They walked as far as they could to a desolate area, a manmade park deserted in the late hour, before taking flight into the starry sky.

And as they soared, he still held her hand, refusing to let go above all else – his soul be damned.

They had decided to fly directly into the 'intruder's entrance' of the Great Pyramid – a side tunnel plunderers once used – providing entrance away from the standard tourist route. Hayden had cast a security bubble to keep their appearance invisible and movements non-existent to any detector outside of the protection's power.

Liv was in charge of the art of a subtle light, casting it only within their sphere, and essentially only for the ground.

Retracing their steps twelve hours later took longer in the darkness than in the previously lighted provisions, courtesy of the Egyptian tourism site.

As they walked through the darkness, slowly, it seemed as if all shadows came alive, all spirits lingered, their presence hovering, suffocating Hayden's conscience as they pursued through the haunted path.

All he could think of was decay. Eyes staring from the darkness that surrounded them, the sadness of the forgotten past and all that its habitants wanted to say. He had directly read from Dionysus's diary that the sarcophagus served as entrances to the afterworld. His skin tingled from the eeriness, like a hundred spiders crawled all over his breathing corpse. Possibly more, depending on exactly how many sarcophaguses resided in this ancient, unknown maze. But after one hundred, what was a dozen or more to the count?

He squeezed Liv's hand; needing her to return the motion and remind him he still remained among the land of the living. Like clockwork, she squeezed back, her hand the only heat source within the deadly cold, stone surrounding. Together, they continued on, farther upward and through the narrowing corridor of the Grand Gallery.

In the dead of night and without the murmurs of other tourists passing through the site, Hayden began hearing the sandy winds from double the distance away. The melodic whispers blowing in the wind called to him, daring him to beckon their call and enter the afterlife. If only he could determine whether it was an invitation, or a warning.

They lightly stomped upward until they met the lowering rooftop that turned their upright ascent into a plateaued crawl.

With the deadly silence, Hayden almost wished a swarm of bats would fly through, just to break up the lack of life surrounding them, *the lack of existence.*

They curled into the King's Chamber. The winds' gust stronger than ever, the accapella voices of beyond growing louder, yet all still barely there.

"Do you think we touch the sarcophagus?" Liv whispered curiously, reaching her hand out.

Hayden grabbed it.

"Whatever we do, we do it together." He warned, after exhaling a sigh of relief from successfully catching her limb in time. It was too close. Both feet stood on the edge of a cliff, unbalanced and uncomfortable.

Everything felt wrong.

Why did he bring her here?

They were in danger. Attempting to venture into a land of the unknown, of the dead. Why hadn't he seen the crazy in this idea sooner?

"The noise seems to grow even louder inside the sarcophagus." Liv studied, carefully bending over into the granite coffin without touching the surface to inspect further.

Her observation made Hayden remember the only consistent note from Dionysus's journals – many depictions about placing the body into the sarcophagus.

And suddenly, it clicked – making it so obvious it was a wonder nobody had pieced it together before, or had been crazy or insane to want to attempt the theory.

"Hayden, I think we have to step inside…"

Liv had also placed the pieces together, the necessity of a burial ritual procedure. Only this time, for their own bodies.

Father, please help us, Hayden prayed.

Rowan's face was brighter and clearer than ever, as if agreeing to honor his wish from the Underworld, their afterlife. Hayden eyed the sarcophagus with a sense of dread. He knew Liv was correct in her theory. The static noises came from one source within.

"We step in, together." Hayden instructed, "Do not let go of my hand, Ollie. If you do one thing, it's to never let go of my hand."

Liv nodded in understanding. "On the count of three."

Hayden started counting as he tossed the cryptic hieroglyphic stencils into the sarcophagus. "One. Two…"

"Three."

Now, levitating above the structure, they both stated the final number and dropped their feet together against the solid base in unison.

A gust of wind rose from the sarcophagus, a desert tornado surrounding them and pulling them down. The acapella music crescendoed, until they collapsed into the sarcophagus and everything went still.

As if the act in itself had died.

TWENTY-FIVE

JOCELYN

"Are you alright?"

It was a common courtesy Jocelyn had been groomed to ask. Although she already knew what Demetrius's response would be.

"Yes, you?" He replied, brushing off dirt from his beige, grey and deep red plaid suit jacket.

"Yes." Jocelyn breathed, squinting her eyes as she placed her hand over them to shield the rising sun's bright rays.

"Where are we?" Demetrius asked.

"The Burren." Jocelyn responded, "The question is... *why*?"

Demetrius turned to the sun, communicating with his own subjected entity and translating its source of knowledge for Jocelyn. She combatted a blurry mind, still unable to gather any visions to address those in which they were trying to seek.

"It's protected. The land is enchanted so only those who enter a specific way are granted access to all it holds within." Demetrius explained, his eyes emblazoned with fire reflecting from the rays of which he spoke.

"All it holds within?" Jocelyn repeated, turning around swiftly, suddenly on alert.

Who was the shadowed creature beckoning her?

"Perhaps it's an alternative route to visit our lovely Danu's residence." Demetrius offered, "Come, so long as the sun is up, let's explore."

His cheery confidence calmed Jocelyn's beating heart. Although denouncing her visions throughout her entire life, they had become a security blanket. From afar, not being able to see the lost deities hadn't concerned her, but now potentially within another's abode, an enemy's territory at that, Joss realized just how much she relied on and needed her powers.

The one assurance that kept her from totally losing it, was the knowledge that she and Demetrius could walk away from the national park and into a version of the world they knew existed.

It felt like one of Hayden's childhood video games that he had forced her to play, capitalizing on her powers to discover an alternative route that granted more coins, powers, time and endless opportunities – but outside the secret path, the level itself and way through remained the same.

Jocelyn started following Demetrius upward, toward a hill filled with rocky crevices that circled around its point.

As they ventured further upward, the sight on the other side of the hill made Jocelyn's jaw drop.

While Joss had been imagining their surroundings as a plus-up video game version of the Celtic world, the sight before them offered something endless, but entirely different. Instead, it was a decrepit sight, that of the villain's destruction, in which you were tasked to save and ressurect.

One with no other optional paths.

TRISTAN

The last few minutes of his eternal life were certainly unexpected.

Or perhaps, the past few hours – depending on how long he had been knocked out cold in the temple of the Emerald Buddha.

Fortunately, however long it may have been, he woke to find a deserted temple empty of international tourists who would have been shocked to find his figure spiral from nothing and crash onto the carpeted ground.

His body and…

Tristan shot up, strategically keeping his gaze away from the pinnacle statue and anxiously searched for the vessel of another deity within the room.

He finally breathed, finding Piper laying in a deep sleep near the entrance.

Tristan quickly lifted up his sleeve followed by another intense breath at the sight of normal-colored green fabric against his creamy skin.

They hadn't dissolved.

He hadn't turned green.

But his reprieve did not last long, realizing the positive state of their being could still be temporary. Ignoring his wicked reality, Tristan slowly lifted his body off the ground and walked toward Piper, bending over to gently tap her awake.

She stirred, turning from her side to her back. Her eyebrows furrowed.

Clearly, she had been knocked out as aggressively as he had been. Fighting his own headache and groggy pain, he greeted her with the celebration Piper deserved.

"I believe you owe me a kiss." Tristan whispered softly, too quietly for his partner in crime to hear, but nevertheless, he nudged her again.

"Ugh, Zeus…" She murmured softly, slowly lifting her delicate arm to place her hand atop her forehead.

"We made it, Pipes." Tristan nudged her again, knowing he could very well stare at that mesmerising face for eternity while she slept, but at the moment, they needed to get the Hades out of this highly secured and protected temple.

Finally, it clicked. Piper went from nurturing her headache to clasping her face, realizing she existed in the flesh.

Her eyes opened first; her body's top-half levered up, as if she were a mousetrap that had just been snapped.

"You..." She reached for Tristan, cupping his face, her touch solid and true.

"We did it." Tristan grinned, nodding his head.

"Okay... good..." She breathed before her eyes rolled to the back of her head and she collapsed onto the floor.

"Piper?" Tristan's eyes went wide. "Piper!"

She was still breathing, thank Zeus. Her pearly skin had been slightly kissed with a pink glow.

Piper looked peaceful at least, but had she actually just fainted?

Tristan jumped up and ran to the door, cracking the temple door only slightly so he could assess the outside situation. It looked clear and bright, meaning the tourist site was opening for vistors soon.

He ran his hand through his hair, thinking through his game plan – although it sounded more insane by each additional notion – before he returned to Piper and wedged his arms between her back and knees and the floor. After lunging upward with her snoozing corpse in his grasp, he made for the door.

She still smelled of rose, plum and pomegranate. And she looked so serene, a subtle smile amplifying her delicate beauty.

"Zeus Piper," Tristan speculated, "you read in the morning of the most nerve-wrecking day of our lives and faint at the direst moment in need. And yet, you have me wrapped around your finger. What on earth am I going to do?" Tristan muttered to himself, working his way back toward the cracked light craving entrance.

He paused before the door, knowing wholeheartedly that passing through the confined threshold was when the true curse's battle began. Taking a moment to acknowledge that as soon as he fully opened that door, he had about a tenth of a degree to set Piper down gently, combat an ancient and cursed deity power, return a shoe to communicate transportation success, grab Piper again and fly at lightning speed, while dodging all mortal and immortal security parameters in the process.

Two hundredths of a degree per activity.

Maybe four hundredths of a degree for Piper-related activities, a hundredth degree for other activities.

One second to combat an ancient and cursed deity…

Zeus, he was so fucked.

"Huh?" Piper moaned, wiggling from his grasp. "What happened? Why are you holding me?"

Oh-thank-fuck.

Tristan set Piper down, although he kept an arm around her waist, just in case she had unexpected plans to feel lightheaded again.

"You fainted." Tristan explained tersely.

He didn't want to dwell on it. They were working off borrowed time and besides, now that she was awake, their predicament improved ten fold.

Not that he would have held it against her if she had remained unconscious.

Or at least not at first.

Tristan smirked at the thought but returned to Piper, once again focused on the task at hand.

"I have to return this shoe." He grabbed the slipper from his foot, holding it up as proof. "And quickly."

"Tristan!" Piper's eyes went wide, making him turn around on defense in case they were under attack.

"What?"

"We're wearing shoes inside the temple! It's sacrilegious!"

Tristan rolled his eyes.

"The slippers were literally given to us by the Buddhist deities. I think our souls will survive. Can we please wrap this up? I'd prefer to not get shot today by a mortal security guard."

Piper nodded, but Tristan had noticed how she slyly slipped off her shoes as he spoke, making him chuckle and terribly ruin his final sarcastic delivery. An angel fighting a devil the two of them made, a duo to fight one another for eternity to keep the cosmos in balance.

"Here's the plan," he shook off his bad delivery and continued on, "We're going outside, I'll look at the Emerald Buddha through the door with the shoe in its light of sight. I'll let go of the shoe and you need to slam the door before I can get sucked through again along with it."

"What?" Piper shrieked. "I just woke up! How did you know I'd be functional to help you?"

"Improvization." Tristan replied swiftly, moving to prepare for step one.

"I, er, I..." Piper stuttered, "I can't do that! What if I'm not strong enough against Shiva's powers!?"

"Piper, you are." Tristan paused, turning to grab her shoulders. "You're incredible."

"No, I'm actually not." Piper combatted, "I'm the opposite of... that."

She wouldn't even say the word.

"You've come this far. If you want what you've never had, you-"

"-Must do what you've never done. I know!" She cut him off, her voice already heightened to panic. "But it's you! I can't put your life at risk like that..."

"You can. And it's precisely why you won't fail."

Tristan pulled her into an embrace.

Truthfully, he wanted to kiss her. That would certainly shut her up and be quite entertaining to watch unravel, but it would also add more pressure to the upcoming task, so he knew he had to wait, no matter how much the impulse grew into a desirous craving, taking ahold of his being.

"I hate this." Piper cried. "I hate this."

It tore his heart in half to hear her sob, her broken words, to feel her clenched fists against his chest. Even if she failed, he wouldn't. He couldn't bear her grief, even more so if he wouldn't be there to console it.

"I'll count to three and we'll go."

So, against the trembling body that magnetized to him, he perservered. With a steady voice, he counted.

"Three... two... go."

He opened the door and followed Piper out before they plastered themselves against the wall. Their shoes from before were still outside, surprisingly.

Piper grabbed his left hand, clenching it with all of her might. She looked up to the sky as if praying to the gods for strength.

"Ready?" He confirmed.

She nodded, but her stare remained upward.

Tristan turned, levitating the shoe directly in front of his eyes. He raised his eyes from the ground, immediately onto the Buddha. It glowed green.

"Now!" Tristan yelled.

The shoe magnetized toward the Buddha and the room erupted into a bright green explosion, but the door slammed shut before he could see if it had been a success. His body crashed against the door, the Emerald Buddha's force pulling him in.

Piper screamed, her eyes now closed in attempt to focus on keeping the pressure against the doors' closure. Her grip tightened against his hand as she pulled him back toward her simultaneously. She slid down as she cried in agony against the battle of the winds.

Tristan refocused his minimal earth power to help her, planting their feet to the ground outside and wrapping their legs in vines, another component for Shiva to fight against.

Finally, a big BOOM erupted, and the pressure evaporated.

Piper collapsed to the ground, crying.

"Piper!" Tristan yelled, again scooping her up into his arms.

She was so small. Her trembles felt weak, tired. Her head fell heavy against his shoulder, his chest. Her skin was clammy and cold.

Piper had depleted her powers. For him.

"I hate this." She repeated with a soft whimper, her eyes closing immediately after, but then she started gagging.

Tristan propelled over the wall with Piper in his arms and returned to the bushes they had hid in only two nights before, just in time for her to throw up.

Her head hung limply toward the ground. She still shook in pulses.

Piper needed rest, water and sustenance. It was going to be a hellish 360° for the selfless deity before him.

Tristan returned to the sky, searching for any resemblance of a hotel. He spotted the King Power Mahanakhon tower in the distance – and figured it would be the best place to begin.

He landed on the deserted rooftop deck within a quarter of a degree.

Within an eighth of a degree, Tristan had cascaded the stairs and blasted open the security door into the tower. Another quarter was spent waiting for the elevator to arrive on the highest floor, and a third of a degree more descending to the property management and leasing offices.

When the doors emerged, he glided through the dazzing entrance, gently placing Piper on a nearby sofa to lay and rest before striding to the front desk and demanding attention.

"How may I help you, sir?" A bright-eyed lady in glasses inquired politely.

"I am interested in purchasing a furnished condo, immediately." Tristan stated, he glanced to her nametag, reading 'ACHARA.'

"Immediately?" Achara clarified, her eyes growing wide and sparkling with intrigue behind her lenses.

Tristan smiled in confirmation before swiftly turning to check on Piper, who remained curled in a ball and still as a lion before jumping on its prey. Yet, in this scenario, Tristan was doing the hunting on her behalf.

He'd buy the whole damn Tower if he had to.

Achara began typing on the computer, before pausing with delight. "We do have a three bedroom and three bathroom furnished condo for sale on the 44th floor for one hundred and fourteen million Thai Baht."

"Fabulous. I'll take it." Tristan confirmed.

"You do not want to see it first…?" Achara glared, pulling down her glasses to study the apparently insane man standing before her.

"If I can drop off my jetlagged friend and leave her in bed sooner, sure." Tristan laughed, trying to brush off his desperation to find Piper a suitable accomodation. "I'd be happy to begin the process of connecting my bank wire as we proceed."

"Let me call in our property manager to assist." Achara nodded speculatively before grabbing the wireless phone.

She started speaking in Thai to her boss, so Tristan took a moment to breathe before beginning to curate his account details for the purchase.

If Piper hated it, he could always sell the condo once she regained the energy to tell him so.

"Malee will be here shortly to assist you." Achara nodded, before making herself scarce behind the desk.

Tristan returned to Piper, who wasn't shaking as much as before, but still looked drained and exhausted as she lay delicately against the couch. He gently picked her up, before hearing footsteps click against the marble floor from behind.

"Hello. Welcome. I am Malee."

Tristan turned with Piper in his arms to find a very sleek woman dressed in a navy suit and eyeing the unconscious Piper suspiciously.

"Hi Malee. I'm Tristan and this is my... wife, Piper." It would seem less creepy if they were married, he determined on the whim. "I must apologize, she's experiencing extreme jet lag, but after having our... assistant tour many properties in Bangkok, we've both concluded we'd love to live here."

Was he sweating? Malee's presence was truthfully a force to be reckoned with – he didn't understand why he felt like he needed to defend himself and concept lies to combat her judgmental stare, but alas, Tristan was now a happily married man looking for a permanent resident in Bangkok with his jetlagged wife. It was better than having to burn the building down to save his honor.

"Of course. Shall we?" Malee stated sweetly, yet with contempt.

What on earth did Achara *tell* this manager?

"After you." Tristan stated, deliberately speaking with his velevety, caramel tone.

She spun and led him to the elevator, using her ID to scan access to the 44th floor.

For only having to travel ten floors north with Malee, ten floors felt like ten decades. Tristan held his breath the entire time, making sure to smile politely, but not *too* forced, whenever Malee turned to his direction and subtly observed Piper through quick glances.

Finally, the elevator doors opened and Malee led them to an entrance on the right, using her thumb to unlock the residence's door.

Holy Hades, it was stunning. Ceiling-high windows bordered the apartment, allowing natural light from the rising sun to make the condo glow. Yet, the sun itself was nowhere to be found, meaning in one of the rooms they would have the honor to view a very stunning sunset every day they concluded here.

Tristan shook his head; he was dreaming of an unpromised future.

An open kitchen greeted them first, white marble counters with gold trims sleekly beckoning them to enjoy a casual cocktail, whereas a long dining table parallel to the bright windows called for a more formal sit-down meal. Perpendicular to the table, Tristan found a built-in bar already filled with rare wines and whiskies to his greatest desire. Through a doorway on the right, a cozy sitting area captured his attention. A plush, navy velvet sectional stood opposite to two cream leather armchairs, both decorated with rich cinnamon and yellow pillows. Beside a bookcase behind the furniture stood a sleek fireplace at the wall's center, and best of all, the ceiling high windows in this space were trimmed with cream and navy plaid shades.

He hadn't necessarily been listening to Malee speaking to all of the accolades of the residence, but he was already sold – even if it hadn't been out of necessity.

"The master bedroom is this way, follow me." She said tartly.

"Wonderful. Thank you." Tristan finally replied.

She brought him, and consequently Piper, across the kitchen and down a hallway, noting a bathroom easily accessible to guests or for the common area, before opening two large doors and entering another impressive room. In the corner of the apartment, it had a 180° view of Bangkok, with a bed centered within it that was beckoning Piper – both name and tired body.

Tristan set her down carefully onto the bed, tucking her into the beige, gold and mauve fabrics that made up the silk sheets, soft comforter and cozy pillows.

"Thank you." Piper mumbled softly, before turning over.

Within moments, subtle vibrations could be heard from her direction with every inhale. A steady beat playing to the tune of a restful and peaceful slumber. Tristan could listen to it all day and night.

More so, Tristan hoped the normal interaction was loud enough for Malee to absorb.

She seemed to be smiling once he turned to her, finding the property manager closing the shades to darken the room for the sleeping beauty.

"If the misses approves, is there anything else you would like to see?" She asked coquettishly.

"Happy wife, happy life." Tristan grinned, handing Malee a piece of paper with all of his monetary account details. "You can request a wire tranfer for the full amount, I've already alerted my banker of the purchase. My number is at the very bottom if you should need any additional information from me."

"We look forward to having you as a resident." Malee nodded, before eyeing the master bedroom once again, "And we will bring complimentary room service to help you both with your *jet lag*."

"Thank you, Malee." Tristan beamed, following her to the door.

"Once the transfer has been received, we will return with paperwork and set you and your wife up for security. Please let Achara know if you do need to depart before."

"We certainly will. Thanks again." He replied, closing the door shortly after.

With the click of the lock and silence of the apartment, Tristan sighed. His chest felt lighter, yet heavier and more exhausted than ever. He stumbled down the hallway and opened another door, fortunately leading into another bedroom, and collapsed onto the bed.

Until Piper woke up, he could breathe. Until Piper recovered, he could rest. Relief quickly languished into oblivion.

It wasn't until his head hit the pillow and his body felt like he was lying among clouds that he realized just how much he needed to recover from the madness.

Until both he and Piper inevitably took on an even more extreme level of madness with their next task.

And he needed to be strong enough to make sure both of them survived.

JOCELYN

Destruction and despair welcomed them, as Jocelyn and Demetrius overlooked desolation. Households made of rocks looked like they would crash with a simple gust of wind, deities crept from one destination to the next, if you could even call *them* or *it* that, all looking weak and tired, and no longer in control of their lives.

"What on earth?" Jocelyn whispered, ducking behind a tall rock to remain invisible as she studied the village from afar. "How did my mother not see this?"

"Did you?" Demetrius questioned.

"Everything related to our foreign deities remains unknown to my powers, but surely my mother has a domineering sight..." Jocelyn debated, her heart breaking for the subjects she witnessed below. "How did it become *like this*?"

A premonition hit her. Somehow, they felt like they were *her* responsibility now, a natural inclination to care for them as if they were her own.

"Unfortunately, Danu may be our only chance to find out, but something tells me she is ignorant to this reality."

Demetrius stood, ready to tackle the corruption head-on. He stared into the sunlight, to test his powers, nodding proudly when the sun shone brighter and broke through the clouds, under his command.

Determined, Demetrius began marching toward the desolated village. Joss stumbled quickly after him.

As they approached, whispers began growing in speculation for the two unknown visitors.

"Not long until Danu is aware of our presence." Demetrius hummed.

"I still can't see her." Jocelyn admitted, stepping closer to Demetrius and grabbing his hand. She had no advantage here.

They passed a woman, her hair in red dreadlocks, filled with feathers, beads, leather and tokens. Possibly even more existed within her mane, unknown to the external eye. Her face was painted and pierced with Celtic markings, and she looked as if she came from the land, a tree folk. Certainly not of the sea, apparent by her clear battle in carrying a pail of water through the streets.

A young girl followed, holding a pint-sized version of the same liquid contraption, stumbling toward a wooden box, in which they seemingly called home.

The woman slipped on the limestone, collapsing to the ground.

Within moments, Demetrius was by her side, helping her upright and asking if she was okay.

"Aye, I'm alright." The lady sighed, "But, me pail ha' seen betta days."

"Let me refill it for you." Jocelyn offered, sending the bucket to the nearest water source, a lake one kilometer away, and within moments returned it full to its owner.

"Mo dhia." The woman cried in happiness. "Who are ye?"

"Can we speak, somewhere private?" Jocelyn prompted quietly, nodding to the woman's cottage.

"O' course!" She limped slowly, an impediment from combatting the decay of centuries working against her immortal powers, and showed them inside her house.

Jocelyn ducked under the entrance; Demetrius nearly had to crawl through.

A simple wood table sat beside a fire, and a small cot with a tarnished quilt resideded in the corner.

"I will ask ye again, who are ye?" The woman prompted, now inside.

She poured the pail of water into a metal kettle and threw another log into the diminishing fire.

"Thank you for inviting us into your home." Joss began, eyeing Demetrius to give him permission to cut her off if he did not agree with her upcoming explanation. "I'm Princess Jocelyn of the Pure Gods, and this is Demetrius, God of the Solar System."

"How in the Otherworld did ye find yerselves here?" The woman commented abruptly.

"We seek Danu but… are hoping to understand a little more about your… community before we approach her." Jocelyn explained half-hazardously. "Can you tell us your name?"

"Ah, pardon me. Not used to seein' new people. Where did me manners go?" The deity chuckled, then coughed. "Me name is Adair and this here is Caitriona."

Caitriona bowed delicately, before plopping onto the cot to play with rocks.

"It's a pleasure to meet both of your acquaintances." Joss offered with a sincere, yet saddened smile.

What had happened to these deities to become this way, living in shambles?

"I hope I'm not coming off too strong," Demetrius inquired softly, asking what Jocelyn did not have the courage to seek, "But, might you shed light onto what happened to the Celtic Gods here?"

"What happened to the Celtic Gods, eh?" Adair repeated with a confused laugh, before gagging and running to the now empty water pail and retching in it.

Jocelyn's eyes went wide.

They were deplenished. All of them.

But how?

"Sorry 'bout that." Adair apologized, lifting herself up from the ground and wobbling to a counter that appeared to be the kitchen. She grabbed a bottle and took multiple sips of liquid, the first swirling it around in her mouth and spitting it out, before gulping down a second and third. "Where were we?"

"What happened to everyone here?" Jocelyn stated, concernedly.

"Oh." Adair shrugged, furrowing her brows to recollect centuries of history and condense it to a few words, as she knew it. "I guess, Christianity took over. We ha' no weight compared to the Christian faith here."

"You're saying that you lost your powers because less mortals believed in you?" Demetrius clarified, although speculative.

"I s'pose so. Although, I dunnae recall havin' 'powers' as ye say?" Adair coughed, "I certainly wouldna walk to the lake twice a day if I could summon the pail like ye did."

"Happy to do so again," Joss offered, sending the vomit pail to the water source, thoroughly cleaning it out and returning it back promptly and full of water.

"Dia dhaoibh." Adair gleamed.

God bless you. Jocelyn translated.

"Where can we find Danu?" Joss asked, knowing that through clean water, Demetrius and she had gained Adair's trust.

Adair shivered, her eyes turning grey. "I dunnae why ye want to go lookin' fer trouble."

"We're hoping to set up an alliance… er, and possibly aid one another…" Jocelyn explained, correcting herself. In truth, she was not sure exactly how much this deplenished village could offer to their cause, but perhaps after a couple weeks of care, they would regain their strength.

"Well, ye can find her in the castle near the border, o' course." Adair offered.

"There's a castle?" Demetrius asked, clearly surprised.

"Yes, where the Queen and her son reside." Adair stated, yawning as she turned to Jocelyn. "Did I not just say that?"

If she was surviving in a deplenished state and with a daughter to care for, Adair needed rest and immediately. It was time to make their leave.

"Thank you, Adair." Jocelyn smiled graciously, taking her hand and blessing her, gathering whatever royal strength she could posess and pass on. "Please, take care."

PEYTON

She stayed behind Rei the entire time they flew northwest, claiming it was due to his knowledge of the terrain and requesting he take her to through the Sognefjord track, in the hopes something would inspire her.

A calculated request. Little did Rei know he was taking her directly to the mouth of Sognefjord.

Directly to the Norse Gods, if she were correct.

The clouds thickened as they ventured toward the fjord, the sky turning from a first snowfall white to the gruesome, muddy slush after the frozen water had sat on the ground for days. It obscured as they flew over the glacier and onto the sea-river path. With the darkened sky lingering over the stunning mountain terrains and arctic blue water, it certainly would be a beautiful place to die.

When the thunder sounded in warning, Peyton knew they were on the right path. Soon, pellets of water slashed through the sky, the wind picking up to throw the bullets horizontally.

"Are you sure we should continue on?" Rei clarified, summoning a protective shield around him for the storming seas.

The glassy water below grew choppier, soon crashing against the valley's rocky terrain. The swirling pellets from the sky turned to hail, each ball colliding against the sea below, riling it up even further.

They were getting closer.

"Yes!" Peyton screamed defiantly, her voice getting cushioned by the howling winds. She casted her own protective shield for a molecule of reprieve.

She saw lightening up ahead, brightening the horizon with its deathly roar.

Suddenly, an idea entered her head, albeit a crazy one.

Pursuing it would be mad. She would be *insane* to attempt it.

Yet the aggravated, golden eyes stared her down further, beneath the surface, mimicking the same lightning she saw ahead.

Liv, give me strength. Peyton pleaded, searching in her mind desperately for a Norse counter to execute the back-half necessity of her deranged plan. *Heimdall, if you're still there. Please allow us safe passage through the threshold.*

Peyton flew up to Rei, close enough for her to grab his hand.

"What are you doing!?" He yelled through both protective shields and windy rain.

"The lightning! I think that's the portal!" Peyton pointed ahead.

"Are you insane!?" Rei angrily screamed. "You want us to actually get *struck* by lightning!?"

"Yes. And YES." She confirmed, refusing to let go of his grip when he tried to gain control of his hand.

If she turned around now, she'd never come back.

Peyton also wondered if Rei saw the same eyes as she did, growing stronger with its penetrating internal gaze, whether with impress or mocking observation.

She fought against the wind trying its hardest to blow them off course, into the side of the mountain, away from the storm. Was it strictly defense, a foreboding warning or a kind gesture to try to save their lives from her ridiculous ideas? Everything and nothing made sense.

The distance between the thunderous roars and flashing lightning grew shorter, promising they were indeed closer to the ultimate destination.

Clenching onto Rei's hand and possibly breaking his bones at this point, Peyton prayed to Liv, pleading that she offer them safe passage through the treacherous light. Simultaneously, she begged to the Norse gatekeeper, whispering on repeat, "We come in peace, Heimdall. We come in peace."

Lightning struck one hundred yards ahead, setting the side of the mountain ablaze.

Shit. Peyton's eyes grew wide and immediately after, the thunder pounded against her ear.

Tristan, protect us from the flame...

They were entering the mouth.

She dragged Rei head first toward the shallow seas, closing her eyes and beseeching to all three gods, and anyone who could hear, to grant safe passage.

As they grazed the surface of the salty water, with the river expanding into a vast Norwegian Sea, she saw the lightning attacking from the sky, its bolt a claw ready to grasp its prey.

And within that instant, Peyton pulled Rei underwater with her, letting the electricity penetrate and capture them completely.

TWENTY-SIX

LIV

Shit.

Liv's eyes fluttered before she grounded herself by placing her hand on the granite floor. Dimly lit chandeliers hung across the expansive room, making the gold accented pillars and wall moldings shimmer brighter but cut the crevices and shadows into an intimidating black.

Her eyes flew open, finally realizing she didn't lay in a dark, confined space, but instead a large and grand hallway. Hayden still slept across what appeared to be a geometric star design.

"Hayden." She whispered, shaking him, weakly. "Hayden!"

He stirred, lifting her own hand in attempt to touch his temples, before gazing at their tightly clasped limbs, still uniting them as one.

"I think we leveled up." Hayden dryly commented, groaning as he lifted his torso upright. "Remind me to bring a pillow, next time."

Liv rolled her eyes, looking around more consciously to take in their surroundings. Nobody greeted them, nobody seemed to *care* about their intrusion. Nobody seemed to be in this distant land – making her the most worried of all.

Hayden and Liv had been so concerned with accessing the afterlife, they hadn't considered the possibility of what would happen if nobody resided within it.

"We ventured into the world of gods and went unconscious upon entrance. They don't see us as a threat, since I suspect we are heavily outnumbered, Ollie." Hayden explained, still rubbing his forehead. "Damn, my skull must have broken my fall."

Liv laughed, her dark humor getting the best of her, before covering her mouth in attempt to quiet herself.

"Here," she summoned ice to her hand, gently placing it atop Hayden's head. Yet, instead of the full blast of a glacier penetrating her palm, only a cold stream ran to the tip of her fingers.

She furrowed her brows, examining the filtered version of her powers before looking up at Hayden with panic.

"Another reason to why we're not considered a threat." Hayden observed blankly. Only those who knew him best would notice his worry breaking through the exterior as he feverishly studied Liv's powers as well as ran trials of his own.

Gently, he lifted Liv's hand from his forehead.

"Save your powers. We'll have to make do with what we have." He nodded gravely, standing himself up.

Using the same hand that linked their bodies, he offered to help Liv upright as well.

"If you need to, pull from me for more impact. We'll combine our powers." Liv offered, nodding her head eagerly, accepting his arm as a lever to stand.

Yet, something seemed off. Like they had entered a manipulative trap, set up to lure them with ease before coercing them into depths of terror.

Footsteps paced from a distant hall; both Liv and Hayden turned their heads towards its source, finding a young woman jump in the middle of the doorway at the sight of them. She caught her breath, her hand placed on her chest as she scurried toward them, eyeing them up and down in wonder.

Her small figure was dressed in all black, clothed from head to toe with a stunning hijab. Bright gold jewelery accented her layered outfit with stacked bangles paired with heavy, statement necklaces that turned into a turtleneck. Beneath a beaded mask that fell over her face and only revealed her eyes, Liv noted bold, black liner that accentuated her golden skin beautifully. The perfect embodiment of Egyptians of the past mixed with the modern fashions of Cairo today.

"Come with me." She prompted quietly, waving them in her direction and prompting them to follow. "His highness has expected you."

She turned back, studying their clothes with wonder; Liv speculated the guide might have even purposely given her 'side eye' if the Egyptian knew what the concept was.

"Expecting us? Are we heading to meet his highness, now?" Liv pressed, curiously.

Had he simply left them on the floor to make a statement?

"We must prepare you to meet him, first." The young woman stated bluntly, leading them down another corridor.

This hallway, still emblazoned with gold, opened up to a stunning courtyard with a pool of water at its center. Palm trees shaded the sunlight for a perfect glow, its brightness kissing the water with glitter sparkling upon the surface.

The view was idyllic. In fact, everything Liv had seen appeared peaceful. So drastically different from the desolate King's Chamber in their world.

The guide led Hayden and Liv past the courtyard and turned down another hallway, leading them upstairs before finally stopping at a door.

"Your room." The guide announced. "You shall prepare to see his highness, a rarity to even our priestesses, but he insists." She glared, apparently still unsure as to why such commoners should be granted such a prestigious right.

She opened the door, revealing a beautiful room accompanied by a personal balcony overlooking the courtyard. A large canopy bed, with black and gold pillows atop a plush white comforter on the left. The space was decorated with intricate candles and moldings across the ceiling, paired with hieroglyphics depicting a story of the gods against the wall. Every piece of furniture looked intricately handmade and of another time; Liv could not wait to study each piece of art when time allowed.

"Thank you, um…" Liv paused, before kindly smiling. "Apologies, I'm afraid we did not catch your name?"

"Fukayna." She replied tartly.

"Thank you, Fukayna." Liv nodded, doing all she could to remain pleasant. "If you don't mind, would you be willing to grace us with knowledge for the best way to present ourselves to his highness? In the most respectable way possible? We do not wish to offend your high priest."

Fukayna turned her head, once again studying Liv curiously. From her golden blonde hair to her bright blue eyes, down to her burnt orange linen and silk ensemble.

"You must cleanse your mouth." Fukayna nodded to the attached bathroom, "Shave all non-essential hair from your body. You will find tools that you can use to achieve both. Wash your body, style your hair and put on makeup as you see fit. There are appropriate gowns in the armoire you may borrow."

"Thank you, Fukayna." Hayden bowed.

"I will wait for you outside and take you to his highness in fifteen degrees."

Thirty minutes.

Liv sighed, both relieved to hear a piece of home but terrified that she only had a half-hour to get ready for the King of the Egyptian Gods, whomever he may be.

Hayden nodded to the bathroom, letting her jump into the shower first. Liv began carefully, but quickly shaved her legs and her arms while Hayden brushed his teeth and shaved his face from across the room by the sink. Within minutes, she jumped out of the water, high fived Hayden with a laugh, and swapped places.

Efficiently wrapping her now clean hair in a towel, Liv began the process of brushing her teeth and applying makeup, finding gold eyeliner to circle around her eyes atop the charcoal shadow. Fortunately, her lips looked rosy enough, so she moved on to accessories, adding a jeweled headband,

and a stunning gold and druzy statement ring, perfectly tying together her druzy necklace and Hayden's gifted bracelet containing their two crests, bonded as one.

As Hayden hopped out of the shower, Liv quickly ran to the armoir, finding a loose silver and gold crewneck sequined dress, with flowy long sleeves and a cascading train. Although heavy from the beadwork, the silk and chiffon fabric would help it breathe, which was all Liv desired at this point in the dry, desert heat. Throwing it on, she ran out to the patio, hoping the light in this world could help serve as a blowdryer to quicken the drying process. She circled her hair into ringlets, expecting the heat and the breeze from the outdoors to set some waves to her golden hair.

Hayden came out and joined her shortly after, wearing a gold, woven high neck crewneck sweater with an Egyptian collar woven with beads around the neckline. The sweater overlapped with two layers at the center and underneath began the beginning of his black and gold-embroidered harem pants.

He too, added charcoal liner around his eyes, transforming him immediately from the King of the Pure to a God of Ancient Egypt.

"Egyptian fashion suits you, your high-pain-in-my-ass." Liv murmured, standing up and fully taking in his greatness with a breath before leaning in for a soft, sultry kiss. She hummed as she relished in the touch of his soft lips against hers.

"Please don't address the Egyptian King with that filthy mouth." Hayden smirked, kissing her back.

"I only save my foul words for you." Liv grinned, before reality set back into their present. She groaned, "I guess it's time…"

"It is." Hayden agreed, sighing as he pulled back, a scowl now replaced on his previously blissful face. Yet, his smile returned shortly when he looked back at Liv with the radiating light outlining her body with gold, like she was a treasure to be cherished. "Although, it is comforting going into this unknown with you at my side."

Liv stepped toward him, grabbing his hand and pressing her forehead to his. "Always."

Suddenly, Liv jumped back, both to her alarm and Hayden's.

"I'm sorry." Hayden apologized, looking bashful.

"No, Peyton." Liv clasped her chest, looking up desperately to Hayden. "She's summoning my powers. She and Rei must be in danger."

"Give her what you must." Hayden advised. "Grant her prayer."

Liv nodded obediently, letting the electricity flow from her body, pulling from Hayden as needed and infiltrating it to Peyton's being, sending her protection and guidance for whatever her friend may be facing.

The opponent was strong. Almost as powerful as Liv in their world.

Possibly even stronger. Certainly more in her current condition.

"Hayden…" Liv croaked, dropping to the ground. She was starting to feel queasy.

"Pull what you need from me."

She obliged immediately, opening the bond more for her to pool all of his powers.

Another blast of energy supplemented Liv, inadvertently strengthening Peyton, making her capable to combat whatever demon she faced.

PIPER

Did Tristan essentially buy her a condo?

Every room they glided through made her fall in love with the residence more, each step comprising the world's loveliest sonnet. And with Tristan's feet acting as her own, each of *Tristan's* steps transformed the sonnet into a romanic declaration, further motivating Piper's soliloquy to announce her undying love for him.

The master bathroom that connected to her room was stunning. White marble filled the floors, walls and counters with a large jacuzzi tub centered in the middle. Three bedrooms, all lavishly decorated (and with a subtle nod to Tristan's iconic plaid incorporated into each space). Beside the living room, there was a den filled with so many books that Piper wanted Tristan to drop her on the exquisite couch and let her live in blissful peace there for the rest of her immortal existence. And honestly, she would have asked if she wasn't enjoying being held in his strong arms (upon his insistence) and recognized the impending doom they both faced with the task of finding the Emerald Buddha. But for now, she felt safe.

If she had been daring, Piper would have asked to have a drink to celebrate the new property. If she had been bold, Piper would have told him the residence was an absolute dream and thank him for making hers come true. And if she had been selfish, she would have told Tristan that she needed him as more than a friend by now.

Alas, Piper was certainly one who didn't take risks and typically followed the path laid out for her, steering clear of passing any boundaries and obediently remaining within the societal rules that guided, *controlled*, her life.

And now not only one deity existence relied on their task at hand, but two. The two-lane highway divided into a oneway path, with no exits or alternative routes for her to consider.

So, Piper sighed and asked Tristan to take her to the nearest library instead.

Yet, unexpected and certainly bold in reply, Tristan set her down, grabbed the kitchen counter for support and roared, "What the Hades!?"

TWENTY-SEVEN

TRISTAN

"What the Hades..." Tristan almost collapsed, feeling the aggressive plea from Peyton of all people, for help.

First, he steadied himself, gently returning the recovering Piper to the floor. Immediately after, he answered Peyton's prayer, sending his flaming protection for her burning corpse, hoping for dear god the smoky tar scent he consumed wasn't an already burnt carcass.

"What!?" Piper squeaked. "Do you really hate the library *that* much?"

"No...It's Peyton, and I think Rei..." Tristan bowed his head, focusing on his powers. He was already depleted from the day before and although Peyton's demand was strong and anxious, the meaning or reasoning remained faint and blurry, as if her summon had been tainted in some way.

"How can I help?"

Piper had grabbed his shaking hand; his whole body was trembling.

Had they jumped into a *fucking* volcano? The heat Peyton combatted was becoming too warm for Tristan's own tolerance.

Piper's cool hand kept him grounded.

"Your touch is helping." Tristan said through a clenched jaw.

Piper nodded, sending a colder breeze through his own body.

Yet the temperature still rose in his mind, his forehead ablaze. A bead of sweat trickled down the side of his head, but he couldn't shift his focus to wipe it away. Tristan had only one thing he needed to keep his full attention on. Keeping his friends from burning alive.

Peyton you fucking idiot... He cursed her, while still trying to keep his flames engulfed around her, combatting the combusting surroundings from whatever deadly poison erupted, consuming her being.

Until he crashed onto the floor, and the connection collapsed.

Only Piper's cool touch and the cold granite floor remained.

LIV

It had taken Liv a few minutes to regain her composure and prepare for the next battle they too, shortly faced. She felt lightheaded but knew she must perservere.

Stepping out of their guestroom, Hayden and Liv found Fukayna obediently waiting outside the door. Her gaze much improved, steering away from obvious judgmental disdain to neutral tolerance.

"You're late."

That was all their guide said, before turning to lead them to the great throne room.

Liv scoffed internally, wondering if their friend Fukayna simply had a personal vendetta against the color burnt orange, and now, apparently gold.

Nobody could dislike any color that you wear, Ollie.

Hayden's voice echoed in her silent mind, a blessing and reminder of their bond and that she was not alone.

Let's just be fortunate that Fukayna is not who determines our fate, for now. Liv huffed.

They followed the small yet mighty Fukayna through many ornately gilded hallways, each one more compelling and mesmerizing than the last. Finally, they curved into a grand entrance, featuring a limestone staircase that took over the entirety of the room. Even with Fukayna steps ahead of Liv and Hayden, the two still towered over their sassy guide by a full head.

A sinking dread overtook Liv's body, knowing they would be concluding the robustly informative tour with Fukayna and facing his highness soon in the flesh. Her heart started pacing as she tried to control her internal shakes.

Remember who you are, Olivia Monaco, Elemental Elite. Hayden's voice echoed in her head, offering an umbrella when standing outside in a storm. *And your accomplice is no ordinary deity, either.*

The smirk near the end of Hayden's statement helped her breathe. There was no reason to fear an equal, no matter the circumstance. No matter the intimidation tactics.

"Enter." Fukayna stopped by two massively ornate doors, two artistic masterpieces in their own right.

Black and gold stripes reminiscent of the infamous King Tutankhamun decorated the heavy thresholds, paired with carvings of the ancient masters and their descendents of Egyptian mythology. The first included Anubis with his pointed ears as a jackal, Osiris with his elongated beak, Hathor with her horns of a cow and Horus the falcon-headed man. The second depicted Set the tricky fox, Ra beholding the sun within a cobra atop his head and Amun the ram-headed king.

Who all began as distant memories taught from histories in Liv's education, had now become all too recognizable, as if reborn within her mind from the search for the afterlife.

And they *had* been reborn with having found the afterlife, whether the Pure Gods wanted to awaken them or not – there would be no erasing these memories from her mind for an eternity. The Egyptian Gods actually existed. The afterlife was an actual destination. Myths of ancient past were once again becoming her present, but this time on such a more formidable scale.

Hayden opened the door, summoning his powers to do the work for him. Even if diluted, the King of the Pure Gods wanted to showcase his strength and make a statement before formal introductions could be made.

He held out his arm, allowing Liv to hold onto it, uniting as one. She began channeling her power to him, if he should need it for whatever they faced.

They entered a room decorated like a modern tomb, with painted dedications to the gods and stunning hieroglyphics depicting a story of the Egyptian deities. Bright colors, ornate gems and mesmerizing architecture adorned the walls of the breathtaking sight. At its center, they approached a magnificent throne, seated within it a stone creature with the body of a male warrior but the head of a gazelle. Beside him sat a woman, with the most impressive caracal headdress, her hair slicked back into a pony reaching towering heights the only giveaway to the mask she wore.

Sending her attention back to the gazelle, Liv noticed now more syndicators that he, too, wore a ceremonial mask in tribute to his predecessors' traditional style.

"Hayden, King of the Pure Gods and Olivia, Elite of the Elements Pillar, we have been waiting for you." The man's voice commanded the room, his voice echoing in ripples around them.

"We thank you for your kind hospitality." Hayden replied, bowing courteously. Liv followed suit, echoing his regards. "We come in peace, seeking only to discuss an alliance in order to protect your people in the mortal realm."

A moment of pause. Liv locked eyes with the gazelle, who studied her curiosly, trying to assess their truth. Swiftly, the gazelle lifted from his seat and marched before Liv, summoning a stunning bouquet of Egyptian Lotus flowers and presenting them to her in a stunning gold and granite vase.

Do not move. Hayden commanded.

"I'm afraid, your highness, Olivia Monaco is already spoken for." Hayden gently reached out his hand to accept the flowers instead, "Yet, they are enchanting. May I?"

The gazelle tensed, before reluctantly handing the welcome gift to Hayden, instead.

Liv tilted her head curiously to Hayden.

A King Ramesses and Goddess Isis precaution, I'll explain later. Hayden quickly shrugged and turned his attention back to the Egyptian King.

"I must ask, how did you find us?" The woman finally spoke, rising out of her own throne and gliding to meet their guests head on.

"We took into consideration the Seven Wonders of the World…" Hayden began, before the caracal cut him off.

"Does she not have a voice?" The caracal inquired, eyeing Liv. "Or do women outdatingly endure a lost seat at the table to speak where you come from?"

Hayden coughed, turning to Liv and encouraging her to oblige by stating "Monaco," before giving her the floor.

"Research accompanied by accessing our archives from the Ptolemaic dynasty, where some ancestors resided among your kind during a previous alliance."

"Your voice is like warm velvet." The gazelle commented; Liv sensed a creepy smile forming underneath the platonic mask.

"I knew that drunkard Dionysis could not be trusted." The caracal sneered, turning to the Egyptian high priest. "We should order his tribute in the Catacombs of Kom el Shoqafa to be eliminated for his betrayal."

"I assure you, the discovery we have made will remain confidential." Hayden offered, his body stiffening. "We mean you no harm."

"For now." The high priestess hissed.

Hayden did not step back, but held his ground. The only shift in his demeanor was polite etiquette to pure shock.

"Shall we start over?" The high priest offered after an awkward pause, pulling off his mask to reveal a perfectly handsome face, his voice lowing to a sultry whisper. "Please excuse our rudeness. Years on defense have embarrassingly caused us to forget our manners. My name is Ahmed, son of Amun, King of the Egyptian Gods and High Priest for the Egyptians. Perhaps revealing our true nature will allow for more cordial conversation."

He bowed to Hayden and extended his hand to Liv, who obliged, allowing him to kiss her knuckle gently. She would be lying if she was not in awe of his glorious features. He had a strong jawline and beautiful grey eyes that perfectly complimented his olive skintone, like finding iceburgs amidst the desert. Without his ornate headpiece, Ahmed's hair was revealed, edgier than she would have suspected. With long pieces styled to fall near his jaw line, a unique combination of messy and smooth, he looked like a rockstar at a photoshoot, making him all the more glamorous in contrast to his simple black sherwani and silk scarf.

When the gazelle did not follow his suit, Ahmed cut in for the high priestess's introduction.

"My partner and equal, Sabra, daughter of Isis, Queen of the Egyptian Gods and High Priestess for the Egyptians."

Sabra bowed, only taking off her mask after Ahmed stared long enough to insist the next step to her vulnerability. Liv immediately understood why she hid behind the intimidation of a caracal, for Sabra was as beautiful as she was stubborn.

Blessed with the fountain of youth, Sabra still looked like a young adult, no more than eighteen in age. Not that Ahmed was old, Liv observed, he just looked more like he had at least graduated university. A perfect, prime, prestine, frozen-in-time, mid-twenties.

I'd appreciate if you'd stop drooling over the male meat. Gazelles may be delicious, but their hearts are small. Hayden joked, catching Liv off guard. When she turned to him, he just grinned with amusement. *And remember, the famous King Tutankhamun died at age 19, after having a wife and two stillborn children.*

Although supposed to bring light to the situation, instead Liv was encompassed with melancholy. In less than a month, Hayden would be nineteen; Liv, turning the same age only a season after. And yet the world of myth and history that surrounded them reminded her that at this time, many not blessed with the life of immortality would see its end within years to come.

"You must be hungry after such a long journey, will you do us the honor of joining us for dinner?" Ahmed offered casually. His eyes sparkled, as if he had heard Hayden's mental teasing, before dangling the true bait. "Perhaps we can further discuss this alliance you speak of?"

Liv blushed, thankful that Hayden nodded, accepting the invitation.

With her soul mate beside her, Liv followed the Egyptian King obediently, although she began to feel wary about the High Priest's welcoming tone. What alternative motives did he have for being so openly kind to his guests?

And although she willingly trailed the powerful Egyptian into the dining room, she was terrified to find out the real truths that lay behind the façade.

PEYTON

Her eyes fluttered open, finding a bright cotton-candy sky ablaze with its departure from the sun. Blackened trees hovered above, in contrast to the picturesque background she floated below. She tried to shade her eyes, but her arm didn't budge. Peyton looked down, to find her wrists shackled against a glass board.

She closed her eyes immediately, unprepared for an interrogation if her captors realized she had awakened.

She tried to piece the clips of her scenic observations within her mind, but found no results. Her discovery powers were mute in this land.

They had ventured into another world. But *which* world?

Minutes later, Peyton heard Rei stir and then buckle beneath his restraints.

He would *kill* her if they survived this.

She snuck another glance to the side, hoping to find him beside her. Whole.

Relief swarmed her as she found him still, binded on a similar crystal platform like her own.

But they had ventured up onto a mountain, apparent with the tree line dwindling. The mix of icy, glacier terrain with rocky patches below presented a breathtaking sight as its spectrum of greys contrasted with the pink hue of the sky.

Yet, Peyton didn't feel the pull of the sun in the sky to determine the time. She didn't feel the heat of the orbiting planet anywhere. The sun did not exist in this world.

Zeus help me. She gulped.

They continued climbing higher, following a path that glittered, as if diamonds grew out of the soil in this unknown land. After another hour of ascension, Peyton and her confined block halted.

"Hva er dette?"

"Inntrengere. Varsle kongen."

Intruders. Alert the King.

Somehow the translation formed in Peyton's head. Perhaps not all of her powers were mute, just limited.

She still didn't like the idea of being weakened.

"Vi kommer i fred."

Peyton's eyes sprung open at the low vibrations of Rei's voice speaking Norwegian in defense of the two.

We come in peace.

He also caught the attention of a Viking god, who swiftly approached him in moments. His tanned face hovered over the Security Elite, rage growing behind his teeth.

"Vi lar kongen bestemme, fange."

We'll let the King decide, prisoner.

Peyton twitched as she heard the guard spit, but Rei did not falter.

"Jeg er Rei. Fortell kongefamilien at Rei, the Pure God Security Elite, er her. Jeg krever å snakke med dem."

Tell the royal family that Rei is here. I demand to speak with them.

The guard took a step back, granting Rei space to breathe. He observed the prisoner with wonder, no longer bearing the all-powerful demeanor from moments before.

With a thick accent, he finally asked. "How do I know you speak the truth, Security Elite?"

"My sword." Rei grunted, summoning his weapon to the air. It sparkled in the light, mimicking the same rainbow spectrum of the colors from the ground below. A true Scandinavian sword, wielded from the mythos land.

Whatever *land* this was.

"Slipp dem." A guard commanded.

Without question, Peyton's plexi glass board shifted upward, inevitably causing Peyton to stand entirely upright before her cuffs released and immediately magnetized together behind her, entrapping her once again.

She stumbled from the shift in weight and turbulent lightheadedness, and caught her balance, before finally taking in the grandiose entrance that stood before her and the giant red-haired warrior who stood beside it.

Metal doors were intricately carved into the mountain, layered with tinted glass pieces to create a mesmerizing chrome design with the nine worlds painted. Asgard, depicted as sunken underwater, snakes and dragons bordering the realm; Midgard, a tall city skyline sparkling beneath a starry sky; Jotunheim, giants hovering over Redwood trees; Niflheim, an icy blur; Muspelheim, a screaming fire world ablazed with flames; Alfheim, tinycottages nestled in the mountain forest surrounding a vibrant stream; Svartálfar, an industrial city beneath the ground; Helheim, a desolate graveyard.

And finally, Vanaheim, a peaceful mountainous wilderness beneath a forever setting sun.

The red-headed soldier blew the Cong in his hand, and the doors opened in response, splitting the Asgard and Vanaheim worlds into two.

Stepping into the mountain revealed a night market, stores lined up on both sides of the main entrance. An art gallery, a couturier, an apothecary, a wine merchant...

Vanaheim had certainly evolved from the documented histories of their world as Peyton and Rei knew it. They trailed the guards, venturing further into what seemed to turn into a metropolitan city. Overhead, dazzling performers put on a show, a DJ putting down tracks with beats that echoed through the mountains, flame throwers and acrobats flew through the air. The backdrop – a rock ceiling, was decorated with tiny crystals of various sizes, sparkling to resemble a stunning night sky.

If it weren't for the missing moonlight, Peyton would have been convinced she was truly staring out into space, not just the cavernous mountain.

It was the strangest and yet most intoxicating scene Peyton had ever seen.

Yet, with one look from a coffee shop barista glancing apprehensively at her shackles, Peyton bowed her head to the ground, ashamed to be greeting such a mesmerizing world in this particular conundrum.

She followed behind the commander of the gods, his long, auburn hair braided down to his lower back – her level of eyesight. Peyton recalled his heavy facial hair; both mustache and full beard in all its glory, but wouldn't dare look up to further inspect his intimidating armor or helmet adorned with two antelope skulls for his own horns. Instead, she followed the blind swing of his falchion sword, its blade larger than her arm, engraved with stunning Scandanavian runes.

Further out into the hills of the mountain, houses glowed, growing more majestic as they stacked above the others. They started ascending upward, marching through streets until the streets turned into cobbled paths and residential neighborhoods, passing by houses with parents cooking meals for their families or drinking wine and reading a book.

Soon, the brightest star in the sky caught Peyton's eye. A modern glass house, buried deep in the mountain, the crown jewel for what could only be the royal residence.

Kongefamilien.

She wished she could talk to Rei. Ask bluntly what his history was with the Norse Gods, prepare for whatever trial awaited them for entering these unknown lands. Figure out how the Hades they'd get out of this predicament with contained powers at best to utilize.

Quickly, Peyton tried to research cultural customs, proper etiquette for Scandanavian royalty, praying it was only depletion that caused her weakness, to no avail – nothing came to mind that felt applicable for the Vanir.

They finally reached the resident jewel. In contrast against the glass frames, a gold-carved door met them at the front of the palace. The fortress to enter.

The red beast struck the flat cylinder opening of the cong against the door in an intricate pattern, before it swung open moments later, revealing another female guard.

She nodded obediently, stepping to the side to allow their captor entrance. And inevitably, his captives that followed behind like heeled dogs.

"You will meet with his royal highness, King Mothi." The security guard explained, his voice a growl, as he quickly led them into the throne room.

Peyton barely had time to admire the sleek, modern Scandinavian interior décor before they were thwarted into the past, a medieval display of dominance with two higher throne chairs to grovel.

"My work here is done." The guard declared, dropping his voice. "For both your sakes, I hope you have an earth-shattering reason for breaking the treaty."

The treaty?

Peyton almost choked.

In all of the weeks of research, the strategy, the speculation, *none* of the Pure Gods had heard or seen documentation of a treaty with the Norse.

Before Peyton could ask about the treaty, before the red-beast captor could depart, another set of doors clicked open, revealing two blonde men in sleek suits.

"King Mothi." The guard bowed, placing his right fist in front of his torso and left behind. Both elbows bent at a 45-degree angle.

Peyton took note.

"Thank you, Heimdall." Mothi nodded, excusing his commander.

Heimdall?

Peyton tried to search the confines of her mind, but nothing but mortal mythologies crossed into her conscience. She hadn't been able to recognize him.

Recognize *them all.*

Weeks of research, wasted.

Mothi's cobalt eyes moved from gratitude to speculation as he turned to his newest visitors.

Blue eyes.

Peyton looked to the other male deity, standing stoically beside the king. The same cobalt hue.

Brothers.

If the identical eye color didn't give it away, the high cheekbones and matching tanned skintone showed they were two of the same kin; however, where King Mothi stood leaner with sharper attributes, the other, most likely Magni, was built with muscle and cat-like eyes.

And although both stared threateningly at their newest victims, neither held the foreboding amber eyes that had haunted her dreams. The eyes she had expected to see once faced with the lost Norse Gods.

Finally, Mothi spoke.

"Traitor. You broke your promise."

While Mothi drawled lazily, his voice remained musical, almost playful, but laced with deceit.

"We come in peace." Rei clarified.

"And who is *she?*" The other brother interrupted demandingly, eyeing Peyton with disgust. "You brought another with you?!"

The look he gave her made Peyton's skin boil. She wanted to kick the brute to where the sun didn't shine – of course, her version of it did not involve this alluring land.

"Peyton. And technically Magni, she brought me." Rei replied bluntly, returning his gaze back to King Mothi. "I have honored the treaty for over seven hundred years, only returning when a matter of life or death's at stake. I come in peace. Nothing has been broken."

"Your promise. Not the treaty." Mothi clarified.

What promise? Peyton's mind was racing.

Rei sighed, eyeing Peyton before returning his gaze to Mothi.

"Perhaps you could stop treating us like prisoners and show us some Norwegian hospitality."

Mothi laughed, before staring Rei down in deliberation.

"Darling, please be kind to our guests."

A dazzling brunette strutted across the throne room, her melodic request singing against the ancient acoustics of the wooden carved walls, her sexy golden pant suit a beacon of light, a lively shimmer contrasting against the gloom of the historical past.

Most impressive of all, were the caramel eyes that locked with Peyton's.

The lioness had arrived.

Immediately, Rei and Peyton's cuffs evaporated.

After kissing Magni's cheek in greeting, the vixen approached Peyton with a genuinely kind smile and a subtle wink that only Peyton could see.

"Hi. I'm Gigi. Welcome to Vanaheim."

PIPER

"Do you think it's really worthwhile exploring the Bangkok City Library?" Tristan speculated as they exited the tower and walked toward the literary resource nearest their new residence. "It contains merely mortal knowledge."

Tristan had requested that instead of flying from the ceiling, Piper make a cognizant appearance on the realtor and lobby floors to introduce herself as a well-being individual who indeed, was simply recovering from intolerable jetlag. Yet, between Piper's quick switch from recovery-mode to pressured and anxiety-driven action-mode, and Tristan's request to sneak in a somewhat propagandous tour to reinstate his honor before departure, little time had been left to actually discuss Piper's makeshift gameplan until they were clear of staring eyes and prying ears as the tower's newest and most mysterious residents.

"I'm not sure." Piper admitted honestly. "But, we're here. So, it couldn't hurt to check before we defer to Puerdios's or the royal library and venture back to our lands."

She didn't mention her dread of potentially returning without having successfully achieved what they were tasked to do. Piper didn't want to be cast aside as one who only partially completed their mission, but someone who could be fully trusted to tackle the immense amount of responsibility warranted among her royal and powerful friends.

Either way, she prayed to Peyton in hopes that the God of Discovery could help her locate the knowledge she needed to find regarding the Nagas – wherever her friend may be.

After an hour of walking through the electric streets of Bangkok, where life seemed to buzz and the air beckoned its habitants to give into a deeper pulse, challenging them to see the beauty in chaos, the two deities finally approached a yellow building with a cylinder façade and bold block letters that claimed, 'BANGKOK CITY LIBRARY.'

And upon entering, Piper's eyes grew wide.

A gold art deco desk labeled, 'INFORMATION,' greeted them immediately, but beyond that, modern black industrial fixtures contrasted against bright white walls. From her recent movie binges with Liv, it was like a perfect blend of *Titanic* and *The Great Gatsby*, resulting in pure literary bliss. Certainly, it was a 180° switch from the ancient historical atmosphere of her beloved Puerdios, but all the same, Piper knew she already loved it here.

The man sitting behind the information desk did a double take from their appearance. Dressed in a casual navy hoodie, jeans and grey shirt, the librarian's jaw dropped in tandem with the magazine he perused when he found Piper, still in her navy silk and gold-bodiced gown courtesy of Buddhist royalty, standing next to Tristan in a sleek new leather bomber jacket, grey trousers and a light grey button down shirt with subtle white tie-dye streaks.

Piper made a mental note to ask Tristan to include her in his personal shopping services next time while she walked up to the desk and smiled politely.

"We'd like a guest pass for the library, please."

The man nodded, apparently still overwhelmed by their presence as he silently handed them two guest badges before leading them through security.

"Thank you." Piper nodded kindly to the young gentleman, making him blush and mumble a mix of various responses with laughter.

"It appears you have an admirer." Tristan whispered, before following Piper's ignorant gaze upward toward the directional sign.

"Tourist information, second." Piper read and determined aloud, before she spoke the words Tristan's eyes had just found on the right. "In honor of Liv, I think we must check out the coffee shop, first. Do you agree?"

"Pipes, are you putting play before work?" Tristan jibed, pretending to be aghast.

She smiled softly, lightly chuckling at the observation. "It's been a long trip. Don't get used to it."

They walked straight down the corridor, Piper sneaking peaks down each small room and staircase, drooling at the stunning fixtures and even more impressive artwork before she nearly ran into a light counter filled with baked goods.

Behind the cashier display were shelves of artisan coffee items and an even larger painted mural that confirmed that this was truly Piper's happy place.

Well, here and the new condo Tristan now owned.

"A black coffee, please." Tristan politely requested, giving Piper time to finally find and read the menu.

"A cold brew, please?" She squeaked, unable to contain her excitement.

She twirled around, loving the oak tables and black stools that matched the family-style elongated rectangle tables sprinkled with intellectual mortals all engaging in literature masterpieces while sipping coffee.

If only they could stay and pretend they weren't divine figures, that they weren't in pursuit of a mythical creature, that they weren't tasked to urgently help restore the greater Buddhist deities.

At least Piper could soak in the wonder of this magical building for minutes longer, so she grabbed her cold brew and followed Tristan to 'Tourist Information' while still trying to appreciate the smaller moments – the bronze art installation flowing in the air, a nod to art deco graphics sprinkled throughout each floor, and finally, the intrigue of the Rotating Reading Exhibition, displaying rare books in Bangkok, where Tristan nearly had to pull Piper away from her natural magnetic desire to explore.

They finally approached the third floor, filled with books and knowledge related to Bangkok such as history, economy, governance, religion and culture.

From their search at the Tourist Information desk, they had pulled over fifty titles that should include information on Nagas. They claimed a table with a beautiful golden lamp, collected a series of textbooks to peruse and began their research.

The first book only listed Nagas among other mythical creatures connected to Hinduism, Buddhism and Jainism. Piper sighed, calming her taunting excitement, and slammed the book closed.

She took a sip of her cold brew and grabbed another text halfheartedly. Perhaps they should have gone back to Puerdios; she knew the school's library like her own personal bibliography. And even if they found relevant information pertaining to the Nagas here, could it be trusted through a mortal lens?

Piper flipped open the pages of *Encyclopedia of Beasts and Monsters in Myth, Legend and Folklore* finding *Nagas* indexed on page 224. Cascading through the numbers, she finally found Nagas listed with contextual information of value.

"Tristan, listen to this." She bent over, even closer to the pages after skimming through the Chola dynasty and its family members' ability to turn into snakes, imprinting the following paragraph within her brain as she read aloud, "'Especially greedy, Nagas hoard jewels.' Well, that certainly fits with wanting to protect the cursed Emerald Buddha." She mumbled, before continuing, her eyebrows furrowing with every word. "'They possess an array of undefined magical abilities from the gem embedded on their head.'"

"Control over an entire deity population seems accurate with the term, 'undefined.'" Tristan rolled his eyes.

Piper smirked in agreement.

Talk about a vague understatement.

"This text mentions Nagas are half cobra, half human." Tristan proposed unenthusiastically. "And that's it."

"Half snake, half man? *Revolutionary*." Piper commented sarcastically, at least feeling lighter with their communal mockery of the situation which presented itself.

Somehow life didn't seem as intimidating when you had someone on your team experiencing it with you.

Finally, turning through pages of an older book titled, *Ancient Mythology and Religion of Southeast Asia Influenced by India*, Piper squealed.

"Tristan! I think I found something!" She squeaked excitedly, once again hovering over the pages. "'Nagas have jewels either in their hoods, necks or heads; however, this jewel is more than just a decoration – though coveted, misfortune would befall anyone who killed a Naga to obtain the jewel."

"I'd appreciate if you didn't discuss our untimely death with such enthusiasm." Tristan dryly observed.

Piper rolled her eyes. "It says here, 'It *is* possible to obtain the jewel by throwing dust upon it once captured.'"

Tristan had circled around the table, now he leaned over her from behind. His left arm lightly rested against her back; Piper could feel his gentle breath warming up her neck and sending chills down her spine. Oh, how she *loved* his cozy cinnamon scent.

"Dust?" Tristan questioned, his eyebrows furrowed as he focused on reading the surrounding text from where Piper's navy and gold painted fingernail pointed.

"The jewel belongs to King Rāhula and Queen Thira – perhaps it would be best to pull dust from their world, their land. You haven't washed our clothes from our visit?" Piper thought aloud.

"No. An extraction spell should do the trick." Tristan agreed, although not entirely convinced. "Can you see if 'dust' is indexed?"

Piper nodded, moving to the back of the book, finding the word 'dust' listed (fortunately) and navigated toward its page.

"'There is a story about a poor young boy who, having nothing to give the Buddha as a gift, collected a handful of dust and innocently presented it. The Buddha smiled and accepted it with the same graciousness he accepted the gifts of wealthy admirers. That boy, it is said, was reborn as the Emperor Ashoka.'"

Piper turned her gaze from the book up to Tristan, eager to gauge his reaction.

Tristan nodded sternly before catching Piper's eyes and pausing.

It was as if his hard-amber eyes had melted into a soft caramel immediately from the shift in sight.

Tristan took a breath, stepping back before returning to his seat across from her.

Piper shook her head; she clearly must have imagined it. Instinctively, she returned to the book, trying to gather any additional details about dust, without any luck. Yet, between the pages, her mind continued to flash back to the brilliant eyes of a bronze hue.

They had moved through dozens more books before the library's natural light began to darken. Piper and Tristan had finished not only their first coffees, but also second and third rounds, only to show a slightly caffeinated energy but no additional information regarding the Nagas to be showed for it.

"Maybe we pivot and try to eliminate locations where the Nagas could reside." Tristan suggested, slamming the final book closed on the table. Without thinking, he levitated it to its place atop a stack of textbooks.

"Tristan!" Piper squeaked, looking around anxiously to see if anyone may have witnessed his lazy reliance on power.

"Piper, nobody is here." Tristan looked around to confirm his statement, before turning back with a grin. "We've been mortal all day. My powers are buzzing on the edge of my skin to be used, released. We can't confine it forever."

Piper had never experienced that feeling before, but now that Tristan mentioned it, Piper realized her caffeine buzz may actually be due to her powers, or lack there of. Before, Piper had gone days without using powers, knowing her sourcepool was low to begin with – but in comparison to how much she had been using her powers during the past few weeks, especially in contrast to being trained to control and contain it, it was almost as if she had built a higher tolerance and now was in withdrawal.

"Okay, what do you suggest?" She hummed with intrigue.

"Follow me." Tristan smirked, returning all the dozens of books back to their destination with a snap, and reaching out his hand.

Piper took it with a shy but exhilarating smile, reveling how their touch cascaded the buzz to electrifying pulses between their grasp.

PEYTON

Queen Gigi was truly Peyton's new favorite person. Deity. Immortal. Everything.

Rei, on the other hand, was *not.*

Her appearance in the royal throne room shifted the atmosphere from intense and accusatory to friendly and welcoming. The first order, imploring Heimdall to release their visitors' restraints. As they walked through the castle's hallways and not downward toward the cells, Peyton was fairly certain their accommodations were entirely due to Gigi's insistence of personally showing Rei and Peyton to their chambers.

"Tonight, you must join us for dinner." Queen Gigi smiled, "It is rare we have visitors from Midgard."

With the hassle it took to get to Vanaheim, Peyton fully understood why. Yet, Queen Gigi's eyes insinuated something greater, deeper.

"Do you not visit the mortal world often, your highness?" Peyton asked, curiously.

"When it's just me, please, no formality is needed. Just Gigi is fine." She waved Peyton off, a natural façade to hide her face, now looking forward. "I'm afraid I have not visited Midgard for quite some time, almost two decades."

Damn. Peyton turned to Rei naturally, eyes wide, before remembering she was mad at him. Rei only shrugged, but remained silent. Precisely the reason why she was angry with him in the first place.

"If you don't mind me asking, Gigi. Why not return?"

"It is safer here." She whispered, before pausing in front of a door. "Here is your room. I hope it is to your liking."

Gigi opened the door and extended her sophisticated, chic smile – one camouflaged with a thousand secrets – before bidding goodbye.

They entered their guest room, *not a dungeon,* to Peyton's final relief as she found a Scandinavian dream equipped with a king bed, stunning view of the mountainous city and sleek bathroom, accompanied with lavender lattes that had soothing 'calm glitter' sprinkled atop.

As soon as the door clicked closed, Peyton shoved Rei to the wall.

"You better tell me *all* you know, sir. Or else I will make a very strong case for sending you to the Underworld if we ever escape this mess."

She was shaking. Peyton gripped his arm tighter.

Rei calmly looked down at Peyton's stronghold, then back up to her stare, his eyebrow raised.

She groaned, releasing him immediately.

When he still didn't speak, she walked over to the bed and punched the mattress.

"Well?" She finally demanded through her teeth.

"Peyton..." Rei sighed. He sat down at the table and placed his head between his hands. A minute of silence passed, before he finally spoke. "After Ragnarök, Thor was mad – a dangerous combination of all the word's meaning. So, King Rowan and Thor signed a private treaty, protecting the Norse Gods in their new world – Vanaheim. They agreed to remain and rule over the separate worlds and designated Midgard lands in peace, with no crossover. It was to remain discreet, so other deities would not become aware of Vanaheim or seek passage to the realm. Only King Rowan, Silas and myself knew of the treaty."

"Why not just tell us, tell Hayden?"

"Speaking of the treaty existence was in breach of the treaty itself." Rei replied tersely.

Peyton paused, thinking about what details Rei had just revealed, testing whether she should believe them as truth. But, unlike Rei, she refused to keep this barrier of secrets between them. Honesty and openness would be the only way to stay sane as they carefully maneuvered against the true opponents: The Norse Gods.

At least, her true opponents.

"No, there's something else." She stated blankly.

Peyton wasn't asking for more information, didn't want to express further disbelief, but wanted to make sure her supposed partner understood she was more perceptive than she ever let on. A subtle warning, whether Rei wanted to reveal it on his terms or wait for Peyton to discover it on her own.

Rei opened his mouth to defend the accusation, but Peyton shook her head. She couldn't have this conversation right now, but as she looked around, there weren't many options for places to retreat, so she turned and marched into the bathroom.

The one thing she caught in Rei's vague explanation was that Silas knew of the treaty. But why didn't Rei originally request Silas to accompany him to visit the Norse Gods? It was a simple solution to keep the treaty a secret.

Your promise. Not the treaty.

Peyton's mind flashed back to Mothi's accusation hours before.

Rei must have had a separate interaction with the Norse Gods since the treaty. One that Silas would have become immediately aware of if Rei had returned with his father. Instead, he had preferred gambling the chance that Peyton would not have been able to find Vanaheim, that his protective measures combined with that of the Norse God King would have been strong enough to combat her discovery powers.

But he had bet terribly wrong, the odds now against him in every way.

That left Peyton with one last question, the scariest of them all.

What the Hades kind of deal did Rei make with the Norse Gods?

TWENTY-EIGHT

LIV

"So, Olivia, tell me about yourself." King Ahmed inquired as wine was poured to all but his own glass, which they filled instead with sparkling water.

Insisting that he sit beside *Olivia*, Ahmed had waved the red liquid away. So, Liv questioned the gesture on her right, prompting a reason before she willingly drank her own.

"I don't drink." Ahmed bluntly explained. "I prefer to remain clear-minded."

When Liv pushed her own wine glass away, Ahmed laughed.

"I mean no judgment, nor do I wish to make you feel insecure – I truly don't mind. Sometimes I have my staff pour me a glass to pretend I'm drinking and make my guests feel at ease. It's not strategic in any way, just a personal preference."

"And why did you choose to steer away from the charade tonight?" Liv purred.

Ahmed leaned in, grabbing his water glass and holding it below his eyes. "I figured honesty would be key to build this relationship."

"Honesty is always key." Liv raised her eyebrow, trying to assess the games this immortal deity was playing, yet came short of recognizing one. For now.

Sabra and Hayden now joined in, a suspicious gaze met Liv with a supportive one.

"I grew up in the mortal world, unknowing of my deity heritage." Liv began, eyeing Hayden to confirm he was aligned with her sharing this story. "For my protection against my uncle, Hayden was placed in school with me, although we both did not understand my immortal potential."

"Fascinating." Ahmed leaned in, prompting for more, before Sabra interjected once again.

"So, what brings you here now?" She inquired, her question blunt and direct, before sipping her wine.

"My uncle, Arlo – who also killed my father – has started an uprising with the radical Dark Gods. He released Kronos from the Underworld earlier this year and now the two have created a new breed of deities – the Soulless – with the goal of conquering the world and enslaving mortals to do whatever bidding they choose."

"And how does this affect us?" Sabra retorted, leaning back in her chair.

"If we don't unite and fight now, there will be no hope in the future." Liv combatted, her voice battling against Sabra's nonchalance. "Kronos is our creator. The most powerful deity of the Pure, possibly of this world and all its realms."

"Then why do you think you can beat him now? If you do not mind me asking?" Ahmed cut in curiously.

"A prophecy. With Liv and my powers connected, together we can channel our strength to duplicate its potential." Hayden chimed in.

"Together?" Ahmed studied the two, his head crossing the table as he evaluated his guests in a new light.

"Kronos will not be able to control our subjects – we too descend from the original deities, our powers equally matching his." Sabra challenged, standing up and pounding her fist against the table, hissing. "When our deities faced an internal war with Isis only a decade ago, we did not cry for help. We fought and did what we needed to do to ensure the good prevailed."

Isis. Liv recalled Ahmed's introduction. Sabra, Daughter of Isis. And now partner to the King. Dread filled her core. Liv had not yet imagined the possibility of killing her uncle (however much she wanted to) – the actual act of being the one to send him to the Underworld. And yet, here Sabra stood, now equal to the King, from a sacrifice Liv did not want to dwell too much on. All she knew was that she now was fucking terrified of the Egyptian goddess before her.

"We would have aided your cause, if you had called. And we would honor the alliance to reciprocate future needs if we prevail." Hayden whispered.

His gaze scanned between Ahmed and Sabra equally, but his words were deliberated toward the fighting warrioress who growled with disgust across the table.

"If you two are strong together, why ask for aid?" Ahmed softly questioned, taking a sip of his water.

"Numbers." Hayden replied tartly, still eyeing Sabra with unease.

"Hayden and I could handle Kronos, easily a handful of deities within our court to tackle Arlo, but the Soulless creates an infinite army that we are unsure we can match." Liv chimed in, finishing his thought.

Thank you. Hayden nodded.

The two deities before them championed equality between men and women; Sabra relished in it. The more Liv could speak, the better chance they had at gaining an ally with this modern duo.

Ahmed eyed both of the Pure Gods suspiciously.

"You two are too strong together. I worry it would become an unbalanced alliance." Ahmed eyed Liv, his eyes clearly admiring the view before him. "Perhaps we can make an arrangement to balance out the powers at hand."

"What do you propose?" Hayden asked, his eyes narrowing down on the Egyptian King.

"A marriage to ally our worlds. Olivia Monaco shall become my betrothed, uniting the Pure and Egyptian together through a blood heir."

Liv nearly choked on her wine.

"Did you just propose!?" She spat, standing up from the table immediately.

"Now, she speaks." Sabra rolled her eyes, unimpressed with the outburst.

Liv hissed at the high priestess, before returning her shock back to Ahmed. "Are-are you *sure* you're not drunk?!"

Ahmed laughed, albeit awkwardly. "Please, Olivia, I do not mean offense. Sit down." He pulled out her chair, beckoning she return to the dinner table. "You need our armies, but if together you are able to defeat Kronos, after having already infiltrated our afterlife, what is to stop either of you from conquering our people?"

He smiled kindly, his eyes and grin both dazzling, as if sunshine perpetually graced him with a golden glow. Liv breathed, catching her composure, before returning to the table and sitting down, stealing a glance from Hayden before determining her next move.

Hayden sat at the table, composed, but his eyebrows furrowed, showing an internal debate being argued within his mind, even if he appeared to be considering the proposal.

Even if it was at Liv's expense.

"We ask for an alliance because we have no choice." Liv pressed, "Even together, Kronos was able to capture me. If I had been forced to remain in that castle one more day, I would not be here right now. He almost broke me."

"Don't use those words so lightly." Sabra sneered.

"I apologize, Olivia. I do not wish to bring up painful memories." Ahmed hushed Sabra, before consoling his guest.

Finally, he turned to Hayden and explained. "In my lands, women have equal rights. That is how my sister Sabra rules with me, in partnership. We do not believe in hierarchy or gender determining who rules, but work in a democracy. If Olivia were to marry me, as queen she could rightfully send my army to support your cause."

Ahmed stood up, pushing his chair against the table before nodding to his staff, "I shall take my dinner in my chambers tonight." He returned his attention to Hayden and Liv, but addressed only Hayden. "In your world, only the King has the final say, so I request you think it over tonight, and we can discuss further in the morning."

He finally turned to Liv, acknowledging her as if nothing bizarre had occurred. He bowed, lifting her hand from the table and kissed her knuckle, before going in and kissing her cheek unexpectedly after.

Liv almost jumped out of her chair again in surprise, but she had to admit, it *did* feel nice to work with a normal amount of apprehension, butterflies and unease, without dealing with the darkness that typically lingered in her subconscious, full of dread and anxiety, hoping not to kill the one she yearned to touch.

That was precisely how fucked up she was, proof finally served up on a platter and slammed against her face. And it didn't taste good.

Before Ahmed exited the dining hall, Sabra stood up, beckoning the same request.

"You must be insane if you thought I'd willingly stay to entertain you two." She curtsied; the entire etiquette gesture laced with mockery, before she stomped out of the room and slammed the door.

PIPER

The sun had fallen below the earth, against a fruit-medley sorbet colored sky, leaving behind an inverse version of mint chocolate chip. Diamonds glistened in the sky among the colorful neon structures that made up Bangkok.

Piper had never felt so *alive*.

She followed Tristan diligently and without question to a large park. Walking through tall shadows of trees, the trail led them to a big lake that perfectly mirrored the city skyline on its glassy surface, covering the unknown abyss below.

"I never imagined the world could be this big, this beautiful." Piper whispered in awe as she spun around and took in every angle of the stunning scenery. She laughed, finally slowing down to face Tristan. "It's as if I fear the worst yet have been so disproportionally wrong by every imagination… it makes me wonder if my view needs adjustment."

She softly whispered the last revelation, suddenly shy from her honest outburst.

Tristan looked across the lake and remained quiet.

Piper was going to try to better explain herself, the declaration was stupid. She turned away to gather her confidence to speak again, but when she opened her mouth, a caramel voice made the next statement.

"You, of all deities, Piper, have an inspirational view on life."

She turned back to find his golden eyes locked to her crystal aquamarine, as if their two pairs of eyes fueled the electric skyline's color surrounding them. She didn't dare speak now.

"You need not adjust anything."

His words were honest, sincere and simple. Yet, they matched the worth of a lifetime of compliments and made Piper finally felt complete – like she may have value in this expansive world.

"Thank you." Piper responded, her statement clear and true.

She hoped her words had a similar influence on him.

Tristan grinned, an unspoken exchange that infectionously made Piper smile as well. She felt lighter, now ecstactic, so she continued turning in a circle to absorb this one-of-a-kind night.

After she felt like she could no longer spin without growing sick, she fell to the ground, taking in the clean scent of fresh grass and enjoying the crisp green blades lightly scratching against her legs. Her body began buzzing with anticipation once again.

"So, Tristan. You wanted to play?" Piper taunted, her voice fluttering into a distant smirk.

Intrigued, Tristan walked over and plopped down beside her, leaning back against his arm and radiating heat that immediately warmed her.

"Okay hear me out. I'm the God of Fire and you clearly have serious wind powers. Why not put on a show for our new Bangkok neighbors?" Tristan proposed casually, but his eyes gave away his masked excitement. He was daring Piper to be reckless, to break the rules.

"A show?" Piper questioned, trying to understand exactly what he wanted to do to test her.

"How does 'fireworks in the park' sound?" He whispered seductively.

"Fireworks!?" Piper squeaked. "You want to create explosives and then make *me* responsible for not blowing up the city?"

Tristan laughed at her outburst. Piper immediately took a breath and reminded herself to calm down. They hadn't blown up anything *yet*, at least.

"To me, it sounds like you get to have the fun while I get all the boring logistics." Tristan drawled in persuasion

"Fun – yet terrifying and terribly consequential part." She rolled her eyes with a sigh, hoping her fear wasn't too obvious.

"You're the ying to my yang, Pipes." Tristan nudged her encouragingly. "And, I purposely chose the lake to host our festivities so there's water at bay if anything were to turn faulty."

"As in, become *your fault*, since this is your insane idea to begin with?" Piper joked, although admittedly, she was growing excited to do something rebellious. She shook her head and mumbled in disbelief. "Freaking pyro."

"I'll take full responsibly." Tristan pledged, placing his hand across his chest. "You ready?"

She considered his proposal, a slight nudge daring her to try something *new* – be something *new*. In this new world and with this new, intoxicating male.

"Hades yes." Piper squeaked enthusiastically, clapping her hands together to seal the deal.

"When you see the sparks start, cast away." Tristan explained with a mischievious grin. "Aim for the sky, not the trees."

He cupped his hands together and began focusing on the empty space within, until a small electric red ball began fuzing into a larger sphere.

Piper cast the ball into the sky and watched as it exploded into a halo of rubies.

Her entire body thrummed with excitement, as if she had just released an energy spike, with many more to go.

Green lit up Tristan's palms shortly after, so she propelled the light over the lake before it erupted into dozens of tiny bulbs with blazing golden sparkles cascading within.

In the distance, Piper began hearing 'ooh,' and 'ahh,' subtle claps and excited shrieks from passerbys now able to enjoy the dazzling production.

A glowing blue popped from Tristan's hands, and as Piper drove it across the lake, it left trails of stars sparkling in the sky.

They continued crafting their masterpiece, each firework a curated artwork in its own right, until finally Piper's energy grew steady, and then a while later, she yawned.

"Last one." Tristan observed, no longer masking his clear concern of her very long day.

"Make it the best one, then." Piper demanded.

Tristan smirked, pausing a moment to think about what he should create, before going back to work. A golden bauble formulated in his palm and he delicately presented it before Piper as if he were serving it to her personally on his own platter.

Piper lobbed the glimmering object into the sky, watching as champagne glitter sparkled against the night's backdrop, diamonds erupting from each liquid trail. Two bright crystal blue eyes exploded into the night, before they turned into caramel and blinked into darkness. As the remaining gold fireworks slowly melted down to the water, they disappeared among the lake's abyss and then the night sky returned to a slumbered peace.

"Anything else, Piper?" Tristan whispered, turning to her.

Gone was the smirk and jovial excitement. Now only a serious face remained.

Piper's heart was pounding so hard, it felt like it was going to jump out of her body, first from the adrenaline and now from the raw way Tristan looked at her.

Like she was the only person in the world who mattered.

Piper watched cautiously as Tristan's eyes explored her lips, testing the water before returning back to her gaze, contemplating whether or not to dive in. She didn't dare move, so her eyes remained precisely on his, and she almost cursed herself when she involuntarily gulped from the anticipation.

He began leaning toward her, slowly, curiously and unsure.

Piper took a deep breath and then gulped again.

"Piper..." Tristan whispered, his eyes finally asking if she wanted more.

Did she want more?

"Swn sāthārna pid!"

Tristan jolted back, refilling the space with air that he had inhaled during the past five seconds.

They heard footsteps from behind and the yelling growing louder.

"We need to go, now!" Tristan breathed, grabbing Piper's hand and launching into the night. His fiery wings blazed aglory as they propelled into the sparkling dark sky, the duo becoming a falling star among the hundreds glistening steady until they finally landed atop the roof of their condo's building.

"That was incredible." Piper breathed, still calming from the adrenaline.

Ignoring what could have been, she hugged him quickly, before gliding toward the building's entry door.

"You deserve nothing less." Tristan whispered, his eyes sparkling as densely and brightly as the sky behind him.

He thought she didn't hear him, but Piper used an ounce of her powers to carry his words in the wind, summoning a breeze to deliver his thoughts quietly to her.

She smiled, wanting to pinch herself to confirm this seemingly alternative reality where the dauntingly cool deity falls in love with the school outcast, but refrained, too terrified to ruin the perfect dream.

PEYTON

She remained in the bathroom as she heard Rei depart for dinner, between the rushing water of a faux shower. Instead, she sat stubbornly in the corner, drooling over the unconsumed lavender latte that beckoned her name hours ago.

Good. Let him go alone and conspire with his Norse friendlies.

Finally exiting her safehaven and reentering the room, she diverted immediately to the warm beverage. Once consumed, Peyton almost summoned her liquid poison of choice, Fireball, to attend a pity party in her quarters, submit to an alcoholic oblivion, and ultimately stick it to Rei for being such an arrogant dick.

But then she remembered the kind eyes of Gigi, echoing a fire sitting in the backdrop of a lake shore, warm and welcoming, and angrily determined it would not be proper political etiquette to flip off her alliance prospects before having a genuine reason to do so. More importantly, she wanted to understand why Gigi had so intimidatingly warned her while in Midgard on the Norwegian lands.

So, grudgingly, she stomped across the room and toward the closet, hoping to find a gown befitting a royal dinner. Surely it was time to retire her monochrome olive suit and take advantage of whatever hospitality the Norse might provide.

And worse case scenario, she could at least focus on indulging in endless glasses of Champagne.

Looking at her options, Peyton decided she might need that glass of Champagne sooner than later. Not entirely her style, the armoire had been filled with silk, minimalist designs. No embroidery, no frills, no bright colors, nothing to make a statement. Peyton chuckled, thinking how much Liv would live for these options. After debating whether to wear a black silk gown (since the color matched her soul), Peyton finally found a taupe slip dress with buttons down the front, having the closest to personality of all the options.

She pinned her wavy hair into a low bun, happy to see her spiked diamond earrings could be visible on her ear. Her collection of mini studs bordered her left ear cartilage and sparkled in sight, helping add some edge to the bleak outfit. Accessories would be her friends tonight, since she clearly had none among the deities here.

And perhaps her décolletage. Peyton smirked, realizing just how low the deep v-neckline hit across her chest.

But overall, Peyton was impressed with how well she cleaned up, considering she had been a traveling vagabond for the past week. Plus, the silk gown was soft, so she could practically sleep in it tonight.

In the cozy bed, with Rei certainly on the floor.

Amused with her internal hilariousness, Peyton finally left the room and slammed the door behind.

Looking down both ends of the empty hallway, Peyton selected to retrace the steps of how she arrived to their living quarters. Although slightly surprised there was indeed not a guard standing outside her door, Peyton finally figured it couldn't be too hard to find the dining hall, even without her powers.

Turning the corner, she nearly ran into another woman, a slender and tall deity, with creamy, pearl white hair, the same hue as Mothi.

"Oh, excuse me!" Peyton exclaimed, taking a step back.

The lady simply turned in surprise, laughing immediately.

"It's not often you encounter strangers in your hallway." She brushed it off with a sweet smile. "I'm Sif. And you are?"

Sif. Wife to Thor and mother to King Mothi. Although, she only aged to look like the King's older sister.

Peyton was uncertain her inventory of knowledge proved accurate in this world, but according to traditional Norse Mythology (however vague the sources may be), it was easy to imply Sif still had some royal association if she considered the palace her living quarters.

"My formal apologies, Dowager Queen." Peyton tested, placing her right hand in front of her core and her left atop her lower back, bowing as she had seen Heimdall address the King earlier. Sif smiled in approval, so Peyton continued. "I'm Peyton, God of Discovery and colleague of Rei, Security Elite of the Pure Gods."

Sif's smile immediately shifted from welcome to suspicion.

"Thor did not inform me we would have guests tonight." She stated tersely, but nevertheless, extended her hand forward as an invitation to follow.

"In all fairness, I think the term 'guest' is still up for deliberation." Peyton joked.

Sif bowed her head, as if trying to contain her burgundy-painted smile while she politely led Peyton down the stairs. The curve of her lip looked like a delicious strawberry against her contrasting blue eyes, porcelain skin and black long-sleeved crewneck gown.

The silence that followed their adventure to the dining room ensured guards would indeed be posted outside her bedroom tonight; not that Peyton would be inclined to try and escape the enclosed mountain city. But explore it? Hades yes.

The two entered the great hall, finding Mothi, Gigi and Magni grouped around the bar and Rei speaking with another new face, although it was easy to assess the man as Thor. His highlighted blonde hair clearly surrendered himself as Magni's father and while Mothi was far from lacking in taking after his mother, Thor's sharp jawline and slender eyes were almost like a reflection in a glass mirror to his brother.

"Thor, I'd like you to meet Peyton." Rei began, his eyes sparkling with pride, lust and everything that made Peyton want to kick him as he gazed upon her admiringly.

"Peyton, what an honor." Thor took a step forward, a golden ray of sunlight in his tailored suiting, but with a cashmere sweater instead of a tie like his two sons. His arms extended outward, walking toward her before naturally embracing her into a welcoming hug.

Peyton stood on her tippy toes to try and peak over his shoulder, barely finding Rei's gaze in surprise at the friendly gesture.

Yet, after the former King of the Norse Gods took a step back, Peyton picked up on a more natural shift, the air less stuffy, the demeanor more calm.

"What a gift you must hold, to have discovered Vanaheim working solely with pure instinct and determination."

"You speak too kindly, Thor." Peyton smiled, accepting the first of many Champagne flutes to be headed her way. "Most would say my stubbornness is a curse, but you are correct in assuming I have found ways to make it nevertheless, advantageous."

"The powers of discovery prove to have endless opportunities, then." Thor grinned, leading Peyton to the dinner table. "Sit! Make yourself comfortable."

Gigi glided over, immediately plopping herself at the head of the table between Peyton and Rei. Now donning a peach gown, Gigi had clearly appreciated the beauty of an outfit change, unlike her husband and brother-in-law. But most of all, Peyton was surprised to find stunning embellishment in her sleeve work, roses among a flourishing garden depicted by beads. She gave her a quiet smile, before returning her attention to the center of the table, where her husband sat down at the opposite end.

Mothi seemed approachable, yet something obviously kept him uneasy. While Thor was laughing and catching up with Rei like old friends to Peyton's left, Mothi remained closed-off, in concentrated observation of the two guests he now unwillingly welcomed into his kingdom.

"Well, once Mothi here found a bride, it seemed to be a natural time to resign from the throne after nearly ten centuries of ruling and take a much-needed vacation…"

In opposition to his father's kindness and like a stubborn boar, Magni dropped into his seat like an oversized beast forcing itself to act civilly, hovering over the table and glaring at Rei like he would be his next meal if given permission. Delicately, his slim mother gracefully sat down next to him, physically and emotionally matching the contrasting space between her two sons.

Mothi and Magni clearly knew something that Thor did not. And although Peyton understood Sif's demeanor to be a mother's intuition, Gigi seemed like a wild card, holding an entirely different secret unknown to the whole group, perhaps even a dozen. There was something strangely familiar about Queen Gigi, which made her certainly the most concerning of them all.

"Oh, I'm terribly sorry to hear about King Rowan." Thor finally concluded, as the main dishes were being served, "Please extend my condolences to Daphne when you see her next…"

"Enough with the pleasantries!" Magni slammed his fist on the table, forcing all the crystal glasses and plates to bounce. "I too, am sorrowful for your loss, but that does not give permission for loose lips. Whether the recipient has the sight or not."

Peyton didn't flinch from Magni's embarrassing attempt at intimidation across the table; she was too intrigued by Gigi's mouth dropping and eyes welling up by Thor's abruptly loud statement. While staring at Mothi, Peyton observed the young, lioness queen grab her glass of wine to sip, but ultimately shadow any true emotion or expression that crossed her face.

"What my brother means, is we wish to discuss why you are here." Mothi clarified, his voice drawling with boredom.

Too much of an uninterested emphasis, meaning he truly was anxious for the answer.

Peyton turned to Rei, insinuating he give as much information as he felt comfortable, grabbing his hand in support.

"Kronos has escaped the Underworld. He builds an army of the Soulless, hoping to regain control of the Pure God throne and enslave mortals. We seek an alliance for the greater good of Midgard."

"An alliance?" Magni laughed in astonishment. "Do you *not* recall when a similar civil war broke out in Asgard between Odin and Loki? We did not call for your aid."

Through his teeth, Rei addressed the untamed beast, "You may not have called aid, but aid came nonetheless." He turned back to Mothi, the seemingly reasonable one, "Those loyal to your family and your friends showed up, *silently*, if you recall," he smirked at Magni, emphasizing the latter phrase before continuing to address the king, "and fought for King Odin, anyways. It simply appears that King Hayden chooses what is best for Midgard before what is best for his pride."

Magni stood up, looking like he wanted to punch the smug look from Rei's face.

"Your aid will always be appreciated and remembered." Thor nodded in agreement, roaring silently at his son to sit down and heel, before continuing, "Having King Rowan, your father Silas and yourself at Ragnarök tremendously helped the outcome; however destructive it turned out in the end." But, Thor turned to Rei apologetically, "If I were still King, it would be an easy decision, before and after deliberating with the gods of war."

"Enough." Mothi tersely commanded, silencing the table with a simple word. "As King and a God of War, I will be making the final decision, and if you recall, Rei," he finally hissed, "loyalty to us and our friends proved to be very different things."

Peyton squeezed Rei's hand, feeling the heated water reaching its boiling point within his bodily control, trying to help control it herself.

If only she knew what the Hades happened those centuries so long ago. Or what had changed since. Any insight of the sort would have allowed her to make some snide remark or funny quip to ease the tension.

"What about keeping Vanaheim a secret all this time? Even from his partner. Does that not demonstrate what you look for in an ally?" After chugging her Champagne, Peyton took a stab anyway, with what angered *her* – an apparent theme of tonight's conversation. She ensured her voice remained melodic and lighthearted as she prompted 'polite' conversation, weaving in politics as angelically as possible and batting her eyelashes for good measure.

"Sure, King Rowan kept the secret to his grave, but King Hayden had *nothing* to do with it. So ultimately, it does not convince me further to justify putting my people in danger on behalf of an unknowing king." Mothi was calm again, clearly preferring Peyton's face to Rei's.

Duly noted. Game on.

She squeezed Rei's hand, subtly letting him know she had an idea formulating.

"King Hayden's soul mate and soon-to-be Queen, Olivia Monaco, is the Element Elite and the niece of Arlo – a radical Dark God who has conspired with Kronos to overtake the thone. Arlo not only killed her father – his own brother, but also King Rowan, all in pursuit to claim the throne. Just like Ragnarök, this is a cruel and vengeful family war, that could grow tumultuous and destroy another world soon enough if not contained."

Both Mothi and Gigi's ears perked, the two magnetizing together as they leaned toward Peyton's explanation. Magni still remained unimpressed, but Peyton decided she nor anyone at this table gave a true shit to his opinion, and as much as Peyton was sure Magni liked to believe he had influence, she knew he truly had no power or stake in the conversation at hand.

"The prophecy is coming to fruition?" Gigi's gaze clasped with Mothi's, intrigue and alarm both simulating on their faces.

Peyton turned to Gigi, surprised to find the Norse Queen had heard of a Pure God prophecy.

"When… you last visited us, Rei – you had mentioned suspicions of the Elements Pillar turning Dark. Is that not the case, anymore?" Mothi interrupted, clarifying the politics the Pure rule faced.

"The Elements Pillar is Pure again, but I'm afraid other Pillars have turned Dark since we last saw one another, including the Humanities Pillar," Rei stated blankly at his untouched plate before turning to Mothi once again and pleaded, "You must understand. I would not risk coming here unless we desperately needed your aid."

Gigi set down her flute, the glass clinking against the table and shaking the table settings nearby.

"I apologize, I must be feeling unwell." She whispered, standing up as she locked eyes once again with her husband and adding apologetically, "I must excuse myself."

Without receiving a formal response, Gigi exited the dining hall. No longer the bubbly socialite but a ghost walking across the room, as if in a trance.

As soon as Gigi left, dinner turned south. It was like she was the glue holding together the broken glass and without her, the entire structure crashed into a million sharp and very painful pieces.

She was on her sixth glass of Champagne when Magni finally erupted.

"Your society are *murderers* – why not let you all kill eachother off and allow our world to remain in peace?"

Speaking of peace, Peyton had given up on trying to keep it around glass five. There was no controlling or convincing Magni with any reason, and it seemed after glass four anything she said simply went in one of Mothi's ears and out the other. Thor and Sif had politely departed after glass three, which she completely understood.

"Because if Kronos defeats us, it won't be long until he forces us to reveal Vanaheim's location. And you can be certain as Hades we won't feel a morsel of regret giving him the intel to wreak havoc on your idyllic mountainous shit for a society!"

Magni was like the younger brother Rei never had, so easily able poke at every aggravating button and know exactly how to get under his skin. If she didn't despise the smug wolf for taking an opposing side, Peyton would have applauded him for getting such unseen or unheard reactions from Rei.

"You ask us to risk everything – our safety, knowledge of our existence, our economy – to uproot and march to war, but offer nothing in return?"

"As I said, we offer strength in numbers, an alliance..." Rei repeated through his teeth.

"And why should we trust you?" Mothi narrowed his eyes, speaking for the first time since Peyton's seventh glass of Champagne.

Peyton sunk further back in her chair, realizing she was now measuring time in Champagne flutes. She was in no position to continue negotiations tonight, not that it would help.

"The lovely Peyton looks like she's about to tip over. I think we've heard enough, either way." Mothi stood up, excusing himself before walking out the door.

"If you are allowed to leave without consequence, I would consider you fortunate." Magni hissed, before marching out after his brother.

Rei buried his head into his hands, taking a deep breath before shaking it.

"What do we do?" He asked, turning to Peyton for comfort.

"We?" Peyton challenged, a little too quickly. "So, we're a team now? Because if I remember correctly, you've lied to me and kept many secrets to which I still have yet to be enlightened."

She stood up, slamming her chair against the table.

"Ask me that question again when you're actually ready to work as a team."

Peyton headed back to her quarters, thinking to herself: *and after glass eight, Peyton lost her shit entirely.*

JOCELYN

"They're deplenished. All of them." Jocelyn explained, trailing close to Demetrius as they continued walking through the destructive village.

Hungry eyes and weakened intenstines confronted them from every corner. The smell of vomit and dirt swallowed them whole, forcing Jocelyn to stop breathing as they made their way to the castle.

"Should we even attempt to ally with Danu?" Demetrious challenged, pulling Joss even closer as he continued to sadly study their surroundings. "You saw Adair's natural instinct, to recoil in fear at the name. Is it worth the trouble if we're going to get shambles for an army?"

"We can't leave these innocent deities to peril." Joss pushed. "Perhaps we offer their support in pay for power and wealth to rebuild the Celtic empire?"

Demetrius considered the idea, studying the Burren and all it had to give, which wasn't promising.

"Twenty gods with souls from natural creation, no matter how burdened, can easily wipe out those numbers of the Soulless, if not more."

"I agree. That's not what I'm worried about." Demetrius explained, tilting his head toward Joss while gesturing to their surroundings, and whispered. "Why not seek aid before?"

Jocelyn took a deep breath, immediately regretting it. She coughed, leaning on Demetrius a bit more for support, and to keep her upright.

"Pride?" Joss offered, releasing her grasp on Demetrius's arm and forcing herself to refrain from relying on him. "Maybe they lost hope. But hope has come at last, and we need to see if they're willing to fight for it."

Suddenly her mind blasted into the unknown. Jocelyn grabbed her head, seeing the face of her best friend plastered against her mind, a vision she had not seen so clearly for almost twenty years. Dazzling caramel eyes, frosted chocolate hair curled into stunning waves and plush lips curved into surprisingly thin lines, revealing such a full smile that you could even see her soft pink gums.

A vision of the future, glistening brightly instead of a dark, fainted memory of past, meaning only one thing...

Jocelyn stumbled, crashing to the ground; Demetrius caught her just in time.

"Joss! Are you okay?"

Shaking, Joss clung to the image of vibrant life.

When she had visited the Underworld and begged Hades for affirmation that her best friend had passed through the veil, the God of Death cruely confirmed that he couldn't see her soul in this world. No emotion, no empathy. He had relished in her grief.

And since then, Jocelyn had taken it as truth. For she had gone searching, hoping to find a vision or prophecy with any sign of her best friend's return.

She hadn't heard her laugh in decades…

At the revelations, her eyes started filling with tears of joy, she found herself laughing along.

Giselle was still *alive*.

TWENTY-NINE

REI

Peyton had retreated back to their bedroom when dinner concluded. Rei thought it would be best to give her space while he took advantage of an open balcony that overlooked the stunning metropolitan of Vanaheim. He needed to clear his head, too.

Now that he stood so obviously between two opposing forces, he needed to make a choice and accept the repercussions. If only his honor didn't reside with both armies, that would have made it a much simpler decision.

He heard subtle clicks gliding toward him, turning to find the only one who might feel as remotely strained as he, a ghost between two worlds, just living on the other side.

"I thought I would find you out here." She smiled, genuinely.

It still took Rei a moment to match the familiar voice with the new face. Giselle had done a mesmerizing job of concealing her natural facial structure, adding water to her cheeks, chin and lips to round out her face, a remarkable disguise in itself to make her unrecognizable. Yet, her eyes commemorated her lost heritage, a mirrored gaze to that of her provoking younger brother, Tristan. He certainly missed her arctic blue gems – her true, stunning eyes – but the amber flames that decorated her face were how he had immediately recognized Giselle upon walking across the throne room earlier that day. A ploy that made Rei grow tenser when she had playfully winked his way, playing into the character of Queen Gigi, but subtly acknowledging her disguise still held strong against Peyton.

But Rei knew Peyton, understanding that they had a finite amount of time before she started putting the pieces together and figured out his deepest, darkest secret.

Fortunately, if anyone could resolve an alliance or revise the existing agreement between the Norse and the Pure, it would be the two who now sat together on the balcony in peace.

Giselle sighed, no longer the dazzling royal socialite but instead the reserved, sophisticated deity he once knew.

"My brother?" She whispered, desperation cutting underneath her calm inquiry.

"Alive and well." Rei smiled, adding, "But annoying as hell."

Giselle smirked before sighing in relief, finally receiving a response to the question that had haunted her mind for the past eighteen years.

"And you honestly believe he's in good hands with the new Elemental Elite?"

Rei nodded, first shocked with his immediate reaction, before explaining, "I'm surprised I'm saying this, because Olivia Monaco is also annoying as hell, but she truly wants to create a better world, with justice, reason and a balance of power for her subjects. Her vision combined with King Hayden's will probably be the beginning of a new age. That is, if they are able to defeat the venom poisoning it."

"I want to help." Giselle stated bluntly, before biting her lip. "I wish I could convince Mothi to ally…"

"Did you pledge obedience to the Norse Gods?" Rei asked curiously.

Giselle furrowed her brows, staring up into the cave's sparkling ceiling. "No, not even with our union. I promised respect and understanding, as you advised."

"Good." Rei nodded, taking a deep breath before starting his final lecture, his only hope for advancing his agenda – to leverage word play and loyalty. "You must remember where you come from, Giselle. Mothi is your *spouse*, your *equal*, but only that. You two fell in love and I don't want you to betray that. But he is not your King. *Hayden* is your true king."

"Cynical Rei diminishes love to a strategic partnership. Should I be surprised?" Giselle huffed. "You forget that I've lived almost two decades with these deities, Rei. My age is not as refined to your two thousand years, so I'll grant you a pass at not understanding how that time here has impacted me. These gods have become my *family*."

"Tristan is your family." Rei pushed.

Giselle paused, scolding Rei with her silence.

"And for him, I will try to persuade Mothi to shift his perspective. But I will not betray my husband."

He had always respected Giselle for her selfless compassion while maintaining her relentless principles. Although she had always been closer to Jocelyn, Rei had appreciated her more sophisticated perspective to balance out Jocelyn's wild one.

"I'll also try to convince Mothi to share our secret with Peyton." Giselle added quietly. "Although I must admit, my motives are partially selfish. As great as it is to be reunited with you and catch up, I do miss her too, and it's growing harder by the minute to remain a stranger when a dear friend is nearby. And that's even with the ability to completely avoid her, at all costs."

Rei shrugged. He had sworn secrecy but at the time had not realized just how bad the consequences could be, but he had already promised to face the consequences head on.

"I would understand if you chose Peyton over me." Giselle whispered softly. "Rei, this secret started as a cut – simple, clean and easily bandaged – but now dirt has infiltrated the wound and the longer it festers, the more dangerous and incurable it may become."

"How do I begin to explain that I've blatantly lied, broken rules, conspired and took part in faking a death? Biggest of all, that you're still *alive* and I knew about it all this time?"

"You start with telling her the truth and… go from there. Improvise." Giselle said, grinning at her lack of great advice.

"And what about you?"

"Exposing me?" Giselle clarified, shaking her head into the unknown. "With Kai dead and Arlo in an open battle against Olivia, the true Element Elite, it seems my safety is no longer the greatest concern."

For now.

"And you are happy here? With him?" Rei finally blurted.

It was what had haunted *his* thoughts, what he craved to know. A yearning desire so compelling it challenged his control and being, turning him from a sensible war Elite to an emotional wreck. Yet, Giselle had always made him act differently; he never had full control around her. It seemed some things never changed, but nevertheless he had to know.

She grabbed his hand, squeezing it assuringly, sorrow longingly hitting her gaze. She removed her glamour, her intoxicating, porcelain face reminding Rei of all that he had lost those years ago.

Giselle almost looked exactly as she had when he left her the last time. Incriminatingly beautiful and tauntingly innocent. But now, she had a certain poise, an elegance that made her soft features a weapon for trickery, especially if one ever underestimated her calculating and sharp intelligence.

"I am." Giselle smiled sadly, but honestly. She was cunning, but she wasn't a monster. "At first, I was a wreck. A ghost. I was angry and depressed and in disbelief that this was my new world. But, overtime, I healed.

"One night, I ran into Mothi at a private wine bar. I hadn't told anybody about my past. Only those who were there the night you and Silas brought me and asked for refuge on my behalf knew my story – Thor, Sif and Mothi and select royal guards. I had ignored all invitations or olive branches they extended as soon as I had run from the palace and sought to get lost in the oblivion the city provided.

"But even after years passed, Mothi recognized me that night and approached me, explaining how he once watched his home burn to the ground and what terror he had unleashed getting acclimated to this new world. He saw me when I was trying to be invisible and made me feel like maybe I could belong. Just like you, we had to acclimate and do our best to move on. We helped eachother survive."

Rei forced himself to stare blankly ahead, clenching his jaw and refusing to break upon hearing the words of her happiness. He was an asshole for wishing she suffered like he had, even knowing that she *had* suffered. But flashes of their last moments together – the tears shed, the final kiss, his heart tearing into two, while the Norse Royal Family simply watched their tormenting final goodbye, indifferent to the ripping of a lost love – still left a bitter taste in his mouth.

Giselle gently grabbed his cheek, guiding him back again to the present, to her fierce glacier eyes.

"It wasn't the plan. For *either* of us."

Rei nodded, gulping. He was scared and sad at how quickly he agreed.

Giselle continued, her eyes glistening. "But, I saw the way you quietly smirked in amusement at Peyton's sassy comments and how your eyes lit up when she walked in the room tonight. Even as obviously pissed she may be at you right now; I still see the strong foundation you both have built together. The life you have built together. It's time you let us go, Rei. Let me go."

His cheek still felt warm as Giselle stood up and departed, impulsively hugging him from behind before leaving him alone on the balcony once again, the ghost of her presence lingering with him as it had for the past twenty years. Yet this time, the shadow of her laugh, curves and scent evaporated entirely.

Rei was finally alone.

LIV

Hayden hadn't spoken a word, shown no opposition to the proposal.

Was he actually considering it?

They both remained silent as they trailed behind Fukayna back to their pyramid suite, a hovering presence sending them back months in progress. Everything Liv had pushed Hayden to pursue, encouraged him to find even against her broken heart, had now been shoved onto her.

Onto them.

Should she be considering it, too?

Liv looked over to Hayden, who showed no obvious concern, a blank canvas waiting desperately to be transformed by paint.

Were they in such a dire situation against the Soulless that this had changed everything with being soul mates?

If that was the case, Liv would do it.

She nodded in affirmation to her choice. For Hayden, she would do anything.

They walked together, but separate. Their unity once again only a façade as they cascaded down the grand staircase, back toward the serene courtyard.

Liv glanced around her, taking in the stunning surroundings and recognizing that although her heart would always belong to Hayden, if needed, she could become fond of this desert oasis.

If needed, she could sell her soul to the devil for the greater good of humanity, for her other half.

When Fukayna led them to their room, the pressure increased twofold. Liv's looming fate to be concreted within moments.

As soon as the door slammed shut and they were alone, Liv immediately turned to Hayden, begging for some inclination to his thoughts. When their eyes locked, he nearly shrugged, disappointment taking over his stoic face.

"Oh god, Hayden." Liv ran into his arms, hoping it would not be the last time he would embrace her, praying he would not decline her upon first touch – she needn't be pure for Ahmed. When he allowed it, Liv melted into him, letting his strength hold her up against her impending worry. "What are we supposed to do?"

"As long as we aren't married, this will be a continual topic." Hayden exasperated softly to himself. "But my perspective will always remain the same – no."

Liv lifted her head at that statement. "Hayden, if this gives us an advantage…"

She needed to approach every angle, make sure *he* was aligned before she gave into her hopes.

"You're actually considering it?" Hayden huffed with bewilderment.

"We've fulfilled the prophecy. We fell in love, and you have my heart, always." Liv stepped back, needing to meet Hayden directly in the eye. "What if our love is the exact reason I appeal to Ahmed? The exact opportunity that helps us win this war?"

Hayden shook his head, unable to comprehend any alternative solution. "Ollie, you're talking about *eternity*. You aren't offering yourself up for a decade, but for a thousand lifetimes. *A thousand lifetimes apart.*"

The inevitability of her circumstance hit her like entering a room without oxygen; she couldn't breathe. Hayden was her air but could no longer save her.

She couldn't contain herself, Liv started sobbing. "I'm offering myself for you."

"No, Liv. No." Hayden insisted, his jaw locking, his voice wavering.

"I'm fucked up, Hayden. You know it and I know it." She needed to state what they both wondered at night. It was time to layout everything with their tormenting predicament, however raw it may be. "What if I'm never able to give you myself entirely again? What if this is how it was always supposed to transpire?"

"I refuse to humor this conversation, Liv. I refuse to make lifechanging decisions on prophecies. They ruin everyone they meet and still come to fruition. Let's make the prophecy fight for its life, instead of disposing our lives on its behalf." Hayden took a step forward, grabbing Liv's hand gently, no longer the passionate grasp forcing her into his arms, but considerate, caring and still all too aware of the horrors that haunted her subconscious.

"I will *never* negotiate our love. We will find another way."

He lifted her hand, softly kissing her knuckle.

With the small gesture, Liv returned to earth, finally able to take a breath of oxygen and calm her nerves. She sighed with a soft sniffle, "It seems our relationship is only hindering our success with defeating the Dark Gods." Muttering softly, she continued, "The prophecy said that our relationship would help our people defeat the Dark Gods. What if choosing eachother over everything else ultimately becomes our cause for destruction?"

Hayden huffed in agreement, angrily mocking the words they had heard all too often since enrolling at Puerdios. "Only when the son of the King falls in love with the daughter of an Elite will the Pure Gods defeat the Dark Gods."

Yet, his echo of mockery quickly turned to consolation, reminding them both of what they had forgotten amidst the competition of winning.

And with that realization, they smiled and grabbed eachother's hands, choosing eachother above all for their cause. And then dreadingly and silently understood what they needed to do next.

"Let's wait to tell Ahmed." Hayden suggested, pulling Liv back into a hug, resting his chin atop her head. "Try to befriend him, work to build a genuine alliance before we decline his offer. Perhaps, with some semblance of a friendship working for us, he may have a change of heart regarding his proposal."

Unsure of where to go from there, Liv instead focused on the relief of their mutual agreement, no matter how guilty she would feel with essentially manipulating the Egyptians. And how to play the fine line between interest and lust? What would happen when they inevitably declined Ahmed's offer? How could she make it so that the Egyptian King didn't feel like she mislead him or refrain from allowing Sabra to become acquainted enough that the fierce warrioress didn't slay them at the first sound of betrayal?

And even if that went successfully, how the hell would they learn how to escape this world?

"Hayden…" Liv pondered aloud, asking the same question that ran through her mind.

"Tomorrow. We split up. I'll look for their library to research our return." He offered, hoping to appease her spinning thoughts.

"And me?" Liv asked, finally lifting her head to lock eyes with Hayden.

He furrowed his eyebrows while pulling a lock of hair from her face, his thumb trailing her jawline and resting it upon her lip. His touch sent chills down her spine; the weight of his lingering finger creating desirous tension she would soon need to appease. But Hayden had another agenda on his mind, as he looked upon Liv with relentless guilt.

"Make sure you're somewhere to be found."

PEYTON

She refused to wallow in self-pity and certainly did not want to be stuck in this room when Rei returned, suffering in suffocating silence and hovering lies. And if Mothi planned to declare his decision tomorrow, what it really meant was that Peyton didn't have that much time left to explore Vanaheim.

So, she grabbed her silk olive green blazer and matching snakeskin crossbody and headed for the door to hit the town.

Yet, before she turned the handle, it turned itself.

The door gently swung open, revealing Rei in the hallway.

"I thought you would be asleep by now... are you going somewhere?" Rei first offered an apologetic tone, but it shifted to accusatory when he assessed Peyton's outfit and freshly curled hair.

"I am." Peyton challenged. "I have a better chance of learning about these people and this culture than I do staying in here, don't I?"

Rei began to oppose, but paused, instead acquiescing by running his hand over his head. "Peyton, can we talk?"

"Oh, now you want to talk?" She mocked. "About what, Rei? What do *you* want to talk about?"

Rei smiled, knowing at long as Peyton mocked him, there was hope. That pissed her off even more.

"Depends, how long do I have before you head off to the land of Fireball and EDM?"

He was trying to be funny and charming, which if Rei was attempting, at least he knew he was clearly on her shit list and in the wrong.

"It depends how long your talking proves to be of interest and value. And right now, sir, you are failing."

Nevertheless, Peyton turned around and sat on the bed.

"Any topics of interest to begin with?" Rei offered.

Peyton squinted her eyes, looking off toward the window, and tapped her chin.

"Okay. Mothi and Magni – why do they despise you?"

"A misunderstanding, or perhaps selective understanding." Rei sighed, sitting down beside Peyton to further explain. "I met Fenrir, the Norse God of Strength, while fighting with Rollo. We became close, after breaking through the suspicions of our relentless power and undefeatable energy. He introduced me to his nephews, Mothi and Magni, and I even brought him to Silas's birthday symposium, to support Zeus's efforts to ally with the Norse. But when he met Daphne, she had a vision and told us that when Asgard burned, Thor needed to inherit Odin's powers in order for their people to prosper."

"I should have known Daphne would be in on this..." Peyton exasperated.

"That was the extent of her involvement, I promise." Rei commented before continuing, "So, we visited Odin and relayed the prophecy, where he demanded that when Asgard burned, Fenrir would need to kill him in order to save his people."

Rei tensed as he relived the memories in his head, but forced himself to continue on. "When we learned that Loki's attack would be the cause of the vision, I offered to kill Odin so Fenrir would not have to so directly betray his father Loki, but he insisted it must be him, claiming an already suspicious and evil Norse killing Odin would cause heartbreak within their community, but a Pure God murdering Odin would instigate a world war for revenge."

Rei took a deep breath, finally turning to Peyton, "You already know what happened to Fenrir, surely."

Peyton nodded, recalling what she had read on Ragnarök, how Vidar avenged his father Odin by stabbing Fenrir in the heart.

"And you defended your friend's tarnished name to those you thought would be sympathetic."

"It started as innocent conversation over mead, but erupted into me slamming Magni's head against the table and possibly calling him a coward."

"I'm surprised a similar scenario didn't go down tonight." Peyton smiled softly, the pieces starting to form together.

"Close." Rei smirked.

"And Mothi?"

"He's territorial of Gigi."

Peyton laughed. "So, what – Thor doesn't hold a grudge?"

"Thor thought nothing of it, he wasn't there to see my friendship with Fenrir nor hear my stupid soliloquies in his defense. He went off proven facts, that King Rowan, Silas and myself aided his people and helped provide refuge in Vanaheim with the Vanir. I think ultimately, he was like his father, and wanted to avoid conflict with opposing forces. So we signed a treaty promising our secrecy to Vanaheim's existence, along with the Aesir and Vanir living within it, and lived in harmony for almost one thousand years."

"Until you returned."

Rei turned to Peyton, grabbing her hands, his eyes pleading. "I returned by myself to protect another. But with King Rowan and Silas both unaware of the visit, Thor became suspicious, most likely with Mothi and Magni whispering conspiracy in his ear. All I can say is I promised to never return, unless Vanaheim was truly at risk."

"To protect another?" Peyton asked curiously, pulling her hands out of his grasp.

"I promised to not speak of the arrangement to anyone, to ensure the protection remained strong. I want to tell you, Peyton, but I'm afraid it is not my story to tell. I have done all that I could to keep my promises to everyone, even if I failed miserably along the way. But as the Security Elite, I cannot proactively breach someone's protection. I can't, Peyton, I can't... I won't..."

He bowed his head, shaking it between his hands. She hadn't seen him this unraveled, ever.

"Rei, it's okay. It's okay." She hummed, immediately wrapping her arm around his shoulder, and held him tightly, slowly rocking him back and forth until he finally relaxed. "I understand. And I trust you, so if you think it's not important, then it's not important."

Rei finally fell asleep twenty minutes later, possibly the first deep sleep he had fallen into since they left Puerdios University. Peyton almost contemplated staying with him, but upon the first sound of a snore, she decided there was no way in Hades that she would miss the opportunity to experience the brilliant nightlife of Vanaheim. The electric lights and intoxicating music was practically calling her name.

She was more surprised to find Gigi sitting in the living room near the front door, no longer in royal attire but now outfitted in a loose grey cashmere v-neck sweater, high-waisted black denim and brown booties.

"About time." Gigi grinned, standing up from the couch.

"For?" Peyton questioned.

Gigi's smile faded from ecstatic excitement to polite composure before explaining, "You mentioned wanting to see Vanaheim in all its glory, so I'll be your official guide for the night." She smirked and kicked her leg back, while framing her face angelically, almost like the equivalent of a socialite bowing before her king.

"Won't people recognize you?" Peyton asked.

"Nah, don't worry about me. I'm in disguise." Gigi winked and then twirled to show off her 'casual' attire.

Peyton chuckled awkwardly. "No offense, but I recognized you almost immediately."

Gigi's eyes blazed, the caramel heating up against the fire, holding a million secrets behind the flame. "Impressive, God of Discovery." She mocked, before nodding to the guards and walking toward the door. She turned back to look at Peyton, "Besides, do you really think the guards would let you leave the palace without supervision?"

Peyton rolled her eyes, following obediently behind Gigi because the queen certainly had a point.

"Lead the way, your highness."

Gigi frowned, turning to show her new partner in crime her pout. "Gigi, please. Even better, 'G,' when we're in the city."

"And where exactly in the city are you taking me first?" Peyton asked curiously, losing her breath in awe at the first sight of the lit-up city from the peak of their descent. It was a mesmerizing circus, full of intrigue and desire just waiting to be grasped.

"I thought I'd start with my favorite bar, *Spetses*. It's chic, but cozy. The people who frequent there are relatively civilized but definitely a fun time – a perfect blend for a first-time visitor."

"Sounds delightful. Is there dancing?"

Gigi's eyes sparkled. "Would I dare take you somewhere that didn't?"

"Perhaps you Norse folk are tolerable, after all." Peyton smirked, looking outward toward the mountain's ceiling, watching all the various artists provide their own unique show from the sky.

"The outdoor ambiance truly baffles me," Peyton observed, her eyes following the talented terpsichoreans sparkle across the city, elegantly dancing intricately between the ceiling scrapers. "I've never seen something so... beautiful."

"Mothi's idea, actually." Gigi smiled in memory. "During the transition, we worried our people would grow tired and melancholy living within a dull mountain, not being able to see the true night sky, surrounded by rock and darkness. We thought providing stunning sights to the faux sky and live entertainment with music, lightshows and more, would increase prosperity."

"I wouldn't have suspected the God of War to have such an appreciation for the arts." Peyton observed quietly, wishing she were granted the opportunity to get to know the deity beneath the barricades.

"Nor did I." Gigi agreed, laughing melodically.

Peyton turned to Gigi, processing the statement, the sound. A blank memory flashed across her mind, as if she had heard the noise before, but she couldn't place it.

Gigi coughed, terminating her joy as quickly as flicking an 'off' switch.

"You didn't know the prince well before you were betrothed?" Peyton switched gears to the other curiosity Gigi's response peaked.

"Not personally, only what I had heard from peers, stories mostly, and had observed from afar." Gigi stated, tighter lipped than before. "I was fortunate to earn his friendship before any discussions of marriage were placed on the table."

"Mothi married for love?" Peyton clarified, once again shocked by Thor's offspring. She considered Magni, then laughed at the idea.

Mothi had the eloquence of a renaissance warrior, refined but rugged. Magni, on the otherhand, was pure arrogant brute.

"Surprisingly, yes." Gigi smiled, "Although, when you are a secret society with no true threats of invasion, there aren't many advantageous prospects to leverage for marriage."

"Touché."

They had exited the long residential path and began turning corners toward the city proper.

"Our king, Hayden, also chose love." Peyton bridged the pause to hopefully encourage some commonality that Gigi could share with Mothi. "The Element Elite nearly drove him mad trying to encourage him to marry for an alliance, despite their bond, support from family and friends, fate and a prophecy. She was determined to find her soul mate a match that could offer more than love – and almost broke her own heart by sending him to the Sirens to ally with their Queen."

Gigi turned away to mask her reaction before replying, "I'm sure that was quite the emotional rollercoaster. But, I'm glad they were able to find one another, in the end."

"It was a shitshow disaster that I never want to repeat again." Peyton agreed, rolling her eyes.

Gigi burst out in laughter. Covering her mouth to mask the noise and a final snort.

Another memory flashed across Peyton's mind.

Staying up late in a bunkhouse-style bedroom at the cabin, giggling under the sheets about Zeus-knows-what with Xander snoring above and Tristan sound asleep in a crib, but needing to remain quiet so their families would not realize they were drunk and awake, and see just how bad of an influence Peyton was on...

Peyton froze. How did she not piece the clues together sooner? The bright amber eyes, identical to Tristan's, the mention of a last visit to Midgard about twenty years ago, the voice so melodic and charming like her brother, the applaudable confidence and sass.

The Goddess of Water may have been able to contort her face, but she had not thought about the other bodily functions, other physical descriptors outside of her control, not realized the simple combination of a laugh and movement to cover her disguise would nearly scream to her family friend that the lost Giselle, was indeed, alive.

Tears starting welling in Peyton's eyes, her body was shaking as a weight lifted from her chest. With so many loved ones she now mourned for and preparing for the number to only increase in the upcoming months, it was a relief to finally close the chapter of an unknown.

"*Spetses* is here on the right-"

Peyton lunged her body toward Giselle, wrapping her arms around the goddess and pulling her into a hug worthy of the thousands of hugs that were long-overdue.

"Peyton?"

"It's you!" Peyton cried, squeezing Giselle tighter. "We all thought you were *dead*!"

She wanted to hit her, scream at her, but most of all, never let her go.

But then it hit her, Giselle was alive.

Did Rei know?

The growing heaviness in her gut suspected Giselle was exactly who Rei had been trying to protect all these years, who he continued to protect and always would.

Peyton pulled away, battling the estactic joy of a family friend returned against the appearance of facing the previously-almost-betrothed of her current boyfriend.

"I knew it wouldn't take much time for you to discover my true identity," Giselle admitted slyly. She opened the door into the bar, grinning mischievously as she led Peyton into the darkened room. White walls were held up by Grecian pillars, all glowing a warm hue from torches that dimmed the light to a cozy, intimate feel. Olive trees meticulously adorned tables surrounding a circular bar. Empty, Peyton would have believed the bar to be sleek, chic and that she underdressed for the occasion, but filled with roudy guests, laughter and a band playing upbeat music, the establishment was exactly the vibe Peyton looked for. Apparently, she had taught her younger friend to have fabulous taste.

And right now, she could go for a shot of ouzo, or perhaps three.

"Here, in the back." Giselle grabbed Peyton's hand, leading her closer to the stage.

The music growing louder would certainly provide the secrecy the two would need to honestly discuss their pasts, presents and future.

"Nikolaos! I ryggen!" Giselle hollered toward the bartender. "To bilder av ouzo og den vanlige forretten min!"

"Ok, kjære!" Nikolaos nodded to the queen without confusion.

Apparently, this disguise was not only for Peyton.

"Takk!" Giselle yelled back, before lowering her voice so Peyton could hear, "I ordered my usual: pita, veggies, hummus and tzatziki, but more importantly, two shots of Ouzo."

"Sounds fabulous. So you come here often?" Peyton slid into the booth, nodding toward the attractive Nikolaos behind the bar.

"When I'm feeling homesick." Giselle sadly smiled, "Nobody here knows our customs, understands the importance of our history. Sometimes, I would sit back here and pretend I was home, that I was simply sitting alone at a bar in Mykonos."

"Why haven't you come back?" Peyton couldn't dwell on the image long, nor think how lonely Giselle must have been these past two decades.

"At first, it was for safety." Giselle replied, as if rehearsed.

"So, will you come back now?" Peyton pressed, ashamed that in addition to pushing for an alliance, a part of her remained curious for personal reasons as well. "Your Element Elite, Olivia, is *Liam's* daughter and will welcome you with open arms. You need not worry about Arlo, at least no more than your brother or any of your peers."

Giselle frowned, guilt painted across her face as she quietly thanked Nikolaos for the quick arrival of their ouzos and appetizers.

"Part of the negotiations that allowed my sanctuary here in Vanaheim include my inability to cross over to Midgard." She finally confessed, taking a sip of ouzos immediately after.

"And Rei's participatory silence to ensure the secrets of Vanaheim were never exposed." Peyton tersely commented, taking a sip of her own ouzos as well. "Cheers."

"Peyton, Rei loves you. Please don't hold this over him. He is a man of his word, that is all this is about." Giselle grabbed her hand, squeezing it tight.

"I understand it all." Peyton plainly stated. "What I truly don't understand is that you plan to take a passive stance during this war, while your only bloodline remains in danger, who willingly fights for the good in this world, in your honor, and you refuse to try to make a difference."

Her grip had tightened around the ouzos, she now spoke through her teeth. She had certainly never wanted to teach her younger friend to be a coward.

"We bargained this demonic idea for my safety." Gigi defended, "I endured isolation, heartbreak, exclusion and never-ending worry for my family, my friends. I separated my life. *Hades*, I sliced my connection with the Pure Gods with a dull knife, slowly but stubbornly, deliberately, until my soul and who I once was no longer existed in my body."

Her voice was terse, cutting. No longer the gentle, jovial younger sister Peyton had known, but now a woman who had hardened through her hardships, whatever they might have been.

"I am fortunate that Mothi suffered as I had, Peyton. How sickening is that to say? To be happy that my partner also knew what it felt like to be ripped out of the only world he knew and thrown into this mountainous hell? I'm thankful for our relationship, but it saddens me that our bond, our love, formed from darkness. It took *years* to forget my life, but I did, as I promised. And after all that Mothi has done for me, these people have done for me? I do not wish to risk it all by throwing away my safety as he so generously offered me twenty years ago. I refuse to betray my husband."

"Safety!?" Peyton retorted with a huff. "And all they have done for *you*? They have been *hiding* for twenty years, while we battle for the world of those they are sworn to protect!"

Her voice crescendoed to a scream. Peyton wasn't proud of it, but at the core and in the back of her mind, she kind of was. It had a damn good effect.

And someone needed to knock some sense into the House of Water. What that power and responsibility represented.

"It was all for my safety, Peyton." Giselle's voice trembled. "And I earned my safety. *Here*. Where there is no threat of my grandfather Henri, Arlo and our original maker Kronos. I am a Norse God, a Norse *Queen*, and now I willingly support my king and what is best for my people."

"You know, the Element Elite is a demi-god?" Peyton had calmed, her heart still raced, but she was losing respect for Giselle with every new word coming out of this brain-washed, lost soul who no longer deserved her care. "And the irony is that she has every power to strip yours, now knowing they did not pass on to another in your supposed passing and that she does not have your loyalty or support. Even more ironic is that she's battled against Kai, Arlo and Kronos countless times and survived, and yet she refuses to let their power intimidate her, to scare *her* from doing what's right, no matter how broken she may be."

Giselle's mouth had dropped, yet she was speechless. Her face dwindled closer to self-destruction, but ultimately, she faced the terror of becoming a powerless immortal being dangled right in front of her.

"It's because Liv believes in the good, the possibility for good in this world and the good within people who reside in it. And the thing that is most ironic, is from all the pain Liv has endured, exponential to yours – I am certainly positive, to all the battles she has faced and has yet to face, she will continue believing in the good. And because of that idyllic belief, when I tell her Tristan's sister, Giselle, Head of the House of Water, is still alive – she will believe in the good and endlessly hope for you to be the older sister that her best friend Tristan deserves. She will never strip that power away from you, even when you no longer merit the opportunity to make amends."

Peyton stood up, holistically over this conversation.

"Peyton, wait-" Giselle reached for her.

"If Kronos wins?" Peyton sneered, "He will demolish this world and the first thing he will do when he sees your traitorous ass is send you to the Underworld, only to strip you of your powers so Arlo can immediately absorb all of the Element Elite Powers – as if your powers would even stand a chance against the two of them to begin with."

Peyton stormed out of the bar, judging Rei even more for ever loving that lost goddess, even more so if he still did.

One more day. Peyton reminded herself.

Only one more day until she could return to the world of the sane.

JOCELYN

They had hidden again, away from the desolate town, to try and regain strength before pursuing Danu; however, even after a night's respite, Joss felt no more rested than when they had first stepped foot on the cursed land.

Yet, she couldn't focus on her weakness, that certainly would not help aid in survival. So, instead, Joss woke up with a stubborn mindset, grabbing Demetrius's hand at first sunlight, and marched toward Danu's lair to finally face the beast once and for all.

Approaching the 'castle' proved to look more like approaching a penetentiary. Rows of windows covered in metal bars greeted them, taunting Jocelyn and Demetrius to enter with the risk of never leaving again.

Tiny faeries scurried within the greenery plants before the stone fortress, whispering between the leaves to report on the two trespassers approaching the estate.

Within moments, the entire Burren would be alert of their presence. Within hours, all of Ireland.

Joss ignored their reality, continuing on. Although secretly, she wished they could have kept the element of surprise, but now knew their only advantage with Danu was quickly slipping with each additional whisper buzzing among the wind.

The door swung open, slamming against the fortress, enforcing its powerful dominance to intimidate its guests.

There were so many paths.

Jocelyn closed her eyes and tried to concentrate.

But everything was blurry.

She was growing weaker.

A flash of limestone passed through her mind.

Was the limestone the cause of her weakening state?

Did it have the same effect on her partner, also too stubborn to admit the possibility, refusing to speak the words in an effort against making it all the more true?

Finally, her eyes opened, having a bit more focus on where the route would lead her. Shadows curved against the foyer, creeping up the stairs.

"This way." Joss confirmed, leading Demetrius through the door and to the left, ignoring the shadow and heading in the opposite direction.

"Do you have a game plan?" Demetrius purred from behind.

Joss paused for a moment, considering which path to take before responding. She turned right, finally replying, "We push an alliance for prosperity. Danu is the goddess of knowledge, so pray we find a common denominator there."

The corridor led to a great stone hall, cold and grey, but nonetheless prepared to greet the unknown visitors. Lines of Celtic deities stood bordered around the room, standing straightforward and with dull eyes, but the feathers, trinkets and braids paired with more painted symbols and tattoos created a savage stronghold.

Joss explored the possibility of waging war, trying to remain unfazed and calm when she only saw darkness and downfall.

She continued on the path that led to survival, although did not guarantee it. The only way out was through.

Her head began hurting. Crafting her powers was draining Joss more quickly here than in her world. She wanted to grab her head to soothe it but did not want to give those who watched her the satisfaction – or worry – of her depletion.

Looking up, she saw a large stone fortress carrying a divine being.

It could only be Danu.

Silence greeted Demetrius and Joss.

Jocelyn bowed, allowing herself and her royal status to feel inferior for the sake of survival. Fortunately, Demetrius interpreted her unspoken queue, following her lead by also lowering himself to the ground and demeaning his worth.

As she rose, Joss raised her chin with dignity, now demanding to be acknowledged.

"You seek an alliance." Danu stated, her voice terse and sharp.

No welcome. No questioning needed.

Well, two could play this game.

"Hello, Danu. I am Princess Jocelyn and Candor Elite of the Pure Gods." She began, ignoring Danu's intentional demand and instead continued at her own pace by motioning to the male beside her, "With me is Demetrius, God of the Solar System."

She paused, politely inviting the powerful goddess to pivot or ask any questions, even if she already had the answers.

Silence greeted her, again.

"We come to warn you and your people of the dark powers brewing. Kronos has escaped the Underworld and is using his return to build an army of Soulless and eradicate the democracy of our divine rule over mortals. We invite you to join the Pure Gods to fight this evil and in return we shall provide reward and partnership for both communities to prosper."

Danu's eyes narrowed as her lips pursed.

Shit.

Joss corrected her proposal immediately, "What is it that you desire? With an alliance, the Pure Gods will promise to fulfill their part in the negotiation."

Danu smiled, although it was delivered with a cruel intention.

"You are not welcome here." She purred delightfully, considering the new predicament. "However, you are lucky that you have what I desire. Knowledge."

Her eyes exploded to Joss, infiltrating her mind and breaking her protective barriers within moments.

"Ah, now I understand who brought you here." Danu's eyes sparkled; her green eyes filled with what looked like lava rocks exploding from a volcano.

Getting high off the suspense, the Celtic Queen finally called out. "Niall?"

Joss saw a shadow erupt from the side of the room, before a young man stepped out of rank and toward the queen.

A Celtic warrior, the man stood firm. His blond hair had been pulled back into a braid that looked as big as Jocelyn's arm but tiny in contrast to his solid frame.

Jocelyn's expertise in knowledge would bring nothing powerful enough to combat the physicality in strength that the beckoned deity radiated.

He finally turned, even daring to stand beside the queen at equal rank.

"My heir." Danu offered with a smirk.

The intellect and the strength. A brute force. Together, they had conquered the Celtic deities.

Now, Jocelyn understood.

Niall bowed his head, such a subtle maneuver it clearly had been planned to demonstrate his lack of respect.

She had been a fool to trust the shadows.

"We offer no more than an alternative. If you choose to support our cause and engage in an alliance, we will be happy to provide food and housing." Demetrius pressed.

Danu ignored Demetrius, turning to the blood soldier at her side.

"Niall, you know we do not welcome visitors." She stated through clenched teeth.

"I led them here for you." Niall confirmed, "You seek knowledge. And I brought the Candor Elite directly to your feet. You can absorb her powers now. Surely, in return you can send bodies to fight. Soldiers for power."

Zeus. This world, Danu's powers, *were* weakening her.

Weakening them all.

They *needed* to lead these poor deities to safety.

"Child, you are mistaken." Danu laughed delightfully, her eyes staring directly at Jocelyn and cutting through the depths of her thoughts with a simple look. "None of my people who live on this earth can hide from me."

Her grin was laced with poison, her glee radiated with horrifying satisfaction.

On this earth.

Joss's mind flashed to Demetrius instantaneously and then she immediately wiped her conscience.

But it was too late.

Danu's gaze snapped to Demetrius, assessing an influx of possibilities that Joss had tried to compartamentalize and hide within the deepest parts of her vaulted thoughts.

Her eyes narrowed toward him.

Joss knew exactly what the goddess was thinking, what ideas rolled through her head, what cruelties she was planning for the God of the Solar System.

The world moved slowly, too slowly, as Joss turned to Demetrius, her jaw dropping as she screamed, "No!"

Joss lept to Demetrius, casting a blocking spell.

It collided with another power, too strong against her waning strength. Joss was shaking, using every last drop of energy within her core, her *being*, to go against the Goddess Danu.

From behind, soldiers grabbed Demetrius, physically restraining him while he tried to fight against their hold.

Slowly, the room went fuzzy. She could feel her defensive wall weaken, shrinking as her own powers deplenished, until there was nothing.

Crashing to the ground, crying, Joss watched as Danu's powers finally penetrated through her protection and attacked Demetrius, soon carrying his soul above the air and to the Otherworld, the Celtic Underworld.

THIRTY

JOCELYN

Joss fell to the ground, crying for the soul of the man she loved. He was gone…

"Jocelyn! What did you see?" Demetrius hissed, his strong hand lifting her up into a hug, cradling her shaking body. "It's okay. We're okay…"

Don't tell him. Jocelyn shook her head, knowing she couldn't tell him something so dark when there still stood a chance of survival.

"We must leave. Now." Jocelyn cried, grabbing the lapel of his suit jacket and pulling it away, back toward the entrance.

"Jocelyn… are you sure?" Demetrius asked softly, clearly wary of pushing for more insights to her visions in Joss's panicked condition.

Jocelyn stopped, seeing a coven of deities approaching the castle, clearly having heard the whispers from the faeries. There would be no escaping now. Images flashed across her mind, ending in blood, death and disaster.

A shadow darkened the wall, demanding attention. It made a gesture to follow it again as it jumped across the wall and up the stairs.

Niall.

Jocelyn knew she couldn't trust the prince. Not after her first exploratory vision.

Heading upstairs proved blurry; she was unable to see the outcome – most likely due to her growing weaker and less powerful by the minute. But, at this point a blurry unknown outranked Demetrius's death.

"Change of plans." Jocelyn corrected, grabbing Demetrius's hand and redirecting him up the stairs.

She paused mid-step and turned around to face the Solar System God, the advantageous two stairs allowing her eyes to meet his directly. With her free hand, she grabbed his neck and pulled him toward her lips, lusting for his bodily warmth, proof he was still with her and whole, even though she no longer knew for how long.

Everything he needed to know, she penetrated into that kiss. The desperation, the longing, the terror, the regret – within moments, he was mirroring the same passion – wanting to make this moment, this kiss, serve as a strong enough memory to be preserved and cherished for the next thousand years if they were to be parted.

Finally, as the marching steps grew louder, they pulled away.

"I love you." Demetrius whispered, his eyes desperately searching for any additional inclination of Joss's knowledge.

Jocelyn choked; she couldn't say it back. Not today, when the words would be spoken out of fear. Danu had already taken so much from her, could take so much more, that she refused to let the Celtic goddess steal a moment that was meant to spark a lifetime of happiness, not bury a lifetime of despair.

She turned, hating herself for letting her emotions get the best of her because of the knowledge she possessed. Again, she cursed her gift for how it always caused pain to those she loved most.

The shadow hurried along the wall, taking a sharp right down a long corridor lined with flaming torches, sparking a warm ambiance against the contrasting cold stone.

The speed of the dark shape quickened, clearly aware that both it, and *they*, were running out of time. It ran down a staircase, leading to a back entrance, and then a large wooden door.

The shadow slipped through the crack, and within seconds, the door opened, pulling Jocelyn's navy arm with Demetrius attached to her other through the threshold, and then slammed shut into darkness.

A match ignited, revealing a large hand before a familiar blonde head.

"For deities looking for an alliance, it sure took you a hell of a lifetime to reach your destination."

Niall stomped quietly over to a candle and lit it, revealing a cozy space that must have been his bedroom. As soon as the candle caught flame, the shadow that had served as Jocelyn's guide reattached to the prince.

"You – how do *you* know of our plans?" Joss spat incredulously.

"You're the Candor Elite, shouldn't *you* already know?" Niall challenged with a playful grin.

"My powers work... differently here." Joss explained tersely.

Oh, how she wanted to lay in that burgundy velvet bed that looked so welcoming for her slumber. Sleep would be a welcome oblivion to her currently pounding headache and shaking limbs.

"Ah." Niall studied Jocelyn curiously. "We must have less time than I anticipated."

Jocelyn snapped her eyes open, refusing to appear weak to this stranger, who very well might want to contribute to the demise of Demetrius.

"Let's get to it. Shall we?" The prince proposed, picking up the candle and leading them to a sitting area.

After Demetrius and Jocelyn sat down across from the prince, Jocelyn anxiously demanded, "Why did you bring us to this cursed place, in the first place?"

"Hope." Niall replied quickly, too quick to be taken as anything other than honesty.

"Hope?" Demetrius's eyebrow lifted.

"I am Prince Niall, God of Truth. Danu is my step-mother." Niall explained, his voice a soft whisper – an unexpected contrast to the size and build of his physical vessel. "Not many would have had the sight to successfully visit and escape our lands without encountering her. Even now, we don't have much time."

Niall nodded to Jocelyn, gratefully.

"How long until she knows?" Jocelyn prompted.

"She already knows." Niall clarified, "And, it's only a matter of time that she begins seeking you out."

"And why are you helping us?" Demetrius asked.

"I hope that we will help eachother." Niall confirmed.

Jocelyn turned to Demetrius, watching him calculate the meaning.

Unlike Jocelyn, Demetrius was used to using his wits to determine friend from foe when negotiating with deities. She needed to trust his wisdom now that hers was diminishing rapidly, soon it would be as if she were completely blind and her reality would blur her surroundings, as well.

"Danu married my father, the King of the Celtic Deities, centuries ago. He was desolate after my mother's time passed on earth too soon. Weak and not thinking straight." Niall's eyes looked dark, as if jumping into the truths of the past were a painful abyss. "Later, I learned that his demise was because she cast a dorcha curse – one to drain his powers so that she could absorb them and become stronger – a spell that even I did not envision she could be capable of. Soon, all of his immortality left and he died shortly after, making Danu the most powerful deity among our community, including me. And that was only the beginning."

"Goddess of land, water, fertility, wisdom, bounty, wind..." Joss murmured, all of the pieces clicking into place. "After your father, she cursed the limestone and inevitably, the people."

Niall nodded in agreement, "The limestone works for her, it has been slowly absorbing everyone's power and memories, only fueling Danu's tyranny with what it steals from others."

"So, we're dealing with an all-powerful deity?" Demetrius confirmed with a sigh. "We come for an alliance and instead find another enemy."

"You'll have an alliance with me and my people... if I can convince them to follow me to safety." Niall clarified.

"And take them *where?*" Demetrius clarified, his impatience growing.

Oh Zeus. Joss knew exactly where Niall saw opportunity.

"None of her people who live on this earth can hide from her." Joss repeated aloud, steering her gaze once again to Demetrius.

His face confirmed he registered the unspoken request.

"Are you serious?!" He stated, exasperated. "Are you god-damned serious?"

"Demetrius, you may be these deities' *only* hope to survive." Joss coaxed, trying to make him see reason between right and wrong.

"These deities may be my only downfall!" Demetrius roared back. "I cannot compete with a goddess who has the powers of hundreds!"

Joss knew they needed to divert the conversation to a more proactive solution. Scrambling, she turned back to Niall. "How do you propose we defeat Danu?"

"Only a few remember, but those who do have trained with me. She may have stolen most of our powers now, but we know we can battle her through brute strength."

"You've been training for an advantage." Joss confirmed, understanding how one so calm and intellectual could also seemingly compete against giants.

"I will safely escort you away from these lands, without Danu's detection." Niall proposed, "All I ask is for a safe haven for those who success-fully escape."

"And then a warzone for when Danu comes for blood?" Demetrius huffed, unconvinced.

Ignoring Demetrius, Joss pressed on. "How will you escape? Can you fly?"

"The faeries are allies of the land, the rightful ruler." Niall explained, "They will help spread word. We can create a ruse and fight off her men to give enough time for my people to ride our Griffins out of this hemisphere. As soon as they pass the fortress and enter space, the limestone curse will no longer affect them. They will recover their memories and began regaining their powers, becoming an asset to the Pure God rule. All creatures involved and who seek refuge will agree to fight against the Dark Gods, and eventually Danu's Dorcha rule."

"If all goes to plan." Demetrius clarified.

"I have spent the remainder of my powers exploring many paths." Niall agreed, "The biggest contender for spinning the wheel of events lies here. Now. With you."

"Demetrius, if Danu comes for war, the Pure Gods will fight with you." Jocelyn reiterated.

"Some help they'll be – the Pure Gods have a much bigger war to focus on, if I remember correctly." Demetrius rolled his eyes, running his hand through his hair. "One that I'm fighting with *them*."

"I'm running out of time." Niall added, desperation lacing his strong voice. "As soon as I forget who I am and succumb to Danu's curse entirely, she becomes omnipotent. Once she conquers Ireland, it won't be much longer until she extends her Dorcha across the globe."

The sight hit Jocelyn like a car accident in the center of the road.

"Demetrius. Once she takes over the globe, she'll have her sights on the solar system." Joss pleaded for him to see reason. "Don't you understand? She is the Celtic version of Kronos. This is no longer about alliances; this is about survival. We have to unite."

Demetrius gave her a long, hard look.

Another element constantly working against them. An inequality of partnership. For in the back of Demetrius's mind, anytime Joss pushed for a choice, he knew it was heavily influenced by consequence but never able to fully know if it benefitted her or him.

"If anything, so we're given the best chance to escape." She implored.

And so, finally, he acquiesced.

Taking a deep breath, he threw his hands in the air. "Fine, you can seek refuge on my grounds. But while you're in my realm, you report to me, princeling."

"Deal." Niall stood, reaching his hand out and allowing Demetrius to shake it in agreement.

He bowed politely to Jocelyn and beckoned to the door.

"You'll only have minutes. Follow my shadow and it will lead you to safety."

"What will you do?" Jocelyn asked, standing up and preparing to run.

"I haven't decided yet, and best you don't know." Niall replied vaguely. "It's the only way Danu will be unable to anticipate our moves, and we need every advantage."

Niall stomped over to his door, "Danu beckons me. When the sun sets behind the mountains, my shadow will arrive to guide you to safety. You don't have long, use your time wisely."

And with that, the Celtic prince blew out the candle, opened the wooden door and slammed it quickly, leaving Demetrius and Jocelyn in darkness.

"How much time?" Jocelyn asked, grabbing Demetrius's hand.

"A degree, at most." Demetrius confirmed.

Among the obscure space, it almost felt more intimate between she and Demetrius. No flamboyant disguises or pressured need to interpret what the other was thinking – and now, unable to see any future in relation to this land – Jocelyn could breathe for once.

"Thank you for offering your kingdom as refuge." She finally whispered.

"You know there was never another option." Demetrius admitted. "I could never allow innocent lives to peril without choice."

"Another act." Jocelyn realized, smiling sadly at his manipulative ways, "It's always a show with you, isn't it?"

"I needed to ensure Niall's tolerance if I were to allow his people to enter my life and make it much more complicated, and dangerous." Demetrius explained, "It's about survival, like you said."

"Do you not trust him?" Jocelyn asked. He had seemed like an honorable man to her.

"I trust *no one*." Demetrius replied tartly.

The words struck Jocelyn's core like a hammer hitting a nail.

"Not even me?"

"Especially you."

Joecelyn let go of his hands.

The room took over silence.

"How could you say that?" Jocelyn finally snapped, her voice filled with emotion and laced with regret.

"Because of everything you never say to me." Demetrius replied. His voice was controlled, straightforward and honest.

Too many times she had hurt him that the feeling of pain had absorbed into a normal one. Now, it was her turn to taste her poison.

Jocelyn began to speak, but a sound from the door caught her offguard, causing her to forget her thoughts and snap her back to the present, reminding her what predicament existed outside the dark space.

"The sun has set. Let's go." Demetrius confirmed, gently grabbing her hand again and guiding her toward the door.

Jocelyn appreciated his guidance because she could see nothing. And although she trusted Demetrius in this particular circumstance, his response posed the same question in her mind. Did she really trust him?

Before, she truly believed he would leave innocents to die for selfish reasons, not even considering his ploy. Were there other occasions – both past and future – that she had believed his words or actions as true, when his intention had or would remain otherwise?

With the burst of light radiating through the door, like water finally rushing through a dam after breaking, Jocelyn's wandering mind again snapped to the present.

It was almost as if with the silence of the future penetrating her skull constantly, her mind had never had the opportunity to breathe and consider her feelings about the facts presented. The cursed land of the Burren had inadvertently given her the gift of exploring her thoughts, so she could finally see the gaps between her blindness.

Niall's shadow greeted them across the wall, beckoning them further along the corridor and down another staircase which led them into the kitchens.

Fairies buzzed across the room, capturing the attention of those preparing the upcoming meal, giving space for Demetrius and Jocelyn to silently sneak by and through the doors, leading them behind the castle.

Already on the border of the Burren, Niall's shadow led them through a rocky trail, encompassing them in its hue so that both Jocelyn and Demetrius were able to hide behind shadows of the growing darkness.

Suddenly, Niall's shadow stopped, but beckoned the two deities to continue.

Jocelyn followed its request, but when she turned around, both the shadow and castle disappeared.

"We've passed the border." Jocelyn whispered, turning to Demetrius with growing relief. "We made it."

She jumped toward Demetrius, solace filling her soul as the vision of Demetrius's demise fizzled into a memory, no longer possible to come to fruition.

But where did they stand *now*?

Without trust, without purpose uniting them together, was this the end?

Selfishly, Jocelyn didn't want *this* memory to be the last before they went their separate ways. Not when she now knew she had so much more to think about and reconsider.

As if her mind selected to aid her emotional breakthrough, a whirlwind of sporatic images penetrated Jocelyn's mind, none of which made sense.

Ancient symbols crashed across desert plains and jungles, a lightening bolt thundered in the distance, a circle of divine creatures marched and prayed to the lands beneath a full moon.

Jocelyn was too weak to see coherent scenes play out, but the core of her powers called for a relative connection, although vague.

The word was not of Jocelyn's tongue. The voice which whispered it was quick and soft, barely audible, but echoed as if a distant vision existed far away in the universe of her mind, buried for now but could become accessible, eventually, with more energy. With more knowledge.

"Orisha." Jocelyn stated aloud, her eyes widening with hope as she looked up to Demetrius. "I think there's another divine community out there, one that we need to find."

"*We?*" Demetrius clarified; his eyebrow raised.

"*We* were tasked to find an alliance." Jocelyn pressed, ignoring the true reason she pleaded to remain in his company. "The Celts are by no means a guarantee, even if Niall does successfully escape with his people. *We* have another opportunity to deliver what we promised."

What Jocelyn really wanted to say was, *I need you.*

Demetrius considered her proposal, still holding her in an embrace, but she could tell he was beginning to pull away.

With the beginning of the end approaching, Jocelyn exploded, her words cascading off her tongue as she tried to transcribe the blast of visions into verbal interpretations. "I saw a lightening bolt, ancient symbols of a written tongue I have never encountered before, images of an expansive desert and luscious jungle, which could be anywhere on the globe or even a world not of this realm and a circle of deities praying beneath the moon."

Demetrius head lifted at the concluding description. "They prayed to the moon?"

"I think so… but cannot be certain. It was only an image." She answered honestly.

Truth. He needed to trust her again.

"I think… I've read about the Orishas before." Demetrius deliberated aloud, "It must have been… a hundred years ago? If they worked with the moon, they certainly must be documented somewhere in our books."

"Can we look into it?" Jocelyn offered shyly, still very aware of her limbs entangled in his.

Demetrius considered the proposal, clearly debating what would be the smartest course of action.

Jocelyn coughed, sensing his hesitation and pulled herself away.

"I'll need to go to Jupiter either way, to make preparations for the potential Celts infiltrating my kingdom." Demetrius stated, organizing his thoughts with the necessary steps against the ambitious ones. "But Joss, what happens if we find the Orishas and get trapped in their prisons like we almost encountered with the Celts? Is it worth the risk? We're more valuable in this realm, for certain."

He made an accurate point, and whether or not he truly planned on helping the Celts, he was now in the predicament because of her.

Jocelyn checked for visions of their friends, most of which remained blank, beside Piper and Tristan walking outside in a foreign city and Dylan, Zayne and Kyril safely reading in Study Hall at Puerdios. She knew she was not allowed to search for Hayden, so stuck with Liv. Yet, the others existed uneventfully in this world, or at least within the distance her sight would allow.

She told this to Demetrius and added the proposal, "Until they're back, let's at least see if we can find out more about the Orishas. No promises. We decide on whether to act or not only if we discover pertinent evidence that shifts our perspective."

Demetrius considered the proposal, eyeing the small but mighty goddess who stood before him.

Finally, he extended a hand. "Okay, we stay together."

Inside, Joss sighed with relief. On her exterior, she remained poised as her mother had trained her to act, emotionless and unreadable.

"Together." She nodded assertively.

TRISTAN

They had promptly returned the next morning to Piper's favorite place in Bangkok: the library. She went straight to work, promising to set up camp upstairs at the same table as before while Tristan offered to return to the café to order and retrieve their liquid breakfast.

And yet, as they departed to tag team the immediate next steps in pursuit of discovering the Nagas, Tristan didn't want Piper to leave as he watched her glide upstairs and away from him. On the otherhand, Tristan needed space from his partner-in-crime to figure out what was actually going through his head.

He had almost kissed Piper last night. Twice.

Sure, he thought she was the sweetest, kindest and purest deity in their fucked-up world – and he envied her wicked intelligence – and yes, he enjoyed making her squirm with the casual flirtacious comments here and there, but he had previously seen her as a little sister, someone needing his care and protection... not his *affection*. He did not want to be the one to corrupt her.

And damnit, she was Liv's *best friend*. Hades, Piper had grown into one of Tristan's closest friends, too. And worst of all, she was Matthias's ex-girlfriend. That alone declared she belonged to his dead friend – a stamp of ownership covered her head-to-toe from that relationship, serving as an eternal reminder of the past.

Tristan shook his head to clear his mind, approaching the café to spit out their order without thinking.

A latte and a dark roast.

Beverages perfectly depicting their souls: Piper's gentle and light, Tristan's dark and bitter. He certainly would corrupt her, there was no way of her saving him instead.

For even when Piper had explored the darker side, admitting she ordered the cold brew to look "cool," they had both agreed the beverage over-caffeinated her as she did accumulate the shakes after drinking it. She couldn't handle, nor did she like the effect, of having the influence of the edgy, stronger substance in her system.

Piper's virtuous body simply repulsed that of Tristan's demeanor. And she was willing to endure torment at her expense just to impress him.

See? The entire notion was stupid. He'd ruin her.

...And he just compared them and their non-existent relationship to coffee beverages.

Tristan rolled his eyes, thankful that the barista had completed brewing his order.

It would never work.

Although, as he grabbed both beverages and began his ascent toward their study lounge, Tristan couldn't help but acknowledge his natural excitement at the thought of reuniting with Piper once again.

And looking at the beautiful latte art depicting a book, he considered ordering her beverage-of-choice for the next coffee round.

Just to get a taste of it…

When he arrived at their little corner of the library, he tried to find the table in which Piper had already sprawled dozens of books, two of which she currently flipped through. Her concentration and determination to uncover information awakened a part of admiration from Tristan – Piper was thoroughly reliable and never went back on her word.

"Your coffee, madame…"

Piper jumped twice, first at the noise, second at Tristan's arm that now extended across the table and right in her line of eyesight.

"Sorry!" She squealed, letting out a deep breath before her lips slightly curved upward, almost as if in a smirk. "I didn't see you there. Apparently, the God of Fire can be light on his feet when he so chooses."

"Have I *never* told you of my dreams to become a prima ballerina?" Tristan retorted, essentially tossing the latte to her as he rolled his eyes.

Without missing a beat, Piper snatched the warm cup and immediately took a sip, humming as she leaned back in her chair and smiled with amusement. "A book? How *cool*."

A scent of pomegranate, plum and rose filled the air, infiltrating Tristan's senses and making his coffee taste a bit sweeter than the day before. He smiled, reveling in her presence and how she made him feel lighter.

Shit.

Tristan shook his head again, ignoring the weird feeling and instead pivoted his thoughts to the task at hand.

"Any luck?" Tristan nodded to Piper's stack of open books, noting that most looked similar to the texts they had already read through from their previous research.

"Miss Piper?" The receptionist from the entrance walked in their direction, today looking notably sleeker with a blazer and buttoned-down shirt, holding a folder filled with paper and handing it to her. "I pulled the requested search phrases and printed out the most relevant websites."

"Thank you, Rune." Piper smiled, causing the young man to blush as she gently collected the folder from his offering.

She opened the file and began flipping through the pages, clearly impressed. "This is excellent, Rune! And so fast?!"

Piper beamed, causing a hint of jealousy to pang Tristan inside; he kicked himself to knock out of it.

Both Rune and Piper turned to him, curiously.

"Thank you, Rune. Really appreciate it, man." Tristan added, slapping Rune generously on the back in an attempt at comraderie.

"No problem… Happy to be of assistance." Rune replied. He then kindly offered to help Piper with anything else should she need it before turning around and walking away. Although Tristan noticed the library employee began rubbing his back before descending down the stairs.

"Rune was able to pull locations around the globe where there is evidence of any Naga reference onsite." Piper explained, "This would have taken us *all day* to filter through with these books. He had inquired why we were pulling the exact same books again, when we had read through all of them yesterday…"

Piper was rambling, her real intent focused on the printed paper she flipped through, her grin reaching ear to ear with amazement.

"The majority of these statue references seem to be primarily at Angkor Wat?" Piper lifted her head, finally meeting Tristan's eyes for the first time all morning.

The crystal gems penetrated through his being, causing Tristan to lose his breath. He was never truly prepared to anticipate how breathtakingly stunning her eyes were. When he had first met her, the world had temporarily lost a treasure when she secretly went undercover as a Dark God and resultingly, wore brown contacts that covered her oceanic eyes.

Ever since, it was like every time he saw them in all their glory, she had just unveiled the cover for the first time and revealed a part of her dazzling soul.

"Let me see." Tristan coughed, taking another sip of his black coffee.

Small figurines popped up in the search, but Piper was right, the majority of images and listings involved Angkor Wat in some capacity.

"What is Angkor Wat?" Tristan asked rhetorically, reaching for a book on Buddhism to his left.

"Rune pulled that research, as well." Piper shuffled to another stapled group of papers, waving it in the air before setting it before her to read aloud. "We really need to look into this computer-internet thing. It seemed too good to be true when we learned about it in class, but now that I'm reaping the benefits firsthand..."

Piper stopped talking and pointed to her paper, already switching gears from conversationalist-joker to hard-facts-to-discuss-detective.

"Angkor Wat is a temple complex in Cambodia and the largest religious monument in the world." She flipped through the pages, cross-referencing her own index. Her head moved like a typewriter, slowly perusing a sentence before snapping back to her own notes on the left. "The temple is located north of Siem Reap, but originally served as the capital of the Khmer empire. It was also originally dedicated to the God Vishnu, before it became a Buddhist temple at the end of the 12th century. Although Angkor Wat remained in use until the 1800s, the site has sustained significant damage, from forest overgrowth to earthquakes to war."

"Three instances of destruction." Tristan observed.

"Shiva." The two confirmed in unison, together.

"What if this is his shrine now... a trap where we encounter him instead?" Piper whispered, finally dropping the stack of paper to take a sip of her coffee.

"Then we encounter Shiva, instead." Tristan shrugged, accepting his fate, whatever was meant to be. "And after, we return to this library, grab another set of coffee and ask Rune to do more impressive research on our behalf."

Piper shrugged, "I already miss Rune and his clever internet."

Tristan rolled his eyes but couldn't ignore the subtle pang of jealousy that resulted from his partner's joke, dripping occassionally into a larger pool of water at his core.

But he kept it contained, allowing Piper to continue thoroughly investigating all options before slamming the last file atop the table. As they finally departed the library, he pivoted back to the coffee shop for a quick detour, ordering a latte, to Piper's surprise. After enjoying an elephant design crafted with the steamed milk, he took a sip.

And it tasted damn delicious.

LIV

After waking up to a stunning sunrise (one with a distinguished flare that could have only been crafted by the master of sun, Ra), sipping coffee beside Hayden on the Egyptian patio and inevitably preparing for the upcoming day and all it would bring, Liv wished Hayden luck searching for escape opportunities while venturing into escapism of her own curation.

She walked over to the serene courtyard oasis, sitting down on the stone edge that hovered over the still body of water, sliding off her black sandals and hitching up her geometric, triangular-printed sheer skirt to dip her feet into the pool. The courtyard seemed to be the center of the palace, with priests and priestesses gliding around from one task to another.

The coolness of the water served as a nice contrasting balance to the dry heat of the sun. Liv was all too grateful she chose a low messy bun to keep her dense golden curls from suffocating her skin in the warm temperature. She pulled up her long, metallic rose sleeves, hoping to provide some sliver of reprieve.

An hour passed. Thankfully, the sun's position in the sky fell behind a palm tree, rotating the necessary 36 degrees to shade her body entirely from the direct heat. A necessity if she were to survive the current climate without using her powers.

She watched as priestesses dutifully walked through their daily tasks, a rotation set like clockwork as she began recognizing faces that repeatedly walked their course, almost precisely every 30 degrees.

The third time Liv spotted Fukayna suspiciously watching her during her own passing, she was surprised to find the priestess carrying a smoothie.

"Courtesy of his highness." Fukayna offered flatly.

Liv knew better than to ask why, or where he was. So instead, she smiled with gratitude, the sweet taste of frozen pineapple and coconut exploding in her mouth, moving like ice down her throat.

"Thank you, Fukayna. Please tell his highness it is absolutely delicious." Liv replied vaguely, enjoying the refreshing treat during the next hour.

Still no sign of Ahmed, Sabra or Hayden for that matter.

Perhaps Hayden has seen more success than me, today. Liv pondered, leaning back onto the shadowed tile and laying down, her feet still in the pool. After another 30 degrees, Liv debated moving to another location. The grand staircase? The throne room?

On one hand, she was sure to run into Ahmed there; but would it feel too obvious?

No. He knew where to find her. And if he wanted to pursue Liv, she certainly wanted *him* to pursue *her*.

Fukayna brought another smoothie an hour later, mumbling criticism under her breath about laziness as she left Liv to continue lounging stubbornly in the courtyard.

Another thirty degrees and the sun began setting, the courtyard shifting from a golden glow to cooler tones. Candles began flickering to brighten the darkened spaces and the pool began to glow. A mesmerizing painting filled with navy and gold and every shadowed palette in between, a masterpiece in the making.

"At this point, I'm half-convinced you may be part siren." A low accent vibrated from behind Liv. She rotated her core, turning to find Ahmed approaching. Seductively smiling, Liv began her act. The one she had been mentally preparing for all day.

"I'm surprised it took you this long to find me." Liv smirked, looking back to the pool and making a splash by lifting her leg into the air.

She looked down at the spot beside her, before demurely gazing to the Egyptian King to request he join her.

"I do have *some* responsibilities, you know." Ahmed joked, sitting beside her. "For instance, today I had to govern a mythological world. Not all of us are able to lounge by the pool and look stunning while doing so, Olivia."

Liv flinched at the use of her formal name, sounding like a snake from Ahmed's accent – but obviously he wasn't a serpent, she was simply on edge from discomfort. Liv scolded herself internally, mentally commanding she remain calm and convincing.

Calculating and cruel.

"I apologize, did I say something to offend you?" Ahmed nodded his head curiously. "I promise my sarcasm and dry humor should be considered harmless."

Liv smiled at the response, truly impressed by Ahmed acknowledging a concern, yet having an ability to keep it lighthearted.

"No, I should be apologizing to you." Liv turned shyly toward him, shaking her head before explaining, "Those we fight, those who captured and tortured me... call me Olivia. So although my formal name, it still sometimes... strikes a chord." She whispered the final phrase, embarrassed.

"Noted." Ahmed replied, studying Liv. "So, to clarify, you enjoy my humor?"

Zeus, this man would give Tristan a run for his money with cockiness.

Liv laughed. "I do, actually. I only hope to match your level in cleverness and equally witty replies." But then she paused, recognizing that in comparison to before, now with only Ahmed – she wasn't scared. In that moment, she was being genuine and not playing a part. Perhaps, she could focus less on the task at hand and instead try to get to know the deity before her, before finalizing their approach to the alliance. So, she added kindly, "My friends call me Liv. I welcome you to do the same."

"Liv." Ahmed tested, his low, raspy pronounciation making it sound more like 'Leaf.'

It wasn't terrible.

"Queen Liv, to you." Liv smirked.

"Thank goodness. The informality was becoming too painful to endure." Ahmed joked, dramatically clutching his hand to his chest with a relieved sigh.

From the distance, they heard footsteps, growing louder as a handful of priests entered the courtyard, presenting a charcuterie board filled with pita, Baba Ghanoush, vegetables and hummus.

"Like clockwork." Ahmed grinned to Liv after expressing gratitude to his priests. "Please, help yourself." He grabbed a plate and handed it to Liv. "If you're surviving off only the smoothies I sent today, you're bound for a sugar hangover any minute."

"Sound the alarms." Liv smiled, dishing her plate with a variety of items, and appreciating the act of chewing more than ever before.

A final servant appeared, first offering a goblet to King Ahmed, before filling it with water.

"You truly don't drink." Liv observed, astonished. She took another bite out of her hummus-dipped carrot.

"Truly." Ahmed confirmed, taking a sip of the pure liquid. He shrugged. "I don't like the thought that you 'have to drink in order to have fun.' I can have the same amount of fun without consuming alcohol. Perhaps even more because I remember it the next day and don't feel like a herd stampeded through my head."

The sentiment resonated with Liv, long had she so heavily relied on wine or whisky to cope with her insecurities, her emotions, to commemorate her successes – the whole spectrum. It was refreshing to hear someone confident enough to not engage with the potentially harmful substance.

The servant returned, handing Liv a glass and lifted a bottle of wine for confirmation.

"No thanks, water tonight." Liv smiled.

"Please, you do not need to do that for me. I don't mind or judge when others drink – there isn't anything wrong with it. Just a personal preference. That's all." Ahmed encouraged the servant to return with the bottle.

"I like the sentiment. And I'm already having fun with you tonight, so I'd like to remember it tomorrow, *sir.*" Liv smiled, genuinely, grabbing her now full-glass of water and lifting it into the air. "To new beginnings."

"Fi sihtik." Ahmed clinked his glass with hers, never moving his intense gaze from Liv.

With the moonlight glowing off his skin, surrounded by twinkling lights and glowing water, his black linen kaftan and matching pants both trimmed with gold, all made Ahmed a truly stunning specimen. His brown eyes sparkled, his sharp jawline relaxing into his smile, revealing pearly white, dazzling teeth.

"What?" Ahmed taunted defensively but with amusement. "Why are you staring?"

Liv blinked, looking away as her cheeks grew warm. He just seemed so *pure* at his core. It was a nice reminder that there still remained *good* among other powerful deities. Even still, she prayed to Daphne that his intentions remained sincere.

"I didn't mean for you to look away." Ahmed pressed, gently grabbing Liv's cheek and bringing it back to his gaze. "Perhaps I enjoy staring at you, too."

Liv's cheeks exploded with heat, yet she was still curious.

"It perplexes me that you and the lovely Sabra can be related." Liv admitted, studying Ahmed and barely containing her grin.

"Ah, yes. Sabra." Ahmed looked in front of him, blankly staring at the bright blue water. "You must have caught on that she has seen darker days."

Gone was the carefree deity, but in his place remained a stoic, quiet and remorseful god.

"She's your sister and your equal. Her days could not be that much darker than yours." Liv challenged. "Yet, on the same rose, you are the petal and she's the thorn."

"She was the one who sent our mother to our version of the Underworld." Ahmed explained, straightforward and concise.

A fact not to be argued. Liv noted the change in tone, so changed the topic, in hopes it could reveal clues as to how to venture through to other realms. To leave the afterlife in pursuit of another world.

"Your version of the Underworld?" She purred, intrigued.

Ahmed lifted his hands, showcasing all that surrounded them. "We took over the afterlife, so naturally had to set up another place to reprimand and house our less obedient deities. Anubus's son, Osiris, controls it now."

"Like a prison? Jailhouse?" Liv pressed, before taking a step back from her interrogation and pivoting her content by humming, "I'm surprised your sister hasn't become a guest with her seemingly rebellious streak."

Ahmed smiled sadly, "She was once kind, lighthearted, care-free... before."

"And you?" Liv whispered. "You forgave her?"

He paused, trying to find the words. Liv could see the struggle as his eyebrows furrowed, so similarly to Hayden when he was trying to organize his thoughts. She waited, granting him the time to formulate his response to such a complicated subject.

"My mother, Isis, was making brash decisions at the expense of thousands." He began, lifting his head up to the sky, and ran his hand through his long hair. "It had to be done."

He stared into the dark night until a twinkle in his eye once again matched the stars above. Ahmed turned to Liv, compassion radiating from his being; Liv swore his skin turned gold. "But the act for good still chipped off a part of Sabra – her spontaneity, her innocence... and carved her into a warrior. Always alert and always aware. Never trusting."

"So, really, now she's even more like you?" Liv teased.

"No. I didn't mention her intelligence, wit and fiercely handsome appearance." Ahmed smiled, not missing a beat.

"Forgive me, I must have misheard." Liv chuckled before rolling her eyes, but her laugh was genuine.

"Sabra did it, so I did not. I not only forgave her, but I applaud her." Ahmed reiterated, "My sister is still there, underneath layers of armor. If you're lucky to be exposed to her true self, you would love her, just like I do."

Liv understood. There was a time not so long ago she too only existed under layers of grief, had asked herself how long it took to act a certain way before it became a description of who she was, a definitive part of herself. When she had been at any moment on the brink of a breakdown, tears at the cusp of her lids, she had hid behind black, books and angry music, scowling at the world while secretly pleading for her return to fully living within it. She wondered if it was harder for Ahmed, watching it happen to a loved one without having any control over the repercussions.

"It'll take time." Liv offered kindly, reaching for Ahmed's hand and squeezing it. "I look forward to getting to know the real Sabra, someday."

"Thanks." Ahmed sighed, "I admit it feels strange talking about this, I don't normally speak of my family affairs with others. Strangers nonetheless."

"Why *are* you amusing my prying questions?" Liv nodded her head, curiously. She had been enjoying this intimate conversation, although perplexed as to why it was happening between Ahmed and herself so quickly.

"You asked." Ahmed shrugged.

Fair response and straight to the point, Liv thought.

Similar to most of his responses tonight.

"Don't get me wrong, it's been an incredible conversation and I have thoroughly enjoyed getting to know you tonight..." Liv added, hoping she hadn't offended the Egyptian King. She'd hate to report to Hayden that after taking ten steps forward, she had been propelled a mile backward.

"Liv," Ahmed breathed, his eyes sternly staring through those of the name he stated, "If you are considering my proposal, I want you to know the real me. No filters. No charades. No lies. We'd be partners. That requires honesty and trust. I only ask the same from you when I start asking the questions."

Shit. The proposal.

Liv gulped.

For a moment, she had become distracted by simply befriending a kind deity who she related to on so many levels. She had forgotten about his motive for being so open and welcoming. Why he had remained so damn *charming* during their entire conversation.

He was courting her, hoping to secure an alliance through marriage.

...And was succeeding.

THIRTY-ONE

HAYDEN

He returned to their room after a sufficiently terrible and forced dinner with Sabra. Their female host quickly proved she was more than comfortable with silence and a fan of threatening glares. Fortunately, Hayden could handle it, but he wished Liv could have at least been there so they could mock the awkwardness afterward.

Even better, Hayden had found the library, researching ancient runes and hieroglyphics along with histories of Egyptian mythology after 800 A.D. to try and piece together any route that would take them home.

Home. He sighed, running his hands through his hair. He felt like he had been a day behind since he started Puerdios, a week behind since being crowned King, and growing further and further behind each consecutive day. He refused to give into the darkness, but Zeus, he was *tired*. He was still pulling himself out of the sinking sand formulated by Liv's abduction and trying to focus on some semblance of a happy future, but as each day progressed, the image became fuzzier, the hope that once was a full moon, now a crescent.

All he could do was power through, consider the advice from his family which sculpted his decisions and do what he could to best benefit his people, to try to do *good*. If he took enough ascending steps, eventually he would land on top, instead of behind.

He kept repeating the last phrase, especially when he was alone. Sometimes, he could hear his father's voice echoing in the shadows of his mind, sharing words of wisdom when he had advised on what to do when times were tough.

Now, it seemed every day, times were tough.

And now his kingdom was abandoned, without his protection, as he remained contained within this vicious world in pursuit of an impossible security dream.

The door creaked open; Hayden instinctively spun toward the entrance, revealing Liv in the doorway, looking as mesmerizing as ever.

Her hair had loosened since departing this morning. Small wisps of layered strands now framed her face, beckoning Hayden to tuck them behind her ear so he could see her beauty. Yet the delicate, lived in hairstyle softened her features, making Ollie look younger. Like the moment during freshman year in high school when she had turned and grinned mischievously at him in algebra after he had left flowers on her desk to ask her to homecoming. Making him melt for her all over again.

That was when he decided he never wanted her to dance with another again, and following the idyllic dance, had asked her to be his girlfriend.

Then and now, Olivia Monaco would forever be breathtaking.

Yet, her eyes looked conflicted, tired, like his. Her gold and black sheer geometric skirt breezed back and forth as she glided across the room, wrapped her arms around Hayden's waist and rested her head on his chest.

"Just hold me." She breathed, leaning her weight against him, clinging to his solid strength.

Instinctively, he pulled his arms around her, absorbing her scent of strawberry, jasmine and violet, finally feeling at home.

So Hayden stood there, holding Liv, his best friend, highschool sweetheart and true love, his soul mate and his queen, soaking in this moment of good to help offset the tougher ones to come.

PIPER

It felt oddly sad saying goodbye to the loft she neither owned nor had been a resident of for two sun cycles. Alas, after they collected the dust from their destroyed attire gifted to them during their previous adventure, Tristan followed Piper out, locked the door, and they both continued on to the next, together.

Piper knew that her heart couldn't physically break, but it felt as if she did leave a piece of it in the beloved city of Bangkok. Perhaps that was her version of the curse, unable to completely leave the mythic lands behind.

But soon, they were soaring in the sky, Tristan a fiery blaze in a dark grey turtleneck and leather moto jacket; Piper a glistening swan in a pearly silk and taffeta crewneck dress equipped with a metallic orange bodice corset and train that bellowed over her matching tangerine miniskirt.

"We'll check in to our accomodations, first." Tristan discussed in flight. "Are you sure you're rested enough for whatever Cambodia may bring?"

Piper giggled, trying to keep a straight face as she squeaked, "You act as if I didn't save *your* sorry ass in Thailand."

She wished her delivery was better, but she had blushed and breathed the curseword as she whispered it aloud.

"Touché." Tristan smirked.

After they had checked into their hotel in Siem Reap, they flew toward the unknown through the light skied abyss, a gentle wind pushed the two along, making incredible speed as it fortunately blew in the exact direction in which they headed. Within degrees, the target was easily identifiable, a majestic fortress carved out among a lush green jungle with five pinecones towered above as the pinnacle statement of marvel.

The structure captured Piper's eye immediately, a mesmerising site that pulled her toward it, soft chants echoed in the wind, as if compelling her to enter, if she dared.

She worried that if she set foot on the sacred ground now, she might never be able to depart.

"Tristan, do you hear that?" Piper whispered, feeling the ancient chants crescendo as the wind picked up, pushing them closer to the temple complex.

"I can't hear you over the wind!" Tristan yelled, pulsing his wings closer to Piper before he grabbed her hand.

United, the winds stopped, and the echoes silenced.

"Well, that's certainly convenient." Tristan looked around, astonished at the change in atmosphere.

"I don't think it's our time to visit Angkor Wat." Piper observed aloud. Now, closer to the structure, Piper saw moving bodies as hundreds of mortals explored the ancient temple. Although, something within her drove her to declare the shift in plan. Finally, she turned to Tristan, an imaginary lock clicking into place. "Do you trust me?"

Tristan cocked his head in disbelief.

"Okay," Piper interpreted his response to 'obviously,' but didn't giggle as she typically would have before. Instead, she remained focused on the task at hand. "Let's go to a nearby temple, stay in the area in case... this feeling... changes."

"...Feeling?" Tristan questioned, his face shifting from arrogance to concern.

"I can't explain it, I just... have an inclination that this is not the appropriate time to engage the Nagas."

Tristan shrugged, unimpressed. "Weirder shit has happened."

At that, Piper smiled, appreciative that Tristan always made sure her thoughts didn't spiral too far from comfort.

So, Tristan led Piper to another temple, one that survived the growth of a majestic white fig tree that had spread its gigantic roots over the ancient stones. The air was misty, creating an ethereal image as they slowly walked through the temple rooted in the dense jungle of silk cotton trees and figs.

Tristan walked over to the domineering tree, examining how its roots probed the stones to shift at every angle, still miraculously upright even against the pressure of nature.

"A state of ruin becomes a state of beauty." He observed softly, placing his hand against the cool stone. "Hauntingly charming."

Piper's gaze drifted from his profile to his hand, to the stone, to the root of the tree, to the base of the tree and upward. The roof had been destroyed and taken over by the mighty timbered force that now propelled into the sky, making it seem as if giants could live among the trees and feel inferior to them.

"They dedicated this temple to Brahma the creator." Piper mentioned, finally gathering the courage to walk over to Tristan and look at the engravings carved onto the stones that battled for survival. "Ta Prohm – 'ancestor Brahma' – and yet it is as if they knew 500 years ago when the trees first penetrated these grounds, that through the destruction would come beauty, a new creation to be celebrated, not condemned."

She smiled at the thought.

Perhaps all destruction eventually led to creation. In time.

At least, it certainly made Shiva seem less intimidating.

When she turned to Tristan, her smile quickly shifted to an inhale of surprise and anticipation.

His caramel eyes met her glacier ones, igniting a flame that warmed her soul. He sparkled in the dewy jungle, his heat radiated against the cool mist and stones.

The hypnotizing charm had enchanted them both, seeking beauty in the chaos, and in that moment, Piper wanted to kiss him. Tristan's lips were only breaths away, and she knew he wanted to kiss her, too. That he too, understood the complication of taking the next step and how their relationship was Ta Prohm personified. Roots had taken over their foundation and now influenced how their structure survived. And as limbs continued to grow, entwining them in more chaos and responsibility, it also created something strong and domineering, that could be beautiful, if given the chance. For now it was just a desire, a charm luring both into dangerous territory, only to encourage a building tension from the prospect of forbidden romance. But eventually, they would need to leave their small, enchanting world and return to reality. And that was where all that had they built over these few weeks would collapse. The fig tree could only survive in this subtropical climate. Not in the regal society of powerful deities.

And that's why Piper pulled back, smiling shyly to not be rude.

Unlike Ta Prohm, if Tristan and Piper's friendship was ruined, they wouldn't be strong enough to survive, there would be absolutely no creation from the self-inflicted destruction.

Shiva would win.

PEYTON

She rolled to the side of the bed, dreading the sound of Rei's alarm clock buzzing. Gods didn't get hangovers, but this was significantly close. Her powers had drained in the process of burning off the robust amount of alcohol she had consumed the night before.

After she left *Spetses* and Giselle within it, Peyton wandered the city, doing what she classified as a "Vanaheim Bar Crawl." After the tenth bar, she found herself dancing with a strange Norse deity, so Peyton (proudly and with better judgment) walked herself home and put herself to sleep.

That was only sixty degrees ago.

Between the argument she had with Giselle and the unspoken words separating Rei and her, topped off with the *lovely* immortal beings that hosted her at the moment, Peyton sarcastically mocked what a wonderful day it would be, dreading every moment to come.

"Fun night?"

Peyton rolled over, spotting Rei sitting at the nook, drinking his lavender latte and looking as crisp as a spring morning.

She wanted to be sassy but didn't have the energy to deliver a combative remark.

Instead, she trudged out of the bed and directly to the bathroom, pausing right before she entered the threshold.

"It certainly was interesting – in fact, I ended up running into Giselle."

And with that, she smugly smiled and slammed the door.

LIV

Waking up in Hayden's arms was the homesick medicine she needed. Although, Liv no longer knew what she considered "home." Certainly not her childhood home, nor Puerdios necessarily anymore, since she hadn't spent much time there in the recent months either. The Elements Pillar's headquarters should feel like her new home, but her rooms hadn't resonated, yet. She craved something entirely hers.

As Liv rolled over onto her back, she glanced over to Hayden's creamy skin, the way that his symmetrical nose perfectly complemented his pouting lips, and suspected that home to her was no longer stationary but now a living, breathing thing.

And it sure looked sexy.

Hayden stirred; stretching his body to wake up before realizing another body still lay in his arms. He looked down with a smile, maneuvering around the bed to re-wrap his arms softly around Liv and kiss the top of her head, sending chills down her spine.

His gentle arms felt like stone, a Greek God in its finest form and entirely hers.

She snuggled further into the side of him, resting her head on his solid chest and slowly trailed her finger down his washboard abs.

"Good morning." Hayden murmured into her ear.

"Good morning, handsome." Liv smiled, kissing his nose in admiration.

"You seem to be in a better mood, using words for one…" He observed.

After she had commanded he hold her and he obediently obliged the night before, she had remained quiet until they slowly crashed onto the bed and fell into a peaceful slumber, entwined and safe in eachother's arms.

"Words are hard." Liv joked.

She felt his cheek muscles shift against her head.

"So, how did your date go with *your prince*?" Hayden casually asked.

Liv rolled her eyes, "It wasn't a date."

"I walked by and instantly felt like I was third-wheeling, so seemed like a date to me." Hayden roasted. "Hades, I was even eager to run away and endure dinner with Sabra."

Liv turned her head to make eye contact, smiling with amusement but glaring with disbelief.

"SABRA." Hayden reiterated.

A silent pause told Liv that Hayden wouldn't pry but wouldn't speak until she answered his question.

So, casually she sighed and replied, "He's nice. Not at all what I expected."

Liv felt her cheeks burning in reflection on the mysterious Ahmed she was able to get to know. Her attempt to downplay the intrigue was failing.

Hayden studied her, grinning.

"You're totally smitten with the Egyptian King!"

"I am not!" Liv cried, cheeks burning even brighter at the accusation.

"Does Liv have a crush? Do I need to be worried?" Hayden mocked, hugging her tighter and emphasizing his position by gently kissing her cheek.

"I do not! And *you* certainly do not!" Liv laughed, shaking out of his hold, and climbed on top of him. She pinched his cheek before kissing him back.

"It's adorable that you think he's cute, and are embarrassed by it." Hayden chuckled.

"Stop. I only have eyes for you!" Liv shrieked, defending her honor by sealing her case with a kiss upon Hayden's lips.

"Maybe you have a thing for kings... but that wouldn't explain Tristan..." Hayden speculated, clearly having too much fun.

The fact that he could even joke about Tristan further entwined Liv's heart with Hayden's. This is what they needed. To build out their past and connect it with ease, it was the only way they could stop tiptoeing around the trials and begin growing together.

"I'm glad you think it's hilarious to identify all of the deities your girlfriend..."

Liv stopped, blushing and unable to finish the outburst. She swore she had a legitimate point when she started the argument...

"... finds attractive." Hayden concluded for her. "And not *girlfriend*. Soul mate. Deliberating who my 'girlfriend' found attractive would not be so amusing."

"Oh, how lucky am I to be eternally paired with a conceited, big-headed ass." Liv declared with sarcasm, dramatically motioning her arm around before landing it upon her chest.

"Ah! Perhaps that's the common denominator to your crushes, then?" Hayden smirked. "Does Olivia Monaco have a type?"

Before Hayden could retaliate, Liv had already smacked him with her pillow.

"My only type is you, your royal pain in my ass."

Knowing Ahmed spent the majority of his day ruling the Egyptian kingdom, Liv instead ventured with Hayden into the library for further research. And she certainly taunted him for his irresponsibility and comparative laziness at every opportunity.

The library was light, carved from old palm tree wood with lines of light shelves and tables and seating to match. Between the room extended a large, bright blue river, to what Liv took as an artistic tribute to the Nile.

If only Piper could see this literary paradise. Liv thought of her tightly wound friend, imagining her soprano voice hitting an even higher octave from excitement, the natural anxiety that would maneuver through her desire to read every textbook available in such a limited time. But ultimately, the thoughts just made Liv realize how much she missed her friend.

In contrast to the sandy-toned history keeper they walked through, Liv stood out, wearing a thick silk tapestry draped into a maxi skirt, patterned with black, burgundy and gold. Her black sheer blouse didn't help blend in with her surroundings, not that Liv ever wanted to be a chameleon. Not anymore.

Surrounded by books, Liv felt more comfortable, more in her natural habitat than lounging by the pool. She hadn't been bred to sit and look pretty and now felt like a part of her had returned, now working next to Hayden, his strong arm occasionally brushing against her own.

"We need to identify when they established the Afterlife as their ruling kingdom, any parameters for that setup must include some form of guidance for moving between the mortal world and this one." Hayden explained, "I've covered culture and society texts in Ancient Egypt yesterday, but that only expands about three thousand years."

"Only." Liv huffed, slamming another stack of books on hieroglyphics to decode. "Access between the worlds has to be personal, a system of codes or secret runes like our emblem for the Underworld. Like the symbols we leveraged for our first transit here. They appeared with purpose. I have a dark feeling that escaping is going to become personal."

"You and me both." Hayden sighed. "But, if we're able to decipher how Egyptian deities transcribe passwords and keys, that helps steer us in the direction for what we may need from the Egyptian High Priest."

"He… can't hold us hostage, can he?" Liv whispered, terror creeping along the back of her spine. "We only gave Dylan a week before sounding the alarm…"

Hayden tensed at the thought, blankly staring at his textbook before shaking his head. "We can't afford another war. Not while we're already in one."

Liv grabbed his hand and squeezed it. "We haven't played all of our cards. It won't come to war if we don't allow it."

Hayden turned to Liv, eyes piercing into hers as he replied directly, "If we're forced to play all our cards, it will certainly come to war."

PIPER

"What do you think the others are doing right now?" Tristan asked as they continued walking through the complex, both cognitively remaining at a strict distance of no less than three feet from one another.

"Rei is probably driving Peyton nuts." Piper offered immediately with a giggle, shocked at how quickly and easily that flowed from her lips.

"For doing exactly as she asks or the opposite…" Tristan smirked. "Dylan is probably worried sick about everything."

Piper laughed aloud, feeling lighter at the thoughts of their friends, and yet still darkly added. "Even more so when we send updates about our safety… or impending deaths."

"With every letter, Dylan's anxiety increases ten-fold. Easily." Tristan agreed.

"Thank goodness for Kyril with his comedic relief and Zayne for perservering calm. They'll need eachother; I'm glad they're together." Piper added softly with a nod.

They remained silent, watching as the sun began the process of saying goodbye to the day by shifting the sky from a muted blue to a progressive pink and purple.

And just as their playful mockery to remember their friends started to conclude, Piper became somber. She didn't want the conversation to end, enjoying the charming, make-believe scenes dancing in her head.

She missed her friends.

"Hopefully by now, Liv isn't attacking Hayden… talk about an awkward introduction to explain with strangers."

Yet, Piper couldn't come up with a equally silly roast. Her mind was somewhere else.

"I hate this." Piper frowned.

"I know. You've mentioned it before." Tristan sighed, sadly.

"No, let me finish." Her mousy voice demanded.

He remained quiet, sorrow filling his soul as he watched the most beautiful, delicate flower wilt from an abudance of sun, water and turmoil in its garden.

"I hate this." She repeated softly, but looked up to him, her bright turquoise eyes capturing his soul and attention, "But I'm glad I have you here to bring light to the darkness."

Tristan nodded, no longer needing to respond with a sarcastic comment or snarky smirk.

She watched his eyes move from hers down to her lips, absorbing every thought running through his head, slowly and cautiously, as he maneuvered back to her eyes in question, before taking a step forward.

But the blazing sun captured Piper's attention as it slowly cascaded below the jungle's horizon. A soft breeze sent windchimes that crystalized into a message. It was time.

"Come with me, now." Piper commanded, shooting up into the sky to chase the sun.

It was time to visit Angkor Wat.

PEYTON

Rei was precisely where and in the state Peyton had imagined him to be from the shower. He stood up on the bed as soon as she opened the door, once again in her monochrome olive-green suit.

"Don't." Peyton stated blankly, silencing Rei before he could begin to speak. He bent his head down, clearly ashamed of being caught in the lie.

"I'm going to ask you once and never again." Peyton pointed, her pointer and middle finger pressed together as one, as if holding a gun to his head. "Do you still love Giselle? Because just as Mothi is territorial over her, I'm territorial over you, so I need to know."

Rei lifted his head, his glacier eyes hiding no emotion.

"I care for her, but no. I don't love her anymore."

"Okay." Peyton sighed, sitting down beside where Rei stood and taking a deep breath.

"You know I-" Rei whispered.

"I know." Peyton nodded, closing her eyes and taking another breath.

Onto the next emotionally draining conversation... she thought to herself, finally standing up and summoning her own latte. Peyton dreaded the impending confrontation to come with the Norse royals; unsure she had the energy to combat the inevitable decline in which she anticipated from King Mothi.

PIPER

"We need to find any Naga symbol or statue or… anything."

Piper was pacing, desperately looking for any sign of the seven-headed snake. She no longer knew what to do with her hands, now picking at her navy and gold nails when she wasn't waving them around uncontrollably as she rambled.

"Okay, take it easy, Pipes." Tristan said calmly, his caramel voice soothing Piper almost instantly. "We're here and can cover ground quickly. How much time do you think we have?"

Piper took a deep breath, turning to what glow remained in the sky. "Until sundown."

"Great. The sun is our time-dial. We have 10 degrees. And good news, the sun comes back tomorrow, so we can repeat this breakdown daily, as necessary. So, let's start with the perimeter and work our way in. You said the temple is astoundingly symmetrical with quadrant patterns, so we can stay in this quadrant and essentially cover four times the ground."

"You're right. I did say that." Piper nodded, surprised that he had remembered her rambling from the library earlier in the day.

Tristan had already ventured outward, not wanting to waste any time.

"The pinecone symbol is one of the most mysterious emblems found in ancient and modern art and architecture, alluding to the highest degree of spiritual illumination possible." Piper mentioned, finding it helpful to continue sharing facts that may be helpful in discovering the Nagas. "Shiva would want to destroy, or tamper with the sacred symbol…"

"By putting a cursed figure in the wake of what was made to protect it…" Tristan finished her thought, jogging faster toward the edge and diverting sharply to a symmetrical viewpoint of the three visible pinecones. "Exactly my thinking."

He stopped, dramatically presenting the view before them.

To the left, remains of an ancient structure stood tall, precisely mirroring its right counterpart – a grand statue, in pristine condition, resembling a monstruous Naga with all seven heads still intact.

"Remarkably preserved for a statue that's nine hundred years old, wouldn't you say?" Tristan smirked proudly.

But Piper remained quiet, and slowly walked toward the figure, responding to a faint hissing that grew stronger in her head with every step.

She knew what she had to do.

"Get the dirt ready, now." Piper commanded, "And aim with precision, Tristan. We only get one shot."

Her gaze didn't leave the statue, but Piper knew Tristan was capable. So instead, she raised her hands and focused on her part in the plan, hovering them above the sandstone where the center snake's neck resided, connecting as one with the other six.

If you want what you've never had, you must do what you've never done.

Piper consoled herself, closing her eyes and letting her sight emerge from an unknown vessel, her third eye.

The hissing grew stronger as the sun's powers diminished and the gravity of the moon pulled the snake into the second lock of its curse.

Symmetry was key, her third eye serving as the anchor to combine the two powers as one. It had been speaking to her since she arrived on these sacred grounds, slowly pushing her toward her destiny.

Piper could feel the sun setting and the moon rising, slowly moving toward the linear plane until they locked into place and Piper knew it was time.

She propelled the sunlight's final rays toward her and cast the moon's gravitational pull to her core, projecting both through her invisible eye, her knowledge of all the Naga was and could be – combining sun, moon, earth and sky – to unleash the inner beast and bring the sleeping monster to life.

She opened her eyes and immediately stumbled back, watching the ramifications of her choice to go against the ancient deities and give them hell.

The sandstone broke off scale by scale, revealing beneath it a bright gold and green skin, until it reached the jaw and unlocked it, a bright red mouth full of sharp, venomous teeth, seven-fold.

Even now back beside Tristan, Piper's eyes grew wide as she continued to look up at the enlarged, growing, monster.

"Do you see the jewel?" She cried, quickly darting her observing eyes from one head to the next but getting lost in her assessment as pure terror took over.

"I think we need to capture it either way!" Tristan snarked back, equally worried. "Any ideas?"

"It's cursed under the moon and the sun – it froze the beast before. I think it's the only way to freeze it again?" Piper lobbed the idea into the air, hoping Tristan would be able to slice it for the win.

"We just unfroze it and you seriously want to refreeze it?!" Tristan yelled, taking another step back as their enemy continued to grow toward the sky.

"Capture it by freezing it." Piper clarified, "Partially freeze it, I mean!"

She wasn't thinking straight, unable to focus on anything but how their situation was becoming more dire with each sandstone flake hitting the ancient grounds. And even if she were able to catapult the earth around the sun so it would be near the moon again, would Liv send her to the Underworld for abusing her elemental power?

Seeing the jewel sparkle from within the center beasts' throat answered that question.

Zeus, she had no choice.

"Here goes nothing." Piper squealed, propelling the galaxy winds to speed up the day.

"What are you doing!?" Tristan screamed, turning to the sky abruptly as the starry night became a meteor shower of stars flashing by in a blink. "You're giving us *LESS* time!"

The Naga had fully erupted, now that night was speeding by.

"You're the god of fire, help me get the sunlight here, stat!" Piper commanded, sweating as she concentrated all of her powers to do the unthinkable.

"Holy Hades, here goes nothing." Tristan tried to summon the sun's rays to reach them, extending them as far as he could. "We're still too far in the rotation!"

"It's working, I can feel it. That's all I need. Do it again!" Piper yelled, barely dodging a snake head that tried to eat her by sliding to the right. Simultaneously, Piper apologized to Demetrius and prayed for support in their psychotic endeavor.

"Okay!" Tristan yelled, building a wall of fire to temporarily barricade them from the monster.

Piper closed her eyes, once again pulling the moon and sun together and commanding the Naga to freeze through her third eye. She was trembling, trying to conquer the ancient beast with an unfamiliar magic of the past, and she was probably crazy, but it was her only hope to create some restraint to capture the beast.

And creation was stronger than destruction.

"Oh Zeus, Pipes – you did it!" Tristan exclaimed, albeit shocked.

Piper collapsed to the ground, shaking, but still upright and cognizant.

Before her stood the Naga in its true form, yet frozen again to resemble a new statue. This time, its mouths ablaze and angry, open and revealing an emerald jewel.

"Tristan. Now." Piper weakly stated, unsure how much longer they had with the moon and sun's remaining in nearby proximity.

The world would continue on, with or without their influence.

Tristan ran up to the Naga and threw the dirt down its throat. The Naga didn't flinch, still stoic in its time vault, but the emerald jewel dropped onto its tongue and rolled out onto the ground before them.

"The Emerald Buddha." Piper's eyes grew wide as she reached for the sacred artifact, turning to Tristan, unsure.

He nodded in agreement to continue.

"Crescere," she commanded, allowing it to grow to its full glory and verify they indeed completed their required task.

The jewel expanded, growing into the iconic Buddha, but shining brighter and stronger than the replica imposter that had taken reign for so many years.

Just then, the sun emerged over the horizon, welcoming a new morning after the shortest night in history, and Piper and Tristan's attention diverted from the sacred artifact back to the Naga, the casted spell quickly seeing its expiration date.

"Oh Zeus..." Piper squeaked, still shaking as she weakly stood herself up and looked to Tristan for help.

"Resilio." He mumbled, also drained of powers. The Emerald Buddha slowly recoiled into a jewel before attaching itself to Piper's ring.

The Naga slowly moved its head, fighting against the fading constraints.

"Now what?" Piper asked. "We can't make the sun and moon to rotate again!"

"Unless you're truly aiming to turn leap day into a literal leap year for these mortals..." Tristan retorted back, before cursing himself. "Sorry, that was uncalled for."

"No need to apologize, this was an idiotic idea!" Piper yelled back.

Trellis would surely have their heads, in line behind Demetrius, Liv, Rei and Hayden. They had broken about fifteen laws, with many more in the foreseeable future. That is, if they survived.

"Can we send it to the Underworld? It can battle Kerberos in Hell or even better, become Hades's problem." Tristan suggested darkly.

Another head started breaking through the casted spell, hissing like thunder across the jungle in relinquishment of its anger.

"As tempting as that sounds, I don't think we're powerful enough to make the genius plan come to fruition..." Piper solemnly replied with a tired sigh. And that had to entail breaking another dozen rules...

She needed to focus, preserve any drop of power that remained within her vessel, clear out her impending anxiety so she could think clearly and constructively.

All that was left was to summon her axe, a cruel token gifted by Rei before departure – the very same one that almost ended her life in Hades's lair.

"*To remind you that you're a survivor,*" Rei had stated when he gifted her the dark walnut and silver Nordic-inspired weapon. "*Remember that and use this well. Keep on surviving.*"

Keep on surviving.

Piper called for her mighty axe and stood at the ready, confident that their journey would not end here. They had come too far for this beast to determine their destiny.

Her arms shook against fighting the heavy weight that refused to stand upright, both limbs trying their best to be ready to attack.

Another head was able to break free of the curse; out of the corner of her eye, Piper saw Tristan configure his own sword made of flames.

They continued to watch, Piper flinching every time another part of the monster broke free of her tether. Then, its head darted near and Piper swung her axe so that it nicked its scales, causing blood to draw and the monster to retreat, to her surprise.

The Naga was not undefeatable. They could do this.

Piper reset her feet, planting them into the shaking ground, until the sun shone over the lush jungle and blazed its light among the beast, making it shriek at such a loud, high pitched roar, it pierced Piper's mind and forced her to drop her axe so she could save her eardrums by covering both ears.

"Piper!" Tristan yelled, lunging in front of her and casting another fiery wall before them to serve as protection against an attack.

The flame was not as intense as before.

The Naga cried, trying to release the devilish pain in any form it could. No longer focusing on its prey, it was as if the Naga forgot about the two deities who crossed its path and instead, continued to only scream.

It fell behind the blazing wall, unable to remain upright and recoiled to the ground, so that Piper could no longer see the beast. But alas, she knew the serpent still remained with the excrutiating noise it made.

Until, the noise stopped.

THIRTY-TWO

JOCELYN

Taking a bath never felt so rewarding. Warm water, the soft lingering scent of pomegranate, lemon and jasmine. A calm wafted through the air and encompassed Jocelyn as she soaked in the refreshing feeling of cleanliness.

After peeling remnants of her torn navy trench and beige gown, she stepped into the marble tub and relished in Ireland's dirt dissolving from beneath her fingernails. Soon, the itchiness from grass on her leg soothed and disappeared from touch and leaves and sticks grudgingly departed from her unraveling braided crown.

As she stepped into a cool, blue silk gown and touched the soft, light fabric weightless on her body, Jocelyn felt like she could soar once again. Sure, the lace and embroidery detailing on her back felt a little too exposed for her preference, but the request and delivery of the gown was also quite conservative to Demetrius's usual taste, so she wasn't going to combat his gracious accomodations, yet.

Jocelyn found Demetrius in his office, already scouring through records of treaties past. Although also clean and now shaven, Demetrius clearly had spent less time pampering and instead had three book logs already under his belt – a purple snakeskin belt at that, which perfectly matched the color of his virgin wool suit, complimented by a turquoise silk shirt.

"Well, aside from a peculiar and mixed plea from Piper and a visit from Trellis to essentially reset time in Cambodia, you haven't missed much..." He stated tersely.

But, of course, she already knew that.

Joss saw him pick up Volume 87 – dusted and faint gold Roman Numerals categorized the spine of the master doctrine – flipping through the pages for almost thirty minutes before he laughed with content and looked up to Jocelyn with surprise, "I found it!"

"If you can go through that pile, Jocelyn." Demetrius pointed, without lifting his gaze from his own personal scanning.

"Of course." Jocelyn obeyed dutifully, "Or if you grab Volume 87, you'll find the Orisha contract on the one hundred and eleventh page."

That caught Demetrius's attention. His gaze penetrated the back of Jocelyn's head, the sight of his stunning eyes so alive it was just as if she faced him head on. She was too much of a coward to meet him directly.

"You would have found it, eventually." Jocelyn rolled her eyes and shrugged, a distracting move on her part. It wasn't as if the choice to share her cunning was going to send a ripple effect with only a few hours or days saved of their time. If anything, she more so saved Demetrius's sight from dwindling from staring at such small, faded text for such a prolonged and tortuous period of time.

Yet, she still checked. Everything seemed to remain on course. For now.

Finally, she turned her statuesque, vision-filled body to find Demetrius placing a new book atop his desk. Faint whispers echoed throughout the room, growing louder as Demetrius flipped and skimmed through each page; histories and stories within the text all pleading to be heard, each overlapping the other and replaying itself within Jocelyn's mind.

It went from whispers to yells, from yells to screams, until a high-pitch so loud scratched against the interiors of her mind that she had to grasp her head for physical support to cast the demands away from her thoughts.

Her declaration of truth had awakened the beasts of history within the Solar System's documents, all commanding to be heard.

"Jocelyn!" Demetrius yelled, drowning below the screams that crashed upon the shore that was her mind.

Arms wrapped around her as she screamed.

The cries diluted as Demetrius rocked her in his arms, enclosing her head against his chest and beneath his hand, until all Jocelyn could hear was the steady beat of his flesh.

Minutes passed, perhaps hours.

Jocelyn was trapped within her mind, playing out every forced memory until she could cast it aside within the vault of knowledge for good.

The Orishas never surfaced. But finally, Jocelyn's realization did, along with guilt and terror.

It had never been that bad before.

"I... I'm sorry." Jocleyn finally breathed. She pulled herself away, snapping the bond of Demetrius's protection.

"What happened, Joss?" Demetrius asked steadfast, taking a step toward her.

Jocelyn took another step back, her head was already so tired, she didn't need the linger of him to confuse her focus even more.

"It's never been this *strong*." Jocelyn gulped, trying to calm her shivering body. She fell. Fortunately, onto a plush couch that magically appeared beneath her.

A rich, red cashmere fleece blanket wrapped itself around her, instantly warming her frightened bones.

"Perhaps not having the sight – your powers temporarily inaccessible – they're now coming in ten-fold?" Demetrius suggested, "A slight retaliation to the senses?"

Joss shook her head, wishing he could be right.

She had weakened temporarily in Ireland, but in this realm, their world, she continued to grow stronger, into her cursed destiny.

Would she soon be like her mom, constantly sifting through visions, internally multi-tasking to see all possibilities in her mind while simultaneously balancing external conversations, so she could never fully be present?

The curse of living a half-life at the behest of living the obligated thousands. A seer within the mind to experience nothing fully in one's own life and everything in others.

Demetrius deserved more than that. More than a partner who soon would only be able to give half of her, if at all.

"I-I think I need to rest." Jocelyn proposed weakly. "Once you find the documentation, I can help search for the next course of action."

She stood up, keeping her head held high as she grasped the cozy blanket around her slim frame. The warmth kept her grounded, her last bit of dignity.

"I'll come down for dinner." Jocelyn confirmed, trying to control her shaking limbs.

"Until then, Jocelyn." Demetrius bowed.

Somehow, he had grasped her hand. Laying tenderly cupped along his, her fingers pressed against his palm as he kissed her knuckle.

She saw a galaxy full of stars, blasting with delight. Years of rocks floating and falling through the abyss.

It was overwhelming, it was stunning, it was beautiful.

It was too much.

It was Demetrius.

She focused on the galaxy, the unknown in space. Bringing a calm to her mind amidst the darkness and the simplicity of one million inadamite rocks shining through the dark chasm, following their uncomplicated truths and journeys and enjoying the spectacle of space.

It coaxed her, soothed her and put her mind at peace. As Jocelyn finally crashed against the plush, golden pillows and mauve silk comforter, her eyes shut, and she joined her vision in a much-needed deep sleep.

LIV

"The king requests your presence for dinner." Fukayna tersely stated.

Liv turned to Hayden, amused. And mostly curious to how he would take to being commanded around. Truthfully, Liv was grateful for Fukayna's request on behalf of the royal highness, for her stomach was on the verge of growling due to 240 degrees passing since lunch. Plus, food triumphed over trying to decipher thousand-year-old hieroglyphics anyday.

Hayden nodded to Fukayna, accepting the invitation.

"We would be honored." Liv added politely, elbowing Hayden behind her with a smooth smile.

Fukayna glared, studying both Liv and Hayden and their wardrobe in the grand library, apparently assessing and approving both outfits as appropriate for her high priest. While Liv sported a dark, gothic tapestry look with matching heavy black eyeliner remiscent of Cleopatra, Hayden instead wore a black suit, with harem pants trousers instead of the traditional tailoring and sported a gold bar in lieu of a tie, looped between two holes upon the collar of his button-down shirt.

As if they still did not know their way around, Fukayna escorted them from the great library down the corridor and past the courtyard oasis, leading them once again to the grand staircase that brought them to the dining banquet.

This time around, Liv focused instead on studying the intricate artwork, many symbols depicting the histories of the Afterlife. It was certainly much more tolerable than Fukayna's judgmental scowls and directed side eye. The last image that caught her eye resided near the banquet's entrance, where two royal deities in headdresses, a gazelle and caracal, were depicted above plebians who rejoiced their crowning and era as rulers. Instead of the royals drawn enlarged in comparison to the people they governed, all individuals were the same size, equal in importance for the documentation of this intended rule.

Liv only hoped the standard remained in present day, that the two Egyptian deities could be convinced this war was for the benefit of their own good.

"Ah, King Hayden and Liv!" Ahmed smiled, greeting them almost immediately with a clap. "Please sit down. We're so thrilled you could join us."

Liv appreciated Ahmed's approach to the situation, pretending the request had been an option. As if they had other alternatives to consider. She sat across from the Egyptian King as intended, nodding thanks to the servant who beckoned her and pulled out her seat.

"The pleasure is ours. The more time we are able to get to know one another, the better." Hayden persisted in politeness as well, his voice a liquid velvet, calmly vibrating yet superior in delivery.

Fortunately, Hayden was instructed to sit beside her and across from Sabra.

Today, the warrioress queen wore a stunning orange velvet dress that popped against her dark olive skin and intensified the deep blue of her eyes, like an ocean filled with rocks on the sandy shore.

If it weren't for the constantly despicable sass, Sabra could truly take the breath away from any suitor.

Similar to Sabra, even Ahmed wore a more casual ensemble, a thick black turtleneck sweater, black jeans and combat boots. Liv smiled as she thought how Ahmed's 'hipster' vibe could give Tristan a run for his money, yet again. The God of Fire certainly had competition among the Egyptians.

Tristan. She felt like she had been thinking about him more, everyday. And Piper. And Peyton and Rei… how *were* her friends doing in their separate quests? Were they safe?

Her thoughts came flashing back to reality when a kind priestess beckoned if Liv would like wine, about to pour a glass of burgundy liquid when Liv lifted her hand to pause the gesture.

"Just water tonight, please." She smiled kindly, letting the small woman in black, dressed similarly to Fukayna but without the jewelry adornments, move onto Hayden.

"No, but thank you." Hayden softly replied, also agreeing to coconut water, similar to the beverage sitting in front of the Egyptian King.

"You don't have to decline on my behalf." King Ahmed insisted, once again.

"I'm not drinking because Monaco's not drinking." Hayden simply replied, pointing his thumb casually in Liv's direction and specifying whom to which he referred to.

"I figured we'd put your 'still can have fun' theory to the test. Are you as entertaining as you claim to be with sober guests as an audience?" Liv hummed tauntingly, challenging Ahmed with a seductive grin.

"You figured me out. Now what am I to do?" Ahmed joked, lifting his hands up in surrender.

"I hate you all." Sabra growled, beckoning a priestess to bring her wine immediately.

"At least we know Sabra will be able to compensate for the two of you with her normal drinking habits." Ahmed stated cheerfully.

Sabra scowled.

From her side of the dining table, Liv speculated that Ahmed and Sabra seemed no different than Hayden and Joss, two siblings graced with the power to lead, but still comfortable enough to tease – the familial bond, a foundation for trust and prosperity.

How two deities could so calmly relax in front of two powerful Pure Gods after spending the past thousand years in hiding honestly perplexed Liv.

"Is something on your mind, Liv?" Ahmed asked, tilting his head curiously.

What *wasn't* on her mind?

Liv studied Ahmed, assessing how he may respond if she started prying too deeply; however, they had already been here for three days and time was ticking on their week-long time bomb.

As a priest began serving their dinner plates, Liv finally succombed to her curiosity. "I was wondering why you choose to rule from the Afterlife and let other gods take center stage in the public with your people?"

She wished to take a sip of her water, a natural move to calm her nerves, but refused, knowing she needed to demonstrate dominance, poise and power, at this request for information.

Ahmed smiled tersely. Whether he was expecting the question or not, Liv couldn't tell. Instead, she kept her gaze locked with his, refusing to back down.

Finally, Ahmed receded, taking a deep breath before beginning.

"'There was a time my ancestors abused the system, allowing kings and high priests and priestesses to spread falsities to their people. They created a standard of needing to sacrifice their livelihoods to the gods in order to remain in our good graces, and therefore, prosperous." His eyes transformed from open to targeted, directing his anger inadvertently toward Liv. "It was *ruthless*. Our people starved while gladly, desperately, handing over their winter's meat to nobility, and donated their finely hand-crafted garments while they wore rags – all with the greedy, false notion it would go to the gods, when instead the nobles reaped the rewards and kept the tainted treasures for themselves."

Sabra chimed in, growling as she shook her head in memory, "It was an abusive system."

"So, our deities cast ourselves to the Afterlife, erased our interaction with the mortals, and in time the concept of our kind disappeared, no longer determining the fates of the Egyptians, and we and the corrupt structure eventually faded into history." Ahmed concluded. "Besides, we do not need recognition to rule justly."

Liv turned to Hayden, unsure how to proceed.

He won't answer any of the questions that I ask. Hayden shrugged.

It was unlike Hayden to remain quiet, but he certainly had a strategic point.

"But, that doesn't explain why *you* have chosen to fade into history even among your own kind?" Liv challenged, "Why do you hide from *us?*"

"Did *you* enjoy your journey between the realms?" Ahmed challenged back, his voice didn't raise, but he remained stern. "It's not a trip I care to take often, especially if only for a social gathering. And, if I recall correctly, as soon as you visited our portal, we gave you the proper code to venture into our world. I would not call that 'hiding.'"

"So, now that we know you exist, you're saying your completely fine with letting us return to our world and be on our merry way?" Liv snickered.

Ahmed's grin grew sinister, pointing to Hayden. "He may leave."

But, then he pointed to Liv, his black diamond ring staring darkly in her direction from his finger. "You will stay, as my bride."

Liv scowled, "I haven't accepted yet."

Ahmed smiled, "You will. In time."

The assurity in his statement sent chills down Liv's spine.

In time?

What the hell did Ahmed have up his sleeve?

She turned to Sabra, who thankfully looked like she was about to fall over from boredom, giving Liv the unintentional confidence boost she needed.

"And what about my studies?" Liv purred, back in the game, batting her luscious lashes in his direction teasingly. "I've only completed a year at Puerdios…"

Not missing a beat, Ahmed replied, "You would study here, of course, at the grand Lilaliha University."

"No." Liv challenged, shaking her head with fury. "NO."

There was no way to control her anger regarding the topic of her choice for scholastics.

"Pardon me, Liv?" Ahmed clarified with confusion.

"You do not control where I attend university. If you reap what you sow, and women indeed are partners, I refuse to attend… Lil-ahl-he-hah-tee… University," Liv hoped she had repeated his title description accurately, but was fuming too elaborately to care. She was breathing faster, her words spitting out like a sprinkler on its highest mode, a pitch worthy of Piper's vocal range. "Puerdios is my home. It is apart of me, and I'll be damned if you take the only place I care about away from me…"

"Liv, it's okay." Hayden whispered, grabbing her hand gently underneath the table, pulling her from the flames with the coolness of his grip and slowly extinguishing the raging fire.

Being the infinite ying to her yang.

"I did not realize academia was so important to you." Ahmed nodded impressively, his voice delicious like ruby chocolate. "Of course, we're speaking in the hypothetical, but hypothetically speaking, I applaud your courage in negotiation."

"If we are to marry, this will be a non-negotiable." Liv stubbornly retorted, still squeezing Hayden's hand.

Ahmed grinned seductively, as if impressing the Egyptian King was a key stakeholder in foreplay. Perhaps he enjoyed the outburst, or Liv's proactive declaration of the potential marriage falsely forming.

The subtle joy radiating from his being wasn't necessarily unattractive, Ahmed was beautiful, no matter how he contorted his face, but it simply didn't make Liv feel anything special in return. Not anymore.

And when she turned to Hayden, his exterior calm demeanor appearing to study Ahmed with a furrowed brow, truly hiding his internal rage toward this topic, made Liv feel warmer – in particular, close to where his cool hand clasped over hers…

Liv gulped, taking a sip of water and reminding herself she needed to be less obvious regarding her infatuation with the Pure God King and remain focused on the task at hand.

Could she turn allying with the Pure Gods into a non-negotiable, too? Just as seamlessly as she had unintentionally marched through an agreement for her education?

Somehow, her plate now stood empty, having habitually fed herself without notice. The chicken curry was a delicious, if not a comforting meal, apparently. As soon as she pushed the plate a centimeter forward – another habit, a priestess glided it off the table and back to the kitchen.

Another had proceeded with Ahmed's plate, before he dismissed himself casually and turned to Liv.

"Liv, will you allow me the honor of a walk?"

Liv smiled, subtly glancing at the table to dismiss herself as well, but first held her gaze with Hayden for a moment longer.

He nodded, encouraging her to attend.

Liv gulped, before verbally saying her goodbyes to Sabra and Hayden and gesturing Ahmed to lead the way.

"I want to show you a place very dear to me." Ahmed whispered calmly, guiding Liv through the dining ballroom and down the grand staircase.

Oh, how strange it felt to falsely court a genuinely decent, attractive and powerful deity.

In another life, she could have perhaps been happy here.

Yet, instead of directing her farther into the castle, Ahmed turned sharply toward the front, exiting the fortress and into the massive desert. Situated outside and to where Ahmed now headed stood a sphinx.

Liv paused, remembering both the times she conquered a sphinx for her Security & Warfare class and then mocked the occasion standing in front of a large statue of one only days before.

"Have you not ridden a sphinx before?" Ahmed asked curiously.

"No, I haven't." Liv studied the creature, a little terrified about getting atop it.

Ahmed laughed, "There's nothing to worry about. This is Phix. He's very sweet and well tamed. You can ride with me. He's *the* sphinx of the kings, so you'll be in good hands."

Remember, sphinxes don't like water, so worst case scenario...

By this time, Ahmed already sat atop the large beast and now extended a strong hand out to Liv to help her up.

She first looked at the hand, then up to Ahmed for more validation. He nudged his hand further forward, insistent.

"I promise it'll be worth the view." He pressed.

Liv bit her lip, then mumbled, "Screw it."

She grabbed his hand and plopped onto the spine of the sphinx. Sitting behind him, she immediately clasped her arms around King Ahmed's extremely rock-solid core, blushing as she imagined what chiseled eight-pack must exist beneath the black chunky sweater.

Ahmed threw on a pair of round sunglasses, the lens as dark as the black ensemble he wore. He lifted another pair behind his shoulders, offering them to Liv.

"It's bright, but also sandy out in the Egyptian wild." He insisted.

Liv accepted, slowly recoiling her right arm to grab the pair and slide them atop her nose. Her eyelids relaxed from the unknown squint and fully relaxed beneath the darker shade.

Suddenly, the sphinx whined, taking a step forward eagerly, ready for its ride.

Liv's eyes grew wide while she simultaneously returned her arm around Ahmed, squeezing him in anticipation for the adventure.

"If you hold on any tighter, you may suffocate me." Ahmed joked, "Then you may be, dare I say, in a more dire situation than if you simply trust me?"

Liv relaxed her grip.

"Adhhab!" Ahmed yelled, clicking his tongue.

Immediately, Phix started into an easy gallop, cruising past the palm trees and into the desert-abyss.

"You can see the outskirts of the mecca down there, near the horizon." Ahmed nodded to his right, where a dark rectangle blurred on the edge of the earth.

"Why so close?" Liv teased.

"We needed at least *one* reason for the sphinx." Ahmed grinned, before sighing and replying truthfully. "Honestly, it's a dark reason. But distance gives us time to prepare for any uprising or attack. Fortunately, the location tactic has not been needed to prove successful, yet. Hopefully, we never have to see its worth."

Liv leaned her chin against his shoulder. "Do you visit often?"

"I was there this morning. Sabra and I have a loft in the city center – most of our council lives there so it's easier for us to visit them than bringing all twenty members out to the palace."

Liv considered the humble gesture – accommodation of his people over his own time. It still felt like the notion of not supporting the Pure Gods to protect his own people did not match up with the clues he had been handing her over the past couple of days. Maybe it was as he said – a simple reason to ride Phix more often.

"Liv, now that we're alone. I must ask – why do you speak so intensely about Puerdios University?"

Ahmed's voice was soft, quiet, as if trepid to cause another outburst.

His approach to the topic pacified Liv, it was unspoken that he simply wanted to understand her more, not reopen the negotiation.

He steered Phix to the left, revealing a stunning vista with what looked like bright white icecaps across a traditional desert. Ahmed slowed the sphinx to a halt, nearby large crystals seemingly growing out of the earth and creating a fence surrounding the incredible snowy desert field.

"What is this place?" Liv whispered, mesmerized by the sight standing before her.

"The Crystal Mountain, which borders the north of the White Desert." Ahmed smiled, looking out into the abyss with pure pride. "The crystals are barite and calcite resting on a subvolcanic vault, which we believed emerged during the Oligocene age. The white desert formed by centuries of erosion and sandstorms in the Cretaceous age – the *unique* white statues that you see are calcium rock formations."

"A place older than our kind. Bigger than you."

Liv understood.

It was rare for a deity to feel small, to encounter something that existed longer on this earth than their immortal life. Ahmed explained that the Oligocene age was over 23 million years ago; the Cretaceous even older, occurring over 66 million years before that.

"It reminds me that however infinite our time may be, we are never as infinite as the higher beings and those of our past. We may not always have the time to undo our wrongs."

"It's beautiful." Liv murmured, speaking to both the view and Ahmed's sentiment.

"If anything, it provides a great view to think." He smiled, taking a seat among the sand. He patted the empty spot beside him before casually swinging both arms across his knees, leaning into them and the view ahead.

Liv obliged, plopping down beside him, now ready to tell her story and reveal more to him.

"I grew up in the mortal world, unaware of my deity heritage." Liv shifted her gaze from the sight ahead to the sand directly beside her, gently carving out an infinity symbol with her hand. "I had an incredibly normal childhood. A loving mother, genuinely good friends, and although I always wondered about my father, I never felt incomplete by not having him involved in my life. I was great at sports, excelled at academics and was truly happy, content with what my life was shaping into. It was *easy*."

Her eyebrows furrowed as she drew an x into the infinite shape, her mind darkening to the period she wished she could forget.

"Until, one day, my world crumbled, and I fell apart. Everything I knew disappeared. I saw black. I felt incomplete. I was lost." She scowled, biting her lip as she brushed away the cursed symbol. A clean slate. "I was weak, hit rock bottom."

"Puerdios pulled you out of the darkness?" Ahmed guessed.

"Yes, and more." Liv agreed, returning her gaze to what stunning sight now stood before her. "It showed me I was capable of so much more and that I had something to work for – a *real* challenge. It revealed a part of me I never knew existed, a part of me that made it the first place I felt entirely whole, that I knew my full potential – that it was *limitless*. It was terrifying, challenging but best of all, it opened the doors to the majestic world that I now exist in today, to this…" She waved her hands to the sight before her. "The ancient castle has become my home and the friends there have become my family. Puerdios University has given me so much; it doesn't feel right to cut down the time I have left with it." A tear slid down the side of Liv's cheek, she wiped it away self consciously, sniffling and commanding she pull it together. "I can't imagine my world without Puerdios University."

Not now. Not ever.

Ahmed nodded his hand in understanding. "You could find I share a similar sentiment for the White Desert. It's provided more guidance and sound advice than I deserve. In all honesty, I'm not sure what darkness I would wrath if anything or anyone intentionally hurt this place." He turned to Liv, "You must enjoy the good blessings while they exist and protect what is important while you can. Memorable experiences are what fills our immortal existence with meaning."

"Does it not bother you that I am half-mortal?" Liv wondered aloud.

"What bothers me is your power." Ahmed admitted. "You two are too strong together, and even if we are betrothed for the sake of the Pure battle, it's an unbalanced alliance. And I have to look out for my people."

He turned to Liv sadly. "I want to believe in your intentions, Liv. That your principles are just. I believe you to be good, but as long as you see your people as the priority, you are a threat to mine. I hope you understand where I come from."

Ahmed's eyes intensely focused on Liv, his vulnerability seeping through his hard exterior. It wasn't every millienia that a powerful king admitted he was scared to a stranger.

"I understand." Liv nodded, thinking about all of the possibilities.

She and Hayden felt the exact same way, and perhaps they could find some commonality there.

But even now, being honest with Ahmed and revealing her inner demons, she still concealed so many alternative motives and kept her secrets hidden from him. Today, she would be willing to protect Ahmed and his people, but how long could she keep a promise that could span decades, centuries or even an eternity?

What if it came down to a choice between Hayden and Ahmed? She, and Ahmed, knew that right now, it would always be Hayden. And although Ahmed hoped one day the balance would turn to his favor, it was never guaranteed. Even if it did, the chances of it remaining that way were never promised, either.

When it comes to the gods, nothing is ever permanent.

Hades's sweetly cruel voice echoed in the confines of Liv's mind.

Would immortality eventually drain out her trust and hope for a better future? Her humanity?

"I worry about the future, too." Liv admitted. "We're doing all that we can – but I can only hope our efforts will be enough to ensure all mortals have a prosperous future."

"Hope is never enough." Ahmed replied cynically.

"Without hope, you have nothing." Liv snapped back quickly.

Ahmed chuckled darkly, looking once again over the expansive desert.

"You know the very same desert and crystals exist in the mortal world." Ahmed stated blankly, giving no notion or explanation to the claim.

Liv repeated the comment within her head during the following silence.

"The *very same* or *similar*?" She finally clarified.

"I thought humans should not be robbed of such a life-changing sight. You'll have to visit the mortal world and report back." Ahmed grinned, "Come on. It's getting late."

Before allowing her to protest, Ahmed stood up, reaching his hand out to help Liv once again.

While Ahmed's all black ensemble revealed no sand accentuating his clothes, Liv shook out her rug skirt by twisting her waist and waving the fabric in the air, inadvertently getting sand all over her hands in the process. She batted her hands against her thighs, scowling as she heard Ahmed's lighthearted laughter at the sight.

JOCELYN

She always despised the moments between the dream world and the real one; it was the only time when she couldn't control her mind nor decipher fantasy from reality. Sometimes she woke in a sweat, shaking from seeing a loved one murdered on a battlefield or with overpromised joy at the thought of a new life being born onto this earth.

When she finally returned to consciousness, her eyes awoke, and she had to organize her memories and dispose of the pretend.

It was always hardest when she awoke joyful with hope.

In this case, opening her eyes to the red hue of Jupiter outside her window brought dread as she remembered the panicked state in which she had allowed Demetrius to witness. As a royal and an Elite, it was absolutely forbidden to show such weakness to another deity, even with one she was once romantically inclined. Jocelyn had let her guard down, and for that, she must be punished.

It was 210 degrees SR. Dinner would be served in 8 degrees.

Jocelyn's stomach growled.

After eating bland Irish biscuits and meats while in the green lands, she couldn't wait for the rich, flavorful delicacy Demetrius would surely serve in reward for being gone for such a long time. The one benefit to the Solar System God was that he had a palette that equally matched his taste in clothes.

After tidying up her blonde curls into another braided crown, she glided downstairs, feeling lighter in her step as she fortified her armor.

A buttery whiff penetrated the air, leaving Jocelyn's mouth drooling as she entered the parlour to find Demetrius pouring himself scotch at the bar.

"Good evening, Demetrius." Jocelyn greeted him; her voice distant but controlled.

"Your majesty." He politely replied with a bow. "Care for a drink?"

"Yes, please." Jocelyn sighed, before immediately straightening her composure. "Er, I mean… yes, thank you."

"French 75?" Demetrius guessed, accurately.

Jocelyn blinked, smiling courteously. "Yes, thank you."

He grinned, swiftly serving the lemon cocktail within moments.

"Thank you." Jocelyn repeated, taking a sip.

She felt like a robot and it crushed her inside.

Jocleyn wanted to laugh, flirt and dance like she once looked forward to when her mind was clear. She wanted to be the wild Joss, with no care or responsibility in the world.

Now, all her energy served battling the cursed visions, leaving her deplenished and dull.

What a dreary existence to live.

Taking a sip of her favorite cocktail, Jocelyn hummed in relief as the sweet combatted the sour against her palette, finishing smoothly with the bubbly Champagne.

It was the refreshing replenishment she needed to survive the night.

"I was able to source more details from the contracted record with the Orishas this afternoon." Demetrius began, leading her to the velvet couches by a blazing fire.

"That's incredible, Demetrius!" Jocelyn exclaimed, her excitement getting the best of her.

And the small mistake, the miniature moment of lowering her fortress, caused a sea of visions to crash against her mind once again. Her brain was at high tide and Jocelyn was once again drowning.

Footage of Demetrius locating the larger detailed document from the Orisha contract he referenced earlier, an image flashed of a Nigerian map, a vision of Demetrius in a desert calling out to nobody in particular, "Look for my aid when the sun returns for its longest day!", and then finally, a blur of hazy images, one of which Joss was sure was Hayden and Liv with Giselle…

She dropped her beverage, the shards of glass now exploding in air, each representing a different, terrifying vision which penetrated her mind, all colliding against the ground in a robust display of aggression.

"Oh no, Hayden…" Jocelyn clasped her mouth, turning to Demetrius in frozen terror. For a moment, she had no voice; the influx of truth stole her emotion as she watched Puerdios burn to the ground.

But then she took a deep breath, calming her body and rebuilding her armor, forcing herself to be strong in the face of the inevitable darkness to come.

Jocelyn stood determinedly, "We've got to get back to Puerdios. Now."

She turned for the door but was restrained when a strong hand grabbed her arm.

"Jocelyn, wait. Take a step back. What did you see?"

Demetrius's melodic voice was burned with worry.

Jocelyn blinked, trying to formulate the whirlwind of images and clips from various points in time, navigating them with the most pertinent. Distinguish some form of narrative and translate sentiment into words.

"Puerdios is in danger. The Dark Gods... are going to attack the university seven sunsets from now."

"Are you sure?" Demetrius clarified softly.

"Have I ever been *wrong!?*" Jocelyn cried.

She needed to find her mother, seek Silas and summon her brother, wherever the Hades he was...

Okay, breathe.

"Will you take me to the palace?" Jocelyn asked bluntly, trying to configure specific next steps. She could only do one thing at a time with so many thoughts running through her head, a frenzy slowly freezing her own body's capabilities. She'd never survive a flight by herself.

"And postpone the Orisha cause?" Demetrius challenged, aghast. "Let me get this straight, I've essentially challenged Danu to a war by opening my domain to powerless, refugee deities, while defenseless because, oh yes, I've already donated the majority of my troops to your cause on earth! And now you want to abandon the *only* lead we have in helping our numbers against this madness? You want to leave me to face this *alone?*"

"I can't leave Puerdios defenseless!" Jocelyn screamed.

The visions, the blood – it was a horror movie replaying in her mind, she couldn't escape. It was *too* much. Her knowledge was both a curse and a gift.

"So, you leave me defenseless." Demetrius retorted.

Jocelyn took a step back, twisting her arm indignantly, forcing him to release his grasp on her. There was nothing she could say to make him understand. There was nothing he could say to change her mind.

She didn't see destruction here on Jupiter; her powers weren't strong enough to see past any attacks by Danu. All she could focus on was what she knew.

"You always choose your family over me." Demetrius finally whispered in resolution, "Over us."

Part of Jocelyn snapped. To Hades with composure.

"And you would have me choose!?" Jocelyn yelled, tightening her hands into fists so that she wouldn't combust then and there. "That is the true culprit and you know it. You ask me to risk something tangible in pursuit of… something fantastical!"

"Well, there you have it." Demetrius pursed his lips. "That is the true culprit. You may go now."

Jocelyn scowled, boiling in the silence.

"You can see yourself out." Demetrius hissed, turning his back and walking away, before he hollered with a rude wave, "For once, your powers may serve useful for that."

THIRTY-THREE

PEYTON

Rei had been gone for most of the day; Peyton didn't care.

He only came back to retrieve her for dinner, anticipating King Mothi's decision to be declared and their fate to be determined. So, they departed their quarters and walked to the throne room, where their first encounter with the Norse Gods all began. It felt like no time and all time had passed, and it still pained Peyton's head to consider it had only been one night in Vanaheim.

King Mothi sat in his throne, sporting a thick black turtleneck that brought out the darkness in his eyebrows and even more strongly contrasted against his bright hair, a hue matching both his brother and mother's who sat casually below him and off to each side. Sif sat beside Thor, who had Giselle on the other side. Giselle kept her head toward Mothi, either too ashamed to face Peyton after the words they had exchanged, or to ensure her betrothed did not get more jealous of her past with Rei. Magni stood up, walked over to his brother and hovered from behind his left shoulder, looking smug as ever.

Peyton's stomach felt like it had rotted. She wanted to curl over in her failure and have Rei carry her home to her bed.

She just needed a day. One day to recover and strategize her next plan.

Finally, the Norse king spoke.

"Thank you both for joining us this morning. We hope your accommodations in Vanaheim have exceeded your expectations."

No mention of hoping to return, for a reunion nor a future encounter.

Peyton gulped, wanting to bow her head but willed her eyes to maintain Mothi's casual stare. *If you don't need us, then we don't need you.* She challenged with her glare.

Rei was more polite. Or perhaps he was simply more invested in these personal relations.

"It is us who should be thanking you for your kind hospitality." He bluffed.

More like for Giselle's persuasion of not housing us in the dungeons. Peyton huffed internally.

"As you know, we take the secrecy of Vanaheim very seriously, in order to protect our people from invaders, so we hope we can rely on your discretion." Mothi offered vaguely.

Rei and Peyton both nodded. After a pause, Rei coughed, signaling the request for Peyton to verbally reply.

"Your highness, it has been a privilege to see your stunning city and spend time with your family and subjects. I am willing to do all that I must to ensure its protection." Peyton smiled curtly.

Mothi's sly smile matched her own.

"I'm impressed by your verbiage; however, I would be more disappointed if a deity of your age had not yet mastered the art of false promises." His voice remained calm throughout the accusation.

Peyton grinned. "Why would I give my word when you have not promised anything in return?" She spoke sweetly, innocently, until her eyes narrowed like daggers and her voice hit its target. "Fair is fair."

Mothi laughed. "A firecracker, you certainly are, Peyton, God of Discovery."

Yet, something shifted. No longer stoic or caged, Mothi spoke with impress. His eyes narrowed on Peyton, assessing her strength.

Giselle sat up straight, tensing even further, if that was possible.

"You will leave today, Peyton and Rei of the Pure Gods." Mothi commanded, snickering in the process. "Be thankful we allow it to be together and in one piece."

Magni grinned cruelly from behind.

Giselle finally shot her gaze to Rei and Peyton, her mouth open, speechless.

"Thank you for the kind dismissal." Rei bowed, turning to leave.

Peyton remained, challenging the king to continue.

Instead, Giselle stood up. Her white, thick shawl-collared cardigan coat and black turtleneck jumpsuit making her look like a giantess in comparison to the sitting king.

"I will join you in five days time." She declared boldly, her chin raising up.

Gold specs shimmered from her defiance.

Mothi stood up immediately after. "Giselle and our men will join you in five days time, under one condition," he clarified, "she is to remain in disguise and the Norse will not commit until we see proof of her living brother, safe and unharmed."

Peyton smiled, more so in response to Magni's clear shock and anger to this change in plans from behind the throne. He should have anticipated the power of blood's influence like Peyton had.

"And shall we anticipate your arrival, your majesty?" Peyton inquired sweetly.

"Where my men go, I go – which includes my family." Mothi stated, stepping toward Giselle and wrapping his arm around her shoulder, once separated but now united as one, again. "Please alert King Hayden to make accommodations for the Royal Norse Family as we have so generously offered you."

"Noted." Peyton nodded, walking toward the King and Queen of the Norse Gods. She placed her hands in front and behind her core, and bowed, trying to contain the tears of joy sparkling from behind her closed eyes. "Does Magni prefer the barn or the woods?"

Thor huffed with laughter; Sif nearly smiled, bemused, nevertheless. Magni was boiling, turning a shade of red to purple.

"Shockingly, he prefers a bed similar to you and I." Mothi smirked, releasing his grip around Giselle and pulling Peyton into a hug. "Safe travels, Peyton."

Giselle followed quickly after, grabbing Peyton and squeezing her into a tighter hug. "Thank you." She whispered, holding back sniffles.

Peyton smiled softly, "I only promised not to tell anyone about you so you can tell Tristan yourself."

Giselle wiped a tear from her eye, pulling back as her body shook. She turned to Mothi, wrapping her arm around his waist for support.

With a final nod, Peyton turned around and joined Rei near the door, muttering under her breath as she departed with a swagger and a clap.

"And that Rei, is *how it's done.*"

DYLAN

"Your mother *visited* while I was away?" Zayne asked, his typically tranquil demeanor broken with disbelief. "Thalia. Here. In the flesh?"

"You're just as surprised as we were." Dylan laughed, handing Zayne a tea.

Accepting the hot beverage gratefully and after taking a sip, he asked, "Why did she come?"

Dylan smiled, eyeing Ammiras, who had accompanied Zayne in his return to Puerdios, which was another unexpected surprise, but an applauded development, nonetheless.

The prince of sirens and brother to Queen Calithya had already begun sipping his tea, the deep oceanic blue velvet suit playing richly against Dylan's burgundy pillow and dark brown leather couch. The grey ceramic glazed mug fit in all too well.

"If you do not wish to speak of personal matters in front of me, I understand." Ammiras responded without missing a beat, his sensual accent and honest delivery making Dylan feel all the more guilty.

"No, of course that's not it." Dylan shrugged, finding Kyril's eyes who knew all too well it was a cover. "It's just, I'm not entirely sure *why* she visited."

"Well, that doesn't surprise me." Zayne sighed sadly, sitting besides Ammiras on the chair's edge. "What did she say?"

"Besides being a disappointment to my family and the inevitable demise of the Pure God rule?" Dylan dryly pondered aloud. "Actually, the darkest thing Mother delivered was warning us that, 'War is coming.'"

Dylan used air quotes as she rolled her eyes.

"I mean, obviously war is coming. But why did Thalia specifically seek me out to tell me what I already know?"

"What else did she say?" Zayne pushed, his voice monotone as his thoughts whirled into piecing together the forever puzzle that was Dylan's mother.

"Er, something about soon not being welcome in both of my homes." Dylan struggled to remember the exact words Thalia delivered. She had been too focused on simply keeping her composure.

Kyril jumped up, "Wait, she said that *after* you said that you wish you would be welcome in your home just as she and your family are always welcome in yours!" He gestured toward her dark, occult-inspired loft.

"War is coming to Puerdios?" Zayne merged the two clues together, speculatively.

Dylan's heart dropped.

No, it can't be...

All of her friends were dispersed around the globe, possibly in different realms. The Dark Gods must have recognized the hole, knowing Puerdios was at its weakest... that the Pure Gods were at its weakest. Certainly, the easiest way to seek change was to infiltrate young minds and brainwash them before they could determine right from wrong on their own. Of course, Puerdios would be the next target in the Dark Gods' agenda. How had they not seen this?

Dylan's mind was spiraling.

She sat down on her navy velvet couch, still wrapping her head around the revelation, grappling with what she needed to do.

She needed to warn Hayden. She needed to warn Liv. She needed to alert the Security Pillar as soon as possible.

Could she even summon Silas?

Or Rei?

Could Rei even be found? Be *trusted*?

For all she knew, Rei could be a traitor to the crown.

Her mind flashed to Peyton's cryptic note; Dylan's stomach started to grow queasy. Shortly after, she felt Kyril's arm extend around her in comfort.

"We'll figure it out." Kyril said sternly, assuringly.

"Together." Zayne confirmed with a nod.

Dylan weakly looked up to Zayne and smiled while squeezing Kyril's hand, appreciating that she still had some here who she could trust.

"If it helps, I can summon my sister to bring reinforcements to the school." Ammiras offered hesitantly, hoping to help but not overstep.

Zayne beamed at his new friend, but the look he gave Ammiras made it seem like possibly more than that.

That's another day's discussion. Dylan asserted, closing that chapter in her mind and moving onto the next.

"Does anyone know where the Security Pillar is?" Kyril asked, receiving silence in return.

Dylan sighed, "Royal palace it is. We can ask Daphne to summon Silas, if she's willing to help."

She turned to leave, but Kyril's arm blocked her from taking a step further.

"Dyl, wait." Kyril commanded sharply, "Wouldn't Daphne already see this? And yet, we have heard no precaution taken to tighten Puerdios's security more than what's been already implemented."

"Are you insinuating we cannot trust Daphne?" Dylan tilted her head accusatorily. She knew Kyril was still on the fence between Dark and Pure, but this was a traitorous conspiracy.

"I'm insinuating that the Candor Queen exists within a fine line of withholding information and duplicitous behavior. For one so truthful, she is not always honorable. Even Hayden, her own son and our king, does not always trust her. We need to be careful."

"I agree with Kyril." Zayne echoed, albeit cautiously. "We should at least try to cover our grounds here before we seek her aid."

"How do you suppose we do that?" Dylan challenged, crossing her arms across her burgundy laced dress.

"As all do when they seek attention from a God." Zayne replied swiftly, "We pray."

HAYDEN

"I don't know, he just mentioned 'the very same White Desert and Crystal Mountain exist in the mortal world,' but he didn't explain or insinuate any ties to linking the two worlds together. What do you think?"

Liv was pacing in their suite and hadn't stopped since she returned from her evening stroll with the Egyptian king. Hayden had to admit, he too was growing restless. It seemed like an oxymoron that what was required of him involved studying how to escape this world when there were such bigger issues happening in his *own* world. But he would be damned if he left Liv here with that slimy Egyptian priest...

Help.

It was faint, but the summoning prayer having broken through the power barrier masked in this world must have meant that from Hayden's world, it was a rallying cry.

"Did you hear that?" Liv whispered, clutching her chest.

She had finally stood still, eyes wide and mouth open.

Puerdios... in danger...

Even weaker than before, the plea again broke through the worlds.

"That's Dylan's voice!" Liv cried, turning around in the room as if trying to find her.

"Exactly." Hayden replied tersely.

Shit. How the fuck were they going to get out of there in time?

"We have to ask. It's the only thing we haven't tried." Liv read his thoughts, replying with his voice. "It's the only option left."

She started heading for the door.

"Liv, no! You can't!" Hayden reached for her hand, pulling her back toward him.

"He said you could go at any time." Liv was spiraling with fear, "Worst case we find out how you can depart. They *need* you Hayden."

"I won't leave you." Hayden pressed his forehead aginst Liv, pulling her into a hug. "It's not an option."

"It may be our only option." Liv whispered, looking up desperately. "Hayden, you have to put our people before me if it comes to it. Promise me."

"I can't…" Hayden gasped, grabbing Liv's neck and pulling her into a deep kiss, letting her absorb all of him, his entire being. He couldn't live in a world where she didn't exist.

Liv succumbed to the delicate gesture, but pulled back within moments.

He watched her throat vibrate as she gulped, fighting back the tears in her watery eyes. Finally, she blinked, resulting in one tear gliding down her face, the trail of dampened eyeliner leaving a trail behind.

"Promise me." She breathed, looking up determinedly, commanding him to oblige.

Hayden closed his eyes, pulling her close to him once again, but nodded his head.

She let him hold her for a moment, letting him be her strength as she regained her composure and prepared to chain herself to the afterlife as its prisoner. Finally, she let out a final sigh and took a step back.

"Okay, let's go find Ahmed."

TRISTAN

Holy shit. Holy shit. Holy shit.

Tristan was terrified, shocked, angry, perplexed and relieved all at once.

Terrified that a Naga resided behind his waning defense of embers slowly depleting, shocked that his friend and partner had an unknown third eye and never mentioned it, angry that they had unleashed a monster without thinking through the repercussions, perplexed that they had seemingly frozen in time for what seemed like a day, and finally, relieved that they were still alive, if only for a few more minutes before the beast regained its strength from the brutal sunlight – or figured out what the concept of 'shade' was.

It was survival of the fittest but even as immortal deities and powerful monsters, all parties involved in this mess were seriously struggling.

Even if he could speak without catching their enemy's attention, Tristan didn't even know what to say to Piper anymore.

So, for the moment, both remained silent.

But in time, the slowly diminishing wall of ash piqued Tristan's attention. With each flake of charcoal debris floating down to the patchy dirt ground, the Naga was unseen.

When the wall only stood four feet tall, Tristan mustered up his strength and finally chose to face their enemy. Yet, instead of the terrifying, seven-headed snake, lay an unconscious man.

His silk robes matched the same colors of the beast's scales, but he was no larger than Tristan and certainly did not look like a monster, but a human.

"Piper," Tristan whispered, trying to get his friend's attention. "Pst, Piper!"

"Huh?" Piper mumbled, slowly opening her eyes, the color drained from her face and her eyes a lifeless grey. She tried to sit up, but the slight movement made her body curve inward as she retched.

Tristan eyed the stranger's corpse, before running to Piper's side. He summoned a couple coconuts from a nearby farm and quickly broke one open, gently handing the shell to Piper to drink.

Her hands delicately wrapped around the tropical fruit as she coughed with gratitude before drinking.

Tristan caught himself from staring with intrigue at the feisty, unknown deity before him. The stranger was certainly not a threat unconscious, but he and Piper would be unable to defend without strength. So, Tristan set aside his mistrust and focused on summoning mangoes, bananas and oranges to help nourish their depleted powers.

After peeling back a banana and handing it to Piper, he heard dirt faintly rubbing against fabric and crisp leaves rustle from a distance.

Their friend was awake.

Tristan lunged toward the man, within seconds binding him with fiery handcuffs that burned him to the ground, and a moment later paused with Piper's axe in his hand and its blade slightly edged against the stranger's throat.

"Who are you?" Tristan commanded.

"I mean no harm!" The man squirmed, cursing as the flames burned his raw flesh.

"Who are you?!" Tristan ignored his plea, "Answer the question."

"Rajaraja Chola III." The man said slowly, now frozen with his eyes staring boldly at the precise flames that controlled his limbs. He looked back up at Tristan with a reflective fear blazing through his eyes.

"What happened to the Naga? How did you defeat it!?" Tristan interrogated, unrelinquishing his grip and position.

"Tristan, he's harmless..." Piper coughed from behind.

Tristan ignored her.

"What happened to the Naga!?" Tristan continued, unsettled like a rabid, wild animal. He pressed the axe's blade further against the throbbing skin. "How did you destroy it?!"

"I did not destory the Naga!" The man yelled. "It destroyed me!"

THIRTY-FOUR

PIPER

"Tristan, let him go!" Piper commanded quietly, standing up and trying to remain vertical without retching. Her voice seemed higher, mousier, from her lack of energy and power. "He's only a human!"

She summoned her axe, snapping it from Tristan's grip and poured the remaining coconut water across his fiery bonds.

"Piper!" Tristan yelled, fury blazing from his eyes.

"He's apart of the Chola dynasty!" Piper explained, although unsure how a member of a dynasty from over seven hundred years ago could be living in the flesh today.

"The what!?" Tristan questioned, still clearly seeing red.

Piper crossed her arms and nodded to Rajaraja Chola III, prompting him to further explain what she already knew, or *supposed* from her previous research.

Either he was somehow the real deal or more plausibly a complete lunatic, but his next words would quickly show his true colors.

"I'm Rajaraja Chola III, son of Kulothunga Chola III." Rajaraja began, looking hesitantly between the stern Piper and flaming Tristan before continuing. "I'm assuming you came to retrieve the Emerald Buddha and restore King Rāhula, Queen Chanthira and their divinities to this world?"

"How do you know that?" Tristan asked, his voice still laced with edge.

"You stole the Emerald Buddha from me and broke the curse." Rajaraja explained, "You see, I was the Naga you fought, before you defeated and returned me to my mortal form."

"You were cursed?" Piper asked softly, sending a coconut to their new acquaintance for him to drink. She was also glad to see her axe wound translated to only a small cut that remained on his arm.

"Shiva." Rajaraja replied tartly, before shrugging and continuing on. "I opposed his curse, so inevitably became apart of it."

"But, if you're mortal, how are you… still alive?" Piper asked awkwardly, her voice going higher than usual.

"What year is it?" Panic returned to Rajaraja's eyes.

Zeus, just as he was becoming comfortable with us.

Piper summoned some carrots and lotus seeds his way to hopefully soften the blow. Food always made her feel better, anyway.

"It's… the mortal year 2017…" Piper whispered, furrowing her brows as she observed the man's reaction. If her calculations were correct, Hades, even if they *weren't*, it had been *centuries* since his family, friends and loved ones walked this earth.

Rajaraja froze, his eyes growing wide as he stared at the ground below him.

"It couldn't be…" He turned behind him, finally looking at Angkor Wat, noticing how the years had aged the once mecca of his world. With chipped pieces and debris, years of natural deterioration marked the aged sandstone with calcite and phosphate, weathering the material that once shone under the Cambodian sky as a marvel to the world.

Piper remained silent, letting the man process his new reality. Although a normal concept for the divine, even she was surprised to find an element of immortal preservance with this human – for only a cruel, heartless deity could impose such a cursed fate.

"Do you know how Shiva was able to keep you alive for… seven hundred years?" Piper bit her lip, hoping her vague historical knowledge was adequate for the sake of this very pressing point.

Rajaraja was still staring at Angkor Wat, so Piper summoned some sliced mangoes and oranges into his hand, smiling kindly as she beckoned him to eat.

Food made her feel better, but sugar always made her happier. Even if only temporarily.

"I suppose it's because I'm a descendant of the Chola King. According to legend, he bred with a female serpent demon as part of the dynasty of Pallavas – her blood must run through my veins, allowing me to turn into a Naga like myth suggested."

Rajaraja softly set down the sliced fruit and ran his hands through his thick brown hair, refusing to touch the comfort food Piper continued to place in front of him.

"So, you're not a god, only a part of an immortal curse." Tristan summarized.

"A very vicious one at that." Piper whispered sadly, but as she pieced the puzzle together, there was still one oustanding hole. "Rajaraja-"

"Please, call me Raj." He insisted hopelessly.

King Raj.

Piper gulped, before continuing. "Raj, you mentioned that Shiva cursed you because you opposed him... were there other Hindu Gods or mythical entities who may have had the same position?"

Raj tilted his head, curiously studying Piper; she debated whether his mortal brain could handle another shock by explaining the battle taking place between Pure and Dark deities.

He sighed, his face now glazed with sorrow and doubt.

For a seven-hundred-year-old man, he certainly aged well. He had a creamy caramel complexion and high cheekbones; his hair was still moderately trim and only a faint five o'clock shadow gave hint to his enduring life.

"Even if they once opposed Shiva, who is to say they remain today?" He concluded solemnly, "Cursed, destroyed, imprisoned... are only a few of the ways the god works." He laughed, darkly. "Where do I even go from here?"

Finally, he turned to Piper, his eyes gold and bright just like his previous Naga form, but now completely exposed.

"You can stay with us." Piper nodded, blocking Tristan's clear opposition from her sight by ignoring him. "At least, until you know where your next path leads. Although, we must warn you... by our side may not be the safest choice."

That felt vague enough to keep his mind from exploding but foreboding enough to sufficiently inform him of the dangers to come.

"Thank you. You are too kind." He said softly, still in a daze.

He was going into shock.

Piper elbowed Tristan, nodding to Raj and then glaring a demand to obviously help the man out when the Fire God didn't budge.

Tristan rolled his eyes dramatically, taking a breath before stepping forward.

"Raj, let's take you back to our hotel, where we can try to piece together all that happened while you were... in your other form and... go from there."

Raj looked up at Tristan, his eyes hazy. "What's a hotel?"

Piper's jaw dropped, before attemping to deliver more descriptors for their next destination. "It's, sort of like an inn, hostel-tavern, thing... but more luxurious and modern?"

"It's a place to sleep." Tristan interjected, extending his hand to help Raj stand.

JOCELYN

Finally, she could behave like the obedient, lackluster daughter her mother had groomed her to be. Without Demetrius... replaying those cruel words in her head... her heart felt obsolete, inadequate, and the final flame that fought for a meaningful life finally burned out, leaving her soul dark and alone.

Her tears froze against her skin in the universe, before returning once again to liquid as she spotted her beloved earth and soared closer to home.

Wiping her eyes, she stumbled upon the palace grounds, wanting to crawl into bed and relish in the dream world, she'd take any uncertain vision over the finite, unforgiving clips that spiraled into domination within her mind.

She slowly stomped up the stairs and to the front door, yet her steps didn't cause the impact she had hoped, it was more of a pathetic trudge.

The door swung open slowly but obediently after she quietly tapped it with her knuckle. Jocelyn continued on.

With her head hung low, staring at the floor as her feet took another step forward, two hands grabbed her arms abruptly.

Jumping in terror, Jocelyn had expected to see anyone but her tall, statuesque mother as the culprit to the hold on her arms, now gripping her even more firmly in response to Jocelyn's reaction.

"I told you *not* to allow visions surrounding your brother, Jocelyn." Daphne stated sternly. "You did not warn him?"

Zeus, Daphne had not only seen Jocelyn's freak out, but she had combed through her powers and *seen* the same vision. Leave it to her mother to first ask about the golden brother's status and entirely ignore her daughter's world collapsing right in front of her.

"I can't control it all the time, Mother." Jocelyn challenged, but her voice came out more as a whine.

"That's weak, daughter, and we both know it is a lie." Daphne scolded. "Did you warn him?"

Jocelyn hung her head even lower than before. "No. I couldn't reach him."

"It's too close, Jocelyn. You will end up destroying *everything*."

Jocelyn nodded mindlessly while a dark thought penetrated the only clear space left in her mind.

What if she already had?

LIV

They ran across the palace trying to find a familiar face, anyone who would be willing to divulge the location of the Egyptian King. But as Liv and Hayden were strange guests visiting the castle, nobody would divulge unwarranted information regarding their high priest.

By the time they walked through the library, Liv was growing desperate. They selected to split up in the library and wander every aisle of books, during which Liv begged that Ahmed hadn't departed for some royal business at the mecca, or worse, elsewhere.

"What is this commotion you are stirring up tonight, sir?! The staff is buzzing with worry due to your insulting shenanigans!"

Liv breathed a sigh of relief, never thinking she'd be happy to hear the scornful tone of the fierce Fukayna. She ran toward the aggressive scolding noise, finding Fukayna with her arms crossed and eyebrows raised toward Hayden.

Her disdain did not hold for long, since she turned to Liv as soon as she approached, sighing with dismay.

"Of course your involved, too! Why would I expect the infamous duo to be causing trouble solo?"

"Fukayna, we're looking King Ahmed. I'm afraid it's an emergency, or else we would have waited until morning. Is there any way you may be able to direct us for an audience with your high priest tonight?"

When Fukayna deliberated the request, Liv added another, "It's urgent."

Fukayna studied both Pure King and Elite, tapping her foot beneath her black linen layers. Finally, she rolled her eyes and sighed, "Follow me."

She quickly led them across the library, looking both ways and behind her for any additional onlookers before pulling a curtain aside, revealing a bolted door.

Fukayna lifted her hand, revealing tattooed hieroglyphics as she brushed her palm in front of the lock, allowing the door to click open and reveal another stunning hallway, filled with golden plates, tall Roman archways and intricate marble flooring.

Perhaps the security system used by the Royal Egyptians was not all that different from the ones implemented by the Royal Pures.

The private quarters of the palace involved a long hallway, with many locked doors that ventured into unknown rooms. Finally, they reached the end, where Fukayna knocked twice and murmured, "Iinaha alalihat alsarifatu. Yagulun 'anah 'amr milahun," before stepping aside.

"Let them in." Ahmed called back.

Dutifully, Fukayna again raised her hand in front of the door, unlocking it with the swift flick of her wrist.

"I hope all is alright-" Ahmed began politely while standing at his desk, before he caught a glimpse of Liv and his demeanor dropped to worry. "What is wrong?"

"It's Puerdios." Liv cried; her outburst unintentional.

But now that they had finally made progress, the small accomplishment let her breathe, relinquishing all the stubborn strength she had saved for finding the Egyptian King.

Ahmed ran over to Liv, consoling her immediately with a hug. He looked up to Hayden for more information.

"We received a plea from our friend. It was weak but the message we both received was that she needs our help because Puerdios is in danger."

"You're requesting to go back." Ahmed interpreted.

"Puerdios needs us." Liv begged, taking a step back and composing herself. "We promise to return, if that needs to be a condition for our temporary release..."

"We'll return either way, as we still need to finalize the discussion of our alliance." Hayden calmly chimed in.

Ahmed looked to Hayden and then to Liv, trying to assess whether or not to trust the two. "Liv, may I speak with you? Alone?"

"If you need me to stay, I will. You said Hayden could leave at any time." Liv was sobbing, but she didn't care. "But, I promise I'll return if you let me go..."

"Shh..." Ahmed hushed Liv, looking to Hayden to honor his request. Hayden understood and walked back to the hallway with Fukayna, giving King Ahmed and Liv privacy.

When the door finally closed, Liv whipped around, staring at the empty room; her heart began pounding and she started breathing heavily at the sight of Hayden gone.

"No, wait... I need him..." She cried, running toward the door.

"Liv, I'm letting you leave with him." Ahmed whispered, "I only wish to show you how."

Liv's eyes finally left the door. She turned her body slowly, now facing the warm study and absorbing all of its greatness that she hadn't noticed earlier, when her surroundings had been a blur.

A robust fire blazed in the center of the mahogancy-carved wall, with a renaissance portrait painted above. Rococo detailing richly warmed the ambiance, with minimal hints to any Egyptian heritage. A cream rug spread across the wooden floor, pulling in the cherry brown hues of the leather couch and chairs, perfectly adding a touch of homeliness in contrast to the Tiffany lamp and robust desk. It was a study of a scholar, a refined historian, honest and designed with genuine care – one with taste and appreciation for the arts and culture. It was entirely Ahmed.

"If we're going to be equals, Liv. I want to treat you as one. Not as some hostage being held against her will." Ahmed explained, walking over to her and reaching out his hand.

She took it and followed him to the large leather couch, behind it a large map of Egypt and shelves filled with treasures an archeologist could only dream of discovering – classic renditions of books and rare artifacts spanning what looked like centuries.

"I had only hoped Hayden would have been willing to depart and allow you the opportunity to negotiate, so he could protect his people instead of remaining away."

He grabbed a box from behind her, inadvertently placing his face only inches from hers. He paused and looked down to her lips, considering a next move, but eventually blinked out of it and handed her the box instead.

"Open it." He insisted.

Liv clicked the box open, finding a solid gold bangle with what looked to be hieroglyphics, carved in shapes just like the tattooed ones Fukayna used to enter his private quarters.

"It's beautiful." Liv admired, dumbfounded and confused.

"May I?" Ahmed gestured toward the braclet.

"Of course." Liv handed the box back to him, hoping he would guide the reason for giving her a bracelet that would allow access to his private quarters, and praying it wasn't another ploy to advance their relationship.

He pointed to a set of hieroglyphics.

"Recognize these?"

Liv used a flicker of her light power to cast it on the bracelet, revealing the symbols that had beckoned her to the Afterworld when they appeared on the Pyramid of Giza.

She nodded, still intrigued.

"Join me in the afterlife with these words," Ahmed interpreted, spinning the bracelet to the other side, pointing to another set of hieroglyphics. "Return to the living with these words."

He slid the bracelet over Liv's hand and onto her wrist, the same that bore her own bracelet and crest, so the two tapped together.

"With these codes, you may move freely between the worlds, my bride."

Liv gulped at the words, instead focusing on the key to escaping. His hand still clasped her own.

"You must protect what is important while you can." Ahmed advised.

This was the moment. If she were going to truly pursue tricking the kind king into a fake alliance, she would need to kiss him now to secure it. The time had come. His head was only inches from hers and as soon as she looked up at him, their lips would be significantly closer and within a touching range.

And yet, she could not deceive him a moment longer. Even if it meant the possibility of relinquishing her freedom to leave. If he were true to the deity he had shared with her over the past few days, he would still let her go and consider the alliance.

And if he turned out to be a monster, well at least it would be revealed with her dignity still intact.

"Ahmed, I'm sorry, but I can't marry you." Liv whispered, looking up to him sadly as she simultaneously pulled away.

"Are you sure?" Ahmed pressed, leaning back into the couch, creating more space between them. Exponential distance compared to where their bodies connected nearly moments before.

"I would never be faithful to you." Liv shrugged.

"I had hoped, overtime…" Ahmed pressed.

Liv shook her head slowly. "It will always be him."

Him.

Always.

Liv smiled at the notion, knowing that whatever obstacles they faced, nothing would deter her adoration, loyalty and love to the deity who stood outside the door, patiently waiting for her.

Waiting for her, always.

"You know what this means?" Ahmed asked.

"Of course." Liv nodded, pulling off the bracelet.

"No. Keep it. You will need it for your return to protect Puerdios." Ahmed gently grabbed her hand, preventing her from releasing her key to freedom back into his power. "And if you change your mind, we can reconsider the alliance then."

Liv wished this wasn't how it was going to end.

"We were once allies, when Alexander the Great united our kind and its people as one. Egypt prospered during the Ptolemaic dynasty…" Liv pleaded.

"He conquered us." Ahmed replied tersely, darkness clouding his eyes. "It was not an alliance."

The fear Ahmed had alluded to was ever present now. Liv's proud declaration of always choosing Hayden, their power, now felt more prominent to Ahmed's concerns. He did not want to fall again to a Greek dynasty. Liv understood that. She, like him, did not want to fall to another conqueror either.

"If you change your mind and want to help us defeat our own Greek conqueror, Kronos, know that your sacrifice and choice will not be forgotten by King Hayden, myself, nor anyone who shall benefit from our future reign." Liv stated, standing herself up and bowing. "Thank you for your kind hospitality, Ahmed. I'm fortunate and glad to have left Egypt with a new friend."

Ahmed stood as well, pulling Liv into a hug.

"Friends don't bow to one another, Liv. They hug."

Liv smiled at the notion, finding amicable comfort in his embrace.

But then Ahmed ruined the moment, continuing with a joking speculation, "Seriously, what kind of friends do you have, Liv? Those who do not allow you to hug them? It makes me wonder who you consider a friend. Is this really a terrible revelation that you have no friends? This is very sad to hear, Liv..."

Liv shook her head, before pushing Ahmed away by hitting his chest.

"Maybe we aren't friends, after all." She raised her hands up in the air in a mocking manner, but could not contain her grin.

"Safe travels, Liv."

"Change your mind, Ahmed."

With that, Liv strutted out of the private royal quarters, swore she heard the high priest smirk with amused impress behind her, and greeted Hayden with a kiss before grabbing his hand and began whistling for Phix to take them to the Crystal Mountain.

PIPER

"My brother supported Shiva, and together they conspired with the Kadava tribe to kidnap me, holding me hostage long enough for Shiva to come in privately and curse me." King Raj explained while quietly sipping his pho in the hotel suite. "My brother must have succeeded my reign and inherited the throne."

Raj had slowly warmed up to Piper and Tristan once he was struck with the reality of the modern world and presented a safe accomodation rightfully fit for the king he was (even if the title beared no weight or influence in present day). But most of all, he opened up to Piper and Tristan because they were the only two who believed his story and understood his predicament.

"I'm not sure if this is good news or bad news," Piper pulled out her research from Bangkok on the Chola family, dreading the information she would need to report. "Although the Chola dynasty was one of the longest ruling dynasties in the mortal world's history, the end of the 13th century and during your brother's rule marked the end of their reign."

Piper gently placed the notes on the table for Raj to keep, read and digest in his own time.

Raj put down his spoon and stared at the typed text, his brows furrowing as he demanded, "How did it happen?"

Piper's insides were trembling, she hated that her knowledge was causing another pain. She just hoped that inevitably these details would help Raj heal and move on.

"The Pandyas defeated both the Hoysalas and Cholas, and at the close of Rajendra's reign, the Pandyan empire was at the height of prosperity." Piper struggled to continue, almost mumbling the next words before pausing and forcing herself to speak clearly, even if her voice was mousier than usual. "The last recorded date of Rajenda III is 1279 – but there is no evidence that Rajendra was killed nor succeeded immediately by another Chola prince. It's almost as if he disappeared."

Raj's hands tightened into fists, before he stood up and turned his back to Piper and Tristan.

Tristan eyed Piper suspiciously but did not dare move or make a sarcastic comment to break the tension in the room.

"He fled to live among the gods, possibly even to Shiva for protection, to continue future destruction." Raj stated tersely, turning back to Piper and Tristan with a rage filled beneath his sorrow.

For all that was lost with no punishment.

It was time to bring the last known & existing King of the Cholas up to speed with the impending war between the modern deities.

"Raj, there is going to be a war." Piper began explaining, keeping her voice level and calm, although she constantly combatted against her pounding heart. "Our maker, Kronos, has returned from the Underworld and he's building an army of darkness to take over control of mortals and the gods who protect them."

"If darkness is involved, Shiva will not be far from that cause." Raj responded intuitively, no longer fazed by the new reality he existed in.

"We've already allied with King Rāhula and Queen Chanthira, releasing them from Shiva's curse and allowing them to return to this world with the promise of joining our side." Piper explained.

After Piper and Tristan further detailed their encounter with the Buddhist deities and an overview of the Dark God War, Piper finally asked, "Do you think it possible that the Hindu Gods would support our cause?"

Raj contemplated the ask but shrugged, "I would not dare seek out Shiva after meddling with his games. I think King Rāhula gave you the best advice, to anticipate making an enemy after releasing the Buddhist Gods against the Hindu. He will rally his armies and conspire with Kronos."

Piper and Tristan turned to eachother with dread. Another conversation for another time, but if releasing King Rāhula and Queen Chanthira only brought more enemies to the warfront, were they really helping the Pure God's cause?

Instead, Piper chose to try and make an ally with who they had in the flesh – a seven-headed snake certainly could help shift the outcome in war, especially if another was to accompany Shiva on the battlefield.

"Will *you* support the Pure Gods?" Piper asked, before adding, "Seek out any remaining deities who oppose Shiva's rule?"

Raj laughed darkly, "That is quite a bold request for an old mortal."

"You owe us." Tristan reminded the man, "We released you from Shiva's curse – gave you control of your body and shifting form after seven hundred years! The least you could do is take us up on the offer for revenge."

"Should we not let karma do the work?" Raj asked genuinely.

That response clearly took Tristan by surprise, he paused for a moment to blink before composing himself in a timely manner to deliver his sarcastic retort. "If all goes according to plan, we'll be the ones serving up karma for all who wronged the mortals and good deities. You're welcome to join the slaughter."

"Tristan!" Piper squealed, her eyes wide.

Tristan laughed, his eyes dazzling with amusement, clearly impressed he could still push Piper's recently cooler and calmer buttons.

Before giving him the full gravitas of impress, Piper turned back to Raj, and concluded, "You've had a long day. We'll leave you to rest – feel free to read more of our research or put on some relaxing television – the soap operas are personally quite entertain…" She paused, unsure she had the energy or time to explain what a television was to this ancient man. It would be like explaining using data to predict the future to Daphne… so instead, Piper smiled, grabbed Tristan and pulled her amused friend to the other room, concluding her farewell speech with a vague, "We'll leave you to it. Good night." and slammed the door.

Leaning against the door, Piper closed her eyes and sighed. She was certainly exhausted and mentally drained from the trip. Only a faint smirk made her open one eye and glare at the other deity in the room.

His smile was infectious, but made her chuckle and then groan.

"Ugh, don't make me laugh. Seriously, what are we going to do?" Piper moaned, finally propelling herself from the wall and using the momentum to land directly on the plush bed. Head first.

The cool silk comforter felt so soothing against her skin, she wanted to sink and lay in this bed for eternity. Impending war be damned.

An unusual contemplative silence forced one eye to open; Piper glared at her counterpart until he finally realized she wasn't asking a rhetorical question.

Astounded, Tristan replied to the accusation defensively. "You think I know?"

Piper sighed, rolling over onto her back. She knew it was going to be an arduous journey, but she hadn't expected it to be *this* tough.

"Releasing King Rāhula and Queen Thira would still give us more allies." She pondered aloud, "Is it worth gambling a secured alliance strictly in fear of the possibility it would create more enemies?"

Tristan contemplated the idea, mindlessly rolling a fireball across his knuckles as he responded, "If all that Raj mentioned proves true, you and I both know it won't actually help our cause, and without knowing Shiva's numbers, could hurt it even more. The real question is, do we really trust Raj, *the freaking Naga*, after knowing him for what? A second?"

"That's valid." Piper agreed, biting her lip. But, as she responded to Tristan's latest question, she already felt one scale weighing down heavier than the other toward her decision. "If he's trustworthy, we know the cards we've been dealt, and we'll play with them accordingly. If he's lying, then, well, it works in our favor. But ultimately, none of this is worth debating further, because we have to do what's right. If we don't give their people freedom, then what do we even stand for as Pure Gods?"

"Playing devil's advocate, since Hades didn't want to join the party tonight," Tristan said dryly, extinguishing his flame and sitting up. "If Raj is correct, do we really want to start *another* war with *another* set of ancient deities?"

Piper sunk, it was too much. She was in no way equipped to make decisions on *this* scale. She needed Hayden and Liv, or Peyton and Rei.

But her friends turned into muses and at the thought of them, a sense of determination, courage and strength set in. Piper clenched her jaw, staring at the ground before her.

"We follow what *we* believe in. Nobody intimidates us to succumb to their cruel intentions. That's what we fight for. Liv, Hayden, Rei, Peyton, Dylan, Kai, Zayne – all of them would do the same."

She turned shyly to Tristan, hoping to gauge his response. If he didn't agree now, she wasn't sure she would be able to declare the same decision again.

He rolled his eyes, "I hate when you're right and being all selfless. But right you are, nonetheless. And besides, between everything we've done in these lands, we're probably cursed now anyways, so why not just add to the list and cement it against Shiva, shall we?"

A darkness lingered in his attempt at lighthearted sarcasm. But that's how they would need to think if they were every going to outplay the kings of evil.

If they were cursed, then they'd make sin a pleasure, as if it were a game.

It was time to gamble, play the cards dealt, and do everything they could to get a royal flush, or bluff their way through it until the end.

THIRTY-FIVE

PIPER

The next morning, Piper woke up feeling heavy. She had convinced Tristan they needed to have faith in Raj, but where she saw a promising full glass, Tristan only saw drops in an empty one.

They found Raj looking like an entirely new man, now showered and in clean silk robes. He looked regal, strong and brave – as if the new sunlight removed a casted shadow to reveal his former self and shed seven hundred years of dead skin.

"Hello divine entities." He smiled, revealing dazzling teeth that looked beautifully bright and sharp. "Just in time, I ordered fruit, Num Banh Chok, Nom Kong and coffee."

Excitedly, he walked over to a table, revealing a large spread of enticing looking dishes, and more importantly, three mugs of dark liquid gold.

"Thank you, Raj." Piper smiled shyly.

She had no reason to flirt, but the unexpected transition from rescued-victim to charming-king-with-a-dark-side made Raj seem excitingly dangerous and extremely attractive. He was *part snake* for crying out loud. Besides, it was harmless, right?

She almost justified it because he was a mortal, and then internally slapped her mind for thinking that way. Him being mortal didn't justify any distinction in treating him differently than her immortal peers.

"Really, it's the least I could do." Raj offered, pulling out a chair for Piper to sit before sitting down himself.

The green silk of his new outfit complemented his stunning olive skintone; Piper suddenly felt inadequate for wearing the exact same dress as the day before. She smiled again, tucking some hair behind her ear, willing herself to speak before intimidating silence took over her body forever.

"We hope you've had some time to consider our proposals from last night?" Tristan interjected, clearly unamused with Raj and Piper's lighthearted banter.

Or so Piper liked to believe, in spite of being aware it hadn't actually taken place, yet.

"Ah, yes. That." Raj nodded, setting down a bowl of dragonfruit. "I didn't realize we'd address that so quickly."

His tone was polite, albeit disappointed.

It was crueler than yelling, Piper concluded, squirming in her chair for his response, nonetheless.

"I have had time to consider your request," Raj began sternly, "And for releasing me of the bonded curse, I offer you my support. How can I be of service?"

He did not seem excited or willing; he returned his response with as much directness as the request was served, clearly his offer was only because Raj was a man of honor.

"Are you sure?" Piper whispered, in awe.

When Raj looked in her direction, he softened.

"You both are my only two friends, and I would be a terrible friend to leave you in the dust after all that you have done for me."

"But we're asking you to potentially go against Shiva." Piper reiterated, ignoring Tristan's scowls and gentle taps from under the table.

"You forget there are other deities, possibly even more powerful than Shiva." Raj clarified, "We may not be lost to him, yet."

"Will you be able to find them? Any gods who may be loyal to our cause?" Tristan speculated, finally intrigued with the King.

"Vishnu is the preserver and guardian of humans; he protects the order of things." Raj explained, "He once was a friend, too. I will look for Vishnu, for he may be my only hope in finding a safe connection to them."

At the mention of Vishnu, Piper remembered a prominent third deity.

"What about Brahma?" She asked optimistically.

Raj's face darkened; Piper knew she had asked the wrong question.

"If Shiva is involved somehow with Kronos, and if the Soulless are truly reincarted vessels, I worry that Brahma is cursed by Shiva too and that he is abusing his control over him. Creating something for the first time is a natural power, but recreating something that has been destroyed is a cursed power that could only be forged with darkness."

Raj's words gave Piper chills, she shivered and rubbed her arms instinctively, yet remained cold.

Softly, a warm hand placed itself on her shoulder, sending sparks of flames through her veins. Piper turned to find caramel eyes casting light into her soul, forever grateful for her eternal flame.

"Now, I must leave." Raj concluded, standing up immediately.

"What? Now!?" Piper questioned, still wrapping her head around everything they had just discussed.

Without thinking, she mirrored both the king and Tristan's actions, now also standing as if she were ready to leave, too.

"There's nothing more to discuss." Raj concluded, nodding to his new acquaintances. "We have rested and determined our marching orders, so now, we're simply playing with borrowed time. Shiva will soon realize a curse of his has been broken. You need to make sure you break another before he does. It's time to leave."

"I'm starting to like this guy." Tristan smirked.

"Well, be safe!" Piper squeaked, "Remember, it's 37-35 – er," Piper quickly did the math again, "2017 A.D. Try to blend in. Get a cell phone… and…" She frantically looked around for a notepad, finally spotting one on the desk. She scribbled Liv's cell number and hoped her Elemental Elite kept it charged. "Call this number when you need to find us."

Raj studied the scribbled numbers, printing them to memory and reciting the 'code' (as he called it) aloud, before handing the paper back to Piper.

"As for blending in, I assure you, I'll be in my element." Raj smiled, his spectacular grin the only thing that remained the same as he instantaneously morphed into a seven-headed snake once again.

But this time, instead of being afraid, Piper remained calm. His eyes sparkled, an open vessel into his soul, and Piper knew he was in control.

"Until next time, King Raj." Piper bowed, in awe of this majestical creature.

Raj mirrored Piper's farewell, and then turned toward the window, shrinking into a reptile no bigger than a garden snake, and began his journey.

"Perhaps we should have mentioned modern transportation would be much quicker?" Tristan commented dryly, after the king had already departed.

Piper smirked, and then she shoved Tristan playfully and sat back down for her final sips of coffee, anticipating the next task at hand.

It was time to return the Emerald Buddha to Bangkok.

TRISTAN

The Emerald Buddha felt like a solid weight cast against him as he flew through the Thailand sky. How King Raj had carried the jewel for so many years without toppling over proved the mortal's strength could surpass that of a deity when in his monstruous form.

Piper had offered to carry the token, but Tristan refused. She had done so much, this was the least he could do as his friend continued to endure on depleted powers. A god wouldn't risk emptying their vessel to such an extent in one decade, and she had risked it all on almost a daily basis this week.

Yet, she didn't complain, and only offered how she could help *more*.

Piper was truly a force to be reckoned with. Tristan had already determined he would not want to go against her in battle when she first overcame the powers of Shiva in Bangkok. The inclination was cemeted when she defeated the ancient powers of Shiva again whilst battling a Naga.

So, as much as Piper offered to help Tristan, it was truly he who was assisting her. She was the hero of this adventure. And he continued to grow even more amazed everytime she surpassed his ever-increasing expectations.

By the time they arrived in Bangkok, stopped by Tristan's apartment and changed clothes, the sun was setting. Again, the two would need to break into Wat Phra Kaew in the night, undetected, and hopefully release an army of deities this time.

When Piper walked out in her new outfit, Tristan almost spit out his whiskey. The goddess had the nerve to walk out in a black velvet blazer and trouser pant, but the top underneath was completely sheer, aside from an intricately woven black snake that covered only the bare minimum of her front side.

"You're going out in that?" Tristan spat.

Piper shrugged, completely unaware of his hunger. "It's the darkest thing I packed for our night adventure."

"And the... snake?" Tristan gulped.

Piper smirked, "It was a hilarious coincidence. Couldn't resist."

Oh Zeus, he was in such hot shit.

Fighting the nerve to offer her his tartan-printed woolen scarf and leather jacket off his own body while combating sneaking glances at her pearly, iridescent skin, Tristan instead declared it was time to depart, slamming his glass snifter against the harsh marble counter and then stomping out.

They had followed the same gameplan as before, its previous success ringing true as they once again found themselves in the darkened room of the mesmerizing emerald statue.

So, while Piper murmured "kalo," Tristan launched the true emerald Buddha to deliver it to its rightful place.

The sound was so quiet that Tristan heard the velvet brush against itself as Piper dropped her arm to her side, clutching the cursed Buddha in hand.

"You didn't look at it?" Tristan confirmed, his mind spinning as he mentally checked to make sure nothing else shifted in the room that stood still in time.

Piper's body remained a statue, only her head shook to confirm she hadn't. Her hand still clenched the curse, and possibly a whole world, within her hand.

After minutes of silence, finally Piper squeaked, "Perhaps they aren't aware...?"

"Do we go through the cursed vessel and carry the original Buddha, or attempt to go through the authentic Buddha and hold the cursed one?" Tristan questioned aloud.

He hadn't taken any classes on ancient curses at Puerdios yet, so he was entirely lost with this next step. A predicament he very much did *not* like to be in.

"I vote the uncursed path?" Piper suggested, staring blankly at the ground.

It was infinitively harder discussing an object when one wasn't allowed to glance at it until a decision had been made.

"Although leaving the true emerald Buddha here undefended and unsupervised seems illogical. Can we place a protection spell on it or can we figure out a way to bring it with us for safe keeping?"

"Wait, what?" Tristan questioned, shaking his head and starting over. "We were able to transit through the cursed Buddha before," he reasoned, "and King Rāhula said they overpowered the curse with the true Emerald Buddha... so I vote the tried-and-true, safe keeping route?"

Having duplicate Buddhas was certainly confusing, but fortunately Piper was brilliant and understood his convoluted plan immediately. At least, she seemed to register what Tristan *believed* they had mutually decided on.

"Roger that." Piper nodded, "So you'll be the 'kalo' to my 'recta'?"

She teased lightheartedly but didn't shift her mood. She was already standing, preparing to cast her next spell in tandem with Tristan.

"On the count of three…" Tristan explained. "One, two, three!"

She directed the cursed Emerald Buddha back to its tainted position. Tristan summoned the authentic statue into his grasp, and after a quick catch of the other's eyes, they both shifted their vision to the curse, meeting it head on.

First, they saw green. Then the world went black, again.

LIV

When Hayden and she first departed Puerdios, the unknown had been daunting. Now that they were heading back to their home, the transit in itself felt all the more unnerving. They were still entering into an unprecented time, but now the uncertainty was personal. The stakes were higher and so, Liv was more overwhelmed.

"We'll talk to Joss, Rei and Peyton. We'll figure out a plan, Ollie." Hayden assured her mid-flight.

"If they're even reachable." Liv quipped back darkly. "And Piper and Tristan? Who knows where any of them are?"

She wanted to cry. But alas, she had already cried enough this season. She needed to save some water for April's necessary showers.

Liv had been so focused on their individual mission, she had barely even thought about her friends and their possible predicaments. It had taken a hail mary prayer from Dylan to force Liv to even think about and consider her people. And now that she had, yes, she worried for her friends but at the cost of still needing something from them all the same.

The guilt was the most unbearable.

"Peyton, Rei and Jocelyn are reachable. I've summoned them to Puerdios." Hayden added kindly, but sternly.

Liv appreciated his sincerity, but even the distance between the two of them remained. So much had transpired in Egypt, they hadn't had a moment to dissect and discuss any of it.

If Hayden and Liv continued marching so fiercly, they were sure to misstep soon.

"I'm trying to get ahold of Piper and Tristan but it's silent." Liv replied with a tremble, as if saying it aloud confirmed her specualtion as fact.

"Think about how long it took us to discover the Egyptian Gods, Liv." Hayden consoled, "And we're the King and Elemental Elite of the Pure Gods. We cannot expect they would complete their task before us."

"What if they're in danger, Hayden!?" Liv cried, flashes of shadows and emerald green attacking her membrane, hissing dark thoughts that would forever live caged in her blackened cell within, a symbolic representation of the hellish reality she had existed in for weeks.

"When a considerable amount of time passes to confirm the case, we'll pursue it then. Until that happens, you can only try to continue reaching them." Hayden advised, firmly looking ahead, his gaze unyielding as a familiar stone castle appeared among the mountains.

Puerdios University.

PIPER

"They've returned!"

Piper had not gathered the energy to open her eyes, but she could hear bustling and excited chatter, and imagined the majestic red and gold grand ballroom entrance once again conglomerate with curious deities.

Oh dear Zeus, please make sure my snakes are sufficiently covering my front side.

Piper tried to move her arm, groaning with agony at how foolish her once amusing joke turned out to be.

"Pipes?"

A soft whisper accompanied a warm hand touching her cold arm.

"Yes?" She mumbled, a flute without air.

She heard a relieved breath, but the hand did not retract.

With coughs and the energy condensing to polite intrigue, paired with a shuffling of shoes, hearing King Rāhula greet them did not surprise Piper in the slightest.

Unwillingly, she sat up and opened her eyes to address her royal hosts.

In a swift movement, Tristan soon hovered over her, his hand no longer on her arm but instead extended in front of her. She wondered if he felt as terrible as she and applauded him for his fortress act.

"Thanks," Piper said quietly, standing upright and immediately checking her chest, relief swarming her core when she confirmed her blazer now covered any indelicacies.

"We were able to retrive the Emerald Buddha." Tristan answered the unasked question proudly, prompting Piper to enlarge and hand it over to its rightful owners.

In a stunning gold and navy gown, Queen Chanthira stepped forward, her eyes opened wide and with a smile so genuine that it lifted her face. After one blink, a single tear rolled down her cheek.

King Rāhula was equally speechless, his hope having been at an all time high, but clearly refusing to acknowledge the confirmation in order to eliminate the risk of being let down again.

"Here." Piper offered, extending the true Emerald Buddha to the King.

King Rāhula gently placed his hands on the statue, accepting the offer. As soon as his skin touched stone, a light infiltrated his soul and his eyes inflamed a deep jade. Instantly, his suit transformed from grey to forest green, all power encompassing his being.

"It is true." He breathed in surprise.

The king turned to his queen, joining the silent happiness of his wife by pulling her into a warm embrace and lifting her off the ground. Piper believed she witnessed a small tear grace his cheek from the discovered joy.

The room blinked closed and smoothly transitioned back to the mortal world, with King Rāhula, Queen Chanthira and their subjects standing alongside Piper and Tristan in the temple of Wat Phra Kaew and surrounding Grand Palace grounds.

"That was a much more enjoyable trip." Piper softly joked to Tristan, lighting up when his grin matched hers.

They both turned to the royal couple, anxious to hear their next steps.

"Thank you, Piper and Tristan of the Pure Gods." King Rāhula nodded, eyeing the cursed Buddha warily from the corner of his eyes. "If you will give us some time to rebuild, we will join your cause as allies, as promised, whenever you need our service."

Piper beamed, "No need to thank us, sir. We are equally grateful for your alliance." She too, eyed the evil Emerald Buddha, like a parasite waiting to attack its next victim. "What will come of Shiva's Buddha?"

Queen Chanthira quivered, taking a step closer to King Rāhula with the authentic vessel of power.

"It will remain here, while we take the true Buddha with us to Chang Mai." King Rāhula explained with a devious grin, "Let Shiva believe we are still trapped – if he thinks something is awry, he will check here first. Best make our release a bit of a surprise, shall we?"

Queen Chanthira chuckled at the rebellious comment, bringing light from the sunrise into the dark temple with her laughter. She grabbed her husband's hand and added happily, "So long as we have control of the real one, we shall forever have control of our destiny."

"Very right, my love." King Rāhula agreed, giving his wife a genuine smile – what would certainly have been a kiss if the two weren't in public.

However, Piper did not have long to admire the adoring sovereigns, for an unexpected tug pounded against her heart, causing her to drop against the ground. She was too weak from the past few days, the mere will to stay put was making her sick.

Tristan clasped his chest as well.

"You feel it too?" Piper whispered, clawing to the ground. She could not combat the summoning much longer and soon expected to be dragged along the floor.

Tristan looked out of the temple, his expression confirming Piper's existing worry.

He grabbed Piper's hand again, lifting her up and wrapping her arms around him as a base. Piper didn't have anything left to fight, instead succumbing to his hold and pressing all of her weight against his anchor.

"Liv is calling for us. We must go." He whispered, before turning to King Rāhula and Queen Chanthira and addressing them properly. "We are being summoned by our Elite, but we will see eachother soon. Until then."

He nodded to his peers, an uncommunicated blessing directed to all who stood before him.

"Until then, indeed." King Rāhula agreed, but spoke quickly. "Go. We will follow you and fulfill our promise. If you need us – we'll be discoverable on the Monk's Trail."

Queen Chanthira nodded, adding, "Travel confidently knowing you have friends in Thailand for your cause."

With one last smile, Tristan shot out of the temple and into the glowing morning sky, Piper nestled in his arms.

They were going home.

PART THREE

THIRTY-SIX

LIV

Her fingers touched the cool granite counter, walking toward the leather couches and assessing the empty fireplace. Her head turned slowly to the only sound in the empty space, echoed footsteps running down the stairs belonging to Hayden after having checked the security parameters of his loft. In the distance, she spotted the Jackson Pollock painting that once made her envious, further distinguishing a memory of the past now combatting the present.

So much had changed, yet so much had remained the same, a prime example of what she once considered home, abandoned and lost in the past.

"It's so quiet in here." Liv murmured with a shiver, sighing as she stepped away from the counter before meeting Hayden halfway in the kitchen.

Her soul sought life like a parasite, attaching herself to Hayden for assurance.

"You once enjoyed the quiet." Hayden recalled, casting his powers to spark a roaring fire to solve the issues at present, both proclaimed and unspoken.

"Tea?" Hayden offered, turning on the stovetop.

"Yes, please." Liv smiled weakly, albeit still worried.

"Peyton and Rei are on their way. You've reached Piper and Tristan who are now en route. There's only fifteen degrees left in Study Hall and soon Dylan, Kyril and Zayne will be on their way. The group is back together, Liv. There's nothing to worry about."

"Except Puerdios University. Our home, Hayden." Liv reiterated. "Arlo realized he cannot break us, so now he chooses to target something dear to our hearts. Will it ever stop?"

"The darkness?" Hayden clarified.

Liv nodded. Hayden sighed, combing his hand through his golden locks. The kettle started whistling.

He hesitated at first but chose to turn and pour the steaming water into two mugs, returning to Liv by giving her one along with his response.

"There will always be darkness, Liv. We can't control everything – night will always come. But I think as long as we have something good, something worth fighting for, then we'll be able to face the darkness together and come out whole, eventually. The key is to never stop fighting. Never stop seeing the light."

Liv nodded again, taking a sip of her chai tea when no words surfaced.

"I'm surprised you aren't more excited to see your friends?" Hayden asked softly, finally sitting beside her and wrapping his strong arm around her shoulders, and then pulled her in and kissed her head gently. His soft grey cashmere felt soothing against her skin, as if he was still innocent as a newborn and her skin had scales of a serpent.

"I am, of course." Liv mumbled, staring at her tea. "I just hope they have better news than we came back with."

"You received a proposal! How is that not lovely news?" Hayden dryly joked.

Liv smirked, instantly easing at the dark humor.

"By the wrong deity!" She shoved Hayden playfully, before giggling and catching her breath, calming down simultaneously. After a subtle pause, Liv still couldn't contain her amusement from the insanity of it all.

"Can you even *believe?*" Liv rolled her eyes, grinning. "What if Piper comes back and she's actually engaged to Buddha himself? Peyton's married to Thor?"

"That Peyton has always been a one-upper. I'd be shocked if she *didn't* come back betrothed." Hayden teased.

"I guess you make a good point," Liv smiled softly, kissing Hayden on the cheek in gratitude as she got up to refill her mug. "If this is the story we have to divulge, I can't wait to hear the tales the others must have."

DEMETRIUS

The fact he was knocking on the wooden barricade still rendered him in disbelief.

Somehow, his idiotic mind had convinced him that since the royal palace was essentially on his way from Jupiter to South Africa, having to get to earth eventually, either way – the only right thing to do was to stop by and ask Jocelyn again to assist him in finding the Orishas.

He had given her a few days to strategize with her mother about the visions she saw. Therefore, by now Joss may have reconsidered the opportunity to strengthen the Pure Gods' and his cause against Danu, Kronos, Arlo… and any additional enemy she probably had made since leaving his residence so abruptly.

So, he had put on his finest suit and suede coat and hoped the woman who captured his heart may have changed her mind. May have chosen him.

The doors opened and Demetrius entered the Pure God Palace; however, before he could declare his arrival to a butler and request Jocelyn's attention, Demetrius was surprised to find Daphne and Hades openly in the parlour.

"Demetrius, we were expecting you." Daphne welcomed him warmly, walking toward him with open arms. Demetrius looked behind him and cast a dream-breaking spell, to ensure the Queen's greeting truly existed in reality.

"You seem rather pleasant considering your academy for the Pure Deities is in peril?" Demetrius questioned while he accepted her unsettling hug.

Unlike Jocelyn, who was warm, small and adorable, Daphne was tall, cold and uncomfortable, like hugging an ancient, weathered statue.

"Demetrius, you know better than to submit to my daughter's pre-emptive stress. Puerdios will not be attacked for at least a week. There is still time yet to celebrate my son's birthday and defend the university."

"Do you really think it worthwhile to throw an extravagant party amidst such chaos and divide?" Demetrius speculated, dismissing a maid who offered him whisky.

"Depends what you consider an extravagant party, I suppose." Daphne replied amusedly.

"Daphne, I don't have time for your cryptic musings." Hades cut in, unimpressed. "And from what you've told me, neither does Demetrius. Just tell the God what we need him to do."

"What? Have I not already done *enough*?!" Demetrius declared angrily. "I'm only here to see your daughter, nothing else." He turned and started walking out of the parlour.

"Wait." Daphne said softly, smoothing out her silk skirt.

Demetrius wished he didn't have to impress Daphne, but the sentiment, 'Possible future mother-in-law,' whispered in the back of his mind. If he wanted a chance with Joss, he would have to appease Daphne.

"We-" Daphne turned to Hades, who glared at her, so she corrected herself, "I..." Then she paused, starting completely over and with a touch of irritation. "It is pertinent that Liv celebrates Hayden's birthday."

"I thought we were working without cryptic messages?" Demetrius demanded; his eyebrow raised.

Clearly, this demand was giving Daphne a run for her money. As he learned from Joss, a simple word or rephrasing could cause a ripple effect of change. And Daphne was not used to partaking in the action of things.

Although, it was fun watching Daphne squirm, however stoically, for once in her life.

"Liv has plans, that she's currently debating on cancelling due to the impending battle at Puerdios University," Daphne explained. "Whether they celebrate or not will not change the outcome of the Puerdios battle. I have seen both play out. But, if they do not celebrate this weekend, it will cause the finite elimination of the Pure Gods. It will be our greatest demise."

With a short breath, Daphne returned to her demure self by concluding with a subtle nod, awaiting his response.

"How can I trust you?" Demetrius glared, staring both at Daphne and then Hades.

"Your anger resides with my daughter, do not take it out on me, Demetrius." Daphne snapped back.

"She's right."

Demetrius turned to find Jocelyn standing in the doorway, looking down at her hands.

"I have seen it, too." Jocelyn said quietly, finally looking up to meet his eyes. Although finely dressed in a tailored tweed jacket and skirt, she looked exhausted, with bags under eyes.

Her visions had not decreased.

He wanted to run to Joss, hold her in his arms and rock her to sleep, assuring her that all would be okay.

But then he heard Hades snicker and for all Demetrius knew, the three were conspiring together and had planned to play on his weakness. Another beat of his heart turned to stone. Besides, he had other responsibilities he needed to see to.

"Then why don't *you* tell your brother?" Demetrius sneered.

He didn't mean to sound so cruel when he addressed Jocelyn, really it was because he needed to make sure Hades would not consider him weak. He did not need another immortal threat on his kingdom.

Joss started crying and collapsed to the ground.

"If I tell… him… he'll know it's because of a vision and that knowledge shifts everything." She pleaded with Demetrius, "Please. It can only be you. And you can only work through Liv."

Zeus, he felt like a dick. A threatened dick.

"And you can't tell Liv?" Demetrius clarified, a little kinder, but still while restraining from pulling the woman he loved into his arms.

"Liv and I aren't on good terms. She trusts you." Jocelyn admitted, crying between words. She had dug her hole and now she was regrettably lying in it.

"So, to be clear, I am supposed to convince Liv and if needed, the king, along with his friends, to selfishly celebrate a birthday before an impending war, without any valid reason to do so?" Demetrius whaled, spinning back to Daphne and Hades for his wrath. "You know, this is exactly why everyone thinks *I'M INSANE.*"

"Precisely." Daphne nodded, "It can only be you."

Demetrius tsked.

"Demetrius, I wouldn't be down here, otherwise." Joss sobbed, "I don't know what else to do."

Demetrius paused at that revelation.

"Come with me." He demanded.

Jocelyn lifted her head, confused.

"I do this for you, then you must come with me and… hear me out."

Joss peered to Daphne, "Mother?"

Demetrius almost sighed then and there. *How did Daphne have Joss wrapped around her finger amd on such a tight rope?*

"It's fine, darling. Just be careful." Daphne smiled, sadly. "Enjoy these moments, while you can."

Demetrius almost lost focus as Jocelyn's demeanor shifted and she beamed to him, but before he fully shifted his attention to the petite blonde, he noticed that Daphne nodded contentedly to Hades, and the God of the Underworld mirrored a similar sentiment to the Candor Elite.

LIV

It was a beautiful sight, seeing all of her friends sitting on the couch or leisurely on the ground, in front of a warm, cozy fire.

Hearing the tales of all the deities discovered and met seemed like mythology was coming to life in the most surreal and overwhelming way. They were casually talking about Nagas, ancient curses, Shiva, Budda's son and now King – Rāhula, Thor and Vanaheim. All real, all intertwined in their present.

Liv snuggled closer to Hayden, wrapping the cozy wool blanket securely around her. Beside the marvelous stories, she had noticed a few things upon the return of her friends.

The first, Tristan's hesitation when Liv jumped into his arms for a hug. She had expected to receive nothing less than pure happiness at the reunion with her two best friend.

The second, Peyton's distance from Rei, who she typically synchronized with so fluidly it was as if she lived to try and lessen his rigid demeanor in a marvelous tango.

The third, with what Liv assumed to be a chemical reaction from Peyton's behavior, was that Rei grew even more terse and unamused with the charming banter taking place within their loft.

And finally, an observation that stung Liv the most, seeing Piper's subtle glare when she did greet Tristan, not entirely understanding why Piper harnessed such anger toward her friendship with the God of Fire.

But after so much time apart, Liv expected things would change. Although her friends had all grown apart over their time and experiences away, she hoped that they'd find their commonalities and come together once again. The question that remained was whether these changes would incur permanent behavior or if whatever had transpired could still be repaired.

The craziest of all, seemed not to be a battle against a seven-headed snake nor Liv's proposal from an Egyptian King, but an unexpected knock at the door, revealing Demetrius and Jocelyn.

To add onto the inordinary even further, the duo shared an outlandish update that neither involved their experiences with the dwindling Celtic Deities nor Demetrius's declaration that he might be facing an additional war against Danu. No, the craziest update was instead the God of Jupiter's insistence that they should continue to celebrate Hayden and Piper's birthday, as planned.

What made the least sense of all, was Demetrius insinuating that although he encouraged the party taking place, he wasn't planning on attending due to the personal and pressing matter of finding the Orishas. Soon, the insinuation transformed into affirmation.

Demetrius was always a peculiar character, but perhaps Liv's time apart from the deity had lowered her delusion of what to expect from such a flambuoyant immortal.

Everyone laughed it off, but throughout the night, Demetrius was unwilling to give up on his insistence, even dwindling down his stance to offer he would indeed partake in the festivities.

"Liv, you know I mean well, right?" Demetrius pressed, cornering her in the kitchen. "I wouldn't ask of this unless it was truly important."

"Demetrius, of course I trust you." Liv agreed, contemplating how she could navigate this request without committing to anything, at least before she discussed it privately with Hayden. "We just have to make sure we're not being selfish or naïve, take a look from every angle, before we decide to pursue such a… *reckless* act."

Liv stupidly paused before using the final descriptor and Demetrius saw right through it. His eyes narrowed and he tilted his head, raising his bourbon and pointing a finger accusingly to her.

"But it wouldn't be 'reckless,' because you've been planning this for quite some time?" Demetrius inquired suspiciously.

Shit.

Liv wished she hadn't turned to whiskey so early in the celebratory evening. She liked to believe she could keep up with the deities, being an Elite and soul mate to the King and all, but her half-mortal vessel always got the best of her when it came to alcohol consumption and competing with her friends' higher immortal tolerances.

"Of course, I've been planning the birthday celebration for my boyfriend and best friend, but it doesn't mean it has to happen before the war." Liv explained, trying to platonically suggest another way.

"But, what if it's the last time we could all be together to celebrate? We may be immortal, but that does not guarantee lives will remain in this realm."

"Okay, morbid." Liv tilted her head down and stared at Demetrius, scolding him and holding her position by crossing her arms.

"While you work with Rei and Hayden on the battle… let me help with planning. That's one less thing to worry about?" Demetrius offered, clearly trying to make up for his previous dark statement.

Liv considered it, and then spotted Jocelyn. "Joss!"

Hollering for her eventual future sister-in-law, Liv figured at least the Candor Elite could provide some honest reasoning to Demetrius's eccentric request.

"Do you know when Puerdios will be evaded?" Liv asked bluntly.

Joss had barely stepped into the kitchen. She froze, eyeing Demetrius for help.

"I'm trying Joss. You've got to help me." Demetrius raised both hands up in the air in surrender, his glittered suede coat sparkling with new beams of light hitting the fabric.

Liv's demanding question caught Hayden's attention, and soon the Pure God King had joined the triangular conversation, now balancing out the discussion to a square.

Jocelyn turned to Hayden and pleaded, "I'm not sure I should say anything. You must ask mother. I-I… I can't."

Jocelyn turned with a weep and headed to the door to exit, Demetrius only a few steps behind the goddess as they departed.

Hayden turned to Liv, the look on his face clearly stating the dreaded request he was about to make in asking what that all was about.

"He wouldn't drop the birthday celebration, Hayden. But the Gemini cycle is in four days and even if you don't want to celebrate your birthday, I promised Piper a birthday party – her first ever celebration – so, if we can confirm when the Dark Gods plan to evade, perhaps we could figure out a way to navigate through the darkness and create something to let us enjoy the good moments in between, like you said? Is that crazy?"

She had rambled, but her guilt combined with the stress and pressure, mixed with whiskey, removed her filter with him. Not that she needed one with Hayden, but the lack of filter was amplified in the moment, nevertheless.

Hayden smiled, sadly. "You drive a tough bargain, Monaco."

He put his arm around her and gave her a hug, kissing her temple softly.

"I'll summon my mother and we'll have a direct conversation with Daphne. I have a feeling she's involved with Demetrius's ploy to some extent."

"Can we trust her?" Liv lifted her head to meet his gaze.

"Still out with the jurors." Hayden sighed, kissing her temple. "But, at least, I'm glad to have you to deliberate with in the meantime."

"It is nice having someone to lean on during the chaos." Liv agreed, instinctively leaning into Hayden and wrapping her hands around his waist. "The true question is if I'll have that person to lean on during class tomorrow…"

Liv looked up mischievously, unable to contain the grin spreading across her face.

"I'll be back by the time Study Hall concludes." Hayden offered with a smug grin.

"Fair enough." Liv sighed, "I can't believe we're supposed to return to our studies as if we hadn't spent the weeks trying to build alliances, and we're still expected to take finals in two weeks?"

"Well, perhaps there's the silver lining if Puerdios gets taken over by Dark Gods." Hayden joked.

Liv swatted him at his indignance.

Hayden was saved from further scolding when his mother opened the door to the loft, sucking the noise in one breath as all guests turned directly to her in awe.

"You called for me?" Daphne ignored the stares and redirected them all to Hayden.

"Let me handle this," Hayden offered to Liv, pulling away from her.

"No, let me talk to her." Liv challenged. "It's your birthday. You shouldn't worry about planning it. Trust me?"

Hayden agreed, letting Liv address his mother head-on.

"Daphne, thank you for coming." Liv welcomed the queen dowager, "Can we chat in private on the patio?"

"Of course, my darling." Daphne smiled, following Liv outside, under the stars that twinkled brightly like her eyes.

"I'm sure you already know why you're here." Liv began, studying Daphne for any clues to her true thoughts, but alas, the Elite's stoic act remained thorough.

For one who wore all white, supported the Pure Gods and led the Candor pillar, it was damn challenging believing her intentions were true.

"I understand your distrust, Liv." Daphne responded swiftly. "I hope to earn your confidence in time. It pains me to see Liam's daughter skeptical of my loyalty."

"Until you give me reason to be skeptical, I will consider your advice as true. What concerns me is the information you choose to withhold." Liv knew she needed to be honest but wanted to keep the peace with her extended immortal family. "For example, why haven't you alerted us about Puerdios's impending war?"

"Ah, that." Daphne nodded her head once. "You have plans for my son's birthday, please know I approve, Liv." Daphne's eyes twinkled with understanding, before hesitating with her next words of advice. "For Puerdios's invasion, you have time. When you return, I will divulge specifics. At the moment, it is not concrete yet. Choices still need to be made."

"Okay." Liv eyed Daphne, trying to imprint her actions, facial expressions and words to memory. Later, she would report to Hayden and they could decide their course of action, together. "And if choices are made that affect the timeline…?"

"I believe Joss will enjoy partaking in the celebration of her brother's birthday," Daphne offered, "And be onsite should anything change. You may deliberate with her as you see fit."

"Thank you." Liv nodded, "We appreciate your support."

"Of course." Daphne smiled politely, "I am appreciative that you understand the predicament the Candor Pillar is in. But we honor the Pure God rule and will do our best to help navigate through the time of darkness."

With that, she delicately bowed, before extending her brilliant white wings, and cascaded into the sky, like an eagle preparing for its hunt.

Liv took a moment, releasing the tension from her body with a deep breath.

Her work was far from over tonight.

TRISTAN

He had forgotten how truly stunning Olivia Monaco was. When he had opened the heavy door into the royal loft, her thunderous aqua marine eyes caught his, making his fiery blaze freeze upon contact.

She dawned a sheer, silver-beaded gown, perfectly complementing her demure complexion, appearing effortless with her hair in a messy braid and essentially no makeup aside from a deep red lip, exemplifying Parisian glam at its finest. She had smiled, glowed with ecstacy at the sight of him, putting down her dram of whiskey and attacking him with an embrace.

Liv felt like home, after so long being a wanderer in an ancient, unfamiliar land.

Liv was certainly familiar, safe.

Tristan enjoyed being in her arms, until he remembered Piper and everything that they had been through. Although they had by no means defined that relationship, nor had he done anything wrong by hugging his best friend, he still felt guilty, like the interaction was wrong and disrespectful to Piper.

Perhaps it was. The action was innocent, but his intention related to it was harmful, unhealthy.

So, he stepped back, rigid. Building a much-needed boundary to divide the platonic and romantic between he and Liv. More so, for himself.

He knew Liv had chosen Hayden. They were *soul mates*, damnit. If he tried to pursue her, he would embark on a miserable, never winning chase, only to hurt him and all those around him in the process. Especially Piper.

Piper.

After she had hugged Liv, his and Piper's *best friend*, Piper's midnight, spiky bob turned, and her two blue fire opals gazed his way. Her eyes dazzled in assurance, equally brilliant. He didn't deserve her as a friend, especially anything that was defined as something more.

She shyly pulled her messy hair behind her ear, unintentionally showing more of her already exposed neck while wearing a stunning, strapless, tan corset gown with mismatched plaid prints grungily mixed together.

From then on, Tristan had done his best to ignore Liv, besides the larger group discussions that occasionally required a response, where he was safely sitting beside Piper on the floor, by the fire. Far away from the intoxicating scent of strawberry, violet, vanilla and jasmine that radiated from his Elite.

It wasn't even that he preferred that scent, although it was simply intoxicating. Truthfully, he preferred the subtle aroma of Piper – pomegranate, plum and rose with a hint of textbook ink.

But eventually, Tristan knew he could not avoid Liv forever. It was only a matter of time that the Element Elite would approach her advisor for safety precautions or implement a meeting with those who volunteered to provide counsel to Liv.

"Hey T." Liv smiled, finally sitting beside him once Piper had left him alone and defenseless to grab another glass of wine.

"Hi Elle." Tristan smiled, appreciating Liv's endless respect for the ever-changing nickname. It at least kept him on his toes.

"So, give me the real scoop on your adventures throughout Thailand and Cambodia." Liv murmured, her raspy, alto voice vibrating smoothly. "You and Piper?"

"Ah, that…" Tristan leaned forward to grab his whisky. "Is complicated and… frankly none of your business."

Liv laughed, nudging him. "Tease."

"You are literally her *best friend*. In any other case, I'm an open book. But come on, anything I tell you is essentially telling Piper, so I might as well skip the 'he-said, she-said' drama and go directly to Piper... not that there is anything to go to Piper directly *with*."

"Uh huh." Liv nodded slowly, unable to contain her growing grin.

"How about you? Pure King... Egyptian King... looks like dear Olivia is in a triangle *yet again*."

Liv smirked, rolling her eyes. "Ahmed is not a contender."

"Well, if the Pure Gods go under, you can always seek sanctuary with the Egyptian Gods and live happily ever after." Tristan pressed on. "Is he cute? Or is he like, old? How do Egyptian Gods age? He's got to be your great-great-great-grandfather's age, at least?"

Liv almost choked on her whiskey. "Ew, when you put it that way..."

"So, he does look like your great-great-great-grandfather?" Tristan's eyes grew wide.

"No!" Liv hit him playfully. "He looks like he could easily be a student here at Puerdios."

"Does he have a sister?"

Liv pushed Tristan again.

"Oh, come on, I'm only joking." Tristan rolled his eyes. "Apparently Egypt made you soft."

"Soft like sand, but beware when you start sinking." Liv retorted. "But yes, Ahmed does have a sister, Sabra. And she's a fierce, feisty and terrifying thing. So, if you're into Piper then I'm team Piper all. the. way."

Tristan huffed as he watched his Element Elite pump her first in support.

"You're insufferable. How did I get into a predicament where I work for you, again?"

"My infectious charm." Liv grinned sweetly, placing her hands beneath her chin cherubically.

"Oh yes, due to the lack of it." Tristan replied, not missing a beat.

He missed this banter. He missed his friend. He was stupid to have all of his impure thoughts and demons twisting his perspective. Liv was his friend, his Elite, and he needed to accept that was it.

And not feel pain from simply enjoying it.

"Okay, so on a less fun topic…" Liv sighed, "Let's plan to visit the Elements Pillar Thursday before we celebrate our Taurus and Gemini friends this weekend. Can you schedule a meeting with the board an hour after study hall?"

"Wait, wait, wait. You're planning to celebrate this weekend?" Tristan's eyes went wide.

"Apparently, Demetrius is quite persuasive." Liv replied swiftly, although not convincingly.

"Okay. We're still planning to host at my cabin?" Tristan confirmed, his eyebrow raised at the shift in plans, but couldn't help but tease. "Cut the cake and then strategize war tactics?"

"Maybe pad in some other, less intense activities in between? Slowly shift from birthday balloons to blood and gore?" Liv sarcastically retorted back. "A birthday piñata is the perfect transition."

"The conversations we find ourselves having sometimes…" Tristan shook his head, laughing.

"What are y'all talking about?" Piper smiled, approaching hesitantly at the two friends laughing together.

"Oh," Liv coughed, obviously letting Tristan take the rein to decide whether it would be a surprise birthday or planned.

"Nothing worth rehashing." Tristan smiled awkwardly.

Piper nodded, even more insecure. Zeus, the worst timing. And the worst cover.

"Elements Pillar nonsense." Liv added, although not convincingly.

After another moment of silence, Liv hit her hands to her knees, catching the attention of both Tristan and Piper.

"Well, I've got to check in with Hayden and see if we're planning to stay here tomorrow or at the palace. And… discuss the Elements Pillar meeting on Thursday." Liv pointed to Tristan, and then Piper, as if that final statement made the ridiculous conversation valid, before standing up, looking pained at the ungraceful adieu, clapping her hands together and walking away.

"What Elements Pillar meeting?" Piper turned to Tristan.

"Just decided, but we're going to get the board together to update Liv on what happened while she was away and discuss security practices for the Puerdios invasion." Tristan nodded, finally happy to have something concrete and non-birthday related to share with Piper.

But now, all the party planning ideas were running through his head, and he knew he needed to write down a list in order to get everything ready for Piper's celebration. She deserved balloons, coffee cake and a piñata – but first he needed to google what all the three things listed were and how he could procure them in a matter of days.

"I've got to go, Pipes. Loads to do, and don't even get me started on homework." Tristan rambled, before leaning in and kissing her on the cheek goodnight.

Then he paused, not sure if that was something he did with Piper, or how she would react to the impromptu action.

"Well, good night then." He stated blankly, still in shock to what he did. He clapped, similar to what Liv had done earlier, and then sprinted away, ignoring Dylan's clear judgment and confusion as he ran past her and out the door.

THIRTY-SEVEN

LIV

She thought her second semester of Puerdios was going to be challenging. Little did she expect to be in the position of having an entire semester to catch up on, a pillar to run, and an impending invasion to prepare for.

As she stomped toward Study Hall with Piper, Liv sported the most comfortable, Puerdios-chic approved outfit inspired by the never-ending studying she would need to conduct, keeping it simple with a jacquard sweater over an oversized white button-down shirt (Hayden's) and black mini skirt. Piper, on the otherhand, wore an academically inspired ensemble that perfectly mirrored her as the dominant in education – a feathered blouse paired with black trousers. It was elegant and put together, exactly how Piper would survive the next few weeks, give or take a number of weekly anxiety-driven breakdowns.

The day had kicked off with Security & Warfare and a relentless Rei and had gone downhill from there. By the time she sat down in Advanced Meteorology, Liv's muscles were jello and she was exhausted, and that was only the beginning. Even Professor Deligne wanted to push their strength to new limits, but of the mind, by spitballing multiple questions about the universe that even Piper drew a blank sometimes. By the time they arrived in Deity Power II, they were useless. Deplenished from both physical and mental factors, the only substance Liv could conjure were tears from the daunting reality that she was royally fucked. Wrapping up the day with Advanced Chemistry started pacifying Liv and Piper's temper as they were mixing elements to create healing potions, until inevitably they accidentally added the Alkaline element Caesium (instead of Lithium) and their entire potion exploded. That was precisely the moment when Piper shifted from worry to frenzy.

"It's fine. Who needs sleep? Or a social life?" Piper shrugged, calculating the gameplan to make up the homework they missed. (Although Hayden had extended an educational pardon for the work, Piper insisted it was necessary to complete in order to properly prepare for their final exams). "We'll study while we eat, we'll listen to audiobooks while we shower, we'll read in bed and we can prepare for tomorrow night's Elements Pillar meeting between classes, and at least we don't have any plans this weekend. We'll focus on catching up this week. Next week will be for assessing improvement areas and the following to focus on new material we missed during the upcoming two weeks, and then voilà, it's finals."

In that moment, Liv almost felt Piper would have preferred *not* having a surprise party this weekend as her birthday gift. She really hoped she was setting up Tristan for success with *that* reveal.

Worst case, they could play study-drinking games and perhaps Rei could spend his free time giving Warfare & Defense tips and exercises?

Liv groaned just thinking about how quickly the fun celebratory weekend could easily turn into a miserable time with one academic suggestion from Piper.

"Here's a chart." Piper whipped out a parcel, filled with notes and colors, giving a specific schedule to what Liv should study and work on to successfully prepare for the upcoming tests.

"Piper, there's not even a break to use the bathroom?" Liv asked dauntingly.

"Simple solution," Piper proposed, "If you finish an assignment *early*, that's your reward."

Liv's jaw dropped, dragging herself to keep up with Piper's pace to the beginning of her personal demise.

She wasn't proud of it, but she had managed to ditch Piper by sprinting out of Study Hall and using her athletic advantage to escape her best friend's impossible study regime.

When she slammed the door behind her, finally finding solace in her loft, she closed her eyes and sighed.

Hayden was right – what a beautiful thing silence could be.

After sixty degrees of reading thematic topline bullets across Meteorology, Chemistry and Deity Power II, exactly 40 minutes for each subject to cover the first two weeks of curriculum, Liv's mind was mush.

"New mindfulness practice?" A silky voice whispered from afar.

Hayden.

Liv opened one eye, happy to see him on the brown leather couch, and determined that planning her special celebration for him would be out of the question tonight. Not that her brainpower could handle any more thinking for the day. Hayden's unexpected visit was the reprieve and excuse she desperately needed.

There was a knock on the door. *Shit.*

"Hide me." Liv whispered, whining to Hayden.

He stood up obediently, considering the request with curiosity.

"I'm joking but thank you." Liv sighed, turning to open the door.

As expected, her incredibly dedicated and wonderful friend who truly only cared for her wellbeing stood outside the door. She was an exhausting sight.

"Liv, we still have to tackle the Solar System Treaties of the first and second centuries for Environmental Science tonight." Piper proposed, pointing to her chart.

Liv smiled kindly, "Thank you, Piper – is it okay if I go through the treaties solo?"

She shifted so her friend could see the king behind her.

Piper's eyes went wide, curtsying, "Of course! I'm so sorry to intrude, your majesty."

"Piper, you never intrude. Thank you for making sure my girlfriend doesn't flunk out of Puerdios, per usual." He hollered from the couch.

"I consider it my royal duty, sir!" Piper squeaked back with a salute, before turning to Liv. "I'll see you tomorrow in Advanced Chemistry?"

"Yes, and then in Advanced Magical Creatures." Liv nodded kindly, before softly shutting the door.

She ran her hands through her hair before rubbing her eyes with a commited yawn.

"Busy day?" Hayden rhetorically asked, walking toward her.

Liv nodded silently, shrugging into his arms and leaning her entire being into him for support. After a moment of content, she lifted her head up. "You?"

"Yes, although, not Piper-level of intensity." Hayden smiled, kissing the top of her head softly; she loved it when he did that. "I fortunately am able to manage the majority of my own schedule."

Liv groaned against his white cashmere turtleneck.

"How am I supposed to endure this tomorrow and then an actual obligation to the Elements Pillar?"

"A lot of tomorrow's meeting will most likely be receiving reports from your team. If they have any questions, have them submit a formal proposal and promise to take a look at it this weekend." Hayden suggested, bringing her to the couch.

"I made fajitas, so take a moment, and I'll dish us up. Don't move."

Liv smiled gratefully, pulling a wool blanket over her as she sat on the pillow and listened to the calming crackling of the fire and the subtle noise of Hayden moving around in the kitchen, preparing dinner. It was blissful, some of the most comforting noises on the planet – simple actions made by someone taking care of their loved one.

"Here you go." Hayden presented a plate in front of Liv, sitting down next to her.

"Do you want to put on basketball or something?" Liv inquired, mid-bite into her fajita.

Zeus, it tasted so good. Simple, yet delicious. Exactly what she needed to reinvigorate her brain cells. And she was proud of Hayden for discovering a dish where it was okay if its ingredients were slightly burnt.

"Baseball?" Hayden offered instead, "Regular pro basketball ended, and playoff games don't start until the weekend."

"Oh." Liv tilted her head, realizing they had never used her Christmas gift. "I'm sorry I never took you to a collegiate game at Oregon, like I promised."

"Ah, don't worry about it." Hayden shrugged it off, flipping the channel to a live game. "I did manage to go to a couple games once you were back, safely, at Puerdios."

"Well, there's always next year." Liv hummed, leaning into Hayden and kissing him on the lips. "I love you."

Hayden smiled shyly, "I love you too, Ollie."

Liv gently grabbed his plate, moving it away from him as she straddled her body across his; Hayden didn't seem to mind the change in plans, since it was apparent Liv had an appetite for something else.

"I think I know how we can help *eachother* decompress from the busy day." Liv murmured, kissing Hayden's neck tenderly.

Hayden grabbed Liv's hips, his hands gingerly rubbing Liv's lower back, moving upward toward her shoulders and massaging her tense muscles.

"That feels incredible," Liv hummed, grabbing Hayden's arm and pulling it in front of her, kissing his palm.

She lifted his turtleneck, revealing the chiseled abs she loved so dearly. He helped her pull off his white sweater, tossing it to the ground beside them.

Swiftly after, she discarded her own jacquard sweater, revealing the oversized white button-down shirt.

Hayden's eyes darkened in realization to exactly what she wore and who it belonged to.

"What's yours is mine." Liv purred, grinning deviously as she slowly unbuttoned the front.

"Take anything you want." Hayden growled back, grabbing a now exposed breast beneath a white lace bra. "Like *my* shirt, off of you."

The shirt slowly fell off her shoulder as she released button by button, Hayden's hand gently shifted to her shoulder as he kissed it delicately, moving up her neck before grabbing her and taking her lips to his.

Liv threw off her white shirt and unclipped her bra, moving again to discard Hayden's clothing by debuckling his belt. Like a whip, she removed it from his pants and threw it to the ground.

With a heavy need, Hayden grabbed Liv and flipped her onto the couch, pulling her skirt and underwear simultaneously down her legs and off her body.

She peeled his pants off while his strong hands glided up her silky legs.

Soon, Hayden hovered over her, asking permission to go further like the sophisticated gentleman he was. But soon, she'd reveal the savage, lustful and wanting man within.

He should have known by now, there was no going back for them, ever.

Liv kissed him deeply in reply, grabbing his ready manhood and guiding it into her.

He plunged into her, filling her entirely and taking control. He electrified her body by kissing a trail against her neck, chest and tummy, before returning to her eager lips and creating friction to where they connected below.

As one, Liv felt invincible. Every part of her body synched beautifully with his while they created a masterpiece, exploding new braincells with pleasure and recharging both with each movement they conducted, each spark another brush stroke created with the other's touch.

The pressure within Liv was building, soon she was yelling Hayden's name with admiration, relishing in the much-needed release.

Until he was moaning from his urgent touch within her, the friction making both bodies convulse with sensual indulgence. Until fireworks exploded and Liv crashed into Hayden's arms, smiling with ecstacy and feeling strong, lightheaded and loved, but most of all, complete.

It was a welcoming sight seeing the bright Elements Pillar sparkle against the contrast of the sea and setting rose gold sun. Pegasus neighed in excitement, after spending the past months at the Royal Palace she too, was finally home.

Although Rei had continued to be silent and angry, he strode ahead. Behind her, Tristan and Piper flew in zigzags for additional protection. When she landed, Liv's feet touching the soil and soul breathing in the air cleansed her. She felt bright and rejuvenated.

After saying goodbye to Pegasus and walking through the entire palace, checking in on familiar departments and saying hello to new ones, Liv walked through wind, water, fire and earth before reaching her own private loft to prepare for the upcoming board meeting.

She was still exhausted, but an adrenaline coursed through her veins, helping her manage through and with a genuine smile.

Hayden and Peyton greeted them from within the Elite residence, Hayden going through paperwork of some sort in the dining room but leaving it behind as he approached Liv to give her a welcoming hug. Peyton jumped up from the couch excitedly, but instead of heading to Rei, she went straight to Piper.

Liv took note of the odd behavior, deciding it would be worth pulling Peyton aside this weekend to better understand what was going on. Hopefully, with her plans of pulling Hayden away tomorrow, Rei and Peyton would have some time alone to figure things out and not worry about security obligations.

"Tonight's meeting in the room of Air should be relatively quick – the proposals submitted don't seem too extroadinary." Tristan began, once everyone had shared their social pleasantries, following Liv into her office. "The biggest question is recruiting volunteers for war, while making sure we have coverage for the day-to-day responsibilities here. Other than that, there are a couple requests regarding water supply and how to help manage mortals' inability to properly reduce their carbon footprint. Of course, I've scaled back fires for a cooler summer and to reprieve from the year before, but that comes at a price of mortals thinking 'global warming' is indeed not a thing. Oh, and you'll meet Cain tonight – he served as your father's advisor. He should be able to help provide historical insight and context."

"What do you know of him?" Liv inquired, quickly scanning over the documents to be further discussed and voted on in the evening. The fortunate result of Piper's aggressive studies is that Liv had become quite the skim reader. Her brain hurt, but now she retained most of the infinite information that demanded residence in her mind.

"He always seemed fair in my recollection of him, and clearly your father trusted him to have placed him in such a high position of influence." Tristan then leaned forward, so Liv caught a whiff of his cinnamon scent. "My only advice is to remember eighteen years has passed, and we do not know what he encountered during this time, nor how it may have affected or influenced his perspective."

Liv rolled her eyes, "Per usual, never trust a deity. Nothing is permanent…"

"Elle, it is not a laughing matter!" Tristan scolded.

"T, I'll only be surprised if one day you advise me that I can whole-heartedly trust a deity, even you." Liv joked back.

In reality, as long as a deity respected her independence and free will, didn't entrap, manipulate or control her, and addressed the same values onto others, she would not consider them a threat or spend time assessing whether to trust them or not.

Deities would do what they wanted – and to try to pinpoint an ever-changing motive was a waste of valuable time.

"I'll give him the benefit of the doubt until proven otherwise." Liv nodded, concluding her perspective, and continued on, grabbing the next proposal to review.

When Liv entered the Room of Air, the white marble fortress seemed almost too large for such an intimate meeting. In the center of the room, a large white stone circular table resided, with a dozen chairs situated around it, all filled with various deities who had stood up in respect as soon as she had entered, aside from two empty chairs designated for the Elite and her advisor.

Tristan followed behind her, but Rei had insisted on remaining outside the room to stand guard at the door and keep the Elements Pillar matters separate from his own knowledge.

"It is only fair, as you do not sit in on the Security Pillar's council meetings." He concluded, not allowing for any discussion on the matter.

Liv nodded graciously to the twelve council members who joined, thanking them for assisting with the running of the Pillar while she had been away, and then politely requested they introduce themselves so she could get to know the team that had managed everything so seamlessly while both Tristan and she had been pursuing alliances for the greater good.

First, Cressida introduced herself as the Goddess of Trees, working directly as a liason with all of the houses – Earth, Fire, Wind and Water – to ensure all worked compatibly with her crop.

Then, Ely began, sharing his histoy with the Elements council and having been apart of the establishment of the periodic table, in which he continued to oversee.

Damion chimed in next, excited to meet Liv and mentioning his work with the ocean ecosystems, as whom Liv presumed to be the God of Oceans.

Lora followed, smirking with a blazing stare as she introduced herself as the Goddess of Lava, lightly elbowing Tristan as she joked, "he had taken away all of her fun in the past year."

Liv laughed at the jest, although curious whether she should ask Tristan to give context to her words and better undersand if Lora could erupt at any time, literally.

Petrov followed Lora, a bit shy and seemingly younger than the others, as he mentioned only recently graduating from Puerdios University but having an interest in politics, so offered any resources he could provide outside of his deity powers, which specialized in hail.

Emilie chimed in eagerly after, explaining she was the Goddess of Gold, which made sense as her golden skin dazzled, and she was dressed in the metal from head to toe.

In contrast to Emilie, Alec dully introduced himself as the God of Rocks and Sand following but said nothing else to give color to his personality, or lack there of.

Georgia spoke next, the Goddess of Blizzards, her demeanor as icy and cold, yet abrupt and demanding, that it perfectly suited her to be in charge of such frosted chaos.

Maeve introduced herself as Goddess of Mountains, regal and divine. She appeared kind but poised.

Relatively jittery, a scholar paused, looking for approval from Maeve before starting his spiel, explaining that he was an Elemental Researcher & Historian, and then stumbled on his words when he realized he had not yet said his name, James.

"Are you Piper's Father?" Liv inquired, although surprisingly he looked nothing like her. Liv figured Piper must take after her mother, since Hades, it appeared her uncle had more of a resemblance to Piper than this sweet man before her. Although, Piper clearly took after James directly in his mannerisms, as he continued introducing himself in a spitting image of her friend.

"Ah, yes. That would be me." He smiled shyly, "She speaks highly of you, so I thought it would be best to offer my knowledge, although I must admit that it may be all I have to give."

Liv nodded with impress, "Your daughter's gifts have served me well, I am genuinely delighted to work with another relative of hers."

"The pleasure is truly all mine, Miss Olivia." James dutifully bowed from his chair.

Lyanna went next, her words delivering wisdom far beyond Liv's wildest imagination and explained she was the Goddess of Fall and sister to Petrov.

Finally, a strong man, his being no older than Silas and Daphne, stood. Only one name remained.

Cain.

He was intriguing, muscular and tall. His bright blonde hair was styled modernly, and he looked like he could have been a European popstar.

"Olivia, it is wonderful to finally meet you." He smiled, his teeth dazzling against the now muted marble that surrounded him. "I am Cain, God of Seasons, and primarily oversee the ecosystems and how they impact one another. I also served as your father's advisor and would be honored to step into the role once again as yours."

Even his voice was musical. What a vision.

Liv blinked a couple of times, taking in the unexpected turn of events – or impression. She had envisioned Cain as a strong warrior, terse and angry, nothing like the charming, impressionable man who stood before her. Perhaps that was his edge, killing his enemies with kindness.

"Thank you, Cain." Liv looked him directly in the eye, warm and welcoming, and reconsidered her skeptical inclinations. "I look forward to deeply getting to know one another and hearing all about your relationship with my father." She then turned to the larger group and addressed them proudly, "As the council knows, Tristan from the House of Fire serves as my advisor, but we look forward to finding the right duties and responsibilities for each and every one of you to oversee."

She grabbed her paperwork, the physical agenda for all that they needed to work through; however, there was a more pressing issue she had purposely omitted but needed to discuss.

The House of Wind.

"Before we get started, I have a personal proposal I would like to address first with the council."

Tristan coughed, clearly thrown offguard with the change in plans.

Liv turned to him innocently, but he did not oppose her request. If anything, the unexpected maneuver would forever keep her council on their toes.

"Wonderful." Liv stacked the papers and hit them against the stone table. "Shall we begin?"

THIRTY-EIGHT

LIV

Liv knew Tristan would give her a piece of his mind, in private, following the meeting. He had been cordial and supportive throughout each proposal, but now it was time to discuss specific ramifications and prepare for all possibilities. But, Liv had more pressing matters to attend to as she kickstarted her boyfriend and best friend's celebratory weekend, promptly following behind the Elements Pillar council meeting.

The first, she needed to get out of the navy minidress she wore and into more casual clothes. The jewels on her couture gown were scratching and poking her skin. So, a date with cashmere this evening sounded absolutely divine.

"Tristan, everyone has their next steps for the next week, most of which pertain to Puerdios University's safekeeping. Anything we need to discuss can wait a week, or at least until after the inevitable battle. Or, Monday – er, I mean One." Liv gave Tristan a stern look, knowing he was only trying to distract himself from his own anxiety with planning and hosting Piper's birthday at his cabin. Or perhaps he was reeling from meeting Piper's father and now having to work with him on an ongoing basis. Either way, Liv concluded Tristan was not in a great mood or mindspace.

Well, he offered his services on both. Liv thought to herself. *He dug his hole and now had to lay in it.*

Liv approached her loft, opening the door without asking if Tristan planned to join.

"How'd the first meeting go?" Hayden hollered immediately from the dining room table still filled with paperwork.

It was as if he hadn't even made a *dent* in whatever he was reviewing.

"Absolutely wonderful." Liv smiled, before eyeing his workload, hesitantly. "I was hoping to kickstart the celebration with you early, but if you still have things to get done...?"

"Celebrate me or labor over endless royal duties..." Hayden considered the notion before his eyes lit up, "I'd much rather celebrate me, obviously."

"I was hoping you would say that." Liv smiled, walking over and giving him a deserving kiss.

"On that note, I'm heading out." Tristan declared, grabbing Piper and saying the appropriate goodbyes before returning to Puerdios.

"Where are you two lovebirds heading to tonight, anyways?" Peyton popped her head above the couch.

Hayden turned his head to Liv, "I figured we were staying here?"

Liv smiled, glad to see she could successfully manage the soul mate connection to contain some thoughts from him. When surprises were involved, at least.

"On contraire, birthday boy, we're heading somewhere near and dear to my heart tonight."

"Tonight?" Hayden dropped an open file, his full attention on Liv now.

"Yes, sir." Liv nodded enthusiastically, summoning a Christmas gift that had not fulfilled its true purpose, yet.

Without warning, she threw the collegiate Oregon sweatshirt to Hayden; the recipient not missing a beat as he caught it in his hand and grinned.

"About time we visit the campus, Hayden. And, as our luck would have it, there's a home baseball game tonight. We leave in five."

Liv nodded enthusiastically and sprinted back to her room, swiftly changing out of her Elemental Elite attire and into her old clothes, turning into the mortal she had always imagined she would be while in college. Tonight, Hayden and she could pretend to be whoever they wanted and live out the life they once thought they would have.

Looking in the mirror, Liv grinned. Back were her leather combat boots, black skinny jeans and a green and yellow flannel button down shirt that she layered with a black Oregon puffervest and topped off with a bright kelly green beanie. She was ready for game day.

When she returned downstairs, Hayden was a sight to see. In the grey Oregon crewneck sweatshirt she had thrown at him minutes before, he had changed out of his typical suit and tie and instead wore dark denim jeans, both items perfectly sculpting his statuesque body and truthfully made Liv want to tear both off and have her way with him in the bedroom right then and there.

But alas, Oregon baseball did not wait for sex-driven immortals. But maybe they could find a dorm later.

"Ready?" Liv smiled, extending her hand.

"Certainly." Hayden grinned, accepting her offer.

They rode Pegasus across sky and ocean, blazing through timezones until the picturesque landscape of tall pinetrees against a cloudy sunset of the Pacific Northwest came across the horizon.

They flew over the Willamette River, spotting the renowned football complex, Autzen Stadium, beside the more humble and newer P.K. Park.

Peyton and Rei reluctantly followed, claiming royal duty called but promised to keep their distance, even apparently, from eachother. Liv huffed as she noticed they stayed far away from one another during the flight, but once they landed on Oregon soil, Liv pushed the duo out of her mind to capitalize on full student mode.

Sitting behind homeplate, Liv and Hayden enjoyed hotdogs, beers, songs and cheers – yelling for players Hayden surprisingly had too much intel on (seriously, did he have ESPNU playing on repeat while he worked?) and Liv happily listening to him spit out rules and strategy tactics during the game.

Oregon won, 8-7, with a double hitter in the ninth inning, causing quite the stressful-but-worth-the-watch-game. Skipping away from the stadium hand in hand, Liv insisted they headed to the campus bar to celebrate with a few drinks among the fellow students.

Hayden obliged, and at the bar even made friends with a group of guys who were in a fraternity, hitting it off to such an extent that they even offered him a bid to pledge in the fall.

They danced, they tried 'Tic-Tacs' (a campus drop-shot favorite), they laughed and eventually they called it a night, leaving the music in exchange for the calm and quiet outdoors.

Looking around at the simplicity of the life she once had been a grasp away from cementing into her future, it was strange returning to it stronger, wiser and having experienced the incredible and terrible things she had encountered since the previous fall. She was greater, more in control of her life than ever before, yet the atmosphere she experienced still had a magical touch to it. A different magic. It was a chapter of her life and surprisingly, Liv wouldn't want to change it, ever. Instead, she wanted to do it due diligence, finally sharing that part of her life with Hayden, her true love.

"It's not raining." Liv observed with a glow. "That seems to be a birthday thing here." She eyed Hayden, unable to contain her smile. "Want to walk with me?"

"Well Monaco, the night is still young." Hayden laughed, looking up at the entirely clear sky and seeing their constellation shining brightly down on them, like a blessing from a higher being, bigger than themselves.

"Why do you call me Monaco?" Liv finally asked, leading Hayden away from the bar and into the main pathway, bordered by captivating pinetrees and stunning academic buildings made out of brick, that were illuminated in the dark by glowing lights.

Hayden hesitated, trying to bring clarity internally before sharing his reasoning aloud.

"I noticed when I called you Olivia, formally, it made you cringe and hurt you on some subconscious level, understandably so. Yet, it didn't feel right to call you by your nicknames – Liv feels too personal and Ollie too intimate for political and public affairs. So, I tested out Monaco."

"I see…" Liv absorbed Hayden's story, the impact of what he must have gone through while she was coping, surviving – what *she* had unintentionally put him though.

"You should be respected, Ollie. Monaco sounds strong, like you. Plus, I kind of like it." Hayden grinned.

Liv smiled back, admitting, "I kind of like it, too."

"So, my Ollie Monaco, you've let me indulge in America's classic sport, consumed a disgusting quantity of hotdogs-"

"Hey, those hotdogs were the best we've ever had. No such thing as too many!" Liv chimed in, poking him with her finger.

"…Danced at the campus bar," Hayden continued, ignoring her comment aside from a laugh, "And got me intoxicated. So, are you going to lure me to your dorm room next and then take advantage of me?"

"Advantage? More like reward you, sir – if anything." Liv huffed, reaching for his hand and twirling into his arms outside of the Business School. "If I recall correctly, my student character rarely conducted such scandalous activities on campus."

She batted her eyelashes innocently, allowing Hayden to twirl her again, dancing with her until she spun back into his arms.

"That's because I wasn't here." He winked.

Liv smirked, soaking in the stillness, the two both becoming silent and one with the trees.

"This moment was how I dreamt of it for weeks last year." Liv sighed longingly, shyly looking up to Hayden's gaze.

"This experience will continue to be a rewarding dream of mine." Hayden offered, pulling her even closer into his arms.

There was a slight chill from the cooler midnight air; Liv reaped in the solace and comfort of his warm, strong body pressed against her.

"Most adults our age are worried about finals, if their resume is strong enough for a summer job or becoming a beer pong Champion." Hayden said, studying Liv. "Ours is saving the world."

Liv nodded, nuzzling her head further into his neck. She loved hearing his heartbeat and feeling the steady rise of his muscular chest.

"Thank you for tonight, Ollie. For being you. And giving me so many extra chances I don't deserve."

Liv finally lifted her head up, "That's where you're wrong, Hayden."

She found his lips, melting against their touch as the impact cast another spell over her. Intoxicated with love, Liv pulled away, stating her finite conclusion.

"You deserve each and every one."

The college baseball game, bar and campus tour were only the beginning of Hayden's celebration. The second part of the night involved another gift, one that was nervewrecking in thought and which Liv desperately hoped Hayden would like.

It was certainly a gamble, if anything.

So, instead of bringing him back to a dorm room as she had teased, Liv whistled for Pegasus to take them to a place even more special and dear to her heart.

When they landed at Hayden's cabin, Rei gave a sigh of relief, immediately marching himself down to the guest room with two twin beds. Peyton smiled awkwardly, squeezing Liv's arm before heading to the other guest room upstairs.

"Do I need to uninvite them to the astrology festivities at Tristan's?" Hayden teased, but then looked back at an unresponsive Liv.

She was too tense, but quickly muttered something ridiculous before sighing to calm her nerves. Laughing awkwardly, Liv apologized.

"I'm sorry, all of the sudden the night has caught up to me." She placed a hand on her chest, hoping to settle down her excitement, but she still had butterflies doing cartwheels in her core. And she couldn't stop smiling.

"We can go to sleep if you're tired?" Hayden offered, taking a step toward her cautiously.

Always thoughtful and alert to Liv's unexpected reaction potential, Hayden had always put Liv's needs before his own. Even when she had doubted him, questioned his motives and thought the worst of him, she continued to be proven wrong. Now, she fully knew and understand that everything Hayden did, was for her – her future, her comfort, her benefit, her joy. At the thought that Hayden was unintentionally willing to self-sabotage the remaining celebratory plans for the night on her behalf, Liv felt even guiltier, which was exactly the motive to her final birthday gift.

"One more thing and then the king can rest." Liv teased, feeling better already as the words left her lips. She stepped toward him and extended her arm. "Follow me?"

"Always." Hayden whispered, taking her hand and letting her take the lead.

Pulling Hayden downstairs and through the kitchen, then outside to the patio and further down to the dock by the lake, she took a breath as the setting became visible for the celebration.

She had queued up small fireballs to sparkle alongside the path to the dock, the floating stage filled with even more candles. In the center, Liv had set up a cream cashmere blanket with a bottle of champagne, tea, a pint of Häagen Dazs Chocolate Peanut Butter Icecream and Hayden's gift, wrapped in a small box.

Liv looked back at the birthday god to gauge his initial reaction, but her boyfriend was rendered speechless. His jaw opened and his eyes glistened as he absorbed the stunning, serene and sentimental setting that meant so much to them both. Directly ahead, and as Liv had planned, they could see Hayden and her constellations sparkling directly among the starry sky.

At this point, Liv was shaking. Her heart felt like it was about to burst out of her chest, but she continued on, breathing and taking one step at a time toward her destiny.

"Ollie…" Hayden began, his head still spinning as he took in the sight.

Liv smiled, hushing him softly by gently placing a finger atop his lips.

"Champagne," She began, her voice shaky. "So, we can toast your 19th birthday and our best year yet to come, together." Liv kneeled, picking up the bottle and trying to concentrate on pouring it into the glass, but the bottle was vibrating.

Gently, Hayden's warm hand covered hers, steadying it, helping her pour the golden liquid into the two flutes, bursting to life with bubbles upon impact, and perfectly embodying the state of Liv's insides.

"Cheers." Liv smiled gratefully, a tear emerging from her eye. Hayden followed suit, taking a sip of his flute.

"Tea, because it's absolutely freezing out here." Liv laughed, opening the canteen and taking a sip of the warm substance.

"And because you won't drink more than one flute?" Hayden smirked, his eyes narrowing in on Liv's playfully before they sparkled with desire, "Perhaps we should have brought whisky as the heating device instead?"

"Clever, but no." Liv tapped Hayden's nose.

Recomposing herself, and laughing in reflection at how times certainly had changed since they were both down on the dock, Liv grabbed the next item on her list.

"Häagen Dazs Chocolate Peanut Butter icecream," Liv handed over the pint. "That I'm willing to share only because it is your birthday, and because I've also brought heated salted chocolate chip cookies to pair with it for *your* favorite dessert."

"Oh, hell yes." Hayden nodded, quickly diverting into the basket to pull out a foiled plate with the warm, freshly baked cookies. He grabbed one excitedly, but paused as he studied Liv before setting it down.

"I'll let you finish your speech before we dig into that."

"How considerate, King Hayden." Liv teased, "You treat your subjects *so* kindly."

"And my equals." Hayden replied quickly, grabbing Liv's hand and gingerly kissing it.

Zeus, that touch still sent warm chills of the best kind down her core. Liv ignored her desire to mount him, instead focusing on her daunting task at hand.

"And finally, your birthday gift."

Liv was trembling, but as Hayden held her left hand with his, she bent down on one knee.

Registering exactly what Liv was about to do, Hayden's eyes grew wide.

"I want to give myself to you, completely."

"Wait, Liv. Wait." Hayden's voice weakened.

Still holding her hand and refusing to let go (although Liv wanted to tear it away and run anywhere private so she could cry of embarrassment alone), Hayden kneeled as well so that he was at the same eye level as his counterpart.

"I should be the one to do this." He consoled her, pulling out a small box from his own pocket, one that was the same size as Liv's gift, matching hers with navy and silver embossing.

He looked up to her shyly.

Now, the king was slightly trembling in her grasp.

"It's *your* birthday!" Liv cried, still shaking but composing herself as she took a deep breath, maneuvering from distraught back to insane exhilaration. She was too excited, nervous and feeling all of the feels. Any longer and she would either faint or explode.

"Ollie," Hayden gulped, lifting his head to gaze directly into her eyes. "I, I… don't know what I did to earn the privilege of having you choose *me*."

Hayden wiped a tear from his eye, laughing embarrassedly before holding her hand again.

"Your intelligence makes me smarter, your love makes me see infinite possibilities and your kindness makes me want to be a better person. Most of all, you make me laugh, over and over," he chuckled at the revelation, "and you create a singular reason to look forward to every day. How did I get so lucky to fall in love with my best friend? My equal? My soul mate?" Hayden was shaking, almost as much as Liv was, but fortunately he furrowed his brows and perservered on. "Every moment I am able to spend with you, Ollie, is one worth fighting for – those of the past, the present and especially those of the future, are all worth fighting for. We are worth fighting for. You give me the courage to persist, the strength to achieve any obstacle and the inspiration and faith to make a better world for you and me, our family and our friends.

I continue to remain in awe of you and that, I am certain, will never change." Hayden smiled, finally popping open the box he had held in his hands.

Liv's jaw dropped, her eyes a blurry mess, waves crashing against the sandy shore of her skin.

"Olivia Monaco, will you do me the immense honor of becoming my queen, my soul mate and most importantly, my wife?"

Liv nodded, while whispering, "Yes!" and then crying even louder, "Yes!" as Hayden slid the immaculate ring onto her finger, before she leapt into his arms.

The gold ring had their princess-cut stone at the center, large and brilliant, with two trillion diamonds on its side. Liv cascaded her light through the ring to find both the royal and her family's crest shining into the sparkling night sky, together. Solidified and concreted as one. The band itself was decorated with ten stunning square stones, making the ring twinkle on her finger, mirroring the ecstatic stars above.

She pulled back from their embrace to kiss Hayden thoroughly, communicating all she couldn't say with her lips. Her desire, her trust, her wonder and excitement for the next stage in their life. One that they had *both* opted to take, together.

Finally, Liv laughed, choking on her tears as she looked down at the sparkling ring.

"You know, you sort of stole my thunder for your birthday gift." She teased, sniffling as she kissed him again, before looking at her ring and then back at him and gazed into his crystal blue eyes. "I love you."

"I love you too, Ollie." Hayden smiled, kissing her cheek.

Liv grabbed the final gift for Hayden's birthday, garnering her internal courage once again to say what was already said but had been planned to be stated with her words. Yet, it didn't feel any easier.

She turned to face him straight on, lifting the box open for Hayden to see her gift to him.

"Hayden, we've been through more than a couple experiences that could fill... an entire lifetime." Liv chuckled at the irony, "Yet, we came out stronger. We always come out stronger, closer and more connected and more in love."

Liv gulped, staring at her engagement ring for courage.

Looking back into his eyes, his gaze said everything. He was hers forever, and she was his.

"From the beginning, we've been set to unite as one. Fates be damned… or applauded," Liv considered that she wasn't entirely mad anymore for whatever cosmic being brought her together with the best man on the planet. "You've been the one constant in both of my worlds. Whether it be our fates weaving our paths intricately as one or the simple fact that I choose you and everyday, you choose me. One thing I know is certain: I want to spend every day, infinitely, with you, Hayden. I want to wake up to your kind smile, I want to roll my eyes at your charming jokes, I want to fall asleep in your protective arms and I want to be selfish with you. Because I want all of you, always. All days."

Liv slipped the ring outside of the box, showing the ten trillion-cut diamonds stacked across the golden band – one diamond for each Pillar in their society – and slipping the metal ring around Hayden's finger.

"Will you marry me, Hayden?"

Hayden grinned, jokingly considering it by looking up to the stars and humming, "Hmmm…let me think about it," as if he were actually contemplating the response.

Liv swatted him playfully.

"Of course I will, Ollie." He laughed, lifting her chin and kissing her tenderly. "You do remember I asked you the very same question only five minutes ago?"

Liv swatted him again.

"Just checking, I'd hate for my fiancée to have already forgotten one of the most memorable nights of her life."

Liv hit him again. But she did like how the word 'fiancée' vibrated off his lips.

She placed her arms around his neck, pressed her body against his and wrapped her legs around his torso so that she sat in his lap, and relished in how her body perfectly sculpted to his.

A few moments later, as the stars sparkled their blessing of the union from above, Liv gently pressed Hayden down onto his back, unable to contain her smile, and made love to her fiancé.

"I can't believe we're engaged." Liv smiled, looking up at Hayden, "Are we insane?"

The two lay entwined in the grey blanket Liv had spread out for their picnic on the dock.

"Crazier things have happened." Hayden replied, kissing the top of her forehead. "And marrying you will certainly be the most sensible thing I do in my life."

Liv looked at her left hand, sparkling across Hayden's sculpted golden chest.

"Were you always planning to propose tonight?" Liv eyed Hayden thoughtfully.

"I was planning to propose earlier," Hayden admitted with a sigh. "But... it never felt like... the right time."

Liv lifted her head, leaning over to kiss him on the lips and stare into his eyes for clarification.

Because Kronos abducted her and abused her mind and body. Liv shuddered at the memory, the pain, the guilt for what her weakness had put Hayden through. He had been planning to propose *months* ago, but she had seen him as a monster. The reality set in and she felt sick.

"Liv, there's no reason to dwell on the past, only to remember that it made us stronger and who we are today. I do not regret practicing patience, it only made tonight all the more blissful. You were worth the wait."

Liv lowered herself, feeling dented.

"Ollie, look at me."

Liv didn't want to, but she forced herself to give Hayden the respect he deserved. Staring into his piercing blue eyes, Liv weakened into his arms.

How had she gotten so damned lucky?

"You were worth the wait." He reiterated, lifting his body to pull her closer and kiss her lips.

Liv smiled, sadly, turning her head to the sky and finding Polaris in the night sky. It sparkled, and then glowed, mirroring the same cascading light her ring now projected to the North Star.

Look to the North Star for direction.

And now the North Star was directing her to Hayden.

She turned back to Hayden, feeling whole once again.

"It was a beautiful night." She leaned her forehead against his.

"It was perfect, Ollie." He whispered back.

THIRTY-NINE

PIPER

In these moments, she wanted to pinch herself.

She had flown over to Tristan's cabin with Dylan, Kyril, Zayne, Ammiras and the owner himself. *Friends*. To meet up with more *friends*, and found Tristan's cabin entirely decorated with balloons and streamers with what ended up being a surprise birthday celebration for her birthday and the Pure God King's.

She was celebrating her birthday with the freaking Pure God King.

And with *friends*.

Last year, she didn't even have friends and the Pure God King certainly didn't know who she was.

Let alone Tristan – and now here he was hosting her birthday celebration.

Piper wasn't entirely sure what to expect from the God of Fire. What they had in Southeast Asia seemed so raw that now, being diluted with competing friends and ex-flings, she had no idea where Tristan's head remained. And as much as she hated to admit it, ever since they had reunited with Liv, Tristan seemed off, distracted.

She hoped it was because they had been secretly planning her birthday festivities, but even still Piper always noticed Tristan. Watching him from the corner of her eye, Piper magnetized to his every movement and reacted to it instinctively, and what she had learned was that while she noticed Tristan, Tristan noticed Liv.

Especially when Peyton finally screamed, grabbing Liv's hand and hollering with excitement upon the Element Elite's arrival with the Pure God King. Piper ran over to congratulate her best friend with pure glee, but still noticed that Tristan's jaw dropped, and a piece of his soul looked crushed at the revelation of the news.

It was a look Piper wished he would only reveal with her, *for her.*

"You must tell us *everything!*" Peyton squealed, jumping uncontrollably as she summoned champagne.

"Of course, I will, in time." Liv beamed, pulling away from Dylan's congratulatory hug and looking to Piper, "But this weekend is about Piper and Hayden…"

"And my first request as the birthday girl is for you to SPILL." Piper squeaked, composing her internal heartbreak and diligently celebrating her best friend by grabbing a flute and raising her glass. "To Hayden & Liv!"

"To Hayden & Liv!" Everyone hollered.

"Okay, okay!" Liv laughed, her eyes growing wide and pulling the goddesses aside. "I'll tell you all of the details but spare the men and Hayden's dignity by divulging all of the romantic, sappy stuff."

"I'm a romantic and damn proud of it." Hayden stated smugly, raising his glass.

Liv rolled her eyes but turned back to her girlfriends, sharing all of the details immediately. From her birthday plans to Hayden unexpectedly hijacking *her* proposal, it was all too sweet and adorable. Convoluted and sincere, it was perfectly Hayden and Liv.

"Okay, enough about me." Liv wrapped up her story, eyeing Piper with excitement. "Now to get back to the festivities." She jumped up, clapping her hands. "I honestly don't think I can keep it a secret any longer." Liv eyed Tristan accusingly, "And you didn't tell her, T?"

T?

Piper's head snapped to Tristan immediately, finding his arms raised with a calm grin. "Scouts honor, I kept my word, Elle."

Liv hushed everyone and stood atop the coffee table.

"We're here this weekend to celebrate two of my favorite people and best friends – Hayden and Piper. As you all know, I've already given Hayden his life-changing gift, *me*." Liv curtsied and then shimmied her body jokingly, stirring small chuckles around the room, "But I have another gift I could not be more honored to bestow upon my best friend, Piper." Liv turned to Piper and grew serious, tears beginning to well up in her eyes as she spoke. "When I joined Puerdios, I had zero friends. Deities were not allowed to associate with me and nobody was even willing to speak to me. I was alone. Except for Piper."

"Hey!" Peyton hollered.

"…And Peyton." Liv added with a nod and a laugh. "Peyton was my guardian angel of course, but Piper took me under her wing. She introduced me to this mesmerizing and intimidating world, and had my back no matter what ridiculous situations I convinced her to pursue or accidentally got us into. She was my rock, my strength and my best friend, and every day I am grateful for her intelligence, kindness, humor and beauty, inside and out."

Piper felt a tear roll down her cheek, she wiped it embarrassedly, wishing she could wear her emotion with pride like her best friend Liv.

"After my induction as Element Elite, I prayed to the gods to consider Piper for a privileged position with much responsibility, knowing that she would be hands down the best contender for this role and hoping they would see the potential that I already saw. And I am so proud to announce tonight what I have observed and felt over the past weeks as an acceptance to my request – that the Elites of the Elements Pillar's past have appointed Piper to the House of Wind and have gifted to her all of the powers associated with such a high-ranking honor."

Piper's jaw dropped.

She turned to Tristan, who was beaming from across the room. He nodded in agreement, that what she heard from her friend's lips were true.

"Congratulations, Piper – Head of the House of Wind." Liv's eyes sparkled as she lifted her glass. "There is no one more deserving than you."

"Th-thank you!" Piper squealed, jumping onto the table and giving Liv a huge hug. "I accept! I, I can't believe..."

"Believe it, Pipes." Tristan stood beside the coffee table, extending his hand.

Liv gave Piper an encouraging nod, prodding her to take his hand.

"You knew!?" Piper shoved Tristan playfully.

"Obviously. I know *everything*." Tristan retorted.

But then he paused and opened his arms, pulling her into a congratulatory hug. And like striking a match, Piper engulfed herself in flames.

"On that note," Tristan smiled, snapped his fingers and turned off all the lights.

Piper turned to the only source of light, two coffee cakes dancing in the air with candles aglow as the entire room began singing, "Happy Birthday," to both Hayden and her.

Holy Zeus. She was the House of Wind. She was the Goddess of Air.

Piper had a title. A responsibility. *A purpose.*

By the time the coffee cake hovered in front of her and the song concluded, Liv hollered, "Make a wish!"

Piper turned to Tristan, whose arm was still around her as he beamed with pride. She returned to the coffee cake and blew out the candle.

Yet, no wish was needed, because all of them had come true.

JOCELYN

She had been avoiding Demetrius the entire evening. Joss was there to celebrate her brother, not try to reconcile a damaged relationship with a past fling.

And now, her duty was to celebrate having not leaked another secret prior to Piper's appointment to the House of Wind.

But, inevitably she saw the leopard print suit approach her and knew Demetrius would want to talk, try to resolve their differences or figure out how to move on.

Quickly, Jocelyn refilled her champagne flute and then walked into the lion's den. It was best to get the scene over with – one that had already played out through her head, ending the same no matter what alternative route she ventured down. Demetrius was certainly stubborn and there would be no shifting his stance nor accepting his decision.

"Come to a birthday party and it turns into a royal engagement and historic appointment." Demetrius lightly commented, taking a sip of his scotch. "You earthlings sure know how to throw a memorable event."

Joss smiled, demurely taking a sip from her flute.

"Are you having a good time?" Demetrius pressed, hoping to get a response, "Considering you're the reason all of this transpired tonight?"

"It's always fascinating when you discover Daphne's intentions, isn't it?" Jocelyn hummed back lightly.

"So, we're just going to continue making pleasantries from now on?" Demetrius sighed, "Do what societal etiquette implores? Come on, we're more than that, Joss."

"*You're* more than that, Demetrius." Jocelyn's effortless façade broke in an instant, a mirror crashing into the ground as she snapped her head in his direction, her voice now tart. "I, on the otherhand, am not granted the privilege of being able to speak my mind or share my worries, as I wish."

"Joss, I don't like how we ended things, how we're *ending* things." Demetrius explained, his voice monotone and dull.

"You don't like it because it is out of your control." Jocelyn bit back. "I on the otherhand, must remain in control at all costs, and you threaten it. End of story."

"Jocelyn, you're angry because I'm leaving to seek out the Orishas – which you think it is for personal gain, but it's not. It's for you. Your family. Your people. Hades, it was your idea! We both agreed to it after practically *giving* my kingdom to the Celts…"

The word sucked in Jocelyn's mind like a flame in carbon dioxide. She saw Niall, in their world, helping others escape into the sky and head toward the stars.

"Demetrius, they did it. They're… on their way to Jupiter!" Jocelyn exclaimed, her voice a whispery breath of excitement. "I… I must go to them and make sure all runs smoothly."

Jocelyn started to step away, but Demetrius gently grabbed her arm.

"Take care of my home for me." He said, not talking about only his palace as he pleadingly looked directly into Jocelyn's complex blue eyes.

The Pure Princess nodded in understanding, a tear sliding down her eye as she realized this was goodbye.

"You too. Be careful, Demetrius." She whispered, pulling him into a hug and then kissing him, rather unexpectedly.

She pulled back, eyes wide, before she let out a soft chuckle and blushed.

"Keep an eye out for me?" Demetrius asked softly, his breath warm on her skin.

"Let me consult the stars about that…" She replied with a weak smile, not needing any sight to confirm the true outcome of his request. She'd look for him, always.

PEYTON

Peyton sat on the patio sipping coffee, enjoying a calm, chilly morning as she watched the fresh sun rise over the mountain, its light discarding golden flakes in reflection atop the still lake.

She heard a door gently shut behind her, knowing immediately who sought her attention.

Well, at least she had a moment of peace before the tide of stress rolled in.

Peyton contemplated standing up and going inside, but she had already pulled that relatively immature move a few times.

…Although she had to admit, seeing Rei clench his jaw in response did bring her joy.

Instead, she'd keep that move up her sleeve if anything they discussed went down a path she did not particularly care for.

"Good morning."

Rei sat down across from her, already changed into his clothes for the day, a grey pinstripe suit with an oversized white button-down shirt layered beneath his jacket and untucked over his trousers.

"Morning." Peyton replied tersely, taking another sip of her coffee.

"Is this how you wish it to be between us?" Rei asked indignantly. "If that is the case, just tell me so."

Peyton wanted to roll her eyes but remained stoic and in control of her emotions.

"Your approach to rectifying the situation makes me truly consider if this is how it should to be."

Rei put down his cup of coffee, tilting his head in confusion. "Do you no longer care for me, Peyton?"

"I'm hurt, Rei." Peyton slammed her coffee onto the metal table, "You lied to me. Multiple times. And, we resurfaced a hidden, past *lover* of yours between those lies. You betrayed me. You deceived me. You manipulated me. So, yes, I care for you. But I don't know if I can trust you. So, for now – this is how it must be between us."

Peyton crossed her arms and legs, and then looked away with a final 'hmph.'

Rei took a deep breath, leaning back against his chair when fortunately, Liv emerged from the cabin to join the duo outside.

"Good morning." She said happily, before registering Peyton's body facing away from Rei's scowl.

Liv eyed Peyton in question, and thankfully registered Peyton's plea to remain outdoors, when she elected to sit beside her friend and enjoy the brisk morning air.

Not too long after, Dylan and Hayden followed suit, bolstering the curiosity of Piper, Tristan and Kyril to join within degrees.

"Is anyone hungover?" Piper whispered, holding her head between two hands.

Peyton smirked, reaching out to her friend and pulling her into a comforting embrace.

"Young one, you soon shall learn." Peyton grinned, petting Piper's luscious midnight locks soothingly and summoning water, vitamins and a hearty breakfast sandwich. "Electrolytes are your friend, hydration is key and make sure to consume something greasy to absorb the remaining alcohol."

"You're my hero." Piper cooed, leaning further into Peyton as she chugged water and started chowing down on a egg and sausage biscuit.

"What happened to Jocelyn and Demetrius?" Dylan inquired, taking a bite out of her own breakfast dish, sausage and scrambled eggs on a plate.

"Joss left to host the Celts on Jupiter, Demetrius left to seek out the Orishas for an alliance." Hayden explained quickly, sitting down beside Liv with a full cup of coffee which caught her attention, immediately.

Handing it selflessly to her, she smiled gratefully. They were too cute together.

"Will either be back before the inevitable Puerdios's invasion?" Tristan asked.

"I don't know." Hayden replied honestly.

It was nice to see the two getting along, especially seeing Tristan not overreact to the news of Liv and Hayden becoming betrothed, although Peyton was certain he was not taking it lightly.

"Sure would have been nice to have Joss's sight for that one." Dylan joked, running her hand through her stunning auburn hair.

In fact, it would have been nice to have any insight to the alliances they had all worked so tirelessly hard to secure, especially understanding if any would prove fruitful for the impending battle.

"Why Puerdios?" Ammiras asked sternly, but curiously.

"It's the heart of the Pure Gods," Hayden assessed, deliberating aloud, "deities at this age are young, influential; it's an easy target to cut off our education processes and easily assuage students to support The Dark Gods' beliefs."

"Kronos and Arlo's beliefs." Tristan corrected him.

"I apologize, I misspoke." Hayden nodded in agreement.

"Egyptians are up in the air." Liv murmured, "But Buddhist Gods are committed, Norse may not support an academic battle but we can call on them if we feel it is necessary, Celts are Dark, but hopefully those on our side can recover soon."

"There is hope." Hayden agreed, grabbing her hand and kissing it gently.

"Should we go back to Puerdios?" Liv asked softly, turning to the group for guidance. "I love you all, especially our Gemini Piper and Taurus Hayden, but don't we all…"

"Feel guilty." Peyton cut in, shrugging.

"I do." Piper yawned, finally sitting herself up. "I'm so grateful for all of you making this weekend incredible, but we celebrated. It would feel insensitive to succumb to another night of debauchery when we should be preparing to protect our school."

"I agree." Hayden added, "Thank you all for the surprise celebration. If anything, you all should continue to enjoy yourself but," he turned specifically to Liv to explain, "I need to get back to the palace to plan with Silas."

Liv nodded in understanding. "We've been young and irresponsible for the past two days, it's time to get back to reality."

With that, Peyton stood alongside the Element Elite and future Queen all too eagerly, ignoring Rei's stare.

She'd follow anyone who gave her a reason to put some much-needed distance between her Security Elite and self.

FORTY

JOCELYN

She could see Niall clearer than ever.

It was a strange transition, moving from not ever seeing or knowing of the divine Celtic prince, to now being able to map out his exact whereabouts and future actions, as if she had been tracking him all his life.

Nevertheless, she paced across the foyer of Demetrius's grand palace on Jupiter. Just because Niall had escaped the wrath of Danu did not mean the Celtic warrior was safe or in any fighting condition.

Ensuring all who wished to leave the cursed land to successfully cross the threshold to safety would involve a bloodbath of fighting loyal soldiers commanded to keep all refugees as prisoners and leave the prince bruised, bloody and weak. The only way out was through.

He no longer led his people to safety, but crawled behind them, praying his final sacrifices would be enough.

"The beds are made and ready?" Joss confirmed with the headmistress of the house, Sloane.

"Yes, ma'am." She bowed, before beckoning other staff members into the room for further instruction.

"We'll assess each as they enter, determine what level of medical attention is required. I should be able to see into each past and future to organize accordingly." Joss stated aloud, more so gathering her thoughts for herself. "I will work as quickly as I can."

She turned back to her team and began to instruct orders.

"Dorian, you will help me filter and assign arrivals. Send anyone to me with whom you are unsure. Bex, make sure we have clean cloth. Maryn – honey water and broth. Sloane, many will simply need to rest; but we'll need to begin rotations of sanitary practices, eventually."

Jocelyn paused, long enough to look at the newest team member, Rhys, the Medicine Elite. "Thank you for coming and helping us out, Rhys."

"My dear Jocelyn, of course." He smiled humbly. "We have everything we need set up in the parlour."

Jocelyn turned around, beginning another repetitive walk across the main floor.

"Lorne, any able-bodied deities will need to be put on patrol." Although anticipating the Celtic Queen's arrival, fortunately Joss hadn't seen any clear visions of Danu. But it couldn't hurt to be prepared. "If we run out of beds, use remaining blankets for mattresses and set them in the dining hall."

"Ma'am, Princess Jocelyn, how many are we expecting?" Maryn inquired softly, but looked worried.

"As many who come." Jocelyn replied softly, turning to the twenty deities who stood at her command because of the Solar System God, ten more from the Medicine Pillar in support of Rhys. "Demetrius selflessly opened up his home to those who seek aid. We welcome all who come. We help anyone in need."

Suddenly, a flash of Griffins stampeding across gaseous orange land burned into Jocelyn's mind. Searching the mass of unrecognizable faces, she did not spot Niall among them. Nevertheless, they were coming.

The knock on the door proved her vision. Jocelyn snapped her head toward the door, nodding to Sloane to open the entry at once.

"Work quickly and kindly. Do not be afraid to ask questions!" Jocelyn commanded, her voice thundering through the palace walls.

A swarm of deities crawled through, skin and bones, dirty and weak. Jocelyn sprinted to the front, beginning her assessments and commanding them to specific hosts and rooms.

So many needed medical attention; the blood was abundant but none were strong enough to heal themselves. Rhys and his pillar had quite the fight ahead of them.

More vessels passed through the entry way, first dozens, then hundreds. So many that Joss lost count of how many futures she had envisioned and pasts she recollected because they were all blurring together and playing into one terrifying horror movie.

"Spear in the abdomen, malnourished and dehydrated." Jocelyn assessed the newest Celtic stranger to enter the palace, "Parlour."

One of the five Shooting Stars from Demetrius's military, who had been rotating and escorting guests to deliver Jocelyn and Dorian's assessments, took the male from her immediately. Another Shooting Star arrived just in time to receive Dorian's next evaluation.

Only fifty Shooting Stars remained from Demetrius's army, they were already so understaffed with protecting the Solar System's realm. Jocelyn's only hope was that their hundreds of guests would recover swiftly to return the favor when Danu inevitably came. To give that monster the fair fight they deserved.

After hours of standing and greeting new guests, Jocelyn's visions were growing weaker, her powers were slowly depleting. She tried to seek out Niall in between evaluations, but between her diminishing powers and only moments between each diagnosis, he remained unseen – perhaps his preference as he tried to dodge Danu's foresight and therefore hers, or so Jocelyn hoped.

"She…" Jocelyn closed her eyes, focusing on the next girl in front of her. A vision of water flashed before her eyes and a recognizable cottage… "Caitriona?"

Caitriona lifted her small head at the sound of her name.

Bruised, swollen and dirty, her face was unrecognizable.

"Where's your mother?" Jocelyn looked out, hoping to find a semblance of Adair among the arrivals.

Caitriona tried to explain but instead, began sobbing.

"It's okay. It's okay. You are safe." Jocelyn bent low so she was eye level with the girl. She looked exhausted and terrified but remained unharmed. "Suzyn here will show you to a bed where you can rest-"

Caitriona shook her head weakly, clinging to Jocelyn's leg.

Joss sighed, turning to the Shooting Star, shrugging. "Bring some blankets and broth, she can rest out here, with me. I'll look after her."

Suzyn nodded, running away to do the inverse of the original plan.

"Caitriona, come over here." Jocelyn grabbed the girl's hand and brought her to the wall, away from the entrance. "You can rest here but if anything happens, do I have your promise that you will listen to any command I may give?"

Caitriona nodded her head, looking more content, before she yawned and sat herself down.

"Good girl. I'll be right over here. You are safe, my darling." Jocelyn sadly smiled, brushing her hand gently through the young girl's copper hair.

With that, she stood herself up and clasped her hands together, spinning her emerald green gown around back toward the entrance, pausing only a moment to yawn and pray to Zeus that she hadn't just inherited an orphan. The thought was too heartbreaking.

So instead, she habitually brushed her beaded gown and adjusted the corset, returning with an unknown strength within her to continue on.

She had just wrapped up with a young man needing a cast for a broken limb, when she heard a low voice growl, "Make way! Make way!"

Fortunately, it appeared the Celts had smartly organized themselves so the most pressing cases had arrived first; Joss began seeing less urgency with medical care as she continued assessing the newcomers.

"Your highness, I'm afraid we've run out of beds." Maryn reported.

Just wonderful timing. Joss thought to herself, but kept a brave face.

"Begin using blankets, as planned. And move those who can sit upright to chairs, or any seating available."

Jocelyn turned her head directly to the commotion, nodding to Dorian that she would handle it as she walked toward the noise. Disorder would not be tolerated.

A strong soldier led a Griffin directly to the castle, the creature carrying what looked like a corpse…

Niall.

Jocelyn's heart dropped.

"Make way for the prince!" The man yelled, splitting the line apart, now close enough to the palace that Jocelyn saw the annihilation that Prince Niall had endured in full from risking his own life to ensure the safety of his people.

He was unconscious, skin turning blue and spiked with a dozen arrows, the blood from his corpse leaving a trail behind him as he was carried through the crowd.

"Over here!" Jocelyn commanded, beckoning the soldier at once while running out to him simultaneously.

She grabbed Niall's hand, focusing on the remaining drops of her powers to diagnose what he needed in order to heal. His hands were cold.

"No, no… no." Jocelyn whispered, entwining his hand with her other and sending heat to warm up his body as she sought any vision to clue her in on what had happened.

Visions began appearing, becoming apart of Jocelyn, with welcome.

Niall had sent fairies loyal to him to lead the people away from Danu's curse and without detection. Telling them no more details than to make their choice sporatically and to only tell people to *follow them to safety, guaranteed by Niall.*

He stood by the edge of the hidden kingdom with the Griffins, dozens of soldiers at hand to ward off Danu's loyalists until all had safely departed. Or combat them until death.

All Niall could grant his people was time and spontaneity, praying it was sufficient enough to safely escape.

Prince Niall, we must go. Now. There are too many!

A bloody and sweaty soldier advised the prince, equally as bruised and drained.

We don't have much time. Ross, you must help as many more on your way out and tell the troops the same.

"*Sir!?*" Ross cried, confused, not daring to leave his master behind.

"*Go!*" Niall commanded, turning just in time to block a sword from behind, held by one of Danu's soldiers.

Reckless. You stupid fool. Jocelyn thought as she watched the scene play out.

After combatting and defeating a dozen more soldiers, finally one gutted him in his core with a sword. That's when the arrows began.

With each hit, Jocelyn physically cringed, as if she was starting to feel the pain and impact of each steel head penetrating Niall's body.

Chaos ensued, less of Niall's soldiers were visible for backup. Soon, only Ross remained, but even he was diminishing into the shadows…

"*Niall! All are out! Pull back!*"

Ross's voice reverberated from the sky.

Niall kept fighting. His eyes were turning red, bloodshot. A sign of poisoning.

"Get out!" Jocelyn cried aloud, no longer remembering this was the past for once, forgetting her need to maintain composure. It felt too raw, too dangerous.

Niall's head snapped behind him, then looked to the sky, stunned.

Then Jocelyn saw the soldier run toward Niall, sword out.

Right toward his neck.

"Behind you!" Jocelyn screamed.

Niall turned, barely blocking the sword, but too weak to keep it held away from his throat. He whistled, calling for a Griffin to rush from the sky, hopping onto it swiftly, and began his ascent.

But with the motion, his attacker had been able to slice his calf open, cutting the prince deeply before Niall darted away from the Irish lands and into the night sky.

Jocelyn stepped back, in horror that he had managed to make it this far. It was an arduous journey even when one was fully recovered and in good health.

"Take him directly to Rhys. He'll need the arrows removed and stitches for his torso." Jocelyn gently lifted the side of his shirt up, blushing when she felt his rock stone abs, and paused when she realized the bloodied gash had dried with the shirt clinging to it.

She searched further to find the source of the poison.

Ricin.

"Ross. Tell Rhys the opponent's blades and arrows were laced with Ricin. He'll know what to do."

"How did you know...?" Ross inquired with wonder.

"Not now. Go!" Jocelyn commanded.

She felt lightheaded and queasy but refused to acknowledge her prince was in a much worse condition. Joss only hoped she had gathered enough information to combat the odds and uphill battle that Rhys and his medical team now faced with Niall.

For one vision was crystal clear. They only had a matter of minutes between life and death for the Celtic prince.

FORTY-ONE

LIV

Stacking a Pure alliance meeting on top of Piper's aggressive educational schedule was at least a welcome yet overwhelming addition to her life. Liv understood that her academics were incredibly important, but admittedly that valued notion had been watered down by her university's impending doom.

Alas, she found herself flying with a grumpy Rei, an excited Piper and an anxious Tristan to the royal palace to greet the Pure Gods' newest allies, King Rāhula and Queen Chanthira.

Truthfully, trying to remember where she was planning to sleep that night and coordinating with Hayden was proving more difficult as they had barely slept in the same location twice since their return from Egypt. If all went to plan and they had to evacuate Puerdios, Liv wasn't sure she could track *another* educational residence to frequent.

But that was a conversation for another day, as long as she spent the night with Hayden, whether at the Puerdios loft, royal palace, cabin or Elements Pillar headquarters, she had no reason to complain. Tonight, she'd remain at the King's palace loft, after a not-so-fun alliance meeting followed by a wonderful engagement celebration, hosted by Daphne.

The fact that her future mother-in-law could have planned such a soiree (and so effortlessly transform it from the King's belated birthday symposium) gave Liv an inkling the Candor Elite may have seen the plans coming to fruition prior to the weekend festivities taking place.

Nevertheless, Liv donned an exquisite white gown armed with feathers and beading to mark the occasion. Fit for a future queen, the dress was gaudy but timeless with a high collared tank bodice and belle sleeves. Although not entirely her style, Liv was willing to appease the Pure subjects and new allies with the detailed couture they demanded for such an occasion, knowing all too well there was no way the powerful society would infiltrate the dress she wanted to wear on her and Hayden's special day.

Riding atop Pegasus and gliding through the night sky, she imagined she looked like a falling star, wondering how many mortals wished upon her in flight tonight.

When Liv and her friends arrived at the Royal Palace, security guards swiftly greeted them, conducting protocol with Rei to confirm both his identity and the others.

"Thank you." Liv nodded politely, wondering if there would ever come a time when the Royal Palace would feel like home. Even as the King's soul mate, and now fiancé, she still felt like it wasn't *theirs*.

When she approached, she felt nervous, like she had to forever prove her worth against the fortress's strong barricade and elevate her being to match the refined power residing within.

"Monaco."

Liv magnetized to the king, finding Hayden standing sexily in a black tuxedo near the parlour. At least she always had a home in him.

"Fiancé." Liv smiled, forcing herself not to drool.

"May I have a moment before the meeting begins?" He asked softly, approaching her and giving her a kiss before whispering, "I have a surprise for you."

Liv took a deep breath, intoxicated by his soothing scent as chills went down her spine. His hand glazed her arm, brushing against her skin and successfully melting her body completely into his.

"I'm all yours." She dazzled, excusing herself politely from the others and escorting him upstairs into his private loft.

Peyton silently followed, wearing a stunning velvet blue gown with a slit that went higher than her thigh. Rei would certainly be drooling tonight, too.

When they finally arrived to his room, Hayden kindly asked Peyton to wait outside. Of course, his security guard retorted back with a classic jibe, "I see how it is now! I thought we were *friends!*" Before laughing it out and shooing them inside, deflecting their apologies as she reiterated, "I was *joking!*"

Rolling her eyes with a grin, Liv leaned against the wall as soon as Hayden shut the door. Her heart began to flutter as she looked at his mouth, it looked so soft and kissable...

Hayden grabbed her hand, playing with the large stone that sat on her ring finger. He took a step toward her, pressing Liv against the cool wall with his heated body.

"Are you still certain you want to be my fiancée?" Hayden asked quietly, "You can still back out before tonight, with no harm done."

"I'm wearing the ring, aren't I?" Liv laughed back, grabbing his waist and pulling him closer. "And you? You're still committed to marrying a crazy, loud-mouthed half-mortal who will never stop giving you a hard time?"

Hayden chuckled darkly, his breath tingling Liv's neck. "I'm never opposed to being *hard* so long as I can do something about it."

He leaned closer to her and bit her earlobe. She certainly had already started giving him a hard time, all right.

"You didn't answer the question." Liv whispered, her breath growing heavy as he continued kissing down her neck.

The heavens, she wanted him to do that soft massage forever.

"I'm wearing the tux, aren't I?" Hayden mimicked softly, before his seductive voice lowered into a lustful purr. "I will be yours however and for ever long as you'll have me, Olivia Monaco."

"Have me now, Hayden." Liv pleaded, spreading her legs wider as she reached down to his manhood and started massaging it. "No tux needed for what I want you to do to me."

The king groaned in pleasure, lifting Liv and walking her over to his bed.

"But, if you ruin my dress I will make your married life a living hell." Liv teased, looking up at Hayden from the velvet-covered bed as he unbuttoned his pants.

"I wouldn't *dare.*" Hayden grinned, climbing atop her carefully and inserting his hardness into her.

She felt whole and entirely filled with him inside her, but wanted more, more of him, more of Hayden. She craved him. Liv started motioning her hips for friction, scaling her hands delicately down his muscular arms and clung to his back, until she grabbed his stone glutes in her hands and continued the motion. He penetrated her deeper, faster, uncontrollably with pleasure. And damn, he felt so good. Their bodies moved harmoniously as one, until quickly, Liv began climaxing, the movement between the two becoming more intense, overwhelming and incredible, until she was yelling Hayden's name with passion and in unison with his own apex.

She collapsed against the bed, giggling as Hayden meticulously stepped away from her, ensuring he did not step on her feathers or rip any fabric with his shoe.

"Oh Hayden, that was a wonderful gift." Liv exclaimed on a high. After a long, stressful day of continuing to slam her brain with facts and spells, a mind-blowing sexual encounter was exactly what she needed to relax before jumping into royal obligations 2.0.

"Why thank you, fiancée." Hayden replied smugly, pulling up his pants and buttoning them, "However, there's an actual reason I brought you up here, *that* was just a delightful bonus."

"Well, I'm satisfied." Liv grinned, finally pulling herself up to begin gathering her gown into bunches.

"Won't that ruin your dress?" Hayden raised an eyebrow.

"*I'm* allowed to ruin my dress if I so choose." Liv clarified, running to the bathroom to clean herself and adjust her gown to be once again ready for a very public viewing.

When she returned, she found Hayden holding a box.

"What's that?" Liv smiled coyly.

"For you." Hayden opened the box, revealing a diamond headband, almost a tiara but not so obvious with the crown design.

Liv was speechless. Her ring was extroadinary, but this? It was a whole new level of extravagance. Yet, it fit her so perfectly – there was no way Liv would wear a tiara for casual gatherings, but this was an ideal blend of tradition and her unique style. Alluding to the responsibility of future queen, but still adding her own personal modern flair.

"Thank you, Hayden." Liv whispered, her eyes sparkling as bright as the diamond piece that lay before her.

"May I?" Hayden asked shyly.

"Of course." Liv smiled, turning around so he could place the headpiece around her signature messy french braid.

Once the jewels were placed, Liv spun around, beaming and requesting Hayden's final approval.

"Stunning." Hayden stated before adding, "The tiara is nice, too."

Liv laughed, swatting him playfully when they heard Peyton holler from outside, "One degree warning!"

"Let's not keep her waiting, your majesty." Liv joked, grabbing Hayden's hand and loving the feeling of his metal band pressed between her fingers.

Walking down the grand staircase, Liv was happy to see so many familiar faces since their last meeting, along with a few new ones as well.

A couple stood beside Piper and Tristan, whom Liv assumed to be King Rāhula and Queen Chanthira.

"Please, call me Thira." The queen smiled kindly as she bowed.

Liv followed suit, but King Rāhula stopped her.

"Your people saved us. You do not bow to us, King Hayden and future Queen Olivia."

Liv smiled endearingly, already admiring the humble royal duo who stood before them.

"We are grateful for your alliance, so will adhere to whatever you request, my friend." Hayden nodded with a smile, before leading Liv to speak with other allies and meet new ones.

Dyoedi congratulated both Hayden and Liv on their engagement, but other than that, the centaur remained as poised and graceful as ever before. Even Calithya nodded stubbornly to Ammiras's kind words, although she did roll her eyes a few times during the encounter. Fortunately, Zayne stood beside the siren prince, bringing a level of calm to Calithya's immature ways. But, overtime, the siren queen began conversing more, mostly in response to Zayne's simple prompting, opening her up to become quite a delight.

They were going to move on and speak to Silas, when the couple standing beside Rei caught Liv's attention. Specifically, the brunette woman who stood beside the tall blonde Norse man.

It wasn't simply the power the guest radiated that Liv could feel, a vibration that she felt she could control if she chose to, but that the stunning visitor had managed to make Rei smile for the first time since his return from Vanaheim.

Hayden caught Liv's distraction, so concluded his conversation with Silas to guide her closer. Liv was grateful for the respite, because the brunette mesmerized her, and she was eager to meet the goddess who had so easily won Rei over.

"Hello, King Hayden and Olivia," the Security Elite began the formal introduction without missing a beat, "please meet King Mothi and Queen Gigi of the Norse Deities."

"The pleasure is all ours. Thank you for coming to our aid." Hayden replied honestly, shaking the king's hand and kissing the knuckle of his wife. King Mothi followed the same motion, gently grabbing Liv's hand and kissing the top of it.

Liv met the gaze of Queen Gigi, her piercing blue eyes seeming so familiar, in fact – her entire being felt familiar.

"It's so nice to meet you." Queen Gigi beamed, extending an arm and pulling Liv into a warm embrace. "Rei and Peyton have told me *so* much about you."

Her smile. In fact, now that Liv thought about it…

Queen Gigi looked just like the female version of Tristan, albeit the blue eyes.

JOCELYN

After she had spent the remnants of her powers fighting to see into Niall's past, Jocelyn was entirely spent. Fortunately, the majority of those remaining to be inspected were relatively stable, mostly dealing with famine and exhaustion. Jocelyn sought to welcome all remaining deities, without using her gift – only a welcoming charm – while Caitriona slept peacefully on a blanket against the wall behind her.

When Joss had greeted the final visitor, she took a deep breath, in a tired daze, not entirely thinking straight as to what needed to be her next step. She turned to face inside the mansion walls and found chaos. Able-bodied deities ran from here to there, carting bandages or soup in a flurry; even exhausted Celts pitched in, recovering strength quickly now that they were separated from Danu's curse and having had a proper meal.

Jocelyn took a step forward to help deliver food and more importantly, visit Niall, but heard a subtle snore behind her.

She spun around, looking at the small child who still had not eaten.

"Well, first things first."

Jocelyn brushed her hands together and then squat down to lift the girl into her arms. Caitriona stirred, opening a tiny, tired eye to glance up at Jocelyn, before taking a deep breath, shifting her body and falling back to sleep.

She walked toward Rhys, knowing he still worked on Prince Niall in the parlour-turned-medicine-ward. It had been an hour and Rhys still had his hands full with the escaped Celts' leader.

Jocelyn went straight to the bar, adjusting Caitriona into one arm so she could pour herself a gin and take a much-needed swig.

Hell to it. She drank straight from the bottle.

"Care to share?" A husky voice growled from behind, followed by a wince. "That would help with the pain, right doctor?"

Rhys chuckled, ignoring the request.

Jocelyn heard another scowl from the patient and then a groaned gasp.

She turned to find Niall conscious, but still bloody and sliced.

"It would seem a waste. If you took one sip, it would simply leak out through your cuts." Jocelyn retorted dryly.

"Kill two birds. Numb the pain and thoroughly cleanse the wounds." Niall shortly inhaled, holding his breath as Rhys continued removing the toxin from each cut before sewing it closed.

Jocelyn kneeled by the prince, gingerly grabbing his hand.

He felt warm, feverish. Jocelyn placed her cool hand against his forehead, it was blazing – an inferno peaking in temperature.

"Iced wash cloths over here when you have a minute, Bex." Jocelyn called, catching one of the palace staff running by. She turned back to Niall, looking him in the eye. "You need to breathe, Niall. You're safe. And I'd much rather enjoy a dram of Irish gin with you alive than dead."

Niall laughed, then flinched as his sculpted torso moved in response. He eyed Jocelyn admiringly, then noticed Caitriona still asleep in her arms.

"Are you… holding Caitriona… or is this another hallucination?" Niall asked speculatively, his voice no more than a whisper.

"My reality." Jocelyn stood up and hopped, lifting Caitriona higher on her hip in response. She turned to the Medicine Elite, calling out her last order before finding a permanent bed for the girl. "Rhys, when you are done, bring Niall to my room – he can rest there."

She looked down to Niall, "And you – no funny business. I'll see you when you're all patched up."

Jocelyn glared at the Celtic prince before spinning and stomping off to her room, first stopping by the kitchens and requesting that two soups and hot teas be delivered for her new roommates: a girl and a prince.

LIV

"Thank you all, for joining us upon such short notice." Hayden announced to the large room, full of allies and supporters from around the world. "We have much to discuss, but we start with the most pressing: An update with alliances forged since our past meeting, an anticipated Puerdios invasion, and what we should prepare to face when we inevitably fight Kronos and Arlo's armies."

"The first," Silas began, standing to begin his report, "we are honored to have gained alliances with the Norse Gods, with King Mothi and Queen Gigi here to represent them, along with the Buddhist Gods, with King Rāhula and Queen Chanthira. Please extend a warm welcome to both."

Applause thundered across the room. Liv turned to Hayden, beaming at what they had accomplished, with more to come.

"We are currently aiding Celtic deities on Jupiter, in which Princess Jocelyn is overseeing for a speedy recovery. We still await the answer from a prospective ally, the Egyptians, and our existing ally, Demetrius of the Solar System, currently seeks out the Orishas to hopefully bring more to our aid, if found."

As Silas sat, Rei stood.

"We want to be transparent to all in this room when discussing these partnerships, opportunities and challenges. We are proud to have the Buddhist deities on our side, but it came with a cost. Releasing them from their enemy Shiva has developed another opponent from the Pure Gods and Buddhist Gods standing united – we must be weary of the Hindu deities; however, we have a loyal Naga seeking out any who oppose Shiva to potentially join our side."

King Rāhula rose at the conclusion of Rei's statement. "We appreciate what the Pure Gods have done for us and are willing to fight Kronos and Arlo, knowing that we may call on you for aid when Shiva comes to seek his revenge."

Rei nodded, agreeing with the terms and continuing on with his war update.

"With the Celtic aid on Jupiter, we gain another threat – the Goddess Danu – who entrapped her deities under a curse and claimed a throne that did not rightfully belong to her. Her tyranny must end, and with the leadership of the rightful heir, Prince Niall, on our side, we accept their alliance knowing we may need to fight Danu and her army to support our alliance with the Solar System."

Hayden thanked Silas and Rei for their honest reports, asking for any questions before continuing onto the next agenda item.

Dyoedi politely raised her concern with the floor open. "So, we must remain in war for the foreseeable future? How will this affect our economy? The mortals in which we seek to protect?"

Hayden addressed her consternation honestly.

"Together, we are stronger. But I will not sugar coat our challenges – tough times will face us. All we can do is control what we can, our perspective, and take every progression day by day. It's no longer a battle against Pure and Dark, but a war for humanity."

Dyoedi sighed loudly in distress, but did not object to his response, and when others didn't chime in with additional apprehension, the Pure God king continued on with his agenda.

"Today's battle to focus on is that Daphne, Candor Pillar Elite, has foreseen a Puerdios invasion by Kronos and Arlo four sunsets from tonight. Too many choices have not been made to deliberate a true victory or defeat. As a precaution, we will send all attending students and faculty to a school in Scotland which specializes in magical education, effective immediately."

Liv turned, trying to remain calm as her mind began racing.

Effective immediately? Hayden I can't go back to Scotland. I can't. I…

She was shaking at the thought. Her hands turned cold. She was having trouble breathing.

Hayden glanced down to Liv, grabbing her hand and squeezing it as subtly as possible so as to not cause a stir.

Ollie, you're not going. He thought quickly, trying to appease her shock and unexpected reaction. *You'll remain here, with Piper as a tutor. You belong here, with me. I'm sorry – I assumed you knew that.*

Liv took a deep breath, the first in what seemed like a minute. She was still shaking, but at least her mind wasn't going to the dark places.

Ollie?

Liv nodded, squeezing his hand.

I'm okay.

Hayden breathed, returning his full attention again to the crowd but not relinquishing his comforting grasp from hers.

"We have grown with our alliances and are grateful to our allies both old and new – but we still need to be strategic with our approach to defend the school. Kronos has engaged restricted powers to create the Soulless – a breed of immortal vessels brought to life without their souls, monsters who attack without thought – so, their numbers are infinite and ever-growing. They are easy to kill but only with Nordic steel that have absorbed destructive venom, so require powers to keep them at bay. They outnumber us, so we need to figure out a plan that does not deplete us all."

"Upon Rei's request, we have brought cursed metal to forge weaponry for your soldiers." King Mothi offered. "We can bring more Norse steel if we have a vessel to penetrate the poison you require."

"Thank you, King Mothi." Hayden replied to their ally, before returning to the larger masses, "Any who seek training in swordplay, archery or combat are welcome to attend Rei's classes here at the palace daily between 300 degrees sunrise and 120 degrees sunset. Now, we discuss strategy."

Hayden sat down, returning the floor to Silas and Rei.

Rei brought up a 3-D image of Puerdios to serve point as a map and visual for their plans.

"We will begin with our best archers, lined within the castle borders to shoot from a distance." Silas explained, tracing in a silver marker the areas they would be positioned and overlooking the lands – covering all surrounding plain, mountain and forest. "The sirens will be equipped with Nordic tridents to protect the bordering sea."

"If deities fly in from the sky, the archerists will redirect there." Rei chimed in, his pen in gold for any conditional tactics.

"We will bury spikes into the ground, to be released upon command to gut Soulless deities in formation."

"How many?" Hayden clarified.

"We brought enough metal for five hundred spears, two thousand arrowheads and one thousand swords, give or take any needed adjustments." Mothi interjected.

"If we're accurate with every device, it leaves us with at least six thousand Soulless to individually stab." Hayden grimaced. "Our best swordsmen – across all allies – will be granted a Viking sword. They will be specifically positioned to combat the Soulless while those without the proper weaponry will be tiered. Less experienced deities will team up with swordsmen to distract and delay the Soulless so our troops are not outnumbered. Those more skilled with their powers will be positioned to combat the Dark Gods."

"And if we qualify for multiple categories?" Tristan speculated.

"Then pick your poison." Queen Gigi replied, eyeing Tristan warily. "And pick it wisely."

FORTY-TWO

JOCELYN

Caitriona was sound asleep in her silk bed, only after Jocelyn forced the girl to sip some soup and drink water. The next round of the child's energy was going to be dedicated to a bath.

Jocelyn chuckled at the peaceful sleeper before quietly exiting the bedroom and checking in on the others, now assigning rooms of patients to her team so they could equally feed, bathe and take care of the Celts, as well as themselves.

She was beginning to see the sun rising after what seemed like an endless night, when a vision of Giselle flashed across her mind, so clear and devastating, Jocelyn dropped to the ground.

Giselle was in the royal palace. She was *at* the royal palace.

And Jocelyn was here, amidst chaos and decay.

Zeus, she looked so happy, sitting beside a beautiful Nordic deity and laughing melodically as she watched her brother with Piper from afar.

Jocelyn could see Hayden and Liv clinking their champagne flutes, properly celebrating their engagement with the Pure God world – oh, how she missed her friends, her family.

Crushing against the wall, a tear emerged from Jocelyn's eye.

She was *so* tired.

Her breath shortened as she sniffled, crouched against the wall. The crying would become uncontrollable and if there was one thing Jocelyn needed to be, or appear to be, it was in control.

"Jocelyn, are you okay?"

Jocelyn blew in air from her runny nose, wiping her eyes immediately before she replied as clearly and calmly as her sinuses would allow, "Yes. Of course, I am."

She stood, taking a breath as she rearranged her gown, turning to find Niall standing upright – well, with the help of Dorian – before her.

"Oh, good. You're alive." Jocelyn spat angrily.

She wasn't sure exactly why she was so mad at the prince. Perhaps it was how vivid his idiocy appeared in her visions from his attempt at getting himself murdered and allowing her to witness it without any restraint from the cosmos.

Nevertheless, she knew her eyes were most likely bloodshot, but she held her head high in the hope that she could actually get away with her small meltdown.

Don't let them in.

Jocelyn knew she could not allow anyone to see her weaknesses, that she had to remain strong. A leader. And burden the pressure of leading these people with insurmountable grace.

Niall remained quiet, looking to Dorian before he spoke.

"Thank you for helping me find Jocelyn, Dorian. The princess can escort me to her room from here."

"But, sir – you surely can't…" Dorian argued in surprise, his eyes growing wider as Niall pulled his own arm from around Dorian's neck and then peeled Dorian's arm from around his waist until he was standing upright, although painfully, with only a cane to help balance his bandaged leg.

"Thank you, Dorian." Niall cut him off, his voice kind but laced with command, compelling him to obedience.

"Of course, let me know if you need anything." Dorian bowed to both Niall and then Jocelyn, before scurrying off.

Now alone with Niall, Jocelyn felt shy and embarrassed of her cracked façade. She needed to be stronger, for Niall and for Demetrius, and especially for their people.

"Come with me." Niall quietly requested, putting his arm around the princess, but not for support, for comfort.

They walked slowly, but he held her close as she inevitably led him to her room.

"I'm sorry about that…out there." Jocelyn whispered, quietly shutting the door before guiding Niall to the empty side of the bed.

"It's okay to feel overwhelmed, Jocelyn. You and your team did more than I could have thought possible." Niall honestly replied, and without judgment, as she helped him get onto the bed. "But you should also feel *proud*."

A relief spread over him as soon as he lay back against the satin pillow. He took a deep breath and closed his eyes for a moment; making Jocelyn feel all the more guilty for her weakness, having relied on him in a moment when he needed her so much more.

"Thank you, Niall." Jocelyn smiled, squeezing his hand before she stood up, "I'll let you rest, but I'm here. If you need *anything*."

Niall looked over to Caitriona, who also slept soundly beside him. He scooted over to the center of the bed, making room for Jocelyn to also lay down.

"Oh, no – I couldn't!" Jocelyn laughed awkwardly at the invitation. "You're sweet, but there's so much more I should do."

"Jocelyn, you're taking care of everyone. But who's taking care of you? You've done enough for now. You can rest." Niall said blankly.

Joss crossed her arms, tilting her head in amazement.

"Look, we're immortal but we're not invincible." Niall explained with a sigh. "We're allowed to hold eachother's hands to get through the tougher times. And tonight was one of the tough ones. So, come here, because I need you to hold my hand."

Jocelyn considered the request, applauding the prince's clever angle and play on her words. It certainly wasn't worth expending either of their energy by stubbornly trying to maintain a façade that she had already broken in the hallway. So, she acquiesced, crawling into her bed with heavy eyes, taking Niall's hand as he wrapped her in his arms, allowing her to feel secure, safe and comforted enough for her tears of relief to fall as she finally crashed into a much-needed sleep.

LIV

Daphne did not spare any expense for the celebration following the meeting. Champagne bottles continued to open and flow, stunning music continued to play while guests danced and powerful Pure deities from across the globe came to celebrate the recent engagement of the Pure God King and Element Elite and a step closer to the famous prophecy coming to fruition.

After she had greeted over a hundred different guests, Liv spotted Tristan approaching her with a flute of an amber beverage too dark to be champagne.

"Don't tell me you've gone all soft, now that you're to be the future queen." He smirked, handing the cocktail over.

Liv tasted the whiskey and then retorted back, "I'm only disappointed this isn't Scotch. You insult me, T."

"Please don't throw me in the dungeon for my offense." He smiled back, spinning toward the dance floor and spotting Piper across the way, chatting with Magni.

His grin turned blank at the sight.

"If you like Piper, here's a brilliant idea: ask her out." Liv dramatically cast her hands in front of her, as if she were revealing an unexpected piece of advice and laying it out before them.

"It's complicated." Tristan muttered quietly before taking a sip of his drink.

"It's complicated only because you both make it complicated. Not because it actually is." Liv rolled her eyes. "You don't want to scare Piper with feelings, so you hold back. Piper is scared of her feelings and too intimidated to do anything, so instead you both pine for eachother from afar instead of actually enjoying eachother's company… which you still somehow manage to do. But with masochistic intermissions. How? I don't know."

"It's easy for you to say. With you and me, it's always been easy. Effortless. We jab at eachother, laugh it off and still genuinely care for one another. I just wish it was like that with Piper."

Liv rolled her eyes again. "First of all, it's easy with us because we're friends. I'm a safezone."

"You weren't always 'just my friend.'" Tristan reminded her.

"Sure." Liv agreed, contemplating exactly how far she wanted to go down *that* path. "But, even taking that into consideration, it still took time for us to develop that comfort. You still can't default our relationship to a standard. Every relationship is beautiful in its own unique way. You've just got to man-up and explore the discomfort with Piper – the first of which is to just tell her how you feel. Peel the band-aid off."

Tristan looked like he was tracking but then became stunned. "What's a band-aid?"

Liv rolled her eyes again, noticing how they had now caught the attention of the topic at hand, with Piper shyly glancing over at the two of them, more so Tristan, between exchanges with the Norse prince. Whether Piper was longingly pining from afar or requesting a secret rescue, it was Tristan's moment to shine.

Wrapping up the conversation quickly, Liv concluded, "That's exactly why we'd never work – now, *go!*"

She shoved Tristan forward, nearly colliding him with Gigi who had walked past, but managed to spill all of his whiskey across her mustard yellow gown.

Zeus, the resemblance was uncanny. But Liv shook it off when Tristan profusely apologized without any acknowledgment, he was essentially addressing his twin without any revelation.

"Are you kidding me, Elle!?" Tristan yelled. "You think knocking down your new alliance is a good way to make friends?"

"Oh, it's fine." Gigi laughed, staring at Tristan with awe before darting back to her gown and its newest tie-dye finish.

"I'm *so* sorry Gigi." Liv offered slowly, realizing how terribly she had just ruined the Viking queen's dress. "Can I offer you something to change into…?"

"You're too kind." Gigi swatted her hand to alleviate the tension, "I think instead we should simply get everyone else *more* drunk in the room so they don't notice!"

Liv offiically *loved* this goddess.

"In all truth, the added color does match your eyes perfectly – it brings out the amber specks." Tristan offered, grabbing a champagne flute from a waiter passing by and extending it to Gigi as a truce. "Soon everybody will be wishing they had whiskey on their evening attire, too."

Liv laughed, "Seriously, Tristan. Combing for a compliment much? I mean, clearly her eyes are blue."

Gigi turned to Liv questioningly, then back to Tristan, her jaw dropped in surprise.

"Sure, Liv." Tristan rolled his eyes, before returning to Gigi, "Okay, you have a filled flute, Liv's showing her true colors and I'm about to head off and do what I was originally planning to before this unfortunate incident. Thanks for being awesome, Gigi. And Liv, you still suck."

He winked as Liv flipped him off, unable to see Liv mumbling, "idiot," as he walked away from them and toward Piper.

"Sorry about that," Liv shook her head and addressed Gigi more directly, "He's my best friend and terribly enough, also my advisor? So, I guess we spend way too much time together and inevitably it's grown into a love-hate relationship, heavy on the hate tonight."

"I love it." Gigi replied happily, watching with intrigue as Tristan walked away. "You both have such a fun banter; I wish the Viking deities shared a similar sense of humor. They're always so serious."

"You speak as if you aren't a Viking yourself?" Liv observed questioningly.

"Through marriage, yes." Gigi replied honestly, but her shoulders tensed, and she started looking around the room, trying to figure out an exit to the seemingly uncomfortable and unintentional interrogation.

This response caught Liv's curiosity; however, she decided it was best to take a step back in sake of a worthwhile alliance.

"When did you marry Mothi?" Liv asked casually, diverting the conversation to hopefully more of an acceptable topic to her guest.

"Oh, about twenty years ago." Gigi answered shortly and sweetly, before spotting Peyton across the room, "Oh! Peyton's waving – I must go say hello…"

Liv stepped in front of Gigi, blocking her for a moment, and then again. She turned to see Peyton now in another conversation with Ammiras and Zayne.

"You're Giselle." Liv accused, piecing all of the clues together.

Truly, it was a gamble. But if Gigi wasn't Tristan's older sister, she would have reacted very differently than the present, and Liv wouldn't have felt the increase in powers buzzing from her anxiety.

"I think you're mistaken." She stated politely, trying to walk around Liv again, but the Element Elite was too quick.

"You're the Elements Pillar's Head of the House of Water. As your Elite, I feel your powers reverberate through my core, just like your House of Fire brother, Tristan, and even more recently, House of Wind's newest Head, Piper. And your powers just increased. The air has changed." Liv pointed her finger into the air, twirling it about her head to confirm her point. "But you don't want anyone here to know that you're *alive*. Hence the disguise, which apparently works for all except the deity who is the master of your powers. Me."

"What do you want from me?" Giselle whispered, no longer the bubbly queen.

"To understand." Liv replied honestly, looking around. "But, not here. Come with me."

She extended her hand, and was appreciative when Giselle took it.

She led the Viking queen to Rowan's old office, which she supposed now belonged to Hayden, although it was apparent, after scanning the royal crest to enter, that he had not touched his father's office since becoming king.

To that, Liv understood. She barely moved anything around in her own father's office, even though he hadn't frequented the Elements Pillar for almost two decades.

"The room is protected; nobody will hear us here." Liv confirmed, shutting the door behind her.

Giselle remained quiet.

"I only need to know a few things." Liv offered kindly. "The first, have you told Tristan you're here, that you're alive?"

Giselle's eyes started watering, but she shook her head.

"Why?" Liv pressed, more so surprised at the response than the tears.

"My protection with the Vikings is only insured by my secrecy. Even with you as the Element Elite, I am once again next in line. So, if something happens to you, I can't risk Kronos and Arlo knowing of my existence – if they know I reside at Vanaheim then I will be banished from the Viking world. They won't risk exposure to their secretive society."

"You don't trust your brother with keeping this secret?" Liv asked.

"I don't *know* my brother." Giselle replied, sniffling.

"Okay." Liv nodded.

"Okay?" Giselle clarified.

"I won't share your secret. It's not mine to tell." Liv explained, "But, as someone who knows your brother very well, I think you should heavily consider letting him know the truth. He still mourns your death, Giselle. He still loves you."

"Thank you, Olivia." Giselle nodded. "I will think about it."

"I'll let you compose yourself," Liv offered kindly. "If you do ever need to talk, I am here. Please know that you are not alone."

"Thank you." Giselle whispered.

Before Liv opened the door, to her surprise, Giselle added another sentiment, speaking directly with words Liv did not expect to hear.

"Peyton was right about you. That you're a trustworthy Elite. I will not forget your kindness, Olivia Monaco. Not only to me, but to my brother. Thank you for looking after him when I could not."

Liv smiled, a little more genuinely this time, before returning to the party.

"Where have you been, Monaco?" Hayden caught her in the hallway outside of his father's office.

"Oh, Gigi needed a moment, so I let her sit in there for a while. I hope that's alright?" Liv took Hayden's hand, and he twirled her into his arms.

"What's mine is yours, darling." He smiled before giving her a kiss.

"Hayden, if we fail at stopping Arlo and Kronos – so many of our people will be in danger." Liv held on tightly to the king as she pulled him into a hug. "I always knew that, but I guess I've just realized the extent of how it will impact not only the Pure Gods, but inherently now the Buddhist, Viking and Celtic deities, too."

"All we can do is fight and be smart." Hayden consoled Liv, "Smarter and better than Arlo and Kronos."

"But, have we considered *all* options?" Liv pressed desperately. "Have we discussed how the prophecy might come into play with this battle?"

Hayden's head tilted, unsure how to respond but trying to understand his fiancée.

"Has my mom's party planning gotten to you, too?"

"No… what?" Liv shook her head, ignoring his question and continuing on her course. "Is there something we need to do specifically in order to help uptick the battle to be in our favor? Should we consult with Daphne for clarity?" She explained, still holding onto him tight but now leaning back so she could look deep into his arctic blue eyes.

"You know how I feel about my mother's involvement in… well anything." Hayden muttered, "She'll tell us what she can, when she can. But that doesn't always mean she has the same intentions as we do, so we must take it all with a grain of salt."

"…And then consult Jocelyn." Liv joked.

"Then consult my crazy sister, yes." Hayden laughed, pressing his forehead to hers. "Oh god, Ollie. Why have you not been by my side all night?"

Liv smiled at the small reprieve, "Don't worry, I'll be by your side for all eternity, instead."

FORTY-THREE

JOCELYN

She rolled over, smelling a delicious chicken stew brewing in the air.

Her eyes snapped open when she realized she had been knocked out bloody cold, and the space that radiated heat as she had fallen asleep was now empty.

Jocelyn shot up, to find Niall sitting across the room, sipping tea.

He lifted his finger to his lips, signaling to their other roommate, Caitriona, who still hummed as she steadily slept.

Jocelyn nodded in understanding, slowly peeling off the covers over her emerald gown before tiptoeing to join Niall at the table.

"You should be resting." Jocelyn commented dryly, sitting across from the Celtic prince who smirked at her first words.

"I feel more energized than I have in quite some time." Niall replied quickly.

Jocelyn glared at the bandages that still held his body together and the cane that helped him maneuver around, most likely quite slowly, to his new location.

"Okay, I'm fine but I wish my body would catch up with my mind. Happy?" Niall smiled sweetly, taking a sip of his tea.

"Did you eat?" Jocelyn asked, pouring herself some soup. "That will help speed up the healing process."

"I was waiting for my lovely host to dine with me." Niall joked, immediately retracting his statement when Jocelyn began scolding him and shoving her full-bowl in his direction.

"Well, now you've earned yourself a second serving." Jocelyn huffed, but then eyed Caitriona anxiously to make sure she did not wake the sleeping child.

"How *did* you inherit Caitriona?" Niall asked quietly, obediently taking a spoonful of the stew to his mouth.

"It's a long story. I recognized her and she attached." Jocelyn sighed. "I haven't been able to find Adair, I'm worried she-"

Jocelyn paused, hearing Caitirona stir. The girl yawned and then slowly sat up, drowsily taking in her surroundings and caretakers.

Her jaw dropped when she realized who dined beside Jocelyn.

"Caitriona, would you like some tea or soup?" Jocelyn offered kindly, walking over and picking up the girl – observing from her stage-fright reaction that Joss would need to instigate the child's next action.

The girl shyly nodded, not taking her eyes off Niall. Jocelyn could have sworn the young deity was *blushing* underneath the natural flush of color from her cheeks.

"Caitriona, do you know where your mother is?" Niall asked kindly.

In response, the girl buried her head further into Joss's neck as the Candor Elite sat down with her at the table.

"Stop it." Jocelyn mouthed, glaring at the prince, even more so when he silently smirked.

Yet, soon she heard a sniffle emerge from the young being.

"Caitriona, what's wrong?" Jocelyn asked softly, running her hand gently through her red curls.

The girl remained silent, but the crying grew heavier.

"Caitriona, you have to use your words so we can help you." Jocelyn prodded, lifting her chin with her finger to gently make eye contact with the darling girl.

"She's... she's gone." Caitriona sniffled sadly.

"Gone?" Jocelyn clarified.

"I left her." Caitriona sobbed, digging her face back into Jocelyn's neck. "She didn't know herself. I had to leave her!"

"Shhh, it's okay... it's okay." Jocelyn patted her back soothingly, bouncing her gently in her arms. Her heart broke for the girl who could have not been older than four. "It'll be okay, Caitriona. You're safe, and we'll figure out how to get your mommy back."

So, Jocelyn sat there, rocking the young deity until she calmed down and fell back to sleep. When she heard the steady humming of breathing, she gently placed her back into the bed and tucked her in tight.

A toddler, leaving her own mother to escape to safety. What had the world come to?

Just thinking about what the poor girl could have witnessed during her escape, the level of danger she had placed herself in, had *risked*, all to find a better world. What happened to Adair? Could the lost mother's soul be recovered? The thoughts swirling within her mind made Jocelyn silently cry, wiping her cheek as she walked away from the sleeping child.

Niall stood, his face breaking as deeply as Jocelyn's, easily reading her dark thoughts with his own recovered powers. Holding his cane for support with one arm, he extended the other and pulled her into an embrace and let her weep into his chest.

She is safer here.

Jocelyn nodded in agreement, although the predicament still weighed heavily against her heart.

So much had happened, it was as if her mind was still trying to play catch up, to organize everything she had discovered and figure out her next steps. The one benefit was that for the most part, her mind had remained calm, clear and collected ever since she had reached exhaustion the day before.

A large, calloused hand gently pulled some loose strands from her braided bun behind her ear, calming Jocelyn's mind even further, so she was able to breathe. Her father used to do the same thing when she was a child, running around wild chasing her younger brother in the fields outside the palace during the summer. She recalled the memory fondly, taking comfort in the worthwhileness of remembering the past.

But then she took an abrupt step back, realizing with shock exactly what she had just allowed the Celtic prince to do to her hair. Joss tried to cover astonishment by making herself look busy, immediately grabbing the tea kettle and refilling her already relatively full cup.

"You should rest." She mumbled to Niall, in attempt to recover her poise.

"I promise I will, after I ask you one last thing." Niall conceded, sitting back down and obediently taking a couple more spoonfuls of his stew to demonstrate his compliance to her instructions.

"Sure." Jocelyn rolled her eyes, realizing he was still entirely in control of this interaction. But she sat back down across from him nevertheless.

His face suddenly turned insecure, his brows furrowing as he played with his soup.

Was the prince of the Celtic Gods… squirming?

"I'm not squirming, although I'm glad to see you get such pleasure from my struggle." Niall rolled his eyes, but clearly now appeared much more comfortable.

Jocelyn snorted unexpectedly, immediately covering her face in horror.

"You need not be afraid of me, Jocelyn." Prince Niall's eyes sparkled at her authentic, adorable outburst. "I am starting to rather like the true princess Jocelyn, without the stoic façade."

Joss ignored his declaration, but could not contain her blush, no less immature than Caitriona's reaction only degrees earlier.

"Your question?" She prompted, trying to deliver the request without interest.

"It's just… I'm not sure if I imagined it or not." His eyes glazed over, looking darker, as if he replayed a memory within his mind, trying to gather evidence before proposing his ask aloud. "When I was fighting Danu's soldiers, alone, trying to buy as much time as I could for the others to escape..." he continued explaining, his eyes growing drearier as he replayed his final moments on Irish land before he looked up and met Jocelyn's eyes straight on, bright green and clearer than she'd ever seen, "Were you... there?"

Jocelyn huffed, then realized he was being serious.

"Me? No!" She cried amusedly, "I was here, pacing the halls and anxiously waiting for you and the chaos to arrive!"

Niall chuckled, although the spark didn't reach his eyes. "Of course. It's ridiculous, I must be mixing my visions, blending the past and future somehow."

"Why do you say that?" Jocelyn tilted her head, intrigued.

"Well," Niall looked out the window, trying to find an accurate explanation, but came up with none. "It's just that, I could have sworn... I heard you, calling out to me."

DEMETRIUS

He had visited a dozen temples. From one dedicated specifically to pythons in Benin, where he had held a snake in his hands in hope of some sign that they were a messenger for the Orishas, to bowing to a number of statues dedicated to Oduduwa – Yoruba's divine king – and then to various chickens, as the creature was a symbol depicted in many myths and represented in the tributing statues he visited.

Demetrius had started with researching who had worshipped the Orishas during the Iron Age, in attempt to try and narrow down potential historical locations or artifacts in relation to the ancient deities. At this point, he was desperate for *anything* that would lead him to the lost gods.

The Yoruba tribe were the key worshippers to the Orishas, but they spread across Benin, Togo, Ghana and Nigeria. Hence how he ended up inevitably talking to a snake and bowing to a chicken, with no success.

By the time he left Oduduwa Grove hot, tired and defeated, he returned to his hotel, knowing he needed to redirect his research to find another option.

What Demetrius had inevitably discovered was that there weren't many options, but every possibility he discovered was a strong one – which made him worry about all of the unknown opportunities that history would never allow him to uncover.

Now, he found himself hiking to the Erin-Ijesha Waterfalls – more commonly known as Olumirin in the wilderness beside the village Abake, where the intelligent hotel concierge had recommended he explore, as it was a historic Yoruba site. Amusedly, she explained that Olumirin meant 'another deity' and so perhaps it would give him some clarity in his journey – he could connect with the ancient gods by first connecting with nature.

Now on his way to the waterfall, the only thing he needed to connect with was a more practical pair of hiking boots – his suede loafers were not equipped for the South African jungle.

He began walking through a long hallway of concrete steps, relatively flat until the path took a steep incline upward, challenging even Demetrius's prime physique. Truthfully, he wanted to fly directly to the waterfall, but it was morning and there were already mortals nearby, and yet somehow the concierge's push to connect to nature resonated with him. For some reason, he felt that the soil was calling to him, demanding he acquaint himself to the land in order to gain privilege to its gods.

He could hear the water running, adding a constant static noise that enhanced his wet surroundings under the now shaded, colder rock that reverberated to a cooler atmosphere. The green leaves glowed brighter and the dark stone contrasted against the vibrant, surrounding palette to make all of nature's mesmerizing colors intensify. Finally, turning a corner, he found the majestic waterfall in all of its glory, crashing into a calm pool of water where many already resided, standing in awe of the sight or taking photos in front of the historical landmark.

A lion to a fawn, the deadly water crashed into the pools until tamed, before slowly rolling out into a trickling rocky river down the hillside and through the jungle.

Yet, as soon as the waterfall became visible, the path leading to it evaporated. To continue moving forward, Demetrius was forced to descend using sporatic rocks and tree roots as leverage to keep from sliding down the dirt hill or falling off entirely and cracking his head open.

That would be a hard one to explain to his fellow bystanders when his skull healed relatively quickly following the crash.

When he reached the watery monster, he observed the layout of the fall and contemplated diving headfirst into the abyss, hearing Jocelyn's guaranteed advice echoing in his mind from their experience in the Dunmore Cave. Instead, he took off his loafer and stepped into the water haphazardly, hoping for some initial response to his immortal powers.

Instead, he cried from the freezing liquid, not anticipating that he would have stepped into the fucking arctic on this trek.

"A little cold for your comfort?" A soft, low voice observed from behind.

Demetrius turned, finding a stunning, tall Nigerian woman sitting on a rock with a kind, but amused look on her face. She wore a white crocheted cover dress with a black swimsuit visible underneath and only a few layered gold necklaces – simple. Her layered hair blew freely in the small breeze.

"More so, unexpected." Demetrius commented dryly.

He observed the woman, intrigued by her beauty, before turning to face her fully as he shook off his leg.

"The waterfall is said to have medicinal properties – people once came from all over the lands to drink the water and be healed." The woman offered, eyeing the other visitors who splashed in the pool, freely and happily. "The natives regard the waterfall as a sacred site and a means of purifying their souls."

"What if I'm not searching for healing or purification?" Demetrius replied vaguely, understanding her clear contempt for those who disrespected the historical site.

"But then, what is it that you seek?" The woman tilted her head, studying him curiously. "You do not look like one who enjoys outdoor activities."

"I don't." Demetrius laughed before considering the answer to her other question. "And, I guess I'm looking to discover if this is the sacred site that can help me find my way to… divinity." Demetrius tried to explain, using the words he had pre-scripted for himself when prodding mortals for relevant information.

The woman's eyes sparkled with delight before nodding to the top of the cliff. "Well, you are only on the second level. If you dare try to reach the top one, you will find the gods you seek in the sky."

"Top level?" Demetrius asked, staring up at the tall mountain before returning his gaze to the mysterious woman. "Of how many?"

"Olumirin has seven falls, however the path is only clear for the first two. Climbing the following five may be a daunting task but rewarding as it gives an awe-inspiring experience. The seventh level is called 'oba òkè' meaning 'King of the Hills.'"

"You come here, often?" Demetrius inquired, impressed by her knowledge of the landmark he could barely find through his own research.

"Yes." The woman smiled, "I want to preserve Nigerian history, so try to enlighten others – only those who are worthy of such knowledge – about the antiquity of the wonder they have traveled so far to find."

"Interesting hobby." Demetrius dryly commented, returning his attention back to the mesmerizing sight.

"Someone must do it." She continued, laughing melodically. "Besides, I like history, travel and nature, so it works for me."

Demetrius turned back to the woman, now wondering if she was the guide he unknowingly needed all along. "What's your name?"

"Akinla. You?"

"Demetrius."

He extended his hand, glad when she took it and shook it politely.

"Do you know anything about the Orishas?" Demetrius finally asked, after staring at the waterfall in silence for a few minutes, deciding he had absolutely no idea what he was doing and wouldn't be able to fly to the top of the waterfall until nightfall.

"Of course. What is it that you wish to know?" Akinla replied simply.

"Do you know about any coveted relics or lost artifacts or other sacred sites related to the ancient deities?"

"Sure, there are many." She stood up, "Starting with the vanished caves nearby. They were originally discovered by the same hunter who found

Olumirin Waterfall, or depending how far you are willing to travel, we can even the visit Ogbunike Caves."

"How far are *you* willing to travel?" Demetrius eyed her warily, surprised the female was so willing to accompany him on his vague quest across Nigeria; however, he reminded himself that mortals were usually drawn to and mesmerized by the immortal powers which deities held – so it didn't seem too abnormal in the scheme of things.

Soon after, Akinla showed Demetrius the vanished cave on their way out of the waterfall complex, telling histories of how natives would celebrate the gods with annual festivals within the spaces until the climate caused it to collapse one thousand years ago.

Secretly, Demetrius placed his hand on the mountain wall, hoping to generate any vision or feeling to lead him closer to the Orisha Pantheon, to no avail.

"Might I suggest we visit the Osun-Osogbo Sacred Grove next?" Akinla offered.

Demetrius was open to the idea, but waited to respond until he understood the reason why.

Akinla raised an eyebrow at his questioning, but inevitably shared the context he desired.

"Not only dedicated to the fertility goddess Osun, it is among the last of the sacred forests that usually adjoined the edges of most Yoruba cities before extensive urbanization."

"Sounds good to me," Demetrius chimed in quickly before assessing both of their attire. With Akinla in a swimsuit, Demetrius's trousers still damp from his walk and his loafers in an abysmal state, he proposed they change into new outfits. And then immediately wished he had bitten his tongue from the look Akinla gave him in return.

"You are joking?" She finally asked, hailing a taxi from the side of the road. He, on the otherhand, had walked up to a cart selling guava, purchasing two of the fruits for a cultural experience and to try a local snack. The hike had certainly left him famished.

"Obviously." Demetrius lied, jumping into the vehicle but desperately wishing he could dry his pants without bringing attention to his powers among the mortal – they were truly becoming quite uncomfortable with the damp jacquard chafing against his legs. "Onto Osun-Osogbo Sacred Grove!"

Akinla jumped into the car beside him, filling the space with a comforting whiff of coconut and herbs. He handed her a guava and started peeling the skin off his own.

"How long until we get there?" He asked casually, taking a bite of the fruit and reveling in its sweetness.

"About 90 minutes, give or take traffic." Akinla confirmed without hesitation.

Demetrius almost spit out his guava when he finally converted the time into degrees.

FORTY-FOUR

DEMETRIUS

They passed the Osun River as they entered deeper into the 185 acres of dense forest and toward the Osun-Osogbo Sacred Grove via an asphalt road. Akinla rambled off facts about how the Osun River helped establish the civilization in the nearby areas for trade with other Nigerian tribes and pointed out various trees that watched over them – ancient kapok, abachi and black afara.

"Every August, the Osun Osogbo festival that takes place here serves as a strong unifier for Osogboland, as many come together to celebrate the goddess, one commonality that everyone focuses on and sets aside different social, economic, religious and political convictions of the people." Akinla continued, walking Demetrius through unique wooden statues intermixed within the forest. "It is truly a beautiful worship – including drumming, dancing, music, costumes, Yoruba language and poetry – a celebration of all beauty in its many forms."

Sculpted faces and figurines poked out of the roadside fence. Demetrius even noted a wall with a keyhole-shaped entrance, as if it beckoned for him to walk through the door and into another realm. It lured in his gaze, the possibility mesmerizing his imagination, until he realized Akinla had not waited for his distraction – her distance gave him a sense of abandon, so he quickly jogged back closer to his guide.

"It sounds spectacular. Do you attend often?" Demetrius asked, trying to keep his breath steady as he returned to a walking pace.

"Oh, no. I have only heard about it." Akinla replied softly, in equal awe of the art and shrines that surrounded them.

"But you so easily joined me here today?" Demetrius asked curiously, walking toward a totem pole.

Akinla nodded in agreement, an elusive smile that hid many secrets beneath the façade as she explained, "The festival belongs to the Osogbo people, to celebrate the special pact between them and the Yoruba goddess. I respect that."

"Seems fair. When was the special pact made?" Demetrius touched the pole in front of him, again hoping for some form of a divine sign.

"Archaeological excavations show that people first moved to the grove about 400 years ago. That was when the voice of Osun, who turned out to live in this river, had advised a settler to move away from the river and into the forest's sacred grounds."

Akinla's back was to him, so she wasn't able to see his slight disappointment to the modern timeline revelation. Unless, the Orishas shifted to a new Pantheon after hiding, in efforts to better secure their secret existence.

Eyeing one of silent temples from the outside, and noticing the intricate geometric 3-D patterns and shapes from within, he asked, "When were the temples made?"

"Most of the statues – like the sculpted two-headed snake sticking from the ground over there – are the works of artists of the New Sacred Art movement, who started embellishing the grove in the mid 1950s. They also built the stylized houses for the gods, established the statues and sculpted the temple doors using wet mud as concrete."

Less than a century old, an infant in relation to the deities he sought.

"Before the New Sacred Art movement, the Sacred Grove was quickly disappearing – termites had eroded the shrines, the roof of the Osun temple had caved in and industrialization from the city of Osogbo was eating up the woodland. We are fortunate for the restoration efforts to preserve this divine, magical place for those to seek and communicate with the gods."

"Is Osun the only Orisha worshipped here?" Demetrius turned away from the temple.

After hearing Akinla's words, he wanted to be respectful to the sacred ground he walked. Demetrius appreciated it more, better understanding the hardship it had endured to have ended up so majestic today.

"No, Osun is not the only deity worshipped in the Sacred Grove." Akinla strolled further into the forest, leading Demetrius to a big-eyed statue.

"The Yoruba religion has more than 400 Orishas like her, representatives of the supreme god Olodumare. Here is Obatala, the Orisha of creation, and over there," she nodded to another figure extending six arms toward heaven, "Iya Mapo – the Orisha of women's crafts, like pottery and dyeing."

Demetrius wanted to reach yet again for the statue, to again determine if there was a way to access the Orishas from this divine forest, but after seeing Akinla appear from behind the Obatala tribute, he realized it would be quite the mess to entirely disappear in front of a mortal, with no guarantee of returning in a timely manner to clean it up afterward.

He would have to come back at a later time, alone, and without his walking encyclopedia of knowledge. But for whatever reason, Demetrius felt that if he said goodbye to Akinla, he would never be able to find her again.

So for now, he asked, "Where to, next?"

The prompt was met with equal excitement from his guide, and Demetrius realized he was truly looking forward to their next destination.

REI

He had been spending most of his spare time trying to figure out where the Hades he went wrong – had taken such a far turn from right and catapulted into unknown territory, before finding himself lost with no understanding of how to return. And with Peyton refusing to merely talk to him, he had no inclination on how to make it right.

Let Kronos bring the Soulless, Rei wanted to *kill* many things.

He was happy for Hayden and Liv, his two close friends, finding their happily ever after – but Rei had low tolerance for romantic celebrations to begin with, even when his life was running smoothly, so respectfully left the engagement party early.

The next morning, he woke early to meet with his father and pillar in the war room to discuss strategy. It had been decades since his pillar reconvened in this space to deliberate battle tactics and mentally prepare to lose lives of loved ones. He had hoped it wouldn't come to this.

He opened the room to find a ghastly looking Peyton sleeping in the conference room. She lifted one eye to see who disturbed her beauty sleep and groaned when she saw his face.

"Did you – did you *sleep* here last night?" Rei demanded.

"It seemed like a brilliant and responsible idea at the time." Peyton spat irritably. "Usually tequila makes me a genius."

"Can I get you coffee? A *new dress*?"

Rei couldn't help himself.

Peyton redirected her gaze to her sexy, velvet dress ensemble from the night before and sighed.

"Yes, to coffee, but I'll summon my own change of clothes. Thanks, asshole."

Rei smirked, hearing sleeping beauty yawn as he left.

When he returned with coffee, Peyton had fortunately changed into a cinnamon rose gown and had been joined by her oldest brother Callos.

"Hair of the dog?" Peyton's brother guessed, dodging his younger sister's shove too swiftly.

Of Peyton's three living brothers, Rei got along with Callos the best. Although Xander was trustworthy and kind (may his soul rest peacefully in the Underworld), Callos brought both elements with a little bit of sass – similar to his sister, Peyton – and as the God of Battle Strategy, was an indispensable addition to the Pillar.

The other two, Andronikos (but everyone called him Andro) and Leon, were younger than Peyton and a handful. Leon had Peyton's confidence but lacked her intelligence (that she had when she didn't drink an abundance of tequila) and Andro was cunning but always too eager to start a fight, whether it was necessary or not.

Soon, Silas joined the room along with his advisor Edwyl and waited until the final remaining pillar strategists and weaponry experts entered the room.

"How is the production of the Viking armory progressing?" Silas asked after initiating the meeting.

"We are tracking on schedule with all spears made, one thousand arrowheads and five hundred swords." Alessia, goddess of weapons, reported. "We're optimistic the viking-steeled horseshoes will work perfectly for the Centaurs."

"Great. And has positioning been determined?" He looked to Callos.

"Yes, sir. We have deliberated with all allies to organize their people's strengths and place them across the Puerdios's borders." The striking man stated, standing rigidly only for his update before sitting down, all the while his hands remained formally clasped behind his back.

"When will I have the final proposal to share with King Hayden?" Rei chimed in.

"End of day, latest." Callos answered.

"We are all in agreement, work hard but do not exhaust yourself." Silas concluded, after walking through the additional updates for the upcoming battle. "Prepare to begin resting two days from now. We work until Three and then prepare to fight on Four, as Daphne predicted. Meeting dismissed. Take care, everyone."

Rei appreciated the quick meeting, but that inadvertently meant less time with Peyton.

He tried to chase after her surprisingly quick departure for one still recovering from the previous night's festivities. Rei didn't even get to call out her name, before she turned, finding him trailing behind her and pointed at him. Stubbornly declaring, "No. Not now.", Peyton then flipped her hair and ran back to her apartment, which Rei could only assume was to restart the morning again, from the comfort of her bed.

DEMETRIUS

Hell had frozen over and he wore the same outfit as the day before to witness it.

Akinla had actually convinced Demetrius to not only drive seven hours south east to Onitsha but to sleep in the clothes he wore during the day and rough it in the same attire for another ten hours before they returned to Osun and went their separate ways – Akinla to her respective residence and Demetrius to repeat every destination the local had showed him, and certainly doing so in new, clean clothes.

But until then, Demetrius would continue to be a good sport. He had met with Akinla in the morning after a night sleeping in separate rooms, finding her in the lobby sipping a coffee.

Now they were approaching the Ogbunike Caves, after a strenuous climb upward on the mountain that held the divine wonder. Upon entering, Demetrius found hundreds of names carved into the cave's stones – whether their writer's first act or last – establishing a creepy, eerie feel to the abandoned sacred site.

Akinla must have noticed Demetrius's change in observance, as she leaned into him and whispered, "Ogbunike Caves – where you experience beautiful fear."

She eyed the names warily before continuing on the trail for her tour.

They started walking through darkness, eventually stepping through a stream where Akinla pointed to the surrounding water and explained, "Many are eager to drink the water because it is believed to be from a divine source."

"Do you recommend I try the water?" Demetrius clarified.

"Do what you want." Akinla huffed, crossing her arms.

Clearly, she did not believe in the common sentiment, so Demetrius withheld.

"The bats will guide us." Akinla nodded after some time in silence, moving her gaze to the top right corner. "The caves contain a large sacred chamber with ten tunnels that all connect to create the shape of a labyrinth. We must walk the predestined path."

"Bats, huh?" Demetrius looked to the same corner as Akinla's gaze. "Where I come from, black birds have a similar role."

Akinla turned her head to Demetrius and tilted it in confusion, precisely as he had hoped, as now he had her full attention as she studied him curiously.

In that moment, he swiftly cast light into the cave, causing the bats to scatter down a tunnel.

"What in the-?" Akinla spun behind her, eyes wide as she watched dozens of bats flap their wings in the cave.

"It seems the bats have spoken." Demetrius observed sweetly. "This way."

Shortly after, the two had to get on all fours, avoiding sharp edges that protruded through the narrowed route in which the bats had deemed the appropriate tunnel, even if they all connected to the same desired destination, anyway.

"We have arrived to the sacred grounds." Akinla announced softly, turning off the flashlight she held in her hand so that they were in complete darkness.

The cave's water glowed from within, reverberating off of Demetrius's divine immortality to instill life within the rocky cavern.

Akinla dropped into the pool of water, praying in her native tongue. Although Demetrius did not understand the words she spoke, they were musical and majestic, and so inspiring that he joined the prayer just so he could take part in her beautiful tribute.

When she finally opened her eyes, they appeared wiser.

She did not fawn over the incredibility of the sacred water glowing or speculate if it were a message from the gods, but instead she stood, walking over slowly to Demetrius, swinging her stunning hips as her white crochet sundress clung to every curve of her chocolate body.

Akinla kneeled down in front of Demetrius, softly placing a hand on his cheek before stroking his wet hair behind his ear. She leaned in and kissed him, letting the energy of the pool collide as the sparks their touch created buzzed through both bodies.

The act was so intentional yet so innocent, Demetrius relished in the surprise and yet felt as if this were his destiny all along.

Until Jocelyn flashed across his mind, and he finally pulled away.

Akinla looked so tranquil, nothing close to the guilty unease spreading through his core. The pool grew darker.

"Why did you do that?" He tried to ask as gently as possible, although his heart was pounding.

Akinla smiled, replying without a hint of doubt, "I have enjoyed my time with you Demetrius. If we never meet again, at least we have this. A kiss, blessed by the gods and a memory I will hold onto forever."

With grace, she continued on, walking slowly away from him and toward the tunnel they had entered. Demetrius followed like a heeled dog, feeling better with every step as Akinla began rolling facts off her tongue again, as if their romantic encounter had never happened. Or at least, impacted her in any way other than an exciting, non-commital experience. And yet, Demetrius couldn't get the touch of their kiss, the memory of it, out of his mind or off of his lips.

They drove back to Ilesa and said their goodbyes outside of Demetrius's hotel – Demetrius turning in for the night while Akinla walked down the street and away from his quarters, until she became a shadow in the night and disappeared.

FORTY-FIVE

LIV

Hayden and Liv had chosen to relocate their headquarters from the Royal Palace to Puerdios for the final days leading up to the impending battle.

After discussing numbers with Rei and acknowledging Liv and Hayden's ability to remain on campus, it was ultimately decided to give students the option to either seek sanctuary at the Scotland school or remain and fight.

Only a handful opted to leave.

And yet, as Liv walked through the empty hall of Puerdios – all had been instructed to rest until Hayden signaled to step into position – it felt desolate, a ghost of its former glory. No longer did Puerdios glow with warmth nor buzz with voices as students bustled from class to class – it felt that the essence of Puerdios Liv knew and loved, had already been lost.

Arlo had wanted to disrupt the Pure Gods' control, starting with the heart of each deity's first home – the one place that united them all.

"If Arlo succeeds in infiltrating Puerdios, he's also in the vicinity of the Royal Palace," Hayden's whisper inevitably echoed down the empty hall. "A much easier base to plan an unexpected attack, versus needing a week for travel."

"Why not go straight for the royal palace, then?" Liv asked.

"That may have been their initial plan," Hayden admitted. "But, Puerdios is a major landmark that stands between them and the Royal Palace. If they went around it, they risk getting trapped between two Pure-dominated locations."

"So, we're choosing to fight here first because we're fighting for time – time to secure the outstanding alliances." Liv saw through Hayden's words, the king dare not admit they were simply trying to postpone the Royal invasion, the ultimate defense.

He nodded in silent agreement, before adding, "Our choice could easily have played into the cards of Arlo & Kronos's plan. But, if we can stop them here, they have to return back to their headquarters or seek out a new camp – a week's time again while investing in additional time to rebuild an army."

"More time." Liv nodded.

It all came down to time. And with immortality in play – who had the stronger power to keep the clock ticking.

She'd never truly grasp the thinking that went behind war strategy, but she hoped there would be infinite time to learn more about the process to become a part of it, versus a bystander who could only observe.

"Are you ready to face Kronos, if it comes to it?" She whispered, grabbing his hand immediately as the words left her body. It was chaos, asking the Pure God King to go against the Creator of their kind.

But that had been the strategy, to leverage Liv and Hayden's connected powers to give the king everything he could to defeat the most powerful deity on the planet, in the universe. Their only hope resided in keeping Arlo occupied long enough so they could properly go after Kronos without being taken out by Liv's uncle, or Kronos himself, first.

Without Kronos, it would be just Arlo. No more Soulless, no more true threat.

"I don't have a choice." Hayden replied honestly. "It's either me or you. And you already know my position on the alternative option."

Liv smiled sadly, squeezing his hand in understanding.

"And if we lose?" She asked darkly.

Hayden sighed, running his hand through his hair, "Then the battle for the world will commence."

JOCELYN

She was pleased to see the loophole around Danu's curse seemed to be working. All those who sought refuge at Demetrius's palace were making slow recoveries, some even able to cast small powers once they no longer felt depleted.

In a few days, most could be ready for battle.

Which led Jocelyn to check in on Prince Niall, now walking without a cane but only a slight limp.

She had left Prince Niall in the morning with the approval to transform her bedroom into his office and now returned to find various deities in her private space reporting to the Celtic prince about the state of their homeland and numbers of their people.

"Good afternoon, Princess Jocelyn." Niall stated loudly, his voice easily thundering over the others who were chattering among themselves.

At the declaration of her presence, all silenced themselves immediately and bowed to her at once, making Jocelyn blush.

Never had she received so much attention singularly on her and so unexpectedly, nonetheless.

"Good afternoon, Prince Niall. Everyone." She smiled back as she walked up to the Prince, not realizing how massive he truly was now that he was not steadily crouching over a cane for support. Looking up to him, as if his head were on the ceiling, she took a step back to help with the angle, all while trying to keep her head held high.

He chuckled at the reality but did not comment aloud to it, instead he beckoned for the others to leave so that they could chat in private.

"What may I help you with?" Prince Niall asked charmingly, "Or should I leave you in peace as well?"

"No, I came to see you," Jocelyn grinned, "…not to change into my tea attire, grab a leisure book to read, or something ridiculous of the sort."

"I would respect any of those reasons, either way." Niall smiled, walking over to the desk and sitting himself down, taking a deep sigh of relief from being able to rest his leg.

"You should take it easy, Niall." Jocelyn glared at his leg, appreciative that his sight now resided below hers. It felt more comfortable – how she was *used* to interacting with this intimidating and powerful source.

Realistically, they were at about the same eye level now, but Jocelyn stood up straighter and ignored the inch in her favor coming from the silk silver shoes hidden beneath her matching lace gown.

"You and I both know there's no such thing as 'easy' when you are royalty." He teased, but the words had a trace of dark reality attached to them.

"True." Jocelyn sighed, still eyeing his leg as she determined exactly how much tough love the stubborn beast before her would need to see reason. "There are some things we cannot control but others that we shouldn't make harder just to feed our pride." She softened her voice, "You're still healing Niall. Don't push it. Your people will understand."

"My people look to me for strength." He explained, stubbornly. "You know that more than anyone."

"Then lean on me for strength, as I did with you." She challenged, her voice strong and commanding.

His jaw tightened, but he did not press further.

Knowing a standstill battle when she encountered one (mostly from her previous arguments with her brother), Jocelyn walked toward the bar cart, summoned a bag of ice and poured a cup of tea, bringing both diligently to the prince and placing the warmer of the two in front of him and the cooler item atop his thigh.

"Elevate your leg while I'm here. At least take care of yourself when you're alone. And do not hesitate to summon for me when you need *anything*. I'll be discrete."

"Understood." Niall nodded obediently, taking a sip of tea. "But I never want you to be discrete, Princess Jocelyn."

The tone and delivery made Jocelyn blush, but she smiled at the request.

"Now, besides berating me like a child, what did you really come here to discuss?"

Jocelyn smirked, although pleased he diligently held the icebag to his leg and took another sip of tea.

She summoned lunch for him while she had his time, sat down across from him and began explaining, "The Dark Gods quickly approach Puerdios, they are only two days out from the premise. I do not expect your people to be ready to fight in this battle, but we must prepare for when the time calls for your people to return to earth."

"We are on the same page," Niall agreed. "I am unsure if it is my powers still recovering, but I cannot see the future clearly – have you been able to see how we work around Danu's curse?"

Jocelyn shook her head, "No, I have not."

Silence filled the room.

"What *are* you able to see?" Jocelyn speculated. "It might help guide my visions."

It was strange openly discussing her powers with another; she had only had these sorts of conversations with her mother. What was even more extraordinary was that for once Jocelyn sought out the visions and felt comfort in them, instead of fear and burden. Sharing this responsibility with another, working together for a common good, brought her peace. She wasn't scared anymore.

"I see a dark figure, hearing a curse in a language I do not understand." Niall closed his eyes as he tried to describe the blurry pictures that ran through his mind. His fists clenched and he started sweating.

"Stop." Jocelyn commanded, summoning a cool cloth and wrapping it gently around his neck. "Do not over exhaust yourself."

"My physical strength is returning, but I feel there is still a hold on my powers." Niall admitted, "Something is off with them and I cannot pinpoint it exactly… but I assume that we are still leashed by Danu's curse to some extent."

The chicken, rice and broccoli arrived a moment after, the plate landing softly in front of Niall. His eyebrow raised swiftly, his eyes sparkling with amusement as he obediently picked up a fork and began eating.

"I'm surprised you manage to go so long without a meal, considering your size must require at least ten a day." Jocelyn teased, rolling her eyes.

Niall huffed and then replied jokingly, "Ten meals is a diet day. My lean, high-energy, warrior body is trained to consume at least twenty or I faint."

"Something's got to nourish that large head of yours." Jocelyn retorted, crossing her arms. A beautiful, large head, indeed.

Niall placed his hand on his chest and replied wholeheartedly, "Finally, someone who gets me."

Jocelyn rolled her eyes again but was unable to contain her smile. The light banter momentarily distracted her from the more daunting thought – they could not find a vision of success, meaning there may not be a workaround to Danu's curse.

No, she refused to succumb to failure.

Standing up, Jocelyn passionately stated, "We'll go to the library. Research possibilities. I'll pair Rhys and his medical team with the researchers of the Elements Pillar – we'll test, trial and continue fighting against Danu, everyday. Until she is *destroyed*."

"Don't you have enough battles to worry about? Is a third one really worth your time?" Niall tilted his head, setting down his fork. "I mean, I appreciate all that you have done for my people, and we do have plans on how to fulfill our promise to fight the Dark Gods…"

"You do?" Jocelyn chimed in.

"Our strength will deplenish under her curse as soon as we return to the Earth's stratosphere, but we believe we can extend our powers as long as we do not touch the ground."

"You're mad." Jocelyn exclaimed. "There is no way I would dare let you or your people risk your lives under Danu's control, enter a battle already weak…"

"We keep our word." Niall fumed. "If it comes to it and we have no other alternative, we will prepare to fight."

"Agree to disagree, for now." Jocelyn argued, "All the more reason to determine a true cure with the time we have left."

She took a few steps away from the desk, turning to Niall one last time with resolve to command, "Eat. Rest. And don't be a royal idiot," before flipping her baroque gown dramatically and stomping out of the room.

DEMETRIUS

He peered out the window of his hotel room, waiting for the final light to go off in the streets, marking the village's complete slumber.

As soon as the last lit room flickered into darkness, Demetrius knew it was time to return to his first destination: Olumirin Waterfall.

This time, he certainly was not going to expend his energy – or another pair of designer shoes – to trek to the top. The second fall was daunting enough, if he was going to make it to the top before sunrise, flying was his only option.

Exiting his hotel room and into the wild dark of Ilesa, he pulled out his wings with stunning peacock feathers and took flight.

He felt like he cascaded through the skies of another world, instead of grids of lights decorating the land, he saw miles of unhabitated jungles and forests still in their natural habitat. The lack of light influenced the night sky, allowing millions of stars to shine brilliantly, screaming their presence louder here than most lands across the globe.

He even spotted Jupiter, pausing a moment to think about Jocelyn and how she was managing – whether she was still waiting obediently for the Celts to arrive or if she was in a flourish trying to heal those who had made it to his front step. He hoped she was doing okay, staying strong and remaining the kind yet stubborn deity he loved so much.

Demetrius had watched Jocelyn's heart, once so boldly cast on her sleeve, shrink in size and then hide within her soul – he understood what caused her reserve – but hoped it was temporary, and that after this darkness, after the hardening of her being came to pass, a piece of her would return to him.

Otherwise, he worried she would spiral to a point of no return, cementing into a duplicate statue of her duplicitous mother.

But that was a matter out of his control, the only thing he could do to help her sanity was secure another alliance, one without strings or parameters, but with a strong community of deities worth fighting for the good in this world. A group of immortals who acted in unison to those like Jocelyn, so they could continue to spread their positive light that the mortals so desperately needed.

He spotted the mystical farmland among the darkness, marking his final destination up in the hills approaching closer. A small lagoon reflected under the moonlight nearby, buried under trees and hard to find, but glowing enough to mark a connection to ancient powers older than itself.

Demetrius landed, retracting his wings and walked up to the small body of water.

Unlike its descendants that roared as they crashed from level to level closer to sea, the originator sat calmly, posing the question if it actually spread its wealth so the other falls could inherit its majestic water.

Somehow the stillness intimidated Demetrius more than the thrashing, dominating falls. The actions below authentically showed its true colors, instead of the lurking mystery of the still, where anything could happen, unexpectedly.

He took a step further, now closer and able to look over and into the water below. Almost immediately, there was no visible ground in sight – his first step could be into an unknown abyss.

"I am surprised to see you here again, so soon."

Demetrius snapped back, startled by the enchanting voice from behind.

Akinla walked in a valley, slowly approaching him. She had changed from her white crocheted sun-dress and now wore a navy and gold printed romper. The gold brought out the sheen on her skin, kissed from the moonlight overhead.

"Akinla." He replied in surprise, "Why are *you* here? "

Akinla smiled sadly, "I never left."

"What?" His head was spinning. "How is that possible? You were just with me at my hotel..."

"I am Akinla." She replied swiftly, "And I know exactly who you are, Demetrius, God of the Solar System."

Demetrius's eyes went wide – for one to make such an accusation only meant...

"You're an Orisha."

Akinla grinned, laughing at the words before pointing at him kindly and replying, "Close. I am the next best thing, though."

"What?" Demetrius was entirely confused and only slightly worried for his life.

Akinla rolled her eyes. "I am surprised my name did not ring a bell if you did any appropriate research on the Olumirin Waterfall."

Akinla...

It finally dawned on him.

"You discovered the Waterfalls in 1140 A.D."

"Correct." She replied, "Olumirin. When translated, it means 'another deity.'"

"So, what are you... exactly?" Demetrius didn't receive any higher-being energy from her, she still felt entirely mortal. But if she was almost one thousand years old...

"I am Oduduwa's granddaughter, blessed by the Orishas to protect the land I helped discover and serve as messenger between the mortal world and the divine."

"So, you knew all along how to contact the Orishas." Demetrius scoffed, running his hand through his silky ink hair. "Yet, you led me on a mad chase across the country."

"I told you exactly how to contact the Orishas during our first conversation." Akinla defended herself, "I told you you could seek the gods you looked for in the sky, on the top level. And here we are." She took a step forward, studying him carefully before she lifted her head, smirking as she nodded with confidence, "But the question is, do you *really* wish to find the Orishas?"

"Of course, I do!" Demetrius replied, his voice too desperate. He paused and took a deep breath, recomposing himself. "That's exactly why I'm here."

Akinla looked at the water, her voice as reflective as the mirror image among the stars flashing before her. "When our people first settled here, they were scared of the waterfall. The intimidating cycle of water was like a mysterious figure that scared people away for fear of being swallowed up."

"Sounds like it served as the perfect inspiration to establish the Orisha headquarters." Demetrius scoffed.

The entire time he was in Nigeria, he had been with the Orisha messenger of this realm. So much time had been lost while he fell pawn to the temptress's games.

"That and Olumirin was believed to be a very tall and huge spirit whose height reached the high heaven. The Orishas rewarded me for finding such a sanctuary, gifting me with powers that matched the same of Olumirin – immortality and a connection to the gods. They deemed me worthy to be the judge of others and guide those of merit to their divine powers."

"Does it get lonely?" Demetrius asked, realizing Akinla was unique, the first of her kind he had ever witnessed in his ancient age.

"Nobody has ever asked me that." Akinla replied, surprised. She looked up to the stars, contemplating her response.

"At first, it was harder than I imagined, seeing my family, loved ones and friends eventually die of age, injury or disease. Then, seeing their children, their children's children, their children's *children's* children… all live and pass through the circle of time.

"Soon, it was harder to remember the names or who belonged to whom, and quickly after, I learned not to get attached. Most who seek my guidance do not return, those few who successfully pass through both worlds are too scarred to want to come back. I have learned to live with my life as a job, a repetitive transaction that I do not grow attached to."

"That sounds pretty lonely to me." Demetrius observed, looking up at the same night sky as she. Akinla was staring at Jupiter, his home. "When did you learn of my true identity?"

Akinla shrugged, "A few clues here and there, but I pieced it all together while we travelled through the Ogbunike Caves, and then I prayed to the Orishas to confirm my speculation with a sign, so when the waters reacted to your divine powers by glowing, it solidified my theories."

"I'm impressed." Demetrius replied honestly.

"I am too. And I have deemed you worthy to visit the Orisha Pantheon, if you should so choose." She stepped aside, illuminating a path that sparkled into the aqua abyss.

"Should I be worried?" Demetrius asked.

"If your intentions are pure, you have nothing to fear." She replied automatically, a phrase the stunning lady must have repeated a thousand times.

Yet, he didn't want to leave her just yet.

Unexpectedly, he stepped off the illuminated path, pulling her lips to his, passionately kissing the stunning, inspiring and uniquely cunning immortal being.

He laughed, glad to see she was finally caught off guard, for once.

"Should I be worried?" He asked again, this time desperately searching for any sign from her brilliantly fierce onyx eyes.

Akinla took a breath, grabbing his arms firmly. "Let Olumirin swallow you whole. Let the sacred water wash over you and take you through all levels of the falls.

"Olorun will be fair, focus on him and do not be distracted by others. He will seek council from his partner Orumila – but do not address Orumila directly. Be weary of Sango's temper, he sparks thunder at the smallest sign of opposition to intensify his case, but he is strong and powerful and an ally you want on your side. If Oya appears, it means change is happening, whether good or bad. Èsu will try to spin your words, do not trust him at any cost. And if something goes awry, seek out Oshosi – he is the avenger of the accused and justice."

"Are you able to visit the pantheon?" Demetrius inquired, trying to remember the rollercoaster of tips his guide just blasted off while trying to remain calm.

"No, my powers are rooted to the dirt of this world. If I cross over, my immortality will be revoked. They can only visit me. My powers begin and end here." Akinla paused, pulling Demetrius into a final hug as she confirmed with a definitive whisper, "I will not be able to save you."

FORTY-SIX

PEYTON

They had all gathered in Hayden and Liv's loft, the final night before the Dark Gods' Soulless army would infiltrate their lands and demand victory. Their estimations deemed the opposing force only five hours away.

As Peyton looked around, it felt like the beginning of the end.

She had fought in many battles before, with centuries of defeated opponents under her belt, but never a civil war of such magnitude – deity against deity. Her family against her friends. Her loved ones, on both sides. She could only focus on fighting for what was *right*, or else she was unsure her body would be able to maneuver with the prowess required to survive a night, day, *week* combatting against those she grew up with, had heard tales of and most terrifying – those who had *created* her.

Determinedly, she focused on the now. It was not the beginning of the end; it was the beginning of the *beginning*. The beginning of opportunity, the beginning of democracy, the beginning of something so incredible, it was worth the dark fight ahead.

She poured herself a glass of Fireball, returning to the circle surrounding the fire. She smirked at Piper sneakily positioned next to Tristan, so obviously into him, that her innocent friend's eyes widened and then she blushed at the unexpected attention.

"What are you up to?" Tristan scowled, noting Peyton's mischievous grin.

"Just joining the fun with a full glass of my good friend Fireball. What are *you* up to, huh?" Peyton glanced at an aloof Piper and raised her brows.

Seriously, what would these fools *do* if she weren't their friend? They'd probably run in circles with their heads miraculously floating in air, detached from their necks.

Peyton plopped beside Dylan, handing Kyril, who sat opposite the vixen redhead, the other glass of Fireball in her hand.

"Cheers to the chaos." Kyril darkly laughed, holding out his glass.

"If this war is anything near chaotic, I resign." Rei muttered, crossing his arms, unenthused. "You all better follow order and stay in your line, or else your blood is *not* on my hands."

"To chaos!" Peyton hollered, returning her glass to his for a majestic and rebellious, *clink!*

Oh, it felt so good to feel Rei's angered glare penetrate the room. Honestly, she had forgiven him – but she didn't want him to know that yet because it gave him something to fight for, to live for – and she couldn't let him feel *comfortable* going into battle. It didn't give him the extra edge he needed to survive. She needed him to keep chaos in order, for everyone, but especially with her.

"I don't understand why you all insist to drink before a very important battle." Calithya scowled, swatting away the glass of wine from her brother's mouth before he could drink it himself. "It's irresponsible."

"We're not getting obliterated." Hayden drawled, "It's statistically proven deities perform better in battle when they are a little looser and less anxious."

Liv chuckled, cozying herself even further underneath his arm, grabbing the whiskey glass from his hand and taking a sip from their shared dram.

"Besides, it'll burn off before we stand in formation." Ammiras scolded, batting away his sister's judgmental arm. "Or, *swim* in formation," he clarified, bursting into laughter.

"You are seriously the worst. That's not even funny." Calithya rolled her eyes, crossing her arms across her blue velvet gown, revealing gold scales across her arms.

"Why so *crabby*?" Kyril chimed in, poking Calithya jokingly.

"She shrimply expects better jokes from us." Ammiras grinned, wrapping his arm around Zayne.

"Shell yeah she should!" Peyton exclaimed excitedly.

"Oh, my, gosh… krill me now." Calithya muttered with a sly smile.

The small play on words erupted the room, everyone hollering with elation at finally breaking down the Siren Queen and her stuffy decorum.

At least they had *one* victory already under their belt as they headed into battle.

Beneath the laughter, Peyton heard a small cough, directing her attention to the kitchen, finding Daphne standing in the doorway.

Her presence only meant one thing.

It was time.

Peyton snapped her head back to Hayden, awaiting his command.

"So soon?" Dylan stated aloud, before muttering, "I don't know if I should be happy or sad."

"Both." Peyton replied honestly with a shrug. "The sooner it starts, the sooner it ends."

Dylan smiled softly, standing and walking over to Peyton to give her a hug.

"This is not goodbye." Peyton declared loudly, pulling from Dylan's embrace and pointing to all who stood in the room, "FOR ANYONE."

Calithya and Ammiras were the first to depart, heading toward the sea where the sirens were to gather and protect the ocean border of the school.

Dylan, Kyril and Zayne left next, followed by Tristan and Piper.

"You ready, your majesty?" Peyton hollered to Hayden.

While Rei commanded the troops, she and Callos were in charge of Hayden, Daphne and Liv.

"Peyton, can we talk?" Rei whispered, acknowledging Hayden's subtle nod as he led Liv away to the kitchen.

"No. We can't." Peyton stubbornly replied.

"Peyton. I don't want to keep things like they are-" Rei tried to explain, pressing for her to acquiesce.

"No, Rei. We're not going to do this." Peyton was boiling, it was water full of heat, passion, lust and anger. "We're not going to magically resolve our issues because we're facing a war tonight. We're not going to kiss out of desperation. We're not going to forgive eachother because of terror for the unknown. If any of those things happen, I want it not to be because of external pressures forcing it. If any of these things ever happen, it will be because you and I both *earned* it. Not by default. Not tonight."

She stomped away, cursing the three words that she wanted so badly to say by flipping off her two friends who stood in shock from her decline and departure.

LIV

In reality, Liv felt like she was existing in a fantasy, a climactic, cinematic scene leading to the final battle of a movie as she looked around and found thousands in armor and positioned for battle. Every window had a body peeping out, bow and arrow at hand. Every balcony was lined with three rows of archers. Troops stood in line in front of the castle, holding over one thousand custom-made Viking weapons. All while Rei, Silas, Magni and Hachiman – King Rāhula and Queen Chanthira's war deity – flew above and yelled out commands.

Her own sword lay heavily against her waist, full sized and ready to be pulled and used in a moment's notice. Her blades had been sharpened by Rei the day before, insisting that she be ready to use it, if their line did not hold. She had no powers today; her powers belonged to Hayden. Her sword would soon become her lifeline if she faced enemies from a broken fortress. She clung onto its hilt tighter, grasping onto her only freedom device for the battle.

But, Zeus, from where she stood, layered deep within the castle's tallest tower and strategically positioned with Hayden, similar to the other royals, thousands would have to be slaughtered if she found herself in combat.

But then again, she wasn't fighting for Middle-earth – her opponents had the capability to fly. Yet, she still wore the intricate armor fit for a warrior, gold plating shielded her core in a modern design equipped for a queen.

Peyton stood behind Liv and Hayden, her role specifically to give Hayden and Liv time to escape, if all hell broke lose.

Callos held a similar position for Daphne, who stood in the opposite tower with King Magni and Queen Gigi, with their respective guards as well.

Piper and Tristan stood near the center of the castle, using their powers to blow away weaponry or burn it to ashes before it hit the Pure God troops.

Dylan and Zayne had opted to be a part of the archery line with the Pure and Buddhist Gods; Kyril a swordsman on the ground with the Vikings.

It was strange having everyone so scattered, they were stronger together, united as one – and separated almost forebode disaster.

Yet only one true strategy remained up in the air, to be discovered today.

Only time would tell if Liv and Hayden's combined powers could stand against Kronos. At the first sight of the first god, she was to begin channeling her powers to give Hayden the strength to fight his ultimate creator. Rei or Silas were tasked with claiming Arlo, whoever saw him first.

So, without her powers, Liv had only her sword to wield off attackers and a loyal Pegasus to swiftly escape.

Yet, unlike the movies, Liv was living through it. So, she repeated the plan seventy-two times, reminding herself of the layout, her loved ones' positions and the strategy for survival. Still far from reality but closer to a terrifying timeloop living out her worst nightmare for eternity.

Then they heard masses marching in the distance.

A slow, but steady *thump, thump, thump* growing louder, like drums queueing in the crescendo at the start of a concert. The silence between the noise deadly.

"Stand guard!" Rei roared, signaling across the fields. "Hold your positions!"

Liv's body was trembling with fear, she grabbed Hayden's hand desperately for something to hold onto.

"These creatures who march toward us are no more than expired, brainless corpses, sadly risen past their time of rest. We show those without souls NO FEAR." His light blue and white wings flapped strongly against the wind, each beat strong and marching to its own rhythm, consuming all previous noise to only his own. "We fight for life. We fight for order. We fight for the good in this world and we fight for those who cannot! We fight for Puerdios! WE FIGHT FOR THE PURE RULE!"

Cheers thundered across the lands, reverberating through the castle, sparking energy and life among the grey unknown.

They were whole. They were ready. They were dauntless.

Hayden squeezed Liv's hand, his position remaining strong and secure.

Black masses started growing over the horizon. The marching demanded presence while more Dark Gods flew through the sky. The blue skies darkened as they approached nearer, an eventual dégradé to black.

"HOLD!" Rei yelled, calculating the distance and when they could successfully shoot the first arrows within target. They needed no more than 500 yards.

"READY. AIM. FIREEEE!!!!" He roared, his voice thundering through the sky as one hundred arrows shot through the darkness and penetrated half of the marching front line.

"RELOAD!" Rei yelled, pointing to the second row of archers already in form, as planned. "READY. AIM. FIREEE!!!"

Another hundred arrows, another fruitful collapse in marchers.

The opposing line started picking up pace. Rei called to the third row of archers, further back on the higher fortress.

"READY. AIM. FIRE!"

From there on out, the first and third rows fired together, the second holding a strong ground between. Rounds of rounds until Soulless collided with Pure God warriors on the ground, combatting with steel as Dark Gods began swarming ahead.

Piper cast a strong wind, holding off the Dark Gods and blowing them out into the sea, where the Sirens would greet them and let them meet their fate. While Piper cast them off-trail, Tristan summoned large fireballs to shoot into the sky and burn wings, forcing any deities Piper missed to join the Soulless on foot.

When the archers ran out of arrows, having catapulted over two thousand into the air and with at least half knocking the Soulless to the ground, they dropped their bows and began summoning powers to help hold the line against the Dark Gods.

So much blood. So much loss.

Liv felt helpless as she continued to search the sky for any sign of Kronos. But he was nowhere to be found.

"Do you think he's not coming?!" Liv called, raising her voice above the grunts and screams, and worst, the cruel cries of pain.

"He's waiting for us to exhaust our power. There's no way he would not witness victory." Hayden yelled back, his eyes anxiously searching the skies.

"Kronos is behind the large black mass in the center. There!" Peyton shouted, pointing directly ahead.

The magnetic strength calling to Liv proved Peyton's discovery correct. She hadn't considered that as the original creator, he would naturally summon allegiance from the Pure. But she didn't have long to deliberate their game plan.

Liv's head snapped when she heard Silas command, "Fall back!", beseeching those with the Viking swords to retract to the castle and cast their swords aside while they secured the fortress and combatted the powerful threats from the skies.

There were still at least two thousand Soulless, soon to begin bombarding the wooden outer gate and demand a rematch. Even the centaurs who stormed across the field, stomping on the Soulless with their Viking steeled-hooves and successfully killing them, could only take out a couple rows of troops at a time.

"Liv, start relinquishing your powers." Hayden advised, squeezing her hand tight.

She closed her eyes, focusing on loosing the tether that boiled inside her core, releasing it through the bond as it followed a trail to another accessible source.

"Down!" Hayden jumped over Liv, pushing her to the ground as a fiery whip blasted the side of the window. He jumped up, casting a spell of attack for his only assigned target.

They had broken Peyton's security powers.

Kronos had broken Peyton's security powers.

"Liv, get back!" Peyton screamed, jumping to the side of Hayden and covering him from any other attacks.

Liv crouched in the corner of the tower, watching gold and red and green and black sparks fly through the sky; Hayden fighting against a fiery chain and spinning one himself as he lassoed his victim into the tower.

"Why, it *is* a party! How rude to have been a last-minute invite." Kronos smirked, breaking the rope that bound him, transforming its pieces into shards of glass and catapulting them in Hayden's direction.

Hayden turned the glass into sand but was still affected by the mini rocks flying at lightning speed in his direction.

"And, the guest of honor! *Ollie*." His eyes turned black, changing into a demon.

Liv wanted to scream, she wanted to torment him, but alas, she felt weak upon his gaze.

"You will not *touch* her!" Hayden roared, levitating Kronos out of the tower and blasting him into the sky.

"Holy shit." Peyton had fallen against the stone wall, eyes wide. "That was Kronos. Holy shit."

"How much time do I have." Hayden breathed, leaning against the wall and closing his eyes.

Liv understood. She was tired – their combined pool of energy was depleting. There wasn't much more she could give him without losing consciousness and becoming obsolete. Hayden, a mirror to her, could not last much longer, either.

Peyton leaped to the window, searching the sky for his opponent.

"T-minus a tenth degree!" She screamed, blasting a curse before collapsing to the ground, her breath was heavy and she was sweating.

"Here we go." Hayden breathed, jumping up again and meeting his match straight on. Their powers collided, a volcano erupting as they intersected.

Hayden could hold his powers, *their* powers, against Kronos. But for how long was still up for debate.

"It is cute believing love conquers all, King Hayden." Kronos smirked, "But did Ollie mention how I defiled your weak, half-mortal bride to be? I ruined her."

Hayden screamed bloody hell, his anger boiling. He was trembling, turning red. Then purple.

No. No. he was depleting...

They were depleting.

Peyton's head snapped to Liv. Her friend's face grew blurrier as Liv yawned, feeling sick to her stomache. Spots started appearing. As more Element Pillar deities were being sent to the Underworld, Liv was starting to feel the loss of each one, more impactful than the next.

"No!" Peyton slapped Liv, capturing her attention immediately.

She looked to Hayden then back at Liv. "You must go. NOW."

"We... we *can't* leave you!" Liv exclaimed, realization dawning over her.

"Oh, to Hades you can and over my dead body!" Peyton yelled, "Rei would *kill* me if I allowed you to stay. Summon Pegasus. You do not have time or energy to waste!"

Liv wouldn't, she winced in pain as she tried to give any last morsel of energy to her soul mate. But he was drowning, and she could no longer help bring him to the surface anymore.

Peyton whistled and within moments a neigh cried from afar, flashing into the tower within a second.

Liv was so weak, she obediently let Peyton throw her on Pegasus – her only focus was Hayden's survival.

"Hayden, on the count of three!" Peyton screamed, dodging and blasting powers as she ran to his side. "One. Two. Three!"

Hayden crashed below the remaining stone as Peyton roared a protective spell, giving Hayden the few seconds he needed to meet Pegasus halfway and crawl onto the winged mare, flying with Liv away from the horror and to safety at the Royal Palace.

Hidden under the shelter of the forest, they watched as Silas demanded more to fall back, and then eventually cried surrender and to get out.

Rei was the first to find Hayden, as many flew through the forest and away from Puerdios, allowing the Dark Gods to claim victory.

"Where's Peyton?" Rei demanded, his voice terse and in a growl.

Liv started crying, there had been no sign of the sassy deity since their departure.

"Where's Peyton!?" Rei roared, looking back to the tower.

He started to head back, but Hayden grabbed his arm. "She followed the plan. Going back for her is a death wish."

Rei shook Hayden off his arm and glared with a hiss, "I can't leave her to die!"

"Rei!" Hayden called for him.

"Don't…" Liv begged, already reading her soul mate's thoughts.

"Rei. I command you to come back and escort Liv and me to the castle." Hayden whispered, a tear falling down his cheek.

Rei turned, fighting the summon, but unable to break the ancient curse.

"Fall back!" Silas's voice echoed overhead. "The grounds are no longer secure!"

A blast of orange lit the sky, the tower in which Liv and Hayden had resided no less than minutes before exploded, tumbling to the ground as hundreds of souls evaporated into the sky, claimed immediately by the Underworld from the power's impact.

Liv's jaw dropped and she screamed, instinctively covering her mouth as her eyes turned from blue to orange.

FORTY-SEVEN

DEMETRIUS

He stirred awake, finding darkness.

His body ached and his clothes still felt damp, but he wasn't sure if it was due to the chilly night or the cold stone his skin rested against.

Lifting himself up, he heard the clash of metal. And then felt the metal around his wrists. And ankles.

His hands were cuffed and chained to a stone wall, and as his eyes slowly adjusted to his surroundings, he realized he was in what sort of resembled a cell.

"What in the world…" He examined his metal bindings, trying to recollect any memory of having met his hosts, but drew a blank.

To his knowledge, he hadn't spoken to or met an Orisha yet. So, what had caused the immediate imprisonment?

"Hello!?" He yelled, hoping to catch the attention of anyone who could explain his predicament.

When silence returned, he took a leap and tried to break out of the shackles himself, delivering the expected result: the cell had been structured to contain powers to eliminate a prisoner escape.

He leaned disappointedly against the stone wall, worried they would not even grant him a conversation – considering his power a threat and immediately casting him as a monster. He refused to give into the darkness, as much as it lurked in the shadows. But, without concrete facts, for now – all he could do was wait.

LIV

She felt blind, numb, careless to wherever Hayden steered them next.

Flashes of an orange cloud, an orange blast, an orange volcano cycled in her mind. All forms, unexpectedly, rapidly, slowly – as if the cloud itself were a monster, slowly consuming the life around it. Yet the visions didn't make it feel any more real, didn't change the outcome.

How many had been lost in the tower?

Was Peyton one of them?

Liv refused to let her mind go there, not until there was proof.

Not until they determined where they had gone *wrong*.

They needed more weapons. They needed more time. They needed more deities.

They needed *more*.

Her body started shaking, her fingers were ice.

But going into shock was not an option for the Element Elite, the future Pure God Queen.

If they survived long enough to fulfill the title. The concept felt obsolete and unimportant in comparison to the horrors she had witnessed to good, deserving deities…

Everything seemed unimportant, except for the only thing that seemed unsolvable.

Kronos.

Puerdios had gone dark.

Who else would follow suit? Select to choose the opposing side of power unknowingly in exchange for their freedom?

She looked up to the sky, finding the stars as scattered as her brain, trying to fight through the smoke to spread light among the desolation.

They were just as weak as she was.

After minutes of blankness while Liv combatted the darkness and desperately clung to Hayden's warm, strong arms wrapped around her, steering the rein and keeping her centered, warm lights beckoned as they sought refuge and arrived at the Royal Palace.

Most of the staff had been at Puerdios helping with the battle; the castle was empty upon their entrance. It caught Hayden off guard, as he began to roll off commands to ghosts in preparation for the inevitable visitors, but stopped.

Silence. Non-existence. Nothingness.

All wickedly greeted their tormented and rotting souls.

He turned to Liv, taking a deep sigh as he ran his hands through his hair in desperation. Hayden, too was on the verge of breaking. Liv ran over to him and caught him in an embrace, already knowing she couldn't be strong enough for the both of them right now, but she would try.

"In here." She whispered, guiding him to the parlour and slamming the doors shut.

He sunk to the floor, sliding against the wall, and began to shake.

"Did I make the wrong choice?" He asked, exasperated as he looked at nothing, his eyes blank and face hollow. Finally, his gaze met Liv's, challenging her will with pain. "Were we fools? Does love not conquer all?"

"Hayden, you can't say that." Liv dropped below to him, grabbing his hands.

They were still warm in contrast to her own and she felt guilty for stealing his heat.

"I only needed a few more moments against Kronos, but I was worried about you... about sacrificing myself and leaving you alone in this world. I was selfish, so we escaped. If I had only held on longer..."

He was rambling, but his words were laced with truth. They both knew that.

"Hayden, you would have *died*!" Liv exclaimed, pulling him further into her arms, needing the physical contact to remind her he was still alive, still with her.

"And instead, Peyton did." He muttered, finally stating the words Liv refused to believe. Looking ashamed, he pulled away from her embrace and sunk further to the ground with grief.

She had no words to combat the reality they faced.

So, instead they sat in darkness and silence.

After a few moments, the fire in the parlour blazed with flames, pulling Liv from her daze as she realized they could hear footsteps outside in the main hallway. She wasn't sure how long the static noise had been there, but now that she heard it, she couldn't *unhear* it.

With their people, friends and allies approaching, Hayden would soon need to prepare to face them.

Liv bit her lip, catching a glimpse of Hayden from the corner of her eye.

She had no idea where to begin, but she had to start somewhere.

"If you had held on longer, we would have both depleted – and then where would our people be? Without hope? Without leaders?"

Hayden didn't respond. Liv didn't expect him to.

"Even if we had the Egyptians at our side and I sold my soul to the afterlife, I don't think that would have changed Puerdios, either." Liv deliberated aloud, although after the words left her lips, she regretted the thought immediately. She had no idea if she was helping or hurting the situation.

Hayden huffed.

"I'm just playing all scenarios here. You would have been distraught, perhaps reckless with heartbreak, and without me as a supporting power vessel connected to you, who knows what would have happened? We stand our best chance against Kronos, together. And we'll get Puerdios back together, too."

Definitely not the right thing to say. It seemed mindless as an inspiring goal when they had just lost so many deities in the process. There was never the right thing to say when you were surrounded by death. All Liv could do was focus on the living.

She turned to Hayden, the only living, breathing thing near her.

Gently grabbing his face, she turned his head toward her, forcing him to reconnect with the living world as well, reconnect with *her*.

"I choose you. And I'll choose you again. In every scenario. I always choose you." Liv rested her forehead against his. "You hear me? As long as you'll have me, Hayden. I'm forever yours."

A few minutes later, Liv heard Hayden take a deep breath. The king began standing himself up, inhaling again before extending a hand to Liv, helping her upright.

Opening the parlour doors, Rei was the first Liv spotted. Hayden walked determinedly up to his friend and pulled him into a strong embrace. The Security Elite grabbed onto his king, his brother, and squeezed him tight with grief.

Behind Rei, Liv spotted Tristan and Piper in the corner, both looking exhausted, but whole. She wanted to run over and give them both a much-needed hug, but instead stood beside Hayden, remaining at his side to show a unified front.

When Rei finally pulled back, Liv caught his eye and immediately started crying. She ran into his arms, sniffling back her tears, but it was too late.

Once the watergates had opened, they flowed all too easily, each time requiring a smaller trigger, and even once her body had drained of liquid, they somehow erupted even more effortlessly, until she was left with a headache, stuffy nose and blood-shot eyes.

Liv was already at the blood-shot eye phase and alas, here she was, crying harder than ever. That would be her punishment for a failed battle.

Wiping her eyes and stepping back, she finally turned and absorbed the room leading into the grand ballroom, where Rhys and his Medicine Pillar had arrived from Jupiter the day before.

Ammiras stood over a cot, patiently holding the hand that could only belong to Zayne.

Daphne and Silas walked up to Hayden, both bearing solemn looks.

In a whisper, Daphne spoke grimly, "We must reconvene with Elites and allies who are strong enough and determine our next course of action. Best to do it sooner rather than later to avoid conclusions to be made preemptively."

For Daphne, the cryptic delivery meant only one thing – loyalty was waning.

"All rooms are being used for recovery and accommodation." Silas explained, motioning to the parlour. "I'll alert the others that a meeting will begin in 5 degrees."

Liv beckoned for Piper and Tristan to join them, giving them both hugs and whispering, "Have you seen the others?"

Piper's head bowed and she sniffled, shaking her head sadly.

Tristan gulped, looking around the room speculatively as he muttered, "Zayne is injured but should recover. Dylan and Kyril are… unaccounted for." He gulped again, looking away for a distraction.

Liv blinked, another tear rushing down her cheek. She wiped it away automatically, willing herself to lock it down and just get through this meeting, somehow. Hell, the next *five minutes* – and then she would focus on the next. She'd learn how to breath again after tonight. Hopefully.

"The allies?" She turned to Piper, who had caught Hayden's attention and pulled him into a hug.

More surprisingly, Tristan pulled Hayden into an embrace right after.

Solidarity and strength.

Liv took a deep breath, waiting for the update.

"Queen Gigi is okay. King Mothi is recovering from a terrible wound. Queen Thira and King Rāhula survived."

If it was possible, Liv felt a weight that she didn't know was there lift from her chest; however, she was still cemented with a guilt that might never go away.

"We were actually doing quite well." Piper whispered nervously. "We eradicated the majority of the Soulless army. Essentially diminishing their numbers by 75 percent." She bit her lip, struggling to say the words, "We lost a lot of good deities, your majesty. And they can never be replaced…"

"But we kept most of our numbers." Tristan chimed in. "The only reason for the final explosion was Kronos's anger at losing so many of his monsters without making a dent in ours."

Piper looked at Tristan, appreciative for him to say what she couldn't, before turning back to Liv. "I'm not an expert, but our strategy *was* working, Liv. Today was hard, those lost insurmountable and the pain we have will never be forgotten, but we have to focus on the good. We have to remain optimistic. Today's battle set up our cause for success next time."

"Next time." Hayden huffed, closing his eyes and leaning his head back.

Liv was exhausted. The idea of facing Kronos in the near future made her want to collapse then and there. From Piper's perspective, they lost Puerdios but in the bigger picture were victorious. But Piper had no idea that without defeating Kronos, their cause was a lost one. Every moment they spent trying to figure out how to demolish him, he created new Soulless – possibly even using the fresh corpses still bloodied from the day's destruction. Every day, the Dark Gods became more powerful with the Pure God chance diminishing. Their enemies were the night and they were the sun's light as it fell behind the horizon.

The sun will return, Ollie. Hayden quietly soothed her dark, numbing thoughts. The thought was weak, but he squeezed her hand gently – giving her all he had, once again.

By now, the room had filled.

Dyoedi took up most of the space by the door, shadowing Calithya who sat by Ammiras on the velvet plush sofa. Queen Gigi sat across the sirens in a chair, staring at Tristan with a secret relief that her brother was okay. King Rāhula and Queen Chanthira stood beside Daphne, looking tired and weak, their clothes torn and burned, skin scathed from what Liv could only imagine was a result of the final explosion.

Rhys of the Medicine Pillar entered last, looking worse for the wear.

"I will start," he stated while wiping his hands with a cloth, "Mostly so I can return to my patients promptly. We have had only ten bodies claimed by the Underworld since their arrival – better here, out of Kronos's reach.

We continue to monitor those injured and will work swiftly and smartly to ensure full recoveries to all." He eyed all in the room, "I advise you all rest after this meeting. Your energy is depleted, and we must prepare to fight again, soon. I have volunteers making nutritional dishes around the clock. Please eat, hydrate and rest. Healing will come in time – both physical and emotional. That is all."

He nodded to Hayden and exited abruptly.

Hayden coughed, turning to Silas for an overview and recap from the battle and where they stand. Out of courtesy to Rei's pride, he added Rei to the request near the end but did not expect him to speak.

"The Radical Dark Gods lost triple their numbers than ours." Silas reported. "They will begin rebuilding, but we have bought time – now it is a delicate balance between necessary preparation and when we begin hindering our odds."

"We obliterated the majority of their Soulless corpses and still have two potential armies at our grasp!" Rei roared, his trauma manipulating his usually stoic and strategic delivery; Liv's heart broke for him. "We can take the school back and we need to do it now, before they can rebuild. The less corpses we have to deplete our energy, the better chance we have at demolishing the radical deities. Once we are fully rested, we easily have the bandwidth to defeat their armies. And we'll have numbers and organization on our side! We must take back Puerdios!"

Hayden nodded politely, but he spoke with reserve. "We must act with intention, not with emotion. I would love to reclaim Puerdios but it does not feel realistic. Not today. Let them have the school so long as they don't have access to our minds."

He turned to the larger room, "We have to find the source and destroy it, or else we're wasting our efforts. We have to focus on finding a way to defeat Kronos and cut the Radical Dark Gods' cause at its core."

"The attempt to combine powers did not work?" Calithya's head peaked up with intrigue.

Hayden guiltily shook his head to confirm. The room erupted in whispers.

The rare, ancient, soul mate connection was their only hope – and the remaining water in the glass had now vanished.

Daphne took a step forward, her statuesque frame immediately catching the attention of all in the room.

"We need to solidify the prophecy." Daphne finally spoke, eyeing Liv and Hayden with an unexpected desperation.

"Solidify the prophecy?" Hayden huffed. "We've seen the prophecy come to fruition. How much more power and lives are we going to invest on a speculative chance?"

"It is two pronged." Daphne dismissed her son's irrational behavior. "First, to instill hope back into your people. They believe in the prophecy. We must unite them with an act that brings optimism, happiness and strength. And secondly, take the final step in uniting the son of a King and daughter of an Elite in love."

Daphne eyed Liv's engagement ring.

"You're delusional!" Liv cried. "Have a *wedding*!? How dare you... even insinuate... how ungrateful, tonedeaf, insensitive can you *be*!? Has eternity made you into a heartless monster!?"

Hayden gently grabbed Liv's arms, holding her back.

Liv was seeing red.

She wanted to *punch* the wall. Hades, she wanted to blow the wall up. Maybe that would remind Daphne of the horror they had all endured.

"We'll consider your... proposal, *mother*." Hayden hissed, before glancing at Silas and softening his tone. "But we must assess the status of our additional allies in the meantime."

"Rhys confimed the Celts are recovering swiftly, and their powers are returning. His research team has partnered with the Elements Pillar to try and discover a cure so that they can properly function on earth without issue. Otherwise, Prince Niall has proposed they will ride griffins and provide aid for as long as it is safe to physically do so." Silas then turned hesitantly to Liv to confirm, "We have not heard any update from the Egyptians."

"We may still be able to convince Ahmed." Liv offered, lifting her bracelet to Hayden, and explained with a whisper, "He said I was always welcome. And he still let us go to aid our people after I declined his proposal. There may be hope."

Hayden nodded, although not optimistically.

"We'll restrategize when we have recovered." Hayden turned to all in the room, "Take care and rest. I open my home to you and your people for as long as you wish to stay. We'll focus on the Celts and Egyptians in the next few days and summon the council with any pressing updates."

Everyone filtered out, slowly and steadily, heads down.

Liv stayed with Hayden, before inevitably they returned to their private rooms.

After making sure Liv was settled, her king asked to check on Rei, and left within seconds when Liv insisted.

Two hours had passed before Hayden returned. Liv hadn't slept the entire time he was away, too worried about her fiancé and close friend. Liv met him at the entrance and comforted him immediately. Softly shutting the door behind her, she dragged her feet to the bed chamber, witnessing Hayden collapse onto the mattress. She followed his steps, crashing beside him, and pulled the comforter over them both.

She anxiously watched him, looking for any inclination of what she could do or say to help.

Hayden sighed, placing his hand on his head and applying pressure to his forehead.

"That was the hardest thing I have ever had to do." He admitted softly, "I pray to Zeus we never have to go through anything remotely close to that ever again. No. I *refuse* to allow going through something like that again. Over my dead body."

FORTY-EIGHT

LIV

"Thank you, James."

Liv smiled softly as Piper's father left her office after reporting they had not yet found a breakthrough on how to control Danu's curse.

She sighed after he closed the door, the back of her mind debating whether her House of Earth powers could help somehow. If she blessed the land...

Liv shook it out of her head, it was too risky.

She pushed aside the thought and instead grabbed the correspondence from Ahmed that had been delivered during her meeting with the recently appointed Elements Pillar Research Lead.

Dearest Olivia,

Give me a reason to visit.

Ahmed

Liv huffed, crumpling up the note and throwing it into her fire.

She leaned her head into her hands, taking deep breaths and focusing on the pattern of inhaling through her nose and exhaling through her mouth. Inhaling, exhaling. Inhaling, exhaling.

It had been a week since they deserted Puerdios. Six days since she sent a larger team to Jupiter to run tests on the Celts. Four days since she wrote Ahmed. Three days since she had seen Hayden and two days since she had returned to the Elements Pillar to try and rebuild.

To try and distract herself.

Liv sighed, walked over to the bar cart in the room and poured herself a glass of whiskey, relishing in its warmth as it slid roughly down her throat.

The first sip always stung the hardest. It was the one she looked forward to most now.

Dylan, Kyril and Peyton still hadn't appeared, recently reported dead among a long list of casualties.

The thought of never hearing Peyton call her, "Roomie!" while bursting through a door unannounced or Dylan sweetly using her reserve to calm anxiety while Kyril mocked it caused Liv to lose it for the fourth time that day. Clouds began hovering in the sky, inadvertently darkening the natural light in her room, and a strong rainfall of pellets started crashing against her ceiling.

"Shit." Liv sniffled, cleaning up her powerful mess.

She took another sip of whiskey, even angrier when it expectedly went down smoothly, but fortunately served its purpose of numbing her once again.

"Liv?"

There was a subtle knock at the door. Daphne gently peeked her head through the entry.

"Oh, hi." Liv smiled weakly, wiping her cheeks, and quickly blotted beneath her eye.

Daphne looked around the office, her eyes sparkling with memories.

"I haven't been in this office for quite some time." She spoke with awe, studying the bookcases Liv hadn't touched. "Not much has changed."

Daphne turned to Liv, kindly not acknowledging her future daughter-in-law's unstable state.

"I'm here to discuss the matter of your nuptials to my son."

Liv's jaw dropped. She took another sip of whiskey, staring down the Candor Elite with astonishment. When Daphne's demeanor did not budge, Liv set down her glass and clasped her hands on the desk.

"What exactly can I help you with, Daphne?" Liv finally asked, but nevertheless still baffled.

"You must convince Hayden that having a wedding sooner is the right move to unite our people and instill hope once again." Daphne stated blankly.

"Convince Hayden? You still have to convince *me*!?" Liv shrieked.

Only three days ago they held a memorial ceremony for those who had passed onto the Underworld from the Puerdios invasion. It was as if Daphne wanted to repurpose the florals to 'save costs.'

"Liv, you know I would not press this matter during such a delicate time unless it was of the upmost importance." Daphne's eyes pleaded, while her voice remained unwavering.

"Showing the prophecy truly coming to fruition and making a bold statement in retaliation to Kronos and the deity universe is the best move you can make." Daphne pressed, "When you unite in marriage, your connection with Hayden will be inpenetrable."

Liv's head tilted at the last noted advice. "The connection will grow stronger with marriage?"

"Marriage is a sacred right, binding two together under the power of the divine. Your connection will be blessed by the most powerful of deities – Aphrodite, Eros, Hymenaeus and Hera."

Liv couldn't believe she was contemplating this nonsense when she and Hayden were both unwhole. But perhaps they could become more whole by committing to eachother and solidifying their partnership. They were certainly never whole, apart.

"If you, Piper or whoever promise to plan it all, I'll talk to Hayden." Liv compromised.

If all she and Hayden had to do was walk down an aisle and repeat a few words, perhaps this could be exactly the distraction they both needed.

"Absolutely not."

Hayden retorted, after Liv laid out the entire proposal.

He turned to Liv, studying her curiously. "How did my mother convince you on this insane and insensitive vendetta?"

"Power." Liv replied honestly. "She started rolling off names of ancient deities and promising it would strengthen our connection, strengthen us."

"Oh Zeus." Hayden rolled his eyes. "She basically 'queened' you."

Liv didn't disagree. Daphne could be very persuasive and inspiring when she chose. Or when they weren't second guessing her manipulations.

"It wasn't just about the promise of power, Hayden." Liv continued explaining softly, slightly embarrassed for what raw truth she was about to reveal. "Honestly, her words gave me hope. A feeling I thought was completely lost."

Hayden turned to Liv; sarcastic judgment entirely washed and removed from his face.

In that moment, Liv knew he had felt the same way, too.

"Maybe it's silly. Maybe I'm naïve." Liv sighed, grabbing his hand and kissing his knuckle. "But we're both living in darkness Hayden, and one of us needs to find the path back to the light. It's the only way we can keep moving forward, keep fighting."

"So, a tuxedo and white dress is how you think we can achieve that?" Hayden whispered.

"Proclaiming our love to the gods can't hurt the effort, either." Liv smirked.

Hayden took a deep breath, thinking through the magnitude of what his fiancée was requesting. "Okay, I'll do it. But let me be clear, I'm doing this because I love *you* and *you* want this. Not to speed up some silly prophecy or appease our allies."

"Thank you." Liv smiled, a tear falling down her cheek. But for the first time in a week, the tear was one of happiness, one of hope.

"Awaken my soul." Hayden replied lightheartedly, kissing away the tear.

Royal Power

"Speaking of allies," Liv took another breath, "I heard back from Ahmed and I think we have to invite him to our wedding."

Hayden paused, clearly taken aback from the request.

"And why are we inviting the immortal who proposed to you to our wedding?"

Liv smirked, turning to Hayden mischievously.

"He told me to give him a reason to visit."

JOCELYN

Her jaw dropped at the wedding invitation she held in her hands.

Her little brother and Ollie. Getting married.

This week.

She ran to her room, finding Niall working on correspondence and dropped the invitation atop his desk.

"What is-"

"My brother, uh-huh, getting married... NEXT WEEK." Jocelyn spun away, pacing across the room. "And of course, I'm not allowed to *look* into my brother's future, so couldn't have even prepared for this crazy news appropriately! What am I supposed to *wear*? Who am I supposed to bring as a *date* on such short notice? And freaking Demetrius chasing the Orishas somewhere..."

"Excuse me. Let's take a few steps back." Niall had stood and silently approached Jocelyn, now gently grabbing her arm to coax her to stop moving. "Your brother is engaged?"

"Yes, to Olivia Monaco. Element Elite. Half-Mortal. Soul mate. Keep up." Jocelyn snapped her fingers at the end from irritation.

She didn't care if she may not have *mentioned* her brother to Niall much, or at least not much outside of a royal, alliance-related way.

"Okay. Do we like Olivia?" Niall clarified.

Jocelyn laughed at his use of 'we,' providing comfort that knowing whatever her response, Niall had her back.

"Yes, we do. Very much." Jocelyn grinned. "She's like the best, annoying, beautiful little sister I never wanted."

"And why can't you look into your brother's future?" Niall asked. "Wouldn't you *want* to know what happens to him? If he's safe… in danger?"

Jocelyn took a deep breath, unsure exactly how to explain it.

"My mother handles my brother to keep me sane. I'm not sure I could handle seeing his demise, I already have too many uninvited deaths penetrate my skull on a daily basis." Jocelyn shrugged, "Although, I have felt more in control of my visions lately."

"Okay, later conversation. We'll work on controlling your visions." Niall tossed it aside as if it would be a simple task, "If you need a date, I'm happy to oblige. And good news, I don't really care what you wear."

Jocelyn's eyes grew wide. She took a step back.

"What? Two birds. One stone?" Niall offered.

"You?!" She exclaimed, crossing her arms in bewilderment.

"Is there someone else in this bloody room!?" Niall retorted, crossing his arms.

"Okay, so I'll just bring Prince Niall of the Celtic Deities to the Royal Pure God Wedding." Jocelyn huffed. "Whole family there, a pending alliance… no pressure… none at all."

"Exactly?" Niall confirmed. "I offered because I thought you'd be happy?"

"Happy to bring a prince to a royal *family* affair? Should we establish our marital arrangement now or announce it after the wedding as to not steal my brother's thunder?"

Jocelyn stormed away, before swinging back around for round two.

"Besides… Danu's curse!? How would you even get around that one?"

"I'm not sure. But hey, a lot can happen in a week." Niall joked, laughing as Jocelyn flipped him off and headed toward the door as he hollered, "Your brother got engaged, fought in a war and now he's getting married!"

LIV

It appeared that death seemed to follow her, but in this case, it was as if she were chasing it.

She flew over the dark marshes and near the mountain that protected the Underworld.

After sending out invitations, Hayden mentioned Hades declined because he was unable to leave the Underworld for security reasons.

She figured that after all they had been through, he would have at least stopped by for a cocktail.

So, reluctantly, Liv was going to meet her Afterworld partner, check in on him and see if anything could be done.

She bowed respectively for the soldiers who lined up by the mountain's entrance, saddened to see Callos in line with the others. He looked so much like Peyton, it *hurt* Liv to see such a strong reminder of her, yet so different, as if his presence mocked the fact that her best friend was no longer in this world. Not to mention he stood where his brother, Xander, once stood only months before.

Surrounded by death, the reminders of those they had lost suffocated Liv. How was she supposed to continue on when so many had perished on her behalf?

Nevertheless, she hugged him, wished him well, and continued on to hell.

The caves typical fortress called her its master, alleviating the obstacles so that Liv could quietly march her way into Hades's lair.

"You're still blonde." Hades said tartly.

"And you're still just as ugly on the inside as you are on the outside." Liv spat back, but with a smile.

"Exactly." He smugly replied. "And congratulations are in order on your engagement. What business can I help you with?"

"Thank you and nothing." Liv honestly replied, "I just wanted to see how you were doing."

"You came all of the way out here to visit? No other agenda?" Hades asked, surprised. "Deities don't usually venture out here and so close to the Underworld without a reason."

"Well now I'm hurt, Hades. You of all deities should know that I'm not a usual god." Liv laughed, truly enjoying this banter. "Truthfully, Hayden mentioned you are typically unable to leave your space, due to security parameters, and since I'm a partner in that sense, I figured I could at least visit every once in a while, to show my gratitude. And even though we work together, I would like to develop a personal relationship, too."

Hades paused, looking confused.

"Well, maybe I did come for something. A drink. At least by now you've usually offered a whiskey." Liv joked.

Hades laughed, his tension lifting. He walked over to the bar area and started concocting cocktails.

"And you aren't terrified of being so close to the Underworld for capture?" He hummed as he poured an amber liquid into his crystal glasses, his words crisp and taunting, and then walked over to Liv with her beverage.

Liv thought about the question while she grabbed the drink and expressed gratitude by clinking her glass with his.

Finally, she answered.

"I guess not. At this point, in my deity life, I feel as if I'm living on borrowed time. And we both know if you wanted me dead, I'd have entered the Underworld that night we originally made our bargain."

"So, you trust me?" Hades tilted his head.

"Yes, I suppose I do." Liv admitted, before adding, "Don't give me a reason to regret it."

Hades nodded in agreement, before his composure softened.

"I am sorry to hear about your friends."

Liv almost spit out her drink from the consideration, but fortunately held it together to not offend the Underworld king.

"Thank you, Hades." Liv replied honestly. "Honestly, it's hard wrapping my head around it."

She looked longingly to the door that led to the Underworld portal. They were so close, yet so far away. Liv hoped they were okay, happier where they were now.

Liv opened her mouth to speak, but then restrained. It felt inappropriate.

"What, darling?" Hades sweetly beckoned. "Trouble for your thought?"

"Er, I was wondering – could you check your log to confirm their passing through the Underworld? It might help me accept the reality, versus wondering."

"Anything for you, my doll." Hades snickered, gliding over to his desk. "I should recall their names for helping fight the Soulless intrusion, but forgive me…"

Liv shook her head; Hades was over a thousand years old. He couldn't remember *every* person he encountered. It was impossible.

"Dylan, Elements Pillar." She offered.

Hades flipped a few pages, scanning the names, before breathing, "Aha!" and nodding his head to confirm her passing.

Liv felt lightheaded but continued on. "Kyril, Elements Pillar."

Hades skimmed the page, before turning it again. After perusing more names, his eyes grew in recognition and finally stated, "Kyril is right here."

"Peyton, Security Pillar." Liv whispered, her eyes wavering.

Hades glanced down, flipped a few pages, before catching Liv's saddened demeanor. He slammed the book shut and then whispered, "Yes."

Liv took a sip of her whiskey, trying to latch onto something, anything, other than the spinning room.

"Olivia. Are you alright?" Hades speculated with intrigue.

"I will be." Liv gulped, turning to Hades softly.

"The first ones are the hardest." He advised, looking off into the distance. "It gets easier with time."

"The downfall of immortality, I suppose." Liv reflected, taking another sip of her whiskey. "Hades, if I passed, would you be disappointed?"

"Greatly." The ancient deity drawled.

Liv's head snapped to meet his eyes.

"Teasing or serious?"

"Serious." Hades replied soundly. "I've grown fond of you, Olivia. Not many young immortals venture to the Underworld so bravely and so often."

A hint of sadness crescented his eyes.

"Hades, is there truly no way you can stop by our wedding?" Liv asked openly.

"If I come to your wedding, then I'll be required to deliver a promised gift." Hades replied ambiguously.

"If you come to our wedding, you might actually have *fun*." Liv teased, looking around the dark office. "Come on, venture out. Live a little."

"Live a little for *Liv?*" Hades chuckled, then defended his pun when he caught Liv rolling her eyes, "Come on, have you *never* heard that before!? Too easy!"

"If I don't roll my eyes at least once because of you, then the whole day will be deemed a waste and you're doing something wrong." Liv shrugged, unable to contain her grin.

"Okay. I'll stop by. For *one* cocktail. But I won't refrain from any judgmental mockery. And I'm out when the dancing begins."

"Wouldn't expect you to stay a moment longer." Liv grinned.

Hades rolled his eyes, "I despise wearing white."

Liv tilted her head, "What?"

As one who always preferred ambiguous dress, so peers constantly questioned his loyalty to dark and pure, Hades's notion didn't surprise her, but the declaration did. Currently sporting a green velvet suit, a silver shirt and black tie with matching leather loafers mixing all three colors into one decadent design, Hades certainly had caught her attention, whether he strategically meant to as a ploy or not.

Hades looked at the bride-to-be confusedly, summoning the invitation. "Traditional wedding attire... ah, yes says right here. It's an all-white affair."

Liv's jaw dropped.

Shit. She may actually need to care *a little* about what her dress looked like, then.

FORTY-NINE

LIV

The room was bright, joyful, softer – full of light and happiness.

Liv had to keep pinching herself to remind herself that this was not a dream. Her mother and her best friend Lacey were both with her, getting ready for a day she had spent her entire life dreaming about.

She spun around, finding light in her eyes as she gazed at her hair and makeup, both done to perfection.

"Oh honey, you look so beautiful." Julia beamed, a tear of joy streaming down her eye.

"Mom, be careful. You can't cry yet!" Liv exclaimed, doing her best to also hold back her tears, laughing as she turned. "Don't look at me!"

Trellis's gift to Liv was manipulating time once again, placing the wedding in the Pure God's natural loop, but five years ahead in her mortal family and friend's lives. A gift from Silas – a glamour so that anything magical would be unnoticeable and unmemorable to those who did not possess immortal power. Not that Liv had many from her world attending today's event – Charles was the only addition to her mom and best friend who would be present among the deities – and Liv knew that Hayden extending this stretch to the divided rule was an incredible endowment for the day.

After this, she would soon need to say goodbye to her mother and best friend, permanently. So, for today, Liv only wanted to focus on the memory being made.

"Liv, the dress is stunning." Piper chimed in, fondly looking at Liv's sleek, white silk gown hanging against the window.

Liv rolled her eyes, choosing the path of mockery rather than emotion; it was the only way her makeup would survive.

"Says the friend also in a white, and equally magnificent dress."

Piper blushed but laughed off the compliment.

As Hades had informed the bride-to-be, Pure God tradition mandated an all-white attired wedding, with all attendees – male and female – to wear a similar color as the bride.

For one, Liv appreciated the opportunity to blend in, but as she took into consideration the exquisite couture gowns her bridal party donned compared to her classic, minimalist style, it would be possible that she wouldn't just blend in, but possibly be overshadowed entirely.

Truthfully, that could be the best wedding gift of all.

Liv smiled, turning back shyly to the mirror. Her hair was loosely curled in waves, but flat like silk near her part and tucked behind her ears so that her hair almost appeared like it had a blonde headband holding the hair from her face. On one side of the sleek part of her head had diamonds built out precisely like the constellation that her husband-to-be and the King of the Pure Gods had once gifted her as a way to stay connected for eternity.

And now, they were going to declare their vows for eternity, strengthening their connection even more.

She blinked, her thick, black lashes bouncing, revealing a shimmer from her eyeliner – half silver, near the inner curves of her eyes, and half black, winged out dramatically.

The only thing left to do was put on her dress.

With help from Daphne and her mom, Liv stepped into the silk gown and pulled her hands through the soft, long sleeves. Lacey zipped up the lower part of the dress and Piper clipped the top neckline together. Her long-sleeved, crewneck mermaid gown clung to her curves, the only part of skin revealed was a teardrop of her full back.

While Liv anticipated everyone wearing lace, embroidery, feathers and more – she opted for a clean, crisp and timeless look. The only details were silk buttons that extended through to her train and the edge of her fabric was finished with a delicate, thin diamond band.

She had been dreaming of a dress like this since she was a child, so felt it would be truest to herself, amidst the chaos and unanticipated summer wedding, to stick to something constant, unsculpted or influenced by the deity world.

"Oh no! Did I miss it?"

Jocelyn's head peaked behind the door, disappointed in her delayed arrival.

Fortunately, she was already dressed in her long-sleeved, old-fashioned silk gown, filled with tastefully layered frills on her arms, hair pulled back in a loose bun. More surprisingly, was the blonde-haired man who towered over her, with raging masculinity and strength, atop a griffin in the doorway.

"Ah, this is Niall." Jocelyn bit her lip nervously, stepping aside for Liv to find a handsomely groomed beast. "Er – I mean, Prince Niall of the Celtic Deities." She shook it off, continuing on her campaign. "Hoping you might be able to do us a solid, future-little-sister Liv, as requested by the research team, to bless the wedding ground?"

Liv tilted her head speculatively.

"It might slow down Danu's curse." Niall explained with a shrug.

"Of course." Liv nodded, "Thank you so much for risking your freedom to be here today. Anything I can do, I'm happy to at least try."

She closed her eyes, praying to Zeus and the Element Elites of the past, honing in her House of Earth powers to bless the wedding ground and protect all those near and far who were loyal to her and the Pure God rule from evil.

Liv opened her eyes, looking to Niall to confirm whether anything may have changed.

He shook his head quietly.

"Let me try again," Liv offered kindly.

She closed her eyes, praying again to her ancestors, calling to her elemental powers, focusing on the land that seemed to have a sheer gleam of darkness surrounding Niall. She could see the curse feeding off his strength, his powers, fortifying it in return. Liv tried to eliminate the residue and cleanse it with pure magic, to no avail.

Opening her eyes, Liv snapped out of the hazy vision immediately.

"I can't penetrate the curse – but I can see its powers." She explained sadly. "Niall, it grows stronger as it feeds off of you, I ask you to not stay long in order to protect yourself and the other Celts."

"Of course." Niall nodded, "I can feel my strength waning – which is why I must apologize for Joss's tardiness. We wanted to postpone our arrival so we could enjoy the wedding as long as possible."

"I am so truly honored that you are here." Liv kindly smiled, walking over to the Celtic prince and giving him a hug, replenishing his powers from her own pool – giving him more energy to fight against his curse, more time to remain on earth.

"Thank you, Liv." Niall smiled, his grin and eyes both sparkling brighter than before.

"Liv, it's time." Julia gently touched Liv's elbow, kindly eyeing Niall to leave, before returning her full attention to her daughter. "If your father were here, he would be so happy for you."

She squeezed her daughter's arms, admiring the mini white pearls adorned with a small diamond that resided on each ear, a wedding gift from Charles and her, before heading out with Lacey shortly behind.

Julia wore a stunning white chiffon gown, layered with lace and satin and structured to perfectly compliment her volumptuous curves. Lacey donned an ivory, corseted off-the-shoulder, long-sleeved gown with a stunning and elaborate silver embroidery to create a whimsical sheen, and her gray-blonde hair in a braided crown. The disguised gowns were a gift from Piper's seamstress aunt, but in the mortal's reality, they both wore colored dresses of their own choosing.

Daphne walked up to Liv, looking admiringly at her best friend's daughter and her son's best friend. Her eyes glistened as she poisedly held back tears. "Your mother is right, if your father were here, he would be *so* happy for you, as am I."

Liv nodded, unable to express the sentiments she wanted to cry for her dad. Daphne's words resonated with her, as one who knew her dad and his entire truth, it was a blessing to hear approval from her father before making such a big, impactful, life-changing choice.

"Thank you." Liv finally whispered, pulling Daphne into a hug.

The Candor Elite's feathers on her elegant dress tickled Liv's neck. Her platinum hair was pulled back into a sleek bun, crystals in a matching feather shape adorning her profile.

Finally, Piper stepped up, handing Liv her bouquet, a larger version to the one she held in her own hand. Liv revelled in smelling her favorite bouquet – white anemonies, peonies, white cherry blossom, eucalyptus, baby's breath and white hyancinth, and laughed at a memory in a dorm room when she had once been so angry at the thought of Hayden gifting them to her for her birthday.

Her best friend looked stunning in a white strapless gown, the front cut low, down her torso and embellished with floral taffeta and silver plating, her gown transforming at the waist with pleats cascading into a large train.

"For Peyton and Dylan." Piper's lips trembled, opening her hand to reveal two pins, the first adorned with a ruby, the second with amber. Looking up with a tear to Liv, who nodded her head in approval, Piper pinned the two jewels into the side of the bouquet's stem.

"I wish they were here, Piper." Liv whispered with a sniffle, pulling Piper into an embrace.

"You know Peyton would be *screaming bloody murder* right now for crying and *ruining* your make up." Piper laughed as she wiped a tear from her cheek.

"Oh Zeus, she would have been a bridesmaid-zilla." Liv rolled her eyes, chuckling.

"Dylan would have been nice to have around." Piper looked around the empty room, "We could have used her calm energy right about now."

"I know." Liv's eyes grew wide in agreement.

"What if I trip?" Piper squeaked.

"What if *I* trip!?" Liv echoed.

"Dylan would say something like, 'take your time, breathe and worst case, we bribe Trellis to turn back time.'" Piper advised.

"Peyton would dare me to shimmy or electric slide down the aisle, and then threaten to do so herself if I didn't 'lock it down.'" Liv added with a smirk.

"Lock it down, Ollie." Piper scolded with amusement, but the words felt weak coming from her mousy voice, more like a request.

"I appreciate the effort." Liv grinned, taking a deep breath. "We should go – as my friend Nike once said... 'Just do it.'"

Piper looked inquisitively to Liv, "Did Nike really say *that?*"

HAYDEN

Flashes of moments implanted into his mind from the day. Buttoning his white, collarless shirt, putting on his white suit jacket, receiving stunning cufflinks with his father's crest from Rei, enjoying a glass of whisky with Tristan and Zayne and spending time with his mother, looking absolutely stunning in her feathered gown with modern cuts, and giving him a proud hug before departing with Silas to greet the arriving guests.

So many other things from the day sped up into a blur, until he was suddenly standing under the stars, the sun slowly setting behind the horizon, hanging lights floating in the air and adding a warm glow to the hundreds of deities sitting in front of him with awe.

He watched with a blink of an eye his mother and Silas walk down the aisle together, followed by Liv's mom Julia and her boyfriend Charles, and soon after his closest friends and family gliding together – Jocelyn and Zayne, Piper and Tristan, and finally Lace and Rei.

But then time stopped.

When he saw Olivia Monaco descend the stairs and walk toward him, each step closer could not be quick enough. While everyone flambuoyantly dressed in ruffles, rich fabrics and over-the-top embellishments, Liv looked entirely like herself – classic, simple and absolutely mesmerizing – inadvertently making her stand out above and beyond everyone else. The white silk perfectly sculpted her curves, each limb accentuated and revealed with every new step.

Olivia Monaco was the most incredibly stunning woman in the world.

What the Hades had he done to deserve such a perfect wife?

Her eyes finally caught his, beaming bright as she smiled, making him grin with excitement as she continued slowly down the aisle. After their eyes met, her arctic blue gaze penetrated his, and never left until suddenly her hand was reaching out to grab his, which he proudly took.

You look beautiful.

Liv smiled shyly, blinking her luscious eyelashes before returning his gaze.

You're quite sexy, yourself. Damn, am I lucky.

Hayden blushed, restraining himself from kissing her right then and there, claiming her as his without need of a formal production.

Instead, he squeezed her hand and looked to Silas, their officiant for the ceremony.

They would do this the right way and they would only do it once.

For Hayden, there was only once.

Silas began speaking, but Hayden didn't register a word the Security Elite said. Instead, he stared at his soon-to-be wife's intoxicating eyes, giving him the strength he needed to remain calm and still.

Soon, Silas was seeding words to Liv for her to repeat. He only caught the silky words vibrating off her soft lips.

"I, Olivia Monaco and Element Elite, take King Hayden to be my divine, wedded husband." She began, her voice trembling in an adorable way.

"With this ring, I give you my heart. I promise from this day forward, you shall not walk alone. May my heart be your shelter and my arms be your home. I stand by your side, as your equal and other half. For better and for worse, we shall rule as one and love as ardently, so long as the gods bless us and our souls remain as one."

She slid a simple gold band onto his ring finger; the piece of metal instantly and willingly locked into place next to his other, a physical representation of Hayden's bonding to Liv.

"Hayden, repeat after me." Silas smiled gently, handing him Liv's wedding band.

Similar to Hayden's, the golden ring was sleek and minimal, perfectly complimenting her ornate engagement ring.

"I, King Hayden, take Olivia Monaco, Element Elite and future Queen, to be my divine, wedded wife." He began, trying to keep his voice stern, but his delivery was shaky and raw.

Liv squeezed his hand in assurance, appreciating his vulnerability.

"With this ring, I give you my heart. I promise from this day forward, you shall not walk alone. May my heart be your shelter and my arms be your home. I stand by your side, as your equal and other half. For better and for worse, we shall rule as one and love as ardently, so long as the gods bless us and our souls remain as one."

He slid the band across Liv's ring finger, feeling it clasp against her engagement ring at once. Solidified and unified.

"The gods bless this royal marriage, I am pleased to not only announce you as husband and wife, but as King and Queen. Long live the Pure God Rule!"

Cheers erupted in front of them, as Silas kindly announced, "You may kiss!"

Liv jumped into Hayden's arms, and as their lips touched, the bond locked in place. Similar to the rings binding to one another, this action cemented their bodies, their souls, as one. Forever.

Still holding onto his wife's hand, Hayden turned in unison with Liv to the crowd that stood before them and strolled down the aisle. He tried to keep his excitement contained, but the influx of powers combined with his already heightened emotions were unparalleled to when their soul mate bond connected earlier in the year.

He could feel the earth call to him, stronger than ever before, the elements buzzing with obedience, but most importantly, the warmth of Liv's love flowing through his veins more intense and rapidly than ever.

PIPER

The wedding was absolutely incredible. Piper continued spinning around on the dance floor, absorbing such a majestic sight.

Rows of long, family-styled tables were adorned with white decorations and golden utensils, glowing underneath the sparkling night sky.

She watched longingly as her two best friends cut a chocolate cake with buttercream frosting, decorated with gold flakes and eucalyptus.

Piper breathed in the fresh air, reeling in the happy atmosphere and clinging to it, praying that those who had not made it to today's festivities were able to feel the positivity all the way to the Underworld, smiling on the new King and Queen's dynasty for the Pure God Rule. Giving them hope from leaving a possibly better world.

Then, she held her breath, as she usually did when she found Tristan approaching. Tonight, looking more untame and dangerous than ever, he had stepped away from his usual dark attire and in contrast wore a white cashmere-silk tuxedo and matching coat. His caramel eyes glowed brighter, intensified and ablaze with the complimentary gold accents surrounding them, as if beckoning her to taste the dark side.

Tristan would certainly be Piper's undoing.

The music slowed as if Tristan had anticipated the shift in dancing. He extended his hand. "May I have this dance?"

Piper nodded, biting her lip, but accepting his request.

She grabbed his warm hand, instantly feeling warmer herself, not realizing she had been slightly chilly in the cooler, night weather. But now she felt perfect.

Since they had returned from Thailand, whatever they had experienced away from the powerful Pure God society had disappeared, their relationship reverting back to cordiality and being friends, at best.

Between multiple Elements Pillar and Royal Council meetings, and Tristan being Liv's right-hand-advisor, to preparing for the Puerdios invasion and *losing* it, to then mourning the loss of three friends – who felt more like family to Piper and certainly even more so to Tristan – plus, hearing the news of his great-grandfather, Henri, also passing to the Underworld during the battle, but not inheriting any Humanity Elite powers to take over the Dark Pillar and revert it back to Pure, they had inevitably grown apart and into leading separate lives once again. No longer united by a common goal, siloed with no competing distractions, it was as if they had both selected to barricade the once compelling but terrifying connection they had explored overseas.

But then again, Tristan hadn't looked at Piper like the way he looked at her tonight.

Had the fire not sizzled entirely?

"You look absolutely stunning, Pipes." Tristan whispered softly against her ear, sending chills down her neck and arm.

"You clean up well, yourself." She breathed back, unsure of exactly what to say.

"I owe you an apology," Tristan's jaw tightened as he pulled back and stared against her glacier eyes, melting them quickly with his flames. "I haven't been in the right headspace to properly treat you the way you deserve to be treated."

He gulped, staring down at the ground, ashamed.

Piper paused moving her feet, trying to understand where his mindset was now.

When Tristan looked up, his eyes were raw, vulnerable – like liquid lava slowly turning into molten rock.

Piper's heart broke, pulling him into an embrace. "There's nothing to apologize for, truly."

Tristan breathed out, squeezing Piper gently in gratitude, his tense posture relaxing at her words immediately.

"If there's one thing I've realized from my idiotic maneuver," Tristan whispered, "it's that I'll probably make many more mistakes." He laughed lightly, but the chuckle didn't fully deliver as he continued on, "But that I've abused the power of immortality, naively believing it gives us time. That it's okay for some things to not be said, or set right, or sacrificed because there would always be tomorrow."

Tristan stepped back, again looking fiercely into Piper's eyes.

"I know now, that tomorrow is not promised. So, damnit, I need to kiss the girl today."

He grabbed Piper's neck, pulling her gently into a passionate kiss.

Piper collapsed into his arms, but then slowly melted into his embrace, after the shock flowed into the enjoyment of their bodies connected as one. The urgency of his kiss transformed into a soft, intentional message, one that Piper understood and continued to enjoy through every level.

Fireworks exploded from his soft lips gently caressing hers, as she pulled him closer – if it were at all possible – his strong torso pressed against hers, making her feel more, *want* more.

Until Tristan pulled away, looking curiously, shyly, at Piper's reaction, before continuing on.

Piper pursed her lips, still fully absorbing the unexpected gesture. She looked from his eyes back down to his sexy pout, wanting to quickly go back to the touching and never stop. But she needed to say *something*. He stared at her sheepishly, waiting for some form of verbal queue to relay her reaction, her desires, her thoughts. So, Piper said the only thought that crossed her mind, and did exactly what she wanted to do for once, insecurity no longer terrifying her true feelings.

"Carpe fucking diem." Piper breathed, pulling Tristan back to her and pressing her lips against his once again, taking control to make sure he understood she was in this and fully committed.

She heard Tristan laugh joyfully, making her smile as their faces continued to press together.

"About time." Piper mocked with a whisper, kissing him one last time before pulling away.

"A fire is at its best when it's been burning for a while." Tristan joked.

Piper rolled her eyes, but Tristan's embers no longer embraced her with a layer of warmth, the contrast causing gooseflesh to appear on her skin – her body's natural reaction to the previously heated events.

"Here," Tristan pulled off his white cashmere coat, wrapping it around Piper's shoulders.

Piper smiled, instantly enwrapped in smoke, leather and whisky, feeling warm once again.

Together, they walked off the dance floor and spotted Raj, who stood by the bar, talking with Queen Chanthira and King Rāhula.

"I was just apologizing for being the keeper of their curse." Raj welcomed Piper and Tristan with open arms.

"Who knew a considered enemy could be so friendly." Queen Chanthira laughed lightheartedly.

It still caught Piper offguard to be on amicable terms with ancient royalty, mesmerized by their wedding attire, both incorporating modern and historical nods to their culture.

Raj wore a striking embroidered sherwani with pearl detailing on its neck lapel, revealing a shirt beneath with pearl buttons, too. The suit was a piece of art, truly transforming the lost Naga into the last Chola Prince.

Queen Chanthira, stunning as always, had a mesmerizing silver headpiece as her crown with dragons adorning her hair, which perfectly matched the entirely jeweled short-sleeved top she wore and complemented her laced silk gown. Her husband, King Rāhula, wore a similar style to Prince Raj, but his was less ornate, and he wore pha chung hang pants in contrast to the prince's traditional trousers.

"I am afraid I don't only bring good news," Raj began, turning to Tristan and Piper, "I haven't had luck finding Vishnu – but I've heard Shiva has joined Kronos's forces and that he's already cursing Pure God prisoners into stone."

The prince quivered as he said the last word; Piper imagined it was a reflection of his own past horror-induced experiences. Her heart went out to those innocent souls who were frozen in time and unable to do anything as they sat in a cold prison cell, or worse, as they watched and heard the terrible things Kronos, Arlo and Shiva plotted.

"Any other leads?" Tristan asked softly.

"I don't suspect Vishnu to stay silent for too long," Raj speculated, "But I have a lead that some of his Puranas were seen in Mumbai, it's where I am headed next."

"Is there anything we can do to help?" Piper prompted, wishing they could do *more, anything* to solidify more power on their side.

"It is I who want to help you," Raj implored. "I have left some vials of my Naga venom for testing with the Soulless upon your Security Elite's request, please ensure it remains in the right hands."

"We will. Thank you. You're doing so much for us." Piper replied quietly.

"Pray to Vishnu and hope I'm able to get to him before Shiva does," Raj instructed, before kindly excusing himself.

"It feels strange discussing such dark matters at a wonderful event." King Rāhula offered, trying to navigate the conversation to more appropriate subjects.

"A wedding can only mask reality for so long." Tristan commented darkly, grabbing Piper's hand, "But perhaps another dance will mask this fantasy for a few moments longer?"

Piper smiled sadly, but graciously accepted, allowing Tristan to guide her back onto the dance floor. Confidently, she chose to add another tease, in hopes of prolonging the bliss for just that much longer.

"And possibly a couple tequila shots, too."

LIV

"So, my *wife*, where do you want to go to celebrate our betrothal properly?" Hayden seductively whispered, spinning her on the dance floor before kissing her hand.

Tristan and Piper danced beside them; Liv was extremely excited to get the dish on *that* development following the wedding and post-celebratory travels. But for now, she knew her two friends needed time to plant the seeds and space to let whatever they had breathe, using the oxygen to grow naturally and without any pressure. Until then, she'd remain blissfully oblivious.

"Did Daphne not handle the post-nuptial celebrations?" Liv teased, allowing Hayden to playfully dip her on the dance floor. Meeting him upright once again, Liv purred in his ear, "Somewhere with you, and a bed, for an uninterrupted amount of time."

Hayden smiled darkly, already envisioning the ways he wanted to discard the thin, silk fabric concealing his wife – the only thing preventing him from seeing her flawless body in all its glory.

Sharing the vision inspired Liv to deliberate how she wanted to remove Hayden's white tuxedo and sheer collarless shirt, making the bride bite her tongue and reactively bring her lips to his.

"Ah, Ahmed and Sabra are approaching." Hayden groaned as Liv trailed kisses down his neck, pulling away before putting on a forced smile, masking his disappointment for the entire scenario.

The question is… do they come in peace?

Liv laughed, turning to find Ahmed in a relaxed, white linen button-down shirt and trousers, Sabra in a lovely saree embellished with gold.

"Hello Ahmed, hello Sabra." Liv smiled genuinely, politely pulling both into separate, sincere embraces.

"Congratulations to you both." Ahmed smiled slyly, eyeing Liv with a smirk.

"Thank you." Hayden cut in tersely, the tension rising. "And thank you both for joining us today to celebrate."

"I plan to celebrate over there, at the bar." Sabra added sarcastically.

"You know what? I'll join you." Hayden offered, "We can mark the occasion properly with a drink."

"You speak my language." Sabra's eyes sparkled at Hayden's proposal before eyeing her brother with disdain.

"I'll bring back champagne for you." Hayden whispered, kissing Liv's cheek gingerly before departing with the Egyptian princess.

When Liv and Ahmed finally stood alone, Ahmed extended his hand, offering a dance with the bride.

"You know, if things played out differently, this could have been *our* wedding."

Liv rolled her eyes. "You know that's not true. Have you not heard of 'the prophecy' by now?"

Between Silas's ceremony scripts, Daphne's welcoming speech, both Rei and Piper's toasts, and perhaps every side conversation in between, the mention of the Pure God prophecy coming to fruition quickly became a dangerous drinking game.

"Of course I heard of the prophecy." Ahmed explained with a shrug, "Even before you visited months ago."

"You did?" Liv raised her brow. "I call bull."

"I did!" Ahmed exclaimed, exasperated.

"Then why the hell did you propose to *me*?" Liv snapped back, equally perplexed.

"I needed to confirm the strength of the prophecy resided with you two. It was a simple test for myself to see what you would give up for eachother's love – in all capacities – before I pledged my loyalty behind it, and especially if I was going to offer my people to fight for you both."

Liv considered his words for some time – it certainly made more sense for his choice to let her go upon her request.

"But you shall always remember, I proposed first." He grinned.

"Sly gazelle." Liv shook her head. "It would have been much simpler if we just started out as friends to begin with."

"But a lot less fun." Ahmed grinned.

He nodded to Liv's bracelet, the one he gifted her the last time they spoke. "The coding still works for the passage, Olivia. It always will. You are always welcome with the Egyptian Gods. And use it to summon us, when the final battle comes."

Liv's head snapped to check the veracity behind the king's final words.

"You'll fight for us?" She clarified; eyes wide.

"Consider it my wedding gift to you." Ahmed drawled unenthusiastically, before his toned changed and he added softly, "I'm sorry for the loss of Puerdios University – I know how much it meant to you."

Liv started getting teary eyed, not just for the school, but more importantly, those souls who were lost with it.

"Thank you." Liv whispered.

The song slowed down, concluding the dance.

"Thank you for the dance, Queen of the Pure Gods." Ahmed bowed respectfully to Liv, before leaving her on the dance floor, alone.

Liv saw Hades in the corner of her eye, wearing a white suit jacket but to his ambiguous flair, paired it with a black bowtie, trouser and pair of loafers. He still blended in well enough with the now darkened atmosphere of night, possibly even more so as half of his body vanished within the shadows.

"Hades." Liv purred, walking toward him with a reprimanding grin.

"Queen of the Underworld and now, Pure Gods." Hades speculated proudly, "Who would have thought a demi-god would achieve so much?"

"It's the future." Liv laughed it off, taking his observation as a compliment. "Glad you could join us in it."

Hades sighed, looking across the flashes of white and laughter. "I must admit, I did not bring a wedding gift." He drawled unenthusiastically, "But, it's all in the stars," waving his hand to the night sky above, "to be redeemed at a later date."

The final phrase was said sharply, as if Hades particularly wanted to enunciate the words for a dramatic effect.

"I shall be waiting ever so impatiently on my toes." Liv replied with a smirk, before noticing Hades's gaze was elsewhere – and his mind possibly not at the table either.

The God of Death was admiring another divine creature, one who equally despised the event she attended as he.

Calithya sat at another table, drinking a margarita and judging all those who conversed around her. Her sequined, more-less-than-covered gown, included a bodysuit with a sheer train, revealing scaly-glittered and long legs, with a regal, ornately structured outer train equipped with feathers surrounding her sheer gown.

"King of the Underworld fancies the Queen of the Sirens?" Liv prompted curiously, reveling in the opportunity to tease the thousand-year-old deity.

"I have not seen Calithya for quite some time, and the last time we spoke it was not pleasant." He speculated softly, sadly.

"Why not talk to her? Have fun, for once." Liv pushed, holding back an eyeroll.

Some deities could be so melodramatic.

"Why would she want to spend time with me? I am the God of Death." Hades admitted, shrugging as he took a sip of his old fashioned.

"The sea drowns many to meet their darkened fate." Liv speculated, hoping to find some kind of connection to give the deity the confidence he typically held in a superfluous amount.

"You think she would be interested?" Hades replied.

"It's a wedding. If there's anytime to catch someone lonely and eager to find love, it's now. Tonight's your best chance, sir."

Hades slammed down his drink.

"Okay." He stood up, eye on the prize. "Here goes nothing."

"I recommend starting with a dance and then perhaps a drink refill thereafter." Liv hollered from behind, the immortal already marching over to play a dangerous game with the siren. Realizing what she had just done, Liv advised responsibly, "And don't get lost in her song!"

The last thing they needed was to get a crying call from Hades, lost on an island with swine. But as Liv thought about that sentiment, she realized there were holes in her assessment, recalling her recent read of Homer's *The Odyssey*, but gave herself a pass since she had consumed an ungodly amount of champagne.

Speaking of champagne, a flute magically appeared in front of her.

"There you are, Ollie." Hayden said seductively, pulling her into an embrace and kissing her forehead. "I'm afraid there are only a couple more obligations we have until I can sweep you away and do wicked things."

Liv's toes curled at the declaration, already feeling serene as she consumed his intoxicating scent.

"I do your bidding and then get punished?" She teased, biting his ear. "I thought we no longer lived in sin, my husband?"

"How virtuous my wife has become, now that we have been blessed by the gods." Hayden smirked, kissing her neck, before pulling away faster than a flash of lightning as his sister coughed, approaching alongside Niall, who now stood on ground and without the griffin.

"Your majesty, I'm pleased to report it worked." Prince Niall stated happily with a grin, pulling Liv into a hug and lifting her high off the ground.

"What worked?" Hayden speculated curiously, patiently waiting for his wife to be returned to him from the handsome Celtic beast.

"My powers are protected from Danu's curse." Niall commented, "As soon as you both exchanged the vows, it was as if some higher power locked into place and she could not reach me within the confines of this sacred space."

"Hayden's royal powers bonded to mine." Liv explained, after first mentally asking Hayden if it were okay to share. "And mine to his – it must have been the combination of my Elements Pillar, House of Earth and now royal powers combining into one, I can now combat and break Danu's equally powerful curse."

"Dia dhaoibh." Niall grabbed Liv's hand and kissed it. "If you do the same to our camps and whatever lands we envision for battle, I can bring our men to earth and prepare for war."

Liv shrieked with happiness, leaping into Niall's arms once again.

Perhaps Daphne was right, this wedding was the hope they needed to ensure the Pure God rule. She just hoped there wasn't an ulterior motive that they were all playing into.

Finally, Hayden brought them to say hello to Queen Chanthira and King Rāhula, before making their way to catch up with Zayne and Ammiras, who both agreed Calithya looked now quite smitten with Hades, although at first they had placed bets whether she would curse him or throw her margarita at him before stomping off. Their royal parade concluded with exchanging pleasantries with the Norse deities, who now stood beside Rei, looking intimidating in numbers with their almost white hair and intense stares. It also didn't help that one of them present was indeed the the very well-known legend, Thor. Liv had to pinch herself that freaking Thor was actually in attendance at her wedding, before forcing herself to calm down and act unimpressed like the Royal Pure God Queen should.

"Thank you for your support and for being here, tonight." Hayden began, shaking Thor's hand with amusement. He completely understood the level of excitement Liv was containing within herself.

"This is my wife, Sif – and as you know, my children, Magni and Mothi, and Mothi's wife Gigi."

Giselle.

Hayden's head snapped to Gigi, clearly having been able to read Liv's initial and instinctual correction within her mind. It appeared her elemental powers had indeed forged together with Hayden's.

Gigi smiled tensely, before diverting the conversation. "It looks as though we both need a refill, King Hayden – might you join me at the bar?"

Liv smiled calmy, letting Hayden question the imposter Norwegian Queen as she continued to distract the others. In all truth, she was pleased she was able to keep it from him *this* long.

Giselle and Hayden returned, the former looking much more relieved and the latter shaking his head at Liv with amusement. After a few more lighthearted discussions, Hayden excused both himself and Liv so they could begin saying their goodbyes.

"Daphne, Lacey, or Julia and Charles, first?" Hayden asked, maneuvering around the party, shaking many guests' hands and assessing the obstacles to get to each target.

"Mortals first, Daphne last." Liv decided, knowing it would be heartbreaking to say goodbye to her mother and best friend, perhaps for the final time, depending on what fate was stored in her future.

"I love you, mom. Please know that." Liv pressed, tightly hugging her mother, before grabbing onto Hayden and saying her final goodbyes.

"I love you too, honey." Julia smiled with affection, looking around at the event with admiration. "What an incredible wedding, even better than I had ever imagined when you two were growing up." She teased, squeezing Hayden's shoulder with a wink. "I'm so glad to finally and officially be able to call you son, although you've always been that to me."

Liv wanted to cry but remained calm so she could face her best friend, next.

"Sorry Hayden, but low key – Tristan is *just* as hot as I imagined." Lacey joked, pulling her friend into a hug. "I'm sad it took me five years to finally get an eye on that piece of meat."

Liv laughed, forgetting the heartfelt conversation they had only months ago. Again, feeling one more level disconnected to her friend who believed they were older, getting married at a more appropriate age for the mortal world.

"At the next wedding together, we'll be celebrating *your* prince charming," Liv offered, sweeping into a much-needed hug from her best friend. The person who kept her grounded, always. "Thank you for being here. I love you."

"I love you, too." Lacey replied with a genuine grin. "Highschool sweethearts – who would have thought? I love you both! Group hug!"

With impressive strength, the mortal unknowingly pulled the King and Queen of the Pure Gods into a final hug, as if they were siblings. No formalities, no royal constraints, only sincere joy.

Hayden chuckled at the irony of letting her do so, infectiously causing Liv to smile and laugh the same.

"Where are you both off to, tonight?" Lacey asked speculatively.

Liv had no idea. She turned to Hayden, hoping for a clue.

"It's top secret." He replied, before leaning into Lacey and whispering in her ear.

"Seriously!?" Liv exclaimed simultaneously as Lacey shrieked, "How romantic!"

"Guess you'll have to practice patience, my queen." Hayden joked. "Shall we?"

They departed among sparklers and fireworks, shooting out bursts of gold under the picturesque starry sky beside the Royal palace. Every step away from the celebration had reality setting more strongly in.

Olivia Monaco, half-mortal, college student and lover of coffee, had married Hayden, the powerful Pure God King – and now she ruled over the immortal Pure God society by his side.

Yet, one thing never felt more certain – she didn't belong anywhere but beside him. Finding comfort in that, she jumped atop Pegasus with Hayden's arms strongly wrapped around her, leaning against him as he clicked his tongue and prompted the white horse to gallop away, into the unknown.

FIFTY

HAYDEN

They didn't have much time, but he'd be damned to take away such a momentous life event from Liv and not do it completely right. He had been working on this gift since Liv confessed her worries at the Elements Pillar about having yet another residence to balance their busy schedule. And within the first week of his mother pressing a wedding, he made an effort to finalize all the details needed to complete the ultimate gift.

He wanted a place to call their own, a constant from moving obligations and separate from duty – somewhere they could make a home.

So, following the wedding, he knew exactly where he wanted to take Liv, to celebrate their first night as husband and wife – to enjoy for once, a new beginning, versus the ongoing trouble and endings they had been so roughly thrown into since he made the stupid decision to try and protect her a year before.

He flew Pegasus up to the mountains beside a lake – a place combining all of their favorite pieces from each previous residence into one, serving as a magical portal to easily transport to their owned properties and obligations onsite through a simple door. Precisely an equal distance from the royal palace, Elements Pillar, his cabin and Puerdios University, and directly underneath the Ollie constellation all year round, it was their homebase, their threshold – a way for them to stay in one place while managing hundreds of duties. He had detached the Puerdios portal after the battle of course, but he'd be damned if he did not reclaim it safely to their collection again one day.

At first, Liv looked innocently at Hayden, intrigued at the stunning palace, but curious to why he brought her here of all places. He remained coy, not wanting to ruin the surprise.

When he carried her across the threshold, he smirked as she spotted his office to the right, precisely furnished exactly as it stood in the King's lair at the royal palace.

To the opposite side, a parlour, decorated with a velvet purple couch squarely facing a fireplace – exactly mimicking her previous loft at Puerdios University.

"Hayden… is this some weird rental you furnished for our wedding?" Liv asked speculatively, unsure of what to expect as he continued to carry her directly to the final destination – the bedroom, but not first without a sneak peek to what was now theirs.

"Not a rental." Hayden grinned proudly, continuing on.

They passed a staircase, leading upward to where Liv would find her office, precisely decorated with the exact furniture as her Elements Pillar office – allowing her to teleport directly to the headquarters and back, a handful of guestrooms, one including her Puerdios armoire and furniture from her dormitory and another with Hayden's. On the main floor, past the stairs and to the left, an industrial kitchen – furnished with Hayden's loft and below, a small dining nook that overlooked the loft's original living room. Below, resided the game room of the cabin, giving them access to the lake whenever they pleased.

On the opposite side of the kitchen lived a separate entrace, filled with a massive dining room and ballroom to host more extravagant parties – the royal palace in all its glory.

"Hayden, is this ours?" Liv finally asked, her eyes wide and vulnerable and her voice shaking.

"Entirely ours." Hayden confirmed with a soft grin, explaining how the secured rooms worked.

"But, how…?" Liv looked like she was going to break, her eyes were watering with joy.

"Honestly? I was just getting annoyed with that damn studio loft at Puerdios and the amount of times you moved back *into* it." Hayden joked, but it was also the hilarious truth.

Liv nestled her head against his neck and laughed, her joy reverberating through the house, filling it with happiness – exactly how Hayden had originally imagined.

"Whatever didn't fit in our loft on campus, I brought it here. But, then it inspired me – why not have all of our favorite residences compiled into one destination? One cumulative home."

"You brought everything here." Liv was speechless, before looking up to him, her eyes open and welcoming. "Hayden, this is the most perfect gift you have *ever* given me."

Yet, to Hayden, it was only the beginning – and he wasn't shy from setting the standards high to compete.

"But, if you hated it so much – you shouldn't have given me the Puerdios studio in the first place." Liv retorted with a laugh, rolling her eyes as she excitedly tapped his shoulder and beckoned him to continue the tour.

"Lesson learned, and I'm growing from it." Hayden chuckled.

"I thought you were going to take me to the cabin." Liv admitted with a murmur, "I wasn't expecting this."

"Could it be home for you?" Hayden asked shyly.

Liv looked around the cozy, yet sleek and minimal designs. It was rich with character but not overly inticate. She turned back to her husband.

"It's perfect. But you're my home, Hayden." She kissed him gratefully, "However, yes, even if you aren't here, I would call this place home, too."

Hayden kissed her back, relieved. "Time to christen the house, then."

Liv grinned, reciprocating the anticipated excitement. "Where shall we start?"

LIV

Somehow the already incredible sex had been intensified on an unthinkably unattainable level now consumating as husband and wife, as one united.

Her toes curled and her skin shot uncontrollable chills to her nerves with each kiss her husband had planted across her body. Her body had yearned to complete the transaction and insisted Hayden rip off her gown without restraint and take her as was intended.

Liv laughed with subtle embarrassment as she recalled tearing off his jacket and using both hands, powers *and teeth* to unbutton his shirt, revealing the sculpted torso that had always made her melt. She had lunged for her husband, laughing angrily as he paused to torture her by gently unbuttoning her dress, making her wish she hadn't senselessly selected the long train of buttons down her lower back. She had been younger then, less wise.

To distract her evergrowing yearning for him, Liv grabbed his back, curving her head so that her neck was exposed, urging him to kiss her. The minute his lips touched her skin, she regretted it – instead wishing he would bite, penetrate and take her at once.

"Having you near our bed but waiting to have you is sucking the soul out of me." Hayden moaned, speeding up his desire to ravish her, appreciate her entirely as his wife.

"It is only because… I absorb your soul." Liv breathed between mind blowing, passionate kisses, "And I give… you mine."

Finally, her silk gown had collapsed to the ground and she faced him with enthusiasm, taking to his pants and swiftly unbuckling his white trousers before pressing herself against him, swinging her legs around his chiseled core. With one muscular arm steadily pressing her against his body, he crawled onto the bed and dropped her among the soft flannel sheets.

He kissed her chest, her torso, her inner thigh – each touch made with intention and admiration.

She pulled herself to him, flipping him over so she now lay on top. Teasingly grazing his statuesque body with her teeth, she kissed and nipped across his chest, his abs, before moving back up to his delectable lips.

Hayden moaned from pleasure, arching his back with desire and pleading she continue and stop all at once. "God, you'll be the end of me."

Liv smiled, kissing him intimately.

"The end of you, and the beginning of us."

Hayden grinned, admiration glowing from his face.

Husband and wife.

"Take me now, Hayden." Liv gasped, grabbing him and switching her position so that she straddled across him. "And don't be gentle."

Hayden smirked, his eyes growing dark with desire. He let her slowly sit atop his hardness, letting him fill her entirely. Liv moaned with the tension building and desperately needing relief.

She leaned forward, placing her hand gently against his cheek.

"I love you, Hayden." She had whispered, indulging in the deep connection his glacier eyes mirrored in hers.

"I love you, too. Ollie." Hayden smiled, before reversing their position and placing Liv again on her back.

Liv took a deep breath, craving more of him, all of him.

He began slowly moving in and out of her, causing her to moan with uncontrollable desire, clawing at his back for the urging release. He began moving faster, building momentum against her body and causing her to gasp his name.

Suddenly, he spun so that she sat atop his lap, still filled with his manhood, but now creating incredible pressure in unexplored spaces within, expanding her desire with each demanding thrust, making her crave more attention in these uncharted, pleasure-evoking territories. She was levitating – mind, body, space be damned.

Her arms wrapped around his neck, lusting for more, allowing him to penetrate her to unseen levels.

She couldn't contain herself, within a few thrusts, she was exploding, he along with her.

Liv tumbled against Hayden, her head spinning with ecstacy.

If this was marriage, she could not wait for a lifetime of marital bliss.

FIFTY-ONE

LIV

Emerald green filled her conscious.

Was she conscious?

Liv tossed and turned in her bed, replaying a diluted memory, uncontrollable and on repeat, in her light slumber.

"Did Daphne ever tell you about our affair, our child?"

More green, more pain.

"Did Daphne ever tell you about our affair, our child?"

Liv couldn't move. She wanted to move.

She tossed in her sleep, but her unconscious remained still.

"Did Daphne ever tell you about our affair, our child?"

Liv wanted out of this nightmare.

"Did Daphne?"

"Did Daphne?"

"Our child?"

"Our affair?"

"Did Daphne?"

"Our affair?"

"Our child?"

Liv sprung up out of bed, breathing heavily as she grasped for her 'now', clutching the flannel sheets and absorbing her bed in the brisk morning light.

"Ollie, are you okay?" Hayden asked anxiously, gently pulling hair away from Liv's sweaty forehead.

Liv looked around, taking a deep breath.

She was safe.

Liv pulled the comforting bedding over her, leaning back into her pillow with a sigh and letting the cumulative warmth take over.

"I'm okay. Just a nightmare." Liv nodded, grabbing Hayden's hand and squeezing it, trying to piece together what memory or dream she had concocted. "Hayden, it was a little surreal... and involved your mother? I hate to cut our time here short, but can we go to the palace? I think I need to see her..."

"Of course," Hayden leaned over, looking worried, but put on a brave face and explained, "The beauty of having an enchanted house of our own is that fortunately, we can easily return whenever we please."

Liv rolled her eyes at his smirk but appreciated his calm demeanor. In the deity world, nightmares were never a good sign. Especially one so vivid and hitting so close to her personal nightmare from only months before. The question was, *what did it mean?*

With a groan, Hayden rolled out of bed with the promise of coffee to be brewing in a matter of minutes. He kissed Liv softly on the forehead before exiting out of their bedroom.

Fully caffeinated, showered and sporting new clothes, Liv was ready to exit the whimsical fantasy and return to their stark reality. Far from their royal wedding attire they donned the day before, Liv chose sleek navy tailoring and Hayden dressed more casually in a black sweater, camel peacoat and gray sweatpants.

"While we're at the royal palace, I've requested Rei to summon our allies, so we can deliberate our next steps." Hayden added, leading Liv to his royal office for their first official teleportation.

It made sense, but a part of Liv wished they didn't have to so abruptly return to the dark reality in full, filled with war, death and pain.

But so long as there was pain, that meant there was something worth fighting for. So instead she turned, looking at her husband, pausing to remember this moment, the calm before the storm.

The moment of sanctuary, in their home, before they once again met the unknown head on. To face the Pure Gods, the Egyptians, the Buddhists, the Celts and the Norse – a rallying cry, united as one, to save humanity and destroy the dark Iron Age, once and for all.

Or die trying.

ACKNOWLEDGEMENTS

First and foremost, thank you to the Young Power fans. Your encouragement, engagement, support and positive reception to the Young Power Series is the reason why I love writing so much and continue to enjoy developing this magical, make-believe world.

Thank you to my husband, Jeremy, for supporting me and letting me continue to explore (and mentally live in) this world on many countless evenings, nights and weekends.

To my parents who have always instilled the belief that I can do and achieve anything as long as I put my mind to it, and that true success is earned through hard work. They've been my champions since day one, and for that I am truly grateful.

To my friends and family, who help me every day on this journey, from content creation to gut-checking my ideas. My best friend Rikki, who champions my literary creativity and encourages me to keep writing this intricate story. My best friend Yana, for being my stand-in model/content curator. My bookstagram family and supportive readers, who bring joy and meaning to this crazy journey – Chelsea, Ann-Helen, Cassandra, Reńee, Adele, Amy, Alissa, Jana, Cathy, Q, Rachel, Ashlee, Maddy, Mia, Allison, Krysten, Jen, Kayla, Rachael, Aria and Leah – thank you for welcoming me to your incredible literary community with open arms and inspiring me every day.

To the incredible female authors out there whose brilliant stories and characters encouraged me to attempt storytelling of my own - Diana Gabaldon, Sarah J. Mass, Holly Black and Jane Austin are names among many whose books I've purged and enjoyed entering their magical worlds created through words, and who helped defined my goals for the type of author I want to become.

And to Halsey, for without her song, "Young God," this series may never have come to fruition.

ABOUT THE AUTHOR

Andrea Blythe Liebman grew up in Sacramento, California, and although during adolescence she attempted various extra-curricular activities from soccer, tennis and piano to diving – one thing remained consistent in what she enjoyed as her pastime hobby: reading and writing.

Fast-forward twenty years – Andrea was able to transition her love of creative writing and fashion into a public relations career. As a creative at heart, her artistic side battled to resurface and after establishing herself in the PR industry, she realized it was time to switch up communicating brand initiatives with media and start telling her own imaginative stories again.

In 2017, Andrea began writing Young Power, the first installment of the Young Power Series, which was published in May 2019. Taking inspiration from travel, fashion, art and mythology, she created a new adult fantasy world filled with mesmerizing characters, intimidating power and turn-paging plots.

Andrea graduated from the University of Oregon with a Bachelor of Arts in Journalism and Parsons School for Design with an Associate in Applied Science in Fashion Marketing.

When she's not writing, she likes to travel the world via coffee shop crawls or sip on whisky with friends, spend time outdoors and pretend to be an amateur photographer, or watch anything U.K.-related, especially pertaining to Scotland.

Currently, Andrea lives with her husband and two Miniature Australian Shepherds in Oregon.

ETERNAL POWER

Coming Soon

*When it comes to immortality,
nothing is ever permanent...*